THE COURT OF THE UNDERWORLD

BOOKS 1 - 4

ALESSA THORN

Copyright © 2022 by Alessa Thorn

All rights reserved.

No part of this book may be reproduced in any form or by any electronic or mechanical means, including information storage and retrieval systems, without written permission from the author, except for the use of brief quotations in a book review.

Editing by F. Sutton

Cover by Damoro Designs

ASTERION

THE COURT OF THE UNDERWORLD I

ALESSA THORN

PROLOGUE

The New Greece

Sing, O' Muse, of the seasons of the world and how all that was lost was found again.

Sing, of how gods and mythical creatures once roamed the lands of Greece, and of how Man became powerful, and the gods were forced into hiding.

Sing, of when Greece's economy collapsed and the land was on fire with the turmoil man's governance had wrought.

Sing, of how the gods returned to build a new world from the ashes.

Sing, O' Muse, of the new city of Styx, and the monsters that govern its underworld.

Sing to me a new song, of a Minotaur, a Labyrinth, and a Woman...

1

Ariadne's hands were aching by the time the man's final breath came out in a wheeze of feta, onions, and sour wine.

"Gross," she muttered, as she unwound the braid of golden threads from around his fat, sweaty neck. She snapped off one of the threads from the braid before she twisted it back around her wrist, turning it into a harmless bracelet once more.

Using the broken golden thread, she tied the dead man's hands together in an elaborate cat's cradle. It was her *modus operandi*, a special way of letting his associates know just who was responsible for this kill. The cradle formed the symbol for 'abuser' in a language only Ariadne and her dead sister knew, her way of honoring Lia's restless shade in the afterlife.

Even gentle Lia would have approved of this death.

Ariadne scattered photos of Botsaris's beaten and raped wife around his body. Botsaris had been a pig of a man, and he'd squealed like one as he died. He'd given names, deals, offered her money, but she had held on until he stopped thrashing.

Ariadne shoved the little black dress she'd been wearing into her oversized designer tote, before pulling out a bundle containing her tights and a singlet top and putting them on. Without looking at the bloated

Botsaris, Ariadne slipped out the back door of the house overlooking Korinthos beach.

Botsaris had been a cheating, abusive bastard, so no one would look twice at the blonde as she walked off the property and into the still busy nighttime streets.

Ariadne dumped the tote bag, and the blonde wig into a bin at the train station and cursed under breath when she saw the red lines across her calloused palms. Botsaris had fought harder than she expected, and even with her calloused, she would end up with some bruising. She had no time to worry about it as she ran to catch her train.

Wedged between a group of teens and two arguing old women, Ariadne settled back into her comfortable anonymity and watched the lights of the city of Styx grow closer.

Almost twenty years beforehand, the ancient city of Corinth had been burned to the ground in the civil war. The collapse of Greece's economy, and the riots and military action that followed, had left many of the major cities in ruined war zones.

Corinth had been one of the worst affected. That was when Hades, the Lord of the Underworld, arrived and claimed the rubble that had been left. In less than twenty years, the city had been rebuilt and was turning a profit again.

Hades wasn't the only Old God that had come out of hiding, but the new city of Styx recovered the fastest, and Greece's new currency, the Nea Drachmae, had come pouring in.

Ariadne had her doubts as to whether the god of the dead thing was true, but she did know they had to be something *other*. Hades had been prominent in the news since the Great Collapse, and whenever the cameras managed the rare shot of him, he still looked like a sleek forty-something businessman.

Whatever Hades was, his media queen Medusa was made of the same stuff. CEO of Serpentine Industries, her skyscraper sat only a few floors lower than Hades's own pillar of black stone and steel. She ran a constant PR campaign worldwide to encourage trade and tourism to Styx, and it worked. Her blood-red hair and green eyes were famous the world over.

As for the rumor that she had snakes in her hair, Ariadne had never seen them in any of Medusa's news programs. She was a recluse, but with the internet at her feet, Medusa didn't ever have to leave Serpentine Tower again.

Like most kids in the Hellas District, Ariadne had grown up in the shadow of those two monstrous towers and with the rumors about the members of the Court of Styx.

There was a running joke internationally that Hades had come back to make the New York City of Greece and had ended up with Gotham instead. The people who lived in Styx didn't find this joke amusing because they knew that Hades Acheron would eat the toughest of Gotham for breakfast before picking his teeth with Batman's bones.

Only the tough survived on the streets of Styx, but despite its dark underbelly, Ariadne still loved the chaotic, violent, and often beautiful sprawl of it.

Ariadne made it back to her apartment just as the sun was rising. It was a tiny one-bedroom in a slightly less dodgy neighborhood than the one she was born in.

It was the one place in the world that felt like home. She had filled it with pieces of furniture and art from thrift shops and even managed to keep a house plant alive. It wasn't much. It certainly wasn't the opulent luxury she'd be living in if she had stayed at the Temple, but at least she didn't feel like every moment she was there, her debt was rising.

Ariadne had a long shower and climbed into bed, knowing she had precious few hours before Minos decided to summon her to the Temple for a full debriefing of the Botsaris job.

"One day soon, you'll never have to answer that bastard's call again," she said to herself like she did every day.

I'll kill him, Lia, I promise.

Curling into a ball under the blanket, Ariadne closed her eyes and let the nightmares take her.

ARIADNE MANAGED to get five hours of sleep before she was in a taxi, heading into the city center. The Diogenes District consisted of six blocks in the very heart of Styx, and it had more money than the rest of the city combined. It housed not only the Acheron and Serpentine towers but also five banks, two courthouses, and more overpriced jewelry and luxury item stores than one city needed.

It never ceased to surprise Ariadne that the city she knew disappeared as soon as the taxi entered the 'Dio Bubble' and everything was clean, shiny, and expensive looking.

The taxi stopped in front of the Temple, and she paid the man a handful of drachmae before climbing out of the car.

The Temple had earned its name thanks to the row of shining marble columns that stretched out along the façade of the mansion. Minos had grasped firmly to the nickname, even going as far as to have bronze lettering bolted into the marble to announce it to the world. What he didn't want the world to know was that the Temple was the training ground for Greece's deadliest assassins.

Those that were rich enough or connected enough knew what the Temple really was behind its pretty architecture. Everyone else thought it was a finishing school for underprivileged girls, run by the philanthropist Minos Karros.

Minos had his grubby hands in a lot of Greece's pies, from the stock market and real estate to oil refinery and shipping, not to mention that all the little priestesses that were raised at the Temple owed Minos a hefty debt. Ariadne felt like she would be a hundred by the time she paid him off.

Schooling her face to pleasant neutrality, Ariadne walked through the polished black and silver doors and into the cold darkness of the mansion.

Girls walked together in huddled groups, all wearing the pleated white chitons with thick black belts that were the Temple uniform. Lynx, one of the teachers in weaponry, gave Ariadne a nod in greeting.

"The master is in the training rooms, Spindle," she said in greeting.

"Thank you, Lynx," Ariadne replied politely, ignoring the watching students' wide eyes.

Once they graduated, they would be able to refer to the other assassins by their chosen names, but until then, they were restricted to titles only. Minos said it was a sign of respect to be referred to by their titles, but Ariadne saw it as just another way to prevent the girls in his charge from developing any personal attachments. If he could've found a viable excuse to give them all a number, Ariadne was sure he would have.

The training room was a rectangle pit of sand in a sunken floor. Minos was still physically fit enough to take on even his best students and liked to oversee certain aspects of their training himself.

Ariadne paused by a wooden pillar to watch him hold a girl's arm in a lock behind her back. She was about ten years old, and her small face was red with anger and embarrassment.

"Think, girl, how do you get out of this without a broken arm?" Minos demanded, sidestepping the kick the girl aimed at his knee.

Ariadne's right arm ached, and she fought the urge to rub the place where he'd broken hers around the same age. Minos still hadn't seen her, but the girl's pain-filled eyes rested on hers, and Ariadne made a small movement with her left hand.

The girl's left hand tightened into a fist and swung it back in a powerful strike aimed between Minos's legs. The strike cracked hard against the cup he was wearing, and he let her go with a jerk of surprise.

The girl rolled and was up on her feet in seconds, the folds of her training chiton smeared with dirt and sweat. Ariadne clapped her hands loudly, and Minos's furious attention turned to her.

"Well done, girl. I've found nothing slows down a handsy man like a good strike in the balls," said Ariadne.

"That's a compliment coming from the High Priestess herself," Minos replied as he straightened out of his fighting stance.

The girl turned to Ariadne and rapped her small chest twice with her fist. "Spindle."

"Go on, you have javelin training with Lynx," Minos said to the girl, and she bowed before hurrying away. Minos watched her go before turning back to his visitor. "If she can keep her temper, she will be good priestess one day."

"A bit of fire is a good thing."

"Only if I can control it," Minos said as he joined her at the top step. "How did the Botsaris contract go?"

"Easy. The man's wandering eye made him a gullible target."

"It was in the news this morning. Your cat's cradle has all of Botsaris's associates shitting their pants and thinking they are next. I can't say I ever approved of you doing it, but it's become a symbol to fear, and *that* I can appreciate."

Ariadne laughed, just as he expected her to. Laugh at his jokes, make him think she loved and respected him, and keep pretending that she didn't want to crush his eyes between her fingers.

"His associates should've taken the photos as evidence that he was killed because he was an abusive fuck, not for his illegal business dealings."

"They are thinking about their own fat hides. I'll let them squirm a bit before I make them pay me for the evidence I have against them."

That was the price Botsaris's own wife had to pay for the Temple's services. Enough evidence for Minos to blackmail his partners and take a nice cut of their future earnings. The man was diabolical sometimes, but Ariadne couldn't deny he knew how to squeeze out every drachmae he was owed. She followed him to his plush office and waited patiently until he told her to sit down.

"I do wish you'd come back to the safety of the Temple, little Spindle," Minos said as he sat down behind an oak desk.

"You know me. I like my privacy and the quiet after living in the dorms with argumentative girls for so long."

"You know I wouldn't expect you to sleep in the dorms! You'd have a lovely space, bigger and much safer than that rat's nest you currently live in."

Ariadne bit her tongue. At least the rat's nest was honest, and no one would try sneaking into her room in the middle of the night.

Minos opened his laptop and put in his password. Ariadne and half of Greece would've loved to get their hands on Minos's laptop. Botsaris's associates weren't the only people he had dirt on, and if they all weren't scared of it getting leaked, or having a visit from one of his priestesses, Minos would've been a dead man years ago.

"The Botsaris contract should prove to be the most lucrative one of the year. Your cut will make a nice little dent in what you owe me, and as always, a little bit extra in my Spindle's account so she can keep her freedoms," Minos mocked.

"Thank you, Minos. You know your Spindle will always come when you call her." She gave him a sugary smile that made him sigh and nod.

"I know, my darling, but a father worries when his favorite daughter is living unprotected in this dangerous city."

Ariadne held out her hand to pat his gently, and he lifted it to inspect the braided gold bracelet looped around her wrist.

"You are going to have to replenish the threads soon."

"Well, someone has been keeping me busy the last few months," Ariadne replied. She slowly removed her hand from his and fought the urge to wipe it down her black pants.

"That's because you are my best, Spindle. Styx is changing, and I'm old enough to feel when the city is restless. I tolerate your freedoms for the time being, but if I start to get worried, I will recall you back to the Temple permanently. Understand?"

Ariadne felt the warning in his words settle like a cold weight in her gut. Was letting her have the apartment just another of his fucking tests? She wouldn't put it past the prick.

"Of course, *pater*. I will always do what you think is best," Ariadne said, ever the dutiful, devoted daughter.

He smiled at her indulgently, and she imagined the day when she'd have her debt paid off, and she wouldn't have to suffer through any more of his bullshit.

It was a favorite fantasy of hers, and it was right up there with the moment she'd wrap her golden braid around his neck and watch him squirm. She would get the revenge that she had spent the last fifteen years cultivating and enjoy every minute it took for him to die.

"I have been working you hard. How about a week off? No summons, just regain your strength."

"That sounds wonderful. Thank you. Is there anything else you need before I head out again?" Ariadne asked.

"As a matter of fact, yes. I've got a gift for you," Minos said, opening the bottom drawer of his desk and pulling out a small black urn. Every thought in Ariadne's head shut down as he offered it to her.

"Lia. I should've given you these a long time ago. I was waiting for the right moment when I knew that I could trust you explicitly."

"I thought you would've disposed of these," Ariadne said, trying to keep the tremble from her voice.

There was a long wall in the Temple gardens that his best assassins got put to rest. Like the majority of the acolytes, Lia hadn't even made it to graduation.

"I was going to, but I knew how much she meant to you. Take them and honor her shade as you see fit."

Ariadne took the cold jar and gripped it tightly. "Thank you, *pater*. Is there anything else you require of me?"

Minos looked her over in a non-fatherly manner. "Maybe stop by the kitchens and eat something. I worry about what you're putting into your body out there."

"That sounds like a great idea. I haven't eaten breakfast this morning."

Ariadne had reached for the door when he cleared his throat. "One other thing, Spindle. If you interfere with my training again, like you did today, I'll break more than the girl's arm. Understand?"

"Yes, *pater*. I'm sorry," Ariadne said and left his office before she climbed over the desk and shoved her fist down his throat.

Ariadne was still fuming by the time she made it back to her apartment in the Hellas District.

With the anger came the inevitable hopelessness that no matter how much money she saved or how hard she fought, Minos was never going to let her go.

Giving her Lia's ashes was just another move in their silent game of wills.

"Don't forget your mail, Aria," the ancient landlady demanded from her desk in the foyer.

"Thanks, Mrs. Contos," Ariadne said politely. It was so rare for her to get any mail apart from the marketing flyers of the local shops that she had a habit of not looking in her box for weeks. She made a show of unlocking the box to appease the still watching Mrs. Contos, and she was surprised to find a yellow package inside of it.

Ariadne stilled when she noticed it was addressed in her full birth name, knowledge she thought only she and Minos had.

It would be impossible for anyone to identify her from fingerprints or DNA left at crime scenes. Minos paid good money to ensure that his priestesses didn't exist in any police or medical databases.

Ariadne had burned her fingerprints off years ago, back when she believed all of Minos's bullshit and wanted to impress him with her devotion.

Ariadne placed Lia's ashes on the mantel of the broken fireplace, turned on her coffee pot, and stared at the package on her kitchen counter. If someone knew who she was and what she had done, then the envelope could contain anthrax or any other number of nasties sent for revenge.

"Don't be ridiculous," Ariadne huffed and tore open the package and tipped out its contents. Inside was a smartphone with a pin code written on a scrap of paper.

"What the..." Ariadne tapped in the code just as the phone rang.

"Hello?"

"We are the Pithos, and we have a job for you, Spindle," a digital voice replied, and Ariadne's safe, anonymous world fell out from beneath her.

2

Ariadne took three deep breaths before she demanded, "If you know so much about me, you know I don't work freelance or take private contracts."

"Minos Karros likes to keep a tight grip on his pretty assassins. Tell me, Spindle, how's that working out for you?"

"I don't know what you are talking about," Ariadne said, even as her pulse raced.

"We are offering you a contract. Your reward will be five million drachmae and a way to keep out from under Minos's dirty thumb forever."

"Why?" It sounded too good to be true, and Ariadne was too smart to bite that bait.

"Pithos wants to get rid of scum like Minos that seek to corrupt Greece."

Ariadne snorted. "Sounds too idealistic to be true."

"I'm sure it does to a woman raised by a monster. We are monster hunters, Spindle. Destroy our monster, and we will destroy yours."

"I'm not dumb enough to take you at your word. For all I know, you are Minos trying to fuck with me and test my loyalty."

"There will be another package delivered to you within the hour. You have until sunrise tomorrow to give us your final answer. Consider what a life of freedom is worth to you."

Ariadne knew she should call Minos straight away, tell him that some jerk gang called Pithos was out to fuck with his business.

Instead, she drained her coffee, stuck the phone into the back pocket of her jeans, and went out. If another package was going to turn up in the next hour, she was going to make sure she saw the face of the person doing the delivery.

"By the saints, I thought you'd died, it's been so long since I've seen you," Dimmi said as Ariadne made it to the food van permanently parked across the road. Dimmi was probably the closest thing she had to a female friend, so Ariadne made a point of giving her business at least once a week. Their friendship was another weakness, like the apartment, but one that she was determined to keep.

"Dim, I was here three days ago. Stop drinking on the job," Ariadne said as she took the bottle of juice Dimmi gave her through the van's serving window.

"My darling, I'm not drinking. I miss seeing your beautiful face. You want your usual?"

"Sure," said Ariadne.

Ten minutes later, Dimmi's curves appeared out the back door of the van, and she sauntered over to the plastic table Ariadne sat at. Dressed in a leopard print dress with her curling black hair pinned up in a perfect sex kitten look, Ariadne knew most of Dimmi's customers weren't interested in her cooking.

"Here you go; veggie kebab with extra hot sauce. You look like you need it."

"Thanks a lot," said Ariadne, with a roll of her eyes.

"I'm serious. Do you *ever* sleep?" Dimmi lit a cigarette and eyed her critically.

"Not well," Ariadne admitted before having a bite of her kebab. The Temple had only fed them strict vegan meals with no sugar or salt, and when she had finally got the chance to eat spice, Ariadne thought she'd die from sensory overload.

"This lack of sleep better not be because of a fucking man. I would advise you to move to women, but they are just as crazy. My last girlfriend stole my good GHD hair straightener and sliced up my favorite dress before she left. Bitch. At least men wouldn't think to steal your hair styling products when you dump them," Dimmi said sourly.

I wouldn't know.

Ariadne had a few brief messy encounters until she found better results doing it on her own. She had occasionally slept with a target to get close enough to kill them, but a real, adult relationship was beyond her experience.

"All sounds way too hard to me," Ariadne admitted. She didn't hear what Dimmi said in reply, as all her focus zeroed in on a bike messenger. She took out her new phone and took a shot of him as he came out of the building.

"Stalker much? What's that poor kid done to earn that death glare from you?" Dimmi demanded.

"Nothing. Some jerk keeps putting creepy messages in my mailbox, and I want to find out who."

"Guys are the worst. At least he hasn't started sending you photos of his dick."

"Not yet, anyway."

"If he does, we'll make a wall of shame, right here." Dimmi pointed at the blank, pink side of the van. "If he's a local, it's bound to flush him out."

Ariadne laughed loud enough for people to turn and stare. "Thanks, Dimmi. I'll keep it in mind."

Ariadne finished off her meal and an espresso before heading back into her building. A box was waiting for her, and when she opened it, she found a thin silver laptop.

"You guys love your tech, don't you," Ariadne said as she turned on the power button. She had to admit it was the smarter way to do it. If you had that much information on a hit, then you didn't want to carry about piles of paper. Handwriting could be tracked, so could the type of paper used if you were desperate. Digital files were traceable, but if Pithos had the stones to go up against Minos, then Ariadne doubted they'd give over anything that could be traced.

There was a single folder on the desktop, and when she opened it, the first thing she clicked on was a photo of the sexiest guy she'd ever seen.

Broad-shouldered and ridiculously tall, the guy had olive-brown skin, sun-streaked dark hair that fell past his shoulders in lazy waves and a short, clipped beard. Even dressed in an expensive suit, he seemed an unlikely candidate for a corporate manager or a banker.

"Gods, aren't you the prettiest contract I've ever been offered," Ariadne told the photo as she clicked open more files.

A full information form came up, including a name; Asterion Dys. Something scratched at her subconscious like she was sure she'd heard the name before but couldn't remember where.

"Have you been a naughty boy, Asterion? Oh my...it looks like it."

Ariadne read through each file carefully. She had to hand it to Pithos. They were thorough. They'd even noted down his weekly schedule and who his closest bodyguards and staff were.

According to Pithos, Asterion Dys was the owner of a nightclub in the Diogenes, and some type of illegal, gladiatorial fighting pit underneath it. It was a place that people died to entertain the rich, and millions were laundered through it every year to the benefit of Styx's worst criminals.

The cops couldn't touch Asterion because not only did he maintain relationships with some of Greece's most powerful people, but Hades fucking Acheron owned shares in the whole operation.

That made Ariadne pause. She'd killed mob bosses, politician's and other high profile people before, but she'd have to be stupid to want to fuck with one of Hades's friends or members of his inner circle.

Besides, if Pithos had all of this on Asterion, why did they need her to kill him? Why not do the job themselves? Ariadne gnawed on her bottom lip as she thought about how she could do it.

Asterion looked like a big fit guy, so he'd be a fighter. It would make him hard for her to take down without the help of a sedative that she'd have to get him to ingest. That is *if* she could get past his bodyguards first who all had the look of ex-military or organized crime about them.

The only time someone like Asterion would be alone was in bed. Just the thought of it filled Ariadne with tense excitement. It would be a nice change to try to seduce someone who was that good looking.

Easy girl, you'd still have to kill him, remember?

Five million drachmae was a lot of money to pass up. She'd been through all the files, and she'd found nothing that would be useful against Minos. If she took the job and Pithos only had money to give, she'd use up that five million just trying to hide from Minos's wrath.

Ariadne woke at dawn, as the cell phone started to ring. She'd fallen asleep at the table, still reading.

"Spindle, what is your decision?" the voice demanded.

"I don't see anything on this laptop about Minos, so this job isn't worth the risk to me," she replied, stifling her yawn.

"Look again," said the voice. Ariadne moved the mouse, so the screen lit up, and sure enough, there was a new folder.

"How are you doing this?" she demanded. The laptop wasn't connected to the internet. She wasn't sure this part of Hellas could even support the network.

"*How* doesn't matter. That folder is only a small part of what we have hacked off Minos's laptop. You'll get the rest when the job is done."

Ariadne opened the file, and her jaw dropped open. Client names, targets, successful hits, ongoing bribes. She already had enough to burn Minos, but not enough to destroy him.

Feeling as if she could see the first glimpse of her freedom in years, Ariadne whispered, "I'll do it."

3

The street in the Hellas District wasn't the kind of place Ariadne expected a rich club owner to frequent.

It was a stretch of sad office buildings left over from old Corinth and repurposed into government housing, or squats in the places too unstable for a developer to want to touch.

The address caught Ariadne's eye because it seemed so out of place. What could be in Hellas's underbelly that would warrant a weekly visit from someone like Asterion Dys? Ariadne decided it had to be a dealer or a lover. Both might be willing to sell him out for the right price.

Fuck this up, and you're dead, Spindle.

If Hades didn't get her, then Minos sure as hell would. She was never nervous before a job because she always had a plan and an exit.

This time, she would have to make doubly sure of how and when she decided to take Asterion down. Meeting a sticky end in a bad part of town wouldn't be nearly as suspicious as if he died in bed.

The address was only three streets away, so Ariadne thought the best thing to do was recon on the way to the gym. She needed to hit some bags to get rid of the anxiety that had settled in her since agreeing to the Pithos contract two days beforehand.

Sitting on a dirty bench, sipping a coffee from a street vendor,

Ariadne watched as a sleek black Mercedes Benz pulled up in front of the building.

It was a slightly less decrepit structure than those on either side of it, and a bronze plaque on the front of it looked newer than the rest of the street combined.

Two bodyguards, one tall and golden, the other short and dark, stepped out of the car first before the back door opened, and Ariadne got her first look at Asterion Dys in the flesh.

Dressed in a tight V neck white shirt and black jeans, he looked more casual and relaxed than he had in the surveillance photos she'd been given.

A few boys playing soccer in the street started calling out to each other before they all descended on Asterion like a plague of dirty shirts, scuffed knees, and boisterous jokes.

Ariadne had expected hookers or hard-faced dealers, not a mob of kids. To top it off, the door to the building opened, and a priest stepped out and shook Asterion's hand.

What was going on?

Ariadne put her headphones in her ears without turning her music on and slung her gym bag over her shoulder.

No one paid any attention to her as she crossed the street and pretended to be looking at a map on her phone.

"Away with you, boys. Asterion and I have things to discuss," the priest said.

"They are okay, Petros. We can talk about the new roof later," Asterion replied, his voice deep and smooth.

Ariadne kept her eyes on the phone as she crashed into him, toppling down with an inarticulate noise of surprise before she hit the pavement.

"Oh my God, I'm so sorry!" she apologized, rubbing at her knee.

"You should watch where you are going," said the blond bodyguard in an irritated tone.

"It's not like I wanted to fall on my ass on purpose," Ariadne snapped back.

Asterion knelt beside her and passed her phone back from where it had gone skidding across the sidewalk.

"Please ignore Theseus. He's still learning his manners." Theseus grunted but wasn't game enough to backchat his boss.

"Thanks," Ariadne said, taking off her sunglasses and looking up at him gratefully from under her lashes. It was a move that she had used a million times, but as soon as his golden-brown eyes reached hers, she was the one that was caught.

"That will teach me to try to walk and read a map at the same time."

"New in town?" Asterion asked, a flicker of interest in his expression.

"Yes, and hopelessly lost every time I step out my door," Ariadne complained. He held out a hand, and she took it with a slight wince as she stood.

"Are you hurt?" Asterion looked down at her scuffed tights.

"Only my pride. Don't worry, I'll walk it off. I don't suppose you know where this gym is?" Ariadne held out the phone, and Asterion bent over it. His aftershave was like spice and wood, but there was something warm and masculine underneath.

Ariadne didn't have to fake the blush that reached her cheeks. He really was the most handsome target she ever had, and her lady parts knew it.

"You are two streets off. There's a quicker way if you take the next right and then a left," Asterion said before looking at her bag and the small scars on her knuckles. "You box?"

"Yeah, I change it up with some mixed martial arts when I can. I love a good fight, and believe it or not, my reflexes aren't bad most of the time," she said with a self-deprecating laugh. It earned her a small smile from Asterion, which was a win.

"This gym isn't in the best neighborhood, but Stavros will teach you right," he said and then added, "Maybe don't leave your headphones in when you're walking this area by yourself. Situational awareness is important."

"Thanks for the tip. Sorry again," Ariadne said, picking up her bag. She looked at the brass plaque. St Paul's Home for Boys.

Shit, it's a damned orphanage.

Ariadne gave the priest a respectful nod before she limped away. She had taken three steps when a warm hand gripped her bicep.

"Here, new girl. If you want a night out sometime, flash this at the door, and they'll let you in," Asterion said, handing her a glossy black card with *The Labyrinth* written in a metallic red font. She flipped it and saw his name printed on the back.

"This better not be some kind of seedy sex club, because I've been warned about those existing in the big city," she said with a raised brow. Asterion gave a surprised laugh that made her think dark, impure thoughts.

"Not officially, though, I find one thing tends to lead to another during the course of a night."

Ariadne tapped the card against his chest and gave him a flirtatious smile.

"I guess we'll have to wait and see, won't we, Asterion?" His eyes flashed with the best kind of trouble.

"Enjoy your boxing, new girl. Try not to knock anyone else over on your walk home."

"How else am I supposed to meet people in this city?" Ariadne called back as she walked away.

She didn't look back, but she felt his eyes on her until she turned off the street. She looked at the card again with a frown.

Why are the hot ones always off-limits?

The orphan in her softened at the thought of him being a benefactor to the boy's home, but the assassin in her drowned that voice out. The fact he donated to an orphanage was a surprise, but it didn't change a thing.

Killing him was the key to her freedom, and that was always going to be more attractive than the sexy smile of Asterion Dys.

4

It wasn't often that Asterion was surprised. His days were planned out for him, and he knew everything that needed to happen to keep his businesses running. And not just the business.

Ever since Hades had brought him to Styx, his life had become one of intensely organized structure in order for him to stay sane. Lately, it had started to chafe him.

He had been thinking of that the very moment he'd been slammed into by a woman. Women who frequented the club knew who he was on sight and knew better than to go anywhere near him without permission.

That clueless woman had nearly knocked him on his ass and then had enough nerve to flirt with him. He had to admire that kind of guts.

Didn't she know how bad Hellas was to attractive women?

An instinct he didn't entirely understand had kicked in, and he'd wanted to make sure she was okay. He didn't go as far as sending one of his men to find out if she got to the gym, but the temptation was there.

"Are you all right, boss?" Theseus asked him for the third time that day.

"Yeah, what's up? Oh right, the order." Asterion looked down at the clipboard in his hands, checking stock numbers before signing off down the bottom. He had people to do that kind of thing for him, but he still liked to know exactly what happened in the Labyrinth even down to consumables.

"The street girl wasn't *that* pretty," Theseus teased him, as he took the clipboard back.

Pretty wasn't a word Asterion would associate with the mystery woman, it seemed too…girlish.

There was a glance in those stormy grey-blue eyes that made the beast inside of him prick its ears up in curiosity. She was attractive with all that straight black hair and long legs, which went without saying, but he could just about *smell* the secrets on her.

"I don't remember asking your opinion," replied Asterion.

"If you had, I would've advised you not to give her your card. She's a Hellas girl, for fuck sake. She could try to take advantage and sue you for bruising her knee."

Theseus was the only one of his men who would be game enough to say such a thing to him, but as his second in command, he'd earned the right and was the closest thing Asterion had to a friend outside of Hades and his Court.

"You've got to have more faith in people, Theseus. Not everyone is out to try and screw you. Besides, I don't see you picking up any pretty girls lately."

"That's because you work too hard to pay attention to what I am doing, boss. If you hadn't noticed, there are a hundred pretty girls who turn up every night who would be more than happy to get naked for you. You just need to say yes to one," Theseus argued.

"Whatever. You've got nothing to worry about, Theseus. She didn't strike me as a club-goer, so I'd be surprised if she turned up anyway," Asterion said dismissively. "How's your mother doing?"

Despite what Theseus said, Asterion *did* pay attention to his men and their family lives. He knew that Theseus's family had lost a lot of money in the crash, his dad had left soon after, and his eldest son had been left picking up the pieces.

"Mom is fine. My little brother is about to graduate, so she's fussing over him at the moment and is off my case, which is good," Theseus replied.

"Even if she's a pain in the ass, you're lucky to have her," said Asterion.

"I'll try to remember that next time she starts complaining that I haven't found a good Greek girl to marry yet."

Theseus left with the order, and Asterion opened his laptop to review the previous night's earnings.

He reminded himself he was too busy to worry about the sexy Hellas woman, but that didn't stop him asking the doormen if she had turned up with his card that night.

And the next.

By day three, Asterion was starting to consider doing stupid things like going to Stavros's gym to track down the mystery woman, when Paulo found him in the private upstairs area that overlooked the club floor.

"Hey boss, I thought you might want to know that a girl just turned up flashing your card," the bouncer said.

"Where is she?" Asterion asked.

"Easy to find, just follow the crowd of drooling men." Paulo grinned and pointed.

A group of five men were standing in a loose circle at the corner of the bar, Christos, his bartender, included. Then one moved out of the way, and he saw the Hellas woman perched on a barstool in the center of them.

She had her long black hair pinned up to better show off the bare back of her stunningly bold red dress.

She laughed at something one of her admirers said, her full lips painted the same bright red. Her only jewelry was a gold wrap bracelet and a single gold and ruby ring on her finger.

She was... perfect.

She had to wear that fucking color, the dark creature he kept locked inside roared, and Asterion gripped the railing so hard the metal bent under his hands.

By chance, she looked up, recognized him, and gave him a smirk before turning back to whatever the man was saying.

"Want me to ask her up?" Paulo said uncertainly.

"No, I'll go to her," Asterion replied, ignoring the bouncer's surprised look as he made for the stairs.

Asterion didn't often walk the floor of the club, too many people stopped him to talk or ask for favors.

The expression on his face must've been enough to warn people off that night because the sea of dancers parted to let him through as he made his way to the bar.

He was standing behind the close press of men when he heard a familiar voice say, "Oh, there you are, honey! I've been waiting for ages for you to turn up."

The man in front of him took one look over his shoulder and jumped out of the way. The other men went pale.

"I'm sorry, I didn't know she was with you-" a braver one mumbled before Asterion tilted his head to the side, and they hurried away.

"Thank the saints you turned up. I swear I was never going to get away from them," she said with a relieved laugh.

"What did you expect when you wear a dress like that," he replied.

"You like it? Honestly, it's not something I'd usually pick, but it's been in my wardrobe forever, and I thought tonight was the night. Not sure about this bit..."

She turned, and he caught a glimpse of pale brown skin and the curve of a hip through a cut out in the side of the dress. He shoved his hands in his pockets, so he didn't reach out for it.

"That's definitely going to attract trouble," he said.

"I'll take that as a compliment. You scrub up okay yourself," she replied, her stormy eyes looking at Asterion's black suit appreciatively.

Christos put a glass of his favorite scotch down in front of him, and he couldn't drink it fast enough.

"So, new girl, are you going to tell me your name?"

She poked him in the shoulder with a red fingernail. "You never asked. It's Kassandra. Kass, if we decide to be friends." Asterion didn't have a second to respond before they were interrupted.

"The Minotaur doesn't make friends, especially not with beautiful women," said an arrogant voice behind them.

"Nikos, what brings you slinking in here tonight?" Asterion asked, swallowing his temper. The short, well-polished man smiled his perfect, greasy smile.

"I have a contender, so I'm here to take your money, Dys." His blue eyes ran over Kassandra and lingered on her breasts. "And maybe your woman too."

"Sorry, shorty, you're not my type," Kassandra said, crossing her legs. Asterion grinned at her attitude.

"You might change your mind after a few hours with this bullish bore," Nikos replied and took another sip of his martini.

Kassandra's smile was lethal. "You wouldn't say that if you saw the size of his dick." Nikos choked on his drink before regaining his composure.

"I'll see you downstairs, Dys," he muttered before heading back into the crowd.

"What was that guy's problem?" Kassandra asked. Asterion stared at her a moment longer before bursting out laughing. "What?"

"You don't realize this, but you just insulted one of the richest men in Styx," he said.

"He was insulting first. What's all this about a contender?" Kassandra leaned closer, and Asterion did his best not to look at the lovely cleavage in front of him. "I heard this place had a fighting pit underneath it, but I thought it was Hellas street gossip."

"And what if there is?" Asterion smiled at the gleam of excitement in her expression. "Interested?"

"Oh, I don't know, I'd have to think about it." Kassandra rolled her eyes at him. "Of course, I'm interested! You know I'm into blood sports."

"Well then, I might be persuaded to show you." He ordered them another round of drinks and caught her staring at the silk banners that hung from the roof, black with a stylized red bull's head that was the logo for the club.

"Why did that guy call you the Minotaur?" she asked, and then something like recognition clicked in her eyes. "Do you *own* this place?"

"Yeah, is that a problem?" he asked, feeling like his good night was about to go down the toilet.

"No, I just feel like an idiot for not realizing sooner. Your name was on the card, so I figured you worked here. The Minotaur is a title or something?"

"Something like that. It used to be my fighting name," he said. It wasn't exactly a lie.

"I knew you had to be a fighter of some stamp when you noticed my knuckles. Most guys don't, and if they do, they automatically assume something bad must've happened, so they never ask," Kassandra replied, and tucked them in her lap like a nervous tick to cover them.

Asterion took her hand and lifted it to his mouth, kissing the criss-crossing white lines.

"Their loss," he said as he let her hand go again. Color flashed along her chest and neck, and he grinned.

"Don't look so smug," she chastised before she downed her drink.

"I have no idea what you're talking about."

"Well, you can sit there without an idea while I go powder my nose," Kassandra said, getting off the barstool in one graceful movement.

"Don't get lost on your way back."

She threw him a cocky smile over her bare shoulder. "I'm sure you'd hunt me down."

"Oh, that I can guarantee, sweetness," he said under his breath as he watched the sway of her hips disappear into the crowd.

5

Ariadne pressed her way into a bathroom stall and shut herself in. Closing the lid, she sat down and tried to get her head together. One stupid kiss on her hand, and she was a fluttery mess.

Don't get emotional. He's a contract. Your body is a weapon and one you can control, Madame Zera's voice echoed in her head.

Zera owned the most prestigious brothel in Styx, and as soon as Minos's priestesses started to bleed, he made sure they were schooled appropriately on how to seduce their contracts.

Ariadne had a special kind of hatred for Madame Zera, and after she was through with Minos, the old bitch would be next.

"What is wrong with you, stupid girl?" Ariadne whispered to herself. She had done this too many times to count, but there was something wrong about getting aroused by a man she'd be killing by the end of the night.

She hadn't exactly planned on getting him into bed that night, merely drugging his drink and finding a quiet corner to finish him off.

Would it be so terrible to take advantage of that lovely body?

She recognized the angry, naughty streak that had started to rear its head, the side of her that had taken the contract because it *wanted* things of its own. Now it badly wanted to be seduced by her target.

You are so messed up, Ariadne. You know that, right?

Damaged or not, she wasn't acting when she flirted with Asterion. She enjoyed his company, even if it was temporary.

"What does it matter? You're already walking the road to Tartarus, so you might as well dance," she said, before slipping off her underwear and putting them into the sanitary bin.

After checking her makeup in the mirror and chewing on a mint, Ariadne stepped back out into the club to see if she could find Asterion again.

Instead, she found Nikos waiting for her.

"Excuse me," she said politely, trying to step around him. A big man that must've been a bodyguard stepped in the way to stop her.

"You seem like a nice girl, and usually I'm not this forward, but I wish to warn you before you get mixed up in something you'll regret," said Nikos, wrapping her arm around his as he maneuvered her towards a wall and out of the way of dancers.

"You want to warn me about what?" she asked.

"Asterion Dys. I know it might seem flattering to get the attention of a rich, powerful man like that, but you have no idea what he is... what he *really* is."

"And what is he?" She had about thirty seconds of patience left in her.

"He's not just a club boss. You know about the fighting pits, yes? That's just the beginning of that violent freak's appetites. People die downstairs, pretty girl. You want to play around with a man like that?"

Ariadne tried to remove her hand from his arm, but he held on. "It's none of your business who I play around with. I don't even know you. I'm not your girl or your sister, so back off."

Nikos licked his lips nervously. "You know about the gods? Did you ever stop to think that the gods weren't the only freaks that crawled out of the shadows the day Greece fell? I make money off Asterion, so I look the other way, but the man is a fucking monster."

Ariadne pulled her arm down and away, breaking Nikos's grip

roughly enough that he jerked forward, and she had to stop him from falling into her.

"Did you ever stop to think he's not the only monster here right now?" she said, with enough of a threat in her tone that Nikos's eyes widened. He made to grab for her again, but he was suddenly pulled back and slammed hard into the wall, Asterion holding him around the throat, his eyes glowing with fury.

"I've warned you before about touching my things, Nikos," he growled in a tone that had the hair on Ariadne's neck rising. Maybe Nikos wasn't as crazy as he sounded.

"We were only talking, you psychopath," Nikos wheezed, his face turning red. Ariadne looked for his bodyguard and spotted him on the floor. He had been dropped without a sound.

Holy shit.

She didn't need Asterion killing someone like Nikos and causing the police to turn up. She took Asterion's other hand and wrapped it around her waist, so his palm rested on her bare skin.

"Hey, big guy, why don't you put the little asshole down? He's not worth the fight," she said into his ear.

"Did he hurt you?" Asterion asked through his teeth.

"Him? He couldn't hurt me if I had both hands tied behind my back." Ariadne pressed her body into his side, and his grip on her tightened. "If you kill him now, how are you going to take all of his money later? Drop him before this alpha male act starts to turn me on more than what it already is."

Asterion loosened his grip, and Nikos fell to the ground, gasping for air.

"Touch her again, and I'll cut that hand off, understand?" Asterion said, standing over him. Nikos managed to nod, but Asterion looked as if he was contemplating doing it anyway. Ariadne threaded her fingers through the buttons of his shirt, lightly stroking the hot skin of his stomach.

"Come on, Asterion. All this manhandling has made me thirsty. We'll see you downstairs, Nik. Right before we take every drachmae you own," she said with a smile, and Asterion finally looked at her.

The fury in his eyes dimmed, and he brushed his knuckles gently against her jaw.

"As the lady wishes," he said, and he turned her away. They headed through the press of people until Asterion opened a door and led her upstairs to his private area.

"I hate that fucking prick," he admitted, once he had made sure she was sitting comfortably. "I'm sorry that you had to witness that."

"Don't be. Nikos was disrespectful. I get it. I could've handled him, but thank you for coming to my rescue. I can't remember the last time a man stood up for me."

Because it's never happened.

The thought made the stupid fluttery feeling return to her stomach.

"What did he want?" Asterion asked as he leaned against the balcony railing and folded his arms. A waiter arrived with fresh drinks like they were watching for him to return. Ariadne took her vodka soda and crossed her legs, the split in the dress flashing enough thigh to make his eyes linger.

"He was trying to warn me off you for my own good. Clearly, I'm too stupid to know better."

"You're something, sweetness, but stupid's not it," Asterion said, his smile widening when she laughed. "You're not concerned that I almost strangled a guy?"

"Should I be? I told you I like blood sports, so a bit of strangulation is hardly going to send me running, especially when it's a slimy little prick being strangled."

"Maybe I'll take you downstairs to the fights after all. They can get messy, but everyone who steps inside the pits signs an agreement. They know what they are getting into, they know the risks," Asterion said, before taking a sip of scotch.

"They volunteer, which means they have a choice to fight and have violence done to them. It's more than some people get," Ariadne replied, her tone soft enough that Asterion's eyes filled with questions. *Damn it.* "Please tell me the winnings make the risks worth it?"

"Gods, yes. A million drachmae to the last man standing," he replied.

"A *million*! That's tempting enough to make even me sign up," she joked, but suddenly, he was beside her, hands holding her face.

"I'd never agree to let you even step foot in that pit," Asterion said, the growl back in his voice.

"Settle that temper down. I was kidding. Remember, I can't even walk down the street without falling over." He released her, brushing her cheeks with thumbs.

"I remember. Hmm, your skin feels nice," Asterion said, sitting down beside her.

"Thanks, I moisturize."

He laughed softly. "You've always got a clever answer, don't you?"

"Sounds to me like you've been hanging out with the wrong kind of women if you think I'm clever."

Asterion looped one of her curls around his finger and let it spring up. "Clever and full of secrets."

"You stay away from my secrets, Asterion Dys. They are what make me so alluring," Ariadne stated firmly.

"Your lips are pretty great too," he said and leaned forward and whispered in her ear. "My guess is that talking isn't the only thing they do well. I wonder how long you'll make me wait to find out." Heat pooled at the base of her spine as he gently kissed the curve of her neck.

"Not very long if you keep that up," she said softly as her pulse raced. A throat cleared, causing Ariadne to jump.

"Sorry to interrupt, but they are waiting for you downstairs, boss," said Theseus, giving her a look of surprise when he recognized her.

"Nice to see you again, Theseus. Your timing is impeccable," she said with enough sarcasm for him to know he was being mocked.

"Who knew Hellas girls cleaned up so well," Theseus replied.

"Careful," warned Asterion as he stood and offered his hand to Ariadne. "Come along, sweetness, we need to watch Nikos cry for the second time tonight."

"Are you sure taking her downstairs is a good idea?" asked Theseus, his golden frown deepening.

"I'm sure it's none of your business who I take anywhere," Asterion replied, and Theseus finally shut his mouth.

Asterion and Ariadne stepped into a small elevator, and as the doors closed, she let out a sigh.

"He seems embarrassed that you're with a girl from the wrong side of town," she said. Asterion pressed her gently back against the wall.

"That's my favorite kind of girl," he replied. Ariadne stood up on tiptoes and kissed him softly, just once.

"Good," she said. Asterion's eyes fluttered open, and they were hot again but not with rage.

He buried his hand in her hair and pulled it, so her surprised mouth tilted up, and he kissed her with a rough force that left her breathless.

Ariadne gripped the lapels of his jacket as one of his knees moved between her legs, and he pressed closer to her. The movement brushed him against her core, and she gasped as the sensation set her on fire.

His other hand curled around her neck and held her pinned to his lips and body until the elevator doors opened again. He released her; eyes wide as if he couldn't believe what he'd just done. She wiped a smear of her lipstick off his mouth.

"That was promising," Ariadne said, meaning every word. If he could do that with just a kiss, she couldn't wait to see what the rest of him would do to her.

Asterion held out an arm to her. She took it as she stepped out of the elevator on unsteady legs. They reached the edge of a balcony as a roar went up around them.

"Holy shit," Ariadne gasped. She had expected a group of rich guys and hard-faced fighters standing around a cage, not a fucking arena.

It was made of white stone and wood, and it looked like a restored version of many of the amphitheater ruins that littered Greece.

The sandy pit in the middle was at least fifty meters long and twenty wide; a small, underground coliseum right in the heart of Styx. It was rigged with enough lights that Ariadne could make out the earth and concrete walls around them.

"I found it when we were building the club, and I thought it would be a shame to let it go to waste," Asterion said as he waved at the assembled crowd.

"How many people know about this place? I'm surprised the police haven't raided you," Ariadne replied. Asterion pointed to a balcony across from them.

"That's the police chief, sweetness. He owns that box with the mayor."

A stocky man smoking a cigar gave them a wave, and Ariadne waved back.

"What about Hades?"

"What about him?" Asterion's eyes narrowed.

"Don't look surprised I asked. Everyone knows Hades is the real boss of Styx," she said, trying to cover her slip.

"Hades was pissed I took an extra year to complete the club after I found the ruins of this, but he recovered his good mood when he saw how much money it was going to make."

Asterion sat down on a large black throne of a chair, looking like a barbarian king, eyes full of violence and lust that appealed too much to her dark and base side. He held out a hand to her.

Ariadne hesitated, knowing that she was hitting the point of no return.

Oh, you know you hit that an hour ago, you hussy.

Ariadne took his hand, and he settled her on his lap. She leaned back against the groove of his shoulder, throwing a leg over his.

A grumble of satisfied male echoed through his chest, not sounding remotely human.

"Where have you been hiding all these years?" he asked.

"Somewhere I hope I never have to go back to," Ariadne replied honestly.

"You'll be lucky if I let you leave that spot," Asterion said, shifting his leg, so she tipped further back into him.

Ariadne didn't have a chance to reply before another roar went up, and a group of ten men entered the arena, most with their hands strapped up.

"Are they all going to fight each other?" she asked.

"The last man standing is the aim of the game," Asterion explained. "Bare-knuckle is usually the warm-up rounds. As the night progresses, things get a bit more serious, and weapons come out."

"They fight to the death?"

"All depends if that's what the bet is. It's a good way to settle disputes. We get a lot of rival gangs, but a death fight doesn't happen often."

"So, the only rule is that there are no rules?" Ariadne asked.

How did she not know about this place? If Minos knew, he'd probably put the priestesses in the arena to test their skill. The training set up at the Temple was far more brutal, and a well-trained priestess could clean up big in the arena.

"There are rules. No animals, no kids, no death unless it's agreed on first by both parties. People have to prove they are good enough before they go into the Labyrinth."

"You have an *actual* Labyrinth?"

Asterion pointed to the huge levers on the sides of the arena. "This top floor can be taken down, revealing a Labyrinth underneath. It's used twice a year at most, and it's a gauntlet. Most aren't good enough for me to agree to let them attempt it."

"Why?"

"Because it's designed to kill people."

"Then why would anyone be dumb enough to attempt it? Money?"

Asterion looked thoughtful before he finally admitted, "Money, fame and a chance to be a guard for me, Medusa or Hades."

Ariadne let out a low whistle. "Least you know you're going to get the best, I suppose."

"You really aren't disturbed by any of this, are you?" Asterion asked in surprise.

Ariadne ran her fingers over the soft stubble of his beard. "The world is ugly and violent. At least this place has rules; the streets don't."

"One day, I'm going to make you share some of those secrets, sweetness," he said softly.

"In your dreams, Dys."

"If you turn up in my dreams, I guarantee it won't be for conversation." Ariadne laughed before turning back to watch the fights beneath her.

Ariadne had to admit that no one entered the arena without having some skill to back them up.

Minos had always encouraged competition amongst the girls, and she had to fight hard to make sure she didn't end up with a dagger between her ribs when she went to sleep at night. She'd loved being the best, loved fighting and winning.

It was a good thing that Asterion had said he'd never let her down there because her cocky violent nature would've loved to give it a try.

When the first fights ended and the second ones began, Asterion leaned forward and whispered, "If I didn't know better, I'd say all of this violence excites you."

"Fighting is exciting, why else do it?" she said.

Asterion ran his fingers lazily down the split in her dress so he could touch her bare skin. When she didn't stop him, he did it again, stroking her and making goosebumps break out along her skin.

He's a contract, remember?

She remembered, but she no longer cared. She shifted back into him, and she felt him hard against her hip.

"Looks like I'm not the only one who finds it exciting," she couldn't resist saying.

"Can you blame me? I have fights to watch, and a beautiful woman's ass pressed up against me," he said, the stroke of his hand going higher, almost as if he were daring her to stop him.

She rested her back against his shoulder so he could look down the front of her dress.

"You are courting danger, sweetness."

"Am I? I thought I was only using you like a comfortable chair." She ground her ass against him ever so slightly, and his hand tightened on her thigh.

"If you tell me to stop, I will," he said unexpectedly.

Ariadne twisted her head so she could kiss the strong column of his neck. "I don't want you to stop."

She turned back to the arena without seeing it, waiting to see what he'd do. His hand on her thigh resumed its slow circles, moving higher and driving her crazy as it carefully avoided the one place she wanted it to go.

His long fingers reached her hip, and he paused when he discovered bare skin instead of underwear. "Aren't you full of surprises?"

"You've no idea," she said, looking across at him.

Without breaking eye contact, Asterion stroked her, his smile widening as he found her slick entrance. Ariadne's heart pounded as he explored her, her eyes fluttering closed at the sensation that was overtaking her.

His other hand moved so he could caress the bare patch of skin at her side before cupping the soft curve of her breast. He was gentle as if he was worried about hurting her. Ariadne rested her hand over his and forced his fingers to squeeze her tighter.

Asterion increased the pressure of his grip on her breast until she moaned. His lips found the curve of her spine, kissing and nipping as his hands worked her. He pushed a finger inside of her, making her shudder hard against him.

"You are killing me," Ariadne groaned.

"You can tell me stop at any time," he reminded her as he thrust his finger in again.

"Don't you dare." He teased her nipple through the thin fabric of her dress until she felt the pressure of her orgasm explode through the base of her spine and rush painfully through her. Her cries were drowned out by the noise of the arena, but she didn't care who heard her.

Asterion loosened his grip on her, but still gently massaging her sensitive breast. She whimpered as he slowly moved his finger from her. She had never had someone, lover or contract, make her come so quickly.

Ariadne could hardly breathe as she watched him study the glisten of her on his finger before putting it to his mouth. Heat seemed to radiate from him. She swiveled in his lap, so she had her legs on either side of him.

"Take me somewhere or take me here, I don't care," she said, gripping his strong face in her hands.

The feral glow in his eyes was back, and his arms came around her as he stood. With impressive strength, he lifted her over one shoulder and made for the door.

Ariadne bit back an unexpected laugh. He was acting like a caveman, and she *loved* it. She should have rebelled years ago.

6

Asterion held tightly to the woman in his arms, the creature roaring to drop her to the ground and take her.

He could smell her arousal, taste it on his tongue, and he wanted more. He needed to plunge deep inside of her, make her scream his name until she wanted no one else but him.

"Boss! What are you doing?" Theseus and another guard were outside the door and looked worried.

"I'll be back when I'm done," Asterion said gruffly.

"It's a Labyrinth night, where are you going?"

"Somewhere you're not invited," the woman over his shoulder replied and then yelped as Asterion smacked her on the ass.

"Don't be cheeky. Theseus, you can officiate, I know you've been waiting to, so now's your big chance."

Asterion could see their confusion. He'd never acted this way with a woman before, but damn, it felt good to let the beast out a little. To do something impulsive, and that wasn't on a fucking schedule.

Asterion's apartment was located on a private floor on a level between the arena and the club. He didn't want to wait for the elevator, so he shoved the door open to the stairs and took them two at a time.

"I can walk, you know," Kassandra said from behind him.

"You aren't going anywhere," Asterion replied, pinning her legs across his chest with one arm, while the other reached out to swipe his security pass and open the door to his apartment.

Only when the door was shut behind him did he lower her back to her feet.

"This place is amazing," she said as she studied the ancient weaponry and sculptures he had on display. He guided her past the plush lounges and fireplace burning in its bed of white crystals until she stepped into his bedroom.

Compared to the rest of his apartment, his bedroom was plain with nothing but a king-size carved bed of black ebony and a door that led to a walk-in wardrobe and his bathroom.

Asterion wrapped an arm around her from behind, his hand stroking her fluttering pulse, causing her breathing to become shallow.

"You still have time to say no," he said, even though he was struggling to keep a grip on his own desires.

"Why do you keep saying that? Are you planning on hurting me?" she asked softly. He shifted so she could see his face, how serious he was.

"I'd never hurt you, sweetness. *Never*. I want you to know that what I said before still stands. If you want me to stop, I will."

Kassandra turned, her big stormy eyes full of desire as she stretched up on tiptoes until her lips were almost touching his.

"Asterion, I don't want you to stop. Tonight is stolen, so let me enjoy it," she said.

He wanted to ask her what she meant by that, but she reached up and pulled the dress straps from her shoulders. The soft fabric slithered down her body and landed on the floor, leaving her standing naked except for the tall black heels on her feet.

"Sweet fucking Aphrodite, you don't do slow," he breathed. Her beautiful face tilted.

"Do you want me to?" she asked. Her hands were already pulling off Asterion's jacket and tie.

"Absolutely not." Asterion stilled as she unbuttoned his shirt and ran her hands down the fine black hairs on his chest, nails gently scraping his scars and muscles until they unclipped his belt.

"You like taking the lead, don't you?" he said, his hands resting over hers to stop her.

"Can you blame me after what you just did to me?" she replied. Asterion could still feel her warm and wet under his fingers, and he wanted more.

"I was trying to act gentlemanly, but if you insist, get on the bed. Now."

Kassandra kicked off her heels, but instead of lying down on her back, she climbed across his bed on all fours. He grew so hard it hurt.

Who was this fucking woman?

If he didn't know the Lord of the Underworld personally, he would've thought she'd been crafted by Hades himself to torment the fuck out of him. He got rid of his shoes and unbuttoned his pants.

Asterion wanted to get underneath her, feast on the perfect piece of wetness between her legs, but he was too far gone. He needed to be inside of her like he needed to breathe.

She sighed with pleasure as he settled behind her, his hands exploring her warm skin, dipping underneath her to cup her soft breasts. He would put aside some time for them later.

He traced fingers over the faded scars over her back, and through his lust, he recognized one or two that had been made by a blade. He would find out the stories behind those later too, and if the person who made them were still living, he'd rip their throats out.

He stroked her low, rubbing her clit in slow pressured circles until she squirmed back against him.

"Stop teasing me," she begged. Asterion gripped her hips and nudged her entrance. He didn't want to hurt her by being too hasty, but as soon as the tip of his dick was inside of her, she pushed backward, forcing him into her hot core so quickly he cursed.

Asterion leaned down so he could kiss her shoulders as he began to move inside of her. Everything about her seemed designed to make him want more of her.

She gripped the black bed sheets, making inarticulate cries of pleasure as he drove into her.

She dipped down to her forearms, her gorgeous ass lifting so he could go deeper. She reached back and grabbed his thigh, holding so tightly that her ring and nails scratched him hard enough to draw a faint line of blood.

He gripped the mass of curls at the back of her head, holding her in place as he lost all thoughts except taking what she offered.

There was nothing gentle or sweet about it. It was animalistic with the reckless, violent need for more, for release.

She screamed his name as she came, her wet sheath squeezing him tight enough for him to cry out and thrust harder. He bit into her shoulder as his own orgasm rushed out of him, hot and urgent.

They collapsed into a heap, Asterion still inside of her as he held her. He didn't know if he was shaking or if they both were, but he clung to her as if she would disappear into a mist and be gone, a beautiful illusion made by the creature inside of him.

"Fucking hell," she said, her breasts rising with her rapid breath.

"I didn't hurt you, did I?" he asked, worrying about how rough he'd been with her. He brushed his thumb over the red mark where he'd bitten her.

"No, of course not," she reassured him, turning her head so she could kiss him. There was a tenderness in it that seemed out of place to the intensity of their lovemaking. "I think I might have caused more damage to you."

Asterion looked down at the marks on his legs and chuckled. "Only a scratch, sweetness. Nothing to worry about."

"Good," she said, kissing him and catching his groan as she shifted so that he slipped free of her.

"Where do you think you are going?" Asterion asked, hand brushing against her breast. The smile she gave him was disheveled and beautiful.

"Hold that thought, big guy. I need to use your bathroom," she said. He released her only so he could watch her lovely naked body walk to the ensuite.

Asterion stretched out onto his stomach, heart still pounding. He was going to enjoy making her scream his name many more times that night. His eyes were growing heavy, but he forced them back open.

He wasn't *that* exhausted. Nevertheless, his limbs were growing sluggish by the second.

The bathroom door opened, and Kassandra was no longer the teasing beauty she'd been all night.

The darkness inside of her that he'd only glimpsed now filled her eyes with violent intent.

"Kass, what's wrong..." Asterion managed before his tongue and lips went numb.

She walked back towards the bed, unclipping the bracelet from her wrist and wrapping it around her hands like a golden rope.

He tried to move, but his body was frozen, limbs paralyzed even as his mind fought what was happening.

"I don't want to do this, but I don't have a choice anymore. I really wish we could've met in another lifetime, Asterion," his dream girl said as she settled behind him, wrapping the garrote around his neck and tightening her grip.

His mind was screaming with confusion and betrayal, but Asterion could do nothing as she choked the air from his body, and his vision went dark.

7

Ariadne held on until the sharp wires cut her palms, and a drop of blood splashed onto the bedsheet. She finally let go when Asterion stopped breathing for a full minute.

She carefully recoiled the bracelet around her wrist and bit down an unexpected sob. The cold sense of justice that she always felt after a hit was nowhere to be found.

She pulled the black satin sheet around Asterion so he would look as if he was asleep if anyone came to check on him.

Unable to fight the urge, she brushed her fingers through the waves of dark, sun-streaked hair.

"I am sorry," Ariadne whispered. Something long forgotten and buried inside of her ached as she stared at him.

Pull yourself together.

She hadn't been upset after a kill since she was sixteen. She pushed that deep and painful memory down as fast as it surfaced.

Beside her, Asterion's body seemed to shiver like heat waves on a hot road.

There is no way he could still be alive.

The waves shimmered again, and his face began to transform.

"What the fuck is happening?" she said as she watched in horror. Horns grew out of the side of his head, and silky black fur burst out from his face. It happened so quickly she couldn't believe what she was seeing.

One moment, Asterion was a handsome man, the next, there was a bull's head sitting on his broad shoulders. His whole body seemed to have grown bigger during the transformation. He was at least a foot taller and broader, and Nikos's words rattled through Ariadne.

Did you ever stop to think that the gods weren't the only freaks that crawled out of the shadows the day Greece fell?

He'd called Asterion the Minotaur, and she thought it had been a joke.

It suddenly made sense why he was friends with the likes of Hades. Adrenaline and fear swamped her as she realized why Pithos had wanted Asterion dead.

They said they were monster killers, but she never thought she meant *actual* monsters.

Get your fucking ass moving, or you're a dead woman.

Ariadne grabbed the dress off the floor and pulled it over her head. It was too obvious in a crowd, so she pulled on Asterion's black shirt around her like a jacket.

Fishing around in his trouser pockets, she cleared the cash out of his wallet and grabbed his swipe card. She needed to get out of the building before Theseus, or anyone else came to find their boss.

She took one last look at the Minotaur in the bed before hurrying out through the apartment.

Ariadne plastered on the satisfied but self-conscious smile of someone doing the walk of shame, and opened the apartment door.

There wasn't anyone around, so she swiped Asterion's card and got into the private lift.

'Club' was written in gold next to a red button, so she pressed it and hoped it didn't open near the dance floor.

By sheer dumb luck, it opened in a foyer that received the deliveries, a space that led into the kitchen and the dock.

Gripping her skirts and hoping there wasn't any broken glass on the street, she slipped out of the back dock, hiding between delivery vans, and ran out into the wet alleyway. She jogged two blocks, ignoring the glances of other partygoers and hailed a taxi.

As soon as Ariadne had locked her apartment door in Hellas, she raced to the bathroom and threw up everything her stomach held.

"Get clean, pack a bag," she told her makeup smeared reflection.

She pulled off her clothes and climbed into the shower. It was cold, as always, but she felt like she deserved it as she scrubbed blood and Asterion's scent off her skin.

She was trained not to feel, and she was the best killer because she never felt guilt over what she did, never shed a tear for the horrible people she took down. Asterion hadn't been horrible, not to her.

You just murdered the first man you ever liked. Well done, Spindle, well done.

Her brain caught up to the fact she'd also just fucked a magical creature, as she bent over trying to get enough air in her lungs.

Not just any creature either, the Minotaur himself.

She knew the fairytale of a king in Crete who had a Minotaur in the Labyrinth under his palace. Minos had told it to her growing up because he liked to boast that his father had named him after that king.

The palace in Knossos was now rubble, but the story never mentioned the fate of the creature that had been locked beneath it. Ariadne thought it had been a theme for the club, not a nod to Asterion's true nature.

You are so screwed.

Ariadne needed to get out of Styx because as soon as his body was found, they'd be hunting the woman responsible. Theseus was too smart and suspicious, and he knew exactly what she looked like.

Ariadne was shoving some clothes into a backpack when the phone given to her by Pithos began to ring.

"Is the monster dead, Spindle?" the digital voice demanded.

"Yes, no thanks to you fucking bastards. You sent me in there thinking Asterion was a club owner, not a fucking magical creature."

"If you had known the truth, you would have never agreed to take the contract."

"Of course not! I'm about to have Hades fucking Acheron and his posse up my ass because of this. You've screwed me," Ariadne hissed.

"If reports are correct, we aren't the only ones that screwed you tonight."

"Are you slut-shaming me right now? You've no right to question my methods, only pay me my fucking money."

"When we have proof of death, the money will be yours." The line went dead, leaving Ariadne shaking with fury.

Her savings weren't enough to get her out of the country, but they were enough to get out of Styx.

She never trusted Minos, so she'd always kept whatever money he gave her hidden in her apartment.

Ariadne was shoving the small cash box into her backpack when the phone rang again.

"You're playing a very dangerous game, Spindle," Pithos said.

"No shit, I just killed Asterion Dys."

"No, you didn't."

"Don't insult me or try to get out of paying me. I'm a professional. I checked Asterion's breathing myself. He's *dead*," said Ariadne angrily.

"Our inside source says that he's damaged but still alive."

"Then they are lying. It's not possible." Ariadne looked at her sliced up palms. No one could've lived through that.

Not unless you are friends with the God of the Underworld.

"Your contract isn't completed. You won't get a single drachmae from us. I suggest you start running, Spindle. The Minotaur isn't known for his forgiveness."

The line went dead, and Ariadne threw the phone against the wall, sending glass and metal flying.

She picked up her backpack, stuffed the jar of Lia's ashes into it, and ran for her life.

8

Time didn't mean a thing inside the Labyrinth. The tunnels smelled of stone, blood, and rotting flesh. The only light that ever reached him was the torches that the sacrifices and the heroes carried, right up until they went mad with fear and pain.

Asterion could still feel the darkness, that endless midnight pit that had been his entire life.

The ground had trembled, and he'd thought that finally, his agony would be over, that the palace above him would come down.

But it didn't. The palace broke apart and sealed the doors to the Labyrinth, left to be forgotten by the world above.

A creature born of magic, Asterion didn't die locked deep in the darkness.

He'd endured, until the day that the Lord of the Underworld found him in the womb of the earth and brought him into the light above.

Those pale, silver eyes of the Lord of Death were looking down at him now with the same expression, black brows drawn together like angry crows' wings.

"Get up, Asterion. You're not going to die today," Hades commanded.

"What..." Asterion winced as he touched the raw pain in his throat.

"Someone tried to kill you. A beautiful woman, if your bodyguard is to be believed." Hades sat back in a chair; his black suit impeccable even at the late hour.

"Kassandra," Asterion replied and tried to sit up. "Did I die?"

"Almost. Vin called me as soon as he couldn't wake you. Smart man."

"Remind me to give him a raise." Asterion rubbed at his neck again, and the black fur and horns melted away to his human form.

"It was lucky for you Thanatos was on this side of town. Otherwise, I'd be getting ready to burn your body. Should I be concerned that the strongest creature I've ever known has almost been killed by a woman? I don't suppose you'd know why?" Hades asked.

"No, but I don't think it was personal."

It was slowly coming back to him. The look on her face when she stepped out of the bathroom. The fear and regret in her eyes.

I don't want to do this, but I don't have a choice anymore.

"A hit? I thought no one would be stupid enough to try after so long."

"Me neither. She was a professional. Drugged me first so I couldn't stop her."

Hades steepled his fingers thoughtfully. "You know there's only one person in Styx that would have anyone that professional on his payroll."

"You don't think Minos was behind this?"

"He's a greedy little maggot, Asterion. If someone offered him enough money, he'd be willing to risk the life of one of his precious priestesses to do the job. Not *any* priestess either. Strangulation is the MO of his favorite."

Asterion searched his memory. He preferred to do his own dirty work, but Minos was a player in Styx, so their paths had crossed. He'd even attended a Labyrinth night, and while he hadn't made any bets, he'd been interested in the course.

Strangulation and the gleam of gold in his memory made his pulse race.

"The Spindle. Damn, they must've paid Minos a gold mine to convince him to let her loose," said Asterion. Rage, frustration, and confusion ran through him.

"She must've been quite something to fool you," Hades commented, reading him far too easily.

"She was. The little minx got me good." Asterion wasn't too proud to admit it even though he felt like he'd got the ass-kicking of his life.

He should've realized she was too good to be true.

"Don't look so glum. The assassin has a soft spot for you."

"She choked the shit out of me. I don't think that counts as a soft spot."

"She slept with you first, even though she didn't have to. Also, her task must've upset her because I can sense the echoes of her grief in the bathroom."

Asterion ran a hand through his hair. "She said she didn't have a choice."

"Minos keeps a tight leash on his priestesses. If he were willing to sacrifice the Spindle just to see you dead, he would've made her afraid enough to go through with it. I've followed her career. She doesn't make mistakes like this."

Hades got to his feet and buttoned his suit jacket. "Would you like me or one of the triplets to handle this?"

The triplets, Thanatos, Charon, and Erebus, would be too noticeable and would likely scare away not only his would-be assassin but whoever had hired her.

"No, keep the inner circle out of it for now. I don't want them getting any unnecessary attention. I'll find out who put out the contract and make them regret it. Maybe let Medusa know in case they are targeting our Court."

Asterion struggled, but he managed to get to his feet and bow. "Thank you, Hades. Please let Thanatos know I owe him a favor. The bastard will love that."

"I protect my own. You know that. Update me on any progress you make, nephew," Hades said, and then he was simply gone.

Asterion sat down on the bed, unable to stand up straight. He had been duped, like some horny teenager with a crush on a pretty girl.

His nose tingled with a scent he knew well. Moving aside the sheet, he found a single drop of blood where it had splashed. He put his nose down to hover over it and inhaled feminine perfume, sex, and the unique signature that her blood gave off.

The growl of a wounded, enraged creature roiled up through Asterion.

"I'm coming for you, Spindle."

THE TEMPLE WAS USED to having Greece's richest walk through their polished halls, but when Asterion and his two bodyguards arrived four hours later, even the fully trained assassins disappeared into the shadows.

Minos Karros turned in surprise and went pale as they filled his office doorway.

"Mr. Dys, this is an unexpected surprise," Minos said.

"Why? Because you sent your pretty priestess to kill me last night?" Asterion demanded.

"Excuse me?"

Asterion grabbed him from the opposite side of the table and dragged him across it. "You had better start talking, you pathetic bastard or I'm going to tear you apart myself."

"I haven't sent anyone after you! I swear it. What would I have to gain?" Minos sputtered.

"Try harder, Minos. I have this pretty necklace this morning, thanks to your Spindle."

Asterion pulled down the collar of his shirt to reveal the red marks that were slowly healing.

"That's impossible. Spindle would never kill anyone that she wasn't ordered to, and I'd never be suicidal enough to take a contract with your name on it. Hades and his Court are untouchable, and you know it," stammered Minos.

"Well, she got orders from someone because it was her golden braid choking the life out of me last night."

"If she's taken a job without my approval, I'll kill her myself. I can't have this kind of rebellion in my Temple. I'll find her and bring her in for questioning."

Asterion could smell the fear on him, saw the real confusion in the man's eyes.

Damn it.

Asterion let him go with a hard shove.

"Do what you have to do, but I'm not going to stop hunting her. If you find her before me and don't hand her over, I'll burn this Temple of yours to the fucking ground."

"I won't be protecting her if she's betrayed me. We are men of business, so let's make a deal. *If* you find her before I do and keep her alive for me once you're done questioning her, I'll give you a million drachmae," Minos said.

"Why?"

"I'll need to make an example of her to ensure this doesn't happen again. You won't have to worry, Dys, I'll make Ariadne's death a slow and painful one."

There was a sick gleam of violent pleasure in Minos's eyes, the kind that told Asterion he liked torture.

Asterion kept his face neutral as he gave a sharp nod. He left the room, knowing if he did find Ariadne, he would never hand her over to Minos Karros.

"We have a location on her apartment," Theseus said once they were in the privacy of Asterion's car.

"Good, we need to go through it before that bastard gets anywhere near it."

The address was located in Hellas on one of the better streets. The apartment block was old Corinthian, but it didn't look as if it was about to drop on their heads, which was more than he could say for the rest of the district's buildings.

Two hundred drachmae was the going rate for the landlord to give up the keys to Ariadne's room.

"I knew she was too pretty not to be trouble." The old woman clucked her tongue and handed over the key.

"Keep a lookout," Asterion instructed Theseus once they found the right door.

Some strange protective instincts had risen up, and Asterion didn't want anyone else looking through Ariadne's things. He blamed it on the reaction the creature inside of him had to her.

It didn't care Ariadne tried to kill him. If anything, that kind of ruthlessness made the Bull want her more.

The contents of the apartment were sparse. There was a shattered phone on the floor that Asterion pocketed, and the bedroom had a new, elegant bed that seemed out of place in its rundown setting.

The red dress she had worn the previous night was on the floor in the bathroom. He picked it up and sniffed it. Her scent was mixed with his, as well as her blood and a lingering sweat of fear. She hadn't been afraid when they had been together, but she had been after.

"What did you get yourself into, Spindle?" Asterion searched through her drawers, knowing that she wouldn't be stupid enough to leave anything behind that could be traced. That was why leaving the phone had him suspicious.

"There's nothing," Asterion said as he joined Theseus, and they headed outside.

"If Spindle is meant to be Minos's best hitter, I wonder why she's holed up in a rat's nest like this?" Theseus asked, looking around the street.

"She's hiding or saving whatever money she gets from the hits for something," answered Asterion.

Few would willingly choose to live in Hellas, not when they could be in a mansion like the Temple. One more thing he'd ask Ariadne when he found her.

A food van across the street caught his eye with a painted sign announcing it as 'Dimmi's Gourmet Kebabs.' A pretty woman was standing with her hands on her hips and glaring at him.

"Give me a minute. You want anything?" Asterion asked.

"Not without following it up with a tetanus shot," said Theseus, looking at the food van suspiciously.

It was bright pink and black and had a funky vibe that parts of Hellas's underground art scene were famous for.

"What can I get you?" the woman asked. Asterion took stock of her menu.

"A vegetarian kebab, no cheese," he said and then passed her an extra fifty drachmae, "and I'm after some information."

"What makes you think I can help?"

"Maybe you can't. I'm looking for a girl."

"Honey, aren't we all?" she said as she made the kebab with deft movements.

"Her name is Ariadne. Black hair, grey-blue eyes."

"Body like Aphrodite?"

"That's the one," Asterion said with a smile.

The woman stopped making the kebab. "You better not be that stalker *malakas* that keeps posting weird notes in her mailbox."

"Do I look like the type of person to do that? I had a date with her last night. We were meant to meet up today, but she never showed," lied Asterion. He filed away the information about the stalker.

"She's a busy girl. Has an imposing boss or father from what I can tell. He keeps her scared and running about. She doesn't sleep enough. I'm surprised she had a date." She looked him over. "I suppose you aren't bad looking...for a man." She handed over his kebab.

"Thank you. I don't suppose if I left you a phone number that you'd give me a call when you see Ariadne next?"

"Ha! If she wants to find you for another date, she'll call you herself. I'm not going to spy for you, even if you look like you can afford me."

"Fair enough," Asterion said.

"If you talk to her before I do, tell her you're not the first person that's come looking for her today. I'm worried. I don't like gangster types in my neighborhood, especially when they are asking about my friends."

"Thanks, Dimmi, I'll find her and let her know."

Once he was back across the street, Asterion told Theseus about what he'd found out.

"If Minos didn't give her the contract, maybe these 'gangster types' did," said Theseus thoughtfully.

"I haven't pissed any of the gangs off. Half the fuckers owe me money and couldn't afford the likes of Minos's girls."

Asterion bit into his surprisingly good kebab. His throat was still sore but was healing quickly, thanks to the magic inside of him. He passed the smashed phone to Theseus.

"Get someone to look at this. I want everything off it. It's the only lead we have."

Theseus pocketed the phone and opened the back door for Asterion. "You sure have a complicated taste in women, boss."

"Just find her and stop busting my balls," commanded Asterion.

He needed to get to her before Minos, and whoever else was chasing her did.

If anyone was going to kill her, it was going to be him, and he was going to get his answers one way or another.

9

The girl sucked on a loose tooth as she stared at the colors of gelato stretched out before her. Ariadne waited patiently with a small plastic cup in her hand.

"You want to know which one is my favorite?" she asked. The girl nodded solemnly. "Pineapple. It's really good on a hot day like this."

"Just hurry up and pick something!" the girl's mother demanded irritably. Ariadne didn't pay her any attention.

A little hand stretched out and tapped the glass in front of the swirl of pale yellow.

"You won't regret it," Ariadne assured her as she gave the girl the gelato and took the three drachmae from her mother.

Ariadne took a moment to scan the stretch of beach for anyone suspicious before admiring the perfect blue water in front of her.

It was another bright summer day in Isthmia. She'd always dreamed of being able to hang out on a beach for as long as she liked, eat too much gelato and get sunburned.

Isthmia was still too close to Styx for her mental comfort, but it was a good place to pretend to be someone else until she got enough money to get out of Greece. She figured Minos would think she'd already tried to leave and wouldn't be looking so close to Styx.

Hiding in plain sight was what Ariadne was good at, and after six weeks and no sign of anyone on her tail, she managed to relax the smallest fraction.

She checked the papers, but there was no report of Asterion's death. She hadn't wanted to believe it when Pithos had told her that she'd failed.

A big part of her told her she was a fucking idiot for being even a little relieved that he was still alive.

Minos would kill her horribly, but if she had to choose between him and Asterion, she'd pick Minos.

The look on Asterion's face when he realized she was going to kill him wasn't the one that kept her awake at night. It was that gentle, teasing expression after their intense tumble in the sheets that really haunted her.

Ariadne didn't think anyone would ever look at her like that. She'd never see it again because there would be no way Asterion would ever let her live long enough.

Ariadne had spent the first few hours after her failed assassination laying false trails of bus and train tickets, and hotel bookings all over Greece.

Whoever was clever enough to follow her would be bamboozled for a few days. That had been more than enough time for her to slip unnoticed out of Styx and walk the ten kilometers to Isthmia in the dead of night.

She had stayed two nights at a rundown hotel before convincing Marina, the elderly owner, to let her live there rent-free if she agreed to clean the rooms every day.

Ariadne didn't know how long her savings were going to last, and taking some cash jobs, like working at a beachside bar at night and the gelato store in the day, made her presence seem legitimate and helped her blend in with the locals.

Four hours later, the sun had almost set over the water. Ariadne was walking to her bar job when a tingle along her spine made her pause and check over her shoulder.

A sunburned English couple was walking hand in hand, and a few locals were sitting on the stretch of beach gutting the fish they'd caught that day. Everything seemed calm.

That serenity didn't stop her from telling the bar owner, Adoni, that she had an upset stomach and wouldn't be able to work that night.

"Too much sun and not enough water will do that," Adoni said with a shake of her head. It wasn't busy, so Adoni made her take two stomach tablets and waved her out the door.

Ariadne made it three streets from the bar before she slipped off her cork wedge sandals and carried them lightly in her hand.

When the first man stepped on the street in front of her, she was already swinging the shoes, hitting him first in the groin and then in the face as he fell.

The second rushed her from behind, his heavy footfalls giving him away and allowing her enough time to sidestep him at the last moment and trip him up.

Ariadne landed a hard blow at the back of his neck to keep him down long enough for her to run.

She didn't stop to think who the men belonged to or how many more might be hiding in the streets. She needed to get to the hotel and get out of Isthmia.

Checking the streets around the hotel, Ariadne slipped down a small path through the gardens.

After making sure no one was in the car park, she unlocked the door to her room. Heavy arms came around her, and she lashed out with all the training Minos had instilled in her since she was eight years old.

Her assailant was big, but she was fast, and she broke his bear hug with a sharp elbow to his kidneys and a follow-up blow to his sternum that left him paralyzed on the carpet, wheezing to try to get air back into his lungs.

The lights still off, Ariadne looked out the curtains scanning for more attackers. Two more men were heading to the front door, so she grabbed the backpack from under her bed and hurried into the bathroom and locked the door.

She shoved her backpack through the window before climbing out after it and dropping straight into the waiting arms of Asterion Dys.

"Hello, little Spindle," he said, his golden eyes glowing with a feral light. His arms held her tightly to his chest.

Enclosed in his strength, all the fight left her. There was no way she could defeat the Minotaur in a fistfight, and he'd probably kill her in the process.

"I don't suppose you'll let me explain myself before you kill me?" she asked, knowing how lame she sounded.

Ariadne could feel the anger radiating from him, but he didn't reply as he carried her out of the garden.

"Boss, she's -" one man said before he spotted what Asterion was carrying.

"Out of the way," he commanded, and the man moved.

Someone turned the light on in her hotel room to reveal Theseus trying to climb off the floor.

"You bitch-" he wheezed breathlessly.

"Nice to see you too," Ariadne said with a sweet smile.

"Get out, all of you." Asterion hadn't put her down, and she was starting to think he'd crush her to death.

"I don't think that's a good idea. Last time I left you alone with her, she almost killed you," said Theseus, and Ariadne saw the concern under the arrogance.

"The keyword in that sentence is *almost*," she couldn't resist pointing out, because her fear always made her say stupid things.

"Let me do it. I can put a bullet in her head right now-"

Asterion's grip tightened even further, making her bite down a gasp as her ribs groaned. "I told you to get out."

Theseus didn't question him further but slammed the door behind him.

Asterion finally placed her down on the bed, and Ariadne tried not to let her fear show. He didn't take his eyes from her face as he dragged a chair over from the small plastic table and sat down opposite her.

Ariadne folded her sweaty hands in her lap, realizing too late that she was wearing the black silk shirt she'd taken from him the night she'd fled Styx.

She had been using it as a summer jacket, seeing how she'd left most of her clothes back in her shitty apartment in Hellas.

Asterion looked at it, with his eyes now holding confusion as well as anger.

You are going to die, Spindle, look how mad he is at you.
"Is that my shirt?" he asked gruffly.
"Yes."
"A trophy?"
"A necessity. I didn't have time to pack properly when I ran for my life. The fabric is nice," she said, feeling like an idiot.
"I know. It's silk."
Ariadne pulled it off and offered it to him. He took it, his eyes raking over the bare skin of her shoulders. Her time wearing summer dresses had left her with tan lines for the first time in her life.
It was a good life while it lasted.
Asterion leaned back in the chair, folding the shirt on his lap. "Do I need to tell you not to attack me?"
"No, I know I'm screwed. Honestly, I thought it would be Minos who got to me first."
"I made sure he didn't."
"Figures. You did strike me as the kind of man that liked to do his own killing."
"Who said I've decided to kill you, Ariadne?" Asterion asked.
Oh, gods, he knows my name, which can only mean one thing.
"You're going to hand me over to Minos to kill me after you're done torturing me." Ariadne let out a long sigh. "I hope he's paying you well."
"A million drachmae."
"So much for fatherly love."
"I wouldn't know, my father was a prick. He was a Minos too. Maybe it comes with the name," Asterion said.
"We should share shit father stories over a bottle of wine sometime," Ariadne replied.
Asterion folded his arms and looked at her in silence for a long time. "You asked for a chance to explain yourself, so start explaining."

10

Six fucking weeks.

That's how long it had taken Asterion to find the woman sitting in front of him.

Smelling like the sea and sugar, dressed in a blue sundress with her hair out in a tumbling mass of darkness, she was the opposite of the ultra-polished woman he'd met at the Labyrinth.

The smart mouth was still the same, and he hated how much he wanted to bury his face in her wild hair and breathe her in. It was his scent combined with hers that had been her downfall.

Frustrated that he hadn't been able to find her through the rest of his contacts in Greece, Asterion had begun the search from the beginning until he'd found traffic camera footage of a woman walking out of Styx on the night of his failed murder attempt. He'd grabbed a few of his men and headed to Isthmia.

For a small town, Ariadne blended in remarkably well. After three days, Asterion had been ready to give up when the salty breeze had carried his own scent back to him. There she was, scooping gelato and talking to the tourists as if she'd been living there her entire life.

He'd been more than a little surprised to see her wearing his shirt with the sleeves rolled up her long arms.

The creature in him had preened with a possessive satisfaction, but the man was torn between wanting to kill her and kiss her with relief that he'd found her again.

Asterion wanted to show how impressed he was that she'd dropped three of his best men as if they were amateur thugs.

Over the past six weeks, he thought he'd be able to kill her or order his men do it, but as soon as he caught her, he didn't want to let her go, let alone allow one of his men to interrogate her.

Sitting in front of him now, the notorious Spindle could barely look him in the eye. He could smell the fear in her sweat, but outwardly, she seemed to calmly accept whatever horrible punishment and death he'd subject her to.

What in all the hells did Minos do to this girl?

"I guess by now you know what Minos and the Temple really is," Ariadne began.

"I have for a while. Hades figured out that you must've been one of Minos's girls. I didn't expect the High Priestess herself. I suppose I should be flattered."

"Minos didn't order the hit."

"I know that too. You must've been offered something more than money to want to cross Minos," Asterion said. That had been the one thing he couldn't figure out.

"Minos *owns* me. Do you think any of the Temple girls are there because of his charity? From the moment he takes you in, he starts an account and keeps track of every drachmae he spends on your upbringing. The contracts we complete mean a percentage of that debt gets paid off. He tells us that once our debt is cleared, we can leave, take our contracts if we still want to be in the life. Do you think that he'd let someone like me pay that debt off when he controls the money?"

Ariadne's stormy blue eyes were filled with a cold fury.

"The girls that fuck up, can't do the job or will never be able to pay off the debt, get given to Madame Zera. No matter how old they are. Minos once sent her a ten-year-old. You know who Zera is?"

Asterion nodded, not trusting himself to say anything. He had no idea that the brothel owner was trafficking children and was sure Hades didn't either.

He was going to kill so many people by the time this business was done.

"Madame Zera gets them if the girls are lucky and Minos can still make a profit off the sale. Those he can't, he gets more creative with his transactions. That's who Minos is, so maybe you can understand why I would consider doing something epically fucking stupid like trying to kill you if it meant being free of him."

Ariadne swallowed hard and looked away from him, but he'd already seen the shadows of regret on her face.

"I got offered a contract by a group called Pithos. They offered me money, but they got me with information. Dirty shit on Minos, which would mean that even if I paid him off, he'd leave me alone to keep me quiet. They said that they were monster killers, and if I took care of theirs, they would take care of mine," Ariadne explained.

Asterion's anger surged. *Monster.* That fucking word made him see red every time.

Ariadne bit her lip. "I want you to know I had no idea who you really were. Are."

"So now you know you fucked a monster. Is that what has upset you? Not that you played me like a fucking drum, but you had *this* inside of you?" Asterion demanded as the change rippled over him.

The beast was loose, and his senses exploded. Ariadne didn't move, though he sensed her heart beating faster. He got into her space until she was forced to lie back on the bed.

He crouched over her, smelling her scent and his own that lingered on her skin, sensing the tremor that ran through her.

"That you're a magical creature isn't what has upset me, so you can stop trying to frighten me because it won't work," she said, her voice steady. She must've had a death wish because she reached up and ran her fingers over one of his soft furry ears.

Asterion was so surprised that the creature retreated in an instant, leaving his human form panting over Ariadne, her fingers still on his ear. She dropped her hand away.

He couldn't keep the snarl out of his voice. "You said you didn't want to kill me, and you did it anyway."

"*Almost* killed you," she corrected stubbornly.

"You're upset that you failed?"

"Upset that I couldn't treat you like another hit. I'm going to die anyway, so you might as well know that I went into the Labyrinth with a plan that didn't involve having sex with you."

"Why did you fuck me then?" he demanded, gripping the bed on either side over her.

"Because I actually liked your company. I gave you a wrong name, but the rest was me, and it was nice being able to talk to someone over a few drinks," Ariadne admitted and turned her head away, so she wasn't looking at him.

"Minos would've trained you to seduce men. You even fooled me. Not many people can do that. You could be saying all of this, so I'll spare your life."

Ariadne's laugh was sad and bitter as she turned back to face him. He could smell the salt in the tears that welled in her eyes.

"I'm not that stupid or naive. I know you're not going to spare my life. I fucked you because I *wanted* to, and then I killed you because I had to. It was all for nothing anyway. Pithos knew you weren't dead. I got nothing but a bag of clothes and the fucking Minotaur hunting me for my troubles."

"How did they know I wasn't dead?" Asterion demanded.

"You have a mole, big guy. Must have. It's the only answer I could come up with, but I couldn't find out who without exposing where I was hiding."

"This could be another lie to distract me from killing you." Asterion could sense a lie, smell it on people, and feel it in his bones. She wasn't lying, and he couldn't figure out if it made things easier or harder.

"Why would I lie? What could I gain? Fucking you was the only bonus I got out of this mess, so hand me over to Minos if you're going to and be done with it!" Ariadne exclaimed, glaring up at him. Her cheeks were red with anger and embarrassment, but she hadn't made a move to push him off her. His hands tightened on the bedsheets.

"I'll *never* give you to Minos Karros," hissed Asterion.

"You can't promise that. He'll have something on you, and you'll be forced to -"

"No, you're staying with me."

"Why?" She sounded so small and confused, and he hated that he was losing control of his anger toward her. He brushed a black lock of hair back from her forehead.

"Because I'm the one you wronged, so I get to decide how to punish you. Also, if what you say about the mole is true, you're my best evidence, so you've been granted a stay of execution, Spindle, until I get what I need from you."

"Don't call me that."

Asterion raised an eyebrow. "I just decided to spare your life, and you're going to argue about what I call you?"

"You just decided to *temporarily* spare my life, and I'd like you to call me Ariadne because I fucking hate being called Spindle. I'm a person, not a code word. Also, who knows what kind of punishment a man who owns a gladiator arena can think up? I might end up dying in some fucked up exotic way like having my nipples eaten off by scorpions," Ariadne argued before realizing what she had said and choked down a bubble of laughter.

"Stop that," Asterion commanded, trying to stop himself from smiling. "Absurd woman, as if I'd get scorpions to eat your nipples. They are the only part of you I don't feel wronged by."

Ariadne stopped laughing and stared up at him. "I'm sorry. Really. For everything."

"You're going to be. You will give me what information you have on Pithos and-" Asterion stilled and looked toward the hotel room door.

Ariadne hooked her arms and legs around him and rolled as bullets ripped through the mattress. They crashed to the floor, and the room exploded with gunfire.

11

Ariadne covered Asterion with her body, shielding his head with her arms.

"Are you insane!" he demanded as he pulled her off him and down to the floor.

"Are you? Minos doesn't use guns, so why are your guys firing at us?" Ariadne shouted.

"They aren't my guys. They must be with Pithos."

Asterion dragged her towards the room's small kitchenette. With a terrifying strength, he pulled the fridge down to use as a barrier.

"Is there another way out?" Asterion asked.

"Only the bathroom and your big ass isn't going to fit through the window. They have to reload at some point," said Ariadne as she reached for the handful of cheap chef knives that she'd bought two days before.

The gunfire went silent, and two men in black gear, kitted with helmets and Kevlar vests, stormed into the room.

Ariadne threw the terribly balanced knives, catching an assailant in the thigh and the other in his shoulder, forcing him to drop his handgun.

Asterion ripped the door off the fridge and slammed it hard into one man, sending him flying across the room.

The second man's head splattered as Asterion brought the door down on top of his helmet. Ariadne gagged but held onto her stomach contents as she relieved the bodies of their guns, a large hunting knife, and two extra bullet magazines that she shoved down the front of her bra.

"Should I ask why you're hiding them there?" Asterion said as he watched her.

Ariadne gestured to her blood-splattered sundress. "I have no pockets because of the patriarchy, so where else am I going to put them?"

Asterion grabbed her hand and maneuvered her behind him.

"Stay close," he said, his shoulders and biceps bulging as he hefted the door like a shield to protect her.

God damn, that's hot.

Ariadne shook her head at the inappropriateness of her mind.

"Where are we headed?" she asked.

"To the cars, so we can get out of here. We haven't finished our conversation yet, Ariadne, and I'm not about to let a few bullets get in the way."

"This is the only time I'm going to be okay with being your prisoner. Better you than Pithos," Ariadne said as she positioned herself close behind him.

"Don't get your hopes up. I'm still hoping to source some scorpions."

"Stop thinking about my nipples in the middle of a firefight."

Asterion's smile was lightning quick. "Make me. I'll draw their fire, and you shoot them when they give their location away."

Ariadne adjusted her grip on the handguns. "This is a shit plan, but I've got your back, big guy."

"Try not to fucking stab me in it this time."

They made for the hotel door, and Ariadne had taken two steps from under the awning before putting a bullet in the head of a shooter on the hotel roof behind them.

"Sneaky bastard," she muttered as another sniper began to take shots at them. Ariadne had another one down in seconds, the shadows under a nearby car giving his location away.

"Two o'clock!" Asterion said. Ariadne fired, and there was a groan from the ornamental garden. "Good shot."

The lights of an SUV flashed as it pulled up in front of them with

Theseus behind the wheel. "Asterion! This place is about to be swarmed. Get your ass in here. Leave the girl. She's not worth it."

"Not going to happen." Asterion dropped the bullet-riddled door and hooked an arm around Ariadne's waist as a flash grenade landed just feet from them.

"Down!" she shouted as their world exploded with light.

Ears ringing and eyes burning, Ariadne didn't have time to complain as Asterion lifted her up, shoved her inside the SUV, and pinned her across the backseat with his body.

"Drive, Theseus!" he shouted. Bullets smashed through the back windows as the car squealed out of the hotel carpark.

"You really do make an impression on everyone you meet, don't you?" Asterion said above her as he kept her pinned.

"What makes you think they were there for me? You're the one they want dead, handsome," she replied, wriggling slightly to stop the seat belt clips from digging into her hip. "They wouldn't have sent that many guys for little old me."

Asterion made a disbelieving sound at the back of his throat. "Little old you, my ass. I just watched you take down their snipers with headshots."

"Minos might find guns inelegant, but we were still trained to use them."

"I'm starting to see why you were his High Priestess," said Asterion.

"Careful, you're getting dangerously close to a complimenting your captive." Ariadne's breath caught as his hand curled gently around the back of her neck and tangled in her hair.

"Easy to do. You know it might soften me up if you start calling me master."

"I think we both know I'm not into soft," she said before her common sense could catch up.

Stop flirting with the man that's going to kill you. His grip on her hair tightened.

"You saved my life tonight," Asterion said.

"I don't suppose that makes us square enough for you to let me go?"

Asterion's deep chuckle rolled up his long body and through her core. "Not even close, little assassin."

"You should think about it. I'm not your enemy, and as soon as Minos knows you have me, he'll make your life hell until you give me back."

Asterion surprised her by brushing his lips feather-light over hers.

"Thank you for saving my life tonight, but I have no intention of giving you up."

Ariadne's hand went under the back of his shirt and touched his hot skin.

"You don't know what kind of war you're starting," she said sadly.

"Asterion, they've stopped following us," Theseus interrupted.

"We are too close to Styx, that's why."

Asterion shifted, and they both managed to untangle themselves and sit up. The lights of the city were getting closer, and fear licked up Ariadne's spine.

There was no way she'd be lucky enough to escape for a second time.

"Are we going to the Temple?" asked Theseus, his blue eyes icy cold as he stared at Ariadne in the rearview mirror.

"Head home. I haven't finished questioning her," Asterion instructed.

"Hope whatever intel she has is worth all of this shit," complained Theseus.

"Me too," Ariadne snapped as she searched around the back seat of the car.

"What are you looking for?" asked Asterion.

"A jacket or something to use as a cover," she replied.

"Why?"

"Because Minos has access to traffic camera feeds, and he'll be watching for your return to the city. If he sees me and you don't take me to him, he'll burn the Labyrinth to the ground or worse."

Ariadne found a black blazer that had fallen to the floor and wedged under the driver seat.

"Perfect."

Ariadne reached down the side of the front passenger seat, lifted the lever, and slid the chair forward enough that she had room to sit on the floor behind it.

"That looks uncomfortable," Asterion commented.

"It is, but it'll be worth it." Ariadne pulled the blazer over her and kept her head down.

A minute later, Asterion's foot moved to touch hers, a small sign of solidarity that she didn't want to think too hard about.

She couldn't afford to get comfortable enough to hope her end wasn't going to be messy, even if Asterion's mouth said one thing and his actions said another.

Trusting him would be trusting another man, and that was something she was too smart ever to do again.

~

ONCE THEY WERE in the cover of the underground car park, Asterion lifted the blazer off his distressed damsel.

Ariadne looked fragile and vulnerable, covered in blood and wild-haired. It was just another thing that made her so deadly. He had suspected, but tonight he'd seen firsthand that Ariadne was about as sweet and innocent as a switchblade.

"Come, little assassin," he said, offering her a hand up. She took it and wriggled out of the tiny space.

"Vin recovered her bag, said there's a laptop you might want a look at," Theseus said, looking up from the message on his phone. "I can take her from here, boss. I'll put her in one of the holding cells under the arena."

Asterion made a point of not looking at Ariadne.

"She'll stay in the apartment's guest room where I can keep an eye on her. Don't argue with me. From what I witnessed tonight, she'll be out of one of the cells within an hour and stolen my favorite car."

"I wouldn't have taken the Maserati, I swear. The Ferrari would have been another matter," said Ariadne.

"We wouldn't leave her without guards, Asterion," Theseus argued over her.

"Oh yeah? Like the three that she brought down tonight with a pair of girlie shoes? I'm in half a mind to throw you all back into the Pit for training because clearly, you've let yourselves go."

Asterion took Ariadne by the arm, and they headed for the elevator. "Tell Vin to put the laptop in the apartment, and I'll be there shortly."

"He really doesn't like me, does he?" Ariadne said once the elevator doors had closed.

"You are intimidating and competent and made them all look bad the night you *almost* killed me. I swear I'm never going to get laid again because they'll be too worried about letting another woman near me."

"I suppose I should be sorry about that too," Ariadne replied solemnly. It was a tone that didn't match the grin that said she wasn't sorry at all that he was now reduced to a life of celibacy.

Asterion let go of her arm and leaned back against the cold steel wall, putting space between them.

"How did you know the Maserati was my favorite?"

"Are you kidding me? Even my dick gets hard when I look at that thing."

"Quite a feat considering I'm intimately acquainted with your anatomy, and you lack the necessary equipment."

Ariadne tried to cover the color flaring up her neck as she pushed a hand through her tangled mane and grimaced.

"Don't suppose you'll let this prisoner have a shower."

"That's a given. I don't want to be smelling unwashed assassin all night."

The creature inside of him did; the combination of feminine sweat, blood, endorphins, and adrenaline made it want to roll in her like a clover patch.

That's why you don't get a say when it comes to her.

Ariadne gave his dirty, blood-splattered appearance a long glance. "You're not smelling so hot either, big guy."

The elevator doors opened to reveal Vin, arms folded and face like a thundercloud.

"You're seriously going to let her stay here with you?" he demanded. He was glaring at Ariadne like he would happily snap her neck. Asterion stepped between them.

"She's cooperating, and I don't trust any of you hotheads with guarding her. Where's the laptop?"

"On the table. She's put a password on it. Want me to get it out of her?"

Ariadne's grin widened as she sized Vin up. It was a look that said, 'I'd like to see you try.'

The woman wasn't the least bit bothered by the man twice her size in front of her. Asterion hadn't seen *anyone* she was afraid of.

He didn't want to imagine what she and Hades would be like in the same room.

"Asterion only needs to ask me nicely, and I'll give him whatever he wants," Ariadne said, fluttering her eyelashes. Vin's hands tightened into fists.

"That's enough, both of you. Vin, can you go up to the kitchen and get us some dinner? It's been a long night," Asterion ordered.

Vin gave Ariadne another disgusted look before closing the door behind them.

"Are all your men this bitchy and disobedient?"

"Only since you came along," Asterion muttered.

"Sounds like they need to learn to share."

"You should know that if you go anywhere without me, they will try to kill you, and I'm not going to tell them not to."

"That's fair. I don't suppose I can have that shower now?"

"After you; you know where it is," Asterion said, following her to the bedroom.

He couldn't help comparing the moment to six weeks ago when she'd dropped that killer red dress to the floor. He pushed the image away before it could cause too much havoc.

Ariadne stepped into the bathroom connected to his bedroom and reached around her back to unzip her dress.

"I wanted to try this shower out when I saw it last time. Funny how the Fates work sometimes," she said.

Asterion had made sure the bathroom could accommodate his Minotaur form, and that included a massive shower with two heads, one down each end, and jets that hit at every angle.

After centuries of living in dirt and stone, there wasn't much in the world he enjoyed more than being clean.

"You know I can't escape from here. You don't have to watch," Ariadne said.

"Who said I was here to watch? This is my shower, and I'm covered in crud," Asterion replied, pulling off his t-shirt.

Ariadne shrugged. "Suit yourself."

She turned her back to him and pulled off the rest of her clothes. He did his best to look away, and got rid of his filthy boots and jeans.

The shower turned on, and the sigh that came from the other side of the frosted glass was almost orgasmic.

"I knew it was going to be good, but this is heaven," she said. He caught a glimpse of her bare back, her arms reaching above her head so the jets could hit her shoulders and wash the blood from the cuts and grazes that covered her.

"Yeah, it is," he agreed as he stepped under the hot water.

"It's so good, it's making me regret trying to kill you on a whole new level. We could've had some great fun in here," Ariadne said, reaching past him to grab some of his shampoo.

"Trying to seduce me again isn't going to convince me to let you go," Asterion argued.

"Who said I wanted to be let go? I have a choice between death by Minos or death by Pithos out there. I've only been telling you to kill me or hand me over to make *your* life easier."

"Why? You tried to kill me, remember?" Asterion asked. Ariadne looked at him over a soapy shoulder.

"If I didn't like you so much, I would've slit your throat as soon as you changed and made sure that you were dead," she said viciously. "Don't worry, Asterion, I'm not stupid enough to think you'll ever forgive me. I'll tell you what I know about Pithos because I've got nothing to hide and nothing to lose. What you do after that is up to you."

"You aren't afraid of dying, are you? You aren't even afraid to be sharing a shower with a Minotaur who could tear you apart with his bare hands."

Asterion passed her the conditioner, and she began to work it into her dark hair.

"I don't want to die, but I'm not afraid of it. I've been raised in it, reveled in it, been the cause of it. Death and I are old friends. Death is kinder than Minos, so I'd rather you kill me than go back to him. At least you won't have an erection as you watch me die."

Asterion didn't know what to say to that. It confirmed about Minos what he already knew, and if anything, it reinforced his decision not to give her up.

"Your Minotaur doesn't scare me either, in case you are still wondering. Magical creatures are rare enough that you're kind of a miracle. I never thought I'd see one in my lifetime."

Asterion was still processing someone associating the Minotaur with a miracle when Ariadne swore.

"What is it?"

"I think I've got something stuck in my side," she said, trying to push water over a cut across her ribs.

"Want me to have a look?"

"Sure, it's stinging like a bitch," Ariadne said, turning towards him and bracing her arm against the dark green tiles.

The cut was an inch long and was bleeding steadily. He crouched down and gently prodded it. In the edge of the gash was a thin sliver of black metal.

"There's something in there. I can try to get it out now, or I can get some morphine to shoot you up and do it pain-free."

Gods save him, she smelled so damn good.

"Just do it, it's not big enough to waste painkillers on. One second of pain is worth saving time on the hassle. It's only a bit of shrapnel, not the end of the world. Just distract me, so I don't tense for it," Ariadne said, frustrated.

"Distract you, how?" Asterion stroked a hand up the outside of her smooth leg, smiling when she trembled.

"That's definitely working," she muttered.

"What if I told you how much of a shame it was when you ran out so early the other night? I had a whole night planned of making you scream and beg." He added pressure to the strokes as he moved his hand to the inside of her thigh.

The air between them hummed, and he knew that she'd been honest when she said she'd really wanted him the night at the Labyrinth.

"You had done enough already. I knew I wouldn't go through with it if I stayed in your bed any longer," Ariadne said, her voice not nearly as confident as it had been seconds before.

"Done enough? We'd barely blown off some initial steam. Six weeks away from you, even wanting to kill you, hasn't made me stop thinking about the taste of you and what a wasted opportunity it was."

He bit down on the curve of her hip, and he pulled the metal from her side at the same time.

"Sonava bitch fuck," Ariadne hissed.

"Got it." He held out the inch-long piece of metal to her, and she let out a shaky laugh.

"Sneaky bastard. I told you it was too small to waste painkillers on," Ariadne said, catching his eyes through the steam.

Whatever Ariadne saw in his glance made her stop laughing. Thirty seconds passed, and then she slowly turned to face him, giving him a full view of her glistening body.

Even with the grazes and blossoming bruises, she was stunningly put together. Logical parts of Asterion's brain shut down, replaced with screaming wants.

"What's the matter, Master? Never seen a naked girl before?" she teased as she ran her hands over her soapy breasts. Asterion stood up again, careful not to touch her.

Sweet Hells, this was a bad idea.

He wasn't about to stop it, though. He might be annoyed she tried to kill him, but it didn't mean he was impervious to his attraction to her.

"You know, you're not the only one who thought about that night as a wasted opportunity," Ariadne said, her hands moving in slow circles.

"Is that so? Haunted your dreams have I, little assassin?"

"Yes. The first night you appeared in them, I woke up covered in sweat, and my hand was..."

"What?" he asked, wanting to test just how far she'd let this game play out. He should have known better than to call her bluff.

Without hesitation, she slipped her hand down between her legs and started touching herself. His dick went so hard at the sight, he almost groaned.

"I have to admit, having the real thing in front of me to draw inspiration from is better than the dreams," Ariadne said, her eyes moving over him as she slipped a finger inside herself.

Blood roared in his ears, and it took all his shredded self-control not to reach for her. Ariadne moved closer to him, eyes heavy.

"Can I touch you?"

"You still want to, even knowing what lies underneath this skin?" Asterion had to ask. No one who knew of his true form had ever looked at him the way she did at that moment.

"Yes," she said and reached out for him.

He caught her hand. "I still don't trust you."

"I don't trust you either. Doesn't mean we can't get off after a stressful night." He let her go, a part of him hating that his self-control wasn't better. Ariadne took his dick in her other hand and stroked him.

Asterion drew her closer, watching her work the both of them. He cupped her breasts, gently pinching and rolling her nipples between his fingers. Ariadne moaned, and he needed more. Asterion pushed her up against the wall, moving her hand away from herself.

"Let me, sweetness," he said, as he stroked her slit. Her leg came up around his hips, giving him more access to explore her.

Ariadne gripped his dick tighter and set a maddening rhythm. She swore as he buried two fingers inside of her, bucking and thrusting against him.

"That's it, take what you need," he said, holding her up as her body shook. She cried out, her nails raking down his back, the pain making him come in her hand.

It was over embarrassingly quick, but there was something about her that made all common sense and control go out the window.

"Asterion..." Ariadne said breathlessly, resting her head against his chest as he kept her pinned, too afraid if he moved, they would end up in a collapsed heap on the tiles.

"Yes, Ariadne?"

"From now on, you get to do all of my first aid."

12

When Ariadne had woken up in Isthmia that morning, she didn't imagine her day would end sitting in a plush men's night robe, covered in Band-Aids and eating a meal with Asterion Dys.

"You must've had some good intel to find out I was vegan," Ariadne said when a plate of pasta was placed in front of her.

"I didn't know you are vegan. They brought it to you because I am," Asterion replied as he sat down at the table opposite her.

"Huh. I guess the stories are full of shit after all."

Ariadne stuck her fork into a piece of eggplant and ate it. It was as good as it looked, and she was suddenly so hungry she wanted to shovel as much in her mouth that she could.

"What stories are they?" Asterion asked suspiciously.

"You know, the old ones about how you used to eat people. You are *that* Minotaur, right?" Vin made a choking sound of horror on the other side of the room.

"It's okay, Vin, she knows," Asterion said before turning back to Ariadne. "And yes, I am *that* Minotaur and no, I didn't use to eat people. I used to kill them."

"And then what?"

"Then my father used to let them rot at the bottom of the labyrinth where he kept me imprisoned," Asterion replied, his face emotionless. Ariadne swallowed hard and reached for her wine.

"I'm sorry."

"Shit fathers, what are you going to do?" Asterion said, trying to shrug off the tenseness that had suddenly filled the room.

"Fuck them," agreed Ariadne. Asterion opened the laptop and looked at her expectantly.

"What's the password?"

Ariadne drank some of her red wine and wondered how to get rid of the frown on his face.

"Try hotminotaur69."

"Fucking with me will get you nowhere, assassin," Asterion said, but there was a glimmer of a smile.

"Oh, fine. It's password."

He gave her a long, disbelieving look before typing it in. "Unbelievable."

"You guys mustn't have tried very hard. This is the laptop Pithos gave me. That's the folder they sent me on you. Notice there is no mention of you being a badass mythical beast that could crush me with one hand. The other folder is a small part of what they got on Minos. You're welcome to do what you like with it. I know of other contracts. I can even tell you which ones I'm responsible for," Ariadne said, pointing out the folders.

"Your contracts are pretty noticeable. I've been wondering about the gold cat's cradle. Why do it?" asked Asterion.

"Why not?" Ariadne replied, the wine churning in her stomach as she heard her sister Lia's hushed whispers in the still dorm room.

There was something about Asterion that made her drop her guard, but he wasn't going to get Lia. No one got Lia.

Seeing that her answer wasn't going to satisfy him, she added, "You can have all my other secrets, but you won't get that one until we trust each other."

"It'll be a mystery forever then," he sighed.

"I guess." Ariadne went back to her food, and Asterion started to read through the files.

No one paid her any attention as she curled up on the couch by the fire after she finished eating.

It had been a long, strange day, made even more confusing by what happened in the shower.

The stress of being caught and almost being killed must've given her brain damage.

You're so fucked up, a voice reminded her as she curled into a ball. This time, the voice sounded like Lia, and that made it so much worse.

∼

ARIADNE WOKE the next day to find someone had tucked a soft grey blanket over her. There was a susurrus of voices trying to be quiet, and she lay still to listen.

"She took down Asterion. She's so little-"

"He shouldn't have brought her here-"

"Total babe, though, can't blame him. Let's wake her up-"

Ariadne opened her eyes and found three men in the room with her, one finger about to poke her in the shoulder.

"Touch me, and I'll bite that finger off," she warned. The owner of the hand smiled toothily. He had curly black hair and black eyes.

"Back off and let her breathe, Erebus," another said, pulling him away. He had straight silver blond hair that hung to his shoulders.

"Don't let Asterion see you looming over her," the third added.

He was sitting on the opposite couch, an arm slung over the back and a gold coin flicking across his fingers tattooed with symbols. He had close-clipped hair at the sides, and a longer top of straight black hair pushed back from his sharp face.

Ariadne sat up as the other two men joined him on the couch. They all had the same black eyes and were dressed almost uniformly in well-cut dress shirts and waistcoats. Somehow, they still managed to look like thugs.

"Who are you three? More bodyguards? Don't worry, I don't plan on trying to kill your boss again," she said, trying to finger comb the snarls out of her hair. All three of the men smirked.

"Asterion isn't our boss, little girl," the blond one said, straightening the cuffs of his grey shirt. "Although it's fortunate for you I was able to save him. Otherwise, we wouldn't be so polite right now."

"Careful, she looks like she'd be able to take you in a fight," the black-haired one said.

"Excellent, you're awake," a fourth voice said, making Ariadne's stomach drop.

Terror coursed through her as Hades Acheron sat down in the armchair near her.

He looked in his early forties with high cheekbones and was greying at the temples of his classic short back and sides haircut.

Ariadne had met powerful men before, but Hades was the first that made her want to submit. His silver eyes were unnerving as they studied her just as carefully.

"You're the infamous Spindle. I wondered how long it would take Asterion to hunt you down. Six weeks is probably the longest anyone has lasted," Hades continued, his voice as seductively rich as hot chocolate. The three men on the couch all sniggered.

"I knew it was pretty pointless, but I had to try...my lord," replied Ariadne, wondering if he was here to turn her into a bloody smear.

"You almost killed him, which leaves a unique impression on a man like Asterion. If Thanatos here hadn't pulled his shade back from the ether, you might have succeeded," said Hades with a nod in the silver-haired man's direction.

The penny dropped, and Ariadne realized precisely who the three men on the couch were. They were a part of the Court of Styx and were seen as rarely by the public as Hades was.

The rumor was that they were brothers and did all of Hades's darkest dirty work. If the silver-haired one was Thanatos, and the curly-haired one was Erebus, then the one with the coin had to be Charon.

You are so, so dead, Ariadne.

She licked her lips nervously. "You don't sound half as annoyed about me trying to kill him as I expected. Are you here to watch Asterion finish me off?"

"You won't be dying today, Ariadne. From what Asterion tells me, you saved his life last night," Hades said.

"I felt like I owed it to him for hearing me out."

"You've made him feel vulnerable in more ways than one. Give him some time, and I believe he'll get over the strangulation, and his admiration will return."

"I don't think his feelings towards me could have ever been described as admiration," Ariadne said. The Lord of Styx actually smiled at her.

"Are you going to help us find this Pithos that's irritating us?" asked Erebus.

Ariadne nodded. "I said that I would, and I gave Asterion everything I had. It's up to you guys to decide whether or not to trust me that the information is any good."

"And why would we do that? You did try to kill him. This could be a ruse to help Pithos take down the Court," said Charon, his coin flicking over his fingers.

"Do you honestly think I would've risked pissing you all off and crossing Minos for the sake of a cause like Pithos? I don't think so. Pithos only got me to agree by withholding information and giving me something I've wanted for the last fifteen years," argued Ariadne. *Where is Asterion?*

"Revenge on Minos," said Hades. His silver eyes flashed unnervingly, and pain pierced through her brain. "For many things but mostly for *her*."

"Get out of my head, you prick," Ariadne hissed viciously.

"Hit a nerve did I, mortal? Perhaps that's what you need to discuss with Asterion if you want him to trust you. Right now, he thinks you did it for money."

"I don't care what he thinks."

"Yes, you do. Are you afraid Asterion won't ever love you if he knows what you did?" Hades mocked.

"Love? Who would've thought the God of the Underworld was such a comedian?"

Hade's smile was infuriating. "Why did you keep his shirt, Spindle?"

Ariadne scowled. "I didn't realize one of your businesses was matchmaking."

"I find humans and their emotions messy and predictable, especially when it comes to sex. There's no point in denying it. I know his other, more interesting side, decided to mark you during your first...encounter. The bruise is gone, but anyone with a drop of magical blood can see the mark and know that to interfere with you would make an enemy of him. I do hope you know what you're doing, Ariadne. Asterion isn't someone who you'd want to play with."

What the actual fuck? A magical mark? Who did that to a person they only just met?

"No shit. I'm not an idiot, Hades. I'm telling him everything he wants to know, and that includes the matter of the mole in his ranks," said Ariadne.

"You believe you can find who it is?" Erebus asked curiously.

"I can try. Only a small group would have close access to him, so it'll be someone he trusts." Ariadne folded her arms. "You know he's not going to be able to view them suspiciously. There is an overprotective bro code between them, and he won't believe that one of them can betray him."

"Then you must find them," insisted Hades.

"How? I can't even take a shower without Asterion following me into it," she said, and Erebus elbowed Charon with a wink. She ignored them and continued, "None of them will answer questions or rat each other out. Even if I do find out who it is, Asterion's not going to trust me enough to believe my word over theirs."

"Then you must earn his trust so he will believe you," said Thanatos calmly.

"As I said...how? As everyone keeps pointing out, I almost killed him. If his guards had their way, I'd be under the arena in a cell right now."

"You could always earn Asterion's respect the way the guards had to," Hades suggested thoughtfully.

"You want me to do the Labyrinth?" A thrill of danger ran through her. The competitive side of her began to goad her at just the thought of it.

"I have a feeling it won't be a challenge for a woman like you, but it's perhaps the fastest way to get them to back off and trust that you're on our side. If you die, then justice is served, I suppose," Hades replied.

"And we could get some good bets in at the same time," said Erebus.

Asterion's bedroom door opened, and he started when he saw who was sitting on his lounge. "Dear gods, what are you lot doing here?"

"We didn't come to see you," said Erebus, with a sly smile. "We came to see the girl who killed you. I can see why you hunted her so obsessively these past weeks."

Asterion's eyes narrowed.

"It's because of my charming wit," Ariadne replied.

"Ariadne was just telling me about how she's going to help us find Pithos and track down your mole," Hades said smoothly.

And giving unwanted relationship advice, Ariadne mentally added.

"I read through the files on the laptop, but I don't know how to track their sources or their origin," said Asterion, sitting on the couch beside her.

"Send it to Medusa. If there's a trail to be followed, she'll find it," Hades said as he stood. He gave Ariadne another thoughtful look. "I want this one to go into the Labyrinth."

Asterion tensed. "Why?"

"I want to know how good she is. When all this dirty business is settled, if she's still alive, then I want her on my payroll. I'm sure Medusa will take her off your hands if you still feel raw about the attempted murder. She always needs more women at Serpentine."

"She has enough women!" Erebus complained. "We should keep at least one pretty one."

"Ariadne is mine," snapped Asterion before checking himself. "I don't think this is a good idea, Hades."

"Your judgement is clouded, and therefore irrelevant when it comes to her. I want her in the Labyrinth tonight. We'll be back at eight to watch," Hades said, the sharp snap of the order making them all straighten.

The Lord of Styx got to his feet, and the three brothers rose to follow him.

"We look forward to betting on you tonight," said Charon.

"For or against?" Ariadne couldn't resist asking.

"For," Erebus said as Thanatos pushed him out of the apartment, the doors shutting loudly behind them.

Asterion swore under his breath. "What did you tell them?"

"Anything they asked me. They are the Court of Styx, aren't they?"

Asterion nodded. "Them, Medusa, and me. I'm sorry that they ambushed you like that. They have problems with boundaries."

Ariadne adjusted her robe and got up. There was no way she'd be going back to sleep after that fucking visit.

"I'm going to need my clothes unless you're going to make me do the Labyrinth naked."

"They are in the top drawer in the wardrobe. I don't want you going in the fucking Labyrinth at all," Asterion said stubbornly like he had a say in the decision.

"Why do you care? I've seen the quality of your bodyguards. If they can survive it, I'm sure I can. They weren't good enough to stop me, after all. I'll happily do the Labyrinth if it means you all stop bitching at me for killing you. Oh yeah, Hades told me about that too. I *did* kill you, and Thanatos brought you back, so I guess that means I was good enough to beat you too," Ariadne replied, and headed for the wardrobe, so she didn't have to see his expression.

She didn't know why she was provoking him, but she blamed waking up to a bunch of gods looming over her. She'd always wondered if they actually were gods, but if Thanatos could bring Asterion's shade back, what the hell else could they do?

Why, oh, why didn't you tell Pithos where to stick their contract?

In the top drawer of a beautifully built-in set of shelves, the clothes that she had kept stuffed into her backpack were now in neatly folded piles.

Who the fuck actually folded underwear? A better question was, who the fuck had folded *hers*?

She grabbed her gym clothes and locked the bathroom door behind her. She didn't need Asterion barging in and having his body making her flustered and distracted again.

"You just back talked Hades fucking Acheron, met his monsters and rubbed the Minotaur's nose in the fact you murdered him," Ariadne told her pale reflection.

She really did have a death wish. No wonder Hades ordered Asterion to put her in the pit.

If you live, you might get to work for Medusa, that wouldn't be so bad.

It was a hell of a big if.

∼

By the time Ariadne emerged from the bathroom, Asterion was gone, leaving Vin to watch over her.

"How many hours do I have?" Ariadne asked as she braided back her hair.

"Two, but I'm to take you to the back of the arena now to where the other contenders warm up. If you thought Asterion was going to give you special treatment because you are a girl, you're wrong," Vin replied.

"You seem to be forgetting who I am, bodyguard. I don't need anyone's special treatment, least of all from your master."

Ariadne was already tired of their macho bullshit. She thought growing up in a house full of murderous girls was bad, but she was starting to think the boys' club was worse.

"We'll see if you're so cocky by the end of the night if you survive that long," Vin said, gesturing towards the door.

"Bet you fifty drachmae that I will be," Ariadne replied and held out her hand.

Vin chuckled. "You're on, girl." He shook it, and Ariadne thought he might be okay under the bullshit.

The arena downstairs was eerie without the roar of the crowds. It was still lit up, with people cleaning and raking away the layer of sand to reveal the doors that would open up to the Labyrinth.

"Don't suppose I get a sneak peek at the set up before I'm thrown into it?" she asked.

"And ruin all the fun? I've seen grown men piss themselves at the very sight of it."

"That's not saying much. I've seen grown men piss themselves when they've seen a pair of tits."

"You talk a lot of shit for a woman," Vin said.

"You can take the girl out of Hellas, but you can't take Hellas out of the girl."

"Thought Minos would've taught you better. Smoothed out that accent and attitude a bit."

"He tried, but I guess he should've picked a younger orphan to manipulate."

"Huh, that explains it."

"Explains what?" Ariadne asked.

Vin gave a lazy half-shrug. "The boss has a soft spot for orphans."

"And you think he has a soft spot for me?" Ariadne laughed. Vin didn't.

"He's had a soft spot for you since you crashed into him on the street. Can't quite figure out why, since you're not the prettiest girl who's ever thrown herself at him. You even tried to kill him, and he's still not mad."

"Hunting me down in Isthmia and making me his prisoner until he decides how to kill me doesn't seem mad to you?"

Vin shook his head. "I've seen Asterion mad. I've seen his bull gore a traitor from his dick to his chin. That's how he usually deals with people who fuck with him. You strangled him, and he still doesn't know what to do with you. It's bad for his reputation."

"I suppose dumping me in the Labyrinth will put the decision in the hands of the Fates. You're all going to have to find someone else to hate if I survive."

"There's always plenty of people to hate." Vin pushed open the doors to a large gym area where a few of the bouncers and bodyguards were working out.

She recognized most of them from the reconnaissance she'd done on the club.

"Looks like the boss has finally come to his senses and decided to let you die," one said from the other side of the room.

"I'm going to enjoy watching the Labyrinth rip you apart," said another.

"Men," Ariadne muttered. Vin pushed open another door that seemed to be an antechamber to the arena.

There was an assortment of weapons positioned in racks against the wall. They were well made but not fancy. Ariadne figured those that were into weaponry would bring their own.

"Don't get any ideas. They aren't for you," said Vin.

"I get nothing? Not even a little baby sword?"

"Hades's orders."

"What a fucker." He really was determined to make her work for it. Vin sat down and gestured at her to get on with it.

Ariadne fell into her regular warm-up routine, letting her body go through the motions as she thought.

Minos had never been one to let them use unnecessary equipment, believing that the weight of your own body was best for working out.

Ariadne tried to go over all the information she knew surrounding the Labyrinth. Asterion had called it a gauntlet. She'd done plenty of those. It was designed to kill people, so she knew that there would be traps.

This is something Minos would enjoy.

It made her wonder all over again why Minos hadn't used the arena as another way to test his priestesses. He had ensured that their entire lives were a constant test.

Ariadne had been poisoned, attacked in the shower, strangled in her sleep...the list went on. All to ensure she was tough enough to survive.

Minos had a devious and violent mind, and his final trial before their graduation probably would have made the assholes in the gym next door blubber. Ariadne had only seen twelve out of thirty girls survive it in all the time she'd lived at the Temple.

A message tone knocked Ariadne out of her meditation. Vin checked his phone and frowned at her.

"You're up in ten minutes, girl. Pray to your god, if you have one."

"Whatever." Ariadne got off the mat and started a final round of stretching. Lia used to pray to Saint Spyridon, patron saint of orphans and other poor bastards, before a fight. It didn't matter how often Ariadne pointed out that if her saint were listening, they wouldn't have ended up in the hands of a prick like Minos. Lia still prayed.

Ariadne didn't think prayers to anyone would help her tonight, not when the God of the Underworld had ordered her punishment.

"I don't know, guys. I think she looks nervous. So much for being a badass assassin," Theseus said from behind her. Ariadne turned to face the group of bodyguards now watching her.

"I'm sorry I'm such a disappointment to you, menfolk," she said sarcastically.

"At least you're going to make it up to us with an entertaining death," Theseus replied.

"You hope. It's going to be fun to watch how much it burns your pride when I survive. Make sure you have my fifty drachmae ready, Vin."

"I should've got you to pay up before we left the apartment," he grumbled as he gestured to the guards to get ready to open the doors.

Ariadne rolled her neck and shoulders. There was nothing outside those doors that could be worse than dying on Minos's torture table.

"You want a kiss for good luck?" Theseus asked.

"You want to be punched in the dick?" she replied.

His smile was cold and vicious. "I hope you die screaming, Spindle."

13

Asterion stood in Hades's personal box, the Lord of Styx sitting casually to watch the show.

Charon stood by the door with arms folded, and Erebus and Thanatos were leaning against the balcony railing.

Asterion had never argued or rebelled against the god that freed him, but he'd argued futilely for the past two hours about letting Ariadne into the arena.

"Sit down and have a drink, Asterion. It's not as if you haven't seen this all before," said Hades, passing a glass of amber liquid to him.

"Go on. I brought this one from home, and you need it."

"Why are you doing this? It's not like you to interfere in this kind of matter," asked Asterion.

"Pithos is why I'm doing this. Monster killers. Like Greece needs their kind rising again," Hades answered. "You know you like the girl. You're too upset and stubborn to admit it. This will make it easier for you and your men to trust her. You weren't strong enough to make the decision to kill her, so I did it for you. Let the Fates decide."

"Trust takes more than almost death in the arena," Asterion said.

"Did you ever stop to think why she gave all her information up to you so easily?" asked Charon.

"She was scared I was going to torture it out of her."

Charon's chuckle was deep and thoroughly amused as he answered, "You don't think Minos trained her to withstand torture? You could have been at her for days and not gotten a thing out of her. She's giving it up because she likes you and because she wants your help. I believe she's hoping you'll kill Minos, even if you kill her too."

"Charon has a point, she likes you," said Thanatos thoughtfully.

"I *am* going to kill Minos. What I read last night is a fraction of the filth he wallows in. That fuck is breathing his final breaths and doesn't even know it. As soon as Pithos is dealt with, I'm going to tear that bastard apart," Asterion vowed.

The bull in him strained, wanting to be free at the thought of violence.

"You see? You've ignored Minos for years, and now you're going to kill him because of what he did to her. Just admit you like the girl," sighed Hades.

"So what if I do? It still doesn't explain to me why you want her down there."

Hades gave him a knowing smile. "Don't you want to know how good she *really* is?"

"I do. I've got a hundred drachmae riding on it too," said Erebus eagerly.

Asterion didn't reply as the drummers began to pound out the steady beat. There were no punters tonight. He wouldn't make a spectacle out of Ariadne any more than what he had to.

The floor opened to reveal the death trap.

Only one way in and out, the Labyrinth had been laid with pressure and time-sensitive traps, and even if Ariadne made it to the middle, she would find three well-trained opponents to kill before she could even begin the second half.

Hades had insisted on the fatality clause that night, and Asterion didn't recognize the three gladiators that now waited in the center.

His guards shouted insults down at Ariadne, gripping the metal mesh that covered the Labyrinth and shaking it, trying to frighten her.

Asterion's heart was in his throat as Ariadne looked at the first trial of time-sensitive spears that were thrusting from the walls intermittently.

Her expression that had a grave seriousness when she'd first entered now changed.

"Is she fucking smiling right now?" Asterion said incredulously, leaning over the edge of the balcony for a better look. She was. A big fuck you grin now stretched from ear to ear.

This woman is fucking insane.

The way she'd handled herself in the firefight and their hurried orgasms in the shower afterward had him wondering if she even knew how to act like a normal person.

Now he had proof Ariadne was nuts as she faced certain death and was smiling.

Erebus laughed. "You expected her to start crying? Sit back, Asterion, this is going to be quite the show."

Asterion didn't sit down. He watched with terror seeping through every part of his being. Even his bull was silent as if holding its breath.

Ariadne didn't bolt through the javelin walls like he'd seen other successful contenders do. That would be too easy. She crouched into a runner's lunge and then launched herself through them in an almost balletic, perfectly timed dive and a graceful roll to clear them.

The men in the lower seats stopped jeering at her.

"Fuck *me*, that was perfect," Charon whistled as he joined them at the balcony.

Ariadne didn't even look up, all her concentration on the obstacles before her. She didn't race through the second section, either. Instead, she picked up a handful of stones from the gravel path and flung them.

Jets of fire shot up where they landed. Ariadne spat on her hands, wiped the excess on the soles of her dusty bare feet and ran up the side of the slick wall, grabbed the metal mesh covering her, and used it to swing up and over the pressure plates and onto the next safe space.

Hades's phone binged. "Medusa is offering two million drachmae for her." Asterion glared at the Serpent Queen's cameras above him and lifted his middle finger.

"Not for sale, you red-haired witch," he said. He knew Medusa would've been roaring with laughter, but it didn't matter. He wasn't going to let them haggle over Ariadne like she was a slab of meat.

"You're missing it," Hades said. Asterion swore. He'd missed two trials by the distraction.

"What happened? Why is she bleeding?"

"One of the darts grazed her. Ah, let's see how she does at the center," Hades said, his silver eyes gleaming with interest.

"You're a real bastard," said Asterion.

"As if I care." Hades was unyielding when he made a decision, and Asterion could swear and threaten as much as he liked, and it would get him nowhere.

Ariadne was moving, ducking quickly under the first gladiator's spear, rolling before tossing a handful of sandy grit into the eyes of the second as she got to her feet.

She took advantage of the distraction to grip him by the arm and twist him around as a human shield, the hatchet the third gladiator threw hitting him in the chest. She shoved the body away and took the dead man's sword.

"I told you she didn't need a weapon, though I'm starting to question the abilities of my men," said Hades.

Asterion didn't reply. He couldn't look away as Ariadne tumbled and sliced, weakening both of her oversized and heavily armored opponents.

The hatchet wielder went down with one of his own blades embedded in his face. The first gladiator swung his spear too wide, and Ariadne charged in and swung up him in a viciously elegant move that had her on his shoulders and snapping his neck in a forceful jerk.

Asterion cringed as she sank to the ground, still riding on the dead man's shoulder. She calmly retrieved the hatchet from the dead gladiator's face and slid the handle down the side of her tights, before lifting the dropped spear.

Ariadne walked out of the center arena, and the curved blades of the pendulums dropped.

After watching them for a few thoughtful seconds, Ariadne took a few steps backward, hefted the spear up in her right hand, ran and threw it with a shout that echoed through the silent arena.

The sharp point of the blade sliced through the first two ropes and shaved the edges of the last two so that the pendulums flopped out of rhythm and fell to the ground as the weave of the rope unraveled.

Ariadne stepped quickly around the fallen blades and came to the last ten meters of a fire pit. A chaotic laugh came from her, and she did a series of sun salutations as if she had all the time in the world.

"What the fuck is she doing?" Erebus asked, leaning back over the balcony.

"Working herself up. She's been trained to firewalk." Hades stood up and joined him.

Asterion could hear Ariadne's breathing patterns change as she rolled her shoulders back.

Gripping the railings of the balcony, Asterion watched as she calmly strode across the fire pit, eyes forward, delicious hips swaying like it was a catwalk.

As she reached the exit to the Labyrinth, she hefted the hatchet and threw it towards the group of ogling guards so quickly that they fell back with a shout even though the weapon couldn't get through the mesh.

"I am so aroused right now," Erebus said. "Are you sure I can't convince you to let me have her?"

"Fuck you," Asterion said, without any real venom. The triplets only laughed at him. Asterion watched as Ariadne disappeared into the anteroom, and his bull roared inside of him.

"I need to go."

"You'd better hurry. My guess is Ariadne has about fifteen more good minutes before the poison from that dart kicks in," Hades said, looking at his phone. "Medusa says, 'If you kill her, I'll turn you into the world's ugliest birdbath' and what looks like a smiling poop emoji."

"I hate you all," Asterion replied before hurrying down the stairs to the elevator. He'd taken two steps into his apartment when he heard the shouting.

"A deal is a deal! Pay up, you ape!" Ariadne shouted.

"You cheated, woman! You cut down those pendulums instead of navigating them and don't even get me started on the fire jets," Vin argued back.

"Don't blame me because you are too dumb to think of a smarter way to do it. Now, you'll pay me my drachmae, or I'm going to beat you like I used to beat up fat, rich kids with too much money."

"Bring it on, you mouthy little-" Vin stopped as soon as he noticed Asterion.

Ariadne was in the big man's red face, ready to carry out her threats.

"If you were dumb enough to bet against the High Priestess, you pay up," Asterion said firmly.

Vin muttered and handed over the handful of bills before heading for the door.

"Good luck to you, boss. I don't know what you see in that harpy," Vin said but gave him a wink where Ariadne couldn't see. Vin knew *precisely* what he saw in her.

Asterion would be surprised if all his men weren't a little in love with her now, not to mention Erebus. Like he needed that headache.

"Decided to finally come back, did you? Enjoy the show from your little balcony with your buddies?" Ariadne demanded.

"The show? You mean watching you break my property and kill Hades's men and almost yourself in the process? No, I didn't fucking enjoy the show," he said as he closed the space between them.

"You were the one dumb enough to put me in there. Don't pout that I didn't die when you've only got yourself to blame-" Ariadne's rant cut off as Asterion lifted the filthy, angry assassin up off her feet and kissed her roughly.

It was filled with all his fear and frustration, and she met him head-on with an almost violent intensity just like she always did.

"Stop talking. Your body is laced with poison, and we need to treat it before you start hallucinating," Asterion said when they broke apart.

Ariadne touched her reddened lips. "I think I already am," she said as she slumped in his arms.

Asterion placed her on the couch, uncaring how bloody and filthy she was.

"You're in for a rough night, sweetness, but don't worry. It won't kill you...and neither will I."

∽

Despite Asterion's reassurances, Ariadne was sure she was dying. Fire raced through her veins, and she couldn't stop screaming.

Through bleary eyes, she could see Asterion injecting her with something and laying cool, wet cloths on her burning skin.

In one eye, she could see the man, and in the other, she could see the Minotaur. He had kissed her, and she didn't know why but she'd liked it and didn't know what that meant either.

"You need to stop making me so confused," she said, her tongue heavy in her mouth.

"I'll stop, if you do," Asterion replied, cleaning the bloody wound on her bicep where the dart had gotten her.

Sloppy! An apparition of Minos shouting at her made her jump backward.

"Don't give me back to him," she begged.

"I'm not letting Minos anywhere near you, Ariadne," Asterion replied as if knowing who haunted her waking nightmares.

Can you trust a creature like him not to betray you? Minos had disappeared, and a beautiful, willowy girl with straight brown hair stood in his place. *Lia.*

Ariadne curled into a ball and moaned. "No, no, not you. Go away, Lia. I can't see you."

Why? Because of what you did to me? You were closer to me than blood. Look at me, Ariadne! LOOK AT WHAT YOU DID.

Warm hands lifted her, and Ariadne cried out when she was lowered into a bath. Her heart was racing as Asterion pulled the clothes from her body.

Look at how he's caring for you. I cared for you like that once. I chased your nightmares away and kept Minos's probing hands from you. I protected you, and you betrayed me, Lia said, refusing to leave her alone.

"I didn't betray you. I didn't know!" Ariadne shouted at the shade.

"Shh, easy, Ariadne. It's just the poison. There's no one here but me," Asterion said, wiping the sweat and dirt away from her face.

"Lia's here. Lia's watching. She's always watching because I failed her."

"You want to tell me about it?" he asked gently.

That's it. Tell him of your great shame, Spindle. Tell him all about how you buried my memory and never honored your promise, Lia goaded.

"She was taken from the orphanage in Hellas, same as me." Ariadne's hands began to move, and she hallucinated a cat's cradle of golden light moving between her shaking fingers.

"We did everything together. Protected each other. We even had a secret language and used the cat's cradles like sign language, so Minos wouldn't know. She was kind. Too kind for Minos. He said that she was being sent to a special school to make her tougher. I believed him. She was always so soft; I thought a special school would help her."

Asterion brushed her wet hair back with his fingers, and she curled her head into his palm like a cat that had been denied too many pats.

"You don't have to tell me anymore if you don't want to."

Lia's shade gave her a cruel smile. *Here's your chance to stop while he still is pitying you, Spindle. Why don't you take advantage of it and suck his cock to keep him from knowing what kind of person you are? Go on. Madame Zera always used to boast how good you were at it.*

"Just go away, Lia," Ariadne heaved, tears streaming down her face.

"It's okay, Ariadne. Just breathe, it won't last long. It's not real," Asterion said.

Ariadne brought her knees up to her chest, trying to force her head to clear. She needed to tell him. If she didn't, he might let Minos go, and she needed to kill him. She needed it more than the air that burned in her lungs.

"M-Minos has a final trial that all the priestesses must face. Part of it is like your Labyrinth — an obstacle course to test our skills, but much harder than what you threw at me today. I was his best student, so he put a lot of effort into it. I have the scars on my back to prove it, but I made it through."

"I thought it was over, but then a person, hooded and cloaked, was brought forward and forced to their knees. Minos gave me the golden braid, knowing that I picked strangulation as my form of kill. I didn't ask any questions. I d-didn't even care. I only wanted to prove myself to be the best. I killed them easily. They didn't even struggle."

"When it was over, Minos removed the hood, and it was my Lia. There was no fucking school, but there was a lesson and one that Minos had repeated over and over. Kill the thing that you love most because it's always going to make you weak. If you love nothing, care about nothing, you never fear to lose it. No fear, no emotion, only duty, and a job done well."

Ariadne looked up to see Lia gone, and she buried her face in her hands and sobbed.

She didn't know how much time passed, but when she stopped crying, Asterion helped her out of the bath and wrapped her in a robe. He carried her gently and placed her in his bed.

"I promised Lia I'd kill him, Asterion. I'll do whatever you want. I'll kill all of Pithos and your mole and everyone you ask, just let me kill Minos. You can even kill me after if that's what you want. Just let me do it, please," Ariadne begged.

Asterion lay down beside her and drew her close, his large body enclosing hers completely.

"I won't be killing you, Ariadne. If anyone tries to hurt you, I'll make sure they don't live long. We're going to get Pithos together."

"You forgive me for killing you?" she sniffed.

"I forgive you, and I'm pretty sure Lia would have too. She would've known you loved her."

"I hope she did. So, we have a truce?"

"Yeah, sweetness, we have a truce."

Ariadne curled her fingers into his shirt. "And Minos?"

"Don't worry, little assassin, Minos is going to die. By my hand or yours...he'll die," Asterion promised, and Ariadne finally fell asleep.

14

Asterion and anger were old friends. It had been a part of him for so long that the new strain of pure fury that was now growing in him was something strange and frightening.

It was tied up with other, more complicated feelings like overprotectiveness that made him question if he was in his right mind.

Looking down at Ariadne, fast asleep with limbs askew, he was filled with a driving need to slay everyone who had ever upset her.

Ariadne could do her own slaying, he knew it, but it still didn't make the feeling go away.

Stop staring at her, you creepy bastard.

Asterion left a glass of water on her bedside, *his* bedside, damn it, and went back to his kitchen to make coffee. The poison had run its course, and she was sleeping peacefully. There was no need to loom over her to make sure she was still breathing.

He needed to take his mind off her, so he poured a coffee and sent a text to Medusa; **Any luck with the laptop?** He didn't have long to wait.

A minute later, his Skype was calling, and Medusa's face appeared on his flat screen. It mustn't have been a filming day because her bouncy red hair was tied up on top of her head, and she was wearing a pair of Doctor Who pajamas.

"Well look who's finally awake," she said irritably.

"Good morning to you too," Asterion replied, sitting down on his lounge chair.

Medusa's wide mouth broke into a grin as she lowered the pair of black-framed hipster glasses from her startling green eyes.

"You don't look nearly as sexed-up as I thought you would be. Did our glorious assassin turn you down?"

"It's not like that. Ariadne caught a dart, so she's been working the poison out of her system."

"She got *grazed* by a dart and only just. Oh, honey, *look* at you. You have a crush on a girl! It only took you being strangled to death to notice they exist," teased Medusa.

"I'm hardly a virgin, Susa."

"Sex wasn't what I was referring to, and you know it. When do I get to meet her?"

"Never if you are going to bombard her like this. The triplets were bad enough yesterday," said Asterion.

"Don't be a bitch. I want her for Serpentine when this is all over. You can't keep a woman like her locked up. She's going to need a job," Medusa said.

"If she works for you, she'll pick up all sorts of bad habits, like back-talking me."

"From what Hades has told me, she already does backtalk. Big ovaries on her to sass the boss, but she did. I'm so in love with her. We are going to be besties in no time. Though I think I'm going to have to fight Erebus for her. The boys are all quite impressed with her."

"Stop trying to get a rise out of me, you know it won't work."

"Look upon me and despair, mortal!" Medusa shouted theatrically, making Asterion jump in surprise.

"Can I despair after I have coffee?" Ariadne murmured sleepily from behind him. "Is there more?"

"Fresh pot in the kitchen," Asterion said, trying not to laugh.

"Thanks, I'll be back to despairing in a minute," she said and shuffled off with a yawn.

"Wow, not even a nibble. No wonder Hades was pouting that his supreme awesomeness didn't affect her," Medusa chuckled.

"Believe it or not, we aren't the scariest monsters she's ever met," said Asterion, the furious, sucker punch feeling back under his ribs.

"Oh, I know that look. If you're about to make a big mess of someone high profile, you better warn me so I can make sure it doesn't turn into a media shit storm," Medusa said with a sigh.

Ariadne came back with a steaming mug and sat on the couch beside him, tucking her feet underneath her.

"Did I miss anything important? Any leads on Pithos?" she asked.

"Look at her, jumping right to it. Well done on the Labyrinth last night, my dear. I don't think I've seen the blockheads so worked up after a contender got through. You made them all look so average I thought their little male egos were going to make them stroke out."

Ariadne laughed, a full belly laugh that Asterion hadn't heard before.

"You should've seen Vin trying to get out of paying the fifty drachmae he bet me."

"Hopefully, Asterion won't give you half as much trouble with the prize money."

"I thought my prize was a truce?" Ariadne said.

"Asterion! If you cheat this woman out of her prize money, I'll come around there and geld you," Medusa hissed.

"I never said I wasn't going to give her the prize money! Why are you putting words in my mouth?" said Asterion.

Ariadne grinned over the top of her mug. "I like you, Medusa."

"Better than Asterion? Because you know, I'd love you to come over and work with me at Serpentine," she offered. Asterion tensed, not wanting to be petty enough to start a bidding match.

"Maybe once I'm done with Asterion, or if he gets annoying and overbearing," answered Ariadne.

"So I'll see you next week?"

"Enough! Ariadne isn't going anywhere until I say so," snapped Asterion.

Ariadne's eyes narrowed. "Is that what you think?"

Medusa laughed gleefully. "Whatever. I did look at the laptop, and they used VPNs and bounced things around, wiped serial numbers, and what have you, but they did connect it to an internet service in the Lethe district. The seedy end, not the nice end," she clarified.

"I looked up who owned the building, but it's leased under a shell company of a shell company, and it might be easier just to go around and have a look. I'll email you an address."

"Thanks, Susa, I appreciate it," Asterion said, his temper cooling.

"Yeah, yeah, I'm brilliant, I know."

"I have another question," said Ariadne.

"Shoot, cutie."

"You're a magical creature too, like Asterion. Can you see a mark?" Ariadne said, pulling down the collar of her robe.

"You mean where our Minotaur here got excited and bit you? Even if I hadn't heard about it from the triplets, you could see that thing from space, and...and Asterion hasn't told you about that."

"No. *Hades* had to. I need you to tell me how to get rid of it," Ariadne said, folding her arms stubbornly.

"Ah, I'm sorry I didn't get that, you're breaking up-" lied Medusa and turned off the call.

Asterion was plunged into the electric silence of female fury.

"I don't suppose you'll believe me when I tell you that it wasn't my intention?" he said lamely. Was he ever going to get on a good footing with this woman?

"Is that how you found me in Isthmia?" Ariadne's eyes were like storm clouds.

"No! I didn't realize I had done it until Hades mentioned it. I tracked you down because you were wearing my shirt, and I could...smell it."

"Smell it? Oh. The bull could. Hades said that it was your bull that marked me, and not you, as such. Are you guys one and the same, or separate?" she demanded.

Fuck, fuck, fuck, how are you going to tell her without freaking her out?

He'd never tried to explain it to anyone except Hades when he'd first released him from the labyrinth. He'd been a half-mad, wild thing that Hades had to tame to even be able to function above ground.

"I see us as being different sides of the same coin. When I'm the Minotaur, I act more impulsively, and more primal instincts come into play. When I'm a man, I can think clearer, control myself better, but sometimes we...leak...into each other during moments of stress or heightened emotion," Asterion said.

"Heightened emotion like sex with a mysterious and beautiful woman?" Ariadne asked.

He managed a small smile. Ariadne wasn't running, so that was a plus.

"Something like that."

"And this stupid mark means that I belong to you or something?"

Yes, the bull said, but Asterion shook his head.

"No, it means you're under my protection and warns off supernatural beings like Medusa and the boys. That's all. It's not some magical binding spell. You're not my slave or my prisoner. After last night, you won't even have anyone guarding you unless you want the extra protection."

"So, I could walk out of here right now, and you wouldn't try to stop me?" There was a challenging glint in her eye that he was starting to become intimately acquainted with.

"You think you have a better chance out there on your own than here with me?"

"That's not what I asked."

Asterion's teeth ground together, but he managed to take a calming breath before he answered, "You're free to leave whenever you like. You'll be safer here, but I can't make you stay."

"But you want me to? Even after what I told you last night about killing the only other person I've ever been close to?" She sounded pissed, but Asterion could hear the unease underneath it.

Is she nervous?

"We've all done shitty things, Ariadne. I'm not about to judge you on what you've done to survive."

"Okay, then, I'll stay," she said as she got up and walked back to the kitchen for more coffee, leaving Asterion confused, which was becoming the norm whenever she was around.

"You'll stay? Just like that? No kicking and screaming?" he asked as he followed her. She was bending over rummaging in his fridge.

"Do you want me to kick and scream?" Ariadne asked as she put a tub of almond yogurt on the counter.

"No, I like it when you're not going for my throat," Asterion replied honestly.

"Then quit your bitching." Ariadne opened the tub and passed him a spoon before she sat up on the counter and dug her own into it. She was already more at home in his kitchen than he'd ever been.

Not wanting to say something stupid, he ate a spoonful of yogurt.

"We need to set up some surveillance at that property, maybe get some cameras in place so we can monitor it for twenty-four hours," Ariadne said thoughtfully.

"Why wait? I could send a group of guys in right now," Asterion argued. Ariadne shook her head as she scooped out more yogurt.

"Because we can't trust them. You're forgetting about your mole. In fact, we shouldn't let them know about the location at all. At least, not yet. I'll do it, that way if the mole turns up, we'll catch them on camera."

"You're not going over there by yourself," Asterion said a little too quickly.

"It's the best plan, and you know it. Besides, you told me I was free to go whenever I wanted."

"I don't want you risking your life just to plant a few stupid cameras," Asterion said.

"I'm not risking anything. It's an easy job, and unlike you, I can blend into a crowd."

Asterion's phone pinged, and he was grateful for the distraction.

"I'm needed upstairs in the club for about an hour. Can we talk about this idea of yours after that?"

"Only if you bring down a really fancy bottle of wine to make it worth the wait," she said as she sucked the yogurt off her spoon. "I'm sure I can kill an hour in your shower with all of those interesting jets."

Asterion had an internal debate of the merits of not going upstairs but knew he couldn't drop his whole life to entertain her, even if he sorely wanted to. He moved past her and put his spoon in the dishwasher.

"It's only a staff meeting. I shouldn't take too long," Asterion mumbled. One of Ariadne's long legs shot out, blocking his exit.

"Before you go, I wanted to say thanks for last night. I was a mess in more ways than one, and you were cool about it. I appreciate that."

"I didn't hear an actual thank you in all of that," he teased.

Quick as a flash, she had him by his shirt front and pulled him in between her legs. She gave him a few seconds to back out if he wanted to and when he didn't, she gave him a long, lingering kiss, her tongue doing wicked things that sent a bolt of excitement straight to his dick.

Her hands slid down his back and gave his ass a surprising squeeze.

"Thank you," Ariadne said huskily, letting him go with a gentle shove.

"Enjoy that shower," he replied as he straightened his shirt.

"You know I will," she replied with a wide smile. "Work hard."

"You're such a terror." Asterion made a quick retreat from the kitchen. It was going to be the fastest staff meeting in history.

15

Ariadne waited until Asterion had left the apartment before she took out the phone she had swiped from his back pocket.

She found Medusa's phone number and sent her a text: *Going to need some cameras to set up around Pithos's building. Help a sister out? Ariadne.*

Does the Bull know you have his phone?

Does it matter? It needs to be done, and we can't trust the blockheads.

Goody pack will be waiting at reception for you. Leave his phone behind. Medusa signed off with a snake emoji, and Ariadne went to get dressed.

Her brush with poisoning the previous night had left her hollow-eyed, but it was nothing that a bit of makeup and a decent ponytail couldn't disguise. Lethe was a more middle-class district, so she made sure her clothes didn't have any holes in them when she dressed in jeans and a t-shirt.

Everything in Asterion's apartment was neat in its perfect place, but his wardrobe was insane.

"You're not half OCD, Asterion," Ariadne said, opening his draws and looking at all his folded clothes.

After a bit of searching, she found a drawer of expensive watches and sunglasses in neat rows. She helped herself to a pair of designer aviators and a watch that probably cost the same amount as the nicest house in Hellas.

As promised, there were no bodyguards outside the apartment doors when Ariadne slipped out ten minutes later.

The club wasn't open, so the elevators weren't locked down to swipe cards only, and the kitchens were empty of staff. Clearly, 'staff meeting' meant everyone.

Perfect.

Ariadne made it out of the building without being seen and walked the two city blocks to Serpentine Tower. The foyer was the combination of a green marble temple and a technological haven. Screens projected a news stream of Medusa in a stunning emerald green velvet suit, scathingly criticizing the current foreign policy.

She seemed the complete opposite of the woman in Doctor Who pajamas Ariadne had talked to less than an hour ago.

"Miss Ariadne?" A cool, polished voice asked. A woman in a tailored black dress held out a heavy envelope to her. "Ms. Medusa would like you to have this, with her compliments. Also, she's instructed me to take you to your car. If you'll follow me?"

"Sure thing," Ariadne said like she knew what was going on. *What car?*

In the underground car park, the woman gave her a set of keys to a small white Renault and left her to it. The package in her arms buzzed, and Ariadne retrieved a smartphone.

Snake Queen flashed on the screen, and she fumbled to answer it.

"You are either insane or brilliant, but I can't make up my mind which," Medusa said.

"Can't it be both? Should I ask why I'm being loaned a car?"

"Because you need to do this quickly and get back to the Labyrinth before Asterion finds you're gone. This was the least flashy car I could organize in such short notice. I trust you know how to drive?"

"Of course, I know to drive. I couldn't take any of Asterion's cars. He would've known I left."

"And would've killed you for taking one of his babies. Okay, in the package is a hands-free headset, so put it in," Medusa instructed as Ariadne got into the car.

"Why?"

"Because I'm giving you remote and emotional support."

"You think I need it?"

"No, but it means I'll be able to configure the cameras you set and also reassure Asterion you're okay when he loses his shit because you left the club without telling him."

"He said I wasn't a prisoner, so he'll have to deal with it," argued Ariadne.

"And you think he'll see it that way? Bless."

Ariadne plugged in her hands-free and wondered if having Medusa involved and running commentary in her head was going to be a good thing.

The building in Lethe was on the edge of an industrial estate that backed onto the Styx port.

Ariadne had to admit, if Pithos was into smuggling, it would be the perfect spot to do it. She parked two blocks from the building, bought a coffee from a local café, and people watched as she waited twenty minutes for the sun to go down.

"Better move that perky ass of yours. You have about another fifteen minutes before Asterion's meeting is finished. He would know he left his phone behind by now, so he'll be heading straight back to the apartment," warned Medusa.

"He'll get over it."

"You hope. Honestly, you could've given him one day to honor that truce of yours."

"Truce and 'not a prisoner' imply I can leave whenever I want. If he doesn't like it, I'll leave permanently."

"Oh, to be a fly on the wall when that conversation goes down," Medusa hooted with laughter.

Ariadne ignored her as she found the fire escape to the nearest building and scaled it soundlessly. There was a tall building facing where the Pithos signal had come from, so Ariadne made a point of checking the roof for any existing CCTV. There wasn't any, which made both Ariadne and Medusa suspicious.

"Doesn't seem right in that part of Styx," said Medusa thoughtfully.

"Unless they know that a certain Snake Queen could hack into them," Ariadne replied. She took out the tiny cameras and began to stick them behind downpipes and under windowsills so that they wouldn't be seen from the street.

"Let me know when we are up and running so I can get out of here," she said. There was tapping in the background as Medusa hummed away to herself.

"These are new prototypes I've been playing with, so the usual camera scanners and signal blockers won't work even if they are clever enough to use them," Medusa explained. "Shit, looks like there is company headed your way. I've picked them up on traffic cams about a block from you."

Ariadne set the last of the cameras, scaled the building and crouched down in the shadows on the roof.

A plain white van pulled up in front of the Pithos building, and three men got out. They were the over-muscled type that Ariadne usually associated with bodyguards who were hired for bulk and not skill.

"Time to get out of there. The cameras are up and running. Don't try to engage them. You don't know who else is in the building, so don't risk it," Medusa said as if knowing what Ariadne was thinking.

She contemplated arguing on principle before relenting to common sense.

"Okay, I'll head back to the club."

"Don't dawdle or detour on your way. Asterion's onto you."

Ariadne let out a long groan. "Shit."

∾

ASTERION FELT the change in the apartment as soon as he stepped into it. It was too quiet, too cold.

He checked the bedroom, knowing he'd find nothing, but was still disappointed when he did.

"What the hell, Ariadne," he said when he found his phone on the kitchen counter. She must've picked his pocket when she'd kissed him.

He'd been so distracted by her mouth he hadn't even felt what her hands were doing.

Why not take it with her if she planned on bailing? He scrolled through his messages, found the exchange with Medusa, and saw red before hitting the call button.

"Two calls in one day? I feel so special," Medusa answered.

"Where is she?" he asked, trying to keep his voice from rising.

"Don't worry. I'm on the other line with her. I've stuck with her the whole time."

"What the actual fuck, Susa? You shouldn't have let her leave at all! Let alone encourage her to go by herself into the enemy's camp."

"You need to get something into that bull head of yours. Ariadne is a capable, kick-ass woman. She's not like one of the ditsy club girls you usually sleep with. She has more experience wading through the filthy underbelly of Styx than the majority of your men. She was born into it, and has lived through the worst of it. You can't treat her like a damsel and expect to keep her."

"I haven't kept her at all! She's fucking gone again, and it took me six weeks to find her last time. I can't keep her here if she doesn't want to stay, but I would've at least liked a goodbye," Asterion said, hating the truth of it.

"That's right. You can't keep her. You can't treat her like a princess when she's an assassin."

"So what am I meant to do? Twiddle my thumbs and hope she decides not to run?"

"You can stop acting like a big baby for a start. Suck it up and wait for her to return. Go to the gym, work off all that sexual frustration. I'll keep an eye on our girl."

"If Ariadne looks like she's about to leave the city, will you tell me?" Asterion asked. Medusa's laugh was delightful.

"Absolutely not," she replied and hung up.

Asterion took her advice and went downstairs to the gym. He had been alone for a long time, and all Ariadne had been was a pain in his ass from the day they met.

Get a grip, man. Three days ago, you were going to kill her, and now you're sulking like a spurned lover.

A few kisses and whatever happened in the shower didn't mean they were lovers. Her debt with him had been cleared with all the information she'd given and by her surviving the Labyrinth. She owed him nothing. She had no reason to stay, especially not for him.

"What? No, Spindle?" Vin asked as Asterion entered the gym.

"She's running an errand," Asterion said. He took off his shirt and stretched his shoulders before pulling himself up the climbing wall.

"Run an errand or run off?" Theseus asked skeptically. Asterion gave him a pissed off glare over his shoulder.

"She's coming back," he snapped.

Theseus gave a lazy shrug. "Maybe it would be better if she didn't. She's caused enough disruption in our lives."

"You're just annoyed that she didn't take you up on that good luck kiss. Poor, pretty Theseus," teased Vin. High up on the wall, Asterion stopped climbing, his whole body tensing with anger.

"You tried to kiss her?" he asked. There was so much threat in his voice that Vin stopped laughing.

"Just as a joke. I wouldn't have gone through with it."

"Don't worry, boss, she offered to punch him in the dick instead," said Vin, trying to smooth the situation.

"That's my assassin," Asterion said with a grin.

"*Your* assassin? Are you fucking serious? Did you not learn from your last round in the sack that she's nothing but a manipulative little bitch, and you can't trust her?" Theseus demanded.

Vin inhaled sharply and stepped away from Theseus. Asterion bounded off the wall and landed on top of Theseus, pinning him to the ground with one move.

Kill him, the bull urged.

"Asterion, don't. He didn't mean it," said Vin urgently.

Theseus's expression was incredulous. "You would kill me...over her? I've been your friend for three years, and I only want you to recognize the truth in front of your face. She's not *good* for you, Asterion. You deserve better than a woman who would be willing to kill you for money."

"You don't get to decide what I deserve, boy. She might not be my lover, but she is still under my protection, and I won't have you or anyone else speak about women in that way. Are we clear?" demanded Asterion, his hands tightening around Theseus's neck.

"We're clear. I won't speak against her, just like I won't say I told you so when she breaks your fucking heart."

The shift to the bull was swift and painful.

"I am the Minotaur," he snarled in Theseus's pale face. "I don't have a fucking heart."

16

Ariadne managed to get to the doors of the apartment before she ran into any guards.

Vin was standing in front of them with his arms folded. Something in his demeanour relaxed when he saw her, and he sagged against the double doors in relief.

"I'm glad you came back, assassin. I wouldn't have liked to hunt you down again," he said gruffly.

"I'm starting to think you like me, Vin."

"It doesn't matter what I like. The boss likes you; that's what counts."

Ariadne bit her lip. "How pissed is he?"

"Very, and keeping it together poorly," replied Vin as Ariadne winced. "Damn."

"You thought he wouldn't be? Listen, girlie, from the moment I saw his reaction to you on the street, I knew you were special. He's not been himself since he met you. Don't know what that means, but he's softer than he seems. He trusts you, even after all the shit you've put him through. Don't make him regret it."

"All I did was go out for a while. He can't keep me locked up."

"He knows that, which is why he didn't come after you. He's not doing it to be a controlling dick. He's trying to protect you. Despite what he says when he's angry, the Minotaur *does* have a heart."

Ariadne waved him aside. "Move. I need to go grab a bull by the horns."

"I don't want to know if that's a euphemism," he complained.

Inside, the apartment was tense with heat and expectation. The air seemed to hum with Asterion's mood, and for the first time, Ariadne felt a flicker of unease lick at her spine.

"You came back," a voice said from the shadows. It sounded like Asterion but deeper and huskier.

"You didn't think I would?" She stayed perfectly still, not wanting to make any sudden movements. There was something behind her, and her heart began to race as her brain tried to warn her of the danger and make her run and hide.

"You had no reason to come back."

"Maybe I like you when you're not trying to scare me. Maybe, a little then too." Ariadne slowly turned to face the Minotaur looming over her. "Hey, big guy."

She couldn't turn away from him, he was so mesmerizing. Huge golden eyes stared down at her with an intensity that made her know that she was prey.

"Why are you so defiant?" he demanded.

"You're not the boss of me," Ariadne reminded him. Maybe if she could get that through to the bull, the man would follow.

"I might not be your boss, but you are still mine," Asterion growled.

"I'm not one of your cars, asshole. I don't care how much you think this Minotaur act is going to scare me into submission," Ariadne said, giving him a hard poke in the shoulder.

He grabbed her hand and pulled her up against him, so her body was flush against his. His head bent down to nuzzle at her shoulder.

"You came back," he repeated, breathing in her scent.

"You can be an overbearing ass, but I still like you."

"I know, I can smell it on your skin."

Ariadne stroked her fingers down the soft fur of his neck before she placed her cheek against his.

"I had no reason not to return," she said, and then very slowly, she put her arms around his neck.

"Even if this is what I really am?"

"Even like this, you're still the best man I've ever known. You could've killed me, but you didn't. I knew the first time I saw you that you didn't deserve the death I was charged to give you. Why do you think I said sorry so many times? I kept the shirt to remind myself that despite the horror, there is some decency left, even in those that others call a monster," she admitted honestly.

It was easier to say those things to the Minotaur instead of the man.

Ariadne stroked the thick black mane at the back of his neck and softened further into him, silently trying to reassure him.

His arms enclosed her, making her feel like a doll beside him. He made her soft and vulnerable, two things she'd never felt in her life. It didn't cause her to panic as she thought it would.

Heat shivered over him, and he shifted until he was a man once more.

"Are you okay?" Ariadne asked uncertainly. Asterion's hands stroked down her back.

"I am now. You can...calm him down."

"You mean, I can calm *you* down. I still see him when I look at you and you when I look at him," Ariadne said, leaning back so she could run her thumbs along his cheek. "Here, in the eyes. Oh look, they are still pissed off around the edges."

"Can you blame me? I was worried all bloody day. I believe the gods designed you as my great test," he said, kissing her cheek.

"Do you think that despite the glorious fuck ups on my behalf that we could one day be lovers, Asterion?" Ariadne asked before she could talk herself out of it. Asterion rested his forehead against hers.

"I think that is inevitable as the sunrise, sweetness. I've tried and failed to fight it, but I can't help that I adore your crazy, violent, smart ass self," he said with a sigh.

"You do? Even after I picked your pocket this morning?" she asked, biting her lip.

"I wish you didn't have ulterior motives when you kissed me, but yeah, even when you do."

"To be fair, I thought of picking your pocket *after* I was already kissing you."

"Makes me wonder what I'm about to lose right now," he said, as he lifted her chin and kissed her slow and sweet enough to cause a flutter in her chest.

Oh, shit, Hades was right. You are falling in love with him.

Ariadne buried the thought, unwilling to give it room to grow. She unbuttoned his shirt and traced the grooves of his muscles, loving the solid strength of him. Gods save her; he was beautifully put together.

"I hope you have something to show for your little rebellion today," he mused before gently biting her bottom lip.

"I didn't engage them. Only set cameras on the building opposite and got out of there," Ariadne replied. She gasped as he slid a hand under her shirt and stroked her spine.

"Hmm, you still should've waited for me to go with you. I can't lock you up, so maybe I need to work on making the thought of you leaving me unbearable."

"Work away. I still won't sit around and wait for the menfolk to do everything," Ariadne said sarcastically.

Asterion nibbled at her neck, making her jump. "I *know*. I hate that the thing that stresses me out the most is also one of the things I admire about you."

"Are you saying you like how rebellious I am?" she asked with mock horror.

"Don't push your luck, assassin."

"Using your growly voice to frighten me doesn't work. It only turns me on," Ariadne said.

"I know," he chuckled darkly. Goosebumps rose along her arms as his roaming hands rested on her hips.

"You want to see what your clever assassin did today?" she asked and then paused over her choice of words. Asterion's grin widened.

Damn it.

She reached into a satchel bag and pulled out an iPad that Medusa had given her.

"This links up to the cameras I set up and also the CCTV in the surrounding block." Ariadne moved out of the circle of his arms so she could try to concentrate.

She set up the iPad on the dining table, but Asterion walked over and knocked the screen over.

"What are you-" Asterion picked her up and put her on the table, trapping her between his knees and placing his hands on either side of her.

"We haven't finished our conversation," he said. His eyes glowed with heat, and her heart began to race.

"But the surveillance on Pithos-"

"I don't care about the fucking Pithos. I care that I thought I'd lost you today, and I didn't, and I want to prove that you haven't made the wrong choice by picking me."

"And how are you planning to do that?" Ariadne moved her hands into his open shirt, nails digging into his sides as she pulled him closer.

She wrapped her legs around his hips and locked his hardness right where she wanted it. He grabbed her hair and fisted it firmly, exposing her neck to his ravaging mouth.

Ariadne groaned against the easy dominance of the position, feeling like she'd agree to just about anything when he turned the intensity of his desire onto her.

She'd had to put up with men who liked to be in charge in the bedroom before, but unlike them, Asterion was always gentle with her, and she knew if she didn't like something, he would respect it and stop. Knowing that made her want him even more.

She needed more of him, to feel that hot skin against her. She pushed the shirt from his shoulders, sighing against his mouth as she explored his powerful body.

Asterion moved his hands down to her jeans, and Ariadne lifted her hips so he could unbutton them and rip them off with her underwear.

Ariadne struggled to pull off her shirt and bra between kisses until she was completely naked on the dining room table. Asterion pushed the iPad and decorative centerpieces out of the way so that she could lie back. His gaze was hot enough to burn as he looked at her bare and vulnerable before him.

"You are perfection, Ariadne. No wonder you've turned me into your creature. This is all I've been able to think about for weeks; you stretched out naked and so, so edible," Asterion murmured.

Her eyes fluttered closed as his mouth moved along her collarbone. Ariadne arched into him, whimpering as his strong hands played with her breasts.

"I didn't get the chance to spend adequate time worshiping your breasts during our last encounter, something I mean to rectify," Asterion said before sucking on her nipple.

She was helpless to fight against the sensations bombarding her, teeth and tongue, and hands making her burn.

Ariadne's hands slipped from his shoulders as he moved down her body, nipping and kissing as he went.

"Asterion," she whimpered, burning to feel him inside of her.

"Yes, assassin?" he asked, hands trailing down her thighs.

"Stop being such a tease and get inside me already."

"No," he said, moving her legs over his shoulders. Ariadne groaned as his mouth lowered onto her.

A growl of satisfaction at her reaction came out of him, and he tasted her again. She whispered his name, and whatever was holding his self-control back vanished.

Asterion devoured her greedily until she saw stars and screamed beneath him. He didn't stop as he slid his fingers inside of her, teeth scraping gently against her clit.

Her orgasm was so powerful that she had to grip the edge of the table to stop herself from falling off it.

Mind and body broken entirely, Ariadne didn't think she could take much more until she opened her eyes and saw him naked and hard, a satisfied smile as he looked down at the mess he'd made of her.

"Please," she begged as he rubbed his dick against her sensitive entrance.

"Promise me that you won't ever leave without telling me first," Asterion said. He eased inside her just enough for her to hiss at him with frustration.

"You're not the boss..." she managed, wriggling in an attempt to push more of him inside her. He placed a hand on her stomach, pinning her down.

"It's not about being the boss or stopping you from having freedom. I only want to know when you're leaving. It's not too much to ask, is it?" he eased inside of her a little further, and she reached out for him. Asterion was quicker, catching her by the wrists and pinning her arms above her head.

"Holy gods, you can be a bastard," she groaned as he thrust slowly, teasing, pushing her self-control.

"Promise me, and I'll give you whatever you want. I'll burn the world to the ground, or I'll lay it at your feet, just promise me you won't run away and scare me again."

"Asterion..." Ariadne cried, her body screaming at his ruthlessness. He leaned over her, kissed the tear of pleasure that had slipped from the corner of her eye.

"Yes, Ariadne."

"I promise."

"You better not be lying," he said, moving further into her, making her arch up against him.

"I'm not. I promise." Ariadne fixed her eyes on his, holding the intensity of his gaze as she said the words that there was no coming back from. "Whatever I am, I'm yours for as long as you want me."

He kissed her roughly and whispered in a voice that was all Minotaur, "What if I wanted you for a very long time? Would you stay?"

"Yes," she admitted.

Asterion was done with games. He slammed into her, and Ariadne cried out. She had dreamed about him all those nights they had been apart, haunted by the feeling of him inside of her, nothing satisfying her craving for him.

He let her wrists go, gripping her hips, dragging her into him with every thrust. She sat up, mouth devouring his, pulling him closer, needing more of him against her.

Asterion snarled and lifted her into the air as she moved up and down him. Pictures fell from the wall as they slammed into it, Asterion holding her tightly against it until she screamed his name.

She could see flickers of the Minotaur in one eye, the man in the other, and both lost in her. She scraped her nails down his back, tightening her thighs around this powerful creature that couldn't get enough of her. She snarled her disapproval when he stopped.

"Don't worry. I'm nowhere near done with you." Asterion carried her to his room, and she gasped as he lay back on the bed, holding her on top of him.

She adjusted to the sensation of him so hard and huge inside of her she thought she wouldn't be able to contain him.

"I know how you like being in control," Asterion teased, folding his arms behind his head. The thought of someone like him submitting to her sent her desire spiraling.

She gripped his chest to steady herself and began to rock against him, pulling up, so he was almost out of her before pushing him back in, slow and hard.

"Fucking hell," he moaned.

"Hmm, I wonder what promises I should squeeze out of you like you did me?" she mused as she pulled up again.

"What could you possibly want that I haven't already offered to give you?" Asterion sat up slowly, taking her face tenderly in her hands. "You've ruined me, Ariadne. I don't want to live without you, and I'll kill anyone who tries to get in our way."

Ariadne kissed him, moving slowly against him until he was at his hilt, their arms and legs gripping tightly to each other until they couldn't get any closer.

"Come for me, Asterion, and then we'll destroy our enemies together." She was on her back in a blink, whimpering as her orgasm broke her. He cried out her name, his own release leaving him trembling in her arms.

"All the gods help Pithos if you fight the way you fuck," Ariadne said, laying her head against his chest.

Asterion laughed, pulling her closer. "For you, sweetness, I'll make their very shades tremble."

17

The next morning, Asterion woke to a steaming cup of coffee, delivered by a very tousled woman.

"Morning," Ariadne said, color staining her cheeks with a self-conscious blush. Asterion took the coffee and kissed her.

"Thanks, sweetness. You're up early."

"I wanted to download the footage from our cameras last night and see if anything exciting happened. You get coffee because I'm nice that way."

"Should I be worried you've put poison in it? Sedatives?" Asterion asked, yelping when she pinched him.

"Don't be a smart ass, or I'll never make you coffee again."

"I apologize," he said, drinking a large mouthful to prove he trusted her not to spike him.

"I'll find some clothes and go see the kitchen about breakfast. You want to start on the footage?"

"Good idea, I'm starving. Someone made me have sex all night, and I missed dinner," she said with a wicked grin.

"You are so full of it. I can't make you do anything," Asterion said, laughing.

"Very true." Ariadne kissed him and got out of his reach, before they didn't end up getting out of bed at all.

Asterion was showered and dressed in record time and headed upstairs. There was no one watching his apartment doors, but he found Vin in the kitchen devouring a plate of bacon.

"Sort that disobedient assassin out?" Vin asked, a knowing smile on his face.

"Ariadne has agreed not to leave without telling someone first."

"I expected you two would have a screaming match, just not *that* kind of screaming match. It's the only time I've left my post from sheer embarrassment."

"Shut up and find someone to put together some breakfast for us," Asterion said and laughed awkwardly.

"Sure thing, boss. I'll make sure it's a big one. Lots of carbs and maybe a few energy drinks on the side."

Asterion lifted his middle finger at him. "Have you seen Theseus this morning?"

"Upstairs, going over last month's takings. He's been snarling at everyone." Vin shook his head. "The kid is good, but he needs to learn when to back off and keep his mouth shut."

"I'll fix it. I didn't mean to snap so hard at him yesterday. Ariadne..."

"Makes your brain all fuzzy with pheromones. I get it. You're lucky you found her before me, boss. I like fiery women."

"She's too much woman for you to handle," retorted Asterion as he headed for the lifts.

"Too much for you too, stud," Vin called back. Asterion was inclined to agree with him. It didn't stop the smile on his face. He caught his reflection in the mirrored sides of the elevator and tried to change it back to his habitual scowl.

You're an idiot. Anyone would think that you've never been laid before.

Theseus was sitting at the bar, staring at a laptop screen. Asterion pulled up a chair beside him.

"I'm sorry about yesterday. I was out of line," he apologized before the other man could speak.

"We both were," Theseus said, swiveling his chair to face him.

"You've been a good friend, and if our positions were reversed, I'd probably feel the same. Ariadne is not what you think she is, Theseus."

"Maybe not. I know you don't trust easily, and yet you trust her. Why? Don't say the Labyrinth, because that's a test of skill, not integrity," said Theseus.

"I can sense when someone is lying to me. I can smell it. She's been honest since we caught up with her and has given us everything she knows about Pithos. As for her trying to kill me, Ariadne was put in a tough position. You have no idea what that bastard Minos has put her through. If it meant freedom from him, from that life, I would've killed me too." Asterion rubbed his neck, unable to keep the grin off his face.

"I *like* her, Theseus. I've liked her since I met her on the street. She's a survivor, and she's not worried about what I am or what I've done."

Theseus let out a huff of laughter. "You've got it so bad, Dys. I knew the day would come eventually. She seems like a good fit for the place. Maybe it's time for a feminine touch."

Asterion gave him a heavy pat on the back. "Good man."

"Tell me about Pithos. Found out anything yet?" he asked curiously.

"We might have found where the rats are hiding. I'll let you know when we are ready to make a move on them."

Theseus cracked his knuckles. "Excellent. I'm ready to take the fight to them after that attack at Isthmia."

"You and me both. I would've been carving bullets out of my hide for a week if it wasn't for Ariadne."

"You gotta love a girl who only does headshots." Theseus smiled widely. "Pithos doesn't stand a chance."

By the time Asterion made it back to the apartment with a tray of breakfast, Ariadne had managed to sync the iPad to the television and was scanning through footage.

"My hero!" she exclaimed when he placed the tray on the coffee table in front of her.

"Anything of interest yet?" he asked, sitting down beside her. Ariadne shook her head, her mouth too full of her vegan croissant to speak.

"I've only skimmed through the first hour, and after the van load turned up, no one has gone in or out of the building," she replied, sinking back on the couch.

"How many hours have we got to go through?"

"Seven, though you can hardly tell in this apartment. This building is ten stories high, why not put a penthouse at the top. Easier to get out of than underground if something goes wrong."

Food caught in Asterion's throat, and he swallowed it painfully. "I had plans to do it. I have space up there. When it came to moving in, I panicked."

Ariadne's face turned from the TV and back to him. "Why?"

"Up until Hades found me, I had spent my entire life in the labyrinth on Knossos. I was a feral thing when he freed me, and even though I've come a long way since then, thanks to Hades's infinite patience and a good routine, I find it hard to sleep above the surface," admitted Asterion.

"How did he find you? I heard the palace at Knossos is nothing but rubble."

"Our blood recognizes each other. My father, Minos, was the product of one of Zeus's many affairs. After the economic crash, when Hades decided that he was going to be in the light once more, he went looking for others like him. The forgotten ones, the monsters. He knew I was trapped from the moment he got to Knossos. He's a tough bastard, but he saved me and Medusa and the triplets. That's why we would do anything for him, back him in war and peace."

"He's family. That explains why he thinks it is okay to give me relationship advice," huffed Ariadne.

Asterion choked on his fruit salad. "He did what now?"

"Never mind. It doesn't matter anymore because everything has worked out. We have a truce and everything."

"What's 'and everything'?" he asked suspiciously.

"Hot sex with a demigod. Vegan croissants. Fancy coffee. A cult to track down and kill. What more could a girl ask for?" she said, leaning across to kiss him. A happy growl came out of Asterion's throat, and she pulled back.

"Oh, don't start that. We have important work to do, so don't distract me with your dick."

"I haven't done anything, and neither has my dick," he protested, but Ariadne wasn't listening.

"Whoa, lookout, we have an SUV turning up," she said. The cameras from the traffic lights followed it and cut out before reappearing on the cameras Ariadne had set. Four men climbed out, guns over their shoulders, and in the same protective gear their attackers in Isthmia wore.

"They must be funded because that kind of gear doesn't come cheap," Asterion commented.

"And who might this be?" Ariadne zoomed in on a fifth person coming out of the car. They wore dark robes with a deep hood, their face covered in a white mask.

"Very theatrical. There's no way to tell if it's a man or woman." She paused it and took a screenshot, before zooming in further.

"What's that painted on it?" Asterion asked, trying to make it out.

"They look like black tears. That must be the boss. Look at how tense those guys are."

The figure waited until the doors to the building were opened for them, and they all disappeared inside.

"That makes potentially nine guys and whoever is in the mask in that building at any one time. Light in numbers, but they will be trained, like in Isthmia," said Asterion.

"Do you have enough guys with experience? The ones you brought with you seemed to take off when the shooting started," Ariadne replied.

"We expected a single woman, not guys with guns. I'll get Theseus to put together some men and make sure they have been in a firefight before."

"Including you and me, we should make a good enough challenge for them," Ariadne said, skimming through the footage looking for any other arrivals.

"And if I asked you not to come?" Asterion was torn, knowing she could handle Pithos and wanting her to be safe.

"You're not dumb enough to ask such a thing," Ariadne replied. She moved so she could curl into his side. "If you go, I go, big guy. Get used to it. We are a team, and while we still don't know who the mole is, I don't trust anyone to watch that gorgeous back of yours except me. Understand?"

She's protecting us? US? The bull demanded. Asterion didn't have the words for what welled up inside of him.

Instead, he placed his arm around her and kissed the top of her head. "Okay, Ariadne."

"No arguing?"

He shrugged. "No point, I know I'd lose anyway."

"Damn straight," she said, pressing her lips into his shoulder.

"Let's hit them tonight. I want this over with, and so does Hades. Monster hunters are bad for business."

Ariadne's expression turned dark. "And then we go after Minos."

18

The night was uncomfortably hot and sticky with humidity and nervous anticipation.

This is why it's better to work alone, Ariadne thought, shifting the blade strapped to her hip.

She looked at the group of ten men that Theseus and Asterion had gathered.

They all were Labyrinth survivors and comfortable around weapons. Despite that, they didn't have the same calm confidence that the assassins had.

Ariadne had never had to worry about the variables involving other people and their actions. She could plan a job, slip in and out, have all her bases covered. Having to work with others made that job so much harder. She didn't dare risk looking too long at Asterion. She didn't want him being anywhere near Pithos, who were so keen on killing his kind off.

Fuck, what are you doing, bringing someone you care about into this shit with you?

She knew his past, knew it involved abuse and murder as much as hers did, but it was a different kind of horror.

He'd escaped from it. Ariadne could only just see a chink of light on her horizon. She hated that he was there because of her and that she had been the one to bring this to his door.

You know Pithos would've found someone else to kill him, Lia's voice said at the back of her head. For the first time since her death, Lia sounded like her old self, like when she used to try to talk Ariadne out of doing something stupid.

Sorry, Lia, I never did learn.

"You five are with me. We'll go through the front," Asterion instructed before looking at Ariadne, Theseus, and Vin. "You three will guard the back door to make sure no one escapes. Give it a few minutes after we make the initial assault and meet us in there. Okay?"

Ariadne kept her mouth closed. Asterion was fine with her coming, but he wasn't about to throw her into the immediate crossfire.

"I can heal my body with magic, sweetness. You can't. I don't want to risk you getting hurt," he'd said so gently that Ariadne couldn't argue with him.

She had agreed, even though she hated being separated from him. She had fought with him by her side in Isthmia, so she knew they made a good team, something that she couldn't say of Theseus or Vin.

"Stay close, and I'll protect you, princess," Theseus said once they got into position minutes later.

"Do you think I'm the one that needs protecting? You're cute," said Ariadne, not taking her eyes off the back door of the building.

"It's not about capabilities. It's about you getting out in one piece. The boss cares for you, which means I'll protect you if you need it or not," he replied.

"Please tell me you aren't going to get soppy on me too, Vin," she said, turning to him.

"You wish. I saw you tear about the Labyrinth. When the shooting starts, I expect you to protect me, not the other way around," Vin answered.

"Don't listen to him, assassin. When things get hot, Vin will jump in to shield you, same as me." Theseus moved his rifle off his shoulder and got into position.

"You both should be more concerned with protecting Asterion. He's the one Pithos wants dead. He shouldn't be here at all," Ariadne muttered. Vin rested a hand on her shoulder.

"Trust me, Ariadne, he'll be okay. He always is."

Ariadne didn't get a chance to argue with him. A loud explosion came from the front of the building, and the sounds of gunfire peppered the night.

Two men exited the building, and she rushed to take them down before they could reach the cars. She was aware of Vin calling out to her, but his voice drowned out from the rush of adrenaline.

Ariadne pulled the knife from its sheath and had it in the first man's jugular before he knew she was there. The second man swung his gun around, but Ariadne's blade was suddenly digging straight through the muscle of his forearm and forcing him to drop it.

Before she could finish him off, Theseus grabbed him from behind in a headlock and held on until he'd passed out.

"I had him," Ariadne snapped as she pulled the knife from the unconscious man's forearm.

"There is no I in team."

Ariadne adjusted her bulletproof vest before crouching low and opening the door.

"I got your six, assassin," said Vin from behind her.

Ariadne crept inside and knew at once they had been set up. There were more men in the building than the surveillance had shown them. *Where the hell had they come from?*

A supernatural bellow shook the building, and she hurried, staying low as she climbed over dead bodies in the darkness.

"They knew we were coming and were waiting," Vin whispered. Ariadne didn't care. A fight was a fight, and they were in it now.

They found a set of stairs, and Ariadne headed up them. She wanted to find the masked figure that was commanding all the men downstairs to die for them.

A part of her wanted to rush to find Asterion and haul him out of there. She told that part to shut the hell up; Asterion could take care of himself. She didn't have to show up like his white knight.

Ariadne found an office and kicked in the door. "Gods damn them," she cursed.

It was a viewing room, filled with screens showing loops of footage from the Labyrinth, the carpark and surrounding streets. They had been watching their every move.

"There's no one here. Let's keep moving," Theseus said and shot at the screens, destroying the workstation.

"Stop! What are you doing?" Ariadne shouted.

"I'm making sure no one can use that footage again."

"You fucking idiot! We could have taken that back to Medusa."

"Stop arguing, you two! We need to get back downstairs and find Asterion and the others," Vin said, getting between them.

Ariadne shoved past them and pulled out her other knife. This was *precisely* the reason she didn't work with anyone.

Ariadne didn't wait to see if they were following as she went back downstairs, searching for the enemy. She counted seven men, using furniture and shipping crates to hide behind.

Like a slice of shadow, she moved behind them, cutting them down silently one by one. She thought she heard Vin praying behind her, but he didn't interfere, and he didn't try to stop her as she slid into the killing calm that was her first nature.

The gunfire died off around her as she picked off Pithos's men that had Asterion and what remained of his crew pinned down.

"I think that's all of them," Vin said. Ariadne risked a glance over her shoulder.

"Where's Theseus?"

"Gone to check the perimeter, so nothing sneaks in to surround us."

The silhouette of a set of horns cut through the smoke and gloom. Ariadne's hearted pounded as she approached him. The Minotaur was covered in gore and looked like he'd climbed out from the Underworld itself.

"Are you hurt?" Ariadne asked, looking him over, unable to tell if any of the blood was his.

"No. They got four of my men when they ambushed us. There was no sign of the masked man," he grumbled.

"Not upstairs either. They must've gotten out before the fighting started. They knew where our cameras were placed, so they would've known how to hide in the blind spots."

"We can talk about this after we get the fuck out of here."

"Theseus has the back secured; let's go that way," Vin said. Asterion placed a hand on the small of Ariadne's back, a reassurance they both needed as they followed Vin through the blood-splattered hallways.

A chill swept up Ariadne's spine as they moved through the car park. She paused, her hands drawing her knives.

"What is it?" Asterion asked.

Ariadne stared up at the figures on the roof above them. "Assassins."

People moved out from the side streets, and Ariadne was thrown aside as a machine gun fired at them. Asterion and Vin went down, followed by the men behind them.

Ariadne crawled to the safety of the cars as a lithe woman dropped in front of her.

"Spindle, you fucking traitor," Lynx spat. Ariadne didn't hesitate. She attacked the other assassin with everything she had. Lynx's clawed gloves caught her vest, tearing the material with a single swipe. Ariadne blocked the follow-up blow with her knives, the claws narrowly missing her eyes.

"You don't have to do this, Lynx," said Ariadne as they squared off against each other again.

"Yes, I do, because I'm loyal to my father, unlike you. You were his favorite, and you betrayed him for the chance at some monster dick. Fuck, you are weak."

Ariadne threw her knife, as Lynx dodged. She was about to make another attack when a black plastic casing dropped from the roof above them.

Ariadne leaped out of the way, but it was too late. The casing exploded in grey mist, and Ariadne struggled back through the cars as the cloying paralytic smoke did its work on her.

Asterion was lying in a puddle of blood, with Theseus standing over him, his gun trained on Asterion's head.

"You fucking traitorous bastard. You were his friend!" Ariadne screamed as her legs gave way.

"Actually, I'm a *loyal* bastard, just not to him," Theseus said calmly.

"Why? What did they offer you?"

"They didn't have to offer me anything. Humankind got rid of these creatures once, and nothing is stopping us from doing it again," Theseus sneered as she crawled towards them. "What's the matter, Spindle? Had your strings cut?"

Ariadne ignored him; her attention focused on getting to Asterion.

Please don't be dead, please don't be dead.

She placed her hands over a gushing bullet wound in his chest, biting down a sob.

"Save your tears, Spindle," a new voice said. A masked figure stood behind her, their voice disguised with a scrambler. It was the same voice she'd heard over the phone when they offered her the contract.

"I'm going to kill you," she swore.

"I'm sure you like to think so. It's such a shame, Ariadne. Pithos would have welcomed a woman of your talents. I could never have anticipated your attachment to this monster."

"You're the fucking monster." Ariadne was shaking with fury and helplessness. Asterion coughed under her as she reached for his face.

"Run..." he gasped.

"She's not going anywhere, except with us," Theseus said his gun pressing into the back of her head.

"Don't fret, Ariadne. The great bull has recovered from worst wounds than this," the masked figure said as they loomed over them. "I'm not going to kill you tonight, Minotaur of Knossos. I will put you back in the darkness where you belong. Theseus, take the girl."

Ariadne threw herself over Asterion, cradling his head in her arms. His golden eyes were wild with anger and fear. He groaned, struggling to move.

"Listen to me, Asterion. You need to get better, and then you need to come and find me. You did it once, so I know you can do it again. Don't make me wait too long, because I'm pretty sure I'm in love with you. Do you hear me?" she whispered, too low for anyone to hear but him.

"Ari..." he managed. She thrashed as she was torn back from him. An assassin stepped forward, and Ariadne recognized her as the owner of the black casing.

"Belladonna, you bitch," Ariadne wheezed. The assassin's smile was cold as Theseus picked Ariadne up and slung her over his shoulder.

"Father sends his regards," Belladonna purred before a mist hit Ariadne's face. Her vision blurred and turned black before she was thrown into a van.

∽

ASTERION'S BODY burned with pain and heat. A pretty nurse with brunette hair hovered over him, scalpel in hand.

"Are you still with us, Asterion?" Selene asked. He managed to grunt in reply, and she went back to work.

Asterion hadn't ever thought she'd have to work on him one day, but Medusa had sent her with a van to retrieve them from Lethe.

His wounded men, including Vin, had been raced to the best hospital in Styx. There was no way that Asterion was going to trust humankind with his medical information, so he got a bottle of whiskey and a woman with a scalpel to dig out his bullets.

"Why is it that whenever I see you lately, you're always wounded?" Hades asked.

Selene didn't pay the Lord of Styx any attention as she began to stitch Asterion back together.

"T-they took her," Asterion managed through his teeth.

"I know, Medusa told me. She watched the whole thing. We sent the triplets, but Pithos was gone by the time they arrived." Hades sat down on a chair beside him.

"I don't believe they will kill Ariadne. Dead bait is no use, and they want you to go after them. What I can't figure out is why? Why not chop your head off while you were lying riddled with bullets? It seems impractical."

"They said they wanted to put me back into the darkness," said Asterion, taking another mouthful of whiskey.

Hades tutted. "And make a show of it so it will be remembered. Fucking humans and their egos. No wonder they are disguising themselves with theatre masks, the dramatic bastards."

"It was Theseus. Three fucking years. Now my men are dead, and Vin is struggling for his life. All for what? Some long game, grudge match? He took her, Hades. Minos is in on it. The assassins were there helping them. I'm going to gut that fucking prick-" shouted Asterion.

"Calm down, Asterion. We'll deal with Minos once we have Ariadne back. You can't rob her of her revenge."

Selene made a clicking sound with her tongue. "I've done what I can, Asterion. Try to rest so your body can heal."

"Thank you, Selene. Charon will drive you home." She packed up her old-fashioned doctor's case and, with a polite nod to Hades, hurried out the door.

"Four bullets. Fuckers." Asterion struggled to sit up and rest against the headboard of his bed.

"There's something else you're not telling me," Hades said, his silver eyes missing nothing.

"Not everything is your business, uncle."

"It is when my family is under attack. Who knows how many people they have recruited into this ridiculous cult? They want to make a spectacle of us—*my* Court. I will not allow that to happen. I won't risk it for a girl. I don't care how valuable she is to you."

"I love her, Hades," admitted Asterion.

The words Ariadne had whispered to him would be burned in his brain forever. He'd never been in love, but it would explain his need of her, his constant desire to protect her.

Mine, the Minotaur said, and he felt the truth of it settle deep inside of him.

"You barely know her, nephew. Don't fall into the trap of human emotions," Hades said, shaking his head.

Asterion took another two large mouthfuls from his bottle. "Doesn't matter. I do. She loves me back. She said so, right before they dragged her off. Now they've taken her gods know where and I'm too weak to go after them."

"You need to sleep. Your strength will return as it always does. Perhaps a bit of space from the woman's many appeals will help you to think things through clearly."

"As soon as I'm able, I'm going after them. You can't stop me," said Asterion.

Hades smiled coldly. "Why would I want to stop you? We will find where they are hiding, and then I fully intend on setting you and the triplets loose on them."

Once Hades was gone, Asterion rolled onto his least wounded side and buried his face into the pillow.

It still smelled of Ariadne, and even with the dull ache inside of him, it soothed him enough to sleep.

19

Ariadne didn't know if it was day or night inside the dark concrete room where she had been placed.

The room was bare except for a bucket in the corner and a bottle of water. She didn't know how many days had passed. She didn't know if they were in Styx or even Greece.

Ariadne had passed out inside the dark, rocking van the night of the attack and woke up in the room with her head pounding and mouth dry, thanks to whatever concoction Belladonna had dosed her with.

She knew from experience that Minos's favorite poisoner could keep her paralyzed for a week or a month, depending on how vindictive she felt.

Minos let them work with Pithos. Maybe he has been a member all along.

But if that was true, why would they work against him and offer her a freelance contract to kill Asterion? Another test of loyalty? It wouldn't surprise her.

Minos only ever looked after his interests, and if becoming a member of a shady, monster hunting cult would give him power, then he'd sign up for it.

Ariadne drank the water, figuring if they wanted to kill her, she'd already be dead. No, some other game was at play, something linked to Asterion.

They knew he would hunt her, and in doing so, he would fall right into whatever trap they set for him.

Please, Hades, don't let him be that stupid.

Ariadne didn't know if the Lord of Styx could hear the prayers of mortals. He didn't strike her as a boon granting kind of god, but she still did it in the hopes he would be powerful enough to stop Asterion from rushing in to try and save her.

Ariadne's head was ringing as she sat back down and rested her sore back against the dirty concrete wall. She'd been shell shocked to see the assassins at the building in Lethe and Theseus's betrayal, but the sight of Asterion gunned down had broken something inside of her that she hadn't known still existed.

She couldn't bear to think that he was dead. Thanatos had saved him once; he could do it again surely.

It took him dying in a pool of blood for you to tell him how you feel.

The truth was she hadn't even been able to quantify what she'd been feeling until that moment when it was too late.

Asterion had always seemed worried and confused that she could want him, knowing that he was the Minotaur. She felt the same way about him wanting her, knowing her reputation and how many people she'd killed.

And how many more she would kill to get out of wherever Pithos had stashed her.

Feelings of revenge were old friends to Ariadne. They were easier to understand than the churning worry and longing she felt for Asterion.

She drank more water and sank down into the dark place in her mind while she waited for Pithos to come.

It didn't surprise Ariadne that Theseus would be the one to come in and have a gloat.

She didn't know how much time had passed since there was no way to tell in the concrete hell box where she was kept. She'd rationed her water and tried to sleep.

Whatever came next, she'd need all her energy. She tried not to think about Asterion's body being covered in bullet wounds.

"You look like shit. That mixture of Belladonna's must pack more of a punch than we thought," Theseus said.

He was heavily armed, and although Ariadne was tempted to beat the ever-living shit out of him, she wasn't sure who else was in the building she was staying. She was still alive, which meant they wanted something.

"Bella's a professional, even if she's a bitch," Ariadne acknowledged.

"A part of me wishes we were able to turn you to our side." Theseus laughed. "I don't think any one of us could've predicted that you'd fall in love with the Great Beast."

"The Great Beast...the guy you were friends with for years, and who you were meant to protect. I thought you were a piece of shit when we met, but I hate that you proved me right," said Ariadne.

She was trying to remain calm. Asterion had trusted Theseus, which made Ariadne vow she would make sure that Theseus never had the chance to betray anyone else.

"Wow, you really have hatred burning in those pretty eyes. Were you falling in love with him? You have no idea what that monster is capable of. The blood that's on his hands. That you lowered yourself to have fucked him makes me want to vomit." Theseus pointed his gun at her.

"Get up. The boss wants to talk to you. I'd ask if you are going to behave yourself, but I know you won't, so I'm going to give you a warning instead. If you try to run, if you try to attack me, or if you even think of looking at me funny, I will put a bullet in your leg. Understand?"

"Sure, don't worry, Theseus. You've got nothing to fear from me. I'm going to let Asterion have the pleasure of killing you. Besides, I'm interested in meeting this boss of yours," Ariadne said and stood up. Theseus waved the barrel of his gun at her, and Ariadne walked from the room.

Her training kicked in, and she counted the iron doors that she assumed led to more cells, ten in all.

She saw a room full of monitors and black and white camera footage in one room. There weren't any windows around them.

As Ariadne walked up a set of concrete stairs, she knew that she'd been locked underground. The concrete stairs became an older stone with the grouting repaired, and the light grew.

"I'm curious to know what you stand to gain out of all this, Theseus. I mean, Asterion paid you well, he probably would've helped you out of any trouble. I don't get it."

"No, I don't suppose an orphan would understand obligations to family and country."

"From what I've seen of it, it's overrated. Did Asterion break your sister's heart or something?"

"No, but his kind hurt all of Greece when they returned and just took what they wanted. Haven't you read any of the stories? The gods always just took and took. Humankind fought them back into the shadows, and we'll do it again."

"Greece was burning, so you can't blame the beings that came to put out the fire," argued Ariadne. She had been eight years old at the time and freshly orphaned because of the rioting in Corinth. The years leading up to the crash weren't exactly the Golden Age.

"Greece should've been kept in the hands of humankind. The country would have bounced back, and the government would have settled," said Theseus.

"They weren't doing a good job. Otherwise, it wouldn't have gone to hell. Lots of rich people were standing on top of the poor people. My parents were both working two jobs to keep us fed and sheltered, so don't preach at me about the good old days," Ariadne said.

"My family lost everything the day the gods returned, so don't think I'm ever going to see the gods as my saviors," Theseus hissed, the barrel of his gun pressing her forward.

"If you still had something to lose by that stage, you were on top of the pile, and so now you've seen how the other ninety percent live, you are going to try to overthrow the gods that made sure we didn't all fucking kill each other?" Ariadne shook her head.

"Fucking spoilt rich kid pouting because he's got to work like the rest of us."

Ariadne expected the blow, but her teeth still rattled as she was slammed against a wall. Theseus's hand was around her throat in seconds.

"That is enough!" a stern voice commanded from the top of the stairs. "I did not recruit you to brawl with prisoners like a street mutt."

Theseus let Ariadne go with a shove, and she turned to look at the newcomer. The man was dressed in tactical gear, and everything about him screamed ex-military.

Ariadne walked the rest of the way towards the soldier, trying to contain the part of her ego that wanted to smirk at them until they were so enraged by her attitude that they did something stupid. She wanted to meet the boss under the mask.

The sun was setting, and Ariadne blinked rapidly at the light. They were in a ruined palace, parts of the walls and roof missing at intervals.

From the gaps, she saw they were on a hill, scrubby brush surrounding them, not great vegetation to hide in if she had to make a run for it.

A camp had been set up amongst the ruins of the palace, and everywhere she looked, there were men and women in black tactical gear carrying big guns.

Pithos has its own army...fucking perfect.

Guards opened a wooden door, and Ariadne stepped into a throne room. The walls were ochre red with frescoes of strange bird-headed lions painted with their heads tilted to the sky. A deep stone basin filled with water had been built into the middle of the room.

Sitting on a stone throne in front of it was the figure in the mask. Black silk robes covered them, but Ariadne saw the slope of a breast. She wore a porcelain mask of a woman, with an exaggerated smile and features, the eyes painted with trails of black tears. Theseus pushed Ariadne to her knees in front of the bowl.

"Hello again, daughter of Minos," the woman said, her voice disguiser still in use.

"Hi.... sorry, what was your name again?" Ariadne asked.

"Still have your sense of humor, I see. I thought a few days beneath the earth would have dampened some of your fire so you could think clearly about your situation."

Ariadne laughed. "My situation? You hired me to kill Hades's nephew, and then you blamed me when everything went to shit. You should've just paid me, and we wouldn't be stuck in this situation."

"Paid you? The beast lived."

"Oh no, I killed him, but Thanatos brought him back to life. So yes, technically, I fulfilled your stupid contract."

"And then you fell in love with the creature. Pathetic."

"He's pretty great if you bothered to get to know him," Ariadne said sweetly.

"He's an abomination born of parents cursed by the gods. He should've been killed at birth, not kept in a Labyrinth to act as an executioner. This palace was built on the sacrifices King Minos claimed from the rest of Greece, and once Asterion is dealt with, it will be bulldozed to the ground."

Ariadne looked around with fresh eyes. "We are on Crete?"

"We are, assassin. Now, I'm going to give you a choice. You can join us willingly and be spared from the horrors that your father is eager to punish you with, or you can watch Asterion die before Minos cuts you to pieces. Those are your options. Be useful or die like a dog."

"My usefulness. You mean as bait for Asterion?" Ariadne burst out laughing. "You seriously think he's dumb enough to come looking for the woman who killed him? Even if he was that stupid, Hades isn't. He'll never permit Asterion to come for me."

"Hades won't get a say in the matter. Asterion is very stubborn when it comes to you, and he has proven his attachment over and over again." The woman pointed to a small camera in the corner of the room.

"He might hold out while he thinks you're dead, but to see you tortured? I believe we'll see just how quickly he comes."

Ariadne was still staring at the camera when her head was shoved into the deep bowl in front of her.

20

It was four days before the bullet wounds in Asterion finally healed over. His muscles would ache for at least another week, but he was done lying around.

It had been a nightmare to sit still, his own mind working against him and filling with all the horrors that Ariadne would be suffering.

Hades's words about Minos training her to withstand torture didn't comfort him. It made him furious enough that he wanted to storm downtown and pull the Temple apart brick by brick.

Patience. Get Ariadne first and then go after Minos together.

He had promised her that no matter what happened, Minos would die. She deserved her revenge.

There was a knock at his door, and he had only just risen when it was kicked open, and Medusa walked in.

"Holy shit, the princess does come out of her tower," Asterion said, so surprised that he sat back down on his couch. "Have you come to play nurse?"

"You wish. I don't like leaving Serpentine Tower, so feel privileged, you bull-headed prick," Medusa said, placing a brown take out bag on the coffee table. "I bought you some spicy tom yum soup to make you feel better."

She adjusted her glasses carefully before sitting down beside him. She had developed the lenses in the early years to deflect the magic in her deadly gaze, but despite that, she very rarely met with people in the flesh.

"As glad as I am to see you, Susa, I get the feeling you're here to bring me bad news," said Asterion as he opened the bag and took out his soup.

He offered her the bag of prawn crackers, and she gave him an approving smile before tearing it open.

"I don't know if I have a mole at Serpentine too, so until we can root out Pithos, anything important I'm keeping off my servers," Medusa explained before biting unhappily into a cracker.

"At least I get to see your beautiful face," he said with a smile as he ate.

Medusa rolled her deadly green eyes at him. "Save it for the assassin."

"Need to get her back first," he grumbled in reply.

"About that...I may have received something in the mail from Pithos. Don't worry, it's not a body part!" she said quickly as he dropped his spoon.

Medusa pulled out a small laptop and held onto it. "This was delivered this morning. I haven't opened it yet, and I don't plan on giving it to you until you've licked that bowl clean. Understand?"

"You're lucky I love you and tolerate your bullshit," said Asterion, staring at the laptop. She waved one perfectly manicured finger at him, indicating not to attempt to snatch it from her.

Asterion always wondered who would win if he and Medusa went toe to toe, but it wasn't the day to find out.

As Asterion ate, Medusa caught him up on the gossip in Serpentine Tower, including the next patch for a video game she'd developed. It had been so successful they were already planning the future three installments.

Asterion had tried and failed to keep up with technological advances since Hades forced him out of the labyrinth. That part of the world always moved too quickly for him.

Medusa was scarily smart with it all and had created a digital online world that was another safe cave for her to lurk in.

"Done, now hand it over," Asterion demanded, and she relented, giving him the laptop.

"Whatever is on it, keep cool, and think about your revenge," Medusa advised.

Asterion opened the laptop, and a black and white security feed flickered to life of Theseus holding Ariadne's head in a basin of water. White-hot rage surged through him so quickly he shifted.

"Don't break it! It's the only link to them we have," Medusa said, taking the laptop back from him and setting it down on the coffee table.

"Those bastards. Notice how they've zoomed this camera in so we can't see the rest of the room? We need to find a way to trace this footage."

Asterion wasn't listening. The bull screamed to tear the rooms apart. To hunt for blood. His common sense was pulling down and away from his conscious mind, leaving only the beast.

"Hey! Stop that! I need you to focus, and so does Ariadne," snapped Medusa.

At her name, the rage eased to an ache. He needed to find her. Then he'd set the bull loose.

~

Two days later, Asterion had gone from fury to nausea.

Medusa hadn't had any success in tracing the feed from the laptop, and it showed 24/7 coverage of Ariadne, alone and in pain, being interrogated by various people, tied up, and getting the shit kicked out of her.

There was no sound, and by the look of continuous frustration on the faces of the Pithos goons, Ariadne wasn't just holding out against their torture but was giving them hell in the process.

Asterion was fiercely proud and utterly sickened at the same time.

Hades turned up on the second day, suddenly appearing when Asterion was almost mad from worry.

"Good evening, nephew. How is your assassin holding up?" he asked, without an ounce of concern.

"She's still alive." Which was the only good news they'd had.

"Of course she is. She's got a will of iron, besides Pithos will damage her but not kill her. They want you coming after her. They are just whipping you into a frenzy before they leak their location."

Asterion clenched his fists. "If you're trying to make me feel better, don't bother. You suck at it."

Hades opened his mouth to reply to him when his gaze whipped to the other side of the room. There were only a few pieces of art but nothing else.

"What is it?" Asterion asked. Hades held up a hand to him and tilted his head, listening. Then he replied in a language that made Asterion's ears pop, a feeling of cold dread and darkness creeping over his skin.

"You are being haunted," said Hades.

"That's not surprising considering how many people I've killed," replied Asterion.

"No, it's a shade of a girl. Brown hair, pretty in a vaguely innocent way. She says her name is...Lia?" said Hades, turning back to the empty space and continuing his conversation.

"Lia is...was...Ariadne's sister," said Asterion. "It makes no sense for her shade to be here."

"Unless she's here because of Ariadne. She can't speak and is trying to mime something at me. Be quiet and let me concentrate."

Hades spoke in the language of the dead again, and Asterion fought the urge to cover his ears. Hades pointed at Asterion as the discussion went on.

Hades turned to him. "She keeps pointing at you and touching her head, lowering something on her head? She keeps gesturing at your head where your horns are and then making a lowering action above it? Like a crown?"

"Bull King," Asterion said slowly, and his world shuddered under his feet.

"She's...clapping her hands at you," said Hades before lifting an eyebrow at his stricken expression. "What is it?"

"Bull King. They've taken Ariadne to fucking Knossos." Asterion shuddered with fear and rage.

"They said they wanted to put me back in the darkness. They have her in the labyrinth where I was meant to stay."

With a bellow that shook the walls in pure animal rage, Asterion tore the laptop in half, flinging the pieces to either side of the room.

"Well, that was an overreaction," said Hades, flicking a non-existent piece of lint from his pressed black trousers. "If you know where they are, we have the advantage, and they won't be ready for us when we go after them."

"I should've blown that place up years ago," growled Asterion as he paced up and down the room.

He still had nightmares about being trapped in the labyrinth, and now he'd have to go back in there willingly. He swallowed down the bile that was already clawing up his throat.

"That place has no power over you anymore, Asterion," Hades said, his voice a whip crack through the panic overwhelming him.

"I pulled you out of there once and did far too much work to make you respectable to lose you to it again."

"Don't ask me to wait any longer. I'm leaving tonight!" Asterion shouted.

Hades pulled his phone from his pocket. "Of course, you are. I'm just calling Charon to bring the helicopter."

Thirty minutes later, Hades and Asterion were on the roof as Charon landed. Erebus and Thanatos were waiting in the cabin.

"What are you two doing here?" Asterion demanded.

Erebus's smile was vicious. "You didn't think we were going to let you have all the fun, did you?"

"And I need to ensure if they kill you, that you don't stay dead," Thanatos said with a disapproving glance at Hades. "You're his favorite."

"Here, take this," Hades said, passing Asterion a dagger. His hand thrummed as he took it. It was made of carved bone, and he knew better than to ask what type of creature it had come from.

"You're not coming?" he asked.

"You won't need me. I'll be with Medusa. She has eyes on the site and is making popcorn," Hades replied. "Find out everything you can on who Pithos is, and please try and keep the masked one alive. If it's another supernatural, use the knife. It'll slow them down without killing them."

"Will do," said Asterion as he climbed into the cab next to Erebus.

"Just when I was thinking life was becoming quiet," he said, smacking Asterion on the back.

"Never thought I'd see the day when I'd be taking you back to Crete," Charon said to Asterion over their headsets.

"I can't say I'm stoked about it," Asterion replied, flipping the bone dagger over in his palms. "I'm not about to let them keep Ariadne."

"Ah, love, it makes it all worth it," Erebus sighed, clutching his heart. "I'm hoping that she dumps you for me when she sees me in battle."

"Stab him if you like. I'll make sure he doesn't die," Thanatos offered. Erebus only laughed harder.

Their stupid banter made Asterion's anxiety lessen, and so he let them joke and carry on for the next hour.

"Drop us on the lower hills. We'll go in on foot to surprise them," Asterion told Charon as soon as Heraklion came into view.

"You expect me to miss out on all the fun?" Charon asked.

"You can come back around after we get in if you like, but not before. I don't want them killing Ariadne because they are getting ambushed," Asterion said.

"And you're about as subtle as a brick, Charon. Leave this to the professionals," said Erebus, cracking his neck. Charon flipped him off over his shoulder before they landed.

Asterion jumped out of the helicopter and headed through the rocky landscape.

The summer air was still hot even at night, and by the time they crossed into a copse of pine and cypress trees, Asterion was already sweating.

Tourism to the palace of Knossos had been shut since Hades had pulled Asterion from the rubble, so it was surprising no one had reported the camp that Pithos had set up around it.

"Look at all those assholes," Erebus said from beside him. The titan let his power release, and the dark shadows at his feet formed themselves into a pack of wolves. It no longer creeped Asterion out, but he hoped it put the holy fear of the gods into Pithos's thugs.

"We'll take the spotlights out first. I take it you still know the way to the labyrinth entrance," said Thanatos in a bored tone as a small scythe appeared in each hand. Like the bone knife of Hades, Asterion could feel the power radiating from them.

The Minotaur rippled its way out of Asterion's skin, and he gripped tightly to the bone dagger as all the humanity burned away until only the monster of rage and violence remained.

21

Ariadne bit down a gasp of pain as she tried to stretch her cramped shoulders. She had seen a brief glimpse of the sun earlier that day as Theseus had dragged her from her cell into the cold, stone walls of the labyrinth beneath the palace.

She had been tied with rough ropes in the center of it, with her arms and legs bound behind her so she couldn't move off her knees.

It had been hours since she'd seen anyone, though from time to time, voices had drifted through the tunnels.

Ariadne didn't know how many days she'd been Pithos's prisoner. Her body was covered in bruises, their colors ranging from sick yellow to purple, so she knew it had been at least a week of getting waterboarded and having the shit kicked out of her.

The tunic she had first woken in stunk of blood and piss, and she was starting to think that maybe Asterion had been convinced to let Pithos have her.

She couldn't blame Hades from wanting to protect his nephew from the fanatics. From what she'd gleaned from snatches of conversation, Pithos was far more organized than she could've imagined, with cells all over Greece.

If —*when*— she got out of there, she was going to enjoy hunting every single one of them down.

Ariadne wriggled in her ropes again, fingers searching for the knot. Minos had loved tying the acolytes up in complex ways and leaving them to save themselves or die of dehydration.

Ariadne was good if only she could find the damn fucking knot. Gunshots and screams echoed through the labyrinth, and her heart rate quickened.

Theseus appeared at the head of a group of men, giving orders and sending them back down the way they came.

"Don't you look spiffy," Ariadne said through split lips. Instead of a gun, he was carrying a sword and a round bronze shield.

"If I'm going to kill a mythical monster, I'm going to do it old school," Theseus said, hand resting on his hilt. "And when I'm done with Asterion, I'm going to love watching what Minos does to you."

Ariadne laughed, a high-pitched mad laugh that she'd been holding onto for days. "Oh, you really are a dumb piece of shit. You've waited too long because you wanted to play games like a ponce. Now Asterion is coming, and you actually think you have a chance."

"I've got more than a chance, Spindle. I've been training for this fight for years. I know his weaknesses and how he moves."

"Much good it will do you," she said sarcastically. Theseus lost his temper and backhanded her, just like she knew he would.

She noticed something sharp was digging into her arm. Would it be sharp enough to cut the rope? She stilled as Theseus came and loomed over her.

"Maybe I won't bother handing you over to Minos. Perhaps, I'll have my own fun with you. Find a better use for that smart mouth of yours."

Ariadne didn't give him the satisfaction of looking scared. She wasn't afraid of being raped. It wasn't like she hadn't spent the past ten years forced to have sex to get targets alone, not to mention all that Zera had made her do.

Theseus turned back towards the tunnels and placed a hand to his earpiece.

"What's happening out there?" he demanded, and when he got no response, he hurried away.

"Dumb ass," Ariadne muttered, her fingers searching and grasping the sharp edge of whatever it was in the sand. Wriggling about her knees, she started to rub her ropes against it.

Asterion is here. Asterion is here. He has come.

A well of energy and adrenaline surged up through her, and she increased her movements until she felt something tear and give way.

Shoving the ropes from her wrists, she rolled her aching shoulders and rubbed her hands together to bring back the circulation.

A shard of bone as long as her forearm was sticking out of the sand, and after prying it free, she used its edge to cut away the ropes around her ankles.

Ariadne ignored the screaming in her limbs as she got to her feet. She'd be damned if she was going to let Asterion have all the fun.

She shredded a length of rope and wrapped it around her wrist, then gripping the bone like a blade, Ariadne followed the tunnels.

"Is anyone reading this?" a voice asked in the darkness, and she froze. Through the gloom, she made out a man in front of her who seemed to be having the same problem with his communications as Theseus.

It's because they are all dead.

Without hesitating, she drove the edge of the bone into his neck as hard as she could. He dropped to his knees with a gurgling sound as he choked on his own blood. Ariadne felt around his body and stripped him of his bulletproof vest and his hunting knives.

A roar shook the walls of the labyrinth, and instead of feeling afraid, Ariadne's heart began beating faster. The mark he'd made on her neck all those weeks ago pulsed with recognition.

Asterion.

With one hand on the wall as a guide, she moved as fast as she could in the darkness. A clang of weapons sounded ahead of her, and she all but ran towards it.

Lit torches had been scattered across the sand, and Ariadne fought her gag reflex. Pithos's men had been torn apart. Those parts were littering the sand, the protective vests doing nothing to stop the horns that had split them open.

This was rage, pure unleashed rage.

And Theseus thinks he has a chance.

Over the smell of blood and shit, Ariadne noticed the air getting crisper and fresher. She had to be nearing an entrance or some kind of opening.

She picked up a torch and held it closer to the ground so she could prevent stepping in anything too disgusting. She was about to go around a corner when she heard Theseus.

"Look at what you've done to these men, and you think you're not a monster?" he asked.

Ariadne snuffed the flames of her torch out in the sand and crept around the corner. Her breath caught when a growl reverberated off the walls, and the sheen of amber eyes flickered in the gloom.

The Minotaur stepped from the shadows. He was covered in black stains that she knew was blood. She could smell it in the air mixed with heat and animal. There was nothing of the man she knew in those golden eyes.

Theseus was standing in a defensive position shield and sword raised.

"Traitor," the Minotaur growled. "Were you treated so poorly that you'd stoop to this?"

"I'm no traitor. It was all a job. You actually thought I was your friend? I told Pithos everything. They know how to deal with monsters like you and your boss and that freak bitch in her tower," Theseus hissed.

The Minotaur lunged, and Theseus's shield clanged again and again as he tried to dodge the lethal blows.

He swung out with his sword, and the Minotaur snarled when the edge of the blade caught his shoulder.

Ariadne could see the bullet wounds and gouges already covering Asterion's body.

No doubt Theseus had used his men as human shields to weaken him before they even came face to face.

Well, Asterion had friends too. Ariadne unwound the rope from her wrist, and her body calmed.

Theseus had been circling Asterion slowly, and once his back was to the tunnel where Ariadne hid, she pounced, climbing up his back and wrapping the rope around his throat.

"Surprise, asshole," she hissed in his ear as he tried to buck her off.

Ariadne drove her knees up between his shoulder blades and pulled harder. Blind instinct took over him, and Theseus dropped his shield to claw at the rope around his neck.

The Minotaur was a blur of shadow and heat, and Ariadne was suddenly falling, tumbling across the sand at the momentum of Theseus being gored.

She was up on her feet in seconds, turning to see Theseus clutching at his chest wound. A hiss of laughter escaped him as Asterion came to loom over him, watching him die.

"D-Doesn't matter that you've killed me. Pithos have c-caught you, and they will get all you other m-monsters," Theseus said as he took one last shaky breath and died.

The Minotaur's head swiveled to Ariadne, and her breath caught in her throat.

For a second, she thought he didn't recognize her, but then he was picking her up and crushing her to his massive body.

"Hey, big guy," she said, looping her hands around his huge neck.

"I'm sorry I took so long," he replied.

"It's okay. Let's get out of here."

Ariadne didn't object as he carried her through the tunnels, his feet sure of their path out. She saw the opening, and the Minotaur halted and placed her down.

"Shit," Ariadne cursed.

A cage the size of a shipping container had been pushed over the only way out. No wonder Theseus had laughed at them. They were trapped.

∾

"Maybe we can push it out of the way?" Ariadne said beside Asterion. She looked small and dirty in her rags, but the determination in her eyes kept him from wanting to hang onto her and not let go.

Get her out.

Asterion reached for the bars of the cage and was paralyzed with pain. With a roar, he let go, and the Minotaur retreated inside of him so fast that Asterion stumbled.

"What the hell was that?" asked Ariadne, her hands steadying him.

"I don't know...it's the cage. It did something when I touched it," he said.

Men were creeping out of the shadows outside, their guns trained on them.

"Get in the cage, beast, and we won't fill her with bullets!" one demanded.

"Excuse me, young man, who do you think you're calling beast?" Thanatos's calm, cultured voice said.

Shadows exploded around the men, snarling and tearing limbs as they screamed. Thanatos's scythes gleamed in the moonlight slicing and cutting.

"Are those wolves?" Ariadne asked, eyes wide but unafraid.

"They are, and I'm here to rescue you!" Erebus said, appearing amongst the chaos.

"Your rescue needs work," Ariadne replied, pointing at the cage.

"One thing at a time, dear lady," he replied, disarming one of Pithos's soldiers and pushing him towards Thanatos's blades. "Can't you shove it out of the way, Asterion?"

"It's enchanted somehow," Asterion called back.

"That's just fucking perfect!"

"Pithos reinforcements are coming," said Thanatos.

"So are ours," Asterion replied. He could hear a helicopter getting closer, and Erebus laughed.

"About time!" he shouted at the night sky. Asterion pulled Ariadne away from the tunnel entrance as the helicopter descended and opened fire.

"Who the hell is that?" she yelled over the noise.

"Charon not wanting to be left out," Asterion said. When the shooting stopped, there wasn't a single man left standing.

Erebus was locking a chain around the bars at the other end of the cage. He was bleeding golden ichor from the bullet holes in his chest.

"Charon needs to work on his damn aim," he snarled.

Thanatos climbed into one of Pithos's trucks and floored it, the chain tightening and dragging the cage away from the exit.

"Come here," Asterion said to Ariadne and picked her up again.

"I can walk, you know," she replied, even as she hung onto him.

"But you're not wearing any shoes, sweetness, and I don't want you any more hurt than what you are," Asterion said softly.

"Aren't you just the romantic hero," Erebus exclaimed dramatically when he spotted them.

"Hurry up, you three," Thanatos shouted as Charon landed on the road leading to the palace. "Don't worry, Hades has a team coming to do clean up."

Asterion placed Ariadne safely inside the cabin before climbing in beside her.

Charon tossed him a blanket from the front seat. "For your girl."

"Thanks for coming back," Asterion said, taking the blanket and wrapping it around Ariadne.

Despite everything she'd been through, she looked up at him, her face smeared with dirt and blood, and smiled at him.

"Please tell me that life with you is always going to be this exciting," she said, her hand finding his under the blanket.

"Probably. Is that going to be a problem?" he asked.

"Not one bit," she said as she leaned over and kissed him.

Erebus and Thanatos laughed at them. Charon's voice came over the headsets, "She is going to fit in just fine."

22

At some point during the flight, Ariadne fell asleep on Asterion and hadn't woken until she was being carried through his apartment and to the bathroom.

She heard Thanatos talking on the phone, and Asterion giving orders before he shut the door on them.

"Here we go, let me help," he said as he undid her stolen vest and lifted the filthy tunic from her. His eyes raked over her bruises and wounds, and the rage-filled his eyes again.

"Asterion, look at me," Ariadne said, holding her hands to his cheeks. "I'm banged up, but I'm okay. You're the one that's bleeding everywhere."

She stumbled into the shower and turned the hot water on.

Oh, God, to be clean again. Blood and filth streamed off her as she lifted her face to the jets.

Asterion joined her, and those hard hands that had committed so much violence that night were tender as they washed her hair and checked the cuts and bruises on her. She'd never felt so taken care of.

Ariadne's energy was draining away, but she still returned the favor. Through some magic in his blood, stray bullets pushed their way out of his body and pinged on the tiles. It must've hurt like hell, but Asterion didn't complain as she washed out his wounds.

"You know this isn't over," Ariadne said as they held onto each other.

"I know. They are after the Court and me. This happened to you because of me," Asterion replied.

"It's not your fault. Minos is involved with Pithos too, somehow. I think they approached him with a deal for me like he tried to broker with you."

Asterion braced his arms on the tiles on either side of her. "I can get you out of Greece, and I wouldn't blame you for leaving. I have the resources to keep Minos and everyone else away from you forever."

Ariadne's heart stopped at the words. Getting out of Greece and away from Minos was all she'd ever wanted. She looked up into his golden eyes and realized as much as she wanted those things, she wanted him more.

"Do you want me to leave?" she asked.

"I want you to be safe," Asterion replied.

"That's not what I asked." She folded her arms and glared up at him. "Do you want me to leave you?"

Asterion's hands balled into fists. "Of course, I don't want you to leave, but it's too selfish of me to want to keep you close and keep putting you at risk."

Ariadne looked around him. "I'm sorry, I was just looking for the damsel you were talking to because you can't be talking to me right now."

"Don't be such a smart ass. I'm serious-"

"So am I! I'm a killer, Asterion. It's what I'm trained for. It's the only thing I'm good at. You don't think Minos has let it slip who the Spindle is? That I don't have enemies of my own? Not to mention all the other assassins he's going to send after me now that Pithos failed to hand me over."

Ariadne rested her hands on his chest and tried to steady her temper. God, she was so bad at talking about her damn feelings.

"Asterion, I meant what I said the night I was taken. I don't care what you are, or that Pithos is going to keep on coming. I...love you. I'm never going to be some tame housewife or gentle-natured lover. I'm always going to be argumentative, and I'll probably make you want to wring my neck at least once a week, but I'm not going anywhere until you tell me to go."

Asterion pressed her up against the tiles and kissed her until they were both breathless.

"You really will be the death of me, woman. As if I could tell you to go! I've loved you since you crashed into my perfectly ordered world and left it in tatters. Maybe we are both killers and monsters, but all I know is that you are *exactly* the woman for me," he said and kissed her again. A growl of irritation rumbled in the back of his throat.

"We need to get out. Hades is here for a debriefing, and we need Selene to see to your wounds."

Selene turned out to be a pretty nurse in her early thirties with light blue eyes and dark brown hair tied back in a braid. She muttered under her breath when she gave Ariadne a shot of antibiotics and plastered up her various cuts and scrapes.

"They did a number on you, but at least they kept you hydrated," she said as she helped Ariadne dress.

"They couldn't let their best bait die, that's why. How did you get to be Hades on-call nurse?"

"Hades has many people on his staff. I help out in the Labyrinth and come when Hades needs me. At least I'm not digging bullets out of Asterion again," she said with a shake of her head. "Try to keep him out of gunfire for a while."

"I'll do my best," Ariadne said with a smile, liking the woman instantly. "They are okay, aren't they? This crew?"

Selene raised a dark brow. "The Court of Styx? They are better than most, but I wouldn't recommend crossing them for any price, and certainly don't try to kill any of them again."

Ariadne laughed. "Don't worry, I learned my lesson last time."

When Selene helped Ariadne out of the bedroom, they found Asterion's lounge room overrun by gods. Hades was whispering with Asterion, and the triplets were sprawled out, passing a bottle of scotch between them. Erebus was up in seconds to help Ariadne to a chair.

"Selene, I've got wounds you need to look at as well," he demanded, and the nurse's eyes narrowed.

"You're a titan, Erebus. Whatever wounds you have will be healed fast enough without my interference," she said as she fixed Ariadne a glass of water and a variety of tablets.

Erebus pointed to his chest. "But I hurt right here, where you continue to break my heart."

"I'm sure you'll live," came Selene's indifferent reply, making Ariadne choke on her water as she laughed.

"One day, you'll say yes," Erebus sighed and reached for the bottle of scotch. Ariadne wondered why she didn't. Erebus, like his brothers, was handsome as hell.

"She knows you too well to fall for your tricks, brother," Charon said.

Ariadne didn't hear the rest of the argument as Asterion came and sat beside her, tucking her under his arm.

"Can we get this over with, uncle? Ariadne needs to rest if she's going to heal," he said to Hades.

"Thank you for coming for me," Ariadne said to Hades. His silver eyes widened just a little as if surprised she'd thanked him at all.

"I don't know how you guys found me, but if I can do anything to repay you, ask it."

"I have a list—" Erebus said, earning Charon's elbow in his ribs.

Hades ignored them. "You're welcome, Ariadne. It was Lia that told us where they were keeping you."

"Lia?" Ariadne frowned.

"Her shade came to haunt Asterion until I saw her," Hades said, explaining how they had gotten a few hours head start on Pithos with the information Lia had given them.

It sounded insane. Had Lia's shade been haunting her all this time? Had she witnessed all the horrible things she'd done for Minos?

Tears of shame filled her eyes, but she blinked them back, determined never to show that kind of weakness to the likes of Hades.

"Tell me what you heard about Pithos operations while you were there. I know a clever girl like you would've gotten more out of them than they got out of you," said Hades, with something that almost sounded like respect.

"I will, as long as you give me two things," Ariadne replied.

Hades's eyes narrowed. "You'd dare to bargain with me, little assassin?"

"Absolutely...my lord," Ariadne said because she knew she'd be able to push her luck only so far.

"What do you want?" he asked.

"The first thing? I want in. I want to help bring them down. These guys are fanatics, and they have enough supporters that they are funded and have cells all over Greece. They went after Asterion, and they nearly killed Vin. I want my pound of flesh for that," Ariadne said, making Asterion's grin widen with male smugness.

"And the second thing?" pressed Hades.

"Before we go after Pithos, you let me deal with Minos," she said.

Lia's shade was haunting her because she hadn't fulfilled her promise. Lia deserved to be put to rest just as much Minos deserved to be put in the ground.

"You say that Minos had dealings with Pithos and others. You can kill him, and I get his laptop," Hades said and stretched out a hand. "Do we have a deal, assassin?"

Ariadne didn't hesitate as she reached out and took his hand. It was warm and firm, but she felt something in the bargain settle in under her skin. It was a deal she'd never be able to break, and strangely, she was okay with that.

"You are going to need to be well to take out Minos. I'm impatient and want the hunt for Pithos to start now, so let's see if I can help," Hades said.

Before she could ask what he was talking about, a rush of heat ran up Ariadne's arm and spread through her body. Asterion's arms went around her to stop her from slumping to the floor.

"It's okay, I got you, sleep now," he said, holding her close.

∽

Ariadne didn't know how long she slept. Her dreams were filled with Lia being trapped in the labyrinth and Theseus's dying laughter.

She opened her eyes and found Asterion asleep beside her. She held out a hand to touch him and hesitated. The bruises that had mottled her skin were gone.

What is going on?

She hadn't slept *that* long. Lifting up the soft blanket, she inspected the rest of her body. Not a single bruise or wound remained.

What had Hades done to her? Not a single part of her ached, not even her knee that she'd once got a knife through.

She felt...good. Then she looked at Asterion again and felt something entirely different. It was an excellent thing to wake up to so much muscle on display.

Asterion's own wounds had healed, and Ariadne stroked a fresh scar over his shoulder where Theseus's blade caught him.

Her fingers moved down the breadth of his chest, along the grooves of his abs, and the V of his pelvis, her face heating as she explored lower and finding him hard.

Grinning with mischief, she slid under the covers and gently licked him. Asterion shuddered in his sleep as she lowered her mouth over him and began to suck. There was no way Ariadne could've fit all of him in her mouth, even with her training, so she wrapped her hand around him, working his shaft. Heat was flooding her core, making her ache, and she wanted to climb on his perfect dick.

Asterion trembled into wakefulness, and he lifted the edge of the blanket up.

"What in all the gods—" he said.

"Good morning," she replied, and then licked him again, causing him to swear. His hands found her, and he stroked her hair.

With a groan, he grabbed her by the shoulders and hauled her up on top of him. The blanket fell back, his eyes staring at her body and mussed hair like she was the most beautiful thing he'd ever seen.

Very slowly, she lowered herself on him, gasping as he filled her in all the right ways. She never thought she'd survive Pithos, and in her concrete cell, the only thing that had kept her sane was knowing that he was safe.

Her only regret was that she didn't have more time with him. She was going to make the most of having him back.

Asterion groaned, his hands going to her hips and squeezing them hard, pulling her down on him until her pelvis ground against his.

In a smooth move, he rolled her, his hands dragging hers up behind her head, pinning her tightly as he thrust back into her. Ariadne screamed his name as she came.

"Again...I want to hear you say my name like that again," he said, kissing her roughly.

He didn't let her up for a second, driving her body insane until he'd gotten another orgasm out of her, before going over the edge with her.

She ended up slung across his chest, with him finger combing the wild knots out of her hair.

"Now, that was a good way to be woken up," she said breathlessly. A deep chuckle rumbled up through his chest.

"I have so many plans for you, sweetness, and none of them involve leaving this room." Asterion lifted her chin. "You're feeling okay after your ordeal?"

"Are you kidding me? I feel like I could take on the whole of Pithos with one hand tied behind my back. Between whatever Hades did to me and you blowing my mind just now, I can't remember ever feeling better." She laughed, moving so she could kiss him. "So...you want to come and kill Minos with me?"

Asterion's eyes filled with violent delight. "I thought you'd never ask."

23

Ariadne was shadow and vengeance as she slipped through an open window of the Temple.

Lynx's eyes were filled with recognition and rage when she woke with Ariadne's golden braid around her throat.

The other assassin tried to scramble backward, her hands trying to claw at her attacker.

Ariadne didn't let go until Lynx breathed her last, fury still in her dark eyes.

Ariadne didn't honor her with a cat's cradle, not this one with no honor who'd let Pithos take her.

Belladonna's rooms stank of fermenting herbs and rotting experiments. One of her victims still lay on a dissecting table where she'd cut them open to see what her new poison had done to their insides.

Belladonna didn't rouse from her sleep until the poison Ariadne had dropped into her mouth was already making its way down her throat.

"You slut..." Belladonna wheezed as lines of black spread out over her beautiful face.

Ariadne only smiled as white foam bubbled out of the assassin's mouth and spread out over her bed.

Not trusting that the poison master hadn't enough immunity built up to survive what she'd been given, Ariadne slit her throat to make sure there'd be no recovery.

The Temple's halls were silent as Ariadne's feet made their way towards Minos's bedroom. She thought that, when this moment came, she'd be filled with nervous excitement, but there was only a deadly calm as her moment of vengeance arrived.

Minos's rooms were lit with candles, the Master of Assassins hating to sleep in the dark. Ariadne had laughed when Lia had told her about it, and then stopped when she realized why Lia would've known what Minos's bedroom was like.

Lia had always protected her, even when Ariadne had been too stupid to understand why her sister would be summoned in the middle of the night.

Old anger twisted Ariadne's guts as she stood at the foot of his bed and looked down at the man who'd been her father, her mentor, her betrayer. The man who'd made her kill her own sister, knowing what it would do to her. The man who had made her into his cold, unfeeling monster.

Her recent experiences had changed her because, as Ariadne looked down at the sleeping Minos in his bed, she didn't see the tyrant that had caused such fear in her over the years, only the pathetic old man who had taken so much from her.

Her time with the Court of Styx had shown her what real power was.

Ariadne woke Minos with a swift punch to his throat. Stunned and gasping in pain, Minos struggled as she dragged him out of bed and into the training atrium in the center of the mansion.

She could see the shadows of the other assassins, woken by Minos's curses.

"This night has been a long time coming, *pater*," she said, heaving him up to his knees.

"You..." he groaned, betrayal and fury in his eyes.

"Yes, me. Did you really think I wouldn't punish you for what you did to Lia? What you did to me?" she said as she wrapped her golden threads around his neck.

"Is this necessary, Ariadne? You've made your point. You want out of your contract? I'll sign it over," Minos said in wheezing breaths.

"Shut up," Ariadne snarled.

Girls were now standing around the sunken floor, watching uncertainly. Some showed fear in their eyes, but most had fire.

"I am the Spindle, the High Priestess of this Temple," Ariadne called out to them. "Tonight, justice will be done for my sisters who suffered and died under the rule of this fucker. If you wish to challenge me, you're welcome to."

No one looked like they were going to step forward, even as Minos cursed them all as cowards. Ariadne didn't hesitate any longer.

"See you in Tartarus," she hissed and then tightened her golden threads.

Minos fought, hands reaching behind him, his blows hitting her ribs, but she held on for all she was worth until his eyes bulged, and blood ran from the cuts in his hands and throat.

Ariadne kicked the limp body into the sand and breathed a deep breath, staring up at the night sky above her.

Erebus sat on the edge of the roof, one foot dangling off, and his shadows curling around him. Asterion and Thanatos stood watching, acting as witnesses and backup should she need it.

A girl stepped forward, her arm in a brace, and Ariadne recognized her as the one she'd helped weeks ago. With her good arm, she beat her fist twice against her breast.

"Spindle," she said, lowering to her knee.

"No stop, that's not-" Ariadne replied as the girls lowered one by one to swear loyalty to her. "No! Stop it! I'm not your new master. Your masters are dead, and you are indebted to no one. Understand me?"

"Then what are we supposed to do?" the girl asked, uncertainty in her eyes. Ariadne understood that fear of having nowhere to go but the streets.

"This place is going to become what it is meant to be. A home for orphans to come and stay and get help. No more killing, no more fighting. You are sisters, and you'll behave as such," Ariadne said and narrowed her gaze.

"This is the only rule I leave you with, and if I hear you've broken it, you'll meet the same fate as the masters."

The girls all bowed solemnly as they took the order to heart.

Ariadne stayed at the Temple until the sun rose. Asterion's men arrived to remove the bodies she'd left and to clean out the rooms that weren't already occupied.

In Minos's study, Ariadne kept to her word and boxed up all his files and laptop and sent them straight to Serpentine Tower for Medusa to go through.

She also found a theatre mask with black tears – proof he'd been in deeper with Pithos than she'd assumed.

"Do you think it's a good idea letting a bunch of little killers loose in the world?" Erebus asked.

Ariadne was standing on the steps of the Temple with him and Asterion, waiting for Charon to arrive.

"They are still kids," Asterion said.

"And they haven't killed anyone yet," Ariadne replied.

"They have the skills, though. You're going to force co-habitation onto them."

Charon pulled up in a bus, and boys started to file out of it, led by Petros in his priest's robes.

It had been Asterion's idea to have Father Petros and the boys move into the Temple. They were all orphans and needed a new building, so it seemed like a perfect fit.

They had already begun sourcing a candidate to look after the girls, thanks to Selene's contacts.

"All these boys are from Hellas, Erebus. They can handle themselves, trust me," Ariadne said, who knew just how tough it was to grow up on the Hellas streets.

If there had been a Father Petros around when she'd been an orphan, she might have never ended up in Minos's grip.

Ariadne was happy for the Temple's blood money to be used for good. It was either that or Ariadne was going to burn it to the ground.

She knew which Lia would've chosen, so she tried to honor that.

Asterion's hand wrapped around hers, careful of her cuts. "Feeling better?"

"Not yet, but I will be. What happened to Madame Zera?"

"I made her cough up all of her secrets before I killed her," Thanatos said calmly. He'd asked to deal with her personally, and

Ariadne had been more than happy to let him cut the child trafficker to pieces.

"What now?" Asterion asked.

Ariadne leaned into him, grateful for his warmth and presence. "Now, I put Lia's shade to rest."

Asterion had mentioned that he had built another apartment in the penthouse, what he hadn't mentioned was the huge rooftop garden.

Ariadne and Lia both liked being up high, so it was the perfect spot to spread her ashes under the trees that looked out over the city.

"This place is incredible," she said, touching the flowering plants that she couldn't name.

"Both Medusa and I were kept locked underground, so we insisted on gardens. If you think this is nice, wait until you see hers," Asterion replied, before giving her a kiss on the forehead. "Take as long as you need. The others won't turn up for another hour."

Alone, Ariadne clutched at the jar of ashes wondering what she would say. She was a bag of tired, mixed emotions, and she didn't know if killing Minos made her feel better or worse.

"I hope that you can be at peace now," she whispered to the wind.

"You know I was never one for peace, but I think I'm going to be okay now. You can move on. You don't have to watch out for me anymore. I have someone else willing to pick me up when I fall. I love you, Lia."

Ariadne watched as the wind tore Lia's ashes away over the city, giving her the freedom in death she'd always wanted in life.

Voices started to echo through the trees, and with a smile, Ariadne turned to join the living once more.

24

Asterion had no way of stopping Medusa as she let out a crow of triumph and wrapped her arms around Ariadne.

"My favorite murder babe is here!" she said, squeezing the life out of a surprised Ariadne.

"Ah, nice to meet you," Ariadne replied awkwardly.

"You'll have to forgive Medusa, she's excitable," he said.

"It's going to be so nice to have some more estrogen around here, that's why," Medusa replied, adjusting her glasses. To Ariadne's credit, she didn't flinch when a tiny snake poked its head out from amongst Medusa's red hair.

"That's different," she said. Medusa pushed it back in with a bashful smile.

"It's curious, ignore it," she replied and took Ariadne's hand and pulled her onto one of the day beds.

Asterion couldn't hide the grin as he watched Ariadne fall into easy conversation. Charon had been right. She really was going to fit in with them just fine.

He'd received a call that morning to say that Vin was recovering and would be able to be released into rehab in the next few weeks, and while his men were still reeling from Theseus's betrayal, they were running the club in his absence.

"You need to come and work over at Serpentine with me, Ariadne," Medusa was saying, and Asterion made a threatening growl in the back of his throat.

"Ariadne doesn't need a job," he said irritably.

"Yes, she does. She isn't going to turn into your live in fuck buddy," Medusa retorted.

"Why are you cock blocking me, woman?" Asterion said as he sat next to Ariadne.

"Don't worry, Medusa, I'm not about to put on my apron and become the housewife. I plan on taking over the fighting pits," Ariadne said.

"What? When did we agree to that?" demanded Asterion.

"Theseus is gone, and I have more training than all of your men put together," argued Ariadne.

"You are all forgetting Ariadne's promise to me," said Hades, appearing in a chair. "She got her half of the deal, and I intend to have this Pithos annoyance dealt with as soon as possible."

Medusa groaned. "Hades, come on, I haven't even had a chance to go through Minos's stuff yet. Ariadne has only just gotten back from killing the bastard."

"And deserves a rest," Asterion added, his arm around her shoulders tightening.

Hades ignored them both and focused his silver gaze onto Ariadne. "Are you good to go?"

"Yes, boss," she said, cracking a grin that was equal parts murder and mischief, and matched Hades's own.

"Excellent. I don't like that these self-stylized monster hunters are rearing their heads again. Going after Asterion was a minor test, not a full-scale attack," said Hades, his long fingers steepled together. "Have you gotten any further with the cage we recovered?"

"My research team has been going over it, and so far, they haven't been able to figure out what about it makes the Minotaur run. They are hesitant to take it apart in case it deactivates whatever it is that makes it so special. It might be magic, but I don't know where Pithos could've learned it," Medusa explained. "I'd really like to know who invented it."

"It seems a bit beyond what's currently on the market, and it's been very specifically keyed to Asterion and his abilities," said Hades.

"Theseus was spying on him for three years. Who knows what he gave them in that time including any of Asterion's blood and saliva," Ariadne added.

Asterion had killed Theseus, but he didn't see it as any kind of victory. He didn't trust often, and yet, he would've said that they were friends.

As if feeling his sorrow, Ariadne rested her hand on his knee.

"With this attack on us, I expect you all to be vigilant and don't dismiss anything, no matter how insignificant," Hades said, fire burning in his eyes. "This game with Pithos is only just beginning."

Asterion leaned over and whispered in Ariadne's ear. "Are you sure you want to be involved with all of this crazy, sweetness?"

Ariadne's smile was dazzling as she kissed him. "Absolutely."

EPILOGUE

Deep in a cave on the other side of Greece, a figure hovered over a worktable assembling his newest invention. Scattered around him were pieces of metal and wires and other flotsam of his craft.

A woman glided in behind him, unclipping the mask that hid her identity from the world.

"How was the hunt?" the man asked, not looking up.

"It was a beginning. We didn't capture the beast, but you proved your worth. The cage you built worked. It scared the beast back into his human form," she said.

"What cage?" he asked, pausing in his work. The madness had long since wiped away his idea of time, but he thought he'd dreamed of a cage once.

He tried to find the memory of making it, but it wasn't there...where had he put it? The man flinched when she draped an arm around his shoulders.

"Don't worry about the cage. We have another move already in play, so you only need to worry about making your toys," she said, voice as smooth as poison.

"Yes, I like to make things," he mumbled, picking up his screwdriver.

The woman and his memory of who she was, of who *he* was, was already slipping away into the darkness.

MEDUSA

THE COURT OF THE UNDERWORLD
II

ALESSA THORN

PROLOGUE

Sing, O' Muse, of the seasons of the world and how all that was lost was found again.

Sing, of how gods and mythical creatures once roamed the lands of Greece, and of how Man became powerful, and the gods were forced into hiding.

Sing, of when Greece's economy collapsed and the land was on fire with the turmoil man's governance had wrought.

Sing, of how the gods returned to build a new world from the ashes.

Sing, O' Muse, of the new city of Styx, and the monsters that govern its underworld.

Sing to me a new song, of a Gorgon and a Thief...

1

Two letters. That's all it took for Perseus's day to go from okay to total shit.

Why did he have to check the mail before he started painting? Now, he was sitting deflated in front of a blank canvas, all of his inspiration ebbing away like the tide.

He held the first letter up close to his face, the magnifying glass hovering over the words, hoping his partial blindness meant he'd read it wrong.

Nope, the letter was still the same, 'Rent increase to Hellas Zone 2 will be implemented from next month.'

"Fuck," Perseus muttered, tossing the letter aside. The gallery was in Zone 2, and he needed it open in order to pay for the rental increase, something he couldn't do if his landlord kept jacking up the price. He could probably make a deal with Markos to square him for the rent after the show.

It was the second letter that really made his guts sink.

'This letter is to inform you that Danae Serpho has been accepted into the early entry program at the University of Athens.' It should've been good news. It *was* good news.

Dany was seventeen years old and a prodigy, and she deserved to leave Styx and have the chance to use that big brain of hers.

As his baby sister's guardian, it was up to him to make sure she had her best chance, and that meant university. It also meant tuition and school fees, not to mention having a place in Athens on campus to live.

Perseus's vision flared in an aurora of color, and he put down the letters and the magnifying glass so he could rub at the band of scarring across his face.

No matter how many years went by, his scars still ached as soon as he got stressed.

"This is what happens when you go legit," he cursed. He couldn't remember ever getting migraines or color auroras when he was thieving. He had given the life up two years ago to give his art a chance and for Dany to have a half-decent role model in her life.

Gods, it was hard to be legit in a city like Styx, especially in the Hellas District.

"You just need the show to go well, and you'll be in the clear," he said to himself as he opened his damaged eyes again and picked up a brush.

A small voice in his head whispered, *One decent job, and you wouldn't have to worry about the show going well either.*

He did his best to shut it out and put paint to canvas.

Painting was the only thing that he loved as much as he loved being a thief. Fuck, he wished he was as good at painting as he was at thieving.

Perseus took three deep breaths and let the colors in the room settle. Then he painted them the best he could. His own aura of anger and frustration tinged the world red and he ran with it. If he painted it out, maybe he would have a clear head by the end of it.

It didn't help that his scars burned with old pain. He was a teenager when it had happened, and it was lucky that the acid that was thrown was meant for another, or he would've been dead.

Now he saw everything differently. It was energy and color auras, like seeing the world through a heat sensor camera.

It had made Perseus do shit at school, but excellent at being able to read security systems and people hiding in the dark.

Growing up as a partially blind kid in Hellas meant getting the crap kicked out of him until he learned to fight back and get damn good at it.

Then his peculiar talents had turned to thieving to survive, and also to get Dany the proper care she needed after their mother, stoned off her face, had fallen into the port and drowned.

Perseus's fist was through the canvas before he could stop himself.

"Fuck," he muttered, doing his best to wipe the paint off his hands. His phone rang, so he fumbled across the worktable for it.

"Hey, Perseus, how's the new painting going?" Cara asked. She was his manager and helped him run the small gallery where he displayed not only his own work but anyone in Hellas with talent.

Perseus had always been a part of the underground art scene that was growing in Styx, and Hellas especially, and he was proud to be able to give other artists a leg up.

"What's up, Cara?"

"What's up is I need another four canvases from you in the next two days, and I need your ass down here to sign off on some invoices for me. Buy you lunch?" she said, not really making it a question.

Perseus looked at the trashed canvas, knowing that he'd never be able to get back into the right headspace to paint that day.

"Sure thing, I'll be down in twenty minutes," he said, far more enthusiastically than what he felt. Maybe the walk would do him good.

He reached for the cane that he didn't need, but was useful in keeping people out of his way. He slipped on his sunglasses and headed for the door.

It was five blocks from the two-story warehouse Perseus and Dany lived in to get to the gallery. Five blocks were all it took to go from squatters' housing to the closest thing to upmarket that Hellas had.

He and Dany had talked about moving, but as she put it, what other place gave them enough space to have a floor each, a gym, and a skateboarding ramp to practice on. He couldn't argue with that logic.

Skateboarding helped her math and programming, painting helped him when he planned illegal heists of expensive and beautiful objects.

Cara was waiting outside the gallery, smoking a clove cigarette that Perseus could smell before his eyes detected the red cherry.

"You're looking pissed, what's happened?" she asked, too good at reading his mood.

"Nothing worth bitching about. A bad painting morning, that's all," Perseus said, pushing his glasses on top of his messy brown curls.

Cara put out her cigarette on the pavement before picking up the butt.

"Well, let's get some food into you and see if it fixes your mood a bit. You're always a cranky bitch when you're hungry."

"So are you," he replied as he followed her through the door of the gallery. It was a neat space of white walls and exposed brick that had an artistic vibe without being snobbish.

The walls were currently stripped in preparation for Cara to start organizing the new exhibition.

"What did you buy for me?" Perseus asked as they headed for the kitchen.

"Kebab and chips," Cara said, heading for the fridge and probably her fifth Coke of the day.

"Seriously! A kebab again. Why don't you just ask Dimmi out, instead of giving all your money away to have the excuse to flirt with her," Perseus replied, reaching into the brown paper bags.

He wasn't really complaining, he loved Dimmi's kebabs. He was just tired of Cara mooning over the woman without making a move.

"I don't know. Dimitria is different. I don't think a screw would be enough, and I don't think my ego could take the rejection this close to a show," Cara replied, strangely honest for once.

She'd never had a steady girlfriend the whole time Perseus had known her and had seemed to like it that way.

"Whoa, Cara has a crush," Perseus teased. "I never thought I'd see the day. Why don't you ask her to the opening?"

"Why don't *you* get a date for the show?" replied Cara.

"Who said I don't have one?" he asked.

"Oh, please, your dry spell is about to have the United Nations calling on international aid for drought relief," she retorted, dodging the chip he threw at her.

The door buzzer rang, breaking up their laughter.

"Must be a delivery, off you go," Cara said, turning back to her lamb wrap. Perseus caved in and hurried back through the gallery to the front door.

"Hi, can I help you?" he asked as he opened it. A man was waiting for him, his aura a distorted blur of color that Perseus had learned to identify with violence.

"Are you Perseus Serpho?" the man asked.

"Yeah, that's me, but if you're looking to buy a painting, we are closed until Saturday night," Perseus said.

"I'm not here about your paintings, Mr. Serpho," the man said, stepping inside the gallery uninvited. "I'm here about your *other* talents."

Shit, shit, shit.

"You don't look like the dancing type, but if you come to the opening Saturday, I'll give you a lap around the dance floor-"

"Stop playing games, Mr. Serpho. I have neither the time nor the inclination to spar with you. My name is Mr. Black, and my organization was given your name because you are apparently the best thief in Greece, and we need you to acquire something of great importance for us." The man straightened his jacket carefully. "We would compensate you generously, of course."

"How generously," Perseus's stupid mouth said before he could stop it

"Three million drachmae," the man replied without hesitation. It took a full thirty seconds for Perseus to start breathing again.

"That's a lot of money for one job. It also makes me think it's so high because no other thief has been stupid enough to take it on."

"It would be easy for a man of your talents if your reputation has any merit at all. Don't you want to know what the job is, at least?"

Perseus folded his arms. "Dazzle me."

"Break into Serpentine Industries and steal a certain necklace from Medusa," Mr. Black said.

Perseus laughed in his face. "You're kidding me, right? Who put you up to this?"

"As I said, my organization-"

"That is who exactly?"

"They are known only as the Pithos."

"Great, well, this has been a fun chat, but unless you and Pithos are going to buy a painting, you can get the fuck out of my gallery and take your suicidal job offer with you," Perseus said, grabbing the man by the shoulder and steering him back out the door.

"Try to think it through, Mr. Serpho. Three million drachmae can go a long way in a place like Hellas."

"Yeah, it could, but you can still shove it up your ass."

"Very well, you have until sundown to change your mind. Think it through before you speak again. A family man like you has a lot to lose," Mr. Black said before turning towards the sedan waiting for him.

Did he just threaten Dany?

Perseus clamped down the urge to smash the smug prick's face into the car window. He quickly shut the gallery door and locked it.

"What was that all about?" Cara asked, sticking her head out of the kitchen.

"Nothing," Perseus reassured her. "Now, what did you want me to sign?"

2

It was late in the afternoon by the time Perseus had finished all the work at the gallery.

He got a call from Dany saying she was going to the skate park and would be home later, and he breathed a sigh of relief at the normality.

The visit from Mr. Black had bothered him in more ways than one. He hadn't been a part of the Styx underworld for two years and hadn't even heard of a new gang called Pithos.

They must have had *big* ambitions to want to steal from the Serpent Queen herself.

Back at home, Perseus turned his music up loud and headed to his gym space to work out. As he hit the punching bag, his mind started to pull apart the logistics of breaking into Serpentine as a purely hypothetical exercise.

He would need to get his hands on some security passes for one. There was no way he could base jump onto the top of the building. The only one higher than it was Acheron, and he wouldn't dare go anywhere near Hades's building.

Stop thinking about it, and start thinking about painting something sellable, he chastised himself in the shower.

He needed to paint every day or the world around him became too loud and chaotic. It calmed him down the way nothing else did.

Pushing aside his destructive thoughts of thieving and creating art purely for money, he picked up his pastels and sketchbook. Maybe a change of medium would help.

He turned on the television for the noise, and the news streamed on with Medusa's velvety voice.

"Shit, bad idea," Perseus muttered as he sketched.

What necklace would be worth trying to cross Medusa and the Court? Even without his vision, he knew that Medusa was a beautiful, powerhouse of a woman. She was smart and would have security cameras all over her tower.

But would she have them in her penthouse? Her most private sanctuary?

Perseus doubted it. There were rumors that she had snakes in her hair and had other special powers. If that were true, she wouldn't want proof of them on camera.

Perseus looked down to realize he had sketched a swathe of red that he always saw as Medusa on screen, while he'd thought of all the ways to rob her.

Shit. He pulled it out of the pad and scrunched it up. That was when he realized how dark it was outside.

Perseus found his phone and headphones, and used his dictation app to send a text to Dany; *Where are you?*

She knew better than to be out on the streets after dark. After ten minutes and no reply, Perseus called her.

"Pick up, pick up, pick up," he whispered, fear mixing with frustration.

"Mr. Serpho, I hope you have thought about my offer," Mr. Black answered.

"What the fuck have you done with my sister?" Perseus asked through his teeth.

"Nothing...yet. Danae, say hello to your brother, please." There was a scuffle of fabric and Dany swearing.

"Dany! Can you hear me?" Perseus asked, his fear for her becoming a living thing.

"Perseus. Are you okay? Some assholes jumped me at the skate park," she said angrily.

"Have they hurt you?"

"No, but they won't tell me what this is about."

Perseus gripped the phone. "They want me to break my promise to you and thieve a necklace for them, sis. I told them to fuck off."

He'd always been honest with her, and he wouldn't start lying to her now.

"They must want it pretty bad to grab me. Are you going to do it?"

"They won't let you go until I do what they want. I'm sorry, kiddo," Perseus said, doing his best to sound calm and in control.

"Yeah, me too, I should've been keeping a better eye out for creepers," Dany replied.

Dany was smart and had grown up Hellas tough. She wasn't going to give those bullies the satisfaction of panicking.

The phone was pulled away from her.

"We do hate to resort to this kind of tactic, Mr. Serpho, but you didn't give us any choice," Mr. Black said.

"I swear to the gods, if you hurt her, nothing will protect you from me," Perseus whispered.

"No harm will come to the child if you get us what we need."

"What is so special about this necklace that you'd resort to kidnapping children?" demanded Perseus. It couldn't have just been about money.

"You know what Medusa *is*, don't you?"

"Really pretty?" A hiss of frustration on the other end of the line told him he'd finally hit a nerve. *Good*.

"Don't be so foolish. Medusa is a creature, a monster who could kill you with one look of her dangerous gaze. The necklace is the only talisman that makes the wearer impervious to her power," Mr. Black said.

Perseus couldn't stop the laugh that burst out of him. "You can't be serious!"

"I am deadly serious. It doesn't matter if you believe me or not. Your job is to retrieve it for me in the next twenty-four hours or we'll start sending you pieces of your sister. Check your emails for further details, and do not dawdle, Mr. Serpho, the clock is ticking."

The phone went dead, and Perseus fought against the urge to throw it in anger.

"Fuck!" he groaned.

He took a deep breath before finding his magnifying glass and opening his emails, something he avoided as much as he could.

Sure enough, there was one waiting for him that contained only one thing, a picture of a copper medallion on a strip of leather.

After he zoomed in as close as it could go, he could make out faint markings or pictograms that had been stamped onto it in a spiral.

You sure don't look worth three million drachmae.

In fact, it looked like something Perseus could pick up at the dockside markets on a Sunday.

Parts of the plan he had been dreaming about earlier suddenly began to fall into place. He was going to need help of a specialized nature, and it was lucky he was friends with the best in the business.

The Graeae Sisters lived on the other side of Hellas in a deceptively pretty house with a well-kept lawn and gardens. Deino, Enyo, and Pemphredo had always maintained their neutrality in the frequent turf wars and gang squabbles that went on in Hellas, selling information and counterfeit products to the highest bidder.

They had dirt on even the cleanest players in Greece, and it kept anyone from trying to take advantage of their good nature.

There were rumors that they were oracles, but Perseus maintained that they were so well connected, they basically could tell you your darkest secrets.

He lifted his hand to knock on the door when it was pulled back, and Enyo greeted him with a smile.

"Bless my soul, Perseus Serpho, on my doorstep once again," she said, straightening her glasses. "Nice to see you haven't run to fat. Though, if you're here, it must mean you are coming out of retirement."

"Enyo, it's been too long," he said, stooping to kiss her cheek.

"Still too cute for your own good. Come on, my sisters will be in the kitchen preparing coffee," Enyo replied, waving him in. Deino and Pem greeted him warmly, the latter casually patting his ass in appreciation.

"Nice to see you back, dear," she said.

"What can we do for our favorite thieving bastard?" Deino asked, passing him a coffee. He sat at their kitchen table and took one of the cookies they offered.

"I was going to ask if you had someone in Serpentine," he said, cutting to the chase. The three women could flirt for hours, and while he could play along, he was running out of time. The sisters shared a loaded look.

"And why, dear heart, would you want to risk going into Medusa's cave?" Pem asked.

"Curiosity?"

"Liar," called Enyo.

"Come now, love, we can keep a secret, you know that," Deino said coaxingly.

Perseus weighed it up and gave in. "A bunch of bastards took Danae, and if I don't get them something from Serpentine, they are going to kill her." The sisters all hissed eerie echoes of disapproval.

"How rude. Did they offer you money first?" Enyo asked.

"Yeah, they did, but it's Medusa. You'd have to be nuts to mess with one of the Court of Styx," said Perseus, reaching for another cookie.

"And if you succeed, you'll be famous. You'll never be able to retire. Still, family is family. They mustn't be from Styx if they are stupid enough to think we'll tolerate child-snatching," said Pem, her fingers tapping on the table.

"I might have a blueprint of when they built Serpentine. Get comfortable, it was twenty years ago."

Her mind made up, Pem wandered off to dig in the basement. It was a hoarder's paradise full of secrets, and no one but the sisters were ever permitted to go down there.

"What do they want you to steal?" Enyo asked curiously.

"A necklace. I'd like you to have a look and see if you have anything similar lying around," Perseus said, before passing over his phone for her to look at.

"Are you worried about foul play, my thief?" Deino asked.

"They will stoop to taking kids to use as pawns, so who's to say they won't kill Dany as I hand it over. Doesn't hurt to have an ace up your sleeve," he replied, hoping he wasn't pushing his luck.

The Graeae sisters could be extremely generous or extremely difficult, depending on their moods, which is why Perseus had always done everything he could to sweet talk them.

"This doesn't look like it's worth the danger of Medusa's tower," Deino said skeptically, her counterfeiters gaze studying the picture.

"I know, right. How hard would it be to make a copy?" Perseus asked. Deino passed him the phone back.

"Not long at all; I could bang it together for you right now if you like. I want to be paid though," Deino said.

"Name it."

Her aura flashed, and Perseus wondered if it was going to be a sexual favor, but Deino said, "I want a new painting for my hallway. Something as pretty as you."

"Consider it done. I'll put together something special for you, or you can swing by the gallery on Saturday and pick the one you like," Perseus said with an encouraging grin.

"Then I'll get to work," she said, moving off.

"Don't you need the picture of the necklace?" he called.

"No need, I emailed it to myself from your phone already," came the reply. Perseus smiled, enjoying the familiarity of the visit despite the circumstances.

"This group that has done this...what are they called, my love?" Enyo asked.

"Pithos. I've never heard of them, which is hard in this town. They turned up at the gallery and knew who I was, which means they are connected."

That they were able to find Perseus bothered the hell out of him. He had always been careful that his real-life and illegal business never crossed lines for the sake of Dany.

"Hmmm, maybe it's time I look into them myself. They are either very organized or very stupid to want to mess with the Court. Let's hope that they don't have bigger plans for you, dear. I'd hate to see you caught up in any of their bullshit," Enyo said, before pouring them both more coffee. "I wonder if it would be worth going to Medusa herself, letting her know that someone is planning against her."

"What? Go to Serpentine and flat out tell her, 'Hey, thought you should know someone is trying to steal from you?' Don't be crazy, Enyo. I'm more afraid of her than Pithos," Perseus said.

Enyo shrugged. "She would be a good contact to have, and she is extremely pretty."

"No doubt, but physical features are kind of lost on me, love," Perseus said, who tended to hook up with women for the way their aura looked.

Two hours later, he kissed the Graeae sisters goodbye and walked out with blueprints for Serpentine, a swipe card for their security doors, and a bronze medallion hanging around his neck.

He had a plan, now he just hoped like hell that his luck held.

If Perseus believed the gods would actually help, he would've prayed to Hermes God of Thieves and Tricksters, but somehow, he doubted the god would've helped him steal from his own kind.

Instead, he sent a prayer up to Dany's favorite, Saint Barbara, patron saint of mathematicians, to protect her. He didn't know where Dany got her interest in the saints from, but as Dany always said, "Couldn't hurt before an exam, right?"

And because Dany's interest had rubbed off on him, he sent his own prayer to eyeless Saint Lucia, patron saint of the blind, because he would need all the help he could get if he were going to pull this job off.

3

Serpentine Tower was a glorious spike of green and gold architecture. Under his khaki overalls, Perseus started to sweat as he used his swipe card on the back entrance of the tower, and he held his breath until the light went green and gave him access.

It was always best not to ask the Graeae sisters where they got such things, but he knew he would be sending them all flowers if he survived the night.

Carrying his bag of tools through the car parks to the storage rooms for the janitors, he found the gardener's trolley in its designated cage.

Picking the lock, he placed his bag on the trolley along with a bag of soil and some seedlings that were growing on the storage benches.

Breathe deeply and calmly, you're meant to be here for some emergency night work while the boss is out filming, Perseus told himself over and over, letting the truth of it settle in his bones.

He tried not to rub at his eyes, the harsh fluorescents overhead making his world brighter and other energy signatures hard to read. The last thing he needed was to crash into something and cause a scene.

Whistling a tune, Perseus pushed the trolley to the service lift and stepped into its canvased sides. Swiping his card again, he hit the top button and hoped for the best.

The lift stopped a few times, and he kept the brim of his cap down and avoided eye contact. The service lift opened to a still foyer of stone, and at the far end, he could make out the blur of double doors.

Next to the lift was a glass door for the gardeners to enter the rooftop garden. He didn't dare glance at the security cameras above him, simply adjusted the gear on his trolley before swiping his card at the panel by the glass door. Nothing happened.

Shit shit shit.

Perseus wiped his sweat off the card and carefully tapped it again and again.

The third time was a charm, and the door buzzed open. He tried not to gulp down the warm night air in relief as he pushed his trolley down the twisting pavement.

The rooftop garden was lit by lamps scattered through the trees, everything smelling like fragrant flowers and earth. The auras of the trees glowed as they swayed in the breeze.

"Wow," Perseus breathed, slowly pushing the trolley further into the garden, momentarily forgetting why he was there. He knew there were parks in Styx, and the council was planning more urban green spaces, but so far none had sprouted in Hellas.

The last time he'd been in a garden like this, he'd been robbing a mansion in the Diogenes District. Perseus shoved the memory aside, pulling his attention back to navigating the gardens.

He couldn't spot any cameras anywhere, but he still planted some of the seedlings and spread the potting mix for appearance's sake.

Everywhere he went, there were statues. He had to use his hands to feel them properly. They were eerily detailed men in warrior gear, and he carefully cleaned leaves off them, so it didn't look like he was feeling up sculptures for the fun of it.

A doorway of light bloomed through the trees and Perseus sighed. It was a private entrance into the penthouse.

He checked for cameras, and finding none, he stripped off the overalls and cap and opened his bag, strapping on a small pack and positioning a set of goggles on the top of his hair.

He rolled his neck, took a deep breath, and headed for the glass doors. His muscle memory overrode his anxiety in seconds.

Gods, he'd missed this feeling. His gloved hands tested the door handle and it slid open, silent as a whisper. His eyes scanned the roof and found no cameras.

His gamble that the Serpent Queen didn't have her private space monitored was confirmed. This was going to make everything so much easier.

Perseus thought that such a prim, polished CEO would have an equally polished apartment, but Medusa's penthouse was like a workshop on steroids. Everything glowed with electrical heat and energy.

Workstations and televisions were playing different shows on mute, and classical music was playing over the hum of electronics. He stepped carefully over cabling and around tables of books.

Following the smell of perfume, he found her bedroom, and thank Saint Lucia, her walk-in wardrobe.

Pem Graeae had assured him that a safe had been put into the wardrobe, and if the necklace had personal value, that's where it would be kept.

He hoped so because there were piles of jewelry stacked on every surface in haphazard piles of glittery gems. He fought his urge to slip a few of them in his pocket.

No, the longer it took for anyone to notice something was gone, the safer he would be.

The wardrobe was a rainbow of color and texture. Through his thin leather gloves, Perseus could feel the silky softness of the garments, the scrape of sequins, and the plushness of fur.

After five minutes of careful searching and feeling like a perve, he found the tiny safe mounted by a wall of jackets. There was a small keypad and lever, and Perseus smiled as he pulled out his small black light torch.

Even his vision needed some extra help, and as soon as he shone it over the keypad, he almost burst out laughing.

There were only two buttons that had fingerprints on them. He wanted to hug his baby sister for forcing him to listen to the audiobooks of *The Hitch Hikers Guide to the Galaxy*.

"Medusa is a nerd, who would've thought," he chuckled softly and then pressed 42, the answer to everything in the universe, including her safe lock.

The safe beeped once, and Perseus opened it, dying to see what someone like Medusa would lock up when a king's ransom of jewelry lay scattered about carelessly.

There were only three things inside the safe; two small female figures the size of chess pieces and carved inexpertly out of olive wood, and the leather necklace with the bronze disc.

Strange.

He tried not to give it too much thought as he put the necklace into a small velvet bag and zipped it into his vest.

Perseus should've left then, but how many people could say that had such a glimpse into the life of someone as famous as Medusa? It was the art that really drew him further into the penthouse.

There were paintings of bleak, beautiful, and alien landscapes that even his color stained vision couldn't make look cheerful. It was such a strange juxtaposition to the colorful wardrobe and furniture.

He followed the walls and stopped dead as a golden haze pulsed from a lounge room.

One huge flat screen TV was mounted on a wall, and a fire was burning in the hearth despite being summer.

There was a book on a coffee table and a half-empty bottle of wine next to a wide purple lounge that was…occupied.

The source of the golden glow was a woman. He had never seen an aura like it, and for the first time since his eyes had been damaged, he saw every feature from her perfect bowed lips, high cheeks, and the slope of her breasts.

He could make out the backlit silhouette of the Slytherin House insignia on her pajamas…and the hand that was moving inside of them.

Perseus didn't move. Didn't dare to breathe. He couldn't tear his eyes away as he watched her touch herself with one hand, the other squeezing her breast, blissfully unaware that she had an audience.

It was the sexiest thing he'd ever seen, making his mouth go dry, and his dick grow hard enough to hurt.

Run, you idiot! A voice screamed in his head, but he couldn't look away. Her aura fluttered in rapid flares of gold and silver, and a sexy moan escaped her luscious lips as she came.

Holy. Fucking. Gods.

Perseus took one surprised step backward onto a game remote control and cursed. Shining eyes opened with a start, followed by a small gasp of alarm.

"Sorry to interrupt, don't stop on my account," his stupid fucking mouth said.

The glowing woman was up in a blink, her golden aura now tinged with red fury and embarrassment.

Perseus took one last look at Medusa's staggering beauty...then he ran like hell.

4

Medusa's day hadn't been great. The new DLC patch for 'Shadow Lords of the Nightlands,' Serpentine's bestselling console game, had been delayed for another month.

Their marketing schedule had been thrown into utter chaos when they learned ARGOS Industries was determined to release their new game on the same day.

On top of that, her team was no closer to figuring out the mystery of the cage Pithos tried to get Asterion in, and the contents of Minos's computer had made her so disgusted, she'd given it to Hades.

It had all been too much, so Medusa had handed the news over to her back up anchor and taken the night off. She needed a good book and a good wine...and everything had been going well until she caught a stranger watching her get herself off. She was so shocked that she froze.

"Sorry to interrupt, don't stop on my account," he said, and then he'd started running.

"Hey! Stop!" Medusa shouted and ran after him. She leaped over a table and tried to tackle him, but he somehow sensed her, and impossibly, managed to dodge her.

He didn't know the maze of the penthouse like she did, so she went through the kitchen as a short cut to try to block his entrance to the outdoor gardens.

Her fingers brushed his tattooed arm as he slipped through the doors. He stopped at the balcony railing, looking at the drop beneath him. She had him trapped.

"Stop!" she called, and he turned slowly with his hands raised. He was tall and well built, curly dark hair blowing in the breeze around a tanned face.

Both of his muscled arms were tattooed in the most amazing designs and colors. He was handsome in a rough way, but it was the strip of scarring that made her pause. It ran from the temple of his right hairline, across his pale blue eyes and down the high curve of his left cheek, and it was the reason he wasn't currently turned to stone.

"You're blind?" Medusa asked curiously.

"You catch a strange man robbing you, and that's your only question?" he asked, his lips curving into a smile, making him go from coarsely handsome to ovary melting sexy in seconds.

Stop that! He's the enemy!

"You have some nerve," Medusa hissed, hating that he was not only a thief but that he was gorgeous.

"I've been told that, but a man's got to make a living, you know?" he said, edging back. "I was never here to hurt you, only rob you."

"Stay where you are, security is on their way," Medusa commanded.

He shook his head. "Don't lie, Medusa. There have been no alarms triggered, no one is coming, it's just me and you, and your sexy Slytherin jammies."

"You shut your mouth about my jammies!" she said, blushing crimson.

The thief clicked his tongue. "Typical, touchy, Slytherin."

"Look, I'm a reasonable lady. Give me back whatever you stole, and I *won't* throw you off this roof? Good deal?"

"I *really* wish I could, but I'm in a jam, and this is the only way out. Don't worry, I'll make it easy for you, babe."

"I'm not your *babe*." She just needed to get him in arms reach.

The handsome thief laughed as he gave her a small bow and stepped over the edge.

Medusa screamed and hurried to the guardrail just as his small base-jumping chute opened, and he disappeared into the night.

"FUCK!" Medusa shouted into the wind. She hurried back inside, and locked the door for the first time since she'd moved in.

"WHAT DO you mean you don't have cameras around your rooftop garden?" Ariadne asked incredulously.

Medusa had called her straight away. She didn't need the triplets rampaging through her penthouse, and she certainly didn't want Erebus anywhere near her lingerie drawer.

It had been a month since Ariadne had officially joined the Court of Styx, and she and Medusa had become fast friends. Girls had to stick together, especially in a group of hot-headed immortal men.

"It's *my* garden! What if I want to walk around it naked? This floor is meant to be my sanctuary, and this - this *man* - has violated my sacred space with his big arms and his testosterone scent," Medusa exclaimed.

Ariadne poured herself a glass of wine and tried not to smile. "Do you know what he took? You have a lot of stuff up here."

"I have no idea!" Medusa grabbed the bottle and had a mouthful.

She was still more embarrassed than angry. He had just stood there and watched her while she...she took another drink.

That look on his face. Like he wanted to fall on his knees at the sight of her. No man had ever looked at her like that.

"Okay, you said you can smell him. Was that for real? Because if you can detect his scent where he has been, then we might be able to figure out what he stole. Maybe retrace his steps to see where he got in?" Ariadne said.

"Good plan." Medusa finished the bottle for courage and went back to the garden. She closed her eyes and tried to search the trail of him. It was like warm skin, sunshine, oil paint, and man sweat that should've smelled bad but didn't. It was mixed with earth, and she soon tracked down the trolley and discarded overalls.

"He came through the gardener's service door," Medusa hissed. "We'll find the footage of the lifts and foyer."

"Smart. He would have gotten a key card from someone, maybe stole it off one of your regular gardeners," said Ariadne, following her.

Medusa followed the scent back to her penthouse doors, slowly tracking the thief's progress.

He went to her wardrobe, and even though he'd touched her clothes, he'd stayed away from her lingerie drawer. Medusa begrudgingly gave him decency points for that.

She opened her safe and hissed. The two statues carved of her sisters remained untouched, but her medallion was gone.

"Son of a *bitch*," she growled, and the small snakes hidden in her hair hissed in unison.

"What did he take?" asked Ariadne.

"Something special to me. If he already had the necklace, why did he go to the lounge room?" She followed his scent to where he'd been standing. Shutting her eyes, she focused on what remained of him in the air and inhaled deeply: oil paint, sunlight, man sweat, and...arousal? He'd watched her and had been turned on. Heat flushed Medusa's face so quickly she couldn't hide it.

"Susa? What is it?" asked Ariadne, her brows furrowing.

"He was standing there watching me while I—" Medusa broke off, too mortified to say it.

Ariadne looked at the title of the romance book on the coffee table and a wide, knowing smile spread across her face.

"He watched you getting yourself off?"

"It's perfectly natural!" Medusa snapped.

"Oh, I know it is, so why are you so embarrassed?"

"Because I can smell that he was turned on!" Medusa exclaimed. Ariadne's eyebrows shot up before she burst out laughing.

"Medusa, honey, you are a very beautiful demigoddess. Any man would be aroused watching you touch yourself. The poor guy...I almost feel sorry for him."

"Fine! Take the dirty thief's side! Just don't feel sorry for him when I hang him from the building by his toes."

"Why not turn him into another ornament for your garden?" asked Ariadne.

Medusa folded her arms irritably. "Because my gaze doesn't work on him. The fucker is blind. Or partially. He moved like he was sighted...I can't figure it out."

Ariadne stopped laughing. "Really? Wow, maybe this could open up a whole new dating opportunity for you. It would be nice for you to be able to hang out with a guy without worrying about accidentally cursing him."

"Are you insane? I'm not going to date a man who robbed me! I don't care how big his arms were."

"Why not? Asterion dates me, and I murdered him."

Medusa rose to her full five foot three inches of height. "Because you and Asterion are psychopaths, and I am a *lady*! I have standards. And if I ever get my hands on him again, I'm going to make him suffer."

"He's got the visual of you masturbating in his head, so I bet he's suffering already," Ariadne teased, completely uncaring about being called a psychopath. "You never know, the visual might drive him so mad he reaches out and asks you for a date."

"I love you, Ariadne, but I will throw you off my balcony too if you keep it up."

Ariadne put a comforting arm around her waist and rested her head on Medusa's shoulder.

"No, you won't, because that would make Asterion sad, and you'd have to deal with all the men without me again. I'm sorry, but this is kind of hilarious. You want to tell me what he stole?"

"I'm going to need ice cream for this," Medusa sighed, and they went back into the kitchen to raid her freezer for her her stash. Ariadne sat up on the bench, and Medusa handed her a spoon.

"I don't even know *how* he knew about the medallion. It doesn't look expensive or valuable."

Ariadne's dug her spoon in. "So what is it really? Magic?"

"It's a talisman that was made by my sisters for me.... right before they were murdered by a so-called 'hero' on some fucking quest," Medusa said, shoving more ice cream in her mouth.

"It protects a wearer from my gaze. I was always the most human-looking of the three of us, the most restless too, and stupidly wanted to fall in love. They made the medallion, so if I ever found a man or woman that was worthy of my love, they could wear it so we could be together."

"That is the most romantic thing I've ever heard. And you never found anyone to give it to?" Ariadne asked.

"No, and now it doesn't matter because I made these," Medusa said, readjusting her glasses. "I kept it though because it reminds me of them and how much they loved me. How did he know to take it? And what would he want it for?"

Ariadne stabbed her spoon back into the ice cream. "Smells like Pithos to me. How did they know Asterion was a Minotaur? I mean, look at the cage. We still don't know how it works."

"Don't remind me. I'll figure it out sooner or later."

"Do you think they will get someone to wear the necklace and then try to assassinate you? I know if I were being sent to kill you, I'd want a magical trinket too," Ariadne said thoughtfully.

"Where are they getting this information? There were never many people who knew of the medallion, and they are all dead," Medusa complained.

Ariadne tapped her spoon against her lip. "We need to find this thief and question him."

"And then you can kill him," said Medusa.

Ariadne's grin was wicked. "It would be my pleasure."

∼

MEDUSA STRUGGLED to treat the next day like nothing had happened. She had shot a text off to Hades, telling him of the security breach and that she was looking into it.

He was in Athens at another business meeting with Demeter, so she didn't want to worry him until she had to. He had a history with Athens, and he was always pissed off when he stayed there.

Not your problem, Medusa, she reminded herself as she got comfortable in her office.

Work was just the thing to take her mind off her thief. Ariadne had stayed late, and a hangover wasn't helping.

She tried to remember the tattoos on his arms because they had been strangely patterned. Maybe they could ask tattooists in the city if the thief was a client?

She wanted her damn medallion back for sentimental reasons more than anything. Ariadne was right; it had the stink of Pithos all over it.

Medusa cursed when she looked down at her legal pad, where she'd drawn the strange patterns of the tattoos she couldn't get out of her head.

"I really need to kill this bastard," she complained, pushing the pad aside and opening her laptop.

Medusa was interrupted an hour later by Kadie, one of the main receptionists. She knocked tentatively on the office door as if sensing Medusa's bad mood.

"Come in," Medusa called without looking away from the monthly financials. Her sensitive nose picked up the smell of flowers, and she looked up.

"These came for you. Would you like for me to find them a vase?" Kadie asked. It was a bouquet of purple and yellow orchids.

"Sure," Medusa said, confused. She didn't know anyone who would send them to her.

"Oh, here, this was with them," Kadie added, passing her a small envelope, and moving to the boardroom kitchen to fetch a vase.

Medusa opened the envelope, her temper skyrocketing as she read the words on the small card.

Lady Medusa, I'm sorry I had to steal from you, but if everything goes well, your necklace will be returned to you by tomorrow night.

There was no name, but when she lifted the card to her nose, she detected the thief's scent.

"*Bastard.*"

"What was that?" Kadie asked, returning to place the orchids on her desk.

"Nothing. Thank you, that will be all." Medusa looked at the orchids, blushed at their weirdly sexual buds and petals, and rang Ariadne.

"Hey, Susa, found your thief?" Asterion answered.

"Not yet, but it's only a matter of time. Where is your better half?" Medusa asked, tapping the card on her desk.

"She's in the shower," he said, with the definite smug tone of someone who'd been laid that morning.

"If you can spare her from your bed for an hour, I need her to come down to Serpentine. There's been a development I need to talk to her about."

"And you can't tell me?"

Medusa flushed. "It's personal. It's a lady thing."

"Ah, huh. Should I be worried about being targeted by this thief of yours?"

"I really don't know. Please just send Ariadne when she's out," Medusa said and hung up.

A%RIADNE and the triplets arrived thirty minutes later, finding Medusa pacing up and down her office.

"What are you three doing here?" Medusa demanded.

"Boss told us to come and check out the apartment," Charon said. Erebus was already touching things on her desk.

"Ohhh, someone has an admirer," he teased, touching the flowers and waggling his eyebrows at her. "Hey, Charon, what do you think these look like?"

"Please refrain from being so vulgar, and just focus," Thanatos chastised, shooting Medusa an apologetic look. "We'll be in and out as quickly as possible. Hades is concerned, and sometimes other eyes will help."

"Fine!" Medusa passed him the penthouse access card. "But you keep Erebus *out* of my bedroom."

"Oh, come on, Susa, I'm not that much of a creeper," Erebus complained.

"Tell that to the orchid's clitorises you just poked at," Ariadne said dryly, pushing the laughing titan away from the desk. Medusa slumped in her chair as soon as they were alone.

"I'm sorry, I tried to tell them that they weren't needed, but Hades was insistent," apologized Ariadne as she leaned against Medusa's desk, arms folded. "You want to tell me about the flowers?"

Medusa huffed out a breath and passed her the card. "They are from him."

"You sure?"

"My nose doesn't lie."

Ariadne read the card, looking thoughtful. "He seems kind of sweet. I wonder what he means about getting it back to you tomorrow."

"What the hell is the point of stealing something if you're only going to return it? None of this makes sense," Medusa complained. Ariadne went to place the card back on her desk and paused when she looked at the legal pad.

"What's this that you've been drawing?" she asked, brows furrowing as she turned the pad around.

"Nothing. The stupid thief had those tattoos on his arms," Medusa said.

"Susa, I've seen patterns like this before," Ariadne replied and reached for Medusa's laptop.

"Where?"

"In Hellas. Oh gods, what was his name?" Ariadne complained as she typed. "Ha! There it is! Hellas's art culture is awesome, I honestly couldn't believe it when I moved back there. Like flowers growing up through the concrete. Anyway, there's a guy slated to be the next big thing in the art scene. His name is Perseus, maybe he drew the tats for your thief."

Ariadne turned the laptop back around to reveal the website of a gallery.

Medusa scrolled down the page, and there he was, wearing sunglasses and standing next to a wall of artworks.

The sleeves of his blue shirt had been pushed up to his elbows to reveal his tattoos, the silver streak of hair where his scars began was tousled in with his dark brown curls.

"That's my fucking thief," hissed Medusa, her heart racing.

"That's...crazy. What would an artist like Perseus be doing stealing from anyone, let alone one of the members of the Court of Styx?" Ariadne said and took a closer look at the photo. "Damn, he's a hottie."

"His hotness is irrelevant. I'm going to annihilate him," snapped Medusa.

Her red lips kicked up in a vicious smile when she read about the event that was happening at the gallery that night.

"I think it's time I buy some art."

5

Perseus took a deep breath and tried to remind himself that he had done exhibit nights more than once.

He pushed his curls back from his face and lightly massaged his aching scar. He barely slept the night before. He was too anxious for Dany, and far too adrenalized from his encounter with Medusa to get the rest he'd needed.

He drank beer and painted and had woken up slumped over his worktable amid a pile of sketches of a glowing goddess, a half-finished painting on his easel.

Perseus had been told that Medusa was beautiful, but it meant nothing to him. After all, beauty was subjective enough if you were sighted, let alone how he saw people. She had been...otherworldly.

He hadn't seen a woman's body so clearly since he'd lost his sight, even if she did glow with golden light.

Medusa was, literally, a goddess. A goddess in Slytherin pajamas. Her glow had backlit the house standard so brightly there had been no mistaking it.

Don't think about what you caught her doing. Too late. Perseus felt like a complete pervert, but he couldn't *stop* thinking about it, to the point he'd ended up having a frustrated wank in the shower after he'd gotten back to the warehouse. And again that morning.

He had also woken up feeling guilty for stealing something that was obviously sentimental in value. He had never felt guilty after a job. Although, he had never been caught by the owners before either.

Perseus's phone rang, and he pounced for it. "Hello?"

"Mr. Serpho, I take it your job last night was successful?" There was no mistaking the creepy Pithos guy's voice.

"Yes, Mr. Black, I got your damn trinket. I'd like to talk to my sister, please," Perseus said, trying not to lose his temper or show how desperate he was to hear Dany's voice.

"Of course, she is an incredibly bright girl. A joy, really. I've enjoyed her company."

Perseus was still swearing under his breath when Dany piped up. "Hey, bro, how're tricks?"

"Dany, are you okay? Please tell me they haven't hurt you," he asked.

"Nope. They have been okay as far as kidnappers go. They gave me a Serpentine console to play, so I have been busy getting all my XP before they release the expansion pack," Dany said, before adding in a less happy tone, "You *know* how seriously I take annihilating my enemies in Shadow Lords."

Perseus let out a relieved laugh. "Yeah, sis, I do. Better let me talk to the douche bag in charge again so we can organize getting you home tonight."

"No probs. Although if it's going to be longer than tonight I'm going to need you to get someone to help you log into my console at home and sync up the game so my changes come across and my caches load up, okay?" Dany asked seriously.

"I promise. Don't worry about it," Perseus said, wondering how he had gotten a sister that was more concerned about her XP than the fact she had been kidnapped.

"I told you the girl wouldn't be harmed," said Mr. Black.

"Thank you. Where would you like me to deliver the necklace?" asked Perseus.

"Tonight, at the gallery, nice and friendly and public. Would that put you at ease? Someone will approach you for the necklace, and once we have it, we'll let Danae go."

"Deal. Don't be late, my sister has never missed one of my shows," said Perseus and hung up before he started swearing at the fucker.

He opened the two small velvet boxes on his worktable. One was Medusa's pendant, and the other was the replica Deino Graeae had made for him.

He brushed his fingers over the markings on both. They were exactly the same in every way except that Medusa's hummed with a low current that he could feel through his fingers.

He'd never felt anything like that before. He was too old to believe in magic, but after seeing Medusa in the flesh, he was willing to believe that she was. It made sense that her necklace would be too, and that was another reason he wouldn't let Pithos have it.

He would pass off the replica, get Dany and give Medusa back her necklace and hope like hell that she didn't bring the entire Court of Styx down on his head.

By lunchtime, Perseus was heading down to the gallery to finalize the exhibit. He hesitated by the florist before going in and sending Medusa a bunch of orchids.

It was cheeky of him, and no doubt he'd regret sending them, but he didn't want her thinking she wasn't going to get her necklace back. He didn't want her to think he was a total prick either, which kind of surprised him.

Dude, aim lower. You'll be lucky if she doesn't vivisect you if she ever sees you again.

BY 8 PM, the gallery was packed, and Perseus was trying his best to keep up his small talk with other artists and interested buyers. He couldn't help but smile when he saw Dimmi arrive, and Cara's energy went from professional to downright giddy.

"Go get her, girl," he whispered, giving Cara a gentle push forward.

"You invited her, didn't you?" Cara asked nervously.

"I did. You're welcome."

"I hate you so much."

"No, you don't."

Perseus was scanning the crowd for anyone that could be Pithos, but so far, no one had approached him.

The replica burned in his pocket, and he kept touching it, making sure it was there. If Pithos were watching, it would look like he was nervously reassuring himself. He needed them to believe it was genuine.

Perseus was getting another beer when a hush descended over the gallery, the background house music suddenly loud.

He turned around as the crowd of people parted, and a golden glow filled the doorway. He felt it the moment Medusa's gaze hit him.

Whispers picked up around him like a susurrus of speculation as Medusa walked across the gallery floor and kissed both of his cheeks.

"Sorry I'm late, *babe*, I got held up at a meeting," she purred.

"The important thing is you're here now, *honey*. Drink?" Perseus said, wondering just how far she'd take this charade.

He passed her a glass of champagne, and the crowd noise rose again, though it wasn't as boisterous as it was before. Cara was going to murder him if Medusa didn't.

"So you're an artist as well as thief," Medusa said, looping her arm around his. "Show me your masterpieces and convince me not to out you as a criminal, right here, right now."

"Sure thing." Perseus took a large mouthful of beer. He was so fucked. "Did you not get the flowers to say that your possession was going to be returned tomorrow?"

"I did, but I was far too curious to find out why you'd want to borrow something so trivial," Medusa replied as they stopped in front of the first painting.

Perseus decided he was more afraid of the woman on his arm than he was of a gang of thugs like Pithos.

"I've been retired as a thief for a while, but I was made an offer I couldn't refuse. I made a replica of the necklace to get myself out of trouble, and you being here right now is completely and utterly fucking me," he whispered urgently.

Medusa's breath was warm against his ear as she whispered, "Dear boy, I haven't even *begun* to fuck with you."

Perseus sucked in a breath, and his senses were assaulted by her perfume of crushed flowers and sex.

"Okay, I'm in equal parts terrified and aroused, but that's irrelevant. The trade-off with the replica necklace is supposed to happen tonight, and if they see you here, I don't know what they will do. Please, leave. I don't want them to back out because they'll think we are working together," he begged.

Medusa leaned further into his embrace, making his heart race even faster as the curve of her soft breast pressed into his chest.

"Tell me, who are *they*?" she asked.

"I don't know. They called themselves Pithos. Please, they've got my sister-" Perseus said before the lights went out.

Cara's commanding voice rose above the cries of exclamations and lit phone screens. "Okay, everyone, stay calm and head to the exit in an orderly fashion until we figure out what's going on. Fucking Hellas power grid, you guys know how it is."

The crowd laughed and filed towards the door. Medusa didn't let her grip of Perseus go as she pulled a phone out of her pocket.

"Charon, honey, we are dealing with Pithos. Can you get ready? Yes, I got the thief, but we are going to need an extraction," she said in a calm voice before hanging up.

"We should go," Perseus urged taking a step forward, but Medusa pulled him back.

"Not that way. Does this gallery have a back door?"

"Why?"

"Because, sweetheart, we are about to be attacked," said Medusa.

Perseus started to protest when something smashed through his front glass windows and pinged loudly. His vision exploded in a wave of white light, and he pulled Medusa down to shield her.

"What are you doing? You're the one that can't see!" she shouted over the noise.

"Not the way you can," he admitted. Perseus's vision cleared, and he saw the heat signatures of men closing in on the front doors. He dragged her behind the bar as gunfire exploded through the gallery.

"Fuck, Medusa! What did you do to these guys?" he asked.

"Existed," Medusa snarled. She grabbed a bottle of spirits from the shelf before ripping off a strip of her shirt and stuffing it in the neck.

Light flared as she lit the bottle and tossed it over the bar. Perseus felt like he was stuck in some surreal dream as shouts echoed through the gallery, followed by more gunfire and the smell of smoke.

Medusa ducked back down beside him and took his face in her hands.

"I'm going to take care of these assholes. You are going to stay here and not move, or I swear to the gods, I'll hunt you to the ends of the earth, and you'll die a horrible, screaming death. Understand me?" Her beautiful golden face hovered in front of his, and he nodded.

"Deal. Just don't get killed before I have a chance to kiss you," Perseus said, wondering if he was possessed.

Medusa's golden lips rose in a smile, and she slid her glasses off. Her gaze landed on him, and he tingled all over. She pushed the glasses into his hand.

"Look after these," she said. She crawled past Perseus and looked around the corner of the bar before pulling her head back as the guns opened fire. "Persistent little bastards, aren't they?" Then she moved in a golden blur of light.

Perseus stuck his head around the corner of the bar and watched Medusa streaking through the group of men with guns. Then there was screaming and gunfire, and all the heat signatures were snuffed out, leaving only Medusa standing in the middle of the gallery floor.

He was so enamored of her that he almost didn't sense the man coming through the back door, his gun already up and aiming at Medusa.

Perseus grabbed a bottle from beside him and threw it hard. It clocked the man in the side of the head, sending him to the ground unconscious. Perseus crawled over to him and relieved him of his knives and handcuffs.

"Perseus! The back door," Medusa shouted, and he was on his feet in seconds. As soon as she joined him, Perseus handed her back her glasses and grabbed her hand. They hurried towards the staff access door.

"It leads out to the alley, watch out for the table," he said, as they went through the kitchen.

He reached for the back door when it was opened, and a man in tactical gear was there, pointing a gun at them.

Perseus stepped in front of Medusa as the man took a step forward and froze.

"Get down on your knees," the man commanded.

"Okay, okay, keep calm," Perseus said as he started to lower down before he feinted, drove his knife into one of the man's kneecaps, then slashed it up his thigh.

Screaming, the man dropped the gun. As he pitched forward, Perseus drove the tip the blade up under his chin.

"So are you blind or not, because I'm now thoroughly confused, thief," Medusa asked as he got back to his feet and tucked the knife back into his jacket pocket.

"It's complicated," said Perseus. Figuring, he was probably about to die for what he would do next, he slid an arm around her waist and kissed her.

Medusa tasted of champagne, lipstick and fire and made Perseus want to drag it out much longer than was sane. She made a startled sound as the tip of his tongue slid against hers, and Perseus snapped the handcuffs over her wrist and to the handle of the fridge door.

"How dare you kiss me! What do you-" she hissed, yanking at her cuffed hand.

"Sorry, babe, I have to run," he said, jumping out of the way of her swinging arm.

"Release me, human, or I swear you'll regret it." Medusa's hair seemed to glow and come alive.

Holy shit, go now! Perseus headed for the door.

"I really am sorry. Pithos has my sister, and if they think we are working together, they'll kill her. You'll get your necklace back, I promise. You just need to stay out of my way," Perseus said and ran out into the night before she broke the cuffs and flayed him alive.

Perseus had made it four blocks before his phone started ringing.

Dany had engraved the screen of his phone, so he could feel the ridges for answering calls, and where to press to hit the record function.

"Hello?" he answered and hit record.

"Mr. Serpho, are you still alive?" Mr. Black asked.

"No thanks to your goons. What the hell, man? You said you wanted to trade this necklace, not blow up my fucking gallery," Perseus replied angrily.

"We got word that Medusa had arrived. Are you trying to play both sides? Because you know that won't end well for sweet Dany."

Perseus let out a frustrated sigh. "Medusa was there looking for a painting, and to support the Styx art scene, something she often does. She didn't even have bodyguards with her! She has no idea who I really am, why would she? And as you pointed out, why would I risk my sister's wellbeing and go to Medusa over a worthless piece of brass. Give me some credit."

"We don't give you any credit, Mr. Serpho, and you know we can't trust you. I didn't want it to be this way, but..." Mr. Black broke off, and a girl started screaming in the background.

Perseus could make out Dany shouting his name and the word 'cache' before the noise was muffled.

"Please, please don't hurt her. I've got nothing to do with the fucking Court of Styx-"

"We are going to give you one more chance, Mr. Serpho. The price of your sister's life has just gone up."

"What are you talking about? I don't have any money-"

"It's not money that we want now or even the necklace. You'll deliver Medusa's head to us, or we'll deliver Danae's head to you."

"Fuck!" Perseus shouted as the line went dead.

He sank to his knees on the sidewalk, trying to breathe as the colors of his vision swarmed. Pithos had him by the balls, and they knew it.

There was no way he could kill Medusa, and she would annihilate him in any case. It was too dangerous to even try...

Perseus's vision settled as an idea occurred to him. It was equally dangerous and stupidly reckless, but it was the only way he could save Dany.

6

Medusa didn't expect her night to turn into such a glorious shit show so early on.

She had planned on going to the exhibit and flat out accusing Perseus, making a scene with her very presence.

Yet, when she got there and saw him talking art in his casual suit that still somehow made him look like a rogue, her solid plan dissolved into fucking with him to watch him squirm. He was quite an adorable squirmer too.

All was going well until fucking Pithos arrived, and you got yourself cuffed to a fridge.

"Susa?" Thanatos's tall figure and broad shoulders filled the door leading out into the alley.

"Here," she said and shook the cuffs. "Not one fucking word of this to the others, you hear?"

Thanatos grabbed the cuffs, and silvery light came out of his hands. Whatever the handcuffs were made of rusted and corroded in seconds and Medusa broke her wrist free.

"Where's the thief?" Thanatos asked.

"Ran off, don't worry about it. We need to get out of here and back to

Serpentine before these Pithos assholes send in reinforcements. Where the fuck is Charon?" said Medusa.

Machine gun fire echoed down the access road, just as a car drifted around the tight corner and screeched to a stop. "Your chariot awaits, my lady," a voice called from inside.

"Back to Serpentine," she said.

"What happened to the thief?"

"Got the slip on me. I don't want to talk about it," Medusa replied as she climbed into the back seat, swearing under her breath.

Charon didn't argue, only put the car in gear, and put his foot on the accelerator.

Medusa should have known Pithos would be watching Perseus, and now Hades was going to be pissed at the attention the attack on her would cause. All she could think about was how the cute criminal had tried to protect her.

Twice.

Perseus had literally stepped in front of a gun, even though he had watched her take down the other attackers.

She didn't know if it made him adorably brave or incredibly stupid. There was more to his involvement with Pithos, and maybe more to him other than a money-grubbing dirty thief.

Medusa realized she was touching her lips, scowled, and dropped her hand away. She couldn't believe he'd gotten the drop on her so easily.

I'm going to kill that damn thief.

All Medusa felt like doing was having a hot bath with a bottle of wine and letting someone else deal with Pithos.

"Susa, you're out of hummus. What the hell?" Erebus called as soon as they walked through the door of her penthouse.

"Get out of my fridge or I'll maim you!" Medusa shouted back. Erebus stuck his head around the corner of the kitchen.

"Where's the thief?"

"Mouse got away from her," said Charon.

"Clever bastard, how did he do it?"

Medusa pulled a bottle of white wine out of the fridge door and drank half of it in one go. "I don't want to talk about it. Pithos turned up to kill me, and we need to find out where they are holed up."

Thanatos pulled out his phone and headed for the gardens. "I need to talk to Hades."

"Better you than me," grumbled Medusa.

"He's going to be pissed," Charon said.

"He's *always* pissed when he goes to Athens," replied Erebus with an eye roll.

"Perseus said Pithos has his sister. What is it with these assholes kidnapping people?" Medusa said, chewing on her lip.

"I did a bit of asking around, and Perseus Serpho has been out of the thieving business for a few years," said Charon, taking a seat at her bar. "The rich and dodgy of Greece wept when he retired, he was that good. Interesting for a blind guy."

"I don't know how blind he is. He said it was complicated. Maybe he only pretends he's blind as a cover," said Medusa.

"You have to love a mystery man. I saw a photo of the scars. There's no way he doesn't have something wrong with his sight," replied Erebus.

Thanatos came in from the gardens looking agitated and drained Erebus's glass of whiskey.

"What did Hades say?" Medusa asked.

"The boss said that this is your mess to clean up. Your thief, your problem. Athens is doing a number on his mood, as usual." Thanatos gave her shoulder a comforting pat. "Let me know when you have a lead. You know how I feel about people kidnapping children."

Medusa knew better than to ask what had happened in the titan's long life to have that particular trigger, but nothing made him go into full berserker mode quicker than violence against children and women.

"Thanks, Thanatos, I'll figure this out, and we'll take them down together," Medusa assured him.

"You want one of us to stay the night for extra protection?"

Medusa shook her head. "No need, Pithos doesn't have the stones to take on my tower just yet."

After they had gone, Medusa finished her wine in the safety of her bathroom, pulled off her filthy clothes, and stepped in the shower to let the steaming water soothe her bad temper.

She wanted to rip Pithos apart for disrupting her life and dragging Perseus and his sister into their mess.

MEDUSA

It was the Court they were after, and they didn't give a shit who they hurt to get what they wanted.

She was pissed off at Perseus for cuffing her, but she also could understand why he would risk the Court's wrath if it meant saving his sister.

Her own sisters, Sthenno and Euryale, had been tortured and killed, and she would've done anything to have a chance to go back and save them.

A small head pushed out of the chaotic mass of her hair and gently nudged affectionately against her cheek, trying to comfort her.

She stroked the small warm body, and it curled back into her hair. Even her snakes were upset, and that was never a good thing.

Medusa's Doctor Who pajamas felt like steady, comforting armor as she headed back to the kitchen to find something to binge eat.

"What happened to your Slytherin jammies?" Perseus asked from her dining room table, making her jump in fright.

"You really do have a death wish," she replied as she closed in on him.

"I come in peace, look!" Perseus said and shook his hands to show her where he had cuffed himself to the chair.

"Who said I wanted peace?" Medusa grabbed him around the throat, her nails lengthening to claws.

"I understand why you are upset, but please hear me out before you kill me," he wheezed and awkwardly held out his phone.

"You're lucky that you're a lead to Pithos," she said, releasing him and snatching the phone. "Why are you here?"

"Because I need your help," Perseus replied and nodded at the phone. "I recorded the last conversation I had with Pithos as proof I never wanted to rob you."

Medusa held up a finger to silence him and went through his phone to find the message.

Of all the shit to happen tonight.

Medusa's stomach filled with ice as she listened to the conversation, Perseus flinching as Dany started to scream.

"It's not money that we want now or even the necklace. You'll deliver Medusa's head to us, or we'll deliver Danae's head to you," the Pithos member said, and the phone call went dead.

Medusa placed the phone down on the table. "I need another drink." Medusa poured herself another large wine and a cup of water for Perseus. She found a bendy straw for him to use and placed it on the table in front of him.

"You should drink something," she said before she sat down opposite him.

"You got anything stronger?" asked Perseus.

"Water and explanations first, and then I'll think about it." He let out a tired sigh but sucked on the straw all the same.

"Okay, tell me everything that happened from the beginning, and I'll decide where we go from there." Medusa sat back in her chair. "*Make* me trust you, Perseus Serpho."

Perseus started talking about the last few days of his life, how he'd been approached by Pithos, and how, when he'd refused to help them, Dany had been snatched.

Halfway through his story, Medusa poured him a glass of whiskey. She was feeling guiltier by the second.

Despite being a thief, he was also a victim. Dany was the one she really worried about. Medusa had watched Pithos work Ariadne over again and again, but she had been trained to withstand torture. Dany was just a teenage girl.

"And then you turned up at the gallery and here we are," Perseus finished. "Trust me?" He looked wrung out and pissed off. Medusa knew the feeling.

"Give me a moment, I need to think," she said and headed outside into the night air. It was almost 1 am, but she knew Asterion would be awake.

"What's up, Susa? Charon said you've lost your thief," he answered after the first few rings. She could hear the club in the background, and she waited until he'd stepped into his office.

"I did, then he showed up again to try to make a deal," Medusa said.

"The guy has big balls, I'll give him that. What did he have to say for himself?" asked Asterion. Medusa gave him an abbreviated version of her last hour.

"Okay, so we have a lead. That is good news, Susa, so why do you still sound so annoyed?"

Medusa hissed irritably. "What made you trust Ariadne? I mean, she *killed* you, Asterion. Why did you decide to spare her?"

"It was because I knew she'd been put into a tough spot, and deep down, even with what Minos did to her, she still had good in her," Asterion said finally.

"I guess I'm going to have to tolerate the thief for a while longer then. Perseus and his sister are also being made to suffer because of whatever Pithos has planned for us. I feel so shitty about it. It was easier when I was pissed off and wanted to kill him," Medusa admitted.

Asterion laughed. "I know how you're feeling. I was the same when I caught Ariadne. Then I couldn't go through with it. In saying that, trust needs to be earned. Give him some rope, if he runs, hang him with it."

"Sounds fair."

"Medusa, you know we need to find the girl even if he does," Asterion added.

"I was planning on it. This Mr. Black called his phone, I'm going to try and trace it. There are a few other stones I can try turning over. I might need your lady," she said.

"You know our number if you need us, Susa. I don't feel like I got half as much revenge on Pithos as I wanted," replied Asterion in a voice that was all Minotaur.

Medusa took a deep breath before heading back inside. Perseus had finished his whiskey and watched her carefully. How much could he actually see? Another question she'd have to ask him.

"Okay, I'll trust you, and we'll help you find your sister," Medusa said.

Perseus's shoulders sagged with relief. "Thank you. I guess I can get rid of these now." He wriggled his wrists, the cuffs falling off him and onto the floor.

"How did you-"

Despite the stressful night, Perseus's smile was roguish as he got up out of the chair. "I'm a thief, honey. I'm good with locks. So what do we do now?"

"Give me your phone back," Medusa demanded, trying not to feel flustered.

"What for?"

"Because I'm going to try to trace where the call came from. This isn't our first brush with Pithos, and as much as I hate to admit it, they are smart. They'll probably have something blocking traces, but it's worth a try," Medusa said.

He passed it over without hesitating. Medusa put it in her pocket and picked up her handset.

"I'm starving, do you like ramen? The building's chef does great ramen."

"You have your own chef? Why?"

"Ah, for ramen at 1 a.m," Medusa reiterated like it was the most obvious thing in the world. "A lot of my designers and programmers work best at night. I like to make sure they are at least eating right."

"That's nice of you."

"Full programmers are happy programmers," Medusa replied and rang the kitchen.

Perseus watched her give the order, amusement lighting up his dirty face.

She turned her back on him and rang another floor. "Hey, Lola, I'm going to need for you to run a trace on a phone for me. Ready for the serial number?"

With promises to call her back in an hour, Medusa hung up and turned back to her unexpected houseguest.

"You are going to need a shower," Medusa said critically. "I'll have laundry come and take care of your things."

"And what am I meant to wear while these get washed?" he asked, emptying his jacket pockets on the table.

"I'm sure we have some Serpentine merchandise that will fit you, although I'm in half a mind to force you to walk around naked," she said.

Perseus raised an eyebrow. "And why is half of your mind thinking about me naked?"

"Considering what you stood around watching *me* doing, forcing you to walk around naked wouldn't even come close to making us even," Medusa replied.

"Look, about that, I'm sorry-" he began.

"I don't want to hear your excuses or your apologies," Medusa said and pointed down the hall. "Shower is that way and clean towels are in the cupboard."

She watched him walk away, wondering how in the fucking Fates she was now meant to cohabitate with a man.

7

Medusa's bathroom was as insane as the rest of the penthouse.

Perseus almost didn't want to put his clothes on the floor because it would be messy.

Everything smelled of crushed flowers and soap, and the type of fancy face product that ladies used.

When he had been sitting on the sidewalk having a panic attack that night, he hadn't expected to be using Medusa's shampoo two hours later.

She could just be putting the vivisection on hold.

She could do whatever she wanted to him after they got Dany back. He pushed his palm against the ball of pressure building in his chest. He had never been the type of man that longed for violence, but he was going to straight-up murder the person who had made Dany scream.

Medusa's entire attitude towards him had softened after playing her the phone call.

What had Pithos done to her? It had to be significant enough for one of the most powerful people in Styx to drop all their animosity and want to actually work with him.

Perseus wished Medusa had let him explain that he was sorry for accidentally spying on her.

Are you though? an unwelcome voice asked in the back of his head. It had certainly added some exotic flavor to his spank bank.

Perseus reached for the body wash and jumped in fright, hands dropping to cover himself.

"Fucking hell! What are you doing in here?" he demanded. Medusa was casually leaning against the bathroom cabinets, sipping her wine.

"I came to bring you some clean clothes, and I decided to just stay and watch...uninvited...like you did to me," she answered pleasantly.

"I didn't mean to walk in on you. I didn't even know you were home. You weren't meant to be," Perseus hurried to explain. "I went into the lounge because I was studying your art, and you were just *there*. I'm sorry. Really, *really* sorry."

"Who would've thought a big tough thief from Hellas would be so shy?" Medusa laughed devilishly as two small snakes curled around the column of her neck.

"Um, is your hair meant to do that?" he asked, wiping the steam off the glass so he could have a better look.

Medusa pushed the snakelets back into her messy curls.

"They are nosey, like you."

"You call me nosey, but I'm not the one watching a stranger have a shower. Something I'm about to get back to if you don't mind."

Medusa lifted her glass in a toast. "I don't mind at all. Go right ahead, I'm not stopping you." She really was going to stay there.

Well, if that's what it took for her to get over him walking in on her masturbating, he would do it.

"Suit yourself," he said, reaching for the shower gel.

"Lola didn't find anything on the phone number we gave her. She knows it was made from within the city, but that's as far as she can narrow it down," Medusa said, clearing her throat. Perseus pretended not to notice.

Despite what she thought, he *wasn't* a shy guy, and if she wanted to start a game of chicken with him, he was determined to win.

"Okay, so what's our next move while we wait for them to call back?" he asked, moving his hands lower.

"They still want the necklace, and they'll have surveillance on the gallery and where you live. In the morning, we'll visit both places to see if it flushes them out. Besides, you are going to need clothes and whatever bag of tricks you have saved for a rainy day. Pithos is going to come at you hard, and you need to be ready," Medusa said and cleared her throat. "You are giving that thing an awful thorough cleaning."

"You are the one that's determined to watch me in the shower. This is what I do in the shower. Besides, I walked in on you, so you can stay and watch me, and then we'll be even," Perseus said.

Despite trying to keep his tone calm, his pulse was racing as Medusa stared at him. He was hard in seconds as he began to stroke himself with more intent.

Oh, gods, she's actually going to stand there and watch me do it.

"We will *never* be even, thief," Medusa said suddenly and flicked the sink taps. Perseus leaped backward with a yelp as his hot water turned freezing.

Medusa was laughing as he fumbled for the taps and turned the shower off. He grabbed the towel off the top of the shower partition, slung it low around his hips, and stepped out.

"Very funny," he said.

"I thought so," Medusa replied, her voice still laced with humor.

The bathroom that had seemed oversized moments ago now seemed too tight for the two of them.

Without her high heels, Medusa was tiny beside him, the top of her fiery head barely reaching his shoulder.

The feel of her lips against his came rushing back. He needed to focus and fast.

"So tomorrow we head to my place and see if they are watching it. Gods, I'm hoping they don't know where I live. Not many people do," Perseus said, looking down at her.

"Pithos is well connected, so you might be out of luck. You should really start hoping they haven't burned it down just for the inconvenience you've caused them," she said. Medusa thrust a bundle of clothes at his chest. "These should fit."

"You don't want to hang around and make sure?" Perseus couldn't resist asking. Her golden aura fluttered, but she shrugged.

"No need. I already have the measure of you," she said smugly.

"If you think that, then gods, do you have some surprises headed your way," Perseus replied with a sly smile.

Medusa gave him a long once over. "I doubt that," she said, before shutting the door firmly behind her.

You're on, gorgeous, replied the voice in his head, the one that dared him to do stupid, risky things.

PERSEUS FOUND Medusa in the kitchen, arranging bowls of ramen at the counter and opening fresh beers.

"I'm sure I gave you a t-shirt to wear," she said as he sat down on one of the chairs.

"It was too small for my shoulders. Besides, I usually sleep naked, so you're lucky I'm even wearing pants right now," said Perseus.

Her aura fluttered again, and he wondered how angry she was going to get when he told her about it.

Her mouth could sass him all it wanted. Her body was telling a completely different story.

"You had better *keep* those pants on too. The last thing I need to worry about is your man junk rubbing against my couch cushions," Medusa replied, sitting down next to him and picking up her spoon.

"You're not used to having guests, are you?" asked Perseus.

"No, especially not...men."

Perseus didn't dare look at her. He skewered something in his bowl with his chopsticks. "That's surprising."

"Why do you say that?" asked Medusa.

"Because you are the media queen of Greece and run a hugely successful company," Perseus said. "And you are fucking gorgeous. I thought you'd have a horde of lovers."

"Who said I don't? I could be keeping the harem on another floor," Medusa replied.

"True, but if that were the case, you wouldn't have resorted to-"

"You don't need to say it," Medusa snapped, her embarrassment radiating off her. "I don't date, are you happy now?"

"Are you?"

"Happy? Yes, I am. It's easier. People are messy. My life is busy enough without the complication of feelings and men and that whole... thing."

"Look at that, we finally have something we agree on," Perseus said before having a mouthful of his beer.

Medusa didn't answer him, so he tried another vegetable floating in his ramen. One chew and he knew it was a mistake.

"Argh, gross. Bamboo shoot sneak attack," he complained, quickly washing it down with more beer. Medusa cracked up laughing.

"You don't like bamboo shoots? What's wrong with you?"

"I have working taste buds?"

"Don't be such a baby about it," Medusa said, leaning over to pick at his bowl with her chopsticks. She fished out all the bamboo shoots, transferring them to her bowl.

"Thanks," Perseus said, surprised. "I forgot to tell you my aversion when you said you were going to order dinner. Dany usually orders for me. She also loves ramen and gross bamboo shoots."

"Well, it's no surprise that the woman in the family has all the taste," replied Medusa.

"All the taste *and* all the brains. She's going to die when I tell her I ate dinner with you."

"Me? Why?"

"She thinks you are the coolest. She's so addicted to the Shadow Lords game of yours, she will rattle on about gaming, coding, and Serpentine console design until your ears literally slide off."

"How old is she?"

"Seventeen and full of cheek. Actually, as far as teenagers go, I can't complain. She's awesome, and I don't have to be on her case about homework or boys," said Perseus.

"You must be missing her," Medusa replied softly, her voice filled with a sadness that hadn't been there before.

"Yeah, I miss her like crazy," he admitted.

"Where are your parents?"

"Dead. I've looked after Dany full time since she was born. It's weird, but most of the time, I feel like her dad rather than her brother. At seventeen, I was a fucking mess of rage and hormones, and she's just so cool and together."

"She sounds it. She's lucky to have you," said Medusa.

"*I'm* lucky to have *her*. Do you have a family?"

"Only the Court. I had sisters, but they...they died."

"Sorry to hear that," Perseus said, the ache back in his chest that even flirting with Medusa couldn't ease. "I honestly can't imagine what I'll do if Dany—"

Medusa's hand covered his mouth. "Don't even say it. We are going to get her back. I *promise* you. You're not going to lose your sister the way I lost mine, you hear me?"

Perseus nodded slowly, and she quickly dropped her hand away.

"Thank you for your help," he said, turning back to his dinner.

"Thank me when we get her back and not before."

Perseus cleaned up the dishes as Medusa disappeared to make up the couch. He joined her in the lounge room, both of them not speaking of the last time they were together in that room.

"You're a tall guy, but hopefully, you won't be too cramped," Medusa said, placing a folded blanket on the end of the couch and quickly stepping away from him when he joined her.

"It'll be fine, really don't trouble yourself," Perseus replied as he stretched out across the cushions. "See? Heaps of space. Room for two actually. You want to tuck me in?"

"Don't push your luck. Good night, thief. Or is it good morning? Never mind," said Medusa, backing away.

"Not even good night kiss?" he called.

Medusa turned the lights out on him. "You already stole one from me. You're not going to get the chance to get another. Sweet dreams."

Perseus was going to be lucky to get to sleep on that couch at all when all he could think about was the feel of her lips and her lying where he was now, her hand in her cute Slytherin jammies. He turned his head and groaned into the pillow.

What the hell had he gotten himself into?

8

The following day, Medusa woke to the distant sound of Ariadne's bawdy, full-bodied laughter.

It took a few minutes for the previous night's events to come back to her: Pithos's attack and somehow gaining a distractingly handsome roommate.

Medusa muttered curses as she slowly sat up in bed and put on her glasses. It had taken hours for her to get to sleep.

She didn't know what had been going through her wine-addled brain when she decided watching Perseus taking a shower was a good idea

She hadn't meant to, but as soon as she was in the bathroom, she found herself reluctant to leave.

Fates save her; the man was *built* and covered in the same beautiful tattoos as his arms.

And he can kiss like there's no tomorrow. She couldn't deny that having dinner with him was also rather...pleasant.

Medusa didn't want to think about that too much, so she stuffed the warm fuzzy emotions down inside of her.

How dare the Fates force her into such a mess. Perseus was a flirt too, but she didn't know how serious he was, and it left her feeling flustered.

Not that she was going to show him he had that effect on her.

Ariadne's laughter echoed down the hall again, causing Medusa to freeze.

How long has Ariadne been alone with him? Medusa leaped out of bed.

If Ariadne turned up at the Labyrinth smelling like another man, Asterion would likely go berserk. Having the Minotaur turning up to disembowel her thief was the last thing she needed.

"No, I'm deadly serious. My gallery manager is completely in love with her," Perseus was saying as Medusa strode into the kitchen. Ariadne was eating Medusa's yogurt with fruit salad and smiling flirtatiously at her thief.

"Oh, hey, look who's awake," Perseus said with a welcoming smile.

He was still shirtless as he poured coffee out of the plunger, and all of Medusa's thought processes seemed to fail her. Instead of responding, she quickly sat down next to Ariadne.

"Susa! You didn't tell me you had a man staying over," Ariadne said, smiling like she had the devil in her.

"It's not what you think. Perseus is my prisoner," Medusa replied, ignoring her implication.

"I did say she could tuck me in, but she turned me down," said Perseus, handing Ariadne a coffee. "It would seem I'm a bit too rough for the princess's palate."

"Oh, I doubt that," Ariadne said under her breath. Medusa elbowed her.

"You want a coffee, gorgeous?"

"Don't call me gorgeous, " Medusa said. "And yes. I'll have a big cup, seeing how it is my coffee after all."

Perseus wasn't fazed by her tone. "Sure thing. You want some sugar, sugar?"

"Yes," Medusa scowled. She *hated* pet names, and she knew he was doing it to get under her skin.

When Perseus turned his back to them, Ariadne pulled a dreamy face at Medusa with a thumbs up.

Shut up, Medusa mouthed at her.

"Perseus and I were chatting about Hellas while I was showing him around your kitchen. We know some of the same people, can you believe that? Hellas really does produce the coolest people, doesn't it, Perseus?" asked Ariadne.

"Coolest, most charming *and* best looking," he replied as he set a steaming cup of coffee and a bowl of fruit salad in front of Medusa.

"Also, statistically, the most criminals in all of Styx," Medusa added.

Perseus let out a low whistle. "You really aren't a morning person, are you?"

"Technically, I'm not a person so-"

"With your manners, I'd believe it." Medusa opened her mouth to savage him when the doorbell rang. "Hold that thought, grumpy, that'll be Kadie with my clothes." Perseus walked out of the kitchen, leaving Medusa muttering under her breath.

"Wow, Susa, you really know how to make a guy feel welcome," Ariadne commented.

"He's *not* welcome. I'm stuck with him as punishment because Hades is pissed at me and wants me to take care of Pithos while he's away."

"It doesn't seem like much of a punishment to have a smoking hot, tattooed babe make you breakfast," Ariadne said.

Medusa didn't reply. She was too busy leaning over to watch Kadie deliver Perseus's suit.

Did she seriously just flick her hair at him?

He turned around and Medusa quickly pulled herself straight.

"What did you say?" she said to Ariadne. The assassin was grinning at her.

"Oh, Susa, you've got a crush on the thief."

"Don't be ridiculous. I don't mingle with commoners," Medusa replied and reached for her fruit salad.

"I'm going to have a shower, are you coming to watch me again, Medusa, so you know I did it right?" Perseus called down the hallway. She leaned over and stuck her middle finger up at him. "I'll take that as a no."

"You had a shower with him?" Ariadne asked excitedly.

"No, it's not what you think," Medusa said, warmth blooming across her cheeks.

"I'm hearing that a lot this morning, but it's sort of seeming like it's *exactly* what I think."

"I was guarding Perseus to make sure he didn't try to escape. There was absolutely nothing sexy about it in the least," Medusa replied.

Aren't you a lying little Gorgon?

"Are we talking about the same Perseus? Because I'm pretty sure absolutely everything would be sexy about it." Ariadne nudged her gently. "What's got you so pissy this morning?"

"I don't like smug people in my space."

"You've got it so bad."

"I have no idea what you're talking about."

"Sure, you do. You two are both so pent up I'm surprised the kitchen didn't spontaneously combust."

Medusa frowned. "I don't think that's true. He flirts with everyone, like Erebus."

"He didn't flirt with me," Ariadne argued. "Why are you surprised that he's into you?"

"Because I don't think he is. He's just flirting because he knows it annoys me."

"Susa, is your nose still working? Because my Hellas bro was oozing so many pheromones that even my ovaries were dancing."

"Not everyone is like you, Ariadne. They aren't interested in fucking monsters," Medusa snapped and regretted it instantly.

Ariadne's storm blue eyes narrowed. "Are you trying to hurt my feelings right now or your own? Because I've never *once* thought you or any of the Court were monsters."

Medusa put down her fork and tried to steady her voice. "I'm sorry. It's different for the others. Asterion can change his appearance. I *can't* change myself to look normal."

"Do you really think a guy like him would give a shit about appearances? He has scars-"

"Ariadne, I have fucking snakes in my hair, amongst other things, I don't expect you to understand."

"You're right, I don't. You are crazy beautiful, snakes and all. You're a magical creature, Susa. You're unique, and any man would be lucky if you bothered to even look twice at them."

"So you say." Medusa drank some of her coffee, wondering why she was even bothering trying to explain. There were things about her that the assassin didn't know about, and while she probably wouldn't care, a man like Perseus, who women seemed to fall all over? Medusa doubted it.

"Susa, seriously. What do you have to lose? You are so killer confident, and as soon as it comes to a cute guy showing genuine interest in you, you act like it's not possible."

"A guy who *stole* from me and kissed me without permission. Surely, I can have higher standards than that," Medusa replied.

"He was in a terrible position, so cut him some slack. Wait, he kissed you?"

"Before he cuffed me and left me for Pithos," Medusa added.

"Wow, he's a quick worker. He's also not a bad guy, and he's going to help us. Don't dismiss him just because you're nervous about having a crush on someone."

"I don't have a crush on him."

That's not entirely true, though, is it, sister? Euryale's voice echoed in her head clear as a bell.

"Please stop stirring me up. I have a long day ahead of me," Medusa added, putting their bowls into the sink.

"Fine, but I know when two people are hot for each other. What are you up to for the rest of the day?"

"Perseus and I are going to check the damage to the gallery and go to his house. Hopefully, we'll find some Pithos guarding the place that we can take for questioning," Medusa explained.

"Be careful and give me a call if you need me," Ariadne said, hopping off her barstool. She pulled Medusa into a hug. "It's okay to be nervous about liking someone. No, don't argue with me and stop arguing with Perseus. Just think about what I said, okay?"

"Okay, now get out of here," Medusa replied with a smile.

"You should join him in that shower before someone else does," Ariadne suggested, waggling her eyebrows at her.

"Go, before I turn you into stone for the peace and quiet," Medusa threatened playfully.

Hellas always reminded Medusa that no matter how hard they tried, there were parts of Styx that the Court and the human leaders had failed.

Corinth had been a smoking pile of ashes when Hades had arrived, and even though twenty years had passed, there were still scars from that time left in the city.

After a minor debate on which car to take, Medusa drove a black BMW SUV from Serpentine Tower heading for Perseus's gallery.

"Even this car is fancy enough to get attention. We'll be lucky if someone doesn't try to steal it," Perseus said from the passenger seat.

"I'm not going to rely on a taxi to wait for us if Pithos decide to attack me again. We need a getaway car, and Charon is busy," replied Medusa.

She didn't want to argue with him, she was already feeling uneasy after her chat with Ariadne. She was barely game enough to breathe too deeply around him in case her nose picked up on something she wasn't ready to admit to herself.

The sooner they got Dany back from Pithos, the sooner they could go their separate ways, and she could have her solitude back. She had spent more time out of the tower in the last few days than she had in the last few months, and it made her feel uneasy and exposed.

Cara was waiting for them when they pulled up in front of the gallery. She had looked radiant the night before, now she was almost grey from sleep deprivation and worry.

"Oh no, please tell me she hasn't been chain-smoking," muttered Perseus. Medusa spotted the pile of cigarette butts on the footpath.

"Out of luck. She looks really upset," Medusa said. "How did you know?"

"Her aura is freaking out," Perseus explained, before climbing out. Cara shot into his arms and burst into tears.

Medusa felt awkward, debating internally whether she should get out of the car. She felt so...noticeable. She had dressed casually in artfully ripped black jeans, ankle boots, and a Captain Marvel t-shirt in an attempt to seem like a regular person on the street.

Hoping that there were no Pithos snipers on the nearby rooftops, Medusa got out of the car.

"They fucking trashed everything! Why would anyone-" Cara stopped talking and stared at her.

Perseus cleared his throat. "Ah, Cara, this is Medusa."

"Yeah, I can fucking see that," Cara sniffed, her eyes wide.

"It's nice to meet you, but we really need to get off the street," said Medusa. Cara nodded, and they walked through the door into what was left of the gallery.

The insides of the building were blackened from the fire Medusa's Molotov cocktail had started and was soaked from the water sprinklers.

The canvases that still remained mounted were ripped from bullet holes and stained from smoke and water.

Medusa knew Hades's men must have been there sometime in the night because the men she had turned to stone were missing.

"Did the office survive? I had most of the business paperwork stored there, including the insurance on the building," Perseus said, his voice expressionless.

"I'll go check, but I did make a backup on my laptop," Cara replied, walking carefully through the rubble to the staff door.

Not knowing what to say, Medusa took his hand. It was warm and huge as he twined his fingers with hers.

"I'm sorry about all of this," she said genuinely. Damn Pithos and their hate campaign.

"It's okay. The space was insured, but it'll be a while before we can get it repaired and reopened. My paintings are fucked, so I'm going to have to start a new collection," said Perseus with a tired sigh.

"Let's hope they have no idea where your house is," Medusa replied. "We'll get revenge for this, Perseus."

"I've had nothing before, Medusa. I'm not afraid of starting again. I only want my sister back."

Half an hour later, they left Cara in charge of calling the insurance companies and headed five blocks to where Perseus said he lived.

"I must have taken a wrong turn, because there are no houses around here," said Medusa as she stopped in front of a derelict warehouse.

"That's because I don't live in a house. I told you, I've always kept where I sleep a secret," Perseus explained.

Medusa followed him through the overgrown yard to a metal door padlocked with a chain. Medusa didn't know what to expect when he opened the door, but it wasn't a graffitied skateboard half-pipe.

"Down here is Dany's domain and the kitchen, the second floor is mine. As long as she keeps my pathway clear of crap, she can do whatever she likes to it," said Perseus, leading her around the old desks covered in pulled apart computers, a variety of skateboards, piles of books and blackboards covered in drawings and math equations.

In one corner, the floor was covered in old carpets and had a massive flat screen TV, Serpentine console, and a battered recliner.

"Please don't let me leave without turning on Shadow Lords and updating Dany's account. If we get her back, she'll be livid if I don't do it for her. Even kidnapped, she was giving me orders to update it because she was worried about her XP dropping too much," said Perseus.

"It makes me happy to hear she likes it," replied Medusa. At least they would have something to chat about when they finally met. Maybe she would give Dany the new expansion early as a 'sorry you got kidnapped because of me' present.

Medusa followed Perseus up a set of metal stairs to a floor that would've once been offices if someone hadn't knocked some of the walls down. It was still split into rooms. One space was a gym, another she glimpsed was a bedroom. Perseus unlocked another door that held equipment.

"I won't take too long to pack," he said, pulling down an empty black duffel bag.

"Take your time, I'm going to do a quick scan to make sure that Pithos haven't set any bugs or cameras." Medusa pulled out her phone and clicked on the new app Serpentine had developed in recent months. It picked up on frequencies, amongst other things.

"Go ahead, but it doesn't look like they've been here," said Perseus.

Medusa walked slowly through the maze of rooms, taking the time to scan them thoroughly while looking at the art and trying to get a better picture of her new houseguest.

There was a neat order to everything that surprised her. Even the laundry was tidy.

She opened a door, her nose detecting fresh oil paints, turpentine, and canvas. She had found his art studio and the creative chaos that she'd expected.

Medusa looked at the piles of sketches on his worktable and froze. They had been sketched with chalk pastels, but they were, unmistakably, of her.

She flicked through them, and something gold flickered in the corner of her eye. A half-finished painting stood on an easel.

Unlike his abstract work that she thought of as his signature style, this painting was of a woman, glowing with golden light, her eyes burning with divine anger and passion.

She was beautiful and powerful, and definitely not how she ever thought someone would think of her.

A strange emotion washed through her, and it took her a minute to finally acknowledge what it was.

Damn it, I do have a crush on him.

"Oh shit," Perseus said behind her. "I can explain."

"Is this how you see me?" Medusa asked, unable to look away from the shining woman on the canvas.

"Yes. I see the world in distorted shapes and colors and mostly blurred images, but you are so clear," Perseus admitted, coming to stand beside her.

"When I saw you for the first time, I felt like Actaeon must have when he stumbled across Artemis bathing in her stream. Like I was a dumb fucking mortal about to be annihilated and still unable to look away, because being able to see something so divine was worth the horrible punishment."

"I'm not a goddess, Perseus. I am a Gorgon. A monster. There's a difference, " Medusa said, her heart racing.

"I've met monsters, and believe me, you're not one. And I'm not entirely positive you aren't a goddess either, no matter what you think. If you had an altar, I sure as hell would worship at it. I could be your high priest, start up a cult, we could all wear matching Doctor Who pajamas, it would be-" Perseus didn't get to finish before Medusa closed the space between them and pressed her lips against his.

He seemed to freeze under the touch, and she almost pulled away, but she finally let herself breathe in his scent. There was paint and warm sunlight, fresh laundry, and coffee, but there was also the scent of his skin and pheromones of pure masculine arousal.

Ariadne was right again.

Perseus groaned as he deepened the kiss and lifted her up onto the workbench. Medusa's hands were in his hair, her legs locking around him as the undercurrent of tension that had been there since they met exploded in a torrent of desperate kisses.

She was on fire, her insides aching with want as Perseus's lips trailed down the curve of her neck to her collarbone, his fingers gentle as they touched her hair, careful of the tiny inhabitants.

His hands stroked down her spine to her ass, and he pulled her closer still. One hand went up to cup her breast, and she gasped with unexpected pleasure. She *needed* more.

Medusa pulled Perseus's shirt open, so she could stroke, touch, and taste all the hard muscle like she'd wanted to since she first saw him.

Somewhere in her mind, an alarm bell rang, and a riddle she'd been puzzling over clicked into place.

"Wait," she whispered, and he froze.

"What is it?" he asked.

"Dany. Something she shouted the other night in the message about a cache." Medusa leaned away so she could think straight.

"What do you mean? I only heard screaming."

"No, she said the word 'cache' but it didn't make sense until just now. You said she told you to update Shadow Lords when she was kidnapped?" said Medusa.

"Yeah, they gave her a console to play to keep her from being too bored and annoying. I don't understand-"

Medusa gave his tight ass a pat. "Out of the way. I need to go downstairs and check something."

"Okay, but just so we are clear, I'm not going to pretend this never happened like the last time," Perseus said, tucking Medusa's hair behind her ear before giving her a kiss so silky it made her pelvic floor muscles clench.

"To be continued, goddess," he said as he helped her back to her feet.

"Looking forward to it, thief."

Medusa did her best to ignore the wobble in her legs as she hurried downstairs and switched on the console. The black and silver load screen for 'Shadow Lords of the Night Lands' filled the TV and Medusa saw a very familiar user name.

"Your sister is NightWitch15?" she demanded.

"Yeah, that's Dany. Why?"

Medusa made a noise of annoyance. "Because she kicks my fucking ass every time our paths cross. I thought she was some next level Korean gamer since her stats are so high."

Perseus laughed. "That's my sister, all right. She's so brutal when she plays that I tend to leave the room. What's this all about?"

Medusa used the controller to click through her stats and found the sync command. "Okay, so Shadow Lords can be played online from any console. You can sync your games up as soon as you get onto a new device, but there is a log in your main console account that gives you a list of the consoles you've accessed. Your sister is a fucking genius to tell you to do this."

"I'm still not following," Perseus said slowly.

"IP addresses are a part of the console log. We can trace it and get a ping on her location, provided they haven't used some kind of VPN to scramble it."

Medusa took a photo of the IP path and sent it through to Lola with instructions. "Okay, let's check her message box and see if she had a chance to leave us some more breadcrumbs while her dumb ass captors were distracted."

"It wouldn't surprise me. As you said, Dany's a genius, especially at this game."

Medusa's heart just about stopped beating when she saw the bunch of messages that Dany had sent back to her own account.

"Is there something there?" Perseus asked.

"Yes, she's sent a few. The first one says, 'Four men with guns. More outside.' She must have been trying to get details out for whoever you sent to rescue her. 'There is someone in a mask' and another message, 'In a warehouse. I can hear big boats.'" Medusa clicked on the last message and felt sick. "There is one more. 'ARGOS labeled merchandise. WTF Grandfather.'"

ARGOS Industries was the second-largest tech company in Greece and was the closest thing Serpentine had as competition.

Before Medusa, they had ruled the whole market and had sent in more than one spy into Serpentine Tower to steal her ideas and sabotage her projects.

"What does she mean by *grandfather*?" Medusa demanded, stepping away from him. "What is ARGOS to you?" Perseus looked like someone had kicked him in the guts.

"Argos was once my surname," Perseus admitted. Medusa gripped the controller, as the betrayal hit her so hard she was breathless.

"Acrisius Argos is your fucking grandfather? Did he put you up to this to get back at me?" she demanded.

"No! I don't have anything to do with the asshole! I haven't for years. It's why I took the last name Serpho, to get away from him," said Perseus, as he reached out to her. Medusa stepped back, unsure that she could trust him.

"Acrisius is one of the richest men in Greece. Do you really think I'm going to believe that you just walked away from all that money and power?"

"I didn't *walk* away from him, I fucking ran!" Perseus shouted and pointed at his eyes. "Right after he did *this* to me."

9

Perseus felt the past crashing on him in a wave of bone-breaking anxiety.

"Get your things and I'll unplug this console. It's coming with us. We are going to the Labyrinth, and I suggest you get your story straight for your own good," said Medusa.

The flirty, sexy bundle of a woman that he'd been kissing only moments before was nowhere to be seen.

This was the Serpent Queen of Styx talking, and the coldness in her voice reminded him exactly who he'd let into his house.

"I don't need to straighten out my story. I'm telling you the truth. Do you really think Acrisius would kidnap Dany if we were all a big happy family?" Perseus replied, but the glow of her aura had already dimmed to something subdued and guarded. She was pissed, so instead of arguing, he went back upstairs to get his bags.

Why would his grandfather bother them now after so many years? Perseus had done everything he could to make sure Acrisius knew nothing about Dany or how talented she was. He must have slipped up somewhere.

Why else would he involve them?

Everyone knew about the rivalry between ARGOS and Serpentine, but his grandfather would have to be insane to think that involving a gang like Pithos would be the answer.

"We are heading over now," Medusa was saying as he went back downstairs. "I don't know, Asterion, I feel like a total sucker. I should've known better than to think I could trust an Argos."

"I'm *not* a fucking Argos," Perseus repeated as Medusa hung up the call and picked up the unplugged Serpentine console.

"Acrisius Argos is your grandfather, so yes, you are."

"You can trust me, Medusa-"

"No, I can't! Go and get in the car. Asterion and the triplets are waiting for us. They want to hear your explanation as much as I do," Medusa said, turning on her heel and heading outside.

It was the most uncomfortable drive downtown Perseus had ever had.

How was he going to get Medusa to believe him?

She had physically recoiled from him, and he hated that most of all because he had *liked* kissing her and the feel of her under his hands and between his thighs.

Now she was never going to let him touch her again. It was yet another way his grandfather had found to fuck him over.

Perseus had only ever visited the Labyrinth once to meet with a client, its pleasures mostly lost on him.

Fighting had its place, but it all became too much when people's energy was up, turning his world into a multi-colored nightmare.

The club was closed, but as soon as they pulled up, the front door opened, and a man made of shadows stood waiting for them.

"Wow, what is he?" Perseus asked.

"Your torturer if you don't come clean," said Medusa, getting out of the car before he could reply.

"So you caught your little thief after all," the shadow man said.

"I came to her actually," Perseus said.

"Medusa has a way of charming even the hardest of men, don't you, beautiful?"

"Out of the way, Erebus. I need to see Asterion," Medusa said, pushing past him. Erebus blocked Perseus's way in.

"I don't envy you, man. Susa looks ready to rip your throat out. Better spill everything while you have the chance," Erebus advised.

"I've got nothing to hide, but she wouldn't give me a second to explain."

"Now's your opportunity because if she doesn't get you, the Minotaur will," he said, pulling Perseus inside and shutting the door behind him.

Perseus was going to ask what he meant by that, but when he looked for Medusa, he *saw*. There was a huge creature of a man talking with her, glowing with a red aura. It was as clear as Medusa's except sitting on top of the man's shoulders was the head of a bull.

"Holy shit," he blurted before he could check himself.

"Yes, you're in it now," Erebus said, taking his arm and leading him around the tables and to the lounges where everyone seemed to be congregating.

"Perseus looks like he needs a drink," a woman's voice said, and he almost sagged with relief. Ariadne was there, at least.

"I really do," he said as he joined them. Lounging on one of the chairs was a man made of silver smoke, sitting next to another that was made of bronze.

"So you are the thief that's causing Medusa's fangs to pop out," the Minotaur said, surprisingly friendly.

"He absolutely has *not* made my fangs pop out," Medusa snarled.

"Wait, you have fangs?" asked Perseus, and her aura flared. "Oops, sorry, I asked."

"It's okay, Asterion is just stirring trouble. We are all a bit tense," Ariadne said, pushing a beer into his hand before going to curl up under the arm of the Minotaur.

Asterion Dys really is a Minotaur.

"I don't mean to be causing anyone trouble, least of all Medusa," Perseus said and sat down in a spare chair. "You two must be Thanatos and Charon."

"Got it in one, thief," Charon replied, and the bronze one lifted a glass at him.

"I will need to update Hades on this new development, so try to be concise as you explain yourself, Perseus," Thanatos said.

"Hades! What on earth has Pithos done to you guys?" asked Perseus.

Who would be insane enough to want to make an enemy of any of these beings?

"Nah, ah, you first, I still have half a mind to toss you into the Labyrinth and let Fate decide," Medusa interrupted.

"Come on, Medusa, let the guy speak. If it's not satisfactory, I'll cut his hamstrings, okay?" Ariadne said like it was a perfectly reasonable next step.

"That's really not necessary. I came to you guys, remember? I have nothing to hide. I didn't mention who my shitty grandfather is because it wasn't relevant. I haven't had anything to do with him since I was a teenager, even then I only met the asshole once, and he fucking threw acid at me," Perseus said, trying to keep his voice steady.

Fuck, he'd *never* told anyone except Dany what had really happened, and only when she was fourteen and old enough to handle the truth. He had a long drink of his beer before continuing.

"You want the whole fucking sad tale of it? Here it is. My mother was Danae Argos. When she was nineteen years old, she was heir to the ARGOS Industries and as stunningly smart as she was beautiful. The way she told it, she never had time to date. She was too busy and wanted to prove to her father that having a female heir wasn't a mistake. That all changed when one night she met a man, and the liaison resulted in two things. She got pregnant with me and she lost her fucking mind," Perseus explained.

"I remember Danae, and I always wondered what happened to her," said Medusa, sharing a look with Asterion. Perseus wanted to know how old she was, but was wise enough to keep that question to himself.

"What happened to her was that Acrisius found out that she was pregnant by a random man. She could never remember what his name was, and Acrisius tossed her out on the street.

"She never told me who my father was. She was such an addict by the time I could ask questions and all she used to say was that he was a god. Used to talk about him in breathy wonder even after he totally left her to raise his kid on her own."

"My mother was smart, but she'd been raised an heiress, so she had no idea how to live in a place like Hellas. I honestly think she got drugged one night at a club by some guy who raped her, and she was too off her face to know what was happening. Whatever it was, it broke her mind completely."

"She used to sit on the kitchen floor and cry because she used to be so smart, and now it was like she couldn't remember how to do basic math," Perseus said and drained his beer.

His earliest memories were of her crying. Always crying for what she'd lost, for a god of a man who never came back for her. It was too fucking sad.

"How did you get burned if Acrisius wanted nothing to do with you?" asked Medusa.

"When I was sixteen, my mother got knocked up again. I don't know by who, because by that stage, I was already thieving wallets and whatever else I could to get by. I was barely at home, so it could have been any piece of shit that was hanging around."

"Anyway, she decided she was going to get us both cleaned up and go to see her father. It had been years, after all, surely Acrisius would have calmed down by then. She was desperate, and that's the truth of it," said Perseus, accepting a fresh beer that Thanatos put in his hand.

"Thanks. We went to ARGOS Industries, and the old receptionist remembered my mother and had a soft spot for her, so she took us to the research floor where good old grandad was working on a project."

"To begin with, he was too shocked to speak, but the lab cleared out of people, almost like they knew he was about to blow his shit. My mother tried to talk to him, shoved me forward, and presented me as his grandson."

"Acrisius saw the visit for what it was, the last chance to get her old life back, or at least, get some fuck off money. He was so angry I thought he was going to have a heart attack. You must understand, my mother was beautiful and a little bit ditzy, but still sweet after what happened to her. I never saw anyone yell at her the way Acrisius did."

"She admitted that she was pregnant again, and then he *really* lost it and decided to throw what he had in his hand at her. It happened to be a sealed glass canister of some kind of acid. Me being the man that always protected her did just that. I knocked her out of the way, and it smashed against my face. I can't remember what happened next, only the pain, and coming to about six weeks later in a hospital in Hellas with this."

Perseus rubbed his aching scars and sipped his beer. There was no way to describe the pain that he had felt; there were no words for it.

"After that, my mother really lost it. I tried my best to work with what sight I had left. I can see heat and auras, and if I'm patient and have a really strong magnifying glass, I can pick out letters on paper even if it gives me a migraine."

"Dany, my sister, was born, and less than a year later, my mother stepped off the port jetty and drowned."

"A man came round a few times looking for us. Lawyer type. I knew it was my grandfather trying to figure out what happened to us. I wasn't going to let him get to my little sister, so I moved us out of there and changed my last name to Serpho. Disappeared into Hellas's underground, where we couldn't be found. I got good at thieving; I did what I had to in order take care of Dany."

"When I told her all of this, she asked me to go legit, and that's what I was trying to do when fucking Pithos turned up and stole her."

Ariadne was the first one to break the tense silence. "What a fucking asshole. Man, I thought I had a shit father. Do you think Acrisius is working for Pithos?"

"He must be if Dany is being held at a factory full of their gear, and she specifically mentioned Acrisius," said Medusa. She didn't sound pissed off anymore, which Perseus figured was a start.

"It also makes sense why they were treating her so well in the beginning, letting her play games and shit. I don't know how Acrisius found us after so long, but I told you, Dany is a prodigy. The day she was snatched, she got accepted into university, and she's not even eighteen," said Perseus.

"You think Acrisius might have staged this whole thing to get her back?" asked Charon.

"A super-smart granddaughter, and me and Serpentine taken out in the process? You can see why he would be a good candidate for a shady cult that wants to kill all of us," replied Medusa.

"Why do they want to kill you?" asked Perseus.

"Because they think we are monsters that ruined the human's lives by coming out of the shadows," said Asterion.

"I remember growing up after the crash. It's not like you would've had much to ruin. Hades saved this city, everyone knows that," Perseus replied.

"Doesn't mean they have to like it. Stupid entitled rich assholes like fucking Theseus with ignorant chips on their shoulders who think they deserve something just by being born," Ariadne grumbled.

Perseus raised his beer to her. "I hear you. I grew up with nothing. I can handle starting with nothing again, as long as Dany is back and safe. It's all I give a shit about."

"Okay, so what's our plan to get her back?" asked Charon.

"Wait, you guys believe me?" said Perseus.

"Your scars don't lie and you haven't either. I would know," replied Asterion, tapping his nose. "We'll help you get your sister back from Pithos and Acrisius."

"Thank you. If Acrisius really is involved with all of this, I swear to all the saints, I'll destroy him and burn ARGOS to the fucking ground," said Perseus.

Ariadne's laugh was delighted. "I like the way you think, thief."

10

Medusa's phone buzzed in her pocket and 'The Dark Dread Lord' flashed up on her screen.

"It's Hades. Looks like you dodged a bullet, Thanatos," Medusa said. She gave Perseus a brief glance before getting to her feet and answering her call. "Hey, boss, what's up?"

"Medusa, what the fuck is going on over there?" asked Hades.

Medusa refilled her drink and found herself a booth on the other side of the club where she wouldn't be overheard.

"The plot thickens, but we might be able to work it into our favor," she said.

"Explain," Hades demanded, his voice deadly soft. Medusa quickly told him about Perseus's fucked up family history.

"You're right. This might be our chance to take out Pithos and ARGOS at the same time. What did Asterion say?" asked Hades.

"That the thief is telling the truth about everything, including that piece of shit Acrisius blinding him," said Medusa.

She was feeling shitty about acting so bitchily towards Perseus, but she had her reasons.

She tried to imagine Perseus as a gangly sixteen-year-old, who would've done anything to protect his mother, and her anger surged again.

"Did Perseus say which god supposedly fathered him?" Hades asked cautiously.

To their knowledge, Hades and Demeter were the only old gods left, but they weren't willing to stake money on it.

"Perseus didn't know. Whoever it was left his mother mad as well as pregnant. She could have just said that because she never wanted anyone to know who the father was," Medusa replied.

"I suppose I'll know the truth of it when I see him. If he's a demigod, there will be no way he can hide it from me. What do you think about it?" said Hades. Medusa had a visceral memory of his muscled, tattooed body grinding up against her.

"He's built like one, but that could be a decent gym membership."

"Susa, I think that's the first time I've ever heard you comment favorably about a human man. Thanatos did say that you were sweet on the thief, but I didn't want to believe it."

"Just because I can acknowledge he's hot doesn't mean I'm sweet on him," Medusa said quickly. Hades's laugh was dark and husky.

"Now, I *am* curious to see him. It's not a crime to like someone, Medusa. Look at Asterion and Ariadne; that *was* a crime and they seem happy," he said.

"They aren't what I'd consider a normal couple, let alone the nature of their courtship. I'm not having this ridiculous conversation with you. We are going to rescue his sister, not have a date."

"Of course, whatever you say. Keep a close watch on him until I get back. I'm curious about which god could have sired him. He can resist your gaze, which is another point in favor of divinity. Also, if another god is roaming about, I want to make sure I find them before they can plot against me," said Hades.

"Paranoid much? There isn't a god that could match you, boss."

"It doesn't mean the dumb fucker won't give it a try. Make sure the Court doesn't do anything stupid in my absence and keep your deadly eyes on that thief of yours at all times," commanded Hades.

"I promise. Go finish up with Demeter. We need you home," Medusa said and hung up.

Keep your deadly eyes on that thief of yours.

It wasn't her eyes that were the problem, it was her treacherous lips that got her into trouble.

She would've shed a skin laughing if someone had told her that she would one day be hot for an Argos, but there she was.

Find the girl, worry about the make-out session after, Medusa.

"How is Lord Dark and Handsome?" asked Ariadne, joining her in the booth.

"Good as he can be. I've been instructed to keep the thief close, find his sister, and make sure the rest of you don't do something dumb and get yourselves killed," said Medusa before draining her wine.

"Better do as Daddy says," Ariadne replied, making Medusa laugh.

"Don't let Asterion hear you refer to Hades as Daddy, or he might take it the wrong way."

"Really? Do you think punishment might be involved?" Ariadne asked, hopefully.

"You're incorrigible."

"That's why you love me."

Medusa tapped the table with her long nails. "What are your thoughts on all of this?"

"I'm glad Perseus told us the truth, so I didn't have to cut up the cute bastard. You?"

"Same," Medusa admitted.

"Then why do you look so disappointed?"

"It's complicated. I kissed him right before I found out about the Argos thing and then reacted poorly after."

Ariadne's stormy eyes widened with shock and joy. "Susa, I'm so proud."

"Shut up. It was only a momentary lapse in judgment at best," Medusa said, wondering why she had bothered to tell her.

"I don't blame you. I would let my judgment lapse all over Perseus," Ariadne replied with a throaty chuckle. "Oh, don't look at me like that. Just because I found the love of my life doesn't mean my ovaries stopped working. He's an adorable, ripped, thieving, artist from my neighborhood. Luckily, I found Asterion first, or I would be giving you some serious competition right about now."

"You'd win because you are normal and I'm not. We kissed, but now thanks to Asterion, he's going to be asking about my fangs," Medusa groaned, wanting to kick the Minotaur right in his stupid bull head.

Ariadne propped her head on her hand. "*Do* you have fangs? Why haven't I seen them?"

"Do you have a weird nipple? I don't know because that shit is *private*, Ariadne," huffed Medusa. The assassin just stared at her. "Yes, I have fangs that will pop out if I am angry enough or...horny enough. Gods, why am I telling you this?"

"Because we are Best Bitches. Wow, fangs when you are horny...was Asterion, right? Has Perseus *popped* your fangs?" Ariadne asked with a waggle of her eyebrows.

"*No*. Gods, it was one kiss in the heat of the moment because he did a nice painting of me."

"He painted you?" Ariadne gasped and battered her lashes. "Did he paint you like one of his French girls?"

"Jesus Christ, I wish I'd never watched *Titanic* with you."

"That isn't a no, Susa."

Medusa thought back of the painting of the glowing goddess that had been painted on the canvas. "It was how he sees me. He will probably see Asterion and the triplet's true forms too. Something to do with their energy or their auras."

"It must have been a nice picture if it made you want to stick your tongue in his mouth. What else happened?"

"Get that smirk off your face. It was just kissing on his workbench."

"Hot. Remind me to tell you what Asterion did to me on his dining room table," Ariadne said.

"I eat at that table!"

"So what? I wiped it down after."

"You are disgusting, the pair of you," Medusa said, trying and failing not to laugh.

Despite Ariadne's upbringing as an assassin, she had maintained her sense of humor and could make Medusa laugh her ass off even when she wanted to be mad at her.

She was about to tell her off again when Perseus broke off his conversation and started to walk towards them. His dark wavy locks were tousled about his face and neck, the streak of white flicking down over his cheekbone.

A part of Medusa preened because she knew he looked so disheveled because it was her hands that had ruffled him so much. Ariadne sniggered beside her.

"Oh, yeah, it was totally heat of the moment," she whispered.

"Hey," Perseus said when he reached them, nervously putting his hands in his pockets. "So, what did Hades have to say?"

"That despite the fact you have Argos blood, we are still going to help you get Dany back," said Medusa, trying her best to keep up her calm facade.

"Thank you. Erebus said I can crash at his place, so I'll grab my bags—"

"That's not necessary. Hades gave strict instructions that I'm to watch you at all times, so you are going to have to come back to Serpentine with me until this is all over. Probably for the best, Serpentine is far more secure, and I have access to the tech we need to track where the IP address was coming from on Dany's console," Medusa said.

"Oh, well, only if it's okay with you," Perseus replied.

"Hades is the *boss*, so you do what he says and go the fuck back to Medusa's like you're told," Ariadne snapped.

"Come on, girl, you don't need to use that Hellas attitude on me. We are meant to be friends, remember?" Perseus said with a teasing smile that made Ariadne crack up laughing.

"Whatever. I *am* your friend, which means I want you to be kept alive, and nowhere is safer for you than wrapped in Medusa's hot coils, understand?" said Ariadne.

I'm actually going to murder her, Medusa thought.

"I don't know about that. She hasn't shown me any of said coils, but I doubt they are very safe for me right now," replied Perseus, with a smile in Medusa's direction that made her feel hot and flustered.

"Go and say goodbye to the sausage party in the corner. I need to get cracking on the console as soon as I can so we can get this over and done with. Then you and Dany can go back to your life of anonymity," said Medusa.

Perseus scratched at the back of his head. "Yeah, okay, whatever you say."

She watched him walk away and was admiring the view when Ariadne kicked her under the table.

"You really suck at flirting, do you know that? You don't have to roast the guy just to show you're interested," she said irritably.

"Not all of us were taught the fine arts of seduction when we were growing up. Besides, we are wasting time," Medusa replied and got up to follow him.

It took until they had stepped into Medusa's private elevator for Perseus to ask the question Medusa had been dreading.

"Is it true that you have fangs, or was Asterion just fucking with me?" he said. He was standing behind her, and Medusa could feel the warmth of him down her back.

"Does it matter?" she asked.

"Not unless they are in your vagina and even then, probably not. Wait, they aren't, are they?" Perseus said.

Medusa bit the inside of her cheek to stop herself from smiling.

"My fangs and my vagina are *none* of your business."

"Fair enough. I'm only curious because my tongue was in your mouth not that long ago, and I didn't feel them."

"They pop out, so no, you wouldn't have."

"Are they venomous?"

"Do you want to keep asking me dumb questions and risk finding out?" Medusa replied.

Perseus's warm breath tickled her ear as he leaned over and whispered, "All depends on whether you're aroused instead of angry."

Medusa gripped the console in her hands so tight one of her nails snapped.

"And who is it that I'm going to kill for telling you that?" she asked through her teeth.

"Erebus told me. I wonder what other interesting secrets you are hiding."

"None that concern you, thief."

The elevator door chimed, and Medusa hurried to get out of the tight space and through the penthouse door.

"You're a hard ass woman sometimes," Perseus said, slinging his bag over his shoulder.

"No, I'm not. You want to know why? I'm. Not. A. Fucking. Woman. And the sooner you get that into your man brain, the better," Medusa snapped. She pulled off her boots and dumped them onto her shoe rack.

"I'm sorry, you are a hard ass female gorgon, Medusa," corrected Perseus coming in behind her. "Saints, I don't know why you are so defensive because I'm curious about you. You're a beautiful, magical creature."

"Because the last time a human man decided to get curious about me, my fucking sisters died!" Medusa shouted at him.

Perseus dropped his bags. "Shit, I'm so sorry."

"*Don't* say it. Just...stay out of my way and let me work so *your* sister doesn't end up the same way," Medusa said before she went into her office and shut the door behind her.

11

Perseus didn't know why he pushed Medusa. He wanted to know more about her, and she was determined to keep him at arm's length.

What had happened to her sisters? Perseus had seen Medusa's aura go warm again as he'd told them his sad tale, so why did she keep shoving him away?

It was stupid for you to think a guy from Hellas would even have a shot with the likes of her.

Medusa had made it clear she didn't need his help or want his company.

Perseus dug in his bag for a sketch pad and chalk pastels, before heading out into the rooftop garden. He needed to sketch out all the irritable energy and anxiety over Dany.

Would they have really hurt her if Acrisius wanted her on his side?

He had thrown acid at his own daughter, so Perseus wouldn't have put it past him.

Perseus found a stone bench in some shade, and as soon as his fingers touched the pastels, something inside of him calmed down.

He flipped open his sketch pad and let his hands take over as his mind went over the past few days.

He missed Dany like crazy. They had never been apart for so long, and he never realized how quiet his world was without her.

How are you going to feel when she goes to university in Athens? The chalk broke in his hand.

The gallery was fucked, and even with the insurance money, he'd need it to be fixed up and turning profits as soon as possible. It wouldn't be quick enough. He would have to take some thieving jobs to help tide them over.

Dany would be pissed that he was breaking his promise to be legit, but he didn't have a choice.

He had to survive, and he would do anything to make sure she did too. Around and around, his current problems went until he heard voices.

"It still gives me the creeps. You know these statues were once people—" a man said. He stopped when he saw Perseus. "Sorry, we didn't know anyone was using the gardens."

"I can move if you guys need to work," Perseus said.

"No, no, not at all, sir. If you're here, it means Lady Medusa is at home, and we don't want to disturb her or her...friend. We'll do the other gardens first," he replied, and the two men hurried back the way they came.

It hadn't even occurred to Perseus that the statues that he had touched and admired the night he came to rob Medusa had once been people.

You saw her turn the Pithos men to stone with her gaze, and it's only now you realize that this garden is a shrine to her fallen enemies?

Suddenly, the gardens didn't seem so lovely and friendly. He knew Medusa wasn't anywhere remotely human, maybe he'd been stupid to kiss her.

Despite how dangerous she was, Medusa didn't seem interested in attacking anyone that hadn't tried to attack her first.

Perseus wondered if the last man that had been curious about her was in that garden with him. Medusa had made it sound like the same man had killed her sisters, so Perseus didn't feel an ounce of sadness over his fate.

Perseus was still sketching when he sensed Medusa walking through the trees. He didn't look up, unsure if she was still pissed off at the sight of him or if she had calmed down.

Medusa straddled the other end of the stone bench, mirroring his posture.

"That's pretty," she said.

"Thanks, it helps me process when I'm overwhelmed," Perseus replied.

"I'm sorry about...about before."

"Don't be. I had no right to push you. Truth is, flirting with you keeps my mind off everything else."

"Is that so?"

"Yeah, well, you are very beautiful when you're not terrifying, but kind of then as well," Perseus said, reaching for another chalk pastel.

"I don't know how to do this," Medusa admitted softly. "My relationships, if you could call them that, have never ended well. So much so that Hades found me in a cave where I'd shut myself away from the world. The Court members are the only friends I've ever had, other than my sisters. The glasses I wear help protect people from my gaze, but I protect myself from everyone most of all. You are suddenly an extra person in my life and I find it overwhelming at times."

"Why are you telling me this?" asked Perseus. His pulse leaped to his throat when her golden hand came and rested over his, stilling his sketching.

"Because despite how insane this situation is, and that it's going against all of my instincts, I actually like your company," Medusa said.

Perseus finally looked up at her. "Me? The dirty thief from Hellas?"

"Yes, the thief from Hellas, though how dirty you are is yet to be determined," replied Medusa, her golden lips curving into a smile that made Perseus's heart pound.

"I like your company too, even though you are determined to fight me about it every step of the way," he said, brushing his hair back from his face.

"I'm not afraid of you, so you need to stop acting like I don't know what you are. It doesn't matter that you have snakes in your hair and fangs and whatever else. You're still Medusa, a total golden goddess who kisses like it's her last night on Earth."

"You're smart and fierce and could crush my dumb mortal ass every time I overstep, but you don't. I broke into your place, stole something important to you, and yet you've put all of that aside to help me get Dany back. You're a special kind of female, Medusa."

"I know I am, feckless mortal. You're just going to have to be patient with this golden goddess, and in turn, I'll try to spare you from my divine wrath when you piss me off," Medusa replied loftily, making Perseus burst out laughing.

"That's fair. I don't suppose one of these statues was the asshole who murdered your sisters?"

Medusa raised an eyebrow. "Why do you ask?"

"I like to think you got your revenge in. If he is and you'd ever like me to smash it to bits with a sledgehammer, let me know. I could use the workout," he said sincerely.

"That's sweet of you. I'll keep it in mind," Medusa replied softly.

"You know if there's anything I can ever do to thank you for helping me, please let me know," Perseus added.

"Dangerous ground, thief. Would you really want to be at the Court's beck and call?"

"I don't know about the Court, but at yours doesn't seem so bad."

Medusa smiled. "You could start by returning my necklace."

"Babe, I did that the night I surrendered to you. It's not my fault you haven't been in your safe," Perseus said.

"What? You were in my room when I was in the shower?" she demanded.

"Only in your wardrobe, I swear. It's not like I could casually peep at you," Perseus said, tapping his scars.

"Not the point! I suppose I should thank you for returning the necklace, though you could've mentioned that earlier."

"And ruin the surprise? Never. Don't suppose we could kiss with this makeup?" he couldn't resist asking. Medusa leaned across his sketch pad.

"Pray harder, mortal," she whispered in his ear. He was about to break into a litany when her phone chimed.

"What-" he began, but she pressed a finger to his lips.

"Hold that thought, handsome, we just got a lead."

Medusa sat down in front of her office laptop while Perseus stayed leaning against the doorway, respecting her sanctum sanctorum.

Hours beforehand, she had locked the office and had regretted her outburst almost immediately.

Medusa hadn't allowed a male to get close to her since her sister's death and was having difficulties lowering her defenses, and not automatically snapping every time Perseus asked her a question even remotely personal.

Once she had sent Dany's console to Lola and had cleared the last two days' worth of emails in her CEO Inbox, she'd realized how overly defensive she had been towards Perseus.

Asterion would've told her if he had even the slightest doubt that Perseus wasn't telling the complete truth to them, and she *did* actually like him.

It was a bitter pill to swallow when she realized she was afraid that Perseus wasn't working an angle and that his interest in her went beyond revenge on Pithos.

No matter how many years you're out of the cave, the beast still lingers under the surface.

And she had reacted like an animal, attacking the first outstretched hands in centuries.

Perseus accepted your apology, so move forward, Medusa, she reminded herself as she opened her email from Lola.

"What is it?" Perseus asked.

"Lola has found an ARGOS warehouse down at the ports that might be a contender for where Dany is being held. She's also pulled the CCTV footage from the night Dany was taken," Medusa replied.

"Won't Pithos just tell me where their location is to bring them your head?" he said.

"We can't rely on that. They might give you a different location for the exchange and not bring Dany to it at all. If they call and it's a different place, we will send teams to both," Medusa replied as she played the CCTV on double speed. "Seriously, though, they aren't going to pick a crowded place to have a head delivered to them."

"Which reminds me, what are we going to give them instead of your head? It's not like getting a necklace replica," said Perseus.

"Don't worry. I've got my girls making something fun for Pithos," she replied, with a touch of murder in her voice. "Wait, I think I have something; come and look – shit."

"Yeah, I'm not going to be any help looking at the footage, goddess," Perseus said.

"Okay, so I'll explain it to you. A white van with no logos, but I can do a trace on the plate number. Four guys...it looks like someone else is with them. A young woman, she's tall...maybe a bit taller than your shoulder? Dark hair tied in a braid and...and she's just stuck the finger up at one of the men."

"That's my sister," Perseus said with a proud grin.

"They are getting out a skateboard too, so it must be her," said Medusa. "We know she was there on the day she was taken, and when she logged into the console, so let's pray they haven't moved her since then."

"Do you think I should try calling them to see if they will want to set a place for the meetup?" asked Perseus.

"Not yet. I know you're desperate to keep things moving, but Pithos is expecting you to be sweating right now and thinking how you could take my head off. It hasn't been twenty-four hours yet, and the surprise head isn't ready either," Medusa said as gently as she could. If their positions were reversed, she knew she wouldn't be taking it all half as well, but she needed him calm and distracted while they got prepared.

"I feel like getting drunk or punching something," Perseus said, rubbing at his scar, a tick Medusa was only just realizing was his stress give away.

"Sorry, but you can't do either of those. We need you sober, and if you put a hole in one of my walls, I will put a hole in you," Medusa said, getting out of her chair. "Look, I can try to find out how long the surprise head is going to be, and then as soon as it is ready, you can call Pithos. Fair?"

"Fair. I don't suppose you have any aspirin?" asked Perseus.

"Sure, come with me. Do your scars always hurt or only sometimes?"

asked Medusa, as he followed her to the kitchen. If he could ask personal questions, why couldn't she?

"They don't usually hurt. Only when I'm angry or stressed out. My vision goes haywire and messes with me too," said Perseus as he sat down at the counter. Medusa poured him a cup of water and gave him the bottle of aspirin.

"Thanks," he murmured and downed a few, before going back to rubbing at his scar again.

"Here, let me," Medusa said, moving his hand away and turning him towards her. "Don't pull that face. I happen to know a thing or two about migraines because of fucked up vision."

"Sorry, it's just...I don't let anyone touch them," he admitted and then shut his eyes. Medusa put her thumbs to his temples and started moving them in slow circles.

"You know, I'm kind of surprised that you haven't tried to kill Acrisius for doing this to you," she said.

"I was just a broke-ass kid from Hellas. I couldn't have gotten close enough to do some damage even if I'd wanted to," Perseus replied, and his expression relaxed. "I hate him, sure, but as messed up as it is, I don't think I would've been as good of a thief without my vision like it is. God, what are you doing? That feels amazing."

Medusa pushed her fingers into his dark hair and massaged his scalp. He made a happy groan at the back of his throat that sounded so sexy, her skin broke out in goosebumps.

"I told you I knew what I was doing. Once all this drama with Pithos is over, I could have my guys try to make some glasses that might help with the migraines."

"Really? You think they could?"

"If I can figure out glasses that stop me turning everyone I look at into stone, your eyes should be a walk in the park," Medusa said and added, "I can't promise anything other than to give it a try." Perseus's pale blue eyes opened, but she didn't stop her massage.

"Thank you, Medusa," he said, his hands moving to rest on her hips. "Is this okay?"

Don't you dare blush, Medusa warned herself and did anyway.

"Yeah," she said, and he closed his eyes again, the faintest smiled on his lips.

Don't you do it! Don't you kiss the thief...oh Hell.

She leaned in and kissed the silver streak in his hair that marked the beginning of the scar.

"Is that okay?" she asked.

Perseus swallowed hard. "Yes."

Medusa could smell his pheromones mixed in with his sunshine and paint scent. She kissed the scar at his temple. "And this?"

His fingers tightened fractionally, but he didn't pull away. "Yes."

She kept moving slowly across his scar, kissing very gently as her fingers massaged. His breathing got heavier, but Perseus didn't tell her to stop.

His fingers moved under the hem of her shirt, and Medusa stilled as he traced a swirl of scales.

"Is this another of your surprises?" Perseus asked.

A part of Medusa wanted to pull away, but he trusted her to touch his scars, so she stayed still as fingers followed another swirl around to her stomach.

"Do the patterns mean anything?" he asked.

"No," she said. "I was born with them, not cursed." Her pulse sped up as he followed the pattern up her ribs and stopped when they hit the edge of her bra.

"I never thought scales would be so soft," Perseus said. "What color are they?"

"Gold," Medusa replied, her breath catching as his fingers continued their exploration. "They curve in the same patterns to my feet."

"Seriously? Is there any part of you that isn't amazing?" he asked.

"My temper?" Medusa suggested, making him smile.

"Even that's pretty amazing. Terrifying but amazing," Perseus replied. "Really makes us poor mortals not stand a chance, goddess."

"Oh, please. Like you don't know how attractive you are," Medusa said.

"Actually, I really don't know what I look like anymore. I'm only happy that Acrisius's aim wasn't worse, and I managed to keep my eyebrows."

"You think every woman you meet flirts with you because you have eyebrows?" Medusa laughed.

"I mean, I hope it's for my charming personality, but it doesn't hurt to have eyebrows." Still laughing, Medusa kissed the frown line between them.

"Silly man, it's because of your beautiful body. No one cares about your personality."

"It's nice to know there is something about me that doesn't piss you off," he said, laughing with her.

"Oh, no, it definitely pisses me off. I'd have a far easier time hating you if you were ugly."

"Shallow, shallow goddess," he tutted.

"Pretty good at distracting you and fixing your migraines, though, aren't I?"

Perseus nodded. "I'm definitely feeling better."

"Good. I'll put it on your ever-increasing number of debts you owe me," Medusa said.

"I'm broke, so I'm afraid they'll have to be paid in sexual favors. Good news is I'm happy to pay in advance," Perseus replied seriously.

Medusa took his stubbled chin between her thumb and forefinger. "You *wish*. I'm not letting you off that easily, thief."

"Have you met you? Nothing about you is easy, I can't imagine getting you off will be any different," Perseus argued. "Luckily, I thrive when faced with difficult challenges."

"Little thief, who always has a clever reply to everything," Medusa purred, the feral part of her rising to the surface and wanting him submitting to her.

Her snakes dropped from her hair and moved to brush against his cheeks.

"Look who's come out to say hello. Can I touch them?" Perseus asked.

"Only if you want to be bitten."

"Are they venomous?"

"No, but I am, and no one touches my snakes," she growled.

"Okay, I'll just sit here and let them touch me. How many are there?" he asked.

"Four."

"That's it? The way the rumors are, you'd think you have an entire head of them instead of hair."

"Anybody could turn their news feed on and see otherwise."

"Except for me, goddess," said Perseus.

"Shit, sorry."

"It's really okay. The snakes shine differently compared to the rest of you, more silver than gold."

"Hmm, we are going to have to talk to Hades about you seeing our true auras," Medusa said.

"Why? It's handy for me to know your emotions, so I know when you're pissed off enough to kill me."

"You don't know that. I could be plotting to kill you right now," Medusa said, wrapping a hand around his throat.

"You're not, though," he said.

Medusa applied the slightest pressure. "No? What makes you so sure?"

"You're shimmering because you're turned on, not angry."

Medusa quickly let him go. "What? How would you- because you saw me- *God's damn it*," Medusa hissed.

Would that night never stop coming to bite her in the ass? She was going to be put off masturbating forever.

"Oh, come on, it's the same as you being able to sniff out my emotions," said Perseus.

"Who told you that?"

"Charon. He said, 'If you lie to her, she'll smell it, so don't lie.'"

"I'm going to murder those boys. I left you alone for twenty minutes, and they spill all my fucking secrets," Medusa complained.

"It has its perks. It means we'll always know if the other one is full of shit." Perseus stroked the pattern of her scales on her back again. "Like when you try to lie about wanting to murder me when you really want to fuck me."

Medusa laughed darkly. "Sweet boy, how do you know I'm not aroused by the thought of murdering you?"

"I suppose I'll just have to live dangerously until you do."

Medusa twisted her fingers into the curls at the back of his neck. "Perseus?"

"Hmm?"

"Do you always take this long to kiss someone?"

"You just told me you want to murder me, and now you want me to kiss you?"

"I don't know what part you have trouble understanding," Medusa said. He hesitated for half a second before his lips were on hers.

Kissing Perseus was like kissing a live wire, her whole body ignited and set her senses burning.

He pulled her closer, his hands dropping from her hips to grab her ass and drag her up against him. Her little gasp of surprise was swallowed as his tongue moved against hers softly, and then again more forcefully.

Medusa gripped his shoulders, and before she could stop it, her nails shot out, and she dragged him on the floor and straddled him.

"Holy shit, you are strong," he said between kisses.

"Yes," she replied, pushing him down. She slid a sharp nail under the collar of his t-shirt, and the fabric tore open, exposing his tattooed chest and muscles.

She leaned back to admire it all, and as soon as her pelvis ground against his, her fangs popped.

"Fuck," Medusa cursed, slapping her hand over her mouth. Perseus sat up.

"Hey, don't do that. They are as gold as the rest of you," he said, wrapping his hand around her wrist. "Don't hide them, show me."

Medusa very slowly let him pull her hand away, so he could see her lengthened canines.

"Cool, just try not to draw too much blood when you bite me," Perseus said and kissed her slowly, his tongue brushing gently against her fangs. The sensation of it ran through her body like a tremor of electricity straight to her clit. Oh, gods, she was going to eat him alive.

Medusa shoved him back down so she could touch all the muscled delight underneath her. She leaned down to kiss his defined collarbone.

There were scars amongst the tattoos, and the feral part of her wanted to kill whoever had hurt him.

Perseus groaned as her fangs scraped across one of his nipples, her nails dragging down his sides. Medusa moved back up his chest and was leaning over to kiss him once more when the penthouse door opened.

"Medusa! Stop! Don't kill him!" Asterion shouted in warning, and she froze. The moment was interrupted by Ariadne's filthy laughter.

"Ah, I don't think she was about to kill him, big guy," the assassin said, patting Asterion's shoulder. Medusa climbed off Perseus quickly, face burning and making her fangs retract so fast it hurt.

"You guys are the biggest cock blockers ever," Perseus sighed, putting his hands behind his head.

"Sorry for the interruption, but we got your email about the warehouse and got some of the guys to do a drive-by. One of them saw your sister," Asterion said.

Perseus's expression changed instantly, and he was up off the floor in seconds.

"Is she okay?" he asked.

Ariadne shared a look with Medusa, and her stomach dropped. "What is it?"

"She was walking, but her face was pretty beat up," Ariadne said. "We can't wait much longer. We know she's there, so let's hit them tonight. Fuck playing by their rules anymore."

12

The port of Styx stank like fish, exhaust, and man sweat. Medusa hated going down there at the best of times, but in summer, it was the actual worst.

ARGOS had three shipping warehouses in Styx and more in Athens, and Medusa was wondering if she shouldn't have been so reluctant to wipe Serpentine's competition off the face of Greece forever.

Get Dany first, then think about how you're going to destroy them.

Medusa looked up from the laptop on her knees to Perseus sitting on the other side of the van next to Erebus.

If he weren't such an intrinsic part of their plan, Medusa would've locked him in the penthouse until it was all over. The last thing she needed was to worry about him getting shot. She shouldn't have been down there either.

Medusa *never* got her hands dirty, preferring to watch from cameras on the other side of the city.

No, Pithos had made it personal enough that she wanted blood on her claws and an outlet for all the rage she was feeling. It wasn't *all* she was feeling.

If Asterion and Ariadne hadn't interrupted them hours beforehand, Medusa couldn't imagine what would have happened.

You know exactly what would've done, Medusa.

The insecure part of her wondered if Perseus would be half as keen to get her naked once they got Dany back.

"Hey, Susa, you with us?" Thanatos asked, beside her.

"Yes, just thinking about if there is a better way to do this," she replied.

"I know the risks, Medusa, I've walked into bigger traps than this," Perseus said.

"And that's supposed to comfort me?"

"Oh, Susa, since when did you give a shit about a human? They won't kill him on sight, they need too much stuff out of him. Just relax," Erebus groaned as he slid a holster of guns over his shoulders.

"Sun's down. If we are going to do this, we do it now," Charon said from the driver seat. "Asterion and Ariadne are in position, and we can't wait around forever."

"Right, see you on the other side," Perseus replied and climbed out of the truck, white box in hand.

"Don't get your ass shot," Medusa snapped.

Perseus grinned. "Worry about your own ass, gorgeous. It's worth more than mine." He was gone within seconds, moving between the stacked shipping containers, heading for the ARGOS warehouse.

"He's right, you know, maybe you should sit this one out," said Erebus.

"Fuck off and get going before I decide to turn you into stone instead." Erebus laughed like a hyena, and he and Thanatos went to get into position.

"Don't let them get on your tits too much. I think it's nice that you care about the thief," said Charon.

Medusa laughed. "You big softie."

"He's genuinely into you, Medusa. That's rare for old monsters like us. Don't let the opportunity pass you by," replied Charon before lighting up a cigarette.

Medusa sighed and went back to her laptop. "I'll worry about it after we get his sister back and deal with Pithos. Damn, here we go…"

∽

Perseus held the white gift box extremely carefully. It was bad enough walking uninvited into an ARGOS warehouse, possibly full of Pithos agents, but he had no idea what the fake head in the box was going to do.

On top of that, he was still worried about Dany, and underneath that worry, was what to do about Medusa.

He had been harder than he'd ever been in his life with her straddled on top of him, and he was starting to think it had been part of her plan to keep him distracted as possible while Asterion and his men got the information they needed.

Now, he was about to walk into a trap unarmed and possibly get a bullet in the head, and he'd never know if Medusa had actually wanted him or not.

Perseus refocused on the task at hand. He hoped that the asshole that had hurt Dany was there tonight because he was dying to get some payback on whoever thought it was okay to beat on a girl.

He'd seen enough of that shit growing up with her mother's dead beat boyfriends. He wasn't about to tolerate anyone laying hands on his baby sister.

Two big guards were standing in front of the staff entrance door of the warehouse. Perseus breathed in and out slowly, getting into the calm headspace like when he was working on a particularly tricky heist.

"Evening, gentleman, please tell your boss that Perseus Serpho is here with a delivery for him," he said.

"Wait," one guard said, taking out his phone.

"He's expecting me," Perseus replied.

"What's in the box," the other guard asked him.

"That's between Mr. Black and me. Trust me, man, you don't want to know," said Perseus. The guard on the phone grunted something in reply before hanging up.

"Pat him down," he said.

"I'm a thief, guys, not an assassin, but go right ahead, and I'll pretend not to enjoy it too much," Perseus replied, placing the box on the ground and spreading his arms and legs. When the search was over, he followed them inside.

"Mr. Serpho, I must say I'm surprised to see you so quickly after our last conversation," a voice said from the mezzanine above them.

Creepy fucker. So they were working with his grandfather after all. Perseus kept his face neutral as he seethed with fury.

"You decided to start beating on my sister, so you didn't leave me a lot of choices, did you? Where is Dany, I want this shit over and done with," he said.

"Carlos? Go and fetch the girl," Mr. Black said as he joined Perseus on the factory floor. "How did you find us?"

"You're not the only one with friends. You think I could have gotten myself into Serpentine Tower without help? I'm good, but not *that* good," Perseus replied and tossed him the replica necklace. "You can take that as a bonus, seeing how it's useless now. You didn't tell me it protects the wearer against Medusa's gaze. Handy, seeing how I had to go back for her head."

"You did what?" Dany said, and Perseus almost fainted with relief when he saw her blue-green aura.

"Are you okay?" he asked.

"What do you fucking think?" Dany made to move towards him, but Carlos's hand came down on her shoulder.

"Not so fast," he grunted.

"He's right. I want proof that you got Medusa's head," said Mr. Black. Perseus shrugged and placed the box on the ground before taking a few steps back from it.

"It's all yours, man. I suppose you know I now have the Court of Styx coming for me because of this, so hand over my sister so we can at least get a head start," said Perseus.

"All in good time, Mr. Serpho," said Mr. Black as he bent down and opened the box. Perseus didn't know what the fake head looked like, but it was good enough for Dany to make a gagging sound.

"Oh, bro, please tell me you didn't..." she said.

"I had to do it if I was going to get you back. You guys have what you want, now let her go," Perseus replied, hating the horror in Dany's voice.

"Release her go, Carlos. Mr. Serpho is a man of honor, after all. I'm starting to think we should've tried recruiting you properly."

"No, thanks. Creepy cults aren't my thing," Perseus replied and gestured a hurry up signal at Dany. She had taken two steps towards him when a heat signature started to glow brightly from the box.

"Dany, tie your shoes!" Perseus said urgently. They both dropped to the ground as the head exploded, and chaos erupted around them.

∼

THE WAREHOUSE WAS full of smoke as Medusa and Charon cut through the Pithos guards inside.

Medusa was vaguely aware of Ariadne and Asterion causing trouble on the port side, and Thanatos and Erebus coming through the roof.

She cut down a man with a machine gun, slicing through his torso with her claws before she scrambled up on top of a pile of wooden shipping crates.

She was wearing goggles, unwilling to risk accidentally getting Dany or Perseus with her vision, but it didn't make her any less deadly.

The others would take care of any of the Pithos and ARGOS men loitering around, Medusa only wanted to get to Perseus.

This is why you don't get attached to humans, she thought as she dodged a bullet, and ripped off a man's hand. *They break far too easily.*

Through the haze of smoke, she could make out Perseus covering Dany's head. He was trying to get her to the doors around crates he couldn't see, hiding her from assailants. Medusa leaped from one stacked crate to the roof of a forklift, and down onto a man with a gun trained on Perseus.

"This way, thief," she shouted over the noise.

"Holy shit, is that Medusa?" Dany's voice said.

"The one and only," Medusa replied, passing Perseus a knife and a baton that she retrieved from a dead guard. "Watch my back?"

"Always, goddess," said Perseus, flicking out the baton. "Stay in between us, Dany."

"Sure thing. I just need to stop dying of shock," Dany said, taking the knife and surprising Medusa by testing its weight and repositioning her grip on it.

"What did you teach your sister, Perseus?"

"You mean, what did I teach *him*," said Dany.

"Bond after we get out of this," Perseus interrupted.

Medusa took the lead, using everything she could to hide Perseus and Dany behind as they made for the loading bay doors.

As they neared them, Medusa held up a hand to make them wait, then she lifted her goggles and turned both guards to stone before lowering them again.

She pushed up the lever, and the unlocking mechanisms whirred to life as the doors started to open.

There was a loud crash behind her, and she whipped around to discover Dany had pushed one of the stone guards over.

"Whoops," she said, and gave Medusa an unapologetic look. "He grabbed my ass. He was like a hundred years old."

Medusa was still laughing when Charon pulled up in a black van. Ariadne waved at them from the passenger seat. "Get your asses in here, we are blowing this joint."

Medusa made sure that Perseus and Dany were belted in before slamming the door shut, and Charon took off.

"Is everyone else out?" Medusa called to Ariadne.

"Yeah, Susa, you're up."

Medusa pulled a detonator from her pocket and offered it to Dany. "Would you like to do the honors? They held you captive after all."

"For real?" Dany smiled wickedly and took the detonator.

Charon lowered the heavily tinted windows. "There you go, little one, I wouldn't want you to miss the view."

Dany hung out the window and pressed the button. The warehouse went up with a loud boom, and fire exploded out the windows and doors.

"Coolest. Thing. Ever," Dany shouted in the wind and tossed the detonator out the window.

"Don't you be a bad influence on my baby sister," Perseus said half-seriously to Medusa.

She smiled and folded her long legs. "Don't worry, thief, I wouldn't know how to be a bad influence if I tried."

Dany climbed back inside the van laughing. Then she wrapped her arms around Perseus and burst into tears.

"Told you, pay up, assassin," said Charon, and Ariadne passed him drachmae.

"It's okay, I got you now," Perseus said to Dany, hugging her close. "I'm sorry about this whole mess, but it's over now."

"No, it's not," replied Dany, wiping the tears off her cheeks. "I heard them talking. Some lady and Grandfather are planning something to take down the Court of Styx."

"As if they could. It's like they don't know us at all," Medusa snorted. Her heart was constricting strangely as she watched them together.

How are you possibly going to protect them, Medusa?

"They *do* know you! There were talking about weapons, some shit Acrisius has been building to hunt you all! You have to believe me," Dany said urgently.

"I do, Dany, trust me. How did you find this out?" asked Medusa. She was doing her best to appear confident to keep the girl calm, but inside, she was seething with rage and worry. *What the fuck has Acrisius been building?*

"Adults can be surprisingly stupid sometimes. I asked to go to the bathroom when Acrisius went into the meeting with the woman in the mask. The bathroom shared a wall with the room they were in, so I tipped the soap out of its glass dish and used it to listen in. As I said, adults are stupid," explained Dany. Perseus kissed the top of her head.

"That's my sis. Did Acrisius tell you who he was?" he asked.

"Yeah, I tried to act surprised. He came in after they gave me this," she pointed to her black eye. "He was acting all shitty that they had done it, but whatever. He told me that you had been hiding me from him because you were as crazy as our mother."

"And what did you tell him?" Perseus asked, his voice tight with anger.

"I was honest and said you are *way* crazier than she was," Dany replied, and they both laughed identical laughs. "Where are we? Holy shit, are we in the Diogenes?"

"You are. This is the Temple, and your new home until we get this shit with Pithos sorted out," said Ariadne, hopping out and opening the sliding door for Dany and Perseus. He hesitated, looking at Medusa. "You're not coming?"

"Go be with your sister, Perseus. Ariadne will make sure you're taken care of, and Selene will be here soon to look at Dany's wounds," said Medusa. Perseus took her dirty hand and kissed it.

"Thank you, Medusa. If there's anything I can do to repay-"

"Yes, yes, I'll take it out of your hide. Don't get soppy on me, thief, I was only just starting to like you," Medusa said, shooing him out and shutting the door on his puppy dog expression.

Charon pulled out into traffic and Medusa collapsed back against her seat.

"Don't say it," she sighed.

"Wouldn't dream of it," Charon replied, and kept his eyes firmly on the road all the way to Serpentine.

13

Perseus had never been to The Temple, but he knew the rumors about it. Ariadne and her terrifying skill set suddenly made more sense.

"I knew someone had killed Minos and taken over, but I didn't connect it with you," he said to her as they walked through the marbled halls.

"I couldn't let it continue, and besides, the girls here needed a home and support, not to be taught to be killers. The boys are from Hellas and needed a new building, so they have the ground floor and the girls are on the first floor. Mind you, be careful not to piss any of them off, Dany, they play rough," Ariadne advised as she waved at a group of teenage girls, watching the newcomers.

"Don't worry, I'm a lover, not a fighter," Dany said, with a devious laugh. "Killer girls in skimpy training togas? Here for it."

"She's more likely going to flirt them to death," Perseus added. "Eyes forward."

"I've just been through a traumatic incident, bro, don't even try to take this from me."

"Damn, she does take after you," Ariadne said with a throaty laugh.

"Yeah, we have a certain rough charm. Doesn't work on everyone, though," Perseus replied, thinking of Medusa. He didn't know why he was feeling so bummed out that she hadn't stuck around.

She's a CEO, she has shit to do that doesn't involve cleaning up your mess.

"Don't look so forlorn, Serpho. Medusa will be around tomorrow morning at the latest to check-in, I've no doubt," said Ariadne, reading him far too easily.

"Yeah, that's something I really want to know. How the fuck did you end up making the moves on Medusa in a few days? I would've gotten kidnapped years ago if I thought that was a possibility," said Dany. "Damn, she's smoking hot in real life."

"Hey, watch your language. And if you must know, I was sent to steal from her and we met. She wanted to help out against Pithos because they have it in for the Court," Perseus replied. "She was the one that figured out that you were leaving messages on Shadow Lords."

"Because she's smart as shit, that's why. The idiot guards had no idea what I could do on an open internet connection," said Dany.

"Medusa couldn't believe you were NightWitch15."

"Damn! She knew who I was?"

"Yeah, she said you annihilate her every time your paths cross."

"Really? What's her handle?"

"No idea, you'll have to ask her."

"You really need to learn to ask the Serpent Queen better questions," said Dany, disapprovingly.

"He was too busy flirting with her," Ariadne replied.

"Couldn't help it," Perseus said with a shrug.

Ariadne opened a set of bedroom doors. "This is you, guys. Selene will be here any minute to check you out, Dany. The shower is through there and there are clean clothes in the drawers."

"Thank the saints. I'll see you on the other side," Dany said and hurried into the bathroom.

Perseus collapsed into an armchair. "I don't know how I'm ever going to repay you for all of your help," he said to Ariadne.

"We are from Hellas, so we only know trades and favors, but the Court really isn't like that when they choose to help out. It's not from the goodness in their monster hearts. You are an asset, and they don't like that Pithos fucked with you and Dany to get at us. They feel like they owe you, not the other way around," Ariadne replied.

She went to a small fridge and got out two beers and passed him one.

"Besides, Susa is hot for you and you could be a demigod. It might be that you fit in with us better than anyone you've ever met."

"I wouldn't put money on that demigod thing. There's no way to tell for sure."

"Hades will know, and it's too late, I already put money on it," said Ariadne. "Medusa thinks you got god blood too."

"If I do, if I don't, it hardly matters. I'm still a street kid deep down. Hanging out with a posher circle won't change that," Perseus replied.

Ariadne laughed and raised her bottle at him. "That I know for sure. I grew up in this place, and the Hellas never washed out, no matter what they did to me. The Court isn't going to care, and neither is Medusa. She's complicated, but she's got it in for you. Don't fuck around with her heart if you don't feel the same."

"I like that you think I've got a shot at getting close enough to her heart to fuck with it."

"I know what I walked in on this afternoon, so don't even try that shit with me, Serpho. You're both crushing so hard on each other it's gross. I only want to make sure that now you got Dany, you won't give up on Medusa."

Perseus couldn't stop the exhausted, frustrated laugh that burst out of him.

"Come on, girl. Stop busting my nuts. It's not me you need to have this conversation with, it's Medusa. She was the one that didn't stick around."

"You didn't ask her to stay either," Ariadne said stubbornly.

"She doesn't owe me shit. I can't ask her for anything, let alone if she's actually into me or not," said Perseus.

"Grow a pair of ovaries, Perseus, and just talk to her." Ariadne finished her beer just as there was a knock at the door. "Come on in, Selene!"

Selene was a nurse with a vivid purple and green aura and must have been beautiful because Dany beamed at her as soon as they met.

"I'm going to go for a shower and give you ladies some space. Don't suppose you got a drawer of clothes for me? All my stuff is at Medusa's," Perseus asked Ariadne.

"You have a single change of clothes. Looks like you're going to have to take a trip to Serpentine tonight after all," she said slyly.

Perseus didn't need to ask if she'd planned that, her smirk said it all. He just didn't know why she was so determined to set him and Medusa up.

They barely knew each other, and they had met under stressful circumstances. Yeah, they were attracted to each other, but how could he not be attracted to Medusa?

Stop thinking about it. You got Dany back. Don't expect more than one miracle at a time.

Perseus grabbed his clothes and went to scrub the crazy week away.

BY THE TIME Perseus got out of the shower, Dany was alone and lying on her bed, flicking through TV channels.

"What did the nurse say?" he asked, flopping down beside her.

"That I'll live. She put some cream on my eye and that was it. They didn't really beat on me as much as they could have. I guess Grandad had some influence on them and I didn't have what they wanted," Dany said, way too cool about everything as usual. "Speaking of which, want to tell me properly what happened this time round?"

Perseus gave in to the inevitable and told her everything that happened minus a few sordid and sexy details.

"Wow, that's a lot. I can't believe Medusa didn't kill your punk ass," Dany said once he was done.

"Me either. She's really amazing and savage and funny," Perseus replied, staring up at the ceiling.

"You hot for her?" asked Dany.

"I'm only human."

"True. Kiss her yet?"

"Yeah. She kissed me first."

Dany lifted her fist for him to bump. "Nice. If she kissed you, it means she likes you, so why are you all hesitant and shit?"

"Out of my league, kiddo."

"Don't be dumb. If Medusa kissed you, she thinks you're in her league. Otherwise, she wouldn't bother. Seriously, do I have to explain women to you?"

Perseus laughed. God, he'd missed her. "Maybe you do. What would you recommend?"

"You got her number?"

"Yeah."

"Message her. Ask her if it'd be okay to come around and get your stuff. Then when you get there, you talk to her and see how she feels. If it's the same, kiss her again," Dany said like it was the simplest thing in the world.

"What if she doesn't and I make a total dick of myself?" he asked.

"Sometimes, you got to be bold and run the risk. Man, if I had a shot at Medusa, I wouldn't be whining about it. I'd be making sure I kept her attention. If she doesn't feel the same, then bow out gracefully, but make sure you stay her friend because I have like a billion questions I want to ask her and I'm not going to waste my opportunity like you're wasting yours," Dany said, passing him his phone and headphones. "Do it or I will."

"Damn, you're a pain in the ass when you're right. I wouldn't mind it so much if it weren't all the fucking time," he said.

"Watch your language," she mocked.

"Very funny, smart ass," Perseus replied. "Find her number for me?"

"What's it under?"

"Serpent Queen. She put it in there like that, not me."

"It's because she's a Boss. Okay, got it. You're good to go."

Feeling like a stupid teenager, he put one headphone in, and using the audio prompts, he sent her a text.

Hey are you still awake?

"See? Didn't kill you, did it?" said Dany.

"Shut up," he laughed as his phone vibrated, and the audio came through his headphones.

Of course, I'm still awake. I've finally got my lounge room back and can play video games again.

"What did she say?" Dany asked.

"She's playing video games."

"Damn, she's my kind of woman. I need my console and her handle, so I know not to decimate her every time our paths cross."

What's wrong, thief?

Nothing. I forgot all my stuff is at your penthouse, and I don't want to cause a riot by walking about The Temple with no pants on. Was going to see if it's okay to come around and get it? It can wait until tomorrow if you don't want the company.

Perseus rolled over and put a pillow over his head. *What are you doing, idiot? She doesn't have time for you.*

He was too wired after the fight to sleep, but messaging Medusa was making his restlessness worse.

"Scare her off, did you?" asked Dany, ten minutes later.

"Probably better I hang out with you tonight anyway. I've only just got you back, and I don't think my heart rate has been this steady since you were taken."

"I'm okay, Perseus. Relax. I'm in a house owned by the Court, surrounded by hot assassins. Pithos aren't dumb enough to attack us here. They probably are only just finding out we blew up the warehouse."

"Acrisius is going to be pissed."

"No doubt. Felt good to blow it up, though," said Dany. They were still laughing when his phone buzzed. "That will be Medusa."

"How do you know?"

"The raids last twenty-minutes and she was too busy to text," Dany replied matter-of-factly.

"It's weird you know that."

"I think it's weird you *don't.*"

Perseus opened the text and listened: *I'd hate to be responsible for you causing a riot. Come round the back service door and plug 777 into the keypad, and it'll let you in. Unless you want to break in again for old time's sake.*

"What did she say?" Dany said, elbowing him.

"She said I can come around and get my stuff. I'm only going to do it because I need my gear. Are you sure you're going to be okay if I go out for a bit?" Perseus asked.

"I'm not a kid, so stop looking at me like I'm going to disappear again.

I'm going to be fine. Spend the night if you get a chance, I don't care. I don't need you hovering around me, and I plan on sleeping late tomorrow. You've never been a clinger before, so don't start now," Dany said irritably.

"I can't help it. I love you, and I was scared out of my brain that I'd lost you."

"You didn't, and you aren't going to. Just like I'm not going to let you pout and sigh here because you didn't talk to Medusa before she left," Dany replied, giving him a sloppy side hug. "If you don't go and make out with her to thank her, *I* will."

"Okay but remember you said that, so if in years to come, you bitch about how I left you the first night you got kidnapped-"

"I won't. God, I just want to go to sleep without someone watching me. Don't make noise when you come back in and bring me back my damn console, would you?"

"Will do, little sis," Perseus said, pulling on his boots.

"I won't wait up," she teased. "Go do the Serpho name proud!"

"You're such a fucking brat," he said, leaning down to kiss her on top of the head.

"Perseus?"

"Yeah?"

"I love you," Dany said and snuggled into her pillows.

"I love you too," he replied, his heart squeezing painfully.

"Also, turn the light off on your way out."

"Will do."

He was shutting her door when she called, "Don't fuck it up."

"I'll try not to," he said with a laugh.

Ariadne was sitting on the Temple steps with Asterion, chatting softly. Asterion's half man half bull shaped aura studied him curiously.

"Running off so soon?" he asked.

"Just going to get my stuff from Medusa's and I'll be back," Perseus said quickly.

"*Sure,* you will. Take your time, Serpho, we are staying the night to keep an eye on things," replied Ariadne. "I won't let anything happen to your sister."

"Thanks, both of you," Perseus said awkwardly.

"Heard you the first fifty times you said it," Asterion replied. "Careful of Medusa's fangs."

Perseus hurried down the steps. "Where would the fun in that be?"

14

Medusa hadn't felt lonely in a long time. However, standing inside her penthouse with a fading post-battle high, her world suddenly seemed too...quiet.

In less than a week, Perseus had turned her life into chaos.

She was ridiculously behind in her schedule, with an increasing CEO to-do list, and instead of getting back to work like she should have, Medusa had a shower and flopped down on her couch with her controller and her new trial expansion of Shadow Lords.

You really should get Dany to play it and find the bugs.

Medusa pushed the thought away. She didn't want to press them into being in her life, and Shadow Lords felt like a bribe to ensure they could still hang out.

Medusa rolled her face into the couch cushion and groaned. It was another bad idea because her couch now smelled like Perseus.

Maybe you should have hung about and made sure they settled in okay, another treacherous thought crept in.

Medusa rolled to face the TV and scowled at it. No, this was her life, not hanging around with thieves that made her hot and reckless and set her body on fire whenever they touched.

Such a relationship could never end well. They got Dany back and would go their separate ways as planned.

Her phone buzzed, and she expected it to be Hades checking in, but it flashed up with 'Dirty Thief.'

Her heart did a weird dance when she looked at it. He wanted to come over to get his stuff? That's all?

She started a raid, determined to kill things, and try to clear her mind. Waiting a bit wouldn't hurt him.

After Medusa had satisfactorily wiped out all her enemies, she took a deep breath and messaged him back, doing her best not to sound too keen.

"You do like him, even if it's a bad idea," she said aloud, and it made something inside her ache and go soft. She rubbed at her chest.

Gods, she almost forgot what this emotion felt like. She went back to playing her game, so she didn't text him again.

Medusa was in the middle of her third raid when a figure appeared in her lounge room archway. She ignored him, pretending she didn't notice him until she finished the raid.

"I see you opted for the break-in option instead of using the doorbell," Medusa said, finally pausing the game.

"It's more fun to keep you on your toes. You really do need a better security system, goddess," Perseus replied.

"How's Dany?" she asked, putting her remote down.

"Really good. Not fazed by her ordeal at all. She's stoked to be in a house full of killer girls to flirt with," Perseus said with a laugh.

"I'm glad to hear it. I've packed up her console for you," Medusa replied, pointing to his bag in the corner of the room, the console sitting on top of it.

"Thanks. Dany wants to know your handle too, so she doesn't kick your ass so hard whenever you meet in the game."

Medusa laughed. "I wouldn't want her to go easy on me." She picked up her empty beer and got up. "You want one?"

"Please. I've been wound so tight for days, I don't know how to chill out now that I have Dany back. Something tells me Acrisius isn't going to drop this either, so it's like the calm before the storm. That make sense?" he said, following her. "Hey, you're wearing my favorite pajamas again."

"How do you even know that?" Medusa asked, getting out fresh drinks.

"Your clothes are backlit by your glow. I can make out the house insignia, and I recognize it because I loved Harry Potter as a kid before I got a face full of acid," he explained.

His head tilted to one side as he studied her. "I know I shouldn't say it, but your jammie collection is fucking adorable."

"Stop acting like they don't turn you on," Medusa said with a grin as she sat down on her couch again.

"Oh, they definitely turn me on," Perseus admitted, sitting at the other end of the couch. "I know I've said it more than once, but seriously, thank you for your help. I couldn't have gotten Dany back without you."

"You wouldn't have even been dragged into this shit if it wasn't for the Court and me, so stop thanking me, because you're making me feel guilty," Medusa said. "And you're right about Acrisius. We need to find out a way to deal with him, but not tonight. You've been through enough, and your prick grandfather can wait a night. Why are you smiling?"

Perseus's sexy grin widened. "You said we, which means you aren't kicking me out of your life just yet."

"You thought I would?"

"Why wouldn't you? You're the Serpent Queen. You don't mingle with peasants like me."

"Well, I'm always willing to make exceptions. Dany is really cool, and I want her to test out my expansions, so I'll definitely mingle with her," Medusa said, as straight-faced as she could. "You're okay, I guess."

"Cold, goddess, cold," Perseus said. He reached for his bag of gear and made sure the console was strapped to the top. "In that case, I should get out of your hair and let you get some sleep."

"You're right. This has been the longest couple of days," Medusa said awkwardly and got to her feet to walk him out.

She didn't want him to go, but didn't know how to ask him to stay either. He stood up but didn't make a move to leave.

Neither of them was moving, and when she couldn't take the suspense any longer, she let out a frustrated sigh.

"What do you want, Perseus?" she asked, finally looking up at him.

She felt so small when she stood close to him, but she loved how tall he was.

"Nothing," he replied and rubbed the back of his neck shyly. "Everything. You. Definitely, you."

Medusa's heart stopped beating. "What did you say?"

"I *want* you. I want you like I've wanted nothing else in my whole damn life. Not a perfect heist, or a painting career or fucking anything," he stumbled on.

"We barely know each other," Medusa replied, not knowing how to process what she was hearing.

"So? What does that have to do with anything? I know enough to know I want you. As far as I'm concerned, the only thing that matters is if you want me back and if you don't? Fuck, I'll learn how to deal with just being your friend."

"Perseus?"

"Yes?"

"Are you always going to take this long to kiss me? Because we will really have to work on that," Medusa said with a smile.

His hands came up to the small of her back and pulled her closer.

"Does that mean you want me too?" he asked against her lips.

"I thought it was obvious," Medusa said, raising up on tiptoes. "You're a train wreck that's going to complicate my life with far too much drama, but yes, I still want you too."

Perseus's thumb's brushed against her cheekbones. "Really?"

"Do you need it in fucking writing?" Medusa snapped, and then he was kissing her.

If she thought kissing him was electric before, nothing compared to the bolt of energy that surged through her. He had to have god blood because the way he was making her feel was unnatural.

She had his shirt off in seconds, needing to feel more of his skin. Perseus sank to his knees in front of her, his hands skimming the edge of her shirt.

"I need to see these scales, I can't stop thinking about them," he said and waited until she nodded her head before he lifted her shirt off. "Damn, they are glowing."

Perseus ran his fingers over their patterns and his lips quickly followed.

Medusa pushed her fingers through his thick hair, a small moan escaping her lips as one of his hands reached up to cup her breast.

His other hand ran up her spine and undid the clasp of her bra.

"Smooth move, thief," she laughed huskily.

"I told you, I've got skills you don't even know about," Perseus replied. He swore softly as she tossed her bra to the couch. "You're killing me, goddess."

"Really? Because I haven't even made it to fucking you yet," Medusa complained playfully, kissing him again. His warm hands found her breasts and he groaned against her mouth.

"Gods, you're so beautiful I can barely handle looking at you," Perseus whispered before kissing her between her breasts.

Medusa's fangs popped as he kissed across one breast, teeth biting gently against her nipple.

Her body was burning, and she didn't know how much more of his teasing she could stand. She wanted him on top of her, inside of her, every part of him underneath her hands.

Perseus's hands covered her breasts, squeezing and teasing as he took the end of her pants drawstrings between his teeth and pulled the bow loose.

Her loose pants slid down her legs, and he made a sound so sexy, her knees shook.

"No underwear to bed? You really are my dream girl," he said, looking up at her with a smile.

"They are uncomfortable," she replied, trying her best not to be nervous.

"You weren't lying about the scales going down to your feet," Perseus said, running his hands slowly up her bare legs, to her thighs and hips.

"What do they look like to you?" Medusa asked, trembling as his fingers traced over the swirls of scales.

"Like you're covered in glowing golden war paint."

"And it doesn't...turn you off?"

Perseus's laugh was helpless. "Fuck no, goddess," he replied, his hand moving up the inside of her thigh. "It's like the gods made you for war and sin."

Medusa gasped as his fingers stroked her, and he swore as they found her clit. She'd never let a man touch her so intimately, and she didn't know how she was going to survive it.

"Fuck, you are so wet," Perseus groaned, and then his mouth joined his fingers, and Medusa had to grip his shoulders to keep herself standing up straight.

"I-I don't think I can stay upright if you keep doing that," she managed to say, her voice trembling.

Perseus looked up, his smile full of wickedness and mischief before he was pulling her to the carpet, her knees on either side of his head.

"I agree, this's a much better position," he said, and Medusa blushed so fiercely she thought she'd spontaneously combust.

She didn't have a chance to reply before his mouth was back on her, hands gripping her hips to steady her. Her breath was ragged, her body aching with the orgasm building inside her.

Medusa reached behind her to run her claws down his sides. She sliced through the hem of his jeans, and his grip on her ass tightened as she stroked his hard dick.

Her body shuddered as he slipped a finger inside of her, stroking in and out as he sucked on her clit. Medusa cried out as she came, her pulse in her throat as the orgasm exploded through her.

Perseus was looking up at her with wide eyes and a smug smile. "Again?"

Medusa growled and moved backward over his chest and tore the rest of his jeans off.

"You keep trashing my clothes, and I'm going to have none left, goddess," Perseus warned.

"Good, that means you'll be naked at all time. I'm sorry, is there a downside to this that I'm not seeing?" Medusa said as she leaned over to kiss his chest. Her fingers traced the tattoos over his muscles. "I love these," she whispered and dragged her fangs and lips over them.

One of her snakes dropped from her hair and sank its tiny fangs into him.

"Holy shit, what was that?" Perseus gasped, looking down at her.

"Sorry, it got a little excited," she laughed. "Don't worry, they aren't venomous, only I am and only if I choose to be."

"Really? So you can bite me, and I won't die if you don't let your venom out?" he asked.

"Why? Does my thief *want* to be bitten?" she purred.

"I'm up for anything in the heat of the moment. I just want to make sure you're not going to kill me before I can make you come again."

"So confident," Medusa said, her hand moving to stroke his dick. Perseus swore as she went back to kissing and exploring his skin.

Another of her snakes bit him, and his back arched, and he grew even harder in her hand.

She chuckled huskily against his skin, and then he moved suddenly, pinning her down underneath him, his dick pushing slowly inside of her.

Medusa gripped his strong forearms, groaning in the place between pleasure and pain.

"Fuck me, you are so tight," he said as he kissed her. "Let me know if I'm hurting you."

"You're not, trust me," Medusa replied, pushing her hips up, so he went further inside of her. "I'm not a fragile human girl, so don't fuck me like I'm one."

Perseus didn't need to be told twice. He thrust into her and she cried out as he filled her entirely.

Medusa couldn't speak as he moved inside of her, her claws raking down his back. He hissed and dragged her legs up over his shoulders, adjusting their position so he could go even deeper.

Medusa thought her heart was going to stop as she came again, but he didn't let up, fucking her all the way through it, so it deepened, and she came apart underneath him.

She kissed him hard, teeth and tongue, her mouth swallowing his groan as he came inside of her. They ended up lying limply on the carpet, Medusa draped over his sweaty chest.

"Are you okay?" he asked, touching her cheek gently.

"I'm better than okay, and you are well on your way to paying off that debt of yours."

"Knew your guilt wouldn't last and the debt would come back to get me," Perseus replied, and he laughed with her.

∼

Perseus knew Medusa would be stunning naked, but as he looked down at her glowing curves, he seriously considered starting a cult devoted to worshipping her.

"Shower?" he asked, stroking her hair gently.

"I don't think my legs are going to be able to work properly just yet," she said against his chest.

"I got you covered, goddess. Hang on," Perseus replied.

"What-" Medusa said and yelped as he lifted her. Her arms went around his neck and her legs locked around his hips, before he carried her carefully to the bathroom.

"I've decided I want to be carried everywhere like this from now on," she said as they stepped into the shower.

"From the goddess's lips to my ears," Perseus replied, turning on the warm water.

"I'm kidding, you can put me down if you want to," Medusa said, reaching up to kiss him.

Perseus pressed her back up against the cool glass to balance her.

The warm water was streaking light over her glorious breasts and he grew hard again. She really was the sexiest creature he'd ever seen, and he didn't think he'd ever tire of looking at her.

"And what if I don't want to? What if I want to keep you wrapped around me just like this?" Perseus said and kissed her.

"You are going to be so bad for my productivity," she complained, pulling him closer to kiss the side of his neck, the sharp points of her fangs gently running against his skin.

"You're the CEO, you'll learn to delegate," Perseus said and lowered her down, so his dick was touching her slick entrance.

She growled in the back of her throat and moved him further inside her.

Perseus turned to press her up against the tiled wall, momentarily afraid that they'd break the glass one, and guided her hips down again.

"You feel so amazing," he gasped, barely holding himself together as her sharp nails dug into his shoulders. Medusa groaned and he slammed into her.

He would never get enough of this feeling.

Fucking Medusa was every crazy, adrenaline-fueled moment he'd ever had rolled into one. It was better than stealing, better than jumping off buildings, better than a fight.

Her golden body flickered with pulsating light, a sure sign she was about to come again. He grabbed her hand and pinned it to the tiles above her head, holding her tightly as he thrust harder into her until she exploded with light.

Medusa's fangs sank into his neck and he came so hard he almost dropped her. Light was flashing so quickly across his vision, he had to shut his eyes to keep upright.

"Fuck me," he groaned and lowered her back to her feet.

"I thought I just did," Medusa said, her hands stroking his back and up to his neck. "Did I hurt you?"

"No, I almost blacked out, it was so good," he replied, his heart still trying to leap out of his chest. "Draw any blood?"

"Not much," Medusa said unapologetically. Her fingers gently touched the bite mark, and he felt it throb all the way to his dick.

"Gods, stop that or I'll have to fuck you again."

Medusa's throaty laugh was pure evil. "How delightful."

"So you *are* still planning to murder me because this is going to do it," he said playfully.

"Hmmm, maybe?" Medusa turned off the shower. The patterns of her scales were glowing over her perfect ass as she wrapped a towel around herself.

He did his best not to stare at her as he grabbed another towel. She headed for her bedroom and he hesitated, wondering if he should follow or if she was dismissing him for the evening.

Medusa looked over her shoulder at him. "Are you coming? Or are you going to stand there all night?"

Then she dropped her towel. Perseus went after her, deciding there were definitely worse ways to die.

15

Perseus woke to a phone ringing on the bedside table. He was momentarily disorientated, wondering where he was, and then his hand found a warm, naked hip, and he remembered.

Elysium, that's where you are.

Medusa rolled over and reached for the phone.

"What?" she answered it sleepily.

"Wake up, you dirty minx, I'm bringing the kid around to Serpentine in an hour, so make sure you and that fine piece of ass beside you is awake and dressed," Ariadne's voice echoed over the line.

"Okay, okay," Medusa said and hung up again. Perseus rolled to his side and pulled her up against him.

"One of these days I'm going to kill that meddlesome assassin," Medusa said. Her hand reached back to run down his side. Perseus stroked her bare breasts, down her stomach to the warm piece of heaven between her legs.

"Dangerous ground, thief, we only have an hour before everyone turns up," Medusa groaned and moved her ass up against him.

Gods, he was so hard already. Everything about her seemed designed to turn him on. He'd always liked women, but something about her short-circuited his brain.

"Plenty of time," Perseus said, kissing the tip of her ear. He rolled on top of her, kissing her bare shoulders and slope of her back, his hand gently lifting her hips and running over the curves of her ass.

He positioned himself in between her legs, his hand going under her to stroke and tease her. She was already wet, but Perseus was gentle as he slid a finger into her, coaxing a gasp out of her.

Medusa swore softly, her hips rising, her gorgeous ass moving back against him. What little self-control Perseus had left vanished and he guided his dick into her.

Medusa gasped and pushed back against him, setting a rhythm he wasn't ready for. He leaned forward to run his hand under her, squeezing her soft breasts as he rode her.

Perseus almost came at the sight of her glowing hand reaching down between them, her fingers touching where they joined before going back to her clit.

"You really are divine, goddess," he said, kissing her shoulder, his hand curling around her neck before going back to her hips.

Medusa groaned, her head tilting back as a glow started to emanate through her. He squeezed her hips hard, slowing their pace, going even deeper into her until she was crying out his name and he was coming with her.

They lay staring up at the ceiling afterward, trying to catch their breath. Medusa looked sideways at him.

"You know I would've also accepted a coffee," she said breathlessly. Perseus leaned over to brush her hair back from her face and kiss her.

"Good morning, Medusa," he said.

"Good morning, Perseus."

"Coffee was it?"

"Yes, please," she said, running her fingers through his hair. "I'll get into the shower while you're at it. I need to be able to focus while I'm in there, and besides, I know where showers with you lead."

Perseus's brow furrowed. "Nirvana?"

Medusa put her hand over his face and gently shoved him away. "Just go and make my coffee, thief."

∼

ARIADNE, Charon, and Dany arrived an hour later to the very minute. Perseus had managed to make coffee and shower, and he and Medusa were fighting over toast when the door to the penthouse opened.

"Here we go," Medusa whispered, and Perseus tried not to look at her in case he got distracted again.

"I hope you made enough toast for me," Ariadne said by way of good morning and stole half of Perseus's last piece.

"Help yourself," he said and sighed.

"She's not hungry, I literally just watched her eat a breakfast bigger than mine," Dany said, before taking his coffee.

"Seriously, are you two in this together?" Perseus replied, but Dany wasn't listening. She was already lost looking at something on one of Medusa's worktables.

"What's this?" she asked.

"Hey, don't go through stuff that doesn't belong to you," Perseus chastised.

"It's fine, Dany, don't listen to him," Medusa said and joined Dany at the table. "I've been thinking about launching a new design for the next-gen Serpentine console."

Dany's whole aura flashed excitedly, and they began talking in a whole different language.

"Here, you might need this," Charon said, passing him a fresh cup of coffee.

Ariadne laughed softly. "Look at those two nerds." Perseus smiled, something about seeing Dany and Medusa getting along made his heart do stupid things.

"You're so fucked, man," Charon said affectionately.

"Literally, if that glow is anything to go off," Ariadne added, nudging Perseus's leg with the toe of her boot. "Surprised you survived the night."

"You and me both," Perseus replied, and she laughed filthily.

"Nice. If you break her heart, and I'll introduce to you a world of pain that you won't ever recover from," Ariadne said.

"That's if you get to him before Hades. Susa has always been his favorite," Charon added. "No one would ever find your body."

"What about her breaking my heart first?" asked Perseus.

"Not something you need to worry about. Us old creatures don't often love, so it's hard to get our attention, but once you got it, you're completely fucked because you're not going to lose it in a hurry. Isn't that right, Ariadne?" said Charon.

"Yeah, but the good news is they make up for their bossy territorial bullshit by being absolute monsters in the sack," Ariadne answered. "Isn't that right, Perseus?"

"A gentleman never tells."

"A gentleman doesn't have to when he blushes as easily as you do."

Perseus's grin widened. "I can't help it, I'm pretty smitten." They were still giving him a hard time about it when Medusa came back over to them.

"I'm taking Dany downstairs to the Research and Development floor...coming?" she asked.

"I wouldn't miss Dany's cries of joy for all the world," Perseus replied.

"We have to get back to the Labyrinth but text us if you need us," Ariadne said and gave Dany a hug. "See you tonight, kiddo, and I'll show you that move I was telling you about."

"Cool! Ariadne is going to teach me how to paralyze people with one punch," Dany said to Perseus excitedly.

"Hellas girls," Charon chuckled before winking at Perseus. "Later, smitten kitten."

~

MEDUSA THOUGHT it would be awkward hanging out with Perseus and Dany, the latter knowing full well what she had gotten up to the previous night with her brother.

Dany was remarkably cool about the whole thing, giving Perseus a sly fist bump when she thought Medusa wasn't looking.

What really surprised her was how beautiful and clever Dany was, not just quick-witted, but that she could keep up with Medusa as she talked design and programming issues.

She *had* to get Dany to the design floors, if for no other reason than to use her as a fresh set of eyes on the issues they had been having with the new expansion pack glitches.

Dany's eyes lit up with sheer joy as they stepped out of the elevator and into the design areas. Screens hung everywhere with people on computers writing code and others in pods on consoles.

Medusa let the programmers have their own way, and one wall was covered in blackboard paint so they could all write their ideas on it or whatever they liked, as well as more beer fridges and bean bags than she could poke a stick at.

"Needs a half-pipe," Dany said critically.

"My kind of girl," Lola called out from two pods over. "I've been trying to convince them to put a roller derby rink in for months." She was a black girl with perfect victory rolled, blue hair, and a killer rockabilly style.

At eighteen years old, she was their youngest, but the best hacker and Medusa had recruited her straight out of high school. "Who's the new girl?" she asked.

"This is Dany. She's going to have a look about and try and help you fix those glitches," Medusa said.

Lola looked Dany over in an interested, yet curious manner. Dany was tall with Perseus's dark curly hair and intense eyes, and from the look Lola was giving her, she liked what she saw.

"Well, get your skinny ass over here, new girl, and I'll show you around."

"I'll go anywhere you want to take me," Dany replied and followed Lola.

"Easy tiger," Perseus whispered, half laughing as Dany ignored him completely.

"She takes after you," Medusa giggled softly. Perseus got a soft look on his face as he watched Dany with Lola and the other designers.

"Only a little. Dany pulls way more chicks than I do, and she is a hell of a lot smarter," he said, and then his smile fell.

"What's wrong?" asked Medusa.

"The day she was taken, she got a letter from the University of Athens telling her she got early acceptance and a full scholarship. I haven't told her yet. I wanted to wait until this whole shit fight with Pithos was over first," he said with a heavy sigh. "The exhibit they crashed? Most of that was to go towards setting her up over there. I'm going to miss her so much, but I have to give Dany her best chance."

"And those fuckers wrecked your gallery...Perseus, I'm so sorry," said Medusa, guilt sitting heavily on her shoulders. It was just another way Pithos had ruined his life.

"I'll deal with it when the time comes. Besides, I got to meet you, so it's not all bad," Perseus said with a smile that made Medusa's ovaries vibrate.

She wanted to kiss him right there in the middle of her employee's cubicles.

"What naughty thoughts are you having to make your aura flash like that?" Perseus whispered to her.

"I'll have to tell you later when there are fewer people around," she said.

Perseus twisted a finger in one of her red curls. "Scared I'll ruin your reputation if they see you kissing a dirty Hellas thief?"

"Scared I won't stop at *just* kissing you," Medusa corrected, and impossibly his smile brightened even more.

Oh, gods, she was a fool for him already, her body wanting him pressed up against her even though it was still sensitive from their night of lovemaking. She was addicted to him in the *worst* possible way. Hades was going to have a field day with her.

Her phone buzzed in her back pocket, and she stepped away from Perseus so she could focus enough to answer it.

"Hello?" she said.

"Medusa, there's a fire in Hellas. I've got Alexa reporting on it, but it's another bombing like down at the port. Happy for us to go live?" Leo, one of her lead cameramen, asked.

"Sure, can I ask where it is?"

"Not near any housing, just an old warehouse on the western side," he said and hung up. Dread coiled in Medusa's stomach.

"Lola, can you get me the news feed up?" she called across the floor.

"Big screen?"

"Yes, please." Medusa went over to the viewing area where they had a small theatre sized screen for viewing completed gaming footage.

"What's wrong?" Perseus said.

"There's been another bombing," Medusa replied slowly. "In Hellas." The news feed flickered to life, and Alexa's pretty face appeared on the screen. Behind her, Perseus's warehouse was a smoking fireball.

"Tell me what's happening," he said urgently.

Dany came to stand beside him. "They found our place. It's burning," she said and took his hand.

"So they knew where we lived after all," he said, his voice hitching.

"Grandfather did. He said that he found out last month. I didn't think he'd bother with the warehouse," Dany replied.

"I'm sorry, kiddo," Perseus said, putting his arms around his sister.

"This isn't your fault, Perseus."

"No, it's mine," Medusa said quietly. "This is because of Pithos and what we did to them down at the harbor. This is on *me*."

"No, it isn't," Perseus and Dany both said at the same time.

"I pushed the button on the detonator," Dany added. "Not that I think they'd care about an ARGOS warehouse. They care about Acrisius's contacts and his money. He is the one that would've ordered our place burned down because he thinks it will make us come back to him begging."

"That's never going to happen, not while I have breath in my body," Perseus vowed.

"No, it's not," Dany said coldly, her eyes staring at the images on the screen. Medusa recognized that look of anger and revenge.

"What do you have in mind, Dany?" she asked, half dreading the sheer fury of a teenage woman.

"We are going to bring down Grandad and take every penny he fucking owns," said Dany, "and then we'll use all of his banking information to turn off Pithos's funding, destroying them one bit at a time until we get to the woman in the mask."

"I like how you think," Medusa said, her smile growing wider.

"I don't. This sounds way too fucking dangerous-" Perseus argued.

"He's not going to stop, Perseus! Now he knows about us, he's never going to stop hunting us even if it's to kill us before we can ruin his good name. We are going to get the bastard before he gets us," Dany snarled. She grabbed Perseus by the shoulders. "I can *do* this, Perseus. I know how, and Medusa has the stuff I need to do it. Let me look after you for once, okay?"

Perseus pulled her close. "Okay, baby girl. We'll do it your way if Medusa will help."

"In any way I can," she promised, unexpected tears burning at the back of her eyes.

"I'm in too," said Lola, as she joined them. "I've wanted to put the boot into ARGOS for ages, and this seems like fun."

Perseus took Medusa's hand, and warmth bloomed in her chest as he pulled her into the hug with Dany. "All right, crazy ladies. You go for it and tell me how I can help."

Medusa's phone buzzed again and she smiled when she saw the text from Ariadne.

Heading back over. Daddy's home.

16

Perseus was slowly starting to get used to the chaotic energy of the Court of Styx. Medusa got a text from Ariadne and her excitement seemed to rocket up. They all seemed to genuinely like each other, even though they pissed each other off.

"Lola? I need you to look into ARGOS, use the dark server, find me all of Acrisius's dirt," Medusa instructed.

"Do we have a time frame?" the woman asked. She was flashing reds and oranges, her energy ramping in anticipation.

"As soon as possible. Hades is coming around for an update, and as soon as I have information for him to work with, the better."

"Hades is coming over?" Dany asked curiously. "Can I meet him?"

"Of course, you can. Hades is coming to get the measure of your brother," Medusa said, her golden mouth laughing at him.

"Should I be worried?" Perseus replied. He had the feeling that he was about to get the 'you're not good enough to be dating my Media Queen' lecture.

"If Ariadne could charm him, which she often does and with enthusiasm, I'm sure you should have no trouble winning him over. He wants to see if you really have god blood," said Medusa, as they got into the elevator.

"Wait, *what* god blood? Are you talking about Mom's crazy rants? You can't be serious," Dany exclaimed.

"Hades is the smartest, most cautious, being I've ever known. He's not going to run the risk of having your daddy turn up trying to use you against him if he is a god."

"But if Perseus had god blood he'd have like superpowers or something. He's good at painting and thieving, but they are skills, not innate abilities," Dany argued.

They got out on the penthouse floor and headed into Medusa's kitchen and dining room.

"You never know with these things," Medusa explained. "He could have superpowers but have never accessed them before. Either way, Hades will know pretty quickly if Perseus is a demigod."

"I feel like it doesn't really matter. Whoever my father was, he never stuck around, so he's a piece of shit just like Acrisius as far as I'm concerned," said Perseus. "Hades is coming to make sure I'm not going to thieve from *him* or break your heart."

"Ew, if you two are going to keep looking at each other like that, I'm going to go play Shadow Lords," Dany interrupted and made a spewing noise.

"Go for it, I'm about to kiss your brother with lots of tongue, and I don't want you to vomit on my kitchen floors before the big boss gets here," said Medusa.

Dany laughed. "I still don't know what you see in him, but I'm here for the perks. Especially Level 7 and the chance to look at Lola."

She disappeared into the lounge room, and as Perseus turned back to Medusa, she took his face in her hands and kissed him. It was hot and desperate and made Perseus's senses spring alight with desire and need.

This fucking female.

"I've wanted to do that all morning," Medusa said.

"Took your time."

"Trying to be on my best behavior in front of Dany."

"If anyone would give you her instant blessing, it would be Dany. She's holding back, but she fangirls over you hard. Though Lola is well on her way to becoming a new obsession."

Medusa's hand brushed up under his t-shirt to run over his abs. "Hmmm, maybe I can convince Lola to give Dany that tour later."

"I don't think it would take much convincing, but you really need to cut that out if you don't want to go for a quickie before your boss arrives," Perseus warned her. Medusa wrinkled her nose adorably and removed her hand.

"A quickie isn't going to be worth my time," she said, and he was just pulling her close to give her naughty mouth another kiss when the penthouse door opened, and Erebus and Thanatos's laughter drifted down the hall.

Perseus straightened his shirt and managed to get one glimpse of a tall man made of silver and black light when he was suddenly standing in front of Perseus. Hades's huge hand grabbed him around his throat and pinned him to the wall.

"Zeus's spawn," snarled Hades.

Medusa was a streak of golden flame and fury as she got between them. She shoved Hades so hard he lost his grip on Perseus and crashed into the opposite wall.

Medusa was a vision of vengeance as she stood in front of Perseus, her snakes out and hissing, her whole body glowing so brightly that he could barely look at her.

"You don't lay hands on what is mine, Hades," she hissed, her voice taking on a supernatural and fucking terrifying timbre that Perseus had never heard her use before.

"Woah, woah, that's enough," Asterion said and put a hand on Medusa's shoulder. "Come on, you two. You are friends, remember?"

"Friends don't fuck with each other's friends," Medusa growled.

Hades was staring at Perseus, and he could feel the weight of the Lord of the Underworld's gaze. "*This* is your fucking thief?"

"Yes, it is, and if you lay hands on him again..."

"Hey! No more threats! Cut it out, the pair of you," Asterion shouted. "Uncle, apologize to Perseus. He's done nothing to cross you."

Perseus half expected Hades to throw down against Asterion, but he only straightened the cuffs of his jacket.

"I'm sorry. I have a...certain reaction when I encounter people who look too much like my brother," Hades said stiffly before offering Medusa a slight bow. "Stand down, gorgon, he's yours, not mine."

"Soooo, Zeus is your daddy? That's...interesting," said Ariadne, her nonchalant tone breaking the tension in the room.

"If you say so," Perseus replied, too stunned to move away from the wall.

"Well, I think we all need to sit down at the table and have a big drink," said Charon, grabbing Perseus and pulling him towards the kitchen. "Come on, big boy, I need you to give me a hand."

"Sure thing," Perseus replied. "Medusa?"

"I'm fine, go with the triplets," she said, carefully moving to ensure she was still in-between Perseus and Hades. "I'm going to talk to Hades for a moment, and then I'll be right in."

Perseus hurried after Erebus, grateful to get away from Hades and the rising tension between the immortals.

What the fuck was going on?

⁓

MEDUSA WAS BOILING with anger and fear as she held Hades's silver-eyed glare. She'd never hit him before, and she was waiting for him to turn around and annihilate her for the offense.

"Stand down, Susa," he said finally. "Really, I'm sorry."

"I am too, but gods damn it, Hades, what is your problem?" she replied, folding her arms.

"That boy is Zeus's, and he looks so much like him under those scars I reacted without thinking," Hades said, leaning his back against the wall.

"I had no idea, boss. Otherwise, I would've warned you. Perseus isn't like your brother, that much I know for sure. He's a good guy who got fucked over by his family and by Pithos," Medusa replied and went to stand beside him.

She quickly told him about what had happened to Perseus's mother and how Acrisius had burned Perseus. By the end of it, Hades was vibrating with repressed rage.

"Fucking Zeus. Danae must have been something rare to get his attention, but to leave her in such a manner? He did that on purpose so she would pine for him forever. He was such a sick fuck," Hades spat.

"At least you don't have to worry about him coming back to fuck with you or using Perseus to do it," said Medusa.

"And why is that?" Dany asked from the archway of the lounge room. Medusa stilled; she'd forgotten that Dany was in there.

"Because I killed Zeus," Hades said, looking her over. Dany's eyes narrowed under the scrutiny.

"Did he deserve it?"

"He drove your mother insane for kicks, what do you think?" Hades retorted.

"Are you sure he's dead? Because I need to know if some god is going to try to mess with my fucking brother," said Dany, arms folded and chin out in an attitude that very much included Hades in that question.

Medusa fell in love with her right there.

"Zeus is dead. I cut his head off myself twenty years ago, and it's the reason I can walk on this earthly plane as I do. He's no threat to your brother, and neither am I, little one," Hades replied.

"Are you sure? Because you just tried to kill him for looking like Zeus."

"Asterion is Zeus's progeny as well and he's my right hand, so yes, I'm sure I can handle your brother looking like him."

Dany looked over the Lord of the Underworld, and Medusa could feel her weighing him up with her blue eyes. "Are you going to help us take down ARGOS or not?"

Hades's mouth lifted in a smirk. "I like this one."

"She's definitely something," agreed Medusa.

"Is that a yes? Because we have shit to do and that fucker Acrisius burned my damn house down. I want to get back at him *now*," argued Dany.

"Patience, little one. You'll get yours; I promise you. We do it right, so there's no way it can fail," said Hades, turning towards the kitchen. "Are you coming? We are going to need you to plan this great coup after all." Medusa smiled at Dany. It was as close to an approving head pat anyone ever really got from Hades.

"Yeah, okay, I'm coming," Dany replied and followed him.

Alone in the hallway, Medusa took three deep breaths and swallowed down the unexpected emotions bombarding her.

She had just attacked her best friend over a man she had barely known for a week. She had gone full territorial animal on him, wanting to protect Perseus and attacking without a second thought. It could only mean one thing.

Finally, you're in love, her sister Sthenno's voice echoed in her mind. Medusa felt the world drop out from under her feet.

"Susa? Are you okay?" Asterion asked, his strong hand moving under her elbow to steady her.

"I think I have a bit of delayed shock from attacking Hades," she said, and let him hug her.

"It's okay. We all have wanted to hit Hades at one time or another," Asterion replied, his laugh a rumble in his deep chest. "Or are you worried because it was defending Perseus?"

"Shut up. Don't analyze me," Medusa said, but without any real venom.

"Come on, Susa, don't shut it down. You care for the kid and it's a good thing. He's a demigod, like us. He's going to need your help dealing with that. He's kind of like...my brother? Gods, this is weird. Fucking Zeus," Asterion replied.

"Asterion? You and Ariadne-"

"Craziest, hardest, best thing I've ever done," he said without hesitation.

"Yes, but she didn't have a child to look after," Medusa replied.

Asterion laughed. "Are you fucking kidding me? Ariadne sees every kid at the Temple as hers to look after. Dany isn't exactly a kid either. She's an adult in every way but age. If you have her blessing, she's not going to be any kind of a problem."

"True. I guess we better get in there and make sure they aren't going to plan anything too drastic," Medusa said.

Asterion kissed her forehead. "Don't worry so much, Susa. He feels the same way. I can smell it on the little thief."

"Are you two coming or what?" Ariadne asked hands on her hips. Asterion picked her up and kissed her before dropping her back to her feet, red-faced and flustered.

"Now, we are."

"Settle down, big guy. Otherwise, you'll get me all hot and bothered, and we'll make a mess of Susa's couch," Ariadne said with a wicked smile.

"Do it, and I'll punt you off my balcony," Medusa replied.

In her dining room, the triplets had covered her table not only with drinks, but they had raided her fridge for food. Hades sat at the head of the table, doing his best not to look at Perseus.

Medusa brushed her hand along the back of Perseus's neck to reassure herself more than him, and then she sat down beside him. He rested his hand on her knee and her nerves calmed.

"So, how are we going to do this?" she asked.

17

Two hours sitting at Medusa's table with the Court of Styx taught Perseus two things: they were all total psychopaths and he liked every single one them.

They were deadly smart, and he only had to sit back and let them talk, and a plan to take down ARGOS formed.

He was glad they didn't ask for his input much because his mind was reeling from all of the morning's revelations.

Medusa had kept her hand in his for the whole time, and that solidarity had made him feel less alone. It was also a very clear demarcation of territory that left him feeling warm and flattered inside.

She might not want you only for a convenient fuck, after all.

"I think this is enough for the moment. Until Lola gets the information we need, there isn't much more we can plan for," announced Hades, getting to his feet.

Charon, Erebus, and Thanatos all rose to follow him without having to be asked. Hades paused by Perseus's chair. "If you want to talk about your father sometime-"

"No need. He was never a part of my past and he's never going to be a part of my future," Perseus said, holding out his hand.

Hades shook it and Perseus could feel the power inside of him.

Hades held on, and something inside Perseus flared to life in response to it. *What was that?*

"I'll be keeping an eye on that too," Hades said, knowing exactly what had just happened. "We'll talk about it after Acrisius is dealt with."

"Fine," Perseus replied and let his hand go.

While Asterion, Ariadne, and Medusa caught up in the kitchen, and Dany had drifted back down to Level 7, Perseus slipped outside to walk under the trees.

His head was burning, his vision going haywire, and he couldn't think straight. He sat down on one of the stone benches and put his head in his hands.

Everything was moving so fast that he hadn't had time to process the loss of the warehouse or the fact that the most powerful people in Styx were about to annihilate his treacherous grandfather.

"Are you okay?" Asterion asked. Perseus looked up and spotted the Minotaur leaning against a tree. For a big man, he barely made a sound when he moved, and Perseus was hard to sneak up on.

"Define okay," said Perseus. "I just found out that Zeus drove my mother insane for the sake of his ego, and I'm about to side with a family I didn't know I had, to take down the side of my family who's made my life hell."

"And you've managed to seduce a gorgon all in one week," Asterion added, and Perseus burst out laughing. It felt good.

"Yeah, let's not forget the Serpent Queen. I should probably have aimed lower, but I'm terrible at knowing my own limits," he said. Asterion came and sat down beside him.

"Look, it's okay to be a bit freaked out, but you should know, although he can be a real prick, Hades has your back. You and Dany aren't alone anymore, but there's going to be times you are going to wish otherwise," he said. "Anyway, the crew needed a decent thief and a genius full of attitude."

"Dany is a good kid. She's just stressed and angry." Perseus couldn't believe the sass she gave Hades.

"I wasn't judging, Perseus. I *like* her attitude. Do you not know who I'm in love with? Smartass Hellas girls are my weakness. Medusa will make sure Dany is taken care of and protected when the shit with ARGOS goes down, that I can guarantee. She adores the kid."

"You think so?"

"I know so. Medusa is a complicated being, but loyal and loving to a fault once you get through her defenses. She might give you a hard time, but she will do right by you if you do right by her."

"Is this going to be a 'you aren't good enough to date my gorgon talk'?" asked Perseus.

"Ha-ha, no. It's not up to me to decide whether you're good enough. You've just found out you are a demigod and your life is going to get complicated. You don't even know how to use the power inside of you. That's going to be a new headache to deal with."

"Any suggestions?"

"Take it a day at a time. Keep loving Medusa, take out ARGOS, and worry about any additional powers later," Asterion suggested.

"Good advice," said Perseus, giving the Minotaur a smile.

"You're not going to deny that you love her?" he asked.

"No point, it would be a lie, and I don't make a habit of lying," Perseus replied. Something in Asterion's demeanor softened, and he gave Perseus a pat on the back.

"You know what? I might learn to enjoy having you as a little brother," he said.

"I'll try not to disappoint you too much," Perseus replied, his heart doing warm and weird things in his chest about the thought of having a big brother. "You don't think me being a demigod is going to turn Medusa off? I mean, Zeus is famous for being a piece of shit. She might not like the idea of dating his kid."

Asterion smiled. "The only way to know is to ask her yourself."

By the time Asterion and Perseus had wandered back into the penthouse, Ariadne was alone and reading in the freshly cleaned kitchen.

"Where's Medusa?" Perseus asked.

"She's gone for a bath. It's been a bit of a stressful day for all of us. I require a massage and I know just the bull to give me one," Ariadne said, her aura flashing with excitement as she looked Asterion over.

"Duty calls, young Perseus. Let us know how Lola goes," Asterion told him.

Ariadne gave Perseus's cheek a loud kiss goodbye, and they headed out, leaving Perseus alone and contemplating whether he should check on Medusa.

After ten minutes of staring at the bathroom door, he gave it a tentative knock and stuck his head in. "Susa? You okay?"

"Yeah," she sniffed. Perseus decided to risk her wrath and walked in. She had her back to him in the huge spa bath, her hair slick against her golden back and her snakes out.

"You sure? If you don't want company, I can go."

"It's fine, thief," she said, not turning around. Perseus sat on the tiled edge of the tub and rested his hand between her shoulder blades.

When she didn't tell him off, he gave her tight shoulders a gentle rub. Her snakes curled against him, and he patted their soft scales gently.

"You know, I almost peed a little when you knocked Hades around," he admitted. "I've never seen you so angry."

"That's because you jumped off a building when you stole from me and didn't hang around to see my murderous rage," Medusa said, and Perseus smiled.

"I'm smarter than I look, that's why. You want to tell me why you're so upset?" he asked, half dreading the answer.

"It's hard to explain," she replied, leaning back against him.

"I got time."

"Then you'd better get in here while the water is still hot," Medusa said.

Perseus didn't hesitate for a second. He stripped and climbed in behind her, gently pulling her back to lean against his chest.

"Okay, I'm in. Tell me what's wrong," Perseus said.

"I know I look young, but I'm a very old monster, Perseus. I like to pretend I have evolved, because Hades has fought for us to be in the light and to be accepted. I'm out of my cave now, that's true, but some days, I'm reminded that despite all of that, I'm still the same old creature at heart. Today is one of those days," Medusa admitted. Her fingers looped around his in the water, and he lifted her hand to kiss it.

"Is it because you attacked Hades?" he asked.

"Yes, I did that because he...touched my property. It doesn't matter the logical part of my brain tells me that you aren't a pretty object that I can hoard away, that you can't *own* other people. I still reacted like a beast when someone pisses on her territory," said Medusa, her voice hitching. "I barely know you, and Hades has been my best friend for decades, and none of it mattered when he went for you. I'm never going to be free of that beast impulse. I'm never going to be like anyone you have ever dated because of it."

Perseus wrapped his arms around her waist and leaned his chin against her shoulder. "Medusa, I *know* what you are. It doesn't scare me, even this overprotective side of you. No one has *ever* protected me, not even my own mother. I'm overwhelmed and unworthy and completely flattered that you stepped in today. If either of us is a train wreck and completely unsuitable partner material, it's me. A broke criminal demigod who might have a power that could go off at any moment as well as a baby sister to look after. I'm not exactly a great bet either, Medusa, let's face it."

Medusa turned in his wet arms to straddle him, her arms going around his neck. "We are both terrible, emotional wrecks."

"Not to mention bad at relationships," agreed Perseus.

"And proper communication," Medusa said.

"This is probably going to be the worst idea both of us has ever had," he replied, looking down at her stunning, glowing face.

"All very true, but at least we are a pair of hopeless cases together," she said, pulling him close to kiss him.

As he always did when she kissed him, Perseus felt a rush of crazy adrenaline, but this time, it was fused with something deeper. His heart rate soared as her wet breasts slid up against his chest, and he pulled her closer to him. Her hand slid between them and she grabbed his already hardening dick.

"At least there's one thing we can always agree on," Perseus groaned against her mouth.

"And what's that, thief?" she asked, guiding him inside of her.

"That you're perfect and deserve to be fucked often, and with a lot of enthusiasm," he managed to say as she thrust against him.

Medusa's hands gripped his hair tightly and said against his lips, "Definitely something I'm never going to argue with."

Perseus squeezed her perfect breasts as he let her set the pace, loving the expression on her face as she gave in to her desire.

He was never going to get enough of the feeling of being inside her, the rightness of it, the certainty that she'd been made to torment and delight him.

She dragged her nails down his chest, and he gripped her hips, pulling her harder against him. He could see her getting closer with every thrust.

"Not yet," he growled, sliding her off him. Her hiss of protest turned into a gasp as he flipped her and dragged her back down on him.

She grabbed the edge of the spa bath, Perseus bracing one arm beside her, the other sliding up underneath her chest to rest on her neck.

"Fuck," she gasped as he moved inside her slower and deeper. He kissed and nipped her neck and shoulder, loving the taste of her against his tongue. Medusa was glowing like a supernova again as they both came together in a burning light that hurt his eyes. He swore when he realized how hard he'd bitten her.

"Shit, I'm sorry," he apologized, gently rubbing the spot.

"Don't be," Medusa said, as she tried to catch her breath. Perseus wrapped his arms around her waist.

"I'm starting to see the appeal of these tubs," he said cheekily. "Very relaxing."

Medusa laughed, leaning her head back against his shoulder. "Definitely better with two."

"I think we've found the perfect solution to every argument we have," he said, lifting her chin so he could kiss her. "It's good to know you aren't as freaked out as I am about being Zeus's progeny."

"You're not the first one I've known," she replied. "You're nothing like your father, so dismiss it from your mind. Zeus may have been a total dick, but you and Asterion are good guys."

"Asterion is different than I imagined him to be," Perseus admitted.

"The way people talk about him, I expected him to be terrifying, but really he's..."

"A total cinnamon roll? Yeah, he is. Don't let how he is with all of us fool you, he can still be terrifying when the situation calls for it," Medusa said.

"It makes me really wonder what Pithos's big deal is to want to go to war against the Court," Perseus replied. "It's not about money or power, Pithos already have both."

"No, it's personal. Whoever the woman in the mask is, she has it in for us in a big way. It's only a matter of time before we find out who and why she's doing this. In the meantime, we take out Acrisius and make sure Pithos have one less supporter," said Medusa, coldly.

Perseus held her a little tighter. "Glad you're on my side, goddess."

18

The following morning, Medusa woke to the sound of Dany banging insistently on her bedroom door.

"Hey, wake up, you two and put some pants on, we have shit to do," she shouted. To her credit, she didn't barge in, which Medusa was grateful for because she was still naked and wrapped around Perseus.

"Okay, we are awake," he groaned.

"Don't get distracted, either! Lola has been busy and I think you'll want to see this," Dany said and then added, "I'll put the coffee on."

"One of these days, I'm going to get that sleep in I've always wanted," he murmured. "You can come too if you want."

"I'll keep that offer in mind. We are going to topple the ARGOS empire today, I hope you are ready for that, thief," Medusa said, sliding out from underneath his arm.

Gods, she liked the look of him in her expensive sheets.

Get out of bed now and stop staring.

She pulled on her pajamas and wrapped a robe around herself.

"You get the first shower. I need to know what Lola has found," she said, and then in a moment of weakness, leaned over to kiss his shoulder. When he didn't reply, she bit him.

"Okay, okay, I'm awake!" Perseus said.

Medusa made sure her glasses were carefully in place before going to hunt for Dany. She was making coffee with the expertise of someone who loved her caffeine.

"Did you sleep at all last night?" Medusa asked. Dany was in yesterday's clothes and had a wild look in her eye.

"I caught an hour or two on a bean bag downstairs, but then Lola cracked their banking records and we've been at it ever since," Dany explained and poured out three cups of coffee, handing one over to Medusa.

"Thanks. Did you find anything on Pithos?" Medusa asked.

"Oh, boy, did we ever. Not only have they been on the Board of ARGOS for years, but a huge part of their funding has also gone into a special projects section. It goes back like seventeen years. I *bet* that was the floor Perseus was on when the bastard blinded him," Dany replied and sipped her coffee. "I know you two are fucking, which you know whatever, but are you feeling serious about him or not? Because I respect the shit out of you, Medusa, fuck I really do, but Perseus isn't really the casual root sort of guy, so don't treat him like one."

"Wow, this conversation took a turn," said Medusa, feeling like she wanted to slide under the table and hide.

"I have about ten minutes to have this conversation without him in the room, so yeah, we are having it. Out with it," Dany replied, looking towards the bedroom door in case her brother appeared.

"I'm not casual either, Dany. Fucking look at me. You really think I would casually fuck anyone? It's new and it's strange, but yes, I want to be serious with your brother if it's something he wants when all this shit with Pithos is over," admitted Medusa and saying the words out loud made them true. "I want you guys to be a part of the Court. You both deserve to have a family, and like it or not, Perseus is Hades's *actual* blood family. You're in that mix too. We look out for each other, and we don't lie to each other, so you know when I say I like your brother, it's for real."

Dany drank more of her coffee. "Yeah, okay, I'm not going to give you a hard time about it, you're both adults. I just needed to say it. Perseus and I have only ever had each other, and as cool as the Court is, I'm not going to believe that we are a welcome part of it without actually seeing it for myself."

Medusa smiled. "That's fair and I wouldn't expect you to. The first step is taking down ARGOS Industries, and getting hold of what Acrisius has been designing for them. We need to make him squirm." Medusa found her phone and called Lola. "You still alive down there?"

"Pumped and ready for action," answered Lola. "What do you need, boss?"

"You have access to all of Acrisius's accounts?"

"Sure do."

"Then hit them hard, bounce the funds around to lead them on a merry chase and then dump the money where they can't get to it," Medusa ordered, and the girl on the other end laughed gleefully.

"Onto it. I have just the program and have already set up a retirement fund for Dany. Speaking of which...do you know if she has a girlfriend?" asked Lola.

"Focus, Lola."

"Yeah, yeah, I am."

"Okay, let me know when the money is gone. I want to know who they call first once they discover the money is missing," Medusa said, and then decided to take pity on Lola. "And I don't think Dany has a girlfriend."

She could very well have six with the amount of flirting she does.

"Sweet. I'll file that away for after this hack is finished."

"Good girl," said Medusa and hung up before going back to the kitchen where Dany was making toast.

"What now?" asked Dany.

Medusa's smile was all danger. "Now, I go and get ready to make a grown man weep."

∽

THE ARGOS INDUSTRIES headquarters was located between the Diogenes and the Lethe district. It was as far away as they could get from Serpentine Tower without being out of the rich suburbs.

Medusa looked across the back of the limo to where Perseus sat. She had him kitted out in an expensive suit for the occasion, and her head was thinking racy thoughts every time she looked at him.

"If you don't get hold of yourself and stop your aura flashing like that, I'm going to have to fuck you in the back of this limo," Perseus said, smiling slyly at her. "And I don't think Charon would like that."

"Oh, I don't know," Charon replied from the driver's seat. "Do I get to watch?"

"Keep your eyes on the damn road," Medusa said, trying not to smile. "We are going to a very important meeting, and I don't want you to ruin my makeup or my outfit with your ardor. I look extremely good right now, I'll have you know."

"You *always* look extremely good, goddess," Perseus said and dropped his voice to a whisper, "especially when you're sitting on my face."

"Shut. Up. I know you're flirting with me because you're nervous, but I don't need you making me all flustered before I get there," Medusa replied.

Perseus's grin grew filthy. "But it's so much fun."

"Behave yourself for the next hour, and I'll-" Medusa leaned over and whispered in his ear.

Perseus cleared his throat, his face going a delightful shade of red. "That's a deal. Game face. On."

"Just in time because we are here," Charon called, and they pulled up in front of the chrome and glass doors of the foyer. "If you two aren't out in twenty minutes, we'll send in the cavalry. Erebus and Thanatos are parked two blocks away, and Ariadne, Asterion, and his crew will be in position in ten minutes."

"Thanks, Charon," Medusa said.

"Try not to make him piss himself."

"No promises," she replied and got out of the limo.

She smoothed her skirt and clutched her leather portfolio in one hand.

Perseus looked like a bodyguard toy boy in his black suit, and the thought made Medusa smile. He really was devastatingly handsome when he smiled, but now his face had an icy calm that she hadn't seen since the night he robbed her, and his sharp savageness shone through.

"Are you ready for this?" Medusa asked.

Perseus straightened his tie. "Where you go, I follow, goddess."

Medusa walked in through the foyer like she owned it because, at that very moment, she did. All of Acrisius's money was gone, and he would've only just been finding out about it.

"L-Lady Medusa, what are you doing here?" The nervous receptionist asked.

"I'm here to see your boss. Oh, don't bother checking if I have an appointment, I don't. Just give me your swipe key, and I'll show myself up to Acrisius's office," she said smoothly.

"B-but I don't think Mr. Argos-"

"It's wiser to be afraid of me than the old man," Medusa interrupted her and held out her hand. The receptionist unclipped her tag and handed it over. "There's a good girl. You'll still have your job by the end of the day, that I can promise. Floor 8 wasn't it?"

"Yes, my lady."

"Very good. Come, Perseus," Medusa instructed haughtily and headed for the elevators. Once they were inside, Perseus ran a hand down her back and grabbed her ass.

"I love when you use your boss lady voice," he growled softly in her ear.

"Good to know that you'll obey when I tell you to get down on your knees," she replied.

"Oh, begging you for favors isn't beneath me, goddess."

"Focus," she warned and made a mental note to never take him to an important meeting again.

Floor 8 was a flurry of nervous activity with lots of old men in suits arguing. Medusa's red smile widened as her heels clicked purposely across the floor, a distinct female sound that made all the men in the room pause uncomfortably.

"Good morning, gentlemen, had a spot of excitement this morning, have we?" Medusa asked conversationally. "Where is Acrisius?"

One man pointed at an office door and blustered when Medusa winked at him. She knocked quickly.

"Ready or not!" she called and pushed it open.

Medusa would have loved nothing more than to take a picture of the horrified, furious look on Acrisius Argos's face when she strode into the room, his face reddening even more when Perseus followed her.

"What are you doing here?" Acrisius demanded. Medusa sat in the chair opposite his desk, Perseus coming to stand protectively behind her.

"I've come to have a tour of my new building, and I thought you might oblige a lady," Medusa said cheerily. Oh, she did *love* making grown men squirm.

"You are no lady and this is my fucking building."

"As of, oh, ten minutes ago, I think you'll find I just bought you out. So glad you've decided to retire in your old age. Don't worry, I'll make sure the company is left in the care of the Argos family's hands...just not yours," Medusa said. That was when Acrisius finally looked at Perseus.

"You. I might have known you'd come crawling like your whore of a mother," he spat viciously.

"Actually, I was quite happy to pretend you never existed, but then you decided to let your Pithos thugs fuck with my baby sister," Perseus said, his tone deadly cold.

Medusa had seen Hades use a voice like that and her heart swelled with dark delight.

"Dany shouldn't be punished for her brilliance and leaving her to live in poverty in a fucking Hellas slum is wasting her talents. Even you can see that, Perseus. You never should have kept her from me. She could be a true Argos heir."

"So, you'd love her and not me because she's smart? Fuck, you really are a piece of work."

"I *had* my heir, and it's because of you that she lost her fucking mind and became an addict. You ruined her. Dany has committed no such crime except to be born after you," Acrisius spat.

Medusa was so angry her claws stretched out and shredded the leather armrests of her chair. Acrisius sneered.

"And the minute I gave you a simple task to prove yourself, you go and fuck this monster instead of destroying her."

"I certainly did, because she's worth fifty of you," said Perseus.

Medusa laughed and opened her portfolio. "I really don't care about what you think of me, Acrisius. I'm here to give you one final deal. Sign this document, and you'll be shipped out of Greece and given enough wealth to quietly live out your days. If you don't, I'll throw your shriveled carcass out on the street without a penny and let Pithos's dogs tear you to pieces." Medusa slid the paper across the desk with a pen. Acrisius looked like he was going to vomit, but his anger was still too hot.

"I should've killed you too the night I pushed your mother into the port," Acrisius snarled at Perseus. "I always knew you were going to be a fucking curse on my family." Perseus grabbed Acrisius by the scruff of his neck and slammed his head against the desk.

"Sign the fucking paper or I'll kill you," Perseus hissed in his ear. Acrisius laughed, a choking gurgle of blood. Medusa was too slow to see the small device in the old man's hand. She lunged for it just as he pushed the small red button and her eardrums exploded.

19

Perseus let go of the old man and sank to his knees, his hands clamping down over the noise that was screaming through his brain.

Acrisius shoved him to the floor as Perseus doubled over in pain.

"It looks like my foolish daughter wasn't lying after all," he snarled. "You really are a waste of life. You're just like the other filth that crawled out of the shadows the day Greece fell."

"F-fuck you," Perseus gasped. "We still have all your money."

"That's something that can easily be rectified," Acrisius replied and turned the sound off. Perseus almost vomited with relief.

"Medusa," he whispered and dragged himself over to her unconscious body.

"Great little device this one," Acrisius said, "We learned that you monsters react differently to certain pitches and tones, and then we weaponized it. But, this is something I'm particularly proud of." Acrisius took something from a drawer and shoved it towards Perseus. "Put it on her."

"Get fucked."

The hammer of a gun clicking back made Perseus freeze. "Oh, you know what that sound is? *Good*. Put the headpiece on the bitch or I'll put a bullet in your head. Then I'll find your little sister, and if she doesn't join me, I'll put one in hers too."

Perseus took the headpiece in his hand. It felt almost like a helm, with half of the face covered.

"Just slide it over her head but do watch your fingers. It can provide a sharp bite if you aren't careful," said Acrisius.

Perseus hesitated, but Medusa groaned next to him. "Just do it, Perseus, I'll be okay. Your piece of shit grandfather has bosses to report to, so he needs me alive for that."

"Listen to the beast," Acrisius instructed.

"I'm sorry, goddess," whispered Perseus as he lowered the mask down over her face.

"Good boy, least I know you're good for something, even if it is just taking orders from your betters." Perseus couldn't see what Acrisius was doing as he bent over Medusa, but there was a beeping sound of a locking mechanism and Medusa screamed.

"Now, now, don't you open those vicious green eyes of yours," Acrisius warned over her cries of pain. "If you do, the mask is designed to sense it and drop some very special acid in them to make sure you don't try it again."

"You fucking asshole," Perseus growled, so angry he could barely breathe.

"Curse at me all you want. I've still beaten you, as usual. Pithos would've been happy with Medusa, but throwing in whatever *you* are is going to earn me a raise," Acrisius said.

Medusa chuckled, even in the agony she must have been in.

"You have a temporary victory, old man. You are so fucked, Death himself is coming for you, and Pithos aren't going to do anything to save you."

Acrisius started cursing them again as the door opened, and something pinged through it. Perseus dived for the small noise device on the desk, as the office exploded in smoke.

He scrambled behind the desk as Acrisius fired the gun. Through the smoke, black shadows reformed to a man.

"You okay, Susa?" Erebus called.

"Get Acrisius," Perseus coughed as he slid around the floor to grab hold of Medusa. "It's okay, love, I got you."

"Get. It. Off," Medusa wheezed.

"I can't see how to unlock it," Perseus said, trying to keep the panic out of his voice as he ran his hands over the mask.

"Little fucker is gone!" Erebus complained. "He had a door behind one of the wall panels. I can go after him-"

"Fuck him! We'll get him later. Help me with Medusa. We need to get her back to Serpentine where someone can get this fucking mask off," Perseus shouted and scooped Medusa up in his arms.

"Okay, this way. Oh, Susa, that new headpiece is hideous," Erebus said, as they walked back out into the office foyer.

"Fuck you, I'm still better looking than you," Medusa hissed and Erebus laughed. All the old men were being cuffed by Hades's men and being led to the elevators.

"Just keep your eyes shut, goddess. We will get that thing off you soon," Perseus said, holding her tightly. He knew *exactly* the agony she was in.

Magical creature or not, acid was slowly eating her face away, and he couldn't do a damn thing to stop it. He'd never felt so powerless in his life.

"Perseus! This way!" Erebus called and guided him into an elevator. "Charon has the car ready."

"Talk to me, distract me, Perseus. Fuck it hurts so bad," Medusa groaned.

"Okay, Acrisius didn't sign the papers, so what does that mean?" he asked urgently.

"It means we have everything and Acrisius gets nothing, no matter how far he runs. As his grandchildren, you and Dany inherit everything," Medusa said through clenched teeth.

"Really? Dany will love the idea of having her own tech company. You might be creating trouble for yourself. She's got a few really good games ideas that could give Shadow Lords a run for its money," said Perseus.

Erebus opened the door to the limo for them and helped get Medusa inside. "We'll clean up here and report back in a few hours."

"Thanks, Erebus," said Perseus.

"You're family, Perseus. We don't leave family behind," Erebus replied and shut the limo door.

Perseus held onto Medusa, scared to jostle her but unable to let her go. She whimpered softly and his panic rose higher.

"T-talk to me," Medusa begged.

"You know, I watched you while you were sleeping last night?"

"C-creepy," she replied.

"Yeah, it is a bit, but I can't help it. Ever since I first saw you on that couch, damn, I can't stop looking at you, and when I can't look at you, all I do is think of you," Perseus admitted, and Charon very subtly lifted the dividing glass up between them.

Perseus put her hand against his face and breathed in the perfume she'd placed on her delicate wrists.

Underneath it, he could smell the blood from under her mask, and he couldn't stop the tears from falling down his cheeks.

Medusa was suffering slowly, and he was sure it was the same acid that he had caught a face full of. He would've done anything to stop it from happening to her, his beautiful goddess.

"Really? Is it because I glow like a firefly?" Medusa asked finally. Perseus laughed softly, and his chest ached.

"Not the only reason. You're the most beautiful thing I've ever seen. I wasn't joking about the cult idea either. I think I could get Hades on board by telling him about the tax cuts you can get," said Perseus.

"Jerk, you can't capitalize on my divinity. What's another reason? You said that it wasn't the only one," Medusa whispered.

"The other one is a bit more complicated," he admitted.

"Tell me," she insisted, her hands twisting in the front of his shirt.

"I think I'm in love with you, goddess."

"You only *think* you are?"

"Wow, even when you're in agony, you want to bust my balls," he complained. "Yes, I'm in love with you, tempestuous gorgon. Happy?"

"All things considered? Yes, I'm happy that you love me. I like the clarification," Medusa said, her lips straining from a grimace into a smile. "Tell me something else?"

"Once that mask is off, I'm going to give you the best head job of your life," said Perseus. "Even though you didn't admit you love me back, I'll rock your world every single day until you do."

"You know you aren't building a good case for me to want to admit my feelings to you," Medusa replied, and Perseus laughed loudly.

"How can I not love you?" he said.

Charon pulled up in the underground parking of Serpentine and helped Perseus get Medusa out of the car.

Perseus carried her close to his chest, the faint tremors in Medusa's body the only sign of the pain she was trying to control.

"Where to?" Charon asked.

"Level 5, where the engineers are," Medusa said.

"And we are going to need Dany. If anyone can figure out how to get this evil fucking thing off, she will," Perseus added. "Not long now, love."

"I-I like that pet name," she admitted.

"Not goddess?"

"Goddess, I can also live with, just so you remember your place in the hierarchy, thief," Medusa said, and Charon laughed beside them.

"You charming old snake," he said.

Perseus only let Medusa go when he could place her down on a comfortable chair. Selene arrived with heavy bags of paramedic gear and steered Perseus into another chair.

"Sit down before you fall down. Are you hurt anywhere?" she asked.

"No, I'm fine. Just...Medusa."

"Yes, yes, I have some solutions here to flush the wounds, but if they are severe, she's going to need a real hospital," Selene said.

"Just get it off and my own body will heal it," Medusa groaned.

"You fucking immortals, you always have to do it the hard way," Selene complained.

"Out of the way, beautiful," Dany instructed, moving Selene away from Medusa. "Okay, over there, bro?"

Perseus sagged with relief. "Fine. Just do your thing. Acrisius did something once the headpiece was on. There was a beep, and it locked down, but I couldn't find a catch or-"

"It's okay, Perseus. Let me have a look." Dany began to mumble under her breath, and Perseus recognized it as Homer's *Odyssey*. Dany had once told him that reciting the stanzas helped her focus and listening to her and feeling the familiarity of it made him calm down a little. His insides felt like they were burning with repressed rage. He should've killed Acrisius years ago and been done with the curse of him.

I should've killed you too the night I pushed your mother into the port. Acrisius's words echoed around his head, making the spark in him burn brighter.

There was nowhere his grandfather could hide now. Perseus would find him and put a bullet in him if it was the last thing he ever did.

"Oh, grandfather, you're a fucker, but you're a clever one," Dany said and then laughed. "But not clever enough. Selene? Do you have a scalpel?"

"Yes, but-"

"No buts, hand it over," Dany insisted. There was a rustle of packaging, and Selene making a disapproving grunt. "Stop pouting, nurse, I needed to cut myself."

"Dany? What's happening?" Perseus demanded.

"Acrisius has a bio lock on this mask. Probably so Pithos didn't kill him as soon as he handed Medusa over," Dany explained. "He obviously didn't account for his granddaughter being all weak at the knees over his enemy."

"I seem to have that effect on Serphos," Medusa said. "Do you know Perseus said he loves me?"

"Is that right? Beat me to it, bro, you fucker," Dany replied.

"Language!" Perseus and Medusa said at the same time. There was a sharp beep and Dany whooped in triumph.

"Okay, it's unlocked. Selene, get ready, I'm going to very carefully open this mask up. No, other side, I'll carry it that way," Dany instructed, and Perseus beamed with brotherly pride at how cool and calm his sister sounded.

He was losing his fucking mind, but as long as she stayed calm, he could be too. It took all the self-control Perseus had to stay in his chair as Medusa started swearing viciously and Dany lifted the mask away.

Selene's aura flared in horror and panic, but she kept it out of her voice as she said, "Medusa, please, you need a hospital."

"P-Perseus, where are you?" Medusa said, ignoring her. Perseus crouched down in front of her and took her hand. The glow about her face was dimmed, the top half twisted in ways that told him just how bad it was.

"I'm here, love, I'm here. You have to go to the hospital," he urged. The spark in him that Hades had poked was growing hotter by the second.

"No, they'll get samples. They can't get them," said Medusa.

"This is fucking insane! I'm calling Hades," Selene snapped and stormed away.

"I'm going to find something to put this mask in. I'll be right back," said Dany.

"Stop panicking, Perseus, I can smell your fear. I'll be okay, it will take a bit, but my healing is very...it's very good," Medusa said shakily. "Looks like we are going to match in another way."

"A perfect pair. There was never a doubt in my mind," said Perseus, the pain in his chest was moving and he gasped.

"Perseus? What's wrong?" Medusa asked urgently. The light was streaming down his arms, making his hands glow, and with a cool and sudden clarity, Perseus took Medusa's ruined face in his hands.

"Nothing is wrong, goddess, I just know what I need to do," he said, and the light exploded out of his hands. It was a rush, like adrenaline and when he was deep in the zone when he was painting. The power of creation surged out of him and into Medusa.

She groaned, and her face began to reform, piece by piece. Perseus could hear people shouting behind him, as the light surrounded him and Medusa.

Then it was fading, sucking back into the hidden part of him that he never knew existed.

"I really do love you," he murmured as he slumped onto Medusa's lap.

"And I love you, little thief," she whispered as his brilliant world went dark.

20

A week later, Medusa was still waiting for Perseus to wake up.

Selene had helped her shower and get dressed after Perseus had healed her, but Medusa still felt like her nerves were on fire even if her body was back to normal and her strength returned.

"Just what I needed, another lunatic nephew who doesn't understand his own damn limits," Hades said, pulling Medusa out of her snooze.

"Hey boss," she said and fumbled to put her glasses on.

"Any changes?" Hades asked as he leaned over Perseus's sleeping form.

"No, he's still out cold."

"The power he used...I felt that all the way across the city. It's still here," Hades said, resting his hand on Perseus's chest. "It's growing again, replenishing what he used."

"You are going to have to help him learn how to use it when he wakes," Medusa said. It was always a *when* in her mind, and never an *if*.

"Undoubtedly," said Hades before looking back to her. "And you? How is my Serpent Queen?"

"Pissed off that Acrisius hasn't turned up. The fucking worm. Apart from my bad mood, I'm fine, Hades. Whatever Perseus did, he healed me and then some. I feel like I'm on fire inside. Do you know if Zeus could do that?"

"Zeus could do a lot of things with his power. We are lucky that Perseus has such a soft heart. Otherwise, he could've gone nuclear and wiped out the city," said Hades, and frowned at the sleeping man.

"You think he'll be that powerful?" asked Medusa.

"I really don't know, Susa. We will have to wait and see. He used it to heal you, and for that, I'm grateful. Will you let me know if there are any changes?" Hades asked.

"Of course, I will," said Medusa, taking Perseus's hand again.

"I never thought I'd see the day when you'd be so worried about a man," Hades teased lightly.

"I love him, Hades."

"You poor dear."

"Laugh all you want. When it happens to you, I'll rub it your face," Medusa replied.

Hades chuckled darkly. "Lucky we are both immortal because I don't see that day coming any time soon. Perseus is going to be fine if you leave him for a few hours. I need you."

"For what?"

"I'm going to take Dany over to present her to the ARGOS Board, and she's asked for you to come with her as moral support," said Hades.

Medusa didn't want to leave Perseus, but she knew what he would want her to do. "Okay, give me an hour and I'll be ready."

THE ARGOS BUILDING was surrounded by press vehicles by the time Charon drove Dany, Medusa, and Hades to its front door.

"You ready for this, little one?" Hades asked Dany.

"I was born for this shit, boss," said Dany, and Hades graced her with a rare smile.

Thanatos had taken Dany to their tailor, and she looked incredible in a dark purple suit and waistcoat. Her hair was out in its full dark locks and Lola had done her makeup.

She didn't look like a girl of seventeen. She looked like a CEO in waiting, and Medusa almost felt sorry for the Board.

Almost.

Half of them had disappeared when Acrisius did, so Hades had appointed other worthies in their place. They would ensure that there were no backstabbing and attempted coups until Dany took over when she turned eighteen.

"Come on then, let me show you how to make men uncomfortable," Medusa said and stepped out of the limo.

She knew how important the moment was for Dany, so she smiled and waved and charmed reporters, all the while her insides were twisting with worry over Perseus.

Medusa stood back and let Dany address the Board with all her usual ball busting grace. The lawyers had provided them with packs of information that ensured that all the relevant paperwork and accompanying DNA tests confirmed Dany's right to be named Acrisius's heir.

The company passing onto another Argos seemed to keep feathers from being too ruffled, and Hades's looming presence ensured that anyone looking to pick a fight decided against it.

In the days after Medusa was healed, they had found horrors on the research floors of ARGOS, prototypes for Medusa's mask and Asterion's cage among them. It had all been boxed up and moved to Serpentine to be studied and destroyed.

Putting Acrisius out of business was a small victory, and all the torture devices he'd designed were a reminder that their fight wasn't over.

Technically, Hades now owned ARGOS, and would until Dany came of age and took it over. In the meantime, Dany would apprentice at Serpentine to ensure she learned everything she needed to about running a large tech company.

Watching Dany carefully charm the Board, Medusa wondered how much she could really teach the girl. Perseus wouldn't ever have to worry about his baby sister again.

Two hours later, when they got back to Serpentine, Dany gave Medusa a brief but tight hug. "Thank you, Susa."

"Don't mention it. It's your birthright after all," Medusa said and kissed Dany's forehead. She bounced away, ready to take Lola out on a date.

Medusa hoped to the gods she wouldn't get too drunk, but she figured Dany deserved to celebrate anyway she wanted to.

Medusa kicked off her shoes and hung up her jacket in her wardrobe. Her hand brushed over the keypad of her safe and it swung open.

Inside, as he'd promised, Perseus had put her necklace. Because he was a cheeky bastard who had a death wish, it was wrapped around a piece of paper with his phone number on it.

Medusa laughed and then tried not to cry as she clutched it to her chest.

"You adorable asshole," she complained out loud.

"Anyone I know?" a voice said behind her. Medusa squeaked in surprise and whipped around.

Perseus was standing in the door of the bathroom, his toothbrush in the corner of his mouth. He was unshaven and sleepy, but he was standing on two feet. Medusa slammed into him.

"Oomph! Damn, woman, don't beat on me just yet," he complained half-heartedly.

"You're okay," she murmured into his chest.

"Yeah, wait, let me spit so I can kiss you," Perseus said with a laugh. Medusa loosened her grip on him long enough for him to spit out his toothpaste and rinse his mouth.

"How long have you been awake? Why didn't you call me?" she demanded angrily.

"I only just woke up, love, and managed to make it the bathroom to brush my teeth when you started cursing at me," Perseus explained. "How long have I been asleep?"

"A few...weeks?" Medusa said, half expecting him to have a meltdown.

"Huh, no wonder I'm so hungry," he replied, non-plussed. "Now, where were we?" He dragged her back to him and gave her a deep minty kiss.

"Are you hurting anywhere?" Medusa asked, running her hands over him to reassure herself.

"No, love, I'm okay, just hungry," he reassured her. "Who knew you'd be such a fusser."

"Shut up. You go for a shower and I'll call the kitchen," Medusa said, shoving him away gently.

"I knew it wouldn't last. I should've played the patient a bit longer," he said and pulled his shirt off. "Woah, don't start flashing that aura around. I don't have the strength for all the trouble it entails."

"Well, you'd better get it back in a hurry. I recall you promising me the best head job of my life, and I haven't forgotten," Medusa said haughtily, before turning on her heel and hurrying away while she still had the strength of will.

Medusa texted Dany to let her know that Perseus was awake and received a thumbs-up emoji back, which she took as a sign that her date with Lola was going well.

Despite her sass, Medusa watched as Perseus ate and forced him to drink a liter of water as per Selene's instructions. He hadn't needed to go on an IV drip due to whatever god blood was in his veins, but Medusa didn't want to risk him getting dehydrated more than he already was.

While he ate, Medusa told him about everything that had happened at ARGOS industries.

"Dany is going to be insufferable," he said with a wide smile. "Thank you, Medusa."

"You don't need to thank me. Dany is the heir, since I figured you weren't interested in the company."

"You're right there. I still have to talk to her about university," Perseus said.

"Do it, but she doesn't need it. Whatever they are going to teach her there, she can learn here, but be on the cutting edge of the tech, not decades behind. Besides, she's on a date with Lola, and I don't think she's going to be interested in Athens," Medusa said, getting up to grab herself another beer.

"A date with Lola! She's so much older than Dany," Perseus said, showing that despite everything, he was a big brother first.

"Only a year! And you're hardly one to talk about dating an older woman," Medusa replied. "They are going to roller derby. It's hardly the sordid sexy affair."

"It will be if Dany gets her way," he muttered, and Medusa laughed even harder.

"Must run in the family," she said, kissing the back of his neck as she wrapped her arms around his shoulders. "I'm so happy you're awake."

"Were you actually worried about me? The dirty thief?" he said, tickling one of her snakes under its belly.

"Yes. You used your weird divine power to heal me, Perseus. Doesn't that worry you?" she asked him.

Perseus pulled her gently into his lap. "No, it doesn't. It healed you, Medusa. It was worth the weeks in bed. I *know* the pain you were in intimately, and I couldn't handle it."

Medusa kissed his scarred face. "When I get my claws on Acrisius, I intend to make him pay for what he did to the both of us."

"I have a feeling we'll have to get in line. His usefulness to Pithos was the company, and now it's gone, they aren't going to protect him anymore. If they don't kill him, I'm sure we'll find him sooner rather than later," Perseus said. He nipped at her lip. "You know I feel like my strength has returned."

"Oh, is that so?" Medusa laughed. "You might be a demigod, but even you have your limits, thief."

"Really? Says who?" he asked and got to his feet, lifting her with him.

"Hades did try to warn me that you are probably a lunatic," she said as he carried her to the bedroom.

"My uncle is a very wise god, but where you're concerned, I'm always going to push my luck," Perseus replied.

Medusa reached up to kiss him. "Lucky me."

∾

It was another two days before Medusa allowed Perseus out of the penthouse. He felt better than okay, but he liked her trying to look after him even if she was in full territorial gorgon mode.

The Court of Styx was rowdy as they invaded Medusa's rooftop garden, where her kitchen staff had organized an outdoor party for them.

"She still not letting you out, is she?" Charon teased as he passed Perseus a beer.

"I'm not in a hurry. Medusa makes a good nurse," he replied, making Erebus laugh filthily.

"Please tell me she has an outfit," he said.

"He wouldn't be able to see it, moron," Ariadne snapped, giving the titan a flick on the head. "And I happen to know that Medusa *is* going to let Perseus out tonight. She just wants us all to eat first."

"Is that so?"

"Shush! I'm not meant to tell you that she has a surprise for you," she whispered.

"You are terrible at keeping secrets, sweetness," Asterion said as he joined them, Dany in tow. She gave Perseus a punch in the arm, her usual greeting hello.

"Little sis, how goes the expansion pack?" he asked, and Dany's aura lit up, and she started talking about features that went entirely over his head. He didn't mind.

They had hung out since he'd woken up, but after making sure he was okay, Dany had spent most of her time on Level 7 arguing with programmers.

"It's good to see you survived your ordeal," Hades said, appearing out of thin air and scaring the hell out Perseus.

"I'm in one piece, and you don't need to lecture me about how stupid I was to try to use my power or whatever it is. Medusa has already given me an ear-bashing over it," Perseus said.

"No lectures. We will have to discuss it further when Medusa has relaxed enough to let you out of her sight," Hades replied. Perseus decided that despite their rocky start, Hades might be okay.

Two hours later, Charon handed Medusa a set of keys, and she took Perseus's hand.

"Let's go for a drive, handsome. The kids can clean up," she purred in his ear.

"Where you go, I follow, goddess, you know that," Perseus said. He was curious to see what mischief she was up to, but he didn't want to ruin the game for her. "I can't believe Charon gave you his keys. He seems intense about his cars."

"He knows what's good for him, and it's his way of making sure I know I'm his favorite," Medusa said, as they drove out into the streets of the Diogenes.

"Is this the part where you take me to an unknown location and get your revenge on me stealing from you? Because I really thought we were past that," Perseus asked.

"I guess you'll just have to wait and see, won't you?"

"So, the suspense can kill me before you do? Perfect date," Perseus said and yelped when she reached over to pinch him. He didn't know where they were going exactly, but he knew the direction. "Taking me back to Hellas?"

"No fooling you," Medusa said and pulled up. "I've got something to show you, and before you bitch at me, your sight has been taken into account."

"Now, I *am* curious." Perseus waited while Medusa unlocked a door and took his hand.

"The Court and I decided to get you something," she said and flicked on the lights. Perseus stilled, his mouth falling open. He was in a brick warehouse that had been refurbished into a gallery.

"I...honestly don't know what to say," he said.

"Oh, this? No, this is just the showroom floor that Cara will run. This is for you, so you keep away from Serpentine long enough for me to get some work done," Medusa replied and pulled him to another door.

She turned the lights on and the room lit up in sharp detail. There were worktables and stretched canvases, paints and charcoal, a couch, and a sound system.

"We salvaged what we could from the fire, but there wasn't much. We figured you'd need another workspace, so Dany came up with the idea to use infrared paint on the tables and walkways so that you can see it. Oh, shit, it's too much, isn't it? I should have totally talked to you first and-"

Perseus was kissing her, unable to speak but needing to express himself in the only way he could. "It's perfect, goddess. No one has ever given me something so thoughtful before. It is way too much, but I'm so grateful."

"Don't worry, I spent Acrisius's money to do it. You didn't think only Dany was going to get all the presents, did you?" she said.

"I wouldn't have cared if she did. Still, this is amazing, and I love you,"

Perseus replied, lifting her up onto the new workbench and kissed her again.

"I love you too, thief. Does this mean you accept my gift?" Medusa asked.

"I'll accept your amazing gift on one condition."

"Oh? And what's that?" she said, her aura flashing in a way that always meant the best kind of trouble.

"You have to be my first model," Perseus replied.

Medusa's lips curved into his favorite smile as she hooked her legs around his hips and drew him tighter to her. "Then, I hope you're good at nudes."

EPILOGUE

In Athens, a van pulled up at the docks and an old man was tossed roughly out onto the asphalt.

"Please, you don't need to do this! I can get the company back easily, I promise you!" he begged as he was led to a wooden box.

A woman in a mask and cloak appeared from the shadows, and the old man got on his knees in front of her.

"Please, my lady! I've served you and the cult faithfully for the past twenty years," he said.

"You have failed me too often, Acrisius Argos. You didn't see your grandson for what he was until it was too late, and you have failed to deliver me the gorgon's head." The woman waved to her men. "I'm weary of you and your lack of results."

The old man shouted and struggled as he was forced into the wooden crate. The woman watched unfeelingly as the lid to the crate was screwed on, and it was pushed off the dock and into the sea, silencing Acrisius's screams forever.

Her hand wrapped around the hilt of the stone dagger in her belt, feeling secure in its power and the death it could wield. The fight against Medusa wasn't as successful as she'd hoped, but she had gained valuable knowledge in the process. A new demigod had appeared, and it was one less she would have to hunt down.

Her eyes drifted up to Lycabettus Hill, high above the city where the goddess Demeter reigned. Some gods, she would wait to destroy, but she wouldn't tolerate them forever.

"My lady, your helicopter is waiting for you at the airfield as you requested," a man said, beside her. At least she had one servant that didn't disappoint her.

With a final glare at Demeter's palace on the hill, she took his hand and let him help her back into the van.

"Come, Vallis, let's be finished with this tiresome business. We have a new project for our mad inventor."

HADES

THE COURT OF THE UNDERWORLD III

ALESSA THORN

Copyright © 2020 by Alessa Thorn

All rights reserved.

No part of this book may be reproduced in any form or by any electronic or mechanical means, including information storage and retrieval systems, without written permission from the author, except for the use of brief quotations in a book review.

Editing by F. Sutton

Cover by Damoro Design

PROLOGUE

Sing, O' Muse, of the seasons of the world and how all that was lost was found again.

Sing, of how gods and mythical creatures once roamed the lands of Greece, and of how Man became powerful, and the gods were forced into hiding.

Sing, of when Greece's economy collapsed and the land was on fire with the turmoil man's governance had wrought.

Sing, of how the gods returned to build a new world from the ashes.

Sing, O' Muse, of the new city of Styx, and the monsters that govern its underworld.

Sing to me a new song, of an unyielding God of the Dead and a Goddess of Life...

SIX YEARS AGO

The club in Athens was a complete dive, but it played the type of dirty blues Hades liked, and the people dancing looked as if they were actually enjoying themselves.

Anything was better than the party he had managed to escape from two hours earlier. He had never been the type to hang around a high society dinner, even on Olympus.

Times had changed...but not that much. He'd never had a problem with Demeter, and now they were business partners as she ruled from her golden and marble tower in Athens, and him from his city of Styx.

It was a decent enough arrangement. Hades had no intention of starting unnecessary fights; he only wished that he didn't have to sit through the fucking social gatherings she insisted on holding every time he came to Athens for a meeting.

It had only taken a simple trick, a slight glamour conjured in the air, and he'd slipped out the back door.

Hades rolled up his shirt cuffs and looked at his watch. He knew his freedom would last another hour before his bodyguards managed to track him down. It was why he paid them, and it was why Asterion trained them so hard.

Sometimes, he really hated pretending he needed them to protect him. It made the humans comfortable to think that the God of Death was vulnerable, so he let them believe the lie.

Hades signaled to the bartender who poured out another two fingers of whiskey.

"Thank you, leave the bottle, will you?" The guy nodded without batting an eyelid.

Hades had managed to avoid the media attention, thanks to Medusa, and outside of Styx, dressed in a white button-up shirt and black pants, he could be any other middle-aged businessman needing a drink after a long week.

He had to get drunk fast, the ichor in his veins would start to filter out the effects all too soon, and he felt like getting drunk.

Anything but the feeling of boredom that had overwhelmed him that evening as glittering women and men with too sharp smiles had crowded him, thrusting business cards and other parts of their persons at him.

Athens was always the fucking same. Styx had its dirty cruel parts, but at least it felt real. Demeter was turning Athens into an earthly Olympus, and he fucking hated it.

"Is that all for you, or are you willing to share?" a voice asked from beside his right shoulder. He looked down in surprise to see a woman with honeysuckle hair looking up at him.

"Excuse me?" he said bristling.

She stood up on the bar's footrest and waved at the bartender, who was chatting up a brunette.

"I swear, if he doesn't come back soon, I'm going to have to owe you," she said, her red lips kicking up into a teasing smile.

"I'd love to give you some, but you have no glass," he pointed out, feeling unsettled by her directness. She laughed, the sound fizzing in his ears before she grabbed his bottle.

"Don't worry, I don't have germs." Ignoring his look of horror, she took a large swig and passed it back to him.

"That's better. Dancing, you know, there's nothing like it to build up your thirst."

"If you're hot, you should take off those gloves," Hades said, looking pointedly at the tight black leather covering her delicate hands.

She took a step back and waved a dramatic hand in front of her red dress. It clung to her generous curves in a way that showed them off to their full dangerous beauty, a black leather belt cinching in her waist before the skirt flared out.

"And ruin my dancing outfit? Not likely."

"I suppose you have a point." Hades looked away from her and took another drink. He expected her to leave, but she just stood there. After an awkward moment, he turned back to her. "Something else you would like?"

The woman took another mouthful from his bottle, her lipstick smearing on the glass. "You know what? You look like the kind of guy I could make some *really* bad decisions with."

Hades smiled in a way that had made men weep in fear. "The *worst*."

"Promises, promises," she sighed, which made him laugh in surprise and then cough in an attempt to cover it up. She held out a gloved hand. "Come with me."

"What do you-" Hades began, but she took his large hand in both of hers and tugged him off the barstool. She looked him up until her head was tilting back.

"Tall as hell too, so maybe tonight isn't going to be a total waste after all," she said, before pulling him through the crowd.

The wide skirt of her dress moved in a mesmerizing way with every swish of her hips, and Hades was just drunk enough to be curious about what this tiny woman was playing at. She pulled him close to a wall covered in buttoned leather.

"What are we doing?" Hades asked over the noise of the band.

She pulled his head down and said in his ear, "Escaping." She pushed at a panel and a door opened. "Abracadabra, mother fuckers!" she shouted, her voice drowned out over the drums.

Hades was grinning again. Maybe Athens wasn't so terrible after all. She gestured at him as she disappeared through the door. He followed, a part of him wondering if he was about to get mugged in the darkness. It turned out to be an empty room with low lounges and soft lighting.

"I know the guy who owns the club, so he won't mind if we are in here," she said, closing the door behind him.

"And what if he comes back?" Hades asked.

"Then I imagine he's going to catch us in a very compromising position," she said, and with a devilish smile, she pushed him down onto the couch.

"You're a forward little thing, aren't you? Are you even going to tell me your name?" Hades asked.

She placed her hands on either side of his face. "Absolutely not." Then she kissed him. Hades stilled in surprise under the force of it. It was like wild summer storms and just as terrifying.

"Look at your face," she chuckled, her breath smelling of whiskey and honey. She threaded her fingers through the speckling of grey at Hades's temples. "You're far too old to be so surprised."

"No one is ever too old to be surprised when a beautiful woman kisses them unexpectedly."

She bit a plump bottom lip. "Is that so? Well, then...what are you going to do about it?"

She squeaked as he grabbed her by her glorious hips and pulled her onto his lap before kissing her just as hard and twice as deep. The same feeling of hissing rain, new things and whispers in the dark rushed over him.

Her hands buried in his hair, pulling just enough that he felt the sting rush through him and become something else.

"You still want this kind of trouble, sunshine?" he asked, coming up for air. Her honey curls were a tangled mass of gold, red lipstick smeared in a tousled way that made him want things. Things he hadn't wanted in an awfully long time.

A gloved finger ran over his two-day stubble, the sensation of leather and heat strangely insensitive and erotic at the same time.

"You're *definitely* my kind of trouble," she said, tightening her legs around him as her pelvis ground against his erection. She lowered her lips to his. "Big, delicious trouble indeed."

Hades wasn't quite sure how it happened, but her hands were under his shirt, and she was kissing him, her tongue in his mouth and her body a maddening tease as she pushed gently against him.

"If you keep this up, I can't be responsible for what happens," he warned.

"How encouraging."

Despite her teasing tone, he didn't want it to go further than she was comfortable with, so he pulled back from her slowly, so he could look into her stunning green eyes.

"Tell me what you want, sunshine, and I'll give it to you," Hades said. "Sound like a deal?"

"That's very gentlemanly of you," she said and lifted his hand to her mouth and sucked on two of his fingers. He felt her tongue brush against them, causing his dick to harden even more.

"This is what I want," she purred and guided his wet fingers under her damp panties.

If Hades would've had a god to pray to at that moment, he would have. She groaned as he slid his fingers into her, slowly exploring her wetness, the scent of flowers, and female arousal filling the air.

Her breath was coming in pants between their kisses as she thrust against him, Hades squeezing her ass with his other hand and pulling her up against him.

"Oh gods, that feels good," she whispered in his ear and then cried out when he increased the pressure. "Never had someone make me come this way."

"Then you've been fucking about with the wrong kind of men," Hades said and kissed the pale column of her throat.

She grabbed his shoulders as she rode him, her gorgeous breasts pressing into his face.

He managed to free one from the low V of her dress, and as soon as he got a nipple between his teeth, she came so hard her whole body shook. She tilted his face up and kissed him.

"You've ruined me, you bastard," she panted against his lips.

"You asked me too, sunshine, and I always make good on my deals," Hades said, slowly moving his fingers from her. Her eyes sparkled with green fire as she smiled at him. She leaned to whisper in his ear.

"You want to know what else I want?"

Hades groaned as her gloved hand gripped his dick. "Tell me, sunshine."

"I want this glorious dick inside of me. I want you to fuck me every which way until we are both too exhausted to fuck anymore."

Hades chuckled darkly. "Oh, darling, I'm going to fuck you so hard you're going to forget your own name."

Hades had one hand bunched tightly in her hair, the other on her breast, when the door opened, making both jump.

"Busted," she said with a forlorn sigh.

"I'm sorry to interrupt, Lord Hades, but you have a phone call. It's Asterion, it sounds urgent."

"Wait outside, Simon," Hades hissed in a tone so chilling his guard snapped to attention, and the woman's green eyes went wide.

It was too late. She'd already heard his name, a wall of coolness coming up over that cheeky, clever face.

"Too much trouble for you, after all, hey sunshine?" he said, tucking a long curl behind her ear.

"I wouldn't say that, but your bruiser doesn't seem like he's going to wait for long," she replied, slipping off him to the couch and straightening her skirt.

"Will you wait? This won't take long," Hades asked, surprising himself that he would request something as opposed to demanding it.

"Maybe," she said and laughed.

Hades lifted her gloved hand and kissed the small skull that was tattooed on the inside of her wrist. It tasted as delightful as the rest of her, the scent of her skin calling out to him.

"Thank you," he said softly. He ran his hands through his hair and tucked in his shirt before stepping out into the club. Simon was looking at him in a mixture of shock and fear as he handed over the phone.

"What?" Hades demanded, pressing one hand over his ear. Asterion was shouting something about getting angry calls from Demeter and the media catching on that Hades hadn't been at the party in his honor.

"Get Medusa to fucking fix it and stop bothering me." Hades tossed the phone to Simon and opened the door back to the secret room.

There was no woman, only her floral and sex perfume in the air, and a single black glove on the low table arranged to give him the one-fingered salute for walking out on her.

1

It had been six years since meeting the woman in the club in Athens, and yet, every so often when Hades was alone, he would catch the faint scent of her skin.

It was maddening that his curiosity about her hadn't left him even after he sobered up.

After the first week, Hades had contacted the club for any footage they had of that night. She had avoided the club's CCTV and those that did get her, her image had blurred out of focus.

Impossible.

If it weren't for Simon confirming the woman had been real, Hades would have thought he'd imagined her. It would hardly be the first time a god had created such an illusion, but madness was something to be cautious of in a god, especially in himself.

"You're lost to the void today, old friend," said Medusa. It was a rare in person visit, not on a screen. She was wearing her glasses that deflected her dangerous gaze, not that it had ever worked on Hades.

"Something like that. I must say I find it strange to see you out and about like this," said Hades, avoiding her question as best as he could. Medusa smiled a sickeningly, infatuated smile.

"Blame Perseus. He's the one that is slowly forcing me out of my tower. It turns out I don't entirely hate being among the humans as much as I thought."

Hades made a disapproving sound. "Now is not the time to be complacent for your safety, my dear."

"You think I don't know that? They sent a thief after me, almost killed Asterion, and hurt my girls," Medusa hissed angrily. 'Her girls' was what she had taken to calling Ariadne and Dany, both full of fire and undoubtedly Medusa's favorites.

"So, what are we going to do about them? I'm tired of Pithos fucking with my business and my family," Hades demanded.

Medusa raised a perfect red brow. "Is that what we are now? Family?"

"You know that we are. A family that each other has chosen, so it's worth more than blood. Asterion ripped through part of Pithos's forces on Knossos, and we've shut ARGOS down, but we still have no idea who is funding them and where they built such a cage to try to house him. If they had gotten him in there..."

"But they didn't. They couldn't get my necklace for immunity so they could attack me, and they didn't get their infernal face mask on me permanently either. We have beaten them when they've come at us."

"Come now, Medusa. You don't believe they were real attempts on us, do you?"

"No, they were tests, and they use other people, innocent people in Dany's case, as collateral." Medusa leaned back in her chair and crossed her legs. "What are you thinking?"

"That their gadgets were trial models for something bigger. What have your tech people figured out?"

All the equipment that they had recovered from ARGOS was now residing in one of the basements in Serpentine Tower. Medusa let out a huff of breath.

"I know that they are brilliant and dangerous. Asterion's cage is letting off a frequency that somehow reacts to his aura. It drains his energy and keeps him weak."

"Is it electronic?"

Medusa shook her head. "That's the part that's brilliant. I don't know *what* causes the vibration. There's nothing electrical built into it to cause the frequency. We are one step closer to taking it apart, but I'm holding off just in case whatever causes it can't be turned on again. If that happens, we'll have lost the way to study it."

"And the mask they managed to get on you?" asked Hades. A soft, dangerous hiss came from Medusa.

"It has two rows of needles which would have kept a dose of acid inside of it, so that when I opened my eyes, it dripped into them." Medusa kept her tone steady even though fury was radiating off her in deadly waves.

"Brutal and clever. I'm extremely interested in knowing who their inventor is, as it takes a singular mind to create such objects," Hades mused.

"They are very specific. I wonder what they have made for you, darling," replied Medusa. She reached into her sleek handbag and pulled out a yellow envelope. "I wanted to see what kind of mood you were in before I gave you this. You're not going to be happy about what it contains, so you must promise not to lose your temper."

"What did you find?" He knew she had to have had a reason to come herself. Whatever was in the envelope, she didn't trust it to go through her own servers.

"I've been tracing the files and history of the laptop that Pithos gave Ariadne. Theseus shot up the Pithos IT room in Lethe, but my girls were able to recover pieces from it and the servers at ARGOS. I won't bore you with details that you won't understand, but I found transactions from certain banking accounts."

"Who do they belong to?" Hades said, his tone icy.

"You must understand how big these businesses are and…"

Hades's power slashed out of him, ripping the envelope from her hands. He tore it open and studied the pile of bank statements.

"They are all in Athens. Someone is funding them, siphoning money out of different companies, usually smaller unnoticeable amounts, but the smaller companies are owned by one big one," Medusa explained.

"Morning Harvest," Hades growled, fighting the urge to crush the documents in his hands. "Fucking Demeter."

"Look, you know I have never liked that vanilla, self-righteous bitch, but we shouldn't jump to her as the perpetrator of this until we know for sure," Medusa tried to reason.

"She's using Pithos to try to destroy us, Medusa. You really believe I'm going to let that slide?"

"No, if you were that weak, I wouldn't have followed you out of the darkness on Lesbos, Hades. I want you to be smart about it, though. Pithos's rhetoric so far has been against the gods and magical beings. Demeter is a goddess and her daughter is a demigoddess. It doesn't make sense that she would help fund a hate group against herself."

"Maybe they don't know who is funding them. A human hate group would be the perfect cover. It means I wouldn't question a goddess's involvement. Demeter might not want to risk open war with me, but she wants the port, she always has, and it's my territory. If I'm weakened enough, she could make a play for it through financial means," Hades said, his mind connecting possibilities. Then another one occurred to him.

"I forgot about the daughter. Her father was human?"

"Yes. Demeter took over his family's company after the crash and married him to keep all parties happy. From what I can tell, it was a good marriage until he was killed trying to stop some muggers. It was in the shady part of Athens, so there were rumors he was there for the hookers. Who knows? Persephone would be...oh gods, maybe thirty-something now? She helps run Mommy's kingdom," Medusa said, tapping her nails against the arm of her chair.

"She always seemed less uptight than her mother, but that's not exactly hard."

Hades frowned. "I don't recall ever meeting her."

"That's not surprising, since you aren't exactly social when you go to Athens. You sign whatever agreements with Demeter, and then you get out of there before she can organize a dinner," Medusa said shrewdly. She would always keep close tabs on Hades's movements, so it didn't surprise him that she knew his agenda.

"Perhaps, I should have paid more attention to treachery at her parties."

Medusa got to her feet. "I can't convince you not to start a war prematurely, and I'll always back every decision you make, Hades, but please try to think this through rationally. Look at Asterion, Theseus was his best friend for years and he betrayed him. Demeter might have moles of her own. Try to get more information before you go after her."

She gave his shoulder a pat before she left his office, her red heels clicking on the polished floors.

Hades read through all the documents, writing notes in a black notebook.

Minutes later, his cell phone started to ring. "What?" he answered.

"Uncle, I've been told you're fixing to do something stupid," Asterion said. There was music on in the background and a feminine voice singing as a pot banged.

"Talked to Medusa, did you?"

"You know, Susa, she has a big mouth. Babe, you're going to burn that if you don't stir it," Asterion called. "Sorry, back to what I was saying..."

There was a scuffle, and a new voice said, "Are you going after Demeter or not?"

"Good evening, Ariadne," Hades said, feeling exhausted by the domestics of his nephew's life.

"Hey. Are you going after Demeter?"

"I'm thinking about it."

"You want some help? I could do with an outing."

"No murdering!" Asterion called in the background.

Ariadne's voice dropped an octave and she whispered, "Seriously, Hades, you need to give me something to do, or I'm going to start terrorizing your nephew in ways he won't enjoy."

"It sounds like he needs to find a way to help you get rid of all of that energy of yours, Ariadne. Shall I tell him you are unfulfilled?" Hades said.

"Oh, we are having plenty of sex, but we both know murder is a different kind of kick, don't we?"

Hades smiled. "We do, little Spindle. If I feel the need for lethal action, I'll call you."

"What about non-lethal? We have to do something now that we know their money is coming from Demeter," said Ariadne.

"What would you do in my position?" Hades asked, curious to see what the ex-assassin would consider.

"Me? That's easy. I'd go for the daughter."

"Ariadne!" Asterion said angrily.

"What? You were thinking it too. I don't mean to *kill* her. At least not yet. She would be the best person to get proper answers from. She runs part of Demeter's business, so she'll have the insight, and she'll be a good bargaining chip should Demeter be the one behind Pithos."

"Hmm, your idea has a lot of merits," said Hades thoughtfully.

"Give me that phone before you start a civil war," Asterion demanded. "Hades, if you take Persephone, Demeter will go ape shit. Aim for someone of lower ranking."

"What if Demeter doesn't know who has taken her? I don't mean to advertise my intentions. Demeter is a billionaire. We can make it look like a kidnapping by some organized crime group for a ransom, and we get what information we need," said Hades, liking the idea more and more.

"You are willing to risk everything to do this, because if you're wrong, Hades..."

"I have no intention of harming the girl, Asterion. I just need to have a talk with her, and if she knows nothing, I'll give her back. I don't suppose I could borrow your beloved to run the team?"

"Absolutely fucking not."

"Fine, put Erebus onto it."

"I respect you more than anyone, Hades, but this is a bad idea."

"Noted. Now get it done," Hades said before hanging up.

2

The place settings were peach and pink, the china was white with a filigree gold trim. Pale yellow and pink roses sat in the center of the table in a decorative crystal vase.

Persephone, in a pair of cream leather gloves, was clenching her hands underneath the table so hard that her fingers were aching from blood loss, from the leashed magic burning in them, and the growing urge to flip the goddamn table over.

She imagined the horrified look on her mother's face and the Japanese businessmen that they were meeting with.

All that perfection; fine china, flowers, and delicate pastries she wasn't allowed to eat, would scatter and smash across the black and white marble tiles...

"Isn't that so, darling?" Demeter said, her tone snapping Persephone out of her chaotic daydream.

"Absolutely. Your investment would double its returns within the year, and it would mean less of a reliance on the Americans and their ever-increasing trade disputes," Persephone said smoothly as she unclenched one hand and reached for her tea. Peppermint, because it didn't have the caffeine in it that made her irritable. God, she hated it.

She smiled her warmest smile, throwing in a little something extra behind it to get the meeting over with. The man's cheeks pinked ever so slightly before he turned back to Demeter.

"Send us through the agreement, and we will have our lawyers do a final review," he said, eyes darting back to Persephone.

The pointed toe of Demeter's high heel nudged Persephone's calf, and she quickly lowered the intensity of her smile.

"Wonderful! Please send through any questions you might have over the clauses, and we can get everything signed and made official," Demeter said, handing the man a white leather document portfolio, and they all shook hands.

The smiles and politeness lasted only as long as they had company. As soon as the private room in the teahouse was empty, Demeter whirled on her daughter.

"What is the matter with you today?" she demanded.

"I don't know what you mean, Mother. You told me this meeting was important, and here I am." Persephone poured out another cup of the infernal tea.

"It was important-"

"And they agreed, so why are you so pissed off?"

"I felt you use...*it*... when you smiled. It was silly and dangerous. You know the humans are suspicious of us enough as it is. We can't afford for them to realize you're playing games with them."

"All I did was smile. Nothing was intended by it. I'm allowed to smile at men, Mother. After all, I'm a thirty-two-year-old woman, remember?" Persephone didn't mean to goad her. It was more trouble than what it was worth with the way her mother held onto petty insults, but she couldn't help it.

She was frustrated and bored, and if she was forced to keep looking at the pastel décor that haunted her life, she was going to scream.

"You're not just a woman, daughter, you're a demigoddess. Thirty-two years is nothing for our kind. I know you find me overbearing and cautious, but it's because I've seen firsthand what man is capable of doing to us, and you have not."

Demeter reapplied her peach lipstick and reached up to smooth one hair into place. Persephone's hands itched to dig into her mother's perfectly coiffured caramel and honey hair and rough it into snarls.

Do you have the devil in you today? Persephone shut down every memory the wayward thought inspired, including that night's previous dream of being back in the club, hands under Hades's shirt, and his tongue...*Don't think about it!*

"You're right, Mother. I'm sorry. I didn't mean for the magic to happen, it leaked out," Persephone said dutifully, knowing the apology would soothe Demeter's mood.

"It'll take time to master it. Perhaps another hour in the pool tonight after the guests leave will help calm it down?" Demeter suggested as she rose from her chair and straightened her pale pink skirt and jacket.

Demeter was scarily beautiful in her perfection, nearly 6ft tall with a slender figure and delicately precise in every movement.

Persephone was half-human, barely five feet tall and everywhere curved, and would never be able to come close to that kind of statuesque, steely grace.

That didn't stop Demeter from trying to make Persephone into a 'better version' of herself.

Persephone gathered her things, and when Demeter had her back turned, she snatched one of the pink macarons from the table and shoved the whole sugary treat in her mouth at once.

She really *was* in a mood that day, and she knew it was the dream's fault.

PERSEPHONE HADN'T ALWAYS BEEN a dutiful daughter. She'd tried to heed her mother's warnings about the magic in her veins and the dangers it brought with it, but that dark part of her needed to get out and play.

Demeter had done her best by keeping Persephone closeted away with private tutors and not letting her mingle too much with human children for their own safety. The gloves had been a fixture in her life since her powers started to manifest.

After they did, Persephone was forced onto a diet of no sugar or stimulants of any kind. There was limited and carefully watched interaction with other children, and the dreaded exercise to keep her adrenaline and magic to a minimum.

That was what Demeter said, but she was privately ashamed that her daughter had a curvy body by the time she was thirteen, and so had always maintained exercise was the best answer to both problems.

Persephone hated everything but swimming, so Demeter had an indoor lap pool built on one side of the compound for Persephone's private use.

She was only doing what she thought was right, Persephone reminded herself as she walked through the gardens, heading for the pool.

It had been another draining night, a business dinner with Morning Harvest's Board members and partners that had dragged on a painfully long time.

Persephone's eyes had drifted too often to the card in front of the only empty place at the long dinner table.

Hades Acheron, the name said in swirled calligraphy. She knew he'd never turn up, which was one of the reasons that she agreed to go. She'd been very, very careful to avoid meeting the Lord of Styx, and she intended to keep it that way.

In her twenties, Persephone would have her moments of quiet rebellion where she would sneak off her mother's compound and down into the streets of Athens.

She had gotten the tattoos on her wrists on one such outing. Mostly she found a lot of cake and club or a bar in the less upmarket parts of town where she wouldn't be recognized.

A night of dancing, drinking, and if she felt like it, a quick fuck with a random guy. Then she would sneak back up the hills to the compound, and her mother would never know she had been gone.

Those nights had kept Persephone sane, she had lived for them, and she hadn't had one in six years.

Persephone opened the glass door to her pool and went into the change rooms. She unzipped her dress that she'd only manage to get one stain on that evening and kicked off the heels that made her feet ache no matter how much she wore them.

Finally, she pulled off her cream gloves, and she almost wept with relief as she shook out her hands.

She tugged out the handful of pins that kept her tumble of curls up and rubbed her aching scalp, moaning aloud at the sensation. She stripped off her purple underwear and pulled on the plain black swimsuit.

Gripping the sides of the sink, Persephone took three deep breaths.

"You're okay," she told her reflection before she dug into the cupboard under the sink for her makeup remover wipes and her dirty secret.

Most rich kids would have kept a stash of coke, but Persephone's tastes were more obscure.

Instead of drugs, she pulled out a tiny packet of seeds. She couldn't go out, but at least she could do this.

The sun tattoo on her wrist flashed as Persephone tipped one seed into her left hand and held it up to the light.

She smiled, and the rush of sweet tree sap, wet black earth, and spring sun hummed through her. The tiny seed twitched and then began to grow.

The green worm of a root shot up in seconds until Persephone was holding a narcissus flower, its yellow center bright in its bed of white petals.

Persephone's smile slipped into a smirk as she passed the flower to her right hand.

It was the hand that Hades Acheron had taken six years ago and kissed her skull tattoo.

She hadn't known it was him until it was too late. It had been on one of her freedom nights that she'd needed so fucking badly.

The hilarious irony of it was that it was meant to be the night that Demeter introduced her daughter to him. Demeter had always been overprotective, but the one person she never dared expose Persephone to was Hades.

Persephone had learned from a young age to fear the God of the Underworld more than any being in Greece. And it was all because of the power of her right hand.

Persephone gripped the narcissus tighter and unleashed the seething darkness in herself. The magic was a rush of danger, like driving too fast, or drinking too much, and kissing dangerously bad men. It was power and shadows and dreams and death. It sucked the life right out of the flower and turned it to ashes.

It was this side of her magic that scared the shit out of Demeter and made her especially careful of Hades. Death was his domain, and all its magic belonged to him.

Demeter was not the kind of goddess to share, especially not her daughter, with a god that was in turns business partner and rival.

Persephone unclenched her hand, carefully turned on the taps and washed the sooty mess down the sink.

Her heart was pounding, and like the seeds, she allowed herself to dwell on the memory she kept hidden at all times. She had never seen a photo of Hades Acheron. He was more careful of the cameras than she was even with the glamour that Demeter had cast over her.

That was why she had no idea who it was that she had tangled with until it was too late.

Persephone had seen him sitting at the bar across the club, her magic and lady parts snapping to attention. Neither had played up that badly at the sight of a man before, so she knew he had to be dangerous. She was in a reckless mood.

Her mother had put so much pressure on her to be perfect for her first meeting with Hades that, when the bastard hadn't shown, Persephone was pissed.

The sight of his back in that white shirt had dragged her straight across the dance floor. It didn't take her long to realize the rest of him was just as pleasing. Dark hair styled in a classically perfect short back and sides cut with a sprinkling of grey at the temples, silvery grey eyes, and cheekbones for days.

Persephone thought all her Christmas's had come at once.

Persephone walked into the warm pool, letting the water soothe the heat that had begun to build inside of her.

The pool was always the safest place to think about the way making out with Hades had made her feel. She should have known something was wrong as soon as her lips had pressed against his beautiful, cruel mouth.

She thought she was going to have fun with a hot guy, and then she had felt something shift inside of her. It was like all the ichor in her veins had heated, both sides of her magic rushing in a haywire burn of life and death and sex and murder.

It was as if all her darker impulses and desires had come to the surface, and she forgot all about her mother's careful years of training.

The way Hades had kissed her had made every other kiss before it seem…lifeless. He had made her come so hard her body had ached afterward. It had rocked her, and she wanted more.

If his bodyguard hadn't broken them up, Persephone knew she would've fucked Hades senseless right on that couch, even if it damned her soul and dignity in the process.

But Simon *had* broken them up, and Persephone's world had frozen from the moment she heard the words 'Lord Hades' come out his mouth.

Hades had seemed just as frustrated and embarrassed by the interruption as Persephone was. He had also seen the fear in her expression, just as she had seen the sadness and regret in his as he had bent to kiss her wrist.

Persephone had a long six years to regret walking out of that room before Hades came back. It was that feral part of her that had left her glove arranged in the one fingered salute just to make him furious.

Persephone had run, literally, from the club and had gone seven blocks before she dove into a cab and got back home before the Lord of Styx could catch a glimpse of her.

Six years was a long time to avoid a business partner, but Persephone had succeeded.

After that night, she'd settled into the role of her mother's heir. She'd stopped her secret rebellions.

She'd done everything she could to forget about Hades Acheron, even as she made sure that the next time they met across a Board room table, she'd be able to hold her own against him and make sure he'd second guess outing her to her mother.

It was embarrassing that every time she ended up oddly disappointed and relieved as she stared at a name card and an empty seat.

Persephone felt the pressure inside of her build up again, so she slipped under the water.

An hour later, after she had done so many laps her shoulders ached, Persephone was feeling almost back to normal.

Using her magic on the seed had been enough to calm it, and her mood, down.

She might even sleep that night without dreaming of Hades fucking her brains out.

Persephone wrapped a thick towel robe over her swimsuit and cut back through the gardens towards her side of the house.

As she closed her hand over her bedroom's doorknob, something pricked her sharply in the neck, and she was unconscious before she hit the wet grass.

3

It was long past midnight in Styx when Hades was informed that his package had arrived at his villa.

Hades had taken Asterion's advice into consideration, but it was Ariadne's he'd chosen to follow.

Demeter's daughter had been her heir and right hand for years; any dirty dealings Demeter had with Pithos would soon come to light, and he would deal with treachery wherever he found it.

Hades had given special instruction that she wasn't to be harmed more than was unavoidable to extract her.

Hades smiled at the thought of the tantrum Demeter would have when she realized her security hadn't been able to stop him from taking what was most precious to her.

Hades left his tower in Styx before dawn, the roar of his Lamborghini drowning out the endless numbers and noise in his mind as he raced along the coast to his beach villa.

After Medusa had revealed all the ways money was being skimmed from Demeter's companies, he had ordered her to go through all of theirs in case of leaks. It was a tiresome job for his forensic accountants, but Hades had enough of Pithos and their games, and any lead was a good lead.

Hades had placed one hand made leather shoe onto the gravel of his driveway when he smelled it...the strange spring smell of the woman from Athens. He looked about at the flowers in the villa's perfectly manicured gardens but couldn't find its source.

You are tired, and your mind always fucks with you when you haven't rested, Hades reminded himself. He didn't always need sleep, he often went days without it, and at that moment he couldn't remember the last time he'd gone to bed. *Well, there you have it.*

Hades dropped his jacket over the back of a couch and his keys into a bowl when a door opened behind him.

"Good morning, sire," said Charon from his place at the kitchen counter.

"How is our guest?" asked Hades, loosening his tie.

"She's awake and very pissed off. There's quite a mouth on her for a posh girl." Charon's smile was as sharp as a blade. "I like it."

"It's probably the first time she hasn't been in control and is taking it poorly."

Hades knew how easily Demeter sulked when she didn't get her way, no doubt her daughter would be the same.

Hades was in the kitchen when strange magic rippled through the house. It was the power of green, growing things, sunlight on streams, and as sweet as ripe peaches.

"Where are they keeping her?" Hades demanded.

"One of the cells beneath us. Why?" replied Charon.

"Something is wrong. I can feel magic that's not mine." Hades pushed open the door to the stairwell, too impatient to wait for an elevator.

"If she's a demigoddess, she's bound to have some abilities," said Charon.

"But nobody knows what those abilities are?"

"Demeter's forced her to live like a nun to make sure no one could have the chance to find out. Believe me, I searched for a clue and couldn't even come up with a decent photo."

"Demeter is too smart for that." Hades opened the metal fire door that led into the row of cells. Why he needed them, his men had never asked, they only knew he used them from time to time.

Hades's steps froze as he looked into the cell's two-way mirror. His prisoner was still hooded, wearing a dirty bathrobe and was cuffed to a wooden chair that had sprung to life.

Roots and branches had grown out from the legs and were whipping about at the guards Demeter's daughter couldn't see but knew were there.

"It appears she has a knack for nature," murmured Hades.

"You good for nothing fuckers better uncuff me or I'm going to let my branches give you an enema you'll never forget!" a woman's voice shouted, and something in Hades stilled.

It couldn't be...

Hades opened the cell door, grabbed one of the branches, and gripped it tight. It blackened like it had been burned, and the stain spread, branches turning to ash as the writhing beast died back into a deformed chair.

His prisoner had stopped struggling and cursing and had gone still, her shoulder's hunching tight like she expected him to hit her. His heart was racing as he reached out for the black hood.

A chaotic mess of honey hair and furious green eyes appeared. She all but vibrated with leashed magic.

"Hello, sunshine," he said, trying his best to keep his cool demeaner.

"How's it hanging, Hades?" Persephone smiled in a way that promised violence. "You know, Demeter has always said you were the smartest god of them all, but taking me is the stupidest fucking thing you've ever done."

Hades heard his men all inhale in shock and fear. None of them would have the stones to talk to him in such a manner.

"Charon? Please get Lady Persephone a new chair, steel this time," Hades instructed, and the rest of his guards left the cell as fast as they could.

Persephone glowered up at him. She had no fear of him whatsoever. He would have to change that.

"What do you want?" she asked.

"Oh, so many things," he said softly, his eyes taking in the curve of her lips. This fucking woman had haunted him for six years. He had a list of things he'd thought about doing to her as repayment for messing with him, and it was *long*.

"You kidnapped me for a date, old man? You could've sent a text like everyone else," Persephone mocked.

"I don't want a date. I want answers about some of your mother's efforts to screw me over." Hades thought he saw a flash of disappointment in her eyes, but he must have imagined it. She had run that night, not the other way around.

"Demeter would never try to screw you over, she's too afraid of you." Persephone started to laugh, it was tired and a little crazy.

"What's so funny, sunshine?"

"This." She waved one finger around, encompassing the destroyed room and them in it. "*This* is hilarious because Demeter has done everything in her considerable power to ensure I didn't end up in this exact spot."

"If memory serves, you sought me out first." Hades smiled, and she looked away.

"It wasn't like I knew it was you," she muttered.

"Why does Demeter want to keep you away from me? What interest would I have in a pampered baby demigoddess with an attitude problem?"

The barb seemed to strike home, but instead of breaking her, it made something harden in her spring eyes.

"Maybe because she didn't want to subject me to a giant asshole with no manners."

Hades chuckled darkly. "What do I care about manners? I'm not one of the coddled rich boys that would fall at your socialite feet or a golden boy of old Olympus that your mother admired so greatly. Your insults are childish, and the only effect they have is to keep you chained to that chair longer than you need to be. You've had a rough night, little princess, I'll give you a few days to cool off and then we will try again."

Hades turned on his heel and reached for the cell door.

"No manners *and* a lousy kisser," muttered Persephone. He pretended not to hear her even if he longed to turn around and prove her wrong.

"What orders, boss?" asked Charon once the door was securely locked. Hades didn't look back at the prisoner.

"We let her stew. Keep her hydrated," he said and then headed back upstairs so they wouldn't see the fury and longing raging inside of him.

Four days later, Hades still hadn't gone back to the woman in the cells, but he'd watched her from the cameras.

The first day, she sat on the narrow bed and stared at the wall.

The second day, she threatened whoever she saw.

By the third day, she began to flirt with them, causing Hades to become so furious, he punched his computer monitor.

Her comments about his kissing skills still smarted, and even though he hadn't left his villa in days, he hadn't felt a moment of restfulness.

In fact, he was more irritable than ever, and he blamed it all on the demigoddess in his basement.

Hades had watched the news, but he saw no mention of the Princess of Athens being kidnapped, only that they had suffered a minor earthquake the night he took her.

Goddess throwing a tantrum. Demeter was smart to keep it quiet, and she wasn't desperate enough to reach out to Hades yet.

By the afternoon of day four, Persephone looked so defeated and bored that Hades felt the stirrings of pity. She might tell him what he wanted to know for a decent meal and a shower.

At nightfall, when his power was strongest, Hades dismissed the guards and entered her cell. She sat up on her bed and stared silently at him.

Despite not having a shower, she had made use of the small sink to clean herself up and braid her snarled hair. She looked less like a vengeful naiad and more like the woman he first met.

"Are you hungry?" he asked, placing a plate on the steel table. Persephone held up her cuffed hands and didn't reply. "Have a seat and let's talk." He pulled out a chair for her, waiting until she had sat down. "Pick a hand to eat with, because you only get one."

Persephone waved her left hand at him, and he fastened the right one down to the arm of the chair before unlocking the left.

She shook out her wrist, and he slid over the plate with the ham and salad sandwich on it.

"How do I know it's not poisoned?" she asked sceptically.

Hades picked up one half and bit into it. "No one is trying to poison you, sunshine. Believe me, I made this sandwich myself. Better make up your mind quickly or I'll keep eating it."

Persephone picked up the other half. "You cut off my crusts?"

Hades looked down at the plate. "I suppose I did. I don't like them, so I just...never mind, eat the fucking sandwich."

Her eyes sparkled in amusement as she bit into it. She made an unexpectedly happy sound as she chewed, and he felt guilty that he hadn't fed her properly in days.

"What's wrong with it?" he asked.

"Nothing, it's just...I haven't had real bread and cheese for six years," Persephone said around a mouthful.

"Why ever not?"

"Where do I start? Bread is full of carbs and gluten, and cheese is dairy, which is very fattening, not to mention the butter you put on it."

Hades frowned. "That is the stupidest thing I've ever heard."

"Tell me about it."

"Why do it then?"

"Demeter thinks a no-carb, no sugar, caffeine, and gluten-free diet keeps my magic behaving itself," Persephone admitted, starting on the other half.

"And does it?"

"Not really."

"Then why deny yourself?"

Persephone shrugged. "Makes her happy, I guess."

Hades didn't like that excuse; he liked the idea of Demeter starving her daughter for such stupid reasons even less.

"What do you want with me, Hades?"

"I want to know if your mother has dealings with a group called Pithos."

"She has dealings with lots of people. Why not call her and ask her?" Persephone said.

"They aren't the kind of group that you'd admit to having associations with."

"Why? They mafia or something?"

"Something like that," Hades said, watching as she licked some stray butter from her thumb.

"Again, why take me? You should just ask her. Demeter is afraid of you like I said. What have these guys done to annoy you?"

"They are fucking with my people and my business, and all the leads I've followed have taken me straight to Morning Harvest," Hades said, trying to keep his voice steady. Persephone swallowed hard.

"That doesn't make any sense," she said with a shake of her head.

"It does to me. Money trails don't lie, and Demeter has wanted to take over my shipping routes for years. I've taken you because if anyone knows what Demeter is up to, it's you."

"I can't deny that, but she wouldn't need to hire thugs like Pithos to do it. She's certainly not dumb enough to tangle with you."

"So you say. You can understand why I'm reluctant to believe you." Hades narrowed his eyes as he studied her. Maybe a kinder touch would loosen her tongue. He didn't know what she knew, but it was *something*.

There had been a flash of recognition in her eyes when he'd mentioned the word Pithos.

"Look, Hades, I wouldn't lie to you about something like this. Maybe you need to talk to Demeter about money going missing."

"What *would* you lie to me about?" he interrupted.

"What?"

"You said you wouldn't lie to me about this. That implies you would lie about other things."

Persephone's brows drew together. "A girl has to have her mysteries."

"I'd like to know the mystery of how Demeter's protected daughter managed to escape from her prison on Lycabettus Hill, so she could go dancing and kissing strange men," said Hades.

Persephone smiled. "I would like a bath and a proper bed to sleep in."

"You seek to bargain with me, girl?"

"Seems only fair."

Hades folded his arms. "And I suppose you think it will make me drop my guard so you can escape."

"Do I look stupid to you? I know I won't be able to leave this place without your blessing. These human guards are all for show. Your power protects this place, so I'm stuck behind its boundaries until you let me go," Persephone said with an exasperated groan.

Hades had to admit, he was impressed that she had felt them.

"Even though you can't escape, do you promise to behave yourself if I agree to this bargain? I treat you like a guest, and you answer my questions?" asked Hades.

"On my honor as a goddess, I swear to answer your questions, if in return, you uphold the sacred hospitality laws of *xenia*."

"Done." Hades held out his hand to shake on it, but she shrank back.

"I won't bite," he lied.

"But I might," Persephone said, staring at his outstretched hand. "You saw what my magic did to the chair. I don't want to hurt you."

"You didn't seem to mind touching me that night in Athens."

"I was wearing my gloves," she said as her cheeks reddened.

"Don't be ridiculous. Give me your hand," Hades demanded. She glared as she held it out.

Hades's hand swallowed hers, and he felt the wild creation burning under her skin. He could tell she was doing her best to keep it under control, so he shook it once and let it go.

"We have a deal," he said in triumph.

Persephone had just made the stupidest mistake of her life.

4

Hades had just made the stupidest mistake of his life. Persephone kept her head down as she followed him out of the cell so he wouldn't see the smile on her face.

Hades would now have to treat her as an honored guest with every courtesy, while she had the opportunity to find the edges of his barriers and use her magic to break out of them.

He didn't know about her right hand, and she needed to escape before he had enough time to figure it out.

When Hades appeared in her cell that evening, she had expected threats and perhaps even some torture.

What she hadn't expected was a sandwich with her crusts cut off. It could have been a tactic to mess with her head, but she had been too hungry to care.

From the stories she had heard, Persephone expected him to break into her mind and rip all of her secrets out of her.

His silver eyes were brimming with questions, she could feel his curiosity and frustration, but he managed to keep his temper. She didn't know what to make of any of it.

"I don't suppose your girlfriend has any clothes I could borrow?" Persephone asked as they rode up in the elevator.

"I don't have a girlfriend," Hades replied coolly.

"Really? Not even like a fuck buddy that left anything behind?"

"No."

"Huh." *Never would've guessed that.* Persephone imagined he would have at least one on call. Most CEO's she knew did.

Hades arched a dark brow. "That surprises you?"

"A little bit."

"And do you have..." he struggled to say the words. "Fuck buddies, ready and waiting for whenever you need them?"

Persephone faced the steel doors, willing them to open. "That's none of your business, Acheron."

"We'll see," he whispered, so low she almost missed it.

"Does that mean you *don't* have any clothes I could borrow?" she asked, not liking his judgemental tone one bit.

"I'll find something you can wear for tonight, and I'll have one of my people bring you something suitable from Styx tomorrow," Hades said as the doors slid open.

The polished marble floor was so spotless Persephone hesitated to step on it with her grubby feet. Then she remembered she was a prisoner and walked over it, hoping she left marks wherever she went.

Persephone had grown up in a house of washed-out pastels and muted golds that were feminine and favored by Demeter.

Hades's villa was almost jarringly masculine with its jewel blues, deep reds, and black accents.

The art on the walls were abstract or impressionism, and Persephone wanted to take her time to study them. Then the hallways opened to a panoramic view of the sea.

"Oh, wow," she breathed.

"Don't even think of jumping off the deck and swimming away. The barriers stretch through the waters too, and you'll drown before you get through them," warned Hades.

"It's not that. I haven't been out of Athens city in ages, and I've missed the ocean," Persephone admitted, resisting the urge to run outside and look at waves crashing underneath them.

"Demeter really did keep you on a tight leash, didn't she?" Hades shook his head in disapproval.

"She did her best," she replied diplomatically. "Your home is very beautiful."

"You seem surprised."

"I am. Take it as a compliment, Acheron. I see a lot of nice homes, and for one to stand out enough for me to notice is an accomplishment."

Hades put his hands in his pockets, his expression genuinely curious. "Can I ask why it stands out?"

"It's very...you. Does that make sense? Many of the houses I see, you can tell that a decorator has made everything just so to show off the owner's wealth. I get the feeling you picked out every painting and piece of furniture yourself simply because you liked it."

"Of course, I did. This is my private residence, so I didn't want it to feel like an office building." Hades tilted his head, studying her. "I get the impression that your rooms wouldn't be as pastel as the rest of Demeter's palace."

"You will never know," Persephone said sweetly. Hades looked as if he would reply when they were interrupted by a deep bark echoing through the villa.

"You have a dog?" asked Persephone.

"Yes. He's another reason you should be cautious about trying to get out of the grounds. He patrols them and likes to bite."

"Puppy!" Persephone squealed in excitement as a huge dog that looked like a mastiff had been crossed with Doberman trotted into the room. The dog froze as it studied her with sharp amber eyes.

"Come on, you big baby, I won't hurt you," she crooned at it and held out her hands for it to smell them. "Oh, look how handsome you are. Such a big, proud puppy." The dog edged forward, its tail starting to wag as it licked her fingers.

"Baby boy, you're so cute, but what's this? Your Daddy has put a glamour on you! Why would he be such a meanie face?" Persephone felt the magical threads of the glamour and gave it a sharp pull.

"Did you just call me a meanie face?" Hades asked incredulously.

The air around the dog's head shimmered, and another two heads appeared, all wearing the same happy smiles.

"Woah! Triple heads mean triple the pats. Come here, baby, you must be so itchy from that binding." Persephone cast an accusing glare over her shoulder at Hades. He looked completely gobsmacked, which pleased her immensely.

"You know animals don't like glamors? Do you, baby? What's your name, it better be something noble."

"Cerberus," Hades said, clearing his throat. "He is a terrifying guard dog."

"*Sure*, he is. Cerberus...you seriously named this glorious creature Spot?" Persephone demanded as her brain caught up on the Ancient Greek. Hades pointed to the patch of gold near the dog's tail. Persephone laughed and scratched it. "That's so lame. Why do you glamour him? Oh, I can feel another one."

"Don't pull it off," Hades commanded, making woman and dog freeze. "He's...very big in his true form. The other glamour on the heads was so he didn't frighten the humans more than necessary."

Persephone turned back to trying to pat three happy dog heads at once. "Peoples are frightened of you? They are so silly. You're just a softie, aren't you? You're not scary at all."

"Stop talking to him like that. You're embarrassing him," Hades said awkwardly. "I really should show you to your room."

"Come and find me later, cutie, when Daddy's not around to pout," whispered Persephone, getting in one more pat before turning back to Hades.

His eyes narrowed as he stared down at Cerberus. "Do you know what I do to traitors?" Cerberus gave him three goofy smiles, and Persephone sniggered.

Hades steered her towards another hallway, and she grinned when Cerberus followed. "The guest rooms are this way. So, you like dogs."

"Love them. Demeter can't handle their hair or the thought of them chewing her furniture, so I was never allowed to have one."

"It doesn't sound like you were allowed to do much at all. How you haven't gone mad or run away, I'll never guess."

"You could try, and never come close," Persephone said, thinking of her stash of seeds.

Hades opened the door to a suite of rooms with its own bathroom and thank the gods, a deep bathtub. "Can I trust you to stay here for a moment while I get you something to wear?"

"I guess you'll find out," Persephone replied as she pulled back a dark blue curtain and sighed at the view.

Persephone was filling the tub when he reappeared at her bedroom door with a black robe and a folded t-shirt.

"These should do for you to sleep in. I should've thought about this earlier," he said, offering them to her.

"They'll do. I'm going to be happy to be clean, and I don't need underwear because I don't sleep in them. Goodnight, Hades," Persephone said and closed the door on his confused expression.

Neck deep in steaming hot water, Persephone reflected that it was perhaps not the politest way to say good evening to her host.

She might be trying to be civil instead of downright hostile, but she wasn't about to forget he had kidnapped her and was now holding her hostage.

Maybe you should tell him what you know about Pithos and go home, the reasonable part of her said.

If what he said about money being stolen from Morning Harvest to fund Pithos was true...saints above, she could barely comprehend the thought.

There was no way Demeter would knowingly give money to people that were trying to start a war with Hades. They would have to be insane to try to mess with him.

Persephone knew she was more sensitive to his aura and magic than the average human, but holy gods, he *radiated* power.

Even with that stinking black hood over her eyes, she'd known Hades was there the moment he opened her cell door.

His magic had touched the branch of the chair, and everything inside of her had stilled under the stroke of his magic. It had radiated through her and made her want to fall on her knees in front of him.

Demeter was an old god, and her magic felt like a drop in a bucket compared to Hades's power. Her right hand had yearned to reach out to touch the ashes of the dead branches, just to feel the fading echoes of it.

"Pull yourself together, he's not that impressive," she huffed at the mounds of bubbles floating in front of her.

Persephone knew they would eventually meet again, and he'd recognize her. She thought he would make a bigger deal out of it than he did.

He had been into it that night just as much she had, and yet she couldn't pretend the way he'd called her a baby demigoddess didn't get to her. Like she was some dumb little girl and not a woman who could hold her own with the most powerful men in the world.

You shouldn't even care.

Persephone slid under the bubbles, holding her breath for as long as she could to take her mind off her wounded pride.

She had bigger things to worry about, like Pithos rearing their ugly heads. If they were after Hades and his Court, all magical beings, did that put her at risk from them too?

Enemy of my enemy is my friend.

Persephone washed her hair twice and contemplated the whole mess she found herself in. She was too tired to decide whether or not she could trust Hades with what she knew about Pithos.

She pulled the soft t-shirt over her head, stubbornly ignoring the ghost of his aftershave that was caught in the cotton and wrapped her hair in a towel.

She climbed into the massive bed that was almost too soft after her days on a narrow mattress and finally switched off the light.

You're in the house of Hades. You should be afraid to go to sleep.

Weirdly enough, she wasn't. There was something about the crusts cut off her sandwich and the fact he'd been very careful not to touch her since he'd uncuffed her hands that reassured her that she was in no immediate danger.

In any case, Hades had also been clear what he thought about her. Remembering how she had daydreamed about their encounter in the club over the years made her cringe with embarrassment.

She was about to shove her head under the pillow to hide her residual shame when she saw shadows flickering outside of her door.

They seemed to hesitate for a long, heart-pounding moment before finally moving on.

With a groan, she pulled the covers over her head and was asleep within minutes.

5

"You know, I've always suspected you'd lost your mind over the years, but now I *know* you are fucking insane." Medusa was glaring at Hades from the laptop screen.

"This from the woman who not only falls in love with the man who stole from her, but starts to play family with him. Who's really the insane one here?"

"No, it's still you. You. Stole. Demeter's. Daughter. You know that unnatural earthquake in Athens was her! People could've been killed. I thought I told you not to do anything rash until we had more information?"

"You did. Then I talked to Ariadne after you, and she said to take Persephone for questioning, and I liked her idea better."

"Ariadne is an ex-assassin and a psychopath who doesn't think like a rational person. You don't ever take her advice over mine! You don't steal people because you want to. You're not fucking Zeus."

"Low blow, Medusa. I'll have you know Persephone isn't my prisoner, as such. I've got her under *xenia*, and she's going to answer my questions. If I'm happy with the answers, I'll send her home to Demeter," said Hades calmly. Two of Medusa's snakes slid out from her curls and hissed.

"It doesn't matter how you spin it, Hades. You kidnapped her. You're a fool if you think she's not going to want payback for that, let alone what Demeter will do to you," said Medusa sadly.

"I told you I'll get answers about Pithos by any means at my disposal, and that's what I've done." Hades fidgeted uncomfortably in his chair. "There's something else."

"Are you serious? Is it worse than what you just told me?" she demanded.

"Yes."

"Well? Spit it out. I need to be filming in twenty minutes."

"She's the girl."

Medusa froze and lifted the screen close to her face. "*What* girl."

"The girl I met...in Athens."

"The one that ran out on you and left you high and dry like a chump six years ago? The actual reason you hate Athens so much is now staying under your roof?"

Hades rolled his eyes. "I knew I shouldn't have told you or the triplets."

"I couldn't find a trace of her when you asked me to look. *Me*. It makes sense that she was glamored from her image being captured." Medusa lifted a red brow. "I suppose this makes things more complicated."

Hades's uncomfortable feeling chilled instantly. "Absolutely not. She's still my prisoner - under my protection – however you want to spin it! I need information from her and then our business is done. She can go home, and I can slaughter Pithos from the face of the earth."

Medusa chuckled deep and dirty. "If you say so, darling. I'll let you know if Demeter calls me to vent her fury."

"Stall her if you can. I'll only need a day or two, and then Persephone will be back home," Hades told her.

"Uh-huh. Good luck with that." Medusa cut off the call, leaving Hades even more disgruntled.

Feminine laughter echoed through the house, and his curiosity pricked up. It was such an alien sound to hear.

Persephone wasn't going to be a sulker, and Hades liked that. He got out of his office chair and went to find out what was going on to make her laugh so loudly.

"Oh, my god, it's so hard!" Persephone said, making Hades freeze.

"Of course, it is, doll," Charon replied.

"Can you show me again? Slower this time, I need to study it."

Charon's laughter was warm and husky. "All right, but we need to be quick before the boss comes out."

Hades's vision swam red and charged into the kitchen, ready to eviscerate the titan.

Persephone let out of a startled yelp, and the coin she was balancing on her knuckles pinged to the marble countertop.

"Good morning, boss, you feeling okay?" asked Charon, sensitive to Hades's fury.

"Yes. I didn't mean to startle you. What's all this?" Hades asked, forcing his voice into neutrality.

"Charon has been teaching me coin tricks," Persephone said, snatching the coin up again. "I had to do something to keep myself amused even though I'm bloody awful at them."

"It's just practice, doll, you'll get it," Charon said, plucking one from behind her ear and making her laugh in delight.

Persephone was wearing Hades's black satin robe, and for some unfathomable reason, he couldn't stop staring at it. It swam on her, but she looked perfectly at ease, perched on a barstool, her waves of honey hair over one shoulder, and with a coffee steaming at her elbow.

Cerberus was lying under her chair, staring up at her with big besotted eyes, and Hades scowled at him. Charon gave Persephone a rare smile, but then he caught the look in Hades's eyes, and it disappeared.

"It was nice to meet you, Persephone, but duty calls."

"Thank you for the clothes," she said, her keen gaze going from Hades to Charon. "I didn't want to wear *his* for much longer, and I'm sure your taste is better anyway." She offered Charon his coin back, but he shook his head.

"Keep it to practice with. I'll come back and check your progress," he said. Hades raised a black brow at him.

Charon, his ruthless fucking ferryman, never *ever* gave any of his coins away.

"Good to know one person of the Court is a sweetheart."

"We aren't that bad, but I'm definitely the sweetest."

Persephone battered her long lashes at him. "No doubt. I'll see you soon, Charon," she said.

"Looking forward to it, princess."

Persephone picked up the bags from the couch and walked past Hades with a small sarcastic smile on her face, Cerberus following faithfully at her heels as she went back to her room.

"She's quite charming when she's not making furniture come alive," Charon said. "You guys have come to an agreement, I see."

"I bound her with the laws of *xenia*," Hades replied.

"Good one. Lots of loopholes and she won't think she's a prisoner when she is. I'm quite sure I got her measurements right, a hell of a body on her, though," Charon said, an appreciative grin on his face.

"Focus. Persephone is Demeter's daughter after all and is bound to be treacherous," Hades replied. "We need her to give up what she knows on Pithos, and then we'll ship her back to Athens."

"She's got plenty of pluck and power, I'll give her that. There's something about her that makes me feel all excitable," said Charon, and his dark eyes glinted.

"You want me to work on her and get some of those secrets out with a bit of honey? I'd be more than happy to seduce her for our cause."

"Charon, she's the girl I met in the club in Athens," Hades admitted, even though he was embarrassed to do it.

Charon choked on his coffee. "You've got to be fucking kidding me. I wondered why you looked like you were going to go nuclear when you came in." He paled slightly. "I didn't mean anything by it...we were just talking, Hades."

"I know. It's fine."

"Yeah, I don't think it is. I know how hard you looked for her. I'll make sure everyone knows she's off-limits, especially Erebus," said Charon.

"She's her own woman, so if she wants to give men her attention, who am I to say otherwise. I've learned my lesson," Hades replied irritably.

He knew she lied about the bad kisser comment, but it still irked him. Clearly, he'd thought about that night in a much different way than she did.

Charon didn't look like he believed his nonchalant act for a second.

"So, what are you planning to do with her? You can't babysit her for days," he said.

"Why not? I have an office and can work from here. Until I get a clear understanding of her powers, I don't want to leave her unsupervised, and I'm not comfortable leaving her in my private residence alone. Who knows what she'll get into."

Charon's grin was wicked. "Hopefully, the pool. I didn't get her a swimsuit."

"Very funny. I don't need my men being any more distracted then they already are," Hades replied with a sharp look. "The sooner we get the secrets out of her and back to Athens, the better it will be for all of us."

"Sure. Whatever you say, boss." Charon laughed and grabbed his car keys. "Let me know if the princess needs anything else."

After Charon left, Hades stared a good ten minutes at Persephone's door. He could hear her in the shower, her faint spring smell still lingering in the air.

He wanted to pin her down and force all her secrets out of her. He wanted to put her back in her cell.

He wanted to know why, for the first time in his existence, he had met someone who simultaneously made him furiously angry and impossibly turned on at the same time.

What is it about her?

Hades had mingled with gods, had seen impossibly beautiful women and supernatural creatures in his time. And this fucking *girl* had him twisted up for six years straight.

It was like the Fates were purposely laughing at him because, for the first time, the bitches dared to.

Hades wanted to kill Persephone. He also wanted to kiss her. Oh, he didn't like this feeling one fucking bit.

The laws of *xenia* made sure that he had to provide food and shelter for her. He thought about what Persephone had said about the ridiculous diets that Demeter had her on. She had literally groaned when she had eaten butter.

Maybe Charon was right, and honey, instead of vinegar, was the way to get all those delicious secrets out of her.

6

Persephone turned the page of her book and tried to ignore the rumble in her stomach. She was lying on her bed and watching the sun go down slowly over the ocean. She couldn't remember the last time she'd had such a quiet day.

Demeter had always demanded a certain level of excellence from her daughter, and that meant always having a full daily schedule.

After she had got her clothes from Charon - the man *did* have decent taste - Persephone had taken a shower and had dressed in comfortable jeans and a singlet.

She had stolen a book from one of Hades's bookshelves, after making sure he wasn't around to see her, and had been in her bed ever since.

This could end up being the easiest vacation you've ever had if you play your cards right.

She was hungry, but she was nervous about coming face to face with Hades again.

This is ridiculous because you've wanted to see him again for six whole years.

"Stupid me," Persephone muttered.

When she had gotten up that morning, she had been determined to remain low level hostile towards Hades, and it had all been going perfectly until she had heard him talking with Charon.

Charon had known about Persephone and Hades's encounter at the club in Athens, but that fact wasn't the one that had struck her dumb. It had been Charon saying, "I know how hard you looked for her..."

Hades had wanted her enough to actually *look* for her, and considering the resources at his disposal, Persephone was surprised he hadn't found her.

The tragically stupid thing was that she had been forcing herself to go to all Demeter's dumb parties in the hope of bumping into him...and he had avoided every single one of them.

"Fucking Fates," Persephone muttered, turning the page of her book before realizing she couldn't remember a single thing she had just read.

She was cursing and flicking pages when there was a knock at the door. Persephone froze but managed to say, "Who is it?"

"The big bad wolf, are you decent?" asked Hades, and he opened the door. He seemed a lot more casual than he had that morning. His suit jacket and tie were gone, and he looked the same as he had the night she met him, a slight dishevel around the edges with his white shirt sleeves pushed up to his elbows.

"You didn't wait until I answered, what if I had been naked?" she said, trying to ignore the way parts of her were suddenly excited.

"Then I would have seen you naked. Are you hungry? Or have you evolved so far in your weird dietary habits that you have decided to go straight to starving yourself?" Hades asked.

Persephone was about to sass him when her stomach growled loudly.

"I could eat," she said, putting the book down. Hades read the title.

"Second book is better. Come on then, sunshine, let's get you fed," he said before turning around and walking away.

Persephone took the time to run her fingers through her hair and straighten her singlet and then hated herself for doing it.

What did it matter what she looked like? She was his damn prisoner, not his date.

She yanked on a pair of thin cotton gloves and followed him. She found her way to the kitchen, her stomach growling the more she smelled fresh bread and garlic.

She had expected to find a chef, but instead, she found Hades Acheron, Lord of the Dead, and Bastard of Styx, pulling the lamb out of the oven.

"Now, there's something I never expected to see," Persephone said aloud before she could check herself.

"What?" Hades asked, brows furrowing.

"I thought you'd have a chef. Demeter wouldn't be seen dead in her own kitchen," said Persephone.

"I like cooking, and I don't like more people in my space than I need to have. Besides, having a chef seems like inviting someone to try to poison me," he replied, carving the meat and arranging it on a platter. "Get the door, would you? It's too pleasant a night to eat in here."

Persephone opened the glass door that led out onto the deck, where a table had been lain out with the rest of dinner.

The moon was coming up over the ocean, the breeze warm and gentle. It *was* a beautiful night, but she couldn't believe Hades wasn't trying to play an angle.

"Why are you acting so nice?" she demanded, getting out of his way so he could put the meat down on the table.

"You invoked *xenia*, so you should know that means I need to be hospitable. This is me doing that," Hades said as he pulled out a chair for her.

Persephone lowered herself into it. "I'm pretty sure being hospitable also involves wine."

"Of course," he replied, not rising to her bait at all. He poured her a glass of red wine that was so dark it was almost black. She lifted the glass to her nose and smelled it.

"What is this made of? I can smell smoke and spice and not cherries, but something other than grapes," she said, her mind struggling to identify it.

"It's pomegranates. It's different, but then so are you, so I thought you might enjoy it," Hades replied as he sat down opposite her.

"By different, you mean a baby demigoddess with a bad attitude?" she asked, still sore over the comment.

To shut herself up, she took a mouthful of the wine. It was surprisingly good, sweet, and smooth instead of dry.

"Your attitude isn't the worst I've encountered, and I think we both know that you're no baby."

"Nice to know you noticed," she replied.

"I had a thorough education when we first met," Hades said, and she almost sucked wine up her nose.

"To be fair, I didn't know who you were. Otherwise, I wouldn't have been so forward." Persephone reached for a pair of tongs so she wouldn't get her gloves dirty. She needed to put food in her mouth, so she stopped putting her foot in it.

"Here, allow me." Hades took the tongs from where she was struggling to grip them and started serving her. "Why are you even wearing those?"

"Because I don't want to make this cutlery come to life accidentally," Persephone said, picking up her fork by its sleek wood handle.

"It's really that bad? I thought Demeter would have trained you to have better control over your power. She seems so keen to control everything else about you."

Hades had a definite *tone* whenever he talked about her mother, and while Persephone couldn't blame him, she also thought it a bit strange that he would care.

"She trained me a little, but she wanted me to be as human as I could be, so I don't really use it except for a stress release. When I am pent up, it kind of leaks out unexpectedly, so she got me wearing the gloves," Persephone explained before trying out the lamb. Like the wine, it was surprisingly good.

"What do you do as a stress release?" Hades asked. It was an innocent enough question, but there was a glint in his eye that made her shift uncomfortably in her chair.

"I grow things," she replied. *And then I kill them slowly.*

"Show me," Hades said. She must have looked incredulous because he added, "Please?"

It was the please that got her. She took a whole olive from her salad and slid off her left glove as she chewed off the olive's exterior. She took the seed carefully from her mouth and held it in her palm.

She hadn't had anyone watch her do her seed trick in a long time, and Hades was studying her with an intensity that made her sweat.

She let out a breath and gently released the smallest amount of her power. It rushed heady and rich through her veins, and her heart began to race as the seed cracked, and a green shoot rose out of it.

She let it grow until it spurted roots, and then she held it out to him. His fingers gently brushed hers as he took it.

"Nicely done," Hades said.

"I showed you mine," Persephone replied with a pointed look at the seed. She thought Hades would say no, but after a moment of considering, his mouth curled up slightly.

Then she felt it, a rolling lick of shadows and darkness and all of the things done in it. Her mouth went dry, and she struggled to keep her eyes on the seedling as it slowly withered before turning to ash.

A thought niggled at her, but she killed it before it had a chance to grow.

"Satisfied?" he asked, brushing the ash away.

Not for six years, Persephone thought but said, "For now."

It took until her third glass of the lovely wine before Hades decided to bring up Pithos.

"Why don't you tell me what you know of Pithos, sunshine?" he asked.

"Why don't you tell *me* why you want to know so badly?" she replied, deciding the third glass was probably a mistake.

"Look, I'm not trying to find out what you know to start a war with your mother, but I do know that Morning Harvest has been funding them whether she's supporting it or not," Hades said.

"Do you have any actual proof to back up that claim?"

"I do," Hades replied, before going back inside.

Persephone really didn't want to talk about Pithos, because it would mean talking about the worst night of her life and she was going to need a hell of a lot more wine.

Hades was back within moments and placed a wad of papers next to her. They were financial reports. Persephone skimmed through the first few pages.

"How did you get these?"

"Medusa is friends with a very competent hacker," Hades said.

"What? Surprised by honesty? You don't seem to understand how badly I want these bastards."

"While we are honest, you want to tell me what they did to you?" she asked.

She wanted to buy time, but she was also interested to see how much Hades would tell her. She had wanted more information on them for years.

"Fine. This is the whole truth..." and Hades told her everything. About Asterion being murdered and Ariadne being tortured, and a cage that stole Asterion's power.

Persephone had known about Serpentine taking over ARGOS but hearing about some of the horrors that Acrisius had hiding in his basement made her stomach churn.

"They are going after anyone that's like us, Persephone. That means it's only a matter of time before they get to you. Your company is funding them to go after my Court, and that's why I took you. It really has nothing to do with making a move to take over Morning Harvest or because of what happened between us in Athens. That night, I had been drinking a lot, you are a beautiful woman, and so it happened. I didn't know who you were either, though I should think that was obvious. There is no hidden motivation. I want your information, and then you can leave," Hades finished, his silver eyes so serious they were almost grey.

"You're worried about them, aren't you?" Persephone said.

"Of course, I am worried about them. The Court is my family. It took me this long to get one I actually like, and I'll do anything to protect them, including throwing you in my jail downstairs," Hades replied. "I like to think we are past that."

Persephone leaned back in her chair and considered the god in front of her. There was an earnestness burning under his calm tone, and she realized how much he was holding himself back out of politeness.

The wind had ruffled his dark hair making him seem a little less intimidating and much more real and utterly sincere.

Maybe you can trust him just a little bit. Cerberus's head bumped against her lap and patted him, resisting the urge to remove the glamour back on him. She let out a deep sigh.

"Okay, I'll tell you what I know. It's not much, so I don't know if it will help. I'd like to go through these banking records, but I can *guarantee* there's no way my mother knows about the money going to Pithos," Persephone said.

"How can you be so sure?"

"Because Pithos killed my father," Persephone replied. "I'm going to need more wine to tell you this."

Hades opened another label free dark bottle and refilled her glass. "I thought your father was killed in a mugging."

Persephone had a large mouthful of her wine. "It *was* a mugging, but it's my fault he's dead."

She should've known better than to think Hades would gasp at that, but she didn't expect his gaze to soften either, and it did, and for some reason that made her heart hurt more.

"Do you want to tell me about it?"

"Not really. I'm going to, though." She held up a one minute finger before draining her glass. It pushed her into feeling sufficiently buzzed and numb. "Okay, so you remember the night we met in Athens?"

"Unforgettable," Hades said, refilling her glass.

"I used to have nights like that to blow off steam. You've met Demeter. She's so perfect *all the time*, so you can imagine what it's like trying to live up to that when you're short and dumpy with weird powers she doesn't understand. I used to sneak out every couple of months. I'd hit the town, do stupid things like drink in dodgy places and get tattoos. It was on one of those nights that my Dad found out where I went and came after me."

Persephone knew she shouldn't have another mouthful of wine, but she did, and it tasted of tears.

"He found me in a club and dragged me out of there. I was drunk and petulant and had enough of my mother's shit. Dad knew how she could get. While we were arguing, men appeared in the street. They weren't some wannabe thugs. They were in suits, and my Dad recognized one of them. He told them that he didn't want to be a part of their Pithos cult, that he wouldn't support what they were planning. One of the guys held up a gun and pointed it at me. Dad stepped in the way and got the bullet that was meant for me. He told me to run, and...and I did."

Persephone drained her wine again, hoping Hades wouldn't detect the parts she was leaving out. It was *mostly* true and that's what mattered.

"Mom blamed me, as was her right. After the funeral, I tried to discover what I could about Pithos, and when she found out, she went mental enough to scare me into dropping it. I've kept an ear out since but haven't really come across anything else. I did my best to behave and not sneak out after that, but I needed the escape too badly because I wasn't allowed to use my magic."

"That's what you were doing that night in the club," Hades said slowly.

"Yeah, I had been groomed up to be presented to Mom's special friends that night like some prized pig. She had spent months and months training me so she could prove to everyone that her perfect daughter was just as perfectly perfect as her and that I was untouchable, and you didn't even bother showing up."

Persephone laughed drunkenly and got to her feet to pace. She felt the rant bubbling up out of her, and she couldn't stop it.

"And then I was so mad that Lord High and Terrible didn't show, I blew that party and found you anyway and almost fucked your brains out. Fucking Fates. Fucking parties. Fucking...*you*. Demeter spent my whole life keeping me away from everyone, but *especially* from you. Then I find you and put my tongue in your mouth, and you fucking disappeared for six years."

"You disappeared first," Hades said, very quietly.

Persephone made a sound of exasperation, and she swayed unsteadily.

"You would've done the same if you had known who I was. I probably did us both a favor."

"Whatever you need to tell yourself," Hades said, getting out of his chair.

Persephone forgot how tall he was and staggered backward. His hand shot out and caught her before she could fall.

"I've had too much to drink," she mumbled and then slumped forward into him. She had forgotten how good he smelled. She had *failed* to forget the feel of his chest against her and hated that it was still just as nice.

"It's okay, sunshine girl, let's get you to bed," he whispered in a voice of night and dark dreams.

Persephone didn't fight him as he gently picked her up and carried back through the house. He placed her gently in her bed and pulled a blanket over her.

"Why did Demeter want to keep you away from me most of all?" Hades whispered in her ear.

Persephone reached up and touched his hair with her gloved hands, finding yet another way to resent the stupid things.

"Because you're dark and beautiful and all the cursed things belong to you," Persephone sighed as sleep began to pull her away. "And I'm so very, very cursed."

7

Persephone didn't know what time it was when she finally opened her hungover eyes the next day. Someone had closed the dark curtains, and she had vague memories of being carried to bed.

How much did I drink last night? Four glasses? Five? Certainly not enough to justify the hangover she was currently experiencing.

"God damn it, Hades, how strong was that wine?" Persephone muttered as she drank the glass of water on her bedside table and took the aspirin that was waiting for her.

"Wait. What?" Persephone stared at the cup of water in her hand that she absolutely didn't have there yesterday, which meant...Hades again.

Through her brain fog, she was oddly touched that he had put them there as if knowing she'd need them.

In the shower, Persephone remembered that she'd told him about Pithos, and she was pretty sure she'd yelled at him at some point.

You are the worst, Drunk Persephone, she chastised herself and rested her head against the cool tiles.

Cerberus was waiting outside of her bedroom door when she finally decided to venture out looking for food.

"You are a good boy, aren't you," she crooned and patted his big head.

"Is Daddy home still? No? Good, then we are going to raid his fridge, yes we are."

Persephone wasn't the best in the kitchen, but she knew how to make an omelette when she was hungover. She was digging in the fridge when she heard a voice clear behind her.

"You must be Persephone."

She yelped in surprise and turned around. A man with curling black hair and a wolf's smile was sitting on the other side of the kitchen.

No, not a man. Persephone's dark magic all but purred in his presence. He *absolutely* wasn't human.

"Which one are you?" she asked, gripping the carton of eggs.

He laughed, a sound as rich as sin. "Erebus. Charon told me a lot about you. It's nice to finally meet you, daughter of Demeter."

"And you. What are you doing lurking around here?" Persephone asked, putting her ingredients down on the counter.

"Hades asked me to come and keep an eye on you while he was in town. I don't think I've ever seen him so agitated. What did you do to him last night?" Erebus asked, propping his head up with one hand. "Tell me all the sordid details."

"I drank all of his pomegranate wine, but he kept pouring, so he only has himself to blame. Are you hungry? I'm making omelettes," Persephone offered.

"I'd love one. Wait, you were drinking Night Wine?" Erebus asked, dark eyes wide in surprise.

"I don't know, it didn't have a label. Tasted good. I think I yelled at Hades. Oh well, serves him right." Persephone searched the kitchen cupboards for a mixing bowl.

The man is way too organized, she thought, looking at all the freakishly arranged kitchen utensils and mixing bowls stored in size order.

"You yelled at Hades? No wonder he was all pissy. The skillets are on the right," Erebus said helpfully. "What did you yell at him about?"

"I don't know, but I'm sure he deserved it," Persephone replied. She chopped chives and grated cheese as Erebus watched her with curious black eyes.

It would've bothered her a lot more if it wasn't for the fact she was so hungry she could have eaten the whole block of cheese on its own.

"You want to tell me what you're staring at, titan?" she asked when the silence became too much for her.

"Nothing. You. A woman in Hades place in general. It's all a bit weird," Erebus said as he came around the counter and switched the hot water kettle on. "Coffee?"

"God, yes," Persephone replied. She could almost hear Demeter shouting in despair in Athens at the thought of her consuming caffeine *and* dairy in the same meal.

"Why is there a woman being at Hades place weird? I'm sure he's had a pile of women around, probably many at once. He's the big boss, after all."

"He is, but no, I've never seen a woman here. Charon said you'd moved in, but I wasn't about to believe it until I saw you myself," Erebus replied. "He also said if I looked at you funny, Hades would throw me back in Tartarus."

"I doubt that. Hades is a weird guy who organizes his kitchen far too much even if he is a good cook, but I doubt he'd throw you into Tartarus," Persephone said, as she poured the egg mixture into the sizzling pan.

"He cooked for you too? Now you're just freaking me out."

"He was the one dumb enough to fall for *xenia*. It's not like I'm a guest here. I'm a *prisoner* until Lord High and Mighty decides to release me," Persephone said irritably.

There was something about the aspirin and closed curtains and general *niceness* of the previous evening that was annoying her for reasons she was sure she would understand if she wasn't so damn hungover.

Now she had yet *another* handsome titan making her coffee, and she didn't know how to take so many immortal's in one week.

"From what I understand, you're keeping yourself here," said Erebus and gave her a flirtatious wink. "Not that I'm complaining at the feminine presence, there are way too many guys around."

"I'm *not* keeping myself here. Hades wanted what I knew on Pithos, and I told him. As soon as he bothers to turn up, I intend to go home to Athens," Persephone said, flipping the omelettes and not looking at the titan beside her.

"You know Hades can detect a lie. If you're still here, it's because he doesn't believe you've coughed up all you know," Erebus replied.

Persephone didn't like that, not one bit. She had told him the important stuff, the bits that mattered to him.

Eat first and unravel the rest after, she prompted herself.

It was oddly easy to be sitting down for breakfast with one of the most feared creatures in Greece. No one could be more intimidating than Hades.

"Is it true that you help Demeter run her empire? You don't seem like the ditsy socialite type," said Erebus as he ate a forkful of egg. "Damn, this is a good omelette."

"Thanks. And yes, Demeter has always been rather determined for me to help her run things. Mostly, she likes to take me to meetings because I look good," Persephone replied and flinched.

She had never been that honest about it before. Her time away was not helping calm the rebellious streak. If anything, it was making it worse.

"Well, you can't blame her. You're very distracting. So distracting that Hades needed to go into Styx today just to be able to get some work done." Erebus poured her coffee, a teasing smile on his face.

"The old man needs to get out more," said Persephone.

"I'm starting to get why he's all frustrated. There's definitely *something* about you that I can't quite put my finger on. Are you sure nature is your only talent?" he asked, his black eyes far too perceptive.

"I'm good with finances, if that counts and an okay dancer, if I get enough drinks in me," she said with a smile to throw him off. She put a little something extra behind it, and Erebus's head snapped up like a wolfhound.

"Oh girl, don't be throwing those tricks around, or you'll get me into too much shit," he chastised, even if he was smiling.

"Can't get anything past you, can I?"

"Nope, not of that nature. As for your dancing skills, I'd be happy to extort those a bit down at Asterion's club if Hades decides to let you out," said Erebus, and they fell into talking about the Minotaur and Medusa and all of the other members of the Court of Styx.

Erebus was as gossipy as an old auntie, and Persephone soon learned all about Perseus, the handsome new son of Zeus that had found his way into their posse after falling in love with Medusa.

It was news to Persephone. Demeter would have been very interested to know that another demigod had surfaced.

"Why are you telling me all this? Seems very unwise," said Persephone.

"We aren't enemies, are we? Maybe I just want you to know some truth instead of rumor about us. We aren't all bad, even Hades," Erebus replied, and then got up and did the dishes.

"Wow, a man cleaning up in the kitchen. Be still my beating heart," Persephone said, fanning herself.

"Have you seen this place? Hades would murder me if I left his kitchen in this shape."

"I noticed he was a neat freak."

"He and Asterion are as bad as each other. It's a control thing. They need the routine and the structure to keep their shit together."

"So, if Hades pisses me off, I should move everything around and watch him have a meltdown."

"Honey, you're cute but not that cute. Try not to poke that bear any more than necessary. One encounter with you and Hades has been an asshole about Athens ever since."

"Oh, yes? And what is it that you think you know about Athens?" Persephone asked. Hades didn't strike her as the type to kiss and tell.

"I know that you two were making out rather hot and heavy. Don't worry, Simon told me, not Hades. He walked in on it and hasn't been the same since. Hades doesn't show off that side of himself very often, and it freaked the poor kid out. Then you walked out on him, and we've had to pay for his pissed off mood whenever he goes to Athens. Thanks for that," said Erebus.

"He walked out on me first," Persephone replied. *He doesn't know just how hot and heavy we were then.* "Good to know I made an impression."

"Wish you hadn't, but I get it now. There's something about you. A puzzle or a riddle. Hades is a sucker for those and no matter what deal you think you've made with him, he's not going to let you go until he figures it out."

Persephone did her best to hide how much that thought worried her. "He just needs me to do his taxes, and the mystery will be solved."

"I'll let him know. You think you can behave yourself while I make some calls? Or do I have to follow you around like Cerberus to make sure you behave yourself?" asked Erebus.

"I'll be good. I'm going to go through those financials Hades got about Pithos. I want to know how the bastards are taking money out of my company," Persephone said, and when he didn't look convinced, she sighed. "Calm down, it's not like I can get past his wards anyway." *Yet*, the feral side of her added.

"True, just don't test Hades's good nature. I like you, so I'd hate to dump your fine ass back into a cell," replied Erebus. He gave her a long look and went out onto the deck with his phone.

"I don't think these boys trust me. Aren't they silly?" Persephone said to Cerberus. The dog seemed to take this as a chance to fetch his chew toy and drop it into her lap. She waggled it at him and took off his glamour, letting his three adorable heads loose. Cerberus sat and scratched at them before looking back at her expectedly.

"Okay, but if we break anything, I'm blaming you." She tossed the toy down the long hallway and laughed when Cerberus scrambled on the polished floors to chase it.

On the third toss, it hit the edge of a door, and Cerberus bowled through it. Persephone waited for him to appear, but he didn't.

Oh shit, he might not be allowed in that room. Erebus's words came back to her about Hades's neatness.

"Damn it, dog." Persephone hurried down the hall and peeked into the room. It was a bedroom. *Hades's bedroom.*

The dark part of her sat up in interest. Did she dare snoop in the Lord of Styx's bedroom?

It's not snooping, it's chasing the dog out so that he doesn't drool on the fancy bed sheets.

"Cerberus? Get out of there," she whispered, but the dog was too busy clawing at something.

Persephone looked behind her to make sure Erebus was still on the balcony before she stepped inside the dark room.

It smelled of Hades's scent, the combination of sexy man and woodsy spice that haunted her dreams. The bed was huge and made with sheets the dark navy Hades seemed to like.

Like the rest of the house, there were interesting paintings on the walls, and the lamps beside the bed were black.

Persephone found Cerberus in the walk-in wardrobe, pawing at a drawer, his slobbery toy resting beside it.

"What's the matter with you? Did he hide something of yours in there?" Persephone asked and opened the drawer.

Something clicked, and a nearby panel slid back on the wall beside her. When no alarm went off, she looked at what Hades preferred to keep locked up and froze.

A helm sat displayed on a stand. It looked a little Spartan and was made with black metal. It was giving off an aura of such power her own rose to meet it.

Before she could think it through, Persephone slid off the glove of her right hand and touched it. Images flooded her mind so quickly that she could barely process one from the other: Hades and two other men casting lots, a forest of black trees, a silver lake.

She pulled her hand back with a jerk, but it was too late. She'd felt Hades through it. Echoes of his emotions, of anger and power and boredom and control. One stood out more than all the others, and it was loneliness.

She was familiar with that feeling, like a deep echo of her old pain. That hurt that she could never play with other children, never go on a date, never be able to touch anything without her gloves in case she lost control and killed them.

Just like you killed all those Pithos men that shot Dad.

The niggling thought that Persephone had kept shut down since the day Hades had used his power in her cell finally came through.

He's like you. Your power is the same. You're not alone.

Persephone stepped back from the helm and tried to clear her head. That was when she spotted the spark of a silver stud.

"It can't be," she whispered. It was. Folded neatly under the helm's stand was the black leather glove that she'd left behind at the club in Athens. Hades had kept it.

"*If he finds out what you truly are, he'll never let you go. Hades Acheron is the only being on Earth that you would never be able to escape from. He will kill you or worse if he finds about your cursed right hand,*" Demeter had said to her, all those years ago when Persephone was struggling so much to contain her magic.

She had foolishly suggested to Demeter that maybe she should ask Hades for help, and it was one of the only times her mother had used her goddess strength to drive Persephone to her knees.

I'll kill you before I let Hades have you, Demeter had spat, full of fury. Persephone had never forgiven her mother for making her go down on her knees in front of her in submission.

It was the night Persephone had taken off into Athens, so angry and powerless. Her father had followed her and met his death along with eight men who Persephone had unleashed her terrible power out on.

You need to get out before Hades pulls it out of you. You can't hide it forever.

Panic seized Persephone, overriding any rational thought, and she turned and bolted from the room.

"Persephone? Where did you get to?" Erebus called, and she hurried down the hall.

"Nowhere, just looking for the dog, that's all. Never mind, I'll play with him later," Persephone said, hating how easy it was for her to slip on the calm lying mask. "I'm going to go lie down and read those financials in comfort."

"Are you sure? Can I get you anything?"

"I'm fine, but my hangover is killing me. Damn wine, you'd think I'd know better," she said, moving towards her room.

"Oh, yeah, that particular brew was made for gods, so it doesn't surprise me it wiped the floor with you," replied Erebus. "I'll be close if you want the company."

Persephone tried not to close the door too quickly to her bedroom.

She looked at the pile of bank statements on her bedside table, pulling out the pages that listed companies she knew were owned by Morning Harvest. Only her mother, or perhaps Vallis her right-hand man, would have a better idea of how their money was getting used to fund Pithos.

She wasn't going to let Demeter shut her down this time. She needed answers, and she needed to get the fuck out of Hades's house.

Outside, the afternoon had set in, the sun making its way down into the water.

Hades is strongest at night, if you're going to make a run for it, now is the only chance you got.

Persephone folded up the papers and stuffed them down the front of her bra. The windows weren't bolted shut, so Persephone opened one and checked around outside. There were no guards under the window, but she knew some had to be patrolling somewhere.

Don't forget about the titan watching TV in the other room.

Persephone slid off her gloves and put them in her pocket. She didn't like the idea of hurting anyone with her power, but she couldn't stay and let Hades dig the truth out of her bit by bit.

If she was honest, she also liked him too much, and he'd be able to charm it out of her sooner or later.

Then you'll be well and truly fucked because he'll kill you.

A smaller voice whispered to her, *You're the same.*

"Can't risk it," Persephone muttered, and then she swung her legs over the windowsill and dropped silently onto the grass.

She crouched low, hiding amongst the decorative shrubs and trees as she hurried through the gardens. She flicked out her finger on her right hand and released some of the dark power inside of her.

Something pulsed back, and she was overwhelmed with a sense of Hades's darkly intoxicating magic. *His wards.*

Persephone took a few hurried steps when suddenly Erebus materialized from the shadows in front of her.

"And where do you think you're running off to?" he asked, voice soft and deadly.

"I'm sorry, I can't stay here. I've told Hades everything he needs to know, so I'm leaving," Persephone said.

"Can't let you do that, honey. I'm sorry, but you'll have to wait for the boss to come back first," replied Erebus, taking a step towards her.

Persephone lifted her right hand. "Please, I don't want to hurt you."

"Sorry, you're going to have to go through me. Whatever has spooked you, we can talk about it with Hades. He's a reasonable-" Erebus tried to say.

"I'm sorry, but I did try to warn you," whispered Persephone, and she unleashed her terrible power.

8

That morning, Hades took one look at Persephone's door before grabbing his keys and heading out to Styx.

He needed to get away from her, so he didn't do something incredibly stupid like start a war or kiss her. He had thought the wine the previous night was a good idea, now he wasn't so sure.

He had kept himself together as much as possible, but he wanted to physically shake Demeter by the end of it. How could she think that stifling Persephone's power was a good idea? She couldn't have passed for a human if she tried.

Persephone had also said 'powers' and not 'power' once she'd gotten a few drinks in her.

What else could she do?

Persephone's information on Pithos hadn't been much, but it had been enough. They had been in operation for a lot longer than Hades had dreamed about, which didn't bode well for any of them.

What else did they have hiding about the place? The collection of fucked up weapons in the ARGOS basement might not have been their only storehouse.

Hades knew only work could keep his mind busy and away from Persephone, so to work he went.

It was late in the afternoon when he got a message from Erebus: *SOS, she's making a break for it.*

Hades had taken one look at it and swore. He thought that dinner the previous night would've lessened some of her animosity.

Apparently not. Hades didn't bother going to get his car, there wouldn't be enough time for that. He fixed his power on Erebus and willed himself to him.

Hades took one step out of his office and into a war zone.

The villa's gardens were torn to shreds, human guards were tangled up in trees and vines, and the earth was scorched black.

"What the fuck is going on?" Hades said as he stared at the carnage. He was going to *kill* Erebus for letting the situation get this out of hand.

"Hades, help me," he heard the titan groan. Hades hurried through the trees and found Erebus, bound in shadows and on his knees. Pain strained his handsome face, parts of his body locked between flesh and darkness. Hades snapped the bonds of strange magic that bound him.

"Are you okay? What the fuck happened here?" Hades demanded, catching the titan before he collapsed.

"Your new girlfriend. She's not what you think, master. Stop her before she drives all the men mad. I'll be fine. Go!" Erebus shouted and shoved him off.

Hades took off at a run, his power reaching out, searching for the signature of spring. He didn't find it. All he felt was death. That was when he heard the screaming.

Hades hurried towards the sound and was suddenly surrounded by shades. He spotted Simon on the ground crying as the shade of older man shouted at him. Hades banished the shade back to the Underworld where it belonged.

"She went...that way," Simon gasped and pointed. Hades had never seen anyone with this kind of power before.

A sharp pain hit him in the chest as something clawed at the warding.

"Got you," Hades hissed and bolted towards it. Persephone was pounding her fists angrily at the invisible barrier that kept her locked in.

"*Stop*," Hades commanded, and Persephone whipped around.

"Let me go!" she shouted.

"Not until I get answers. What the fuck did you do to my men?"

"I told them to stay away from me like I'm telling you right now," hissed Persephone.

Her gloves were literally off, and for the first time, Hades saw the shadows lingering like lace around her right hand. *What is that?*

"You think you have the power to take me on, little goddess?" Hades asked, voice smooth as silk. Persephone turned and ran, and Hades took off after her.

The earth under his feet boiled and the nearest rose bush exploded into life, thorny vines tearing at his skin as the brambles tried to stop him.

His own power lashed out to kill them off and he dove, grabbing his prey around her waist and tackling her to the ground.

Persephone twisted in his arms and brambles wrapped around him, but Hades held onto her as they pierced through him.

"Get off me," she snarled.

"No," Hades hissed and fought to pin her.

"You asked for it, prick," Persephone replied and grabbed him around the throat with her right hand.

Instead of the raw, rich power of spring, sweet glorious darkness and death enveloped him. Shadows of her magic wrapped around him, and he shuddered with the feel of it, so perfect, so powerful.

"Oh, sunshine, you've been holding out on me," Hades chuckled and looked down at the tousled beauty on the grass beneath him. Her eyes were wide with surprise.

"I-I don't understand," she stammered. Hades let his own darkness rise and wrap around hers. She trembled beneath him, a small groan escaping her beautiful lips.

"I do." Hades smiled down at her. "You have my power."

"No, I don't! You need to let me go," Persephone whimpered.

"Don't go. Let me help you. This power is the reason Demeter has kept you so far away from me, isn't it?" said Hades. *How dare she?*

"She said that you'd take it from me or that I'd be a slave to you because Death is your domain and there's no way you'd ever let me be free," Persephone said, her eyes filling with tears.

"Death *is* my domain, yes. But you'll never be my slave, Persephone, I promise you, and I'd never, *ever* take this power away from you. No wonder I haven't been able to be free of you."

Hades touched her cheek gently, leaving a streak of golden ichor where her vines had ripped his skin to shreds.

"Don't run, let me help you. I can teach you how to control it, so you'll never have to wear those fucking gloves again."

"You don't understand. I *killed* all those Pithos agents that shot my father. I lost control for a second, and eight people died. I'm cursed, no one can help me. Demeter couldn't. No one can."

"*I* can, sunshine. I promise you. Let me prove it to you. Please, don't go," Hades whispered. He didn't care that he was begging. He would do anything to keep hold of her.

The vines of the rose bushes were surrounding them, shielding them even as they trapped them.

Hades didn't care that they were ripping apart the mortal form he took. The only thing that mattered was the woman beneath him.

"Why? Why would you help me? I won't side with you against Demeter if that's what you want," said Persephone, uncertainty flickering in her green eyes.

"I don't give a fuck about Demeter. Don't you see, sunshine? We are the *same*."

Tears tracked down her cheeks, and he bent to kiss them.

"Don't cry. I'll never hurt you, Persephone. Give me ten days, and I'll prove to you that I can help. If I can't, I'll let you go. I promise."

Persephone softened underneath him and whispered, "Six days."

"Still trying to bargain," Hades laughed softly.

"Of course. Anything else you want to say, Lord High and Mighty?" she asked.

Hades unleashed his dark power, letting it pour over her as he pinned her hands over her head.

Persephone moaned as her own magic tangled with his. They called out and fed off each other, magnifying their strength and intensity.

"Yes. I'm *not* a bad kisser." Hades didn't know who moved first, but their lips were suddenly together, and everything went still inside of him.

He had thought in depth about the feel of her lips over the years, convincing himself that it was the alcohol that he'd consumed that made him think they were so good against his. That was a lie. Persephone's lips were perfection.

He didn't notice his skin tear as he grabbed her by the hips and lifted her so he could feel all of her luscious softness against him. Her tongue flicked against his, and he groaned.

This is not the place to do this, his common sense reminded him.

Reluctantly, Hades pulled back and reined in his power.

"Okay," Persephone sighed.

"Okay, what?"

"Okay, I'll stay for six days... and you aren't a bad kisser," she said with a shy smile. "And I'm sorry if I hurt your men. I did try to warn them."

"They'll get over it. Kill any of them?"

"I don't think so?" she said.

"Then, they'll be fine." He glanced around at the brambles they were trapped in. "Would you like to do something about this, or will I?"

Persephone traced the fingers of her right hand down his neck, her spring eyes going black. "Show me how you do it."

"As the lady wishes," Hades said, and shadow began to pour out of him.

Everywhere it touched, the brambles died, reducing them to ash. Persephone's breathing quickened underneath him, and it wasn't from fear.

It took only a moment before the vines were gone, and Hades moved off her. Persephone made a small sound of alarm.

"You're bleeding. Oh, shit, I never meant to hurt you."

Hades glanced down at his clothes stained with golden ichor. "I'm fine, Persephone."

Erebus appeared as Hades was helping Persephone off the grass.

"Well, *that* was exciting," he said, eying them both warily. "Are we good, or do I get to throw her back in a cell?"

Persephone was covered in dirt and ichor, and she still smiled threateningly at him.

"Do you think you could?"

"You got the jump on me, I won't be surprised again," he argued.

"That won't be necessary, Erebus. Persephone and I have come to a new arrangement," Hades replied.

"Thought you might have. Charon's on his way with Selene to help with cleaning up. Sweet goddess, if you wouldn't mind releasing the men, it would be appreciated," said Erebus.

Hades didn't leave Persephone's side as she walked back through the gardens, apologizing to people and making the garden release whatever snares they held them in.

Thanatos arrived through the crowd of shades, silver hair gleaming in the night.

"You must be, Lady Persephone," he purred, taking her hand and kissing it. "Would you like me to help you with all of these shades?"

Persephone sagged with relief, giving Thanatos a huge smile.

"Please. I don't know how to make them go away. I have never been able to figure that part out."

Thanatos looked at Hades for permission, and he gave him a nod.

"I'll take care of this, my lady, go with Hades and see to your wounds. I'll show you another night."

"Thank you, I'd like that. I'm feeling a little woozy..." Persephone said and swayed on her feet. Hades caught her up before she could hit the dirt.

"It's okay, sunshine. Let's get you inside."

"I can walk," she said stubbornly. "This is the second time you've carried me in two days, it's embarrassing. Your titans are going to think I'm weak."

Persephone was making his titans think something, but it wasn't that she was weak. All three of them got dreamy besotted expressions on their faces when they looked at her, even Erebus, who had been literally driven to his knees by her.

Yet another mystery to solve.

Hades took her into the lounge room and set her down. Her knees and forearms were bleeding from where he had tackled her, grass stains and dirt all over her.

"What are you grinning at?"

"You look like a filthy hellion," he said, sitting opposite her.

"Like you can talk. You were the one that wanted to play lions like some damn beast," she argued, with the beginnings of a smile.

"It was fun. We should play again sometime," Hades said, meaning every word.

"You wish, old man, I'd annihilate you," Persephone replied, laughing.

Charon and Selene interrupted them moments later. The nurse took one look at Hades and the frown line between her eyes deepened.

"Don't look at me like that, I'm okay. Persephone first," Hades said, waving the nurse away.

"Dare I ask how this happened?" Selene took out antiseptic wipes. "Charon? Would you get a bowl of hot water and some clean towels for me?"

"Sure thing, doll," he said and hurried away.

"Hades had a tantrum; that's how this happened. I'm Persephone, by the way," she said.

"Selene. I'm the one that gets called in whenever one of these boys hurts themselves," the nurse replied and carefully began to clean the cuts on Persephone's forearms.

"Don't let her doe-eyed innocent look fool you, Selene. She was the one that had the tantrum first. I just put a stop to it," Hades explained.

"Well, I'm sure you had it coming," muttered Selene.

Persephone's smile widened in Hades's direction. "He really did. I like you, Selene."

Hades only laughed, which made Selene give him an odd look. It wasn't until Persephone was cleaned up before he gave Selene permission to see to his own wounds.

"Where are you hurting the most?" Selene asked hands on her hips.

"My side is irritating."

"Shirt off, so I can see what I'm dealing with," she demanded. Hades made a point of not looking in Persephone's direction as he pulled off the tattered ruin of shirt.

"Oh, my god," Persephone gasped, but it wasn't in ecstasy.

"What?" Hades looked down and saw a rose vine had pierced through him and came out the other side. He was about to say it was nothing, but she was off the couch in a blink.

"I'm so, so sorry, I didn't mean to do that," she said, her fingertips resting on his skin.

"You did so," Hades replied, and her concern changed to mischief.

"Maybe a little bit, but you were the one that jumped on me."

"Can you get it out? The only way I can is to cut it out," said Selene, as she studied the tracing of vines before stepping away from him.

"What do you think, sunshine? Want the opportunity to hurt me again?"

"Only because you asked so nicely," Persephone said, her fingers stroked the line of tattoos down his back. "These are unexpected."

Hades was about to give her a charming reply, but she took the exposed end of the vine between the fingers of her left hand, and pain shut him up.

"I don't know if this will work, so stay still," she said.

"It will. I trust you," Hades said through gritted teeth.

"Your mistake, Acheron," Persephone said, and Hades swore as the vine whipped around under his skin, and she pulled it free.

"You could've warned me," he said when he'd finally stopped swearing.

Persephone had the nerve to reach up and pinch his cheek. "Where would the fun in that be? Do you still need me? Because I want a shower."

"It'll be fine, I can handle it from here," said Selene pulling out needles and thread. "Have your shower and then get some Band-Aids over those scrapes."

"I will, thank you, Selene."

Hades watched Persephone walk away, his perfect golden handprint on the ass of her jeans.

Right where it belongs.

"Be careful you don't bite off more than you can chew with that one, boss," advised Selene. "She won't tolerate any of your schemes."

"Wise Lady Selene, are you worried about me?" asked Hades. She raised a dark brow and went back to stitching.

"You know me, I care, and you've all been getting hurt far too much lately. I do have another job, you know," she said.

"I've offered you to come work for me full time, you keep saying no."

"There are other people in this city that need help too, ones that aren't as privileged as you. I like you and the Court, you know that. But you don't need me like they do," Selene replied, tying off the ends of a knot and snipping it.

She dug about in her bag and produced an aqua colored tin.

"After your shower, rub this on your wounds, and it will heal you quicker. Play doctor with Persephone if she's hurting. She's a demigoddess, so it'll help her too."

"Thank you, Selene. I promise you a bonus for this."

"Just play nice for a week, will you? I get tired of patching you guys up."

Hades gave Charon a nod, and he helped Selene with her gear. He liked the nurse; there was something of the old healers about her, but no matter how much he offered, she still refused to join them full time.

She knows better than to get involved in this shit.

Hades got to his feet and made for his bathroom. He had bigger things to worry about... like how to teach a goddess to use her powers in six days without them killing each other.

9

Persephone decided she had never hurt as badly as she hurt standing under her steaming shower.

She was covered in cuts and scrapes, with clumps of dirt falling out of her hair and golden ichor all over her.

Despite that, she was...smiling. For the first time, in the longest time, the constant pressure and fear that lived inside of her was gone. Hades finally knew about her right hand - the absolute worst had happened, and she had nothing left to fear.

You have six days to figure it out.

Persephone didn't know if she'd ever give up her gloves, but the thought of one day not needing them? She was almost giddy at the possibility of it.

Now she only needed to figure out how she was going to keep a straight face when Hades used his power to teach her about her own.

It was distracting, intoxicating, and made her want to run in the other direction and rub herself all over him simultaneously. That was something she would have to learn to live with.

Persephone was going to put their kiss down to the heat of the moment as well. It was more out of anger than passion. His lips were as hot as she had remembered from their night at the club, which didn't help her one bit.

Magic first, kisses later. One thing at a time.

She wanted to know about the tattoos inked down Hades's back too. They were unlike anything she had seen before, like words or symbols that she couldn't read. She wanted to know what they meant. She wanted to know what they tasted like…Persephone flipped the taps to cold and stood under the freezing water until she couldn't handle it anymore.

Persephone managed to get pajama shorts and a singlet on before her hunger pains nearly doubled her over.

"What now?" she complained. She had never been hungry after using her magic.

You've never used so much at once, either. She wrapped her hair up in a towel and went looking for food.

Selene was gone, and the couches were clean and organized once more. Hades found her minutes later with her hands in the fridge and shoving grapes in her mouth.

"I knew I'd find you in there," he said.

Persephone stood up quickly, so she wasn't poking her ass at him.

"Sorry, I'm starving, and I couldn't wait to ask politely."

"It's completely fine, eat whatever you like. You used a lot of power today in your escape attempt, your body needs to replenish itself," Hades said.

He was in a pair of grey pajama pants and a t-shirt, his hair still wet and tousled from his shower. Persephone swallowed hard.

"I don't suppose I could convince you to make me one of those really nice sandwiches. Or would that be pushing *xenia* a little bit too hard?" she asked.

"If you get out of my kitchen, I will," he said, and she removed herself from the fridge.

"You're a bit uptight about your kitchen, you know that, right?"

"I don't like people in my way while I'm cooking," he said unapologetically.

"Your containers have all their lids. That's unnatural, Hades," Persephone teased as she sat down on one of the couches.

"I *am* unnatural, Persephone," he argued. She watched as he made sandwiches with intense precision. "You said that you killed all of the Pithos agents the night your father was shot. Would you like to elaborate on that?"

Persephone pulled the towel off her head and shook out her wet hair. "I wondered how long it would take you to ask."

Hades placed a plate of sandwiches on the coffee table in front of her with a glass of juice.

"Just tell me, sunshine, I'm not going to judge you."

Persephone picked up one half of her sandwich and had a bite.

"After Pithos shot my father, he told me to run, but I couldn't. It was like darkness spewed out of me, this crazy despairing rage. I couldn't stop it. They tried to run, but it wrapped around them and killed them. It wasn't like when you killed off the brambles and turned them to ash. It was slow. They died in a lot of pain *before* they turned to ash, and then there was nothing left."

"What did Demeter do when you told her?" Hades asked, sitting on the other end of the couch.

"What do you think? She actually loved my dad, and he was dead because of me. She lost her fucking mind."

Persephone's shoulders hunched in slowly. Demeter had used her power on Persephone in anger for a second time that day, and if it wasn't for the fact that she was demigoddess, she was sure she would've died. Golden power had surrounded her like vines and had slowly crushed her until she was burning down to her bones.

Persephone had passed out, and when she woke, Demeter had healed her, but she had never apologized for doing it.

Hades's voice was barely a whisper. "What did she do to you?"

"It doesn't matter," Persephone said, eating more of her sandwich. "I tried to find out what Pithos was after that. I had a hope that if I found them, maybe it would make up for Dad's death. That we could get some justice. Demeter found out about it, and she made me drop it. She was going to take care of it, she said."

Demeter hadn't used her power on Persephone then, but when Demeter had threatened to do it again if Persephone didn't drop her search, she obeyed quickly and without argument.

"I don't understand. If Demeter knew Pithos killed your father, why would she give them money?" asked Hades.

"I don't think she knows, which means there has to be someone in her company doing it. There's no way she'd support them, and there's no way Vallis, her head of security, would betray Demeter or do anything to endanger her. Demeter is a bitch, but she wouldn't support anyone stirring trouble with you. You are the only thing she fears," Persephone replied. "I'm sorry, I can't tell you more. Really, I am."

"You've told me enough. Pithos will come after us again, it's only a matter of time. Medusa is still running leads. We'll find them, you don't have to worry about that."

Hades took an aqua colored tin from his pocket.

"Selene said to put some of this on your grazes before going to bed."

"What is it?"

"Some salve she made. She's a nurse, but her natural remedies work better than anything I've seen. They'll heal you," he explained.

Persephone put her scraped up leg on the couch between them.

"I'm eating, help a girl out. Pretty sure it's under the laws of *xenia*."

"You're pushing your luck, you know that?"

"That's okay, I'll find one of the triplets to do it. They all seem very lovely and obliging," Persephone said, but as she went to move her leg, Hades's hand came down around her ankle and clamped it to the couch.

"Stay still," he grumbled, and she hid her smile. "Why do you insist on provoking me?"

"I'm simply making the most of this *xenia* deal. You were the one silly enough to agree to it." Persephone wriggled her toes at him.

"Besides, I think you like having a pajama party with me."

"Is that what we are doing?" Hades asked, unscrewing the lid of the tin. The salve was pale yellow, and it smelled of honey and lavender.

"We are both in pajama's, aren't we? If you have any nail polish around, I'll get you to..." Persephone lost her train of thought as Hades gently massaged the salve into her chapped skin.

She sighed as the stinging went numb, and she leaned back against the couch.

"Wow, that stuff works quickly."

"Selene is the best, which is why she is on my payroll," Hades said and gestured for her other leg.

Persephone wriggled around and got comfortable as he worked on her other scrapes. "Hades?"

"Yes, Persephone?" he said, not looking up.

"Thank you for taking care of me," she replied.

"You're welcome. Arm next," he said, and he rubbed the salve on her cut forearms.

"Do you really think you can help me control my power? You saw what I did today. I called up all of those poor shades and had no idea how to release them."

"Has that ever happened before?"

"Once, when I was about ten years old. It hung around the house for two years before it finally disappeared. Only I could see it," Persephone said softly.

"Demeter should have swallowed her pride and asked me to help you. You were only a child. You should never have had to suffer through that," Hades replied through gritted teeth. "I *will* help you, Persephone. I don't know how you're not mad."

"Seeds mostly."

"What do you mean?"

"You know how I grew the olive tree? That's my coping mechanism. Growing flowers with one hand and then killing them with the other," Persephone explained.

"I'm surprised that it was enough to keep it under control. I felt what you wielded today, Persephone, that power was deep. Something that would challenge Demeter's and then some. She's kept you under her perfect high heel not because she's afraid of me, it's because she's afraid of *you*," said Hades.

"That's not true. She's an Olympian and I'm a half breed, Hades. She's not afraid of me," Persephone argued. She didn't want to believe it. Her mother could be a bitch, but she still loved her in her way.

"Just be careful when you go home. Demeter was always hungry for power, even in the old days. She won't like her daughter being able to challenge her, and when I'm done teaching you, you'll be more than a match for her." Hades lifted her chin.

"And she'll never be able to hurt you again the way she did after your father died."

"S-she didn't mean it," said Persephone, moving her face away.

"Yes, she did. I'm sorry if it hurts you to hear the truth of it, but no immortal releases their power by accident. I don't need to know details. I can see in your eyes how much it hurt you. She's kept you scared and chained up like a trained fucking poodle."

"Unlike you? You're keeping me prisoner here, Hades!" Persephone argued.

His eyes narrowed. "You agreed to stay."

"So, you can train me to contain my magic, so I don't lose control, just like Demeter said she was going to."

Hades gripped her shoulders, anger flaring in his silver eyes. "I'm not interested in teaching you to contain your power, Persephone. I'm going to fucking *unleash* you so you can be who you were meant to be."

"What if you do and I destroy more than your garden? What if I wreck everything around me," Persephone asked. She'd had nightmares about going nuclear and wiping out Athens.

"Then I'll rebuild it," said Hades, as if it was as simple as that. He loosened his grip but didn't let her go. "And you can create me a new garden. I was getting tired of the old one anyway."

Persephone tried not to smile. "What if I make one that's super ugly and isn't perfectly ordered the way you like it?"

"Then I'll kill it and make you do it again. It'll be good practice for you," Hades replied, settling back down on the couch. "Can I ask you a question?"

"Sure," said Persephone.

"Why did you run today? Am I such a terrible host?" he asked softly.

Lie, Persephone. Don't ruin this peaceful moment, her common sense commanded her as her mouth said, "Why did you keep my glove?"

Hades's expression snapped closed. "You went through my things?"

"No, I was playing with Cerberus, and he wouldn't get out of your room. I went to chase him out and I saw it. I didn't go through your stuff, Hades, I'm not like that," she said quickly, as he got to his feet and headed for the hallway.

"Don't walk away. Just tell me why you kept it!"

Hades didn't turn around. "To remind me that it happened," he said, and then he was gone, his door shut firmly behind him.

10

The next morning, Persephone woke to a quiet villa. She didn't see Hades anywhere, though she doubted he would've left her alone after the previous day.

You should have kept your mouth shut about the glove, she chastised herself for the hundredth time.

She had lain awake for hours the previous evening, wondering if she should go after him.

And say what? You have nothing to apologize for. So, she had left the awkward moment alone, and had gotten intimately acquainted with the plaster moldings on her bedroom ceiling.

Persephone made a coffee as quietly as she could and slipped out of the door and into the gardens.

In the light of day, Persephone was stunned at the devastation she had wrought. Huge furrows of earth crossed the manicured lawn like whip slashes, trees were torn in half, hedges and flower beds were exploded, and every now and again the ground was scorched black.

She was contemplating where to begin her repairs when a Ferrari roared down the driveway, and Medusa stepped out. She spotted Persephone, and her red lips smirked.

"I have to say I love what you've done with the place," Medusa said as she joined Persephone out on the lawn and didn't lift her sunglasses.

So, she doesn't want to kill me yet, that's a good sign.

"Hello, Medusa, lovely to meet you at last," Persephone replied, and they shook hands.

"You too. I do wish it were under more pleasant circumstances, but Hades ignored *my* advice." Medusa's disapproval radiated off her as she took in Persephone's scraped forearms.

"Please tell me that he didn't do that to you or I'm really going to lose it."

"If it makes you feel better, I gave as good as I got," said Persephone.

Medusa looked around her. "I can see that. I'm quite sure Erebus is in love with you, Thanatos was thoroughly impressed, and Charon, well he gave you one of his coins. I thought it past time that I came out and saw you for myself and give you some female company. I would've brought Ariadne too, but she was the one that suggested Hades kidnap you and Asterion...let's say he's protective of his little assassin."

"Understandable but unnecessary. I wouldn't hurt Ariadne for something Hades did. After the stories Erebus told me, I'm actually looking forward to meeting her," said Persephone. It was true. She had never met an assassin before, and to be able to take on the Minotaur? That was impressive.

"Is that so? I can't help wonder what the gossipy little titan said about me," Medusa replied.

"That you're formidable, which I knew, and that you're dating a demigod painter who has an amazing ass," said Persephone, making Medusa laugh.

"Well, that's true. Perseus's ass *is* perfection. I suppose you're going to tell Demeter about his demigod nature?" she asked, a challenge in her tone that Persephone didn't fail to miss.

"She'll find out eventually, especially because she knew Zeus and will recognize one of his kids when she sees him. I don't think you'll need to worry about my mother's interest in him. As soon as Demeter knows where I am, she'll be too busy having a meltdown to worry about your sexy artist," said Persephone.

Medusa folded her arms. "Do you think she'll try to challenge Hades for you?"

"It won't matter if she does. I agreed to stay for another six days with or without her permission," Persephone replied, straightening her shoulders.

"Is that so? I knew Hades must have a charming bone somewhere in that body of his."

"I'm not sleeping with him," Persephone said, a little too quickly. "He's going to help me with my power."

"How uncharacteristically generous of him," Medusa replied slowly and looked back at the garden. "You want to show me what you got? I have to admit I'm curious after the triplets gushed about you."

"They aren't nearly as terrifying as their reputations make them out to be," said Persephone with a laugh.

"Actually, they are. Why do you think they are so attracted to you? Because you're so pretty? It's because you are a death bringer, and they are creatures of darkness," said Medusa.

"Well, I should try to fix some of this damage first," Persephone replied with a grin. "Before I kill it again anyway."

She tried not to think of her audience as she bent down and placed her left hand onto the wet earth. Persephone shut her eyes and focused on all the green and growing things, sweet sap and flowering seeds.

The ground shuddered, and she opened her eyes as the broken fissures sealed, grass grew, trees healed and bloomed.

"This is...incredible," Medusa breathed, and Persephone reined in her power. "Are you strained at all?"

"Not really, no," admitted Persephone bashfully.

"Have you ever tested your limits?"

"Um, no? Demeter never would allow it, and it's not like I could just walk into a desert just to see if I could make it bloom."

Medusa put her hand on her hip. "Why not?"

"It would draw too much attention," Persephone said. It was one thing Demeter hated and had fought hard to protect their privacy.

"It could also save a drought-stricken nation," Medusa argued, looking about at the wild trees around them.

Persephone was about to reply when she felt it; a rush of dark shadows and whispers of death rolling across the grounds.

Medusa didn't give any indication that she felt the change, but Persephone knew Hades was coming.

Might as well make him feel welcome.

Persephone held out her right hand and let the death power out of her. Medusa swore, but Persephone didn't stop as the ground around them withered, cutting a path to where she felt Hades moving.

His power wrapped around hers, gentle as a kiss, and everything crumbled to ash, leaving only the God of the Underworld strolling towards them in the morning sunshine.

Hades was in his usual perfectly pressed black trousers and a button-up shirt, and Persephone really wished she could get the visual of his tattooed body out of her head.

She would've felt a lot steadier if he had been wearing a tie, and she couldn't see the curve of his collarbone between the undone buttons of his shirt. But no, the Fates just didn't want to throw her a bone.

Hades fixed her with his silver eyes, and her heart rate went up, the taste of his power burning her mouth.

God, you're so hopeless for him.

Persephone knew it, but she still forced her face into pleasant neutrality and refused to drop his gaze for a second. She wasn't going to give him the satisfaction. If he wanted a staring competition, he could bring it on.

"Well, this is awkward," whispered Medusa.

"Susa, I didn't expect you this morning. Did we have a meeting?" Hades asked, finally moving his eyes to the gorgon.

Persephone couldn't stop the small victorious grin that he had lost their little stare-off.

Hades noticed it and gave her a frown that said, *Don't test me, baby demigoddess.*

Persephone made an amused sound that made his nostrils flare.

"I'll let you talk business," she said, turning away. "Let's catch up soon, Medusa."

"You will fix my fucking garden first," Hades shot back.

Persephone lifted her middle finger up as she walked away, leaving flowers blooming in her wake.

~

Hades bit down his frustration as Persephone disappeared amongst the trees.

That fucking finger reminded him of the night in the club, and her attitude made him want to pounce on her again and spank some manners into her.

"Earth to Hades. If you keep staring at her like that, she's going to catch fire," Medusa said, snapping her fingers in his face.

"Good," Hades muttered, focusing on her. "What are you doing here?"

"The triplets told me what happened last night, and I thought I'd better come and check things out for myself."

Hades folded his arms. "I've got the situation under control."

"Hmmm. Doesn't look like it," Medusa replied, surveying the wrecked landscape.

"Don't make that sound at me. Persephone is fine. I'm not mistreating her even if she likes to purposely irritate me."

Medusa laughed softly. "I don't think that is irritation you are feeling, old friend. She was perfectly pleasant until you turned up and started throwing your power and sexy glares around. The triplets said her power was like yours. I thought they were exaggerating. How is it possible?"

"I don't know. Her father was human. Persephone's spring abilities could've easily been inherited from Demeter, but that death power? I feel like the Fates are fucking with me," said Hades.

"It does explain why you've been obsessed with her for the past six years, and why you were so drawn to each other to begin with," Medusa replied.

"Demeter should've come to me to help Persephone, not hide her away from me," he growled.

"Maybe she knew you'd act like this and try to claim her as one of yours."

"She *is* one of mine," Hades snapped before he could stop himself. "All death belongs to me."

Medusa gave his arm a pat. "Good luck telling Persephone that. She's not just death, buddy, she's radiating life."

"I know, and Demeter hasn't taught her to use it either. Just kept her locked up and hoped it would go away." He wanted to throttle the goddess so much his hands hurt.

"So that's why you made the six-day deal to help Persephone. You actually like her," Medusa said with a smile.

"When she isn't provoking me. You saw her just now! I hadn't said a word to her, and she was just-"

"Eye fucking you?"

"She was throwing her power around to get a rise out of me," corrected Hades.

Medusa shrugged. "She was doing both. I don't know why you can't flirt without killing everything in the process."

Because it feels so fucking good when she uses her power.

Hades didn't say it, but Medusa laughed as if she could read his mind anyway.

"I'm no love expert, but maybe try to lose the attitude if you want to win her over. Don't forget we aren't Demeter's enemy, and we don't want to be. Persephone will have to go home to Athens eventually, and we don't want Demeter to pull out of all of our deals," she said.

"If she's been working with Pithos against us, I'll grind her into the dirt," Hades replied.

"You'll lose Persephone if you do."

"I don't *have* Persephone in order to lose her. She swears Demeter wouldn't work with Pithos, which means you need to dig into her inner circle," Hades instructed, and Medusa nodded.

"Can I offer you some feminine advice in regard to the girl?"

"If you must."

"Don't act like another Demeter. Don't keep her locked up and isolated from people like her. Do some training with her as promised and bring her out to the Labyrinth. She's lonely, Hades, like we all were before we had each other," said Medusa. She gave his arm a reassuring squeeze. "I'll look at Demeter's cronies and let you know what I find."

"Thank you, Susa," he replied, and she walked back to her Ferrari.

"Be the charming bastard I know is in there somewhere!" she called out her window before driving away.

Hades sighed and pinched the bridge of his nose. He could feel Persephone's power on the other side of the property, and like a siren song, he gave in to the inevitable and followed it.

HADES FOUND Persephone laughing as she threw a stick for Cerberus, then grew obstacles in his way to confuse the hound.

Hades knew he needed to find Pithos and be done with the ugly business. He needed to go back to his office and deal with the million things on his to-do list.

Instead, Hades smiled and leaned against a tree to watch them play. Persephone yelped as an over-exuberant Cerberus bowled her over and started licking at her face.

Persephone wiped the dog slobber off her cheek with the back of her hand.

"You are the worst, dog, stop that," she complained.

"Leave her be," Hades told the dog and moved to help her off the grass. Persephone hesitated.

"Allow me," he said, and she took his hand.

"Thanks, he's massive but adorable. What happened to Medusa?" she asked.

"She had to get back to work," Hades replied, and then remembering Medusa's suggestion added, "You'll see her at the club tonight."

"The club?"

"She wants to give you a night out with the Court," he said. "Only if you want to. I'm not going to force you to socialize with them, especially not the triplets."

"I *like* the triplets, they are all handsome and charming," Persephone said, removing her hand slowly from his. Hades ignored that comment and looked out at the ocean.

"Are you going to show me how to use my power or just pick fights with me?" she asked eventually.

"All depends if you're going to behave yourself."

"You'd be too bored if I did that," Persephone said.

"I'm too busy to be bored."

Persephone looked him over. "You keep yourself busy *because* you're bored, and you hate it. I could see it all over you the night at the club, and six years later, you're still the same."

"And you have such an insight into my personality?" he said irritably.

"No, it just takes one to know one," Persephone replied softly.

Hades's expression softened. "You don't like being Demeter's CEO in training?"

"It has its moments, but it's...tedious. Seriously, I don't know why you came back and revealed yourself to the world only to become a CEO," she said and then reddened. "Sorry, that came out more judgemental than I meant it to."

"It's fine. I didn't really plan on creating an empire, but then it became necessary to protect the Court, and here we are," he said.

"Why *did* you come back?" she asked. "I thought you couldn't leave the Underworld."

"How about you do some training without fighting with me and I'll tell you," Hades said. He was enjoying the moment, and he didn't want her to look at him in fear when he told her the truth of what he had to do to get free.

"You love your deals, don't you?" Persephone said.

"It's good for both parties to have a clear understanding of what each other gets, so there's no confusion," he replied, even though when he looked at her, all he felt was confusion.

"Very sensible of you," Persephone said with a smile. Hades wasn't sure if she was laughing at him or not, then he decided he liked her smile, so it didn't matter. He reached into his pocket and pulled out a packet of seeds.

"Shall we?"

11

Persephone tried to get her professional face on as Hades handed her the packet of seeds.

They looked like black, dried lemon pips, but she couldn't be sure what they would grow into.

"What did you have in mind?" she asked.

"I've been meaning to grow an orchard of special pomegranates from the Underworld, and I want you to help me. You've already done half the job by demolishing a space on the western side, so we'll start there," Hades replied. Without waiting for her, he turned and began walking away.

He clicked his tongue, and Cerberus abandoned his stick and fell into step behind him.

Persephone followed, even if it were only to keep an eye on his ass and not because he told her to. At least they had stopped arguing for the moment.

She didn't know why he brought out the brat in her, but she loved stirring him up.

Maybe because you want to press more than his buttons.

Hades stopped at the edge of the lawn where they had ended up in the brambles.

Persephone looked at the scorched ground and thought of their angry kiss covered in dirt and golden ichor. Hades didn't smile, but amusement lit his silver eyes as if he knew exactly what she was thinking.

"This will be an excellent spot, seeing how it's mostly clear already. Can you make six rows for me, please?" he asked, one hand casually resting on Cerberus's head.

"Sure, but I can't guarantee that they will be perfectly straight," said Persephone, crouching down.

"That won't matter once the trees are in," he replied. "If it does, I'll just make you do it again."

"Your teaching method needs work."

"Really? How would you *like* me to school you, sunshine?" he asked, looking down at her. She ignored the innuendo in his tone and placed her left hand onto the earth. She focused carefully on releasing a controlled amount of power and drew six careful lines in the ash beside her. Hades was about to say something, but she held up her hand to silence him. Then the ground trembled, and six rows tore into the land in front of them.

"Very nice," he said and held out his hand. "Give me half of those seeds."

"I'm more controlled with the life and growing side of things. It's the right hand that I struggle with," Persephone explained, tipping seeds out for him.

"We'll get to that, trust me." Hades took the far three rows and Persephone the others, and they quietly dropped the seeds evenly in the furrows.

"Now what?" Persephone asked, and Hades moved to stand beside her.

"May I touch you?" he said.

Persephone's mouth went dry. "If you need to."

"I need to feel out how you use your power," he replied, and slowly took her left hand. His gaze lingered on the sun on her wrist. "Your tattoos make a lot more sense now."

"That's what happens when you're young and impulsive." Persephone focused on the earth in front of her and not the warm heat down her back or the hand wrapped around hers.

"I want you to grow the trees, but not to full maturity," Hades instructed, breath tickling the tip of her ear. "Release slowly, so I can get the feel of your power and how it flows."

Persephone released a breath and focused on the link between her left hand and the ground in front of her.

She could sense the small seeds in their furrows and let her power flow. Hades stroked her sun tattoo.

"Slower. Think of a trickle, not a river," he said.

Persephone did her best to shut down how distracting he was and do as she was instructed. She closed her fingers slowly, trying to visualize choking the flow of life and creation.

Sweat broke out on the back of her neck as she held it, and then small green shoots began to sprout and curve, before rising slowly into saplings and thickening to trees.

"Stop there," Hades said, and Persephone closed her fist.

It was still vibrating with power, and she steadied her breathing until the pressure in her hand eased.

"Why is it harder to do that than just release it?" she asked, shaking out her left hand.

"Having control isn't about stopping going nuclear. True control is being able to reserve that power, use it only as much as you need to, so you don't burn out in a confrontation or be too pent up for not using it at all. Less is more, so you have a deep reserve for when you need it," explained Hades.

"Like in a fight?" she asked.

"Yes. Believe it or not, I don't want Pithos ever getting their hands on you. If they attack you, I want you to be able to defend yourself in order to get away. Not panic and hurt yourself or innocents around you. Only the bastards who are trying to hurt you," said Hades, moving a fraction closer.

"If you keep saying things like that, I'm going to start to think you like me, old man," Persephone replied.

Hades right hand slid slowly down her arm and wrapped around her wrist, his thumb stroking her skull tattoo.

"You already know I like you. Probably too much. Do you think I'd bother with any of this if I didn't?"

"I guess not," Persephone said.

Hades's voice turned to black velvet as his lips moved against her ear. "Do you really have to guess?"

Goosebumps flew down her arms, and she hoped he wouldn't notice them. She cleared her throat.

"What's next, you want to kill them off?"

Hades lifted her right hand towards the young trees. "Yes, but the same principle applies, slowly remove the life drop by drop. I'll tell you when to stop."

Persephone let the power in her right hand go, and trickles of darkness curled around her fingers like smoke. She sent it out towards the saplings, and their leaves started to slowly droop, then curl and brown.

There was a rush, and they began to turn black rapidly, but Hades wrapped his fingers around hers.

"Rein it back in," he said, and Persephone tried to slow the dark power.

It was begging to be unleashed, to suck out life and destroy, like a rush of adrenaline and a rough kiss by a bad man.

Hades sensed the change in her, and his power released just enough to drag her's back. Her shadows snapped away from the trees and wrapped around his arm where it touched hers.

"Damn it, why does it do that?" said Persephone.

"Because I'm still a God of the Dead, and it recognizes it," Hades replied.

"Does it feel the same as yours? Or different?" Persephone leaned back against him a little, and his left hand came up to rest on her hip.

"It's hard to explain. It is like mine, but it feels... like you. I can sense you in it, even if the abilities are similar. What does mine feel like to you?" Hades asked.

Like all the forbidden things I want, Persephone thought. She let her shadows out a little more to touch him.

"It's bigger, deeper." She licked her too dry lips and tried to find the words. "Stronger, like a masculine version of mine. It's overwhelming when you use it."

Just to torment her, Hades released some more of his power, and it moved up her arm and down her body. Her heart fluttered wildly as it caressed her.

"How is it overwhelming? Explain it to me," he said.

Persephone closed her eyes, her bare neck tilting in silent invitation.

"It's sensations more than anything. Feelings of things, like being lost in a dark wood, or the thrill of when all the lights go off in your house at night, and you need to find your way to your bedroom. It's satin sheets on bare skin, and the gleam of a silver knife in shadows, and that call to go outside at night to stare at the stars..."

Hades's lips brushed the curve of her neck, and she lost control of the death power. It poured out of her, decimating the saplings and the grass under her feet.

"Focus, sunshine, I don't need you losing control and killing everything," Hades said.

"You're distracting me on purpose," she complained as she closed her right hand.

"You should be able to handle your magic, no matter what is happening. You wanted me to train you, didn't you?"

"Yes," she admitted, her voice not nearly as strong as she'd like it to be.

"Would you like me to stop?" A question...and an invitation.

Persephone knew that playing with Hades Acheron would probably be the most dangerous thing she ever did. She also knew he was the most distracting thing she'd ever encountered, and if she could use her power properly when his hands were on her she could handle anything.

"No, I don't want you to stop," Persephone said softly. She felt, rather than saw Hades's smile, and her own lips twitched. Maybe he liked touching her as much as she did.

"Then grow the trees back," Hades replied. She lifted her left hand and let life and spring come from it. The blackened saplings crumbled as new shoots began to rise.

Hades's hand moved from her hip, fingers sliding under the hem of her singlet.

Persephone tried to shut down all the exciting signals racing to her brain as he stroked her skin, tracing the lines of her ribs and lingering on the fluttering of her heart.

She frowned with the effort to keep the slow trickle of life feeding the earth around her.

The competitive side of her was rising up too, and she was determined not to give him the satisfaction of making her lose control.

Besides, she was curious to see just how far he would go before he gave up.

Persephone focused her power wider, making it grow a garden beside them and repair the grass, patch by patch.

This is easier than I thought.

Her confidence wavered as Hades's fingers brushed against the soft lace cup of her bra, her nipple hardening as his thumb moved in slow circles over it.

She grew the tree saplings higher, focusing as each leaf burst.

"Your scent changes when you are using your spring power," Hades whispered, nuzzling at her neck.

"It's citrus and floral and green things and warm summer nights. It's life and creation and fucking under the stars. I used to dream about it. I thought I was going crazy every time I went to Athens, and I would catch your scent on the paperwork that Demeter gave me or in meeting rooms. I hated Athens from the moment you walked out of the club. Why did you leave that night?"

Persephone kept growing each bloom on the trees. She knew he deserved a real answer from her.

"Because I was afraid of staying. I wanted you so badly, but when I found out who you were, I panicked."

"Why? Did you think I would hurt you?" he asked, his hand stilling on her breast.

"No, I never thought that, and I certainly don't now."

Persephone tried to sort out all the complicated thoughts and feelings she had about that night and decided to go with honesty.

"I was taught from the cradle to fear you. When I finally met you, I wasn't afraid of you like I should've been. From the second I saw you sitting at the bar I wanted you, and when you reciprocated, I couldn't keep my hands off you. I panicked not because I didn't want you the same way once I knew you were Hades Acheron. It was because of who *I* was. If you found out I was Demeter's daughter, I thought you wouldn't want me anymore, and I wouldn't have been able to handle that. That's why I never called or revealed who I was to you."

"And now I know exactly who you are," said Hades, his other hand went to her hip, and he pulled her ass tight up against him so she could feel how hard he was. "Does it feel like I don't want you anymore?"

Persephone's power surged so quickly the buds on the trees went from flowers to fruit in the blink of an eye, and she struggled to pull it back in.

Hades chuckled huskily, his power trembling over her skin and making the thin straps of singlet and bra slide down her arms.

"You play dirty, Acheron," Persephone complained, once her own power had steadied and she could talk again.

"Oh sunshine, you have *no* idea," he said, teeth and stubble scraping against her bare shoulder. "Kill things for me, Persephone. It feels so fucking good."

It took a few moments for Persephone to draw in the spring and release her shadows. Instead of letting them out into the garden, she let them curl around Hades, spreading the smoky tendrils over him, sneaking them in under his clothes.

"Now, who's play dirty," he said, and she bit back a gasp as his hand tightened on her breast.

"Focus on the landscape, demigoddess, instead of playing this very dangerous game of chicken with me, or you might regret it."

Persephone doubted that, her body was getting hotter by the second. His other hand went to her shorts and popped the top button.

Would he really go that far when anyone could come through the gardens and see them?

Persephone sent a part of her shadows out to start killing the flowers in the new garden beds but kept a part of it tangled around Hades.

She thought about where she would like to touch him, and the shadows slid down the grooves of his muscled chest, down his abs, and undid his belt buckle.

"Now look at how much control you're using in such a short period of time. Maybe you only needed the right kind of motivation," Hades said, the slightest waver in his voice that wasn't there a moment before.

Persephone was liking this game more and more. Hades's power wrestled with her and managed to get his belt done up again.

Persephone bit down a curse as he laughed, and she went back to killing things in the gardens. She was making rose petals blacken one at a time when his hand slipped down the front of shorts and cupped her.

She couldn't stop the tremble that ran over her body as his fingers stroked her, running over her slit. His other arm pulled her tight against his chest.

"You can pick fights with me, pretend that you don't want me, but *this* doesn't lie. You're so, so gloriously wet, and it's because it's me that's touching you, isn't?" Hades whispered, his fingers moving in slow circles. "*Answer* me, Persephone."

"Yes," she groaned, her head tipping back against his shoulder. Her hand reached behind her until she touched the toned curve of his ass and gripped it tight.

"Did you think about me in the past six years?" Hades asked, his fingers moving gently around her entrance.

"You know I did." Persephone moved her hips, rubbing her ass against the hard line of his erection.

"Did you think about me when you touched yourself like this?" Hades slipped two fingers inside of her, and her thighs pressed together. "Did you imagine what it would feel like to have me do this to you again?"

"Fuck...yes, I did, all the time," gasped Persephone.

"Did it feel as good when you did it to yourself?" Hades asked as he thrust his fingers harder and rougher inside of her until she was gripping his forearm, her fingernails breaking his skin.

"N-no, it never was the same no matter what I did," she said.

"Have you let anyone *else* touch you like this since you met me?" Hades asked, his voice dropping to a deadly whisper.

"No," Persephone admitted.

"Why not?" Hades's strokes slowed as his teeth nipped at her ear. "Don't you *dare* think about lying to piss me off."

"B-because they weren't you," groaned Persephone. Hades thrust a third finger into her and she cried out.

So close. Oh, Gods, she was so close.

"I knew that no one else could make me feel like this."

Hades licked the sweat dripping down her neck.

"Good to know it wasn't just me having sleepless nights, thinking about the things I would've done to you and this sweet wet cunt if you hadn't run away. I wouldn't have been gentle and meek, but that's not the kind of lover you like, is it, Persephone?"

"No, it's not," she said, pulling him tighter to her as the pressure between her legs made her groan. Hades's hand tangled in her ponytail, pulling it down so her mouth tilted up.

"Good," Hades said and kissed her. His thrusts quickened, and as he pressed his thumb hard against her clit, Persephone screamed against his mouth and came all over his hand.

Hades lifted his mouth from hers and slowly licked her bottom lip. She was trembling as he pulled his hand gently from her shorts.

"I'm *so* glad we got that cleared up. Now, I've got some business I need to attend to in town, so I'll see you tonight at the club," Hades said. His silver eyes were burning as he lifted her chin with one finger.

"Now fix my fucking gardens, Persephone. Don't make me ask you again."

And then he vanished.

Persephone stumbled without him to hold her upright, and she leaned over to grip her knees to stop herself from landing on her ass.

"You *bastard*," she growled as she did up her shorts with shaking fingers. "You want a garden? I'll give you a fucking garden."

She lay back on the grass, her new control measures forgotten as she unleashed herself.

CHARON ARRIVED at the villa late in the afternoon when Persephone was admiring the veritable forest she had created.

"I'm glad you left the driveway alone. Otherwise, I'd have been screwed. I almost drove past the entrance," he said with a devilish smile. "Hades pissed you off, didn't he?"

"Something like that. Honestly, his arrogance is astronomical," Persephone replied. "What are you doing here? Making sure I don't run away again."

"No, I come bearing gifts, doll, so you can put the claws away," Charon said, reaching into the back seat to bring out a large box and a gift bag.

"Hades said we are having drinks at the Labyrinth, so Medusa and Ariadne picked you out something to wear."

Persephone's eyes narrowed. "Hades said Medusa had wanted us all to meet each other tonight, not him."

Charon laughed. "Susa wouldn't have been so pissed off at short notice if that was the case. She got a hold a few of the beauty places she likes who put some makeup and girlie shit together for you too."

"I see. So, Hades wants to test me, does he?" Persephone said, folding her arms.

"I don't think that's it. He wants you to meet everyone but is too emotionally stunted to tell you that," said Charon. Persephone stared at him until he caved in.

"And yes, it's undoubtedly a test. Hades loves his Court and probably wants to see if you can handle all our strong personalities. He doesn't want you to go back Demeter pissed off and ready to start a war."

Then maybe he should stop blowing hot and cold and being a handsome jerk.

She was still annoyed that he'd just left her in the garden, her body aching and temper hot. It was like she couldn't get one with him without the other. She wanted him, he knew it, and she hated it.

Persephone took the bag Charon offered her. His devilish smile was back.

"You know, the dress the girls picked out for you is an absolute knock out so maybe get your revenge in a way that only a beautiful woman can; by making a grown god weep at what he can't have," Charon added, and then bit his bottom lip suggestively. "Let me know if you need your zip done up, darling."

Persephone grinned. "I just might, titan. How much time do I have to get ready?"

"Two hours, though I doubt you'll need that long," he replied as they walked inside. He poured himself a drink and stretched out of the couch. "Give me a shout if you need any assistance, I'm an excellent hair washer."

Once alone in her bedroom, Persephone opened the dress box and looked at what Medusa and Ariadne had picked out for her. She smiled wickedly and hurried to get ready.

12

Hades sat in his office in Acheron Tower and tried to focus on the email he was writing.

He had to get some work done, but his thoughts were still at the villa, his hands on Persephone, her spring scent in his nose, and the taste of her in his mouth.

What are you doing with this girl? You're acting like a horny beast. Are you no better than Zeus?

His hand curled into a fist. He was better than that piece of shit.

For starters, whatever he did with Persephone was consensual, Zeus wouldn't have even taken that into consideration. He would've seen her, wanted her, fucked her, and left her mad and broken like Perseus's poor mother.

You stopped him doing that forever. That counts.

'Serpent Queen' flashed up on his phone, and he opened his message.

Dress sent to the princess. I hope you know what you're doing. Don't fuck her around too much.

Hades had no idea what he was doing when it came to Persephone, and Medusa knew it. He wanted Persephone to like his Court. They had more in common with her than the fucking hideous socialites in Athens.

He didn't like that Demeter had isolated her and kept her alone either.

Kept her from you, you mean.

Hades ran a hand through his hair. Maybe Demeter was right to do it.

Persephone made him feel possessive and frustrated, and he simultaneously wanted to hold her close and send her back to Athens for his own sanity.

He wanted her to go out tonight, so he wouldn't have to spend another night pretending he didn't want to push her up against the wall and fuck her senseless.

So much for his legendary control. She admitted that she hadn't been with anyone since him, and he knew he had no right to press that confession out of her.

She was her own woman; she could be with whoever she wanted. Just the thought of it made his fists curl again.

She's like you.

He would never have to worry about the power under his skin hurting her. She had proven that more than once.

He needed advice.

Hades picked up his phone and rang Perseus. His newest nephew was no longer looking like Zeus to him.

Yes, there were similarities, but the more he got to know the man, the less like Zeus he reminded him.

"Hades, this is unexpected," Perseus answered.

"Hello, nephew, do you have a moment?" asked Hades.

"Of course, I do, what's wrong?"

"Is Medusa with you?"

"No, I'm at the studio on my own," said Perseus. Hades was silent for so long Perseus asked, "Are you okay?"

"Yes. No. I don't know. I need advice. You're the most human of us, the closest to his -" Hades almost gagged on the word, "emotions. I need you to tell me what you would do."

"Is this about Persephone?"

"Yes."

"You kidnapped her, Hades. That's not a great start to a relationship," said Perseus.

"Ariadne killed Asterion, and you stole from Medusa. Clearly, good starts to relationships aren't our forte. I don't think Persephone and I even *have* a relationship. This conversation feels stupid now."

"Wait, don't hang up on me just yet. You rang for advice, remember? Do you *want* a relationship with Persephone?" Perseus asked.

Hades squirmed. "I believe I might consider it if she is amenable to the idea."

"And you think she might be? Has she said anything that made you think she could be into you, despite the kidnapping?"

Hades thought of Persephone's breathy confession, *I knew that no one else could make me feel like this.*

"She could be. It's hard to tell when she's sweet one minute and downright infuriating the next," Hades said.

"Yeah, well, in my experience, you are all a mercurial bunch at the best of times. I still don't know if Medusa wants to rip my throat out or fuck me half the time," Perseus said with a laugh. "It makes life interesting; don't you think?"

"That's one way to put it. She's not boring, that's for sure. I don't know if it's possible. Her mother would never allow it, and Demeter is important to Acheron Industries."

"Look, Hades, maybe you just need to admit that you like her. Really it doesn't matter what her mother thinks. She's not a part of this. All that matters is if Persephone likes you back. You are both adults, and if you want it, then you'll make it work," replied Perseus. "Is this seriously your first crush?"

"A crush isn't what I have. A crush implies that it's a mild flirtation. I don't feel that way," argued Hades.

Perseus sighed. "Okay, then you need to figure out what you feel. I can't do that for you, but here's the last of my advice; you let her get away from you once, can you live with it happening again? Think about your answer and then...tell her."

"I will consider what you have said. You will be there tonight?"

"I wouldn't miss meeting Persephone for the world. Especially with how the triplets are talking about her. I think you might have some healthy competition on your hands tonight, Hades. Better figure out your feelings quick. Otherwise, she might think you're not interested and go with someone who is," said Perseus and hung up.

It didn't leave Hades feeling comforted in the least.

∼

By the time Hades arrived and slipped up the side steps to Asterion's private balcony, the club was packed.

Ariadne looked stunning in a deep purple dress as she came over to greet him.

"Don't you look dashing this evening," she said, looking him over before going up on tiptoes to kiss his cheek.

"I always look dashing," he replied.

"True. I don't think you and Asterion know how to look unattractive," she said. "You can relax, Hades, Persephone's not here yet."

Hades straightened his cuffs. "I don't know what you mean."

"You look nervous," said Asterion, passing Hades a glass of ice and vodka as he joined them.

"Where is Medusa?" Hades asked, ignoring the comment. Ariadne pointed towards the dance floor.

Medusa had her arms around Perseus's neck as they danced. She looked happier than he'd ever seen her.

"They will be up in a moment, she promised him the first dance of the night," Ariadne said. She slipped her arm around his.

"I can't wait to meet your girl, Hades. Medusa liked her, so I'm sure we'll get on famously. If she can get over you kidnapping her, I'm sure she'll forgive me for suggesting the idea."

"You'd want to hope. She's a force when she's pissed," Hades said, draining his vodka.

"Well, maybe you should consider stop pissing her off and let her see how adorable you are under your grumpy bastard exterior," teased Ariadne.

"I am the God of the Dead, I am *not* adorable," he grumbled.

"Hmm, not when you pout like that," Ariadne said, taking his empty glass and breezing away to refill it.

"Remind me again why I tolerate such insolence from her?"

Asterion laughed. "Because she's fucking cute and you like that she's not afraid of you."

"Is she here yet?" Erebus asked, appearing out of nowhere. He was the neatest Hades had ever seen him, his hair carefully styled and wearing a three-piece suit.

"She tried to kill you, Erebus. I worry that you're this excited," said Asterion.

"She wasn't trying to kill me! She just managed to make me hold still. It made my shadows all excitable," Erebus replied with a dramatic shiver. He turned to look at Hades.

"Charon said that you said that Persephone is her own woman and can give any man her attention if she wants. Is that true? Because I'd like to give her some of my attention."

Hades wished he had a god to pray to for patience. "Persephone is a demigoddess. Five seconds with her and you'll realize that she's determined to make her own choices. She's capable of telling you if she's interested in your attention or not," he said, trying not to give the titan a smacking.

Erebus downed a shot. "I'm going to take that as a yes. Whoo! Tonight is going to fun." And then he disappeared again before Hades could throttle him.

"Don't mind, Erebus, Master. He's never had a woman defeat him before, I think the novelty has gone to his head," said Thanatos calmly.

Hades glanced across at his reaper who, like Erebus, seemed to have taken extra care in his presentation that evening, wearing his favorite gunmetal silver suit.

"Oh, Thanatos, you too?" Hades asked. He hoped that at least one of his titans could maintain a clear head.

"She is very lovely, Master. She can summon shades and control them as easily as I. There is something about her abilities that calls to us. Surely, you have felt it?" Thanatos asked, his silvery brows drawing together.

"Oh, he's felt it all right," Ariadne said, laughing bawdily, and pressing a fresh vodka into Hades's hand.

"She is.... like us," Thanatos said slowly, and then his head tilted to one side. "She is here." And then he disappeared.

"Remind me again why I don't send them all back to the Underworld?" Hades muttered.

"You can't blame them for something you're also suffering from," Asterion argued. He joined Hades at the balcony.

"It's okay to be nervous. Don't worry, we'll make sure she has a good time and doesn't go back to Athens hating us all."

"Thank you, Asterion." Hades's senses prickled, and he spotted Charon leading Persephone through the crowd towards Medusa.

She was...breathtaking.

"You like the dress I picked out for her?" Ariadne asked, leaning her arm against his shoulder. "Damn, she's a looker for sure, boss."

That was an understatement. Persephone looked like a queen. The dress was a deep blue that bled out to black and moved like dark water around her. The shoulder pieces were made of black leather and matched the leather belt around her waist.

Her honeysuckle hair was pinned up in a tumble of curls, and Hades wanted to bury his hands in it. He wanted to trace his fingers across her collarbone and down the deep v of the dress's neckline to where her perfect breasts rested.

Get it together, he cursed himself.

Persephone's beautiful mouth lit up in a smile as she greeted Medusa and Perseus, both of them leaning over to kiss her cheek.

Charon's arm was looped around one of Persephone's, and Erebus appeared beside her, taking the other with a charming smile.

Thanatos was trailing behind her, making sure none of the dancers got too close to her.

Instinctively, Persephone seemed to know where Hades was as she glanced up at him. The ichor in his veins heated, but he forced himself to remain calm as he raised his glass to her.

She gave him a sarcastic little curtsey before turning her attention back to Medusa.

Ariadne let out a low whistle. "Damn Hades, what did you do to piss her off?"

"No doubt there is a list of things," Asterion said, moving his arm around her waist. "They are coming up, try not to be a bastard for one night, Hades. This was your idea."

Hades did his best to look relaxed as Persephone came up the stairs, the triplets hovering behind her and making her laugh.

Ariadne and Asterion went forward to greet her, but Hades didn't hear a word of what was said. He couldn't look away from Persephone and the silky dark material swishing gently around her curves.

"Hello Hades, how was work?" she asked.

"Dreary," he said.

He took her gloved right hand and kissed the skull tattoo on her wrist, grazing his teeth against it where no one could see. Her pupils dilated as he let her hand go.

"Dare I ask how my garden turned out?"

"Well, it's not so much of a garden—" Charon began, but Persephone silenced him with a glare.

"Don't ruin the surprise! I'm sure Hades will love it," she said quickly. "He was very firm on what he wanted before he vanished so abruptly this afternoon."

There was mischief in her tone, which told him he was going to be killing a lot of plants in the near future. She was also pissed he had left her.

Surely not.

He had left because he'd been worried he would drag her to the ground and fuck her on the grass if he didn't.

Maybe you should have.

"I'm glad you're here, Persephone," said Perseus to fill the awkward silence. "It means I'm not the newest god to the group. I'd love to ask you about your magic, I've only made mine manifest the once and I've been too worried about trying again."

"Persephone needs a drink first!" Ariadne interrupted and dragged Persephone towards the bar.

"She is quite charming, Hades," Medusa said, sliding up next to him. "And she's far too good for an old monster you."

"I know," he replied.

"You need to stop staring at her."

"I can't."

Medusa stepped into his line of sight. "Seriously, don't be creepier than usual. Are you feeling okay? You look like you want to level the place."

"He's fine, love, he's just trying to process all of those complicated emotions he's having," said Perseus.

"*What* emotions?" Medusa demanded.

"I want to keep her," Hades admitted, and saying it aloud alleviated some of the pressure in his head.

"Then you're doing a shit job of it," Asterion said and pointed to where Persephone was leading Thanatos down the stairs by his tie, Charon and Erebus following obediently.

"The lady wants to dance, the boys are obliging her," Ariadne said, rejoining them. "I like her, she's feisty."

"Hades wants to keep her," said Asterion, hiding his smile behind his glass.

Ariadne gave Hades's shoulder a playful punch.

"Good for you, boss. The triplets feel the same way. You can be one big polyamorous dark lord family."

"*They* are not invited," Hades growled.

Ariadne laughed. "Do they know that?"

She looked down where the triplets were dancing with Persephone, twirling her between them as she kept up with them step for step.

"Certainly is the prettiest orgy in the making."

"Why do you insist on saying such things to piss me off?" Hades asked.

The assassin gave him her deadliest smile.

"Because you need to stop being so passive and go after what you want. Six years is a long time to wait for someone, only to have them snatched away because you are chicken shit."

"Ariadne, honey, maybe don't—" Asterion began with a nervous look in Hades's direction.

"She's right," Medusa said.

"I didn't ask you all here to gang up on me," Hades muttered.

"No, you asked us here to tell you it's okay if you hook up with her, even though she could be the enemy. Congrats, we like her, and it is okay. Now, go get her, tiger," said Ariadne and gave his ass a smack. Hades pushed his empty glass into her hand.

"My patience has limits, assassin," he warned.

"Someone has to push your buttons and get you moving. Now grow a pair of ovaries and go after her before she goes home with the triplets," Ariadne said.

Hades straightened his tie and headed downstairs.

13

Persephone decided that the Labyrinth was her new favorite place to dance in Greece.

It was her first night out in six years, and she was going to make the most of it.

She had downed the martini that Ariadne had offered her and had hit the dance floor before she picked a fight with Hades if for nothing else but biting her wrist and looking so damn handsome she wanted to push him off the balcony.

Persephone was delighted that the triplets were all excellent and willing dance partners. She had been tempted to ask Hades for a dance just to see the annoyance on his face.

She took her dress as being a success by the way the muscle in his jaw had clenched and the fact he wouldn't stop staring at her.

He probably thinks you're going to get lost in the crowd and make a run for it.

As far as plans went, it wasn't bad, but Persephone was enjoying the club.

Besides, she'd promised him six days, and she always kept her promises.

"Dip me!" Persephone shouted to Charon, and laughing, he obliged her, dropping her low enough that her hair almost touched the floor.

She rose back up and collided with a chest that definitely didn't belong to Charon.

Hades was holding her, and she took an awkward step back in surprise. The triplets had been pulling swapping stunts all night, but she didn't think that Hades was going to play.

"Where's Charon?" she blurted out.

"He's gone to get you a drink," Hades said, his hand sliding over the small of her back and bringing her closer. "Problem, sunshine?"

"No, I just didn't expect you to dance," Persephone replied, placing her hand on his shoulder.

Hades smiled. "Who do you think taught them?" The track changed to something slower, and Persephone did her best not to get too close to him.

"That dress...it suits you," Hades said.

"Thank you." Persephone's hands were going sweaty in her gloves.

She didn't know why she could fight with him so easily, yet a slow dance undid her cool. She wished that any of the triplets made her feel half of what she did when she looked at him.

"Are you angry with me about what happened in the garden? Because you know you could've stopped me with a word," Hades said.

Persephone swallowed hard. "I'm confused, more than angry. Half the time, I honestly don't know if you like me or hate me."

"I don't know either," he admitted and twirled her before drawing her close.

Persephone tried to ignore the feeling of her breasts pressing into his chest, the silk of her dress too thin to stop her feeling the warmth coming off him.

"I believe I like you. No, I *know* I do. I hate whose daughter you are and that there are four days left. I don't think it's enough time," Hades continued.

Persephone looked up at his silver eyes to see if he was teasing her. He wasn't. She had never seen him so serious.

Saints above, don't fall for him. Persephone leaned her face against his chest, so she stopped looking at him.

"I like you too, even if you're a grumpy old bastard." Persephone slid her hand underneath his jacket and stroked his lower back.

"You know, it doesn't matter that I'm Demeter's daughter and that we've only got four days left of our deal. I live an hour away from Styx, it's hardly the other side of the world. Unless you do something to really piss me off, I don't see why we can't stay friends and get Pithos together."

Hades's hand moved to touch the bare skin of her back, and she arched into him.

"Is that what you think I want to be? Friends?" he purred in her ear. Goosebumps exploded over her shoulders and down her arms.

"Well, it's either that or we are enemies."

"I do not want to be your enemy, Persephone."

"They are the only two options," she replied irritably.

"Is that so?" Hades chuckled huskily before he dipped her low and placed a kiss on her chest between her breasts, his stubble pricking her bare skin and making her shiver.

When he lifted her again, the air was as charged as a thunderstorm, Hades's eyes like molten quicksilver.

"Dangerous ground, Acheron," Persephone said into his ear before giving his ear lobe a not so gentle bite of warning.

"We are death deities, Persephone. Danger is what we are," he replied.

"Okay, you've hogged her enough, it's my turn again!" Erebus interrupted them. Hades grip tightened on her before he released her.

"Excuse me," Persephone said and moved through the press of people before either of them stopped her.

The Labyrinth was the first club she had been to that had an adequate number of bathrooms, so there was no line for the ladies. Persephone retreated to the safety of a cubicle and clutched her head.

What are you doing? Is Hades suggesting what you think he is?

There was never a clear way to tell with him. One minute they were arguing, the next his hands were all over her, then they were arguing again. She needed to talk to him.

Tonight, when you've had some drinks to give you courage.

She was hot, her heart racing, and she had no pool for her to sink into and cool down.

Breathe through it.

"Persephone? Are you in there?" Ariadne's voice came from the other side of the door.

"Ariadne, you have no concept of personal space," said Medusa, and then added, "But are you in there?"

Persephone opened the door to find the two women standing next to the basins.

"Was Hades worried I was trying to escape through a window or something?" she asked.

Ariadne laughed. "Hades didn't send us. I saw you walk off the dance floor."

"We wanted to make sure the knuckleheads didn't say something to upset you," Medusa added, and her eyes narrowed. "If they have, I'll-"

"They didn't, and I can handle them," replied Persephone.

"So, what's going on with you and Hades?" asked Ariadne, ignoring the look Medusa gave her. "I've never seen him so flustered."

"Hades isn't flustered. He wouldn't know how," said Persephone.

"Oh, he's definitely flustered," said Medusa. "I can tell them all to back off if they are making you uncomfortable. The triplets especially can be overbearing, and they have never met anyone with your abilities before. It's made them a bit giddy over you."

"No, they have all been genuinely nice. Even Hades, in his way."

"Then why are you hiding in the bathroom?" asked Ariadne. "I'm not judging you. It wasn't so long ago I was hiding in this bathroom too."

"I'm not hiding, I'm overwhelmed," Persephone said, before removing her gloves and running her hands under the cold water trying to calm the power yearning to get out.

"Hades will do that to you. If he starts to annoy you too much, I can bring you over to stay at Serpentine if you like," suggested Medusa.

"That's kind of you, but I know I can't hurt Hades, and I don't trust my power around other people when I'm sleeping," said Persephone, drying her hands and putting her gloves back on. She didn't like the way her chest clenched at the thought of leaving him either.

Four more days...

"You look like you're going to be sick," Ariadne said.

"I'm okay, I'm just not used to being around people like...like me," Persephone replied.

"Demeter kept you away, but we've never been your enemies, Persephone. No matter what happens with Hades, you're always going to be welcome in Styx," said Medusa.

"And we aren't just saying that, either," added Ariadne.

Persephone smiled at the women, a weird sense of belonging moving through her. "I would like that. I must go back to Athens in four days, but I'd like us to be friends. Let's hope Hades and I don't kill each other between now and then."

"He'd probably love for you to try it just for the challenge. He's sweet on you, you know that, right?" said Ariadne. Medusa whacked her. "What? He *is*. You saw them dancing just now, I'd be coming in here to cool off too. Damn, I knew he had it in him."

Ariadne fanned herself shot a wink at Persephone.

"I don't know about that. I'm sure he just likes to fuck with me," she said honestly.

"Hades doesn't fuck with people like that," said Medusa. "Hades understands rules, so if you just want to fuck him, tell him, and he'll do it. Don't let him think whatever is happening between you is something more if you don't feel the same way. He's my best friend, and I don't need him moping for another six years and being shitty and difficult every time he goes to Athens because you shut him down."

Persephone shook her head. "You are reading too much into this, Medusa. He wants me because I can get the information on Pithos for him. I'm not an idiot, I know I'm a pretty dalliance until he gets what he wants."

Medusa's expression softened. "I've known Hades longer than I'm willing to admit, and I can tell you right now, he doesn't 'dally' with anyone."

"Why do you think he's so awkward at flirting with you? He doesn't know how to do it," said Ariadne. She put her hands on Persephone's shoulders.

"Listen to us or don't, but let's get out of here and get another drink. Hades will tell you what he wants and then figure it out from there."

"Sounds like an excellent plan," said Persephone, liking the assassin's attitude.

THEY ENDED up in a private dining area, all sitting around a large table laden with food and Persephone telling them what she knew of Pithos.

Strangely, after already telling it once to Hades, she found it easier and easier to talk about. None of them looked surprised or judgemental that she had killed the men who had shot her father.

"Do you think if you called Demeter, she would be able to look at who is siphoning the money from your accounts?" asked Asterion, opposite her.

"I like to think she wouldn't lose her mind because I'm hanging out with the Court of Styx, but she would. She doesn't trust Hades, and every time I've mentioned Pithos in the past, she has been furious," said Persephone, toying with a martini glass.

Hades sat on her right, at the head of the table, letting them all talk and rarely offering his opinion. Medusa sat on the other side of her and was tapping her nails on the table.

"We are going to have to tell her where you are eventually. Otherwise, she'll get the police involved, and I'm not keen on dealing with human law enforcement. With your help, we could hack into Morning Harvest's servers and check for ourselves," she said.

"Let me have one more night, and then I'll call her and ask myself. If she objects, then I'll help you, but only to get Pithos. I expect you to stay out of our other business," Persephone replied.

She knew that they weren't rivals, but the company needed to have some secrets, at least. She didn't want to feel like she was selling out her own company either.

"I can agree to that," said Medusa with a nod. "We only want Pithos, not to take over your empire."

"Good, because Demeter will probably try to kill me when she learns I've agreed to help you," Persephone replied.

Under the table, Hades's long fingers brushed against hers. The cool expression on his face gave nothing away, but the hard line of his mouth softened as she tangled her fingers around his and held on.

14

It was almost midnight when Persephone said goodnight to the Court and sat down in the passenger seat of Hades's black Lamborghini.

She wasn't drunk but buzzed enough to roll down the window and let the cool night breeze rush over her.

"You're quiet," Persephone said as she slipped off her high heels.

"I have a lot on my mind," replied Hades as he shifted gears.

"Did I pass the test?" she asked, leaning back against the leather seats and shooting him a teasing grin.

"None of you decided to kill each other, we have all agreed to go after Pithos. I count that all as progress."

Persephone propped her feet up near the open window, and he looked at her exposed calves but didn't complain about her feet on the upholstery.

"I like them too," she said, and when she placed a hand on his thigh, he didn't move it away.

They were still sitting in comfortable silence when Hades pulled off the road into his long drive and cursed under his breath.

"It's a forest, Persephone," Hades said, looking out at the tall trees.

"It's nice, isn't it?" she replied and then burst out laughing. "Oh, it's not that bad. I thought you'd appreciate the privacy."

"I promised myself that I wasn't going to fight with you tonight, so we'll discuss this tomorrow, demigoddess," said Hades when they finally pulled up in front of the villa.

"How terribly ominous," Persephone replied sarcastically.

"Keep up that attitude of yours, and I will bend you over my knee to teach you some respect," he warned.

"I'm trembling in fear," she said and got out of the car.

Persephone dropped her shoes by the door and greeted an excited Cerberus with head pats.

Hades placed his keys and cuff links in a glass bowl and took off his jacket. He was looking at her with such an odd expression she straightened.

"What's wrong?" Persephone asked, her hands still resting on Cerberus's head.

"Nothing. The moment just seemed oddly domestic, that's all."

"Oh no, is the dark lord getting used to a girl in his house?" Persephone teased, heading for the kitchen to get some water.

"You are tolerable company," Hades said.

Persephone batted her lashes at him. "I'm flattered, I'm so *tolerable*. Someone leaving you presents?"

There was a white box tied with a gold ribbon on the marble counter.

"That is from my favorite bakery in Styx," Hades said. He went to the knife block and used one of the blades to slit the golden ribbon.

"I have a hopeless sweet tooth after a night out. Thanatos must have remembered to organize the order. What?"

"Nothing, it's just kind of unexpected," Persephone said, hopping up on the barstool. "You better be in a sharing mood, Acheron."

"I could be persuaded."

He opened the box to reveal two rows of chocolate ganache cupcakes frosted with gold decorations. He took out small plates and knives and forks.

"What are those for?" Persephone asked.

"To eat with."

"Hades, you are not seriously going to eat a cupcake with a knife and fork."

"Why not?" he asked, placing one on each plate and setting it in front of her.

"It's just wrong, that's why!" Persephone said.

"I was thinking of your gloves," he said and sat down beside her. "You shouldn't be wearing them anyway. You can control your magic a lot more than what you think you can."

"Gloves or no gloves, I'm not eating a cupcake with a knife and fork," Persephone argued, tugging the black satin gloves off and tossing them in the direction of the couch.

He let out a sigh when they didn't make it and landed on his perfectly clean floors instead. Persephone put her hand over his to stop him lifting a forkful of cupcake to his mouth. "No, you can't eat it like that."

"Why are you trying to cause an argument with me over something so small?" Hades said exasperatedly. "How do you plan on eating it?"

"Properly." Persephone peeled back the golden paper and bit into it.

"And by properly, you mean as messy as possible?" Hades said.

Persephone purposely smeared icing on her lips and grinned at him. "Why? Is my messiness bothering you?"

"It is," he said and started laughing. "Stop it, you ridiculous delight, before you get it all over yourself."

It was too late for that. Her fingers were smeared in icing and cake crumbs. She ignored him as she reached into the box for another one.

"Are you sure you're not a chaos deity as well?" he asked.

"Maybe," Persephone said and tried to lick the icing off her fingers before reaching over to smear some on the back of his hand. He grabbed her by the wrist before she succeeded.

"Why must you insist on pushing your luck? You might not like what it gets you," Hades warned her, but there was amusement gleaming in his eyes, so she waggled her dirty finger at him.

"Why? Are you threatened by a bit of mess? Oh no, not a chocolate smear on the perfect Hades Acheron." Her teasing words died in her throat as he put the offending finger to his mouth and sucked the icing off it.

"Mmm, they are good," he said. With his other hand, he lifted her chin and carefully licked the chocolate from the corner of her mouth. "You're right, I should definitely explore other ways to eat cupcakes."

"H-Hades?" Persephone whispered, her eyes fluttering open.

"Yes, sunshine?"

"I don't want to be your friend either," she admitted, and his eyes widened.

Hades brushed a thumb along her cheekbone. "That's going to make things more complicated."

"Without a doubt, but you wouldn't consider it if it were easy. Neither one of us likes *easy*. Otherwise, we would've been with other people in the last six years, and you haven't, right?"

"No, I haven't."

"Why not?" she asked.

"Because you made me feel extremely and unforgivably *alive*. I touched you, and you have been the only thing I've wanted to touch since," Hades admitted, honest as ever.

Persephone leaned her cheek into his hand. "Me too, but you've already wrung that confession out of me, amongst other things, before you vanished today. You really know how to confuse a girl that's for sure. It would help if I knew what you wanted."

Hades's smile was unguarded for once. "What I want is also complicated. Right now, I want you in my bed, but I don't know how to ask you."

"And what would going to your bed cost me? What kind of deal would you make for that—"

Hades placed a finger against her lips. "No deals. No bargains. Never for this. All that matters is if you want to. I'd like it, but only if it's what *you* want with no obligations."

Persephone slowly undid his tie and tossed it over her shoulder.

"I want you to come for a swim with me while the stars are still out." She hopped down from her chair and turned. "Unzip me, would you?"

He obliged, running his fingers down her spine where the dress opened.

"It is a nice night," he said by her ear.

"Then come with me," Persephone replied and opened the door to the deck before she brushed the shoulders off her dress and let it drop to the floor.

She knew if she waited to see if he were following her, she would lose her nerve, so she didn't turn around to see his reaction. She slipped off her underwear and stepped down into the cool water.

When Persephone did turn, he was standing in the doorway, holding her dress and staring at her with a helpless expression.

She swam to the edge of the pool and leaned her arms against the sides.

"Are you going to stand there all night?" Persephone asked. Hades tossed the dress and vanished. "Where did-?"

Persephone let out a cry of surprise as she turned, and he was sitting in the pool opposite her. "You cheated!"

"You were getting insistent," Hades said, shrugging his broad bare shoulders. "Although you were right, a swim was a good idea."

"The water has always calmed me down when I've been nervous or when my magic is playing up," she replied and moved towards him.

He was giving her lots of space, letting her take the lead, and she was doing her best to remind herself that they had been far more compromising positions.

"You're not nervous now, are you, sunshine?" Hades asked and held out a hand to her.

"Yes, though probably not for the reasons you think," she said, staring at his hand. "I don't want to hurt you."

"You can't," Hades replied, taking both of her bare hands and placing them on his shoulders. "See? Now, tell me why you are nervous." Hades ran his hands down her back and rested them on her hips, tugging her gently toward him, and her legs went around him.

"I have varying levels of control over my power, especially when I'm around you, and you're touching me. I'm nervous that I'll blow up your villa," said Persephone.

Hades chuckled deeply. "Oh honey, if I ever make you orgasm hard enough to blow up my villa, then I'd count it as a win and simply build another one."

Persephone shook her head. "If you keep offering to make new villas all the time, I'm going to start thinking you want me to blow them up."

"You don't think you've caused enough destruction to my property already?"

"I fixed it, didn't I?" she said, her hand stroking the fine hairs on his chest before reaching around to touch the line of tattoos down his back. "Tell me what these mean?"

"Once, they were the magic that bound me to the Underworld. After Zeus, Poseidon, and I cast lots for what realms we would rule, Zeus went one step extra and shackled me to the Underworld where I couldn't leave without his permission. Poseidon ruled the seas, but he could travel wherever he chose, but Zeus wouldn't tolerate any such allowances for me," Hades explained, and her grip on him tightened.

"Why would he do that to you?" she asked, a lump in her throat.

"Because my power more than matched his and he was afraid I'd use it to overthrow him. Tyrants who overthrow others always worry that they, in turn, would be overthrown," said Hades.

"How did you break free of it?"

"I killed him. Well, more accurately, someone dealt him a killing blow, and as the God of the Dead, I was drawn to his inevitable death. Zeus had been stabbed through the heart and was dying in the dirt, helpless as a human. He begged me to save him, promised to lift the bonds on me, promised me anything I wanted," Hades continued, his voice going cold.

Persephone moved so she could look up at him. "What did you do?"

"I cut off his head and scattered his body throughout the Underworld where it could never be reassembled or resurrected. As soon as I did it, the shackles holding me, Charon, Thanatos, and Erebus broke. We were free, and I could finally bring them back into the light," said Hades, his hand moving to tangle in a loose curl of her hair. "Does that frighten you?"

"That you killed him? No. From what I know of Zeus, he had it coming," Persephone replied honestly.

The thought of Hades being trapped in the Underworld filled her with a new strange rage. He didn't need her protection, but she felt the urge to do it all the same.

"Then that what happened?"

"I went searching for others. Those that had been labeled as monsters from the likes of my brother and the other Olympians, the cursed ones, the unloved ones. I found Medusa on Lesbos and convinced her to come with me. I looked for Asterion and found him still buried alive in the Labyrinth on Knossos."

"That's why you get so angry with Demeter," Persephone realized. "She kept me locked up."

"Partly. I take *issue* with anyone being caged because they are different. I especially take issue when they can be helped to live a real life and are denied that help. Demeter is like Zeus, afraid of what we are and the power we possess. No matter what happens between us, don't let her keep you caged," Hades said, voice hardening. "You are too special to be kept locked up like some fucking trinket."

Persephone's heart ached. This fucking god. This complicated, hard, beautiful god. She reached up, her lips hovering over his. "I promise."

And she kissed him slow and gentle.

It was so unlike every other passionate, angry kiss they'd had. It was true and honest and without motivation.

Hades pulled her against him so that their wet bodies were pressing against each other, making Persephone's pulse leap up to her throat.

She wanted all of him, his secrets, and his body and his difficult heart. His hand went to the back of her neck, tilting her head up so he could kiss her deeper. He broke away so he could nuzzle her neck softly.

"Come to bed with me, Persephone," Hades whispered. "Please, let me have you, even if it's only for tonight. Please say yes."

Persephone lifted his face so she could look into his sincere quicksilver eyes. "Yes."

Hades's grip tightened on her, and then the pool vanished, and she was in his bedroom with him still holding her up.

"This is much better," he said, lowering her down on the dark sheets of his bed. He ran a hand down the side of her breast, the dip of her waist and curve of her hip. "I've thought about you being naked on my bed an awful lot."

"And?" Persephone couldn't resist asking.

Hades's expression turned wolfish as he grinned at her. "My imagination wasn't up to the task of conjuring the reality of you, sunshine." He nipped the generous curve of her stomach, swirling his tongue over the bite to take the sting out of it.

"Don't you hold back your power either, you can't hurt me."

Hades let his power trickle from his fingertips as he stroked and explored her bare skin.

Persephone trembled as her magic rose to meet it, pulsing under her skin, and mixing with her desire, yearning for the touch of his dark energy.

"That's it, let it out. Don't play coy."

Hades's shadows wrapped around her bare legs, exploring her like extra fingers, brushing and teasing, making her wet with desire.

Persephone's hands gripped the sheets as she tried to contain the raging power inside of her.

"Fighting me, even now," Hades growled in frustration. He quickly grabbed her hands and pinned them above her head. She held on to her magic, a part of her still in the alley watching men die because she lost control for a moment.

But Hades isn't a man, and he'll never die if you lose control...You are the same.

Hades's shadows hung onto her wrists as he lifted her hips, his dick pressing into her slick entrance.

"Let it out, *now*, Persephone," he said in an unearthly voice that demanded her to obey, and he pushed hard inside of her.

The room exploded into shadows, and Persephone laughed as the dam of power inside of her shattered. She looked at the god above her, smiling with dark joy as he moved in her.

"*There* she is. There is my goddess. At last, I can see all of you."

Persephone's last shred of control left her, and with a power she didn't know she possessed, she flipped Hades onto his back. His strong hands grabbed her hips tight enough to bruise as she rode him, her hair out and wild around her, lifting with the unseen power in the room.

Hades sat up so he could kiss her roughly, her hands pulling his hair as she thrust harder and harder against him.

She had never felt more powerful, more desirous, more herself as her teeth dragged down his throat, her body so full and complete.

The locked away part of her was suddenly thrown open, and on the other side of it was darkness and death, life and light with no beginning or end.

Hades's laugh was a savagely delighted sound as his hands clutched her face.

"Do you see now my Goddess of Life and Death? You are answerable to *no one.*"

Persephone fell into the ocean of his power, let it envelop her, and instead of fear, she felt recognition and belonging. She grabbed his shoulders, dragging her nails sharply down his back and pushed him so deep inside of her that they ground together.

They couldn't be any closer as they moved, sharing the same breath and heartbeat. Darkness was wrapped around them, entangled as they were and pulsing with the same familiar power.

"We are the same," Persephone panted against his lips as she rocked against him.

"We are, and I wouldn't settle for anything less from my consort."

Hades's grip on her ass tightened, and he rolled her onto her back, thrusting into her so hard that she screamed his name as they came.

Hades rested his forehead against her heaving chest, his lips kissing her thrumming heartbeat.

"You are my equal, Persephone. Never act like you aren't ever again."

Persephone's hands trembled as they stroked his bare back, her body full and aching and feeling more alive than it ever had before.

"I promise, though, you might regret it next time we meet across a negotiation table."

"If you try to fight with me over a negotiation table, I'll just fuck you on it until you see things my way," Hades replied, gently moving his hips against hers so she could feel him hardening again inside of her.

"You would miss me fighting with you," Persephone said, hands gripping his shoulders.

"I wouldn't like to rob you of your favorite hobby," Hades replied, leaning to kiss her again. "I'm a gentleman in that way."

And then to Persephone's delight, he showed her all the ways he wasn't.

15

Persephone didn't know what time it was when she finally woke. The curtains were closed, and Hades was asleep beside her, his strong arm over her waist and face pressed into her shoulder.

He looked so peaceful that she kissed the top of his dark hair and enjoyed the moment.

Hades Acheron is a cuddler, who would've thought it? Persephone grinned.

The need for food overpowered her, and she carefully slid out from under his embrace, before wrapping herself in a black and gold satin robe she found hanging on the back of his bedroom door.

She took a moment to admire him sprawled across the sheets, biting her lip to keep from smiling like an idiot.

Persephone expected to find Cerberus outside the door; she didn't expect to find the triplets pacing the villa.

"Finally!" Erebus exclaimed when he saw her.

"What's going on?" Persephone asked, patting at her wild hair.

"Why don't you tell us, doll?" Charon said his smile widening. "Hades warded up his room so intensely that we have been trying to get through to him for hours."

"Here you are, Persephone," Thanatos said, passing her a coffee. "You are going to need it."

"Why?" she asked, her stomach sinking.

"Your mother called this morning," Erebus said irritably.

"Someone managed to get a photo of you dancing with Hades last night at the Labyrinth. Those glamours she put on you must've worn off. She knows you're here, and she says if you don't contact her by midday, she's going to the media to say that Hades has kidnapped you."

"Shit," Persephone muttered, sitting down at the end of the couch.

"Our thoughts exactly. We couldn't get through to Hades, and his warding on that room kept even us out. Where is he?" Charon asked.

"Asleep still," replied Persephone.

The triplets all shared a look. "That can't be right. Even when he does sleep, he's usually up before the dawn," said Thanatos.

"You guys blind? Clearly, she wore him out," Charon replied, shooting Persephone one of his wicked smiles.

"Oh, goddess, tell me this isn't so," Erebus said dramatically. "My heart, it's actually breaking that he won you over."

"You really are thick. She was in the bedroom with him, idiot," Charon said.

"How angry did Demeter sound?" asked Persephone, clutching the cup in her suddenly cold hands.

"Really angry. I tried to tell her you were fine, but she wasn't in the right mind to hear it," Erebus replied.

"You don't have to talk to her if you don't want to," Hades said, appearing behind her. He had managed to put on some long pajama pants, but he was shirtless and tousled.

"Good morning, master, we have been trying to inform you of the situation," Thanatos said, in a teasing tone.

"Yes, I heard you." Hades knelt in front of Persephone, his hands resting gently on her knees. "You don't have to call her back. I can deal with it. I caused this mess after all."

"Don't worry, I can handle Demeter," Persephone said, leaning forward to kiss him on the lips and pass him her coffee. His frown didn't go away, but he didn't argue with her either. "I'm going to need a phone."

Charon offered her his cell phone, and she got off the couch to take it.

"Hades, I'm borrowing your office. I'll fix it."

Hades's office was exactly how she imagined it would be with a large desk of dark wood, beautiful melancholy art on the walls, and buttoned leather chairs to sit on.

She had a mouthful of the strong whiskey from one of his crystal decanters before she sat down in an armchair and dialed Demeter's number.

"I thought I told you I didn't want to talk to another one of you flunkies," Demeter's voice snapped as she answered. Her tone was vicious enough for Persephone's shoulders to hunch inward.

"Hello, Mother," Persephone said.

"Persephone! Where have you been? What the fuck are you doing in Styx?" demanded Demeter, her voice rising an octave.

Be calm and breathe, Persephone.

"I needed to get away for a few days, so I came to Styx to blow off some steam. You don't need to get worked up about it," she said.

"Not worked up? There are photos of you dancing with Hades! They are all over the internet, and I've had media companies calling me all day about it."

"We bumped into each other at a club, it's no big deal."

"It *is* a big deal! It's Hades! I thought you had grown out of these ridiculous rebellions. Partying in Athens occasionally, I can deal with but going to Styx? Why don't you just slap me in the face next time rather than betray me to him!"

Persephone's temper flared, and she gripped the phone tighter.

"Fine, you want to know the truth? I'm here because I'm looking for Pithos because *you* refuse to help me. I found out they have been taking money from our company, and I knew you wouldn't talk to me about it, so I came to find information out on my own."

"So, you went to Hades! Are you insane? Of all the stupid things you could do," Demeter shouted. "Come home, and we can sort this out."

"No," said Persephone.

Demeter's tone went from fire to ice in a split second. "What did you just say?"

"I said, no. I'll come home in a few days."

"If this is about Pithos, we can talk when you are back in Athens, and we will work it out together. You don't need to crawl to Hades Acheron for information," said Demeter.

"Hades wouldn't want me to crawl anywhere. He's offered me *xenia*, so I'll learn what I can before hearing what you have to say."

"I'm not a fool, I saw how you were looking at him in that photo. You better not be fucking him, Persephone, or there will be consequences," Demeter snarled softly.

"Goodbye, Mother," Persephone said and hung up the phone.

∼

HADES STARED at the door of his office from the end of the hall. He didn't want to intrude on the phone call, but he also didn't want Demeter upsetting Persephone either.

Or worse convincing her to go back to Athens.

"She can handle herself, Hades," Charon said, dragging his attention back to the triplets in the kitchen. "If she can tolerate your mood swings, she'll be able to manage Demeter."

"I know," Hades replied and finished her coffee. "I should have foreseen that someone would notice us last night, it was reckless."

"It's a good photo," Erebus said, holding his phone up for Hades to see.

Persephone was radiant, staring up at him with her sphinx smile that he loved. Hades wore an expression he had never seen on himself. The only word that he could find to describe it was... adoring.

"I trust Medusa is managing this," Hades said, handing the phone back.

"She is onto it until you can go in, don't worry. It might be good for business to see you two playing nice. Least they don't know *how* nice," replied Erebus.

"Something you want to say?" Hades said.

"We are happy for you," Thanatos answered with a smile. "She is perfect for you."

The tension in Hades's shoulders eased a little. "She is. Let's hope her mother doesn't convince her otherwise."

Charon laughed. "Even Demeter isn't that powerful. Unless you showed Persephone an exceptionally lousy night, you have nothing to be concerned with, boss."

Except her going back to Athens and leaving me to go mad.

Hades patted Cerberus's heads and tried not to look towards the office door. "I need some air," he said and headed out into the forest that Persephone had created.

Small paths already cut through the trees, and Hades wondered if Persephone had managed to convince a witch to move into it as well.

It wouldn't surprise me.

He huffed out a laugh. He would never be able to predict what she would do, and he loved it even though it frustrated him at the same time.

You can't keep her forever, if she chooses to leave you, you're going to have to accept that.

He wouldn't be like his brothers. Women were not property, especially not ones that equaled his power.

He knew Persephone had been holding back, but last night confirmed all his suspicions. Her abilities were as powerful as his, perhaps even more so because she could give life as well as take it.

"Hades? There you are," said Persephone. She walked across the grass towards him, lifting the edge of his oversized robe, so she didn't drag it on the ground.

Her lips were red from a night of kissing, her hair still a gloriously messy tumble. She looked so perfect he felt like he'd been kicked in the guts.

Are you actually in love with her? Zeus's voice asked in his head, full of disgust. Hades smiled that he could infuriate even his brother's memory.

"I was just admiring your handiwork," Hades said, pointing at the trees. "How did it go?"

Persephone bit her lip. "Not great, but hopefully it will stop her spreading lies to the media."

"If you want to go back to Athens, I'll arrange it," Hades said, almost choking on the words.

Persephone's golden brows rose. "Do you want me to leave? What about our deal?"

"Fuck the deal. It doesn't matter what I want. I won't be your jailer, Persephone, not for anything," said Hades.

Persephone placed her hands on his hips, tugging him closer. "I want to find out more about Pithos, and I don't want to go back to Athens. I promised you six days. Besides, you're growing on me," she said, a spark of mischief back in her green eyes.

"Like a fungus?" Hades asked, earning a laugh from her.

"Something far worse than fungus. I'm starting to worry it's going to be permanent, and without a cure," Persephone replied, stretching up on tiptoes, tilting her head to one side to offer her mouth to him. "Not even amputation would be enough."

"I know the feeling," Hades said and kissed her slowly. He tried and failed not to show how utterly relieved he was.

Maybe this feeling is love after all.

"Thank you, Persephone."

"What for?"

Hades stroked the curve of her jaw with his fingers. "Giving me a chance when you know it's going to be difficult, that *I* am difficult. I won't forget it."

"I should think not," Persephone replied, taking his hand. "Come on, handsome, I think we earned our breakfast before we need to go and see Medusa about this photo business. I delegated the task to the triplets, and I am starving."

Hades groaned. "Oh, my poor kitchen. Whatever they create better be edible."

"If it's not, I'll find some clever ways to torture them as punishment," Persephone said as they walked back to the villa.

Hades lifted their hands so he could kiss her fingers.

"You really are the woman for me," he replied, meaning every word.

16

Persephone had been into a lot of office buildings over the years, but she didn't need to hide her delight as she walked through the green and gold foyer of Serpentine Tower with Hades at her side.

He was dressed in a black three-piece suit with a deep red shirt, and she couldn't risk looking at him for too long without vividly carnal thoughts overrunning her brain.

She felt hopelessly casual beside him in her knee-length purple sundress. It was the first time she had been out in public without gloves, and she was trying hard not to think about it.

There's an emergency pair in your pocket, don't panic.

"Words out now that you are in town, we might as well not try to hide it and add extra fuel to the bullshit fire," Hades said, refusing to take her in through the back like some guilty secret. He swiped a black card at the lifts.

"This place is beautiful, Medusa has done an amazing job," Persephone said, looking around as they waited.

She was so used to seeing the pale pastels and aluminum favored by Demeter that seeing so much color in a workplace was blowing her mind.

The elevator binged, and they stepped in together, Persephone's pulse jumping the instant she was trapped with him and his powerful energy in such a small space.

"Stop it, Persephone," Hades warned irritably.

"Stop what?"

"*Stop* looking at me like that. You're killing my self-control as well as my focus, and we have business we need to take care of today."

Persephone was relieved it wasn't just her that was struggling.

Might as well take advantage of it.

"I *can't* stop looking at you, that's the problem. That suit makes me want to push the stop button on this elevator so you can fuck me up against the wall while you're still wearing it," she said, just as the doors opened again, revealing Medusa on the other side.

Persephone stepped out and took the other woman's hands. "Medusa, I *love* your building, you must show me everything, it's simply gorgeous."

Medusa waved the compliment away. "I work with creatives, darling, what kind of terrible boss would I be if I didn't have an inspirational space for them to work in. That's a cute dress."

"Thanks, Charon picked it out. It has pockets," Persephone said, showing her. "I think I'll let him do all my shopping from now on."

"He must've been paying attention to my rants about women's clothing after all," Medusa replied and then frowned at Hades, who was still staring daggers at Persephone. "What on earth is wrong with you?"

"Oh, don't mind him, it's been a weird morning, and he's in one of his moods. Is this your game design floor?" Persephone asked, looping her arm around Medusa's and risking a glance behind her back at the glowering god.

Hades gave her a look that promised retribution later, his nostrils flaring when she shot him a wink.

Persephone thought a game design floor would be made up of boring cubicles, people behind desks, and minimal eye contact.

What she got was a chaos of designers all talking and drawing and coding and eating.

"All right, calm down, you animals, we have a visitor, so try not to embarrass yourselves," Medusa called, and everyone's eyes zeroed in on Persephone.

A tall, pretty young woman with dark brown hair appeared over the top of a divider, and her face broke into a familiar grin.

"Wow! Perseus told me you were a babe, but he undersold it," the woman said, coming towards them. She was dressed in slim-cut cargo pants and a waistcoat and tie but only wearing a singlet top underneath.

She was effortlessly cool in a way that Persephone had always longed to be at her age.

"Persephone, this Dany Serpho, who has no social filter," said Medusa.

"Nice to meet you, I've heard a lot about you and your takeover of ARGOS," Persephone replied and shook Dany's hand.

"Oh, I haven't even *begun* to take over that place. Medusa says I have to break the old boys on the Board in gently. Speaking of old boys, what are you doing here, Hades?" Dany said.

"I was going to see if you wanted to help hack into Morning Harvest, but I'm rethinking it after that comment," Hades replied, folding his arms.

"Who's hacking?" a black woman said, appearing over the top of cubicle. She had bright blue hair done up in a stunning retro style, complete with dark purple dragonfly hair slides.

"Good morning, Lola, have you had your green juice yet?" asked Hades.

"Ready to rock, boss. Step in my office and tell me what you need," Lola said, waving him over to her desk.

"He seems to trust her abilities enough not to include us in the conversation," Persephone said.

"She's the one that helped us with ARGOS and found all the bank statements from Morning Harvest with the Pithos transactions," Dany replied proudly, staring at the blue-haired girl in open admiration. "She doesn't know it yet, but I'm totally going to make her my girlfriend."

Dany waggled her eyebrows at them and headed over to stand with Hades, listening in. Persephone watched them together and tried not to smile.

"He's very good with them, Dany especially," Medusa said, following her gaze. "If Dany has her way, he will mentor her, and then she's going to truly terrify her Board of Directors. She will give Hades a hard time, but she worships him. Looks like she's not the only one."

"Hmm? What? I don't worship him," Persephone replied, tearing her eyes away from Hades.

Medusa's eyes were bright with humor behind her glasses.

"It's okay, Persephone, I'm not judging you, I'm congratulating you on getting through his defenses. Erebus called me as soon as the idiots figured out that you were in Hades's bedroom. Honestly, after six years, I'm surprised you two held out as long as you did," Medusa said, as Persephone blushed. "Anyway, to business, how was Demeter?"

"Furious. She knows more about Pithos than what I imagined. She promised to tell me everything if I return to Athens," said Persephone.

"And are you going to go? Because if you are, I need to start damage control with Hades now," Medusa asked, her smile vanishing.

"No, I'm not going yet. I hate to admit it, but I can't trust anything Demeter says regarding Pithos. I've wanted to know more about the assholes who killed my father for years, and if she's known all along and done nothing? I don't know how I'm going to deal with that," Persephone admitted, a pain back in her chest at just the thought of the confrontation.

"If I get you and Hades to look into it, I can go to Demeter with some facts backing me up and call her out if she's trying to lie to me. Hades can be a prick, but at least he's honest about it."

"For your sake, I hope this doesn't force you into picking sides," sighed Medusa. "Pithos's bullshit aside, Hades will fight to keep you, and while he *is* honest, he's not beneath playing exceptionally dirty to get what he wants."

"Oh, I know that too." Persephone's lips twitched. She knew *exactly* how dirty he played. Medusa read her expression and gave an unladylike bark of laughter.

"Gods have mercy, I don't want to know," she said with mock horror, breaking up the tension.

"You had best go and tell them the easiest way to break your firewalls before this conversation goes any further downhill."

After they were done at Serpentine, Hades cast a glamour over them, and they walked hand in hand the two city blocks to Acheron Tower. He didn't let go of her even when he removed the glamour inside the building.

Persephone wondered if he noticed or didn't care what assumptions people made.

He took a pile of folders from a receptionist with a smile, and he let Persephone into his huge office.

"Now, that is a view," Persephone sighed, going to the wall of windows that looked out over the city.

"I have an aversion to feeling trapped even in my own building," said Hades, sitting down behind his large mahogany desk.

Persephone walked around, admiring the books on the shelves and the few photos of him and the other members of the Court before she went back to sit on the edge of his desk.

"What are you thinking about, sunshine?" he asked.

Persephone folded her arms so she wouldn't reach out and touch him. "What I'm going to do if I find out Demeter has been working with Pithos."

"As much as she irritates me, I don't believe she would willingly fund monster hunters."

"She might not know about the money, but she knows something, I can *feel* it. I hate that she's never trusted me enough to tell me, or even try to get justice for what happened to my father. It's like she doesn't give a damn at all that the people responsible for his murder are just walking about," said Persephone angrily.

Hades held out his hand for her, and she relented, loving that he wanted to comfort her.

"We don't know what her motivations are. Demeter might have been trying to protect you, Persephone. Trust me, I know the instinct. Something you must also understand is that the Olympians used to hoard their secrets to use as weapons against each other. I have no doubt it's one of the reasons Demeter kept you from me and hid the extent of your abilities. She's your mother, but never forget she's a god."

"Like I shouldn't forget that you are a god, and you could be using me as much as her?" asked Persephone.

"I would find other, more interesting ways than petty political intrigue to remind you that I'm a god, Persephone," Hades said, his other hand sliding up her thigh and under the hem of her dress.

"And I plan to use you every which way *except* as a pawn."

Persephone grabbed his tie and pulled him closer with a hard jerk. "If you break my heart, Acheron, you'll have to go back to the Underworld just to get away from my wrath."

"I get so hard when you threaten me," Hades growled, and his lips were about to touch hers when a loud ringing sound echoed through the office.

Persephone managed to see "Morning Harvest" flash on his desktop screen before she was suddenly shoved under the desk.

"She can't see you here," Hades said and then answered the call in a cold voice. "What do you want now?" Persephone expected Demeter's voice, but it was Vallis.

"Hello, Hades, thank you for *finally* answering one of our calls. We have a situation on our hands, I'm sure Medusa has debriefed you by now?" Vallis demanded.

"Could you really call a single photo a situation?" Hades asked in a patronizing tone.

"I consider any threat to Persephone's security as a situation."

"Don't you think Demeter is overreacting? Persephone isn't in danger. All I did was dance with her because she was in one of our clubs. If I thought the girl wasn't wise enough to have a sufficient glamour on her to ward against photos, I wouldn't have gone near her. It's hardly a fault of mine she was so ill-prepared."

Under the desk, Persephone's anger rose. *Did he really just call her an unwise girl?*

"Where is Persephone now? Demeter said you have given her *xenia*. She worries that she's staying...with you. Is she?" asked Vallis, a touch of embarrassment creeping in.

"I gave her *xenia* while she's in Styx, Vallis, as a sign of the friendship between us. A friendship I'm starting to question the longer Demeter acts like I've done something horrible to her daughter," replied Hades.

"Have you?"

"All depends on what you'd consider horrible. I let her drink for free if that counts. What does Demeter think I've done to her precious Persephone?"

"She thinks you've seduced her in order to turn her against us," replied Vallis.

Hades's laughter was gloriously bored. "What interest would I have in seducing a girl that has barely been let out from under her mother's wing? Demeter is thinking of the wrong god if she believes I could have any interest in virgins."

Persephone bit down her outrage. She knew rationally that he was trying to throw Vallis off, but she was no longer thinking rationally.

His belt buckle glistened in front of her, and her anger turned to vengeful glee.

Dark power poured out of her hand, wrapped around Hades's legs, and pinned them to the floor. Then she undid his belt.

He hadn't been lying, threatening him *had* made him hard. *Perfect*.

"Look, Hades, just send her home. I know nothing would happen in your city without you or the Court knowing. Please, for the sake of her mother's sanity and mine, find her and send her back to Athens," said Vallis.

"What's the real issue here, Vallis? It can't be only because Persephone...wanted a holiday," Hades replied, his voice faltering ever so slightly as she took his dick in her mouth.

She gripped his thighs tightly as she felt him trying to wriggle out the bonds she held him with.

"Has she come to you and asked about Pithos?" said Vallis.

"Pithos? Not that I can recall. Although the name is familiar to me. What business do you h-have with them?" Hades replied, his voice slipping as it went from boredom to anger.

"We *don't* have business with them. I'm afraid it's all a misunderstanding. Persephone thinks they are responsible for the murder of her father, and we don't want her to get into trouble asking around about them. As I said, her security is mine and Demeter's main priority."

"Fine! Yes! I'll look for her and tell her to reach out, but I won't send her home like she's a scolded child. No matter how much she may *deserve* a scolding," Hades said through his teeth, his hand coming down to bang on the desk as a warning.

Persephone didn't stop. She moved her right hand so she could work him, letting the dark killing power trickle out of it, and Hades grew even harder.

She had wanted revenge, and now she was so aroused she just wanted him.

"Thank you, Hades, Demeter is also planning to come and visit you tomorrow to discuss this further. Are you happy to meet with her?"

"Yes. Goodbye," Hades said, hanging up before he tore free of the bonds on his legs.

Persephone squeaked as he grabbed her by the shoulders and pulled her out. Before she could fight him, he slung her over his lap, and gave her a hard slap on the ass.

"Hades! What the fuck—" she protested.

"*That* is for back chatting me non-stop since I met you," Hades said before smacking her again. "And that is for the ridiculous shit you just pulled while I was on a *phone call.*"

Persephone groaned, but it wasn't in pain. His hand stilled, and then he reached into her damp panties, running his finger over her wet clit.

"Fuck!" Hades exclaimed.

Files, pens, and organizers were pushed off his desk. He bent Persephone over it, tearing her panties off her.

Persephone cried out as he bit the curve of her ass before gripping her hips and thrusting his dick inside of her. She grabbed the edge of his desk and pushed back against him, loving the feel of him filling her up.

Her power leaped out of her, and half of his desk sprang to life, pushing branches up through his computer while the other half turned to ash.

"Shit, Hades, your desk," Persephone tried to say as it wobbled under her.

"I don't give a fuck about the desk!" he hissed, shifting position so he could move even deeper inside of her. Persephone cried out and the desk collapsed in two. Hades managed to grab her and hold her up before she fell with it.

Hades was out of her only long enough to spin her about to face him, pick her up, and slam her up against the wall before pushing back into her.

Persephone locked her legs around him, and haphazardly tore at his shirt and waistcoat.

"More, I need more," she gasped, heedless of her nails scratching at him.

Hades ripped the front of her dress, freeing her breasts so he could kiss them roughly. His hand came down hard on the wall above her, and something cracked.

Books, photos, and paintings fell from the shelves as the wall shook with each thrust.

Persephone bit his chest to hide her cries, his dick hitting her in the right spot. Hades's mouth found hers, smothering her scream of pleasure as she came loudly.

"Fuck, Persephone," he gasped against her lips, clutching at her hips as his own orgasm shook him.

They sank to the carpet, panting, Hades still holding her tightly on his lap.

"I-I think we broke your office," Persephone said, her hand covering her mouth. She looked at the destroyed desk and long crack in the plaster of his wall.

"I think you broke *me*," Hades replied, eyes wide. He brushed her hands away from her mouth so he could kiss her softly. "I didn't hurt you, did I?"

Persephone shook her head. "Only my heart rate."

"Good," Hades said, and then surveyed his wreaked office. "Must you always break my things?"

"Yes," Persephone replied, and he made a noise of exasperation. "How else are you going to make room for me in your perfectly ordered life?"

The annoyance vanished instantly, and Hades pulled her close, kissing her forehead, temple, and cheek.

"Trash whatever you like," he said softly. "Although we need to have a discussion about phone etiquette."

Persephone leaned back from him and shook her head.

"No, honey, we need to discuss the fact you just agreed to let Demeter visit tomorrow."

Hades put his arms around her protectively. "Fuck."

17

Demeter's entourage arrived at Acheron Tower at precisely 9 am.

Persephone stood in the Board room, and she sensed the moment her mother stepped into the building.

Maybe it was because she had spent the last week around Hades and the others, learning more and tuning into her abilities, but she could feel Demeter's power getting closer with every step.

Persephone let out a tight breath and straightened the red blazer Medusa had given her.

She hadn't wanted to meet her mother in one of the casual outfits she had been getting around in, it would just be another kind of fuel to her fire, so she had been kitted out in pressed pants, a cream silk button-up shirt, and a blazer.

She had taken one of Hades's black and silver silk ties to wear because she wanted a little piece of him close.

Hades had seen it, re-tied it with precision, and said nothing about it, his face steely calm all morning.

She can't force us apart, Persephone reminded herself.

Hades had said those words to her the previous evening when they had drunk wine and watched the ocean waves, her anxiety about facing Demeter almost overwhelming her.

It might not have been goodbye, but it definitely was going to be the death of the responsibility-free holiday she'd been enjoying.

Asterion and Medusa had opted out of the encounter but were in Hades's office next door, the triplets keeping an eye on the streets around them and on any men Demeter had brought with them.

They weren't going to take any chances if Demeter had called in Pithos out of spite.

Persephone glanced at Hades, sitting at the head of the table, his silver eyes focused on her.

"Remember, you are answerable to no one. Demeter might be your mother, but she is *not* your god," Hades said.

The elevator doors chimed open, and Demeter and Vallis walked into the Board Room.

Demeter was a vision of perfection, as usual, her caramel hair in a beautiful updo and was wearing a peach and cream skirt suit. Her eyes widened when they saw Persephone.

"What are you doing here?" she said, placing her handbag down on the table.

"I heard you were harassing Hades to deliver me, well here I am," Persephone replied.

"Good morning, Demeter, are we skipping pleasantries already?" Hades asked.

"I'm just a little shocked you convinced my daughter to see sense," replied Demeter.

"I can't take the credit. You should know by now that you can't convince Persephone to do anything she doesn't want to."

Vallis inclined his head politely in Hades's direction. "Thank you, all the same, you assured us that she was safe, and we appreciate that she has come to no harm in your city."

"Persephone would *never* be in danger in Styx," Hades replied, smiling to hide the tone that had begun to creep in.

Demeter stepped closer to Persephone, and the sense of her influence rushed over her. Persephone could feel it trying to claw its way into her for the first time.

"You've had us all worried while you were away, but you've had your fun, and now it's time to come home," Demeter said.

"I told you yesterday, I'm not going back to Athens yet. There are things I need to do," replied Persephone. Demeter's eyes widened fractionally, surprised that her influence had no effect on her.

I wonder how many times she did it to me without me knowing? Persephone swallowed down her anger.

"We can discuss *those* things later, Persephone."

"No, we are going to talk about them now," Persephone said and looked over at Hades.

"Can you please give us the room for a moment. Vallis? Hades has excellent coffee, so do help yourself to cup."

"Of course, Persephone. Please call if there's anything I can get you," Hades replied, getting to his feet and steering Vallis towards the door.

Persephone took a small measure of enjoyment from the look of surprise and horror on Demeter and Vallis's faces.

"I do believe that is the first time I've seen Hades actually do what he's told," Demeter said.

"Hades is extremely accommodating and polite once you get to know him," replied Persephone. "It does make me wonder why you were so determined to have me be afraid of him my entire life."

"Because I have known him long enough to have the sense to keep my distance from him. Do you know even Zeus was afraid of what Hades was capable of?"

"Is that why he thought it was okay to imprison him in the Underworld?" Persephone asked, a protective edge creeping into her voice. "Is that why you thought it was okay to give Pithos money to help them put him into another one?"

"You have no idea of what you're talking about. You have been in this city, for what? A week at most? And you are going to trust fucking Hades's word over mine?" Demeter hissed angrily, the infamous calm finally slipping.

Persephone slid a portfolio of papers towards her.

"You can stop lying now. I've seen the proof," she said calmly.

Demeter rifled through the first pages and shut it again with a bang. "These are clearly forgeries by Hades trying to drive a wedge between us.

You are far too old to have fallen for such a thing, and I'm disappointed you have."

"What could Hades possibly gain from driving a wedge between us?" Persephone asked. She wanted to shake her. She was *still* lying to her, even with all the evidence in front of her.

"He wants the company and to take everything away from us," Demeter said stubbornly, refusing to back down.

"Look around you, Mother. Does it look like he needs our company?"

Demeter started to pace. "If he finds out about your power, what do you think will happen? I won't have my daughter being one of his subjects. I know you don't believe me about this, but some agreements in this world are beyond even us gods to break. Death and all its kingdoms belong to Hades. That means your right hand *belongs* to Hades and being here puts you in unnecessary danger. All for what? So, you can get drunk and make a fool of yourself in front of him?"

"This isn't about Hades, Mother, it's about Pithos. I'm giving you a chance to tell me the truth. Help me understand, or I will find out the truth on my own. They *killed* my father."

"No. *You* killed your father," Demeter replied, and Persephone flinched. "If you would've done as you were told and stayed home, neither of you would've been on the street that night."

"Pithos was there to kill me, and he stopped them. He didn't want to be a part of their plans, and here we are, involved in their plans anyway. Do you even know what they are? They tried to kill Asterion and Medusa!" Persephone argued.

"They are monsters, what business is that of ours," replied Demeter.

"Do you even hear yourself? If they are monsters, then so are we, Mother."

Demeter grabbed her arm, her nails digging in tightly. "*We* are gods, not monsters. We are not like them."

"I am," said Persephone, wrenching her arm away. "Pithos tried to kill me, and the only reason they haven't killed you is that you are giving them money to try to hurt Hades."

"Fuck, Hades! He's the biggest monster of them all."

"I love him," Persephone said, surprising herself enough that she didn't see Demeter's hand come up to slap her across the face.

"You little bitch. You have sold yourself out to him, and me as well. Pithos has left us be because we have kept our distance from him. Now, I've got to go and clean up your fucking mess again. We are going back to Athens," said Demeter grabbing the portfolio.

"I'm not going with you," Persephone repeated, standing straighter.

"You are mine, Persephone, not his."

"I am *no ones.*"

Demeter's power spiked, and a vine of golden light appeared in her hand. "If I have to use force to drag you out of here, I will, Persephone. Hades won't stop me, because gods never interfere in other god's business."

"Siding with Pithos against him sure seems like interference to me," Persephone snapped.

The golden vine whipped from Demeter, but Persephone was faster and grabbed it with her right hand.

"You won't be using this against me anymore either," Persephone growled, and shadows and death began to turn the vine to ash.

Demeter stumbled back in surprise, the golden vine vanishing.

"W-Where are your gloves?" she stammered, only just realizing they were missing. "What has Hades done to you?"

"Shown me that I don't need them anymore," Persephone replied.

"He has you under some kind of enchantment. You have to believe me —" Demeter said, panicking.

"I can't believe anything you say right now."

Demeter made to reach for her again, but the door to the Board room burst open, and Hades's strode in, his expression colder than Persephone had ever seen it.

"Touch her again, and I'll remove that hand," he said, and Demeter took an involuntary step backward. Hades's expression didn't change as he looked at Persephone. "Are you okay?"

"I'm fine. Just...disappointed. I'd like to leave now," Persephone said, walking to his side.

"Charon is waiting downstairs to take you wherever you wish to go," replied Hades.

"Persephone! You can't leave me," Demeter began.

"Actually, Mother, I can. Just like I can find Pithos and stop them from hurting anyone else because I am *not* like you. I'd rather be a monster," Persephone said, and walked from the room.

Her hands were shaking as she pressed the button to the elevator. She waited until the doors had closed on her mother and Vallis before she burst into tears.

Charon was standing beside a black Aston Martin Vantage waiting for her as Persephone stepped out into the car park. He took one look at her and pulled her into a hug.

"I take it things didn't go as well as you'd hoped, doll."

"Will you take me home, Charon? I can't be here right now," Persephone sobbed into his chest.

"You still want to go back to Athens after all this? I mean I'm happy to drive you but—"

"No, I mean home as in the villa," Persephone corrected as she stepped back.

Charon took the silk handkerchief from his breast pocket and offered it to her with a small smile.

"Of course, my lady. Get in and buckle up. I think we both need to drive really fast right now to help us feel better."

Persephone knew if she left now, she would most definitely be picking a side.

I'd rather be a monster like the Court than a monster like my mother, she thought, and got in the car.

It wasn't until they had cleared the city that Persephone felt like she could breathe again, and then her world exploded in gunfire and screaming metal.

18

Hades wasn't responsible for half of the violent things he had been blamed for over the centuries but looking at the Olympian goddess before him made him wish for a depth of carnage that it would've made even his Court worried.

Demeter was trying not to cry as she watched Persephone walk away from her, and Hades made damn sure that the path between them was blocked so she didn't try going after her.

Hades sat down back at the head of the table.

"I hope you're happy," Demeter snarled. "This is what you wanted all along, well congratulations Unseen One, you've succeeded."

"I'd like to be able to take the credit, but unfortunately, you isolated Persephone all on your own. Now that she is gone and you have no reason to keep lying, let's get down to business," Hades replied, his grip tightening on the arms of his chair. "Sit."

"Vallis-"

"Is sitting outside like a good boy while the adults talk," replied Asterion, entering the room from a side door with Medusa.

"Trying to fight this conversation would be unwise, Demeter, now *sit*," Hades snarled softly.

Demeter sat.

"Excellent. I'll start," said Medusa, opening an identical portfolio that Persephone had given Demeter. "As the summary on page 3 shows, currently, your company Morning Harvest has given the organization known as Pithos over twelve million dollars over the past fifteen years. This money has been distributed through various shell companies of their operation; the complete list outlined on page 2."

Hades tuned out as Medusa went through all the details their hack during the night, his mind lost on Persephone's words.

The Board room had always had microphones in it, and Hades had listened to the conversation from his office. Medusa and Asterion hadn't said a word about Persephone's admission. *I love him.* His heart, his mind, his world had stopped. *I love him.*

Then Demeter had attacked her, and Asterion and Medusa had to stop him intervening because he was ready to tear Demeter apart.

"She's handled it, Hades, she doesn't need you," Medusa had hissed.

"Medusa, she..."

"I *know*, but Persephone needs to make this choice on her own," she said, and Hades had held himself together long enough to try to think straight again.

"If she's strong enough to love you, uncle, she's strong enough to stand up to her mother," Asterion added, with a gentle pat on his shoulder. "Congratulations, now you can stop giving us both a hard time about being in love too."

Hades had wanted to carry Persephone off, to kiss her, to keep her safe from her bitch mother's savage words.

Instead, he'd let her walk away even though she looked like her heart had been shattered.

Asterion cleared his throat, bringing Hades back to the conversation and the squirming goddess in front of him.

"We would like to know why you thought this attack on us is justified, Demeter," said Asterion, letting just enough of the beast to show in his eyes that the goddess paled.

"I did it, so they wouldn't kill Persephone," she replied.

"That's it? They were blackmailing you?" demanded Medusa.

"I don't expect you to understand. You are not a mother, Medusa, even if you like to pretend to be one with that Hellas brat, Dany Argos," Demeter said. Asterion's hand went down on Medusa's shoulder to stop her leaping across the table.

"That is enough insults, Demeter. Do it again and I'll make you regret it. This is not the Court of Olympus, where such games are tolerated. This is the Court of Styx, and we are monsters who won't hesitate to damage your worthless carcass," Hades growled.

"Tell us about Pithos, and I might consider letting you leave today. It's only because of the love and respect I have for your daughter that you are still alive enough to speak."

"Fine, you want to know the truth, here it is. Pithos came to us when Persephone started to show her power. They were horrified at the thought there would be another creature walking around Greece with a power similar to yours," Demeter said angrily.

"We told them she wouldn't harm anyone, but then she lost control and nearly killed someone. That was when they came to us and threatened to take her away, to put her somewhere that she wouldn't be able to hurt anyone or anything."

"My stupid human husband told them that there was no way he would let them touch his daughter. Then she foolishly went out, and he ended up taking a bullet that was meant for her. It didn't matter that she would've survived it, he did it anyway and died for his one act of heroism."

"And you thought it would be better to send her away to be locked up?" Asterion demanded.

"No! Pithos and I came to a new agreement. I'd give them money in exchange for keeping Persephone and teaching her to control her abilities on my own," Demeter explained.

"But you didn't teach her. All you did was shut her up and keep her under your fucking heel. She was trapped and screaming on the inside because you made her fear what she was," hissed Hades.

"Did you ever stop and think what that would've been like for her? Did you even ask what Pithos were going to do with the money that you were giving them?"

"I didn't care because my daughter was safe from them and from you," snarled Demeter. "Now you meet her once and manage to convince her that she's in love with you. Gods don't love, Hades, we aren't capable of it."

"You're wrong. *You* are not capable of it," he said, and his phone started vibrating. He looked at the screen and saw Persephone's new number and photo flashing.

"What's wrong?" he answered, and gun shots fired in the background.

"Hades! We are being attacked!" Persephone shouted over the noise. Hades was on his feet and out of room in seconds.

"Are you okay? Are you hurt? Where is Charon?" he demanded, panic coursing through him.

"He's beside me, but they hit our car, he's not moving!"

"He will be okay, don't worry," Hades said and heard someone talking through a megaphone and the word 'Pithos.' *Fuckfuckfuck*. "Talk to me, Persephone, what's happening?"

"They said I have to get out of the car. We are out of the city, on the main highway towards the villa," she said quickly. "Hades, they are trying to cut their way in."

"Listen to me, Persephone. Do you trust me?"

"Yes."

"Then listen to what I'm going to say very carefully and don't use any of your power on them. Keep it hidden for as long as possible. This is what I need you to do," Hades said, and as calmly as he could, he gave her a list of instructions.

"Did you get all of that?"

"Yes, Hades," she said, her voice steadier.

"Good, one last thing I need you to do; don't doubt for a single second that I'm not coming for you, sunshine."

"Hades? In case I don't get to see you again, I love you," Persephone whispered.

Hades gripped his phone. "I love-" he said before the line went dead.

Dark energy exploded from him, and as he stepped back into the Board room, it already had Demeter gagged and pinned up against the windows so tightly the glass was beginning to crack.

"They attacked Persephone and Charon on the coastal highway. Asterion, get Thanatos and Erebus," Hades instructed, closing in on the weeping goddess. "Did you know they planned this?"

Demeter shook her head, and the shadows slipped from her mouth.

"I had no idea, Hades, I *swear* it! I'd never condone violence against my daughter," Demeter said, gasping for breath

"Except the kind you inflict on her yourself. No one knew she'd left here except you."

"And Vallis!" Demeter shouted, squirming against the power holding her. "He's always been the middleman between Pithos and me in our dealings." Shadows covered her mouth again.

"Medusa," Hades said.

"On him," she replied and hurried out of the room. Hades turned back to Demeter and stroked her perfect cheek, leaving a trail of dying flesh, his power smothering her screams.

"Pithos will make contact soon, it's their style, and they are nothing if not tedious with their demands," said Hades before leaning close to whisper, "What to do with you now that I know you betrayed me?"

"Hades, that's enough," Asterion said. "We'll put her in a cell until this is all over. Thanatos and Erebus are waiting for you downstairs. Please don't waste fresh leads on Pithos with petty acts of revenge. Torturing her mother won't keep Persephone on your side for long."

Hades snarled, dropped an unconscious Demeter to the floor, storming away before he tore her apart.

"I'll get the helicopter in the sky and get into CCTV to pick up a convoy leaving the site," said Medusa, intercepting him by the elevators.

"Vallis is gone. Security footage has him leaving the building right when we sat down with Demeter. I have Lola running the license plates."

"Thank you, Medusa. Keep me updated," Hades replied.

"I will. You just focus on keeping your temper and getting our queen back, okay?" she said.

Hades managed a smile. *Our queen, not His queen.* He liked that.

Now all he had to do was get her back and annihilate Pithos.

Stick to the plan.

Thanatos and Erebus looked as agitated as Hades felt as he met them outside and slid into the back seat of the car.

"Have you got Charon's car yet," he said as they sped out into the streets.

"GPS coordinates are already locked in," Thanatos replied from the driver's seat.

"I swear, if they have hurt him," Erebus began and quickly shut his mouth. There was no point in saying what they were all feeling.

"Persephone said he was unconscious. They might have thought him dead and left him," said Hades.

"Only if they are stupid enough to think he can die," Thanatos murmured.

The remains of the Aston Martin were still upturned and in a gully by the side of the road.

Sirens wailed in the distance as they pulled up and got out.

"Charon!" Erebus shouted, and they heard a groan. Erebus climbed down through the scrub, racing towards the sound.

"He's down here!" Erebus said, and Hades and Thanatos hurried to find them.

"The fucks," hissed Hades.

They had used metal stakes to pin Charon's bullet-riddled body to what remained of the bonnet. A piece of paper was nailed through one arm and had Hades's name written on it.

"It's okay, brother, we'll get these out," said Erebus softly, nodding to Hades. "Think happy thoughts like...like the lines of a Zenvo ST1."

Charon screamed as Hades's power ripped all four spikes from his body at once. Thanatos caught him and lifted him over his shoulder.

"I've got you, Charon, don't worry," he whispered as he carried him out and back onto the road.

Hades bent down to pick up the fallen letter. It was soaked with gold ichor, but he could make out the line of co-ordinates and the words.

Surrender yourself.

Such a ploy would have never worked in the past, but as soon as Vallis had seen Hades's reaction to Persephone, Pithos had the trump card.

Hades walked back through the scrub and to the passenger side of the Aston Martin. They had used some kind of tools to cut through the door to get to Persephone inside. He touched a smear of golden ichor on the side of the seat.

She is okay. She talked to you, remember? You told her not to use her power and to let herself be taken.

Hades was regretting that decision now as he stared at Persephone's blood.

You are no good to her standing here.

Hades climbed out of the ditch and went to find Charon. Thanatos had lain him out on the back seat of the car and was murmuring to him softly in the language of the dead.

"Out of the way, I've got this," said Hades and knelt down.

"I'm sorry...I couldn't stop them...Persephone," the titan groaned.

"Don't worry, we will get our revenge, ferryman," Hades whispered and placed a hand on Charon's forehead.

Hades shut his eyes and sent his power into Charon's body, healing the damage that Pithos had done to him.

The titan groaned but managed to hold himself still until it was done, and he was gasping in large gulps of air.

"Fuck, I hate how much that stings," he complained as he slowly sat up.

"He lives!" Erebus called and climbed into the driver's seat.

"Won't be for long if you are driving," Charon complained.

"Where are we headed, Master?" Thanatos asked Hades.

"We go and get the helicopter and find out where the fuck this is," Hades said, holding up the letter. "We've been given an invite to their hideout."

"Those dumb fucks," Erebus laughed, and they all joined in.

"What a great opportunity to kill them all," said Thanatos.

Charon managed a crooked smile at Hades. "That's if Persephone has left us any."

"I asked her nicely, but let's be honest, she's never obeyed me before," Hades said, entering the GPS coordinates on his phone. He hissed when he saw the location. "Those bastards."

"Where are they?" asked Charon.

"Fucking Crete all along." Hades held out the phone to him.

"Mount Juktas? They must have been using the caves there. I

wondered where all those soldiers seemed to scatter to after we freed Asterion from Knossos," said Charon with a frown.

"That's not all that mountain is known for," Thanatos replied, glancing at Hades in the mirror.

The other two titans stared blankly at Hades. Only Thanatos had been there that night.

"It's where I killed Zeus," Hades admitted, "and it's where I am going to kill whoever is responsible for fucking with us."

19

Persephone woke to the smell of earth and rot. Someone was throwing small, coin size discs of metal at her.

"Hey, wake up, new girl," a male voice said.

Persephone opened gritty eyes and sat up. Her head was pounding from whatever was in the syringe that she had been jabbed with.

"Where am I?" she mumbled and tried to stop her vision from spinning.

"Cave. Why do you smell like someone I used to know?" the voice demanded.

There was a rock wall on three sides of her cell, and through the one side with bars, she could make out a man sitting on a wooden stool next to a worktable covered in bits of metal and wires.

He had long tangled hair and a beard, and he was wearing filthy jeans. She got up and walked to the bars and looked up at the cavern above them.

"I'm Persephone," she said as the man tossed another disc at her. "What's your name."

The man puffed out his cheeks and shrugged. "I don't know. Don't remember. Didn't seem important to remember. She never mentioned a name. Some of the others whisper when they think they can't hear, and they call me the Inventor."

"Really? What did you invent?" Persephone asked, giving the door of her cell an experimental rattle.

"Can't remember. Stuff. Lots of stuff."

"Okay, then who is the 'She' that you mentioned? What's her name?"

The man frowned and picked up a bundle of wires and began to detangle it. "The Many Gifted One. I think I gave her gifts too," he mumbled. "I think I regretted it. I'm sure they all did in the end."

"What's her gift?"

"Being a real bitch," the inventor said, before turning his desk lamp down and studying something she couldn't see.

This guy is totally crazy.

Persephone shook her head and tried to lock down the power in her hands that could've broken down her cell door in seconds. She tightened her fists. No, she had promised Hades.

Persephone was going to have to have a serious conversation with him about his crazy plans when she was free of the place and had him in her arms again.

"Don't worry, inventor, we won't be trapped here for long. I'll get you out," promised Persephone.

The man's golden-brown eyes saddened. "I'm sure I said that too."

"The princess wakes at last," a voice said from the cavern mouth.

The inventor's shoulders hunched, and he instantly became hyper focused on looking as busy as possible.

A figure in a cloak and drama mask walked towards them, two men with guns following behind her.

"Please don't talk to my inventor, it upsets him."

"Looks like *you* upset him," snapped Persephone.

"*Life* upsets him, but such is the nature of his curse," the woman said, lifting a hand. One of the men came forward and unlocked the cell door. "Please don't try any heroics or I'll be forced to shoot both of your legs."

"What do you want from me?" Persephone asked, walking carefully from the cell.

"Why to use you as bait, of course. That doesn't mean we can't have a discussion first. Follow me," the woman replied, her dark robes whirling as she turned.

"I'll see you soon," Persephone said to the inventor, and when he looked up at her, she felt a flash of power from him.

What was he?

Persephone didn't have a chance to find out as one of the men poked her in the back with the barrel of his gun.

"This way," he said, and Persephone followed the masked woman through a tunnel and out another door made of metal bars.

Everywhere Persephone looked, she saw men and women in tactical gear, loading, and checking weapons.

"Are you terrorists?" Persephone asked, making the woman laugh.

"Oh, my dear no. We are monster hunters, amongst other things," she replied.

"And you think I'm a monster?" Persephone said when they stopped in another cavern containing two wooden chairs and a small table.

Someone had placed a bottle of wine and three glasses on it. Persephone had a pleasant thought of making the chair come alive and letting the vines choke them all as she sipped her wine and watched.

You promised, Hades.

"Perhaps not a monster, but you're certainly unnatural, aren't you? Sit down," the woman instructed, and Persephone did.

"Are you going to take off that mask, and talk to me face to face like big girls?" Persephone asked.

"Why not? After tonight, there will be no need to hide anymore," she said.

Because Hades is going to turn you to dust if I don't get to you first, Persephone thought but tried to smile politely.

If nothing else, Demeter had taught her to be polite when faced with an egotistical asshole.

The woman pulled back her hood and lifted off her mask. Underneath, she was stunningly beautiful with glossy black hair, amber-brown skin, and vivid blue eyes.

"Better? I have to say it is for me. The damn thing is useful, but it does itch. Wine?" she asked and began pouring.

"Only if it's not poisoned. So, who are you?" Persephone asked, accepting the offered glass. Like the inventor, there was a low hum of power coming off the woman, but nothing like the members of the Court.

"I've gone by many names over the years, and none really matter anymore. So, Persephone, what to do about you. Your mother assured us that you were going to stay away from Hades, and yet, Vallis tells me you are in love with the Great Unseen One," she said, sipping her wine.

"Sounds to me like Vallis has been telling tales. As for my mother, she was in no position to promise such a thing," Persephone replied.

Vallis betrayed her to this psychopath?

"It appears there was some truth in the tale because Hades's helicopter landed about ten minutes ago, and my men are bringing him to us as we speak," the woman said with a smile.

Persephone laughed loudly. "Your big plan was to bring him to your hideout so he can kill you all? That has to be the dumbest thing I've ever heard."

"No, Persephone, we used you as to bait to bring him here so we can kill him," the woman replied. Men started to file into the cavern and appearing on rock ledges above them, their guns all pointing down at her.

Persephone felt Hades's power coming towards her like a tsunami. Her heart was pounding with the intensity of it before he appeared through the cavern in a pristine black suit and with silver eyes shining.

She had never wanted to kiss him as much as she did now.

"Pandora, well, this *is* a surprise," he said, looking at the black-haired woman with his usual bored expression. "How are you, Persephone?"

"In one piece," she replied.

Pandora? Surely, he didn't mean the Pandora?

"What's this all about, Pandora? Why are you so determined to be a pain in my ass? What did I do to you?" asked Hades.

"This is about righting my wrongs, Hades, so don't take it personally," Pandora replied and filled the third glass.

"Don't take it personally? You tried to kill Asterion and Medusa, and then you very stupidly took the only woman I've ever loved. How do you think I'm going to take it?" Hades said coldly and then laughed.

"*Pithos*. Of course, this is about trying to put all the evil in the world away again all because you couldn't keep the damn jar closed."

"I was set up by the fucking gods from the start," hissed Pandora.

"Of course, you were, they were gods. Zeus sent you in as a weapon, and as you well know, I had nothing to do with it," Hades replied.

"It doesn't matter. You and your freaks should've stayed in your holes where you belonged." Pandora smiled unpleasantly.

"While it has been fun to parry with you over the past few months, I'm afraid we are going to have to get serious now. You are going to die tonight, and all of your monsters will join you soon enough."

"And you think you can kill me?" asked Hades.

"Actually, I thought Persephone could kill you using this," Pandora said and pulled a long primitive-looking blade shaped like a sickle from the inside of her robes. It looked like it was made of stone.

Hades's expression changed from annoyance to true surprise as he recognized it.

"You were the one that got Zeus before I finished him off," said Hades, and Pandora laughed.

"I did indeed. I left him out there to suffer for a while, and then you arrived and cut off his head, vanishing with the body before I even got a chance to spit on it," she said, twirling the sickle knife in one hand.

"I didn't believe I had actually found the real blade until the moment I was fucking Zeus and sank it into his chest. He always thought with his dick rather than his brain. Really, I'm surprised someone didn't kill him that way sooner."

"And how did you managed to find Gaia's blade?" asked Hades.

"You aren't the only one who has friends, Hades, and there is a thriving market for such artifacts. Now get on your knees or I'll fill Persephone with bullets," said Pandora. "Don't forget she's only part god, and a few well-placed shots will be more than she'll be able to regenerate."

Persephone looked down the tiny red dots that were now covering her.

Fuck Hades, this wasn't part of the plan.

She thought he'd arrive with the Court and blast them out of here, not this.

"Hades, don't," Persephone whispered.

"Why make Persephone do it? Why not kill me yourself?" asked Hades.

"Because the gods don't know what real love is, Hades, and I'm disgusted that a creature like you thinks he's worthy of it," said Pandora and offered the blade to Persephone. "I'll give you three seconds to take this blade before I shoot you."

"Take it, Persephone," Hades growled as Pandora started counting.

Persephone leaped up and grabbed it, her skin recoiling from the feel of the stone against her skin. Whatever the blade was, it had been made by a god, and it was pure evil.

Pandora stepped away from them so that there was no way Persephone could use the blade on her.

"It's okay, Persephone. You are the only being that I'll ever willingly kneel to, my queen," Hades said, lowering to the earth in front of her.

"This wasn't part of the plan," Persephone said, hands shaking as tears slipped from her eyes.

"I know, and I'm sorry."

"Save us the sentimentality, Hades, it doesn't suit you," Pandora complained. "Persephone, kill him, and you'll walk free right now."

"Hades, let me-"

"Don't, sunshine. It's not worth risking your life, it's too precious to me," Hades said, silver eyes calm as ever.

"I love you. I *can't* stab you," replied Persephone.

"I love you too, and I know that you can. I wouldn't love you if I didn't think you were capable of it," he said softly.

"Save your tears, daughter of Demeter. Hades deserves this death, as do all the others. You are part human, so I'm willing to be lenient on you if you do this one simple task," Pandora called from the safety of her guards.

Persephone gripped the blade with both hands, and Hades took her arm and brought her close enough for the stone tip to touch his chest.

"Better make it through the heart, you've already broken it anyway," Hades said with a small smile. "Right here should do it."

"Hades, please don't make me," wept Persephone.

"This is getting boring," sighed Pandora. "Five seconds, Persephone! Five! Four!"

"I love you," Persephone whispered.

"I know, sunshine. It's okay, I'm ready," Hades replied.

"Three! Two-"

"I'm sorry," Persephone said, pulling him close to kiss him as the stone blade sank deep into his chest.

Hades let out a choking gasp, and Persephone grabbed his shoulders to lower him down to the earth. Golden ichor spread out over his shirt.

"Well, well, you did have it in you after all," Pandora said, her words sounding distant under the roaring in Persephone's ears.

Vicious, hot power rolled up through her veins as she leaned down to cradle Hades's head close to her chest.

She kissed his face softly, brushing his hair back. She stilled as his lips moved against her ear.

"Go, get them, baby," he whispered.

20

Pain, unlike anything Hades could imagine, raced through his veins as Persephone pushed the stone deep into his chest.

This is the stupidest plan you've ever had, he thought as he sank to the earth. *But not as stupid as Pandora's.*

Persephone's lips were tracing over his skin, a vortex of power swirling inside of her so strongly he could taste it on the air.

"Go, get them, baby," he said, and the world stilled as if time itself had stopped. Persephone exploded into a cloud of shadows and light.

Through hazy vision, Hades could see men screaming as their flesh melted away, the walls around them exploded with vines that pulled them back into the earth.

Gunshots were fired, but none of them hit him. No one was paying any attention at all, as Thanatos appeared beside him.

"Charon was right, Persephone isn't going to save anyone for us," he said and grabbed the knife. "Deep breath, Master." Hades roared as Thanatos pulled the blade free.

"Fucking give me that infernal thing," he wheezed as he sat up. He could feel the wound in his chest already starting to close. Thanatos passed him the knife and helped him stand.

"Where are the others?" Hades demanded just as alarms started blaring throughout the caves.

"Sounds like they are making their presence known," Thanatos said as two scythe blades appeared in his hands. "Will you be all right on your own?"

"Fuck off," Hades said, half-heartedly, and the titan ran to join the fray. Hades gripped the stone blade and looked for Persephone.

There wasn't a single person left alive in the cavern, but there was no sign of Pandora. He shut his eyes for a second, zeroed in on Persephone's power, and followed it.

"Damn stupid stone dagger," he muttered as he walked down the pathway to the left.

He didn't have the power to heal and shift himself to Persephone's side. He almost tripped over more than one body.

"Hades! Are you okay?" Ariadne appeared like a shadow from the darkness, blood sprays on her face.

"I'll live. Have you seen Pandora? The woman in the mask?" he demanded.

"No, I haven't," Ariadne replied and then touched the plug in her ear. "Medusa, keep your eyes out for a woman in a mask exiting the caves. Hades says it's Pandora?"

Hades could hear Medusa shouting expletives from the other side of the tunnel. There were loud gunshots nearby, and Asterion appeared, horns covered in gore.

"Help me get to Persephone before she brings this place down around her ears," Hades said.

"I can smell her trail. It's this way," Asterion replied and slung one of Hades's arms around his shoulder. "Ariadne, watch our backs."

"Of course, honey, I wouldn't want you to get a bullet in your lovely asses," she said, raising her gun with a cheeky grin.

"Don't accidentally put one in mine, waving those things around," Hades added.

"How dare you. I'm a professional. I'm also the one not stupid enough to get stabbed in the chest," said Ariadne, and Hades managed a tired laugh.

"Fair enough."

They followed the myriad of tunnels, but every time they turned into one another three appeared.

"Fuck, this place feels like another labyrinth," Asterion complained.

"This is maddening, put me down," Hades said, and Asterion helped him sit on a chair. They were in some kind dining mess hall with overturned tables and food and dead Pithos agents everywhere.

"Damn Persephone! That girl is *pissed*," Ariadne whistled. "Respect."

"Just make sure no one comes through," Hades said and shut his eyes.

The hole in his chest had stopped bleeding, but his whole body was aching. He released his power, letting it seep out of him and shoot through the stone and earth around him.

Persephone, stop. I'm here. Find me.

His shadows found her in the distance, her power freezing as soon as he touched it. Then it was moving toward him, fast as lightning.

He opened his eyes as the mess hall filled with gold light and shadows before reforming into a wild-eyed woman.

"Sunshine, I do believe we have discovered another one your abilities," Hades said.

"How?" she whispered.

"I'm the Lord of the Dead and all of its domains. Do you really think anything can kill me?" Hades answered.

He groaned as Persephone slammed into him so hard, he nearly fell off his chair.

"You fucking prick," she said, arms locking around his neck. "I thought I'd killed you."

"I'm sorry, my love, I had to keep them distracted while the others snuck in."

"Don't you dare 'my love' me, you bastard, you made me *stab* you," she said, gripping his face tightly between her hands.

Her expression shifted, and she was kissing him hard, hands in his hair. Dark delicious power was flowing into him, healing his wound and replenishing his power.

"Stop, sunshine, you'll hurt yourself," he gasped, and she cut it off instantly.

"*Never* pretend to die on me again, or I'll kill you for fucking real," Persephone said.

"What did I tell you about threatening me?" Hades replied with a grin.

Persephone whacked him and then stepped away from him, her cheeks flushing.

"Get up and help me find that bitch Pandora, I lost her in the skirmish," she said.

"By skirmish, do you mean crazy-ass god massacre?" Ariadne asked.

"That's the one," Persephone replied.

"One sec," said the assassin holding up her hand. "Medusa, can you hear me? Any sign of Pandora?"

Hades got up and took Persephone's hand, her power swirling around inside of him. He wanted to fuck her right there.

"Focus, Acheron, we have business to attend to," Persephone warned, reading the look in his eye.

"Medusa hasn't seen her, and the triplets have said that what remains of Pithos has scrambled or are dead," Ariadne said. "It's over, the caves are ours."

"Good, now let's get the fuck out of here, this place makes me twitchy," Asterion growled.

"Wait, there's another prisoner I promised to free," Persephone said.

"Asterion, you and Ariadne go and find the triplets and secure the perimeter around the caves as best you can before the other mercenaries arrive to take care of the rest," Hades instructed, seeing the beginnings of panic in Asterion's eyes.

"I'll help Persephone get her prisoner."

"Thank you, Uncle," the Minotaur said.

Ariadne waved a finger around the room before giving Persephone two thumbs up.

"Well, done on your first big night out, babe, I owe you a drink."

"Deal," Persephone said with a laugh. When they had left the cave, Persephone leaned over a table and vomited on the ground. Hades rubbed her back gently.

"It's over, sunshine, just breathe," he said.

"Don't you dare tell them I threw up," she muttered, wiping her mouth on the back of her sleeve.

"Not a word," Hades promised. He found a bottle of water in an overturned cooler and passed it to her. Persephone downed a few mouthfuls, and color returned to her cheeks.

"The inventor is this way," she said, taking Hades's hand.

"The inventor?"

"My prisoner, that's who it is. He's Pandora's inventor," Persephone explained.

"Let's hope she didn't shoot him on her way out," Hades said.

"I doubt she would've had time. Besides, he felt...strange. I don't think a simple bullet would be enough. You'll see what I mean."

Hades didn't question how she knew her way through the system of tunnels. Apart from Erebus, he had never seen another god be able to turn themselves into shadows the way she had done.

How many more tricks did she have? Hades wondered and then smiled at the fun they would have to try to find out.

They came to a gate, and Hades placed a hand on the lock, his power eating away at it until it opened.

"You'll have to teach me that," Persephone said.

"Don't worry, I have a very long list of things I'm going to teach you, my love," Hades replied.

"All in good time." Persephone led the way to another cavern.

A man was hunched over a worktable, and as soon as Hades saw him, he felt the pulse of old, bright power.

The man at the table whipped around, screwdriver raised like a dagger.

Hades sucked in a surprised breath and then smiled. "Hello, Hermes."

21

Persephone didn't want to get out of bed for a week, but she knew that she had to do one more thing before she could get her wish.

Charon drove her into Acheron Tower, where Demeter was waiting. So much had happened in the last few days, that confronting her mother no longer held any fear for her.

"Hades has had her in a cell in the building's basement since you were taken. I don't think it would've softened her mood," said Charon as he opened her door for her.

"My mother doesn't know what a soft mood is," replied Persephone. Charon held out a hand to help her from the low car and then held onto it.

"I'm sorry I failed to protect you, Persephone," he said softly. "I shouldn't have let them take you."

"Hey, stop that. Hades told me to let them take me. You didn't do anything wrong, Charon. You were in no shape to stop them either," Persephone replied, giving his hand a squeeze.

"Don't apologize again about it, or you'll really be in trouble."

Charon gave her a crooked smile as he bowed. "Understood, my queen."

"What is it with all this 'my queen' business?" Persephone asked as they got into the elevator.

"You'd best ask Hades, he started it," Charon said.

Despite being held prisoner for three days, Demeter had showered and was dressed neatly.

For the first time since Persephone could remember, Demeter had dark smudges under her eyes, and her hair was out.

Persephone didn't know what Hades had said or done to her, but Demeter had never looked so meek and defeated as she sat on one of the couches in Hades's office.

The Lord of Styx sat opposite her, dressed in black and looking like the decadent dark king he was.

God have mercy, could he not look so handsome just once?

"Persephone, are you all right?" Demeter asked.

"I'm fine, Mother. No thanks to you," she replied, moving to stand behind Hades and resting her hands on his shoulders. Demeter visibly flinched.

"Has there been any sign of Vallis?"

"None, though I still have men cleaning out the caves," said Hades. "It's time you find yourself a more reliable head of security, Demeter. I can recommend one if you like."

"I don't need your help," Demeter replied straightening. "Are you coming home to Athens with me, Persephone?"

"I will return to Athens soon, but not yet. There are things I need to work out with my power first, and I know Hades can help," Persephone replied.

"You aren't just my daughter. You are the Company Secretary. I need you back at work even if I can't convince you to come home to the mansion," Demeter said urgently. "Can't we work out some kind of...commuting at least? Like joint custody?"

"She isn't my child, she is my queen, there will be no joint custody," Hades growled.

There's that phrase again. Persephone gently squeezed his shoulders.

"Get someone else to look after my responsibilities for a while, mother. I'm overdue for a holiday. After I have had one, we can come to an arrangement, but I can tell you right now, I'll never live under your roof again," Persephone said as gently as she could.

"But you'll live under *his*?" Demeter said, her voice cracking. She got to her feet.

"I'd like to go home now, Hades. Persephone might be able to let her responsibilities lapse, but I cannot. I trust the business side of our arrangement is still good?"

"Of course, Demeter. Pithos is destroyed for now, and Pandora is on the run, but if you try to give them a single payment or communicate with them after today, we will know, and we'll be having a very different kind of discussion. Are we clear?" Hades said.

"Crystal," Demeter replied, giving him a smile that Persephone had seen her use a million times to close a deal. Demeter's smile faltered when Persephone moved around the couch.

"I know you're angry with me, but what I did, I did to protect you."

"I know you believe that, Mother. It's still going to take me a while to trust you again," said Persephone.

Demeter nodded, and her expression softened. "Are you going to give me a hug goodbye, at least."

"You've never wanted one before, but sure," said Persephone and let Demeter embrace her.

As she went to step back, Persephone held on to whisper in her ear, "If you lift a single finger to get revenge for this on Hades or the rest of his Court, I will go into our fields, and I will destroy every crop, blight every piece of land, and sink every ship we own. I will tear down Morning Harvest and leave your world in ashes. Do you understand me?"

"Yes, my darling. You are my daughter after all, and I did teach you well," Demeter replied, and Persephone finally released her.

"Goodbye, Mother, I'll be in touch," she said, and Demeter walked out, slamming the door behind her. Persephone turned to see Hades smiling at her.

"That went well," he said, pulling her into his lap. "I especially liked the last bit when you threatened to bring her down."

"You do love a good threat, don't you," Persephone replied. "Do you think she will listen?"

"For a little while, at least. Don't worry, Medusa will have people monitoring her. Now, what would you like to do?" Hades asked.

"Find Pandora and the rest of her maggot men," Persephone replied. "I also would like to know where this 'my queen' business is coming from?"

Hades's smile widened. "It's a title you earned, and honestly, I couldn't make the Court stop saying it now even if I wanted to." He lifted her hand and gently bit the skull on her wrist.

"And I don't want to. You *are* my queen. They recognized it all on their own."

"You don't think maybe we should take it slow, maybe date for a while in case we want to see other—" Persephone yelped as Hades twisted and pinned her to the couch underneath him.

"There will be no seeing other people," he growled and then realized she was laughing.

"*Still* trying to piss me off."

"And it works every time," Persephone said. "Oh, Hades, I love you, but you are gullible."

"You are my favorite nightmare," Hades replied and kissed her until she melted underneath him. "And you *will* be my queen."

"If that's your proposal, then it was terrible. Think it through and try again," she said.

"I will when you learn not to be so difficult. Right now, we have bigger things to worry about, sunshine." Hades slowly let her up, so she was back to straddling him.

"Find Pandora, annihilate Pithos, check," Persephone said, running her hands under his jacket. "And let's not forget the mad god in our basement."

"As if we could. He's the best source on Pandora we have if we can get him thinking straight," he sighed. "Who knows what's been done to make Hermes that way."

"We will figure it out or find people who can," Persephone said, and then to throw him off balance again, she asked, "But do you really want to marry me?"

"Yes," Hades said and then kissed her when she started protesting.

"I was joking," she replied as she realized what she'd done.

"You can't fucking take it back, it's too late," Hades argued. "We have an agreement."

"You are the worst," Persephone complained even though she was smiling.

"I am," Hades replied, lifting her stubborn chin so she could see the gleam of love and victory in his eyes. "And you love it."

EPILOGUE

Selene gripped her medical bag in her hand and tried not to show how nervous she was.

He's just another patient that needs help, it's not like it's the first god you've met.

Hades opened the door to the cells, and she heard people arguing. They had renovated the space into one large room, complete with a private bathroom, and filled it with furniture.

Despite that, it looked like Hermes was still sleeping on the floor. According to Hades, he was also fighting with every person that tried to do a medical examination on him.

"Are you sure this is a good idea?" Selene asked.

"I trust you, and you can handle gods, so a perfect combination," Hades said confidently.

"Pandora was drugging him with something, and now it's worn off he can remember his own name at least, but something else has happened to break him, and I need to find out what."

"I'm a nurse, not a shrink, Hades," Selene argued.

"One step at a time," he replied before calling, "Hermes? Put the man down, there's someone I want you to meet."

The shouting stopped and Hermes appeared from the bathroom. He was wearing a clean pair of pajama pants but no shirt, his body still muscled and tanned despite being imprisoned.

Selene had expected a wasted away hermit. She should've known better after dealing with gods for so long.

"They are trying to cut my hair," Hermes hissed in a deep voice.

"You should let them. You can be a crazy person without looking like one," Hades replied. "I've asked this lady to help you, and you will treat her politely, or there will be consequences. Understood?"

Brilliant golden-brown eyes fixed on Selene like a hunting hawk. "Interesting."

Selene put her bag on the table and sat down before taking out some forms.

"Please join me," she said politely.

"I'll be close by, I need to make sure he hasn't hurt the other nurse too badly," Hades said, leaving her alone with the deranged god. Hermes sat down opposite her, head tilting as he studied her.

"Was it you that washed me down while I was sleeping, cold nurse?" he asked her.

"No, that was the guys," Selene replied, taking the lid off her pen and starting to flick through her checklists.

"They better not have scrubbed too merrily at my dick."

"From the stories I've heard about you, I didn't think being handled by a man would make you blush," she replied.

"Cold nurse has a streak of fire after all." Hermes leaned across the table, his long nimble fingers touching one of the forms.

"If you had paid attention to those stories, you would've remembered I'm the god of tricks, not dicks. That's Apollo's purview."

He laughed at his own joke before turning his laser attention to the small watch pinned to her scrubs.

"I remembered enough to know you're a god of thieves too, so I'll be having my paperclip back now."

"Clever, cold nurse. A paperclip for a name?"

"You can't trade something that already belongs to me," she pointed out. Hermes's eyes twinkled with equal parts mischief and malice.

"Are you afraid I'll take it and make it into something else?"

"You're not cuffed and Hades will let you leave whenever you like. You've no need for a lock pick," Selene said.

"I wasn't talking about the paperclip, cold nurse. I do wonder if I turned your name into something would that change you as well? I do wonder yes, yes, I do," he whispered.

"And what would you turn me into?" Selene asked, her pulse jumping in her throat.

"Someone less cold, I think." Hermes started to straighten the thin paper clip. "You can tell me your name. I can keep a secret. Or are you afraid?"

"Selene," she said to prove that she wasn't. Hades was more frightening than the sick man in front of her.

"Selene." He dragged out the word, changing the stresses as his fingers continued to move. "Selene, the Lady Moon, is that why you are so cold and distant with me?"

"You're a patient, I'm not cold and I'm professional."

"I think you're lying, Lady Moon," Hermes whispered, leaning forward again. "I won't tell if you tell me true, why are you so cold, Lady Moon?"

"Maybe another time," Selene said and gathered her papers.

"Don't forget your paperclip." Hermes held out his hand. In his palm, the paperclip had been bent into a crescent moon with a small star hanging from its tip. She picked it up, a small smile escaping before she could hide it.

"Thank you, it's lovely," she said.

"And that's just what I can do with a tiny piece of metal...just imagine what I could do to you if you let me."

Hermes, the god of thieves and tricksters, smiled savagely at her, and Selene finally found a god that frightened her more than Hades Acheron.

∽

HERMES

THE COURT OF THE UNDERWORLD
IV

ALESSA THORN

PROLOGUE

Sing, O' Muse, of the seasons of the world and how all that was lost was found again.

Sing, of how gods and mythical creatures once roamed the lands of Greece, and of how Man became powerful, and the gods were forced into hiding.

Sing, of when Greece's economy collapsed, and the land was on fire with the turmoil man's governance had wrought.

Sing, of how the gods returned to build a new world from the ashes.

Sing, O' Muse, of the new city of Styx, and the monsters that govern its underworld.

Sing to me a new song, of a Healer and a Mad Man...

1

It had been a long night in the Emergency Room.

The hospital at Lethe was already full, and Selene had been run off her feet triaging patients, stitching up head wounds after an epic brawl at the nearby pub, and dealing with the ever-constant flow of food poisoning, fevers, and imaginary illnesses.

Selene changed out of her scrubs and into some street clothes, pulled out her ponytail, and slipped on her favorite silver bangle. Her neck and shoulders ached as she slung on her satchel and headed for the exit.

She was going to have a long bath with lavender when she got home if it was the last thing she did.

Selene opened the staff entrance door and found a handsome, tattooed man and a sleek black car.

Selene let out a tired sigh. "Shit."

"Sorry, doll, but we need you," said Charon, opening the passenger door for her.

"Bullet wounds or mad gods?" she asked, collapsing on the comfortable leather seat. Charon had a fresh soy latte waiting for her, and she took a grateful sip.

"Mad gods," Charon replied as he turned the car on.

"I already told Hades that physically there doesn't seem to be anything wrong with Hermes. He needs a proper psychiatrist, not an ER nurse," argued Selene, knowing that it was hopeless. Charon didn't have a say in the matter.

"You barely spent ten minutes with Hermes last time. Hades trusts you like he's not going to trust anyone else," the titan said.

"That's flattering and all, but within that ten minutes with Hermes, I realized I wasn't qualified to help him."

And because he scares the shit out of me, she didn't add. She wasn't going to admit to the ferryman of the Underworld that she was afraid of anything.

"Hermes talked to you. Quietly. Coherently. That's more than he's done with anyone else. I've known him for a *very* long time, and he doesn't recognize me most days."

"I thought he was an Olympian, what was he doing hanging out in the Underworld?" asked Selene.

"Hermes is -was- a psychopomp. He used to guide souls to their Afterlife. Some, not all. Also, he used to hang out with us because the Olympians all sucked. He was the smartest of all those bastards, and to see him like this breaks my fucking heart. I'm sorry that we keep interrupting your life, but I want my friend back too badly," explained Charon. He smiled his most charming smile at her. "Besides, he's been asking for you."

"You were friends, and he struggles to remember you but knows me? That doesn't make sense, I only met him once," said Selene.

"Selene, love, I've always told you how unforgettable you are, and now we have proof."

"Shut up," she said and laughed. The triplets could *always* make her laugh, even after an eighteen-hour shift.

Charon tapped his tattooed fingers against the steering wheel. "He's refused to eat for two days, and Hades is getting worried. If you can convince Hermes to do that, at least, we'd all be grateful."

They turned off to Hades's estate, and Selene had to admit, the forest that Persephone had made was eerie and beautiful in the early dawn light.

She thought Hades would get rid of it, but he adored Persephone too much to do it.

Like Asterion and Medusa, seeing Hades with besotted love in his eyes made Selene disturbed and jealous in equal measure.

She didn't have a love life; in fact, if it wasn't for her shitty ex-boyfriend, she would've never been involved with the Court of Styx.

Mixed blessings, to say the least.

Selene liked the Court, which made it hard for her to constantly be digging bullets out of them and stitching them back together.

It had been too much of a regular occurrence in the last few months for her to happy about.

Thanatos was waiting for them and opened Selene's door with a courteous, small bow.

"Good morning, Selene, I do apologize for inconveniencing you this morning."

"That's okay, Thanatos, I know it's not your fault. Where's the boss?"

"In the lounge room. Go on through, he's waiting for you," Thanatos replied.

Hades looked irritated and then relieved when he saw her. "Ah, Selene, thank you for coming."

"It's not like you gave me a choice."

"I could apologize, but it would be insincere. You know, if you came and worked for me full time like I've requested, you wouldn't have to be pulled away like this," said Hades calmly.

"We've talked about this before, and my answer is still no. There are not enough nurses to go around as it is," she replied stubbornly. "Charon says Hermes isn't eating."

"Not eating and generally being difficult. The only time he calms down is when he asks why you haven't been back, so I've had little choice but to call you in."

"Can't you just threaten him into eating?" Selene asked, only half-joking.

Hades smiled his famous cold bastard smile. "I've been tempted to, but Hermes has been forced to do too much against his will since being captured by Pandora. I don't want to put him through that again."

Selene ran a tired hand over her face. "Okay fine, but if you're cooking breakfast, you better make enough for two because I'm famished."

"Thank you, Selene," Hades said, and pointed towards the small elevator. "Go ahead, I'll put something together and get it brought down."

Selene hesitated. "Am I safe with him?"

"Hermes is many things, but he's not unnecessarily violent. You've managed to get his attention, and he never breaks things that he finds interesting," said Hades.

"That was a lot of words when a simple 'I don't know' would've sufficed," she grumbled, making him smile.

She stepped into the elevator anyway. She had dealt with plenty of drunk and high patients to be able to take care of herself, but none of those had been gods.

The doors opened to the underground apartment, previously a group of jail cells, and the first thing she noticed was someone had moved all the furniture around.

"I told you I'm not hun..." Hermes started to complain from a couch when he saw her. "Cold nurse. I didn't expect you."

"Good morning, Hermes, would you mind if I sat down? I've had a really long night," said Selene, trying to keep her voice steady.

Hermes nodded; his hawk eyes as intense as she remembered them. They reminded her a little of Asterion's, a sure sign that Zeus's bloodline was strong, but Hermes's eyes were more gold and unnerving.

Selene took off her bag and sat down in an armchair.

How was she expected to help him?

"How have you been feeling?" she asked, settling for politeness.

Hermes collapsed back on the couch. "Bored."

Selene looked at the stacks of books around the room. "You've read all of these already?"

"Yes."

"You should've said something to Hades, he could get you more if you wanted them."

"Why are you tired?" Hermes asked.

"I'm a nurse, I work in a hospital. I was going home, and Hades invited me over for breakfast," she replied.

Hermes's expression darkened. "Carrot."

"Pardon me?" asked Selene.

"You are a carrot. Hades thinks I'm a donkey, so he's offering you up as a carrot to get me to behave before he decides on the stick. I know a carrot when I see one," Hermes snarled.

"You want me to leave? Fine with me," Selene said and got up. She wasn't going to hang around. She wanted to go home and go to bed. She reached the elevator door when Hermes suddenly appeared in front of her, blocking the button.

"I didn't say that," he said, folding his arms over his bare chest. "Don't be a cold carrot as well as a cold nurse. Stay."

"Why? You don't need me. You're not hurt," asked Selene, too tired to remain polite.

"I *am* hurt!" Hermes declared, taking her hand and putting it on his head. "Here. Here. Can't you feel it?" His skin was feverishly hot under her palm, golden eyes wild. Selene softened like she always did in the face of suffering.

"I can feel it," she said gently.

"Stay. Be a carrot, so I behave." Hermes lifted her hand off his head and pulled her slowly back to her chair. "I like talking to you."

"Why?" she asked, sitting down again.

"Because when you look at me, your eyes don't expect to see someone else. They all do, and then they are disappointed because I'm not him," Hermes said, pulling at a button on one of the couch cushions. "Not anymore."

"You might not remember, but they are your friends, Hermes. They want to help you," Selene replied. The button came off the couch, and Hermes twirled it between his fingers as he studied her. Then he flicked the button at the other side of the room and took a piece of his long hair and started plaiting it.

"I like how you say my name. You make it sound so...permanent and disapproving," he said.

"I don't disapprove of it."

"There is definite disapproval when you say it," Hermes argued. Selene was saved by the elevator opening and Thanatos appearing carrying a tray.

"I told you I wasn't hungry, titan," growled Hermes.

"They heard you, Hermes. This is for me. It's dawn, and I'm starving," Selene said, and Thanatos set the tray down on the small table beside her.

"There you are, Selene. Once again, I'm sorry for pulling you out here so early in the morning," he said.

"Thank you, Thanatos, this looks perfect," replied Selene with a smile. "Are you going to join us?"

"I'm afraid other duties call. Perhaps next time, Selene," said Thanatos before disappearing. Selene turned to her tray and found Hermes glaring at her, eyes narrowed.

"Oh, Hades made me omelets. He must be in a good mood, he usually only makes them for Persephone," she said, ignoring him and picking up her plate and a fork.

"Why do you smile at Thanatos?" asked Hermes.

"Because I like Thanatos, especially when he brings me so much breakfast. I don't know if I'm going to be able to eat it all, but I'm going to give it my best shot," she said, munching a mouthful of toast.

"Do you not smile at me because you don't like me?" Hermes demanded, watching her mouth too intently as she ate.

"I don't know you like I know him," Selene replied with a small shrug, focusing on her plate.

"You are getting to know me right now. You should smile for me too," argued Hermes.

"You can't make someone smile for you because you want it," said Selene.

"Yes, I can," Hermes said, voice dropping maliciously.

"Not me," replied Selene. She wasn't intimidated by Hades. She sure as hell wasn't going to let Hermes get under her skin. "How about instead of threatening me, you help me eat this fruit salad, and I'll *think* about smiling."

Hermes snatched up the other fork and took the bowl of fruit.

"Clever carrot," he grumbled. He studied a piece of orange skeptically before putting it in his mouth and chewing.

"So why don't you like eating?" Selene asked.

"Food makes me foggy, and the bad dreams come."

Selene swallowed hard. "Hades told me that Pandora was drugging your food. I can see why that would make you not like eating," she said. "You don't ever have to worry about that happening again, Hermes, but it's okay if it takes a little while to get used to it again."

"Maybe you're right, carrot," sighed Hermes as he ate a strawberry. His expression brightened. "I liked that one."

"Strawberries are my favorite, so don't eat them all," Selene said.

Hermes frowned but then skewered another piece and begrudgingly offered it to her. Selene bit it off his fork with a wide smile. "Thanks."

"Knew I'd get that smile eventually," he said triumphantly. "I told you I could."

"Well, Charon did warn me you were clever," Selene replied.

"I used to be, not anymore."

"Hades will find a way to fix what was done to you. You should talk to him about it, so he can figure out a way," she said.

Hermes toyed with a grape. "Don't remember."

"You remembered me after we only met once. That's got to be a sign that you're getting a little bit better. It might come back," she said, trying to reassure him.

"You're different. When you are close, things seem...clearer," admitted Hermes. "Words come easier. Thoughts dance less. That's why Hades turned you into a carrot."

Selene didn't know how to answer that, so they ate in silence, Hermes taking half of her omelet when she offered it. She yawned, her body clock protesting despite Charon's latte.

"You should go to sleep, carrot," Hermes said. "I release you from carrot duties."

"Thanks, Hermes. You should try to sleep too," Selene replied, picking up the tray of dishes.

"Can't. Nightmares," he said.

"Maybe I can figure out something that could help you calm down enough to sleep, and Hades could give it to you," she replied.

"You calm me down. You should stay here and sleep with me. That way, we will both sleep," Hermes suggested with an unexpectedly playful grin.

"Nice try, but I'm not sleeping with you," said Selene.

"You need to learn how to be a better carrot, Selene," he replied as he walked her to the elevator. "You should come again so I can show you."

"I'll think about it if you talk to Hades about how you are feeling," Selene said as she stepped inside the elevator. "See? I'm not such a stupid carrot, after all."

"Cold, cold, Lady Moon," he replied, and the doors closed on Hermes's hunting hawk eyes and too sharp smile.

Upstairs, Persephone was awake and pouring biscuits into Cerberus's bowl. She gave Selene a megawatt smile.

"Selene! I didn't know you were here."

"I was summoned to have breakfast with Hermes," she said, placing the tray next to the sink.

"And you actually got him to eat?"

"Yes, not much but a bit," Selene said.

"Thank you. I've been getting worried about him. He won't come out of the basement either, no matter how much I try to cajole him," Persephone replied, a frown appearing.

"Who knows how long Pandora held him in that cave? It might take him a while to feel comfortable enough to risk outside open spaces," Selene replied.

"He behaved himself, I trust?" said Hades, appearing out of nowhere.

"Hermes was tired but fine otherwise. Give him more books, Hades, he's bored. He's nervous about eating because the drugs he was given made him foggier than usual. He likes strawberries, so bribe him with those," Selene replied. Hades was giving her a stern look. "What?"

"You got more out of him in half an hour than I have in the past week," he grumbled.

"Glad I could help. I'd like to go home to bed now."

"Hermes likes you. This is good, seeing how it's now officially your new job to help restore him to his right mind," said Hades decisively.

"I already have a full-time job! I don't have time," Selene argued.

"Quit. This is important, Selene. Hermes could know where Pandora is hiding, and we need that information to stop her. He's also my nephew and I want him back. If this is about money, I'll double what they are paying you."

"It's not about the money," Selene said and rubbed at her eyes. She was too tired to spar with Hades.

"Then I don't understand what the problem is."

"Hades, my love, maybe let Selene have a rest before you start trying to negotiate with her," Persephone said, putting an arm around him. "You think about what you want in exchange for helping us, Selene, and next time we see you, we'll talk about it."

"Thank you, Persephone," said Selene, and headed for the door. "Give him more books, Hades. I also said I'd visit again, but only if he talks to you first. Be patient, and he might just open up."

"Thank you, Selene, I'll be in touch. You know I don't like it when people say no to me," Hades replied.

Of course, you will be, you're not going to stop until you get what you want.

Selene knew better than to argue.

Charon pulled the car around as soon as she stepped outside the front door.

It wasn't until they were almost back in Lethe, that Selene realized her silver bangle was missing.

2

Hermes's world was a broken montage of screaming, light, and blood. He could hear Zeus shouting at him, see the rage in his eyes when Hermes had disagreed with him. Then there was the cave.

For so long, he didn't know when time started or finished, or when the sun rose or fell.

He forgot time, the ocean and music, and everything he used to love until his whole world was the worktable in front of him.

You are my inventor now. You don't need to remember anything else, Pandora's honey voice dripped soothing poison in his ear.

Hermes woke with a start, the couch damp with his sweat, and his heart pounding in his ears.

"Hades's house. Hades's house," he repeated to himself. He wasn't in the cave anymore.

Hermes got off the couch and noticed the silver bangle on the rug. He'd been playing with it before he'd fallen asleep, contemplating the woman it belonged to.

He picked it up and held it tight as he walked into the bathroom and turned on the shower.

Some things came easier after his imprisonment. Hermes couldn't fall asleep in a bed, and wearing a shirt irritated him after so long, but he loved being clean.

He sat on the floor of the shower, lost in the sight of the water on the silver bangle.

"Lady Moon," Hermes murmured and lifted the silver to touch it to his forehead.

When she had her hand on his head, he'd felt something...open. It was a split second, but then it was gone again.

Then *she* was gone, and he didn't like it though he didn't know why he didn't.

"Fuck, focus already," he hissed.

He was thinking clearer without the drugs, but there were too many parts, like a house with all the important doors locked so he could only run up and down in a single hallway.

But he *had* felt something open, just for a second, and that second had been long enough for the memory of Zeus to slip through.

Talk to Hades, a voice said.

"Okay, Lady Moon, I will," he answered it and turned off the shower. Selene was a key of some sort. Hades would know what kind of key she was.

Hermes pulled on a pair of clean pajama pants just as Hades appeared with a bottle of something amber and a wooden case.

"Good, you're awake," Hades said and sat down at the table.

"Lady Moon said I needed to talk to you, or she won't come back and visit," Hermes replied, sitting down opposite him. "What's in the case?"

"I need a half-decent chess opponent, and even in your current state, I know you will present more of a challenge than the triplets," Hades said. He opened the case and started setting up the carved wooden pieces.

"The queen doesn't want to play with you?" asked Hermes. He knew that he knew her name, but it was slippery and just out of reach.

"I tried to play Persephone only once, and she cheated using her feminine wiles to distract me, so I've refused to play with her again," Hades replied.

"More like she beat you, and now you won't play with her again," said

Hermes with a grin. Hades scowled but didn't refute it as he poured a glass of the amber liquid.

"Do you want some?" he offered, and after a moment's hesitation, Hermes nodded. "It's strong, you might not like it."

He pushed the half-filled glass towards Hermes before conjuring another one and filling it for himself. Hermes sniffed it, had a mouthful, and smiled.

"I remember liking this," he said.

"Good, hopefully, your memory will come back in time," Hades replied, setting up the white chess pieces on Hermes's side of the board.

"Selene is a key, but I don't know what kind of key. We need to find out, Hades," Hermes said.

"What do you mean she's a key?" asked Hades, his dark brows going together.

"Keys and locks and rooms and hallways." Hermes tried to articulate, hands moving in frustration before Hades stopped him.

"Have a breath and a drink, and then try again, Hermes. We've got all the time in the world."

Hermes rubbed his face, took a drink, and put the silver bangle on the table. It reminded him of Selene and the water hitting it in the shower, and the thought came back. He tapped his forehead.

"Broken. Like a house with locked doors, and I'm trapped in a hallway. Selene touched," he said, holding the bracelet to his forehead. "And a room unlocked."

Hades drained his glass and refilled it. "I know she has healing abilities, but I've never pressed to find out what she can do with them."

"Selene makes things...clearer," Hermes said, drinking again, "and she smells nice."

"I'll take your word for it. The room she opened; do you remember what was inside of it?" Hades moved one of his pieces, and even though Hermes didn't understand the impulse, he moved one of his own.

"Zeus," Hermes said after a while. "Zeus was in the room. He was...angry. I think he wanted something or wanted me to do something. I said no. He got even angrier, and then it all...shattered."

"Fuck," sighed Hades. "He must've done this to you. I've met another one of his children recently, and Zeus did the same thing to his mother. Broke her brain for the fun of it."

"Another child of Zeus? Does he know? Hades, you must hide him. Don't let Zeus find him," Hermes asked, rocking back and forward in his chair.

"Hermes, it's okay. Zeus won't ever find Perseus or you. I killed him," Hades replied softly. Hermes stopped rocking.

"You finally did it."

"I did. That's how I'm not bound to the Underworld anymore. You didn't think it was strange that I am living among the humans now?" asked Hades.

Hermes smiled big and wide. "Ohhhh, I didn't think about it, uncle. Zeus is dead."

"He is."

"You've made me very happy. *Don't* let me forget this," Hermes begged.

"I won't. I still like to remind myself every day, so I can remind you too," replied Hades. "Now, my next question, what happened to your staff?"

"What staff?" asked Hermes, taking one of Hades's pieces.

"Your fucking staff. You used to use it to open the doorways to the Underworld, amongst other things. Had two snakes on it in gold?" Hades pressed, but Hermes shook his head uncertainly.

"I don't remember," he said, gnawing on his bottom lip. "Selene is a key. Maybe it's in a room that's locked."

"It's another thing to add to my list of worries. If your staff is in the hands of a human, who knows what they will do. Pandora had Gaia's knife, so maybe she has your staff too," Hades replied and then looked down at the board. "You sneaky bastard, you've checkmated me."

"What's a checkmate?" Hermes asked, and Hades let out a frustrated laugh.

"Even mad, you are the smartest person in the room, and I hate that," he said. He was smiling, so Hermes figured he wasn't angry.

"We have been talking a while," he said, turning the glass. "Does that mean I will see Lady Moon soon?"

"You will see her as soon as she stops being stubborn and agrees to come to work for me full time. You like her, don't you?" asked Hades.

"Yes, I don't make her sad, though I think sometimes I make her annoyed, and then she gets a frown. I did make her smile, so maybe I also don't annoy her too much. She makes things...less broken," Hermes struggled to explain. "Everything is noise and shouting and heat, but when she's close, it's cool and quiet. I think that's why I remember her."

"Don't worry, Hermes, she will return. I've known Selene for a few years now, and no matter how much she tries to resist it, she can't handle not being able to help," Hades said, leaning back in his chair with a confident smile.

"All we are going to have to do is wait for her to talk herself into it, and for her own sense of morality to bring her back."

3

Selene woke the following evening as the sun was slowly going down. She mixed leaves and brewed tea before going out into her small garden.

Night work always made her disorientated, and dealing with a mad god straight after a shift had made the surreal feeling even worse.

Hermes.

He made her feel off-balance, and if he wasn't crippled by madness, he'd be an absolute force of nature. Even with a shattered mind, his energy got up in her space, and she didn't like it one bit.

Selene watered her herbs and succulents as she sipped her tea. She wondered if she should email one of the psychiatrists at the hospital, or if she should put together a list of mental health nurses that she could give to Hades as suitable alternatives than herself.

Are you afraid? Hermes's voice echoed through her head with sharp clarity.

He'd asked her that when they had first met, and even though she would never admit it aloud, Selene *was* afraid of him. She was afraid she'd never be able to help him, that her inexperience would make him worse, and that she'd get attached to him because no matter how many red flags went up, she cared about the broken creatures.

She had always been unable to walk away from those that needed her help, even her shitty ex-boyfriend. They had been broken up for years. She had worked off her debt to Hades, and yet she still went when Hades called because she knew that the Court trusted her, and they needed help.

Now, Hermes needed her. In her mind's eye, she could see his twitching hands pulling buttons off the couch, and randomly plaiting pieces of his hair because they couldn't stop moving. Books wouldn't be enough to keep him amused for long.

Selene pulled out her laptop and started researching post-traumatic stress and subsequent memory loss and repression.

Three hours later, she came back to reality with notes scrawled over a pad, her half-drunk tea cold beside her.

You aren't actually considering doing this, are you?

She was tired of working crazy shifts and dealing with arrogant doctors. Her boss was an asshole and she would be able to get a normal sleep pattern again, which would be amazing.

Selene was never motivated by money; she would've chosen a different profession if she was. What *did* she want, and could Hades give it to her?

Outside, the moon had risen, and Selene went to stare up at the night sky and breathe.

Should I do this? she asked it. Selene didn't expect the stars to give her an answer, but she already knew the answer, so they gave her comfort instead.

Selene pulled her phone from her pocket and found Hades's number. **Get someone to pick me up tomorrow at 11 a.m**, she wrote, hesitated a long moment, and pressed send.

SELENE WAS LOCKING her front door when Thanatos arrived the next day. She had already gone out and stocked up on a few things that morning, and he took her bags from her.

"Let me carry those," he said, ever the gentleman. "What is all of this?"

"Ideas mostly."

"You're going to help Hermes after all," Thanatos replied with a small smile.

"I'm going to *try* to help him, but there are going to be caveats that Hades will have to agree to first," she said and got into the silver sedan.

"I'm sure he'll love that. For what it's worth, I know you'll do everything you can to help Hermes. He told Hades last night that being around you calms his mind and helps him think clearer. That is a gift, Selene."

"Hermes actually talked to him? That's a good sign."

Thanatos laughed. "It is. Although I'm sure, he only did it because you threatened not to visit until he did."

Selene flushed. "I didn't threaten him! It was only a suggestion. Hades is his uncle, so it's better that they talk because he might be able to figure out what happened to Hermes."

"Zeus happened," Thanatos said his tone darkening.

"So, it's a curse?" Selene couldn't believe the words came out of her mouth, but working for the Court for the past two years had shown her magic could be just as damaging as a loaded gun.

"It is. We need to figure out a way to break it, and if you can keep him calm and focused as much as possible, I'm sure we will find a way. Hermes might have the answer trapped inside of him for all we know. He is beyond brilliant; if anyone could break a curse on himself, it's Hermes," said Thanatos.

When they arrived at the villa, Selene went straight through to the office to where Hades was busy on a call. He waved her to sit while he wrapped it up.

"Well, back already. This is a surprise," Hades said, not looking surprised in the least. "Have you decided to come work with us full time?"

"I have. Though you might not like what I'm asking for," Selene replied and sat up a little straighter.

"Name it, Selene, don't be nervous about it."

"I want you to fund another ten nursing jobs in the Lethe Hospital. You know throwing money at me won't work, but they need more staff, Hades, and desperately. I can't in good conscious leave such an understaffed job knowing that it will be made even worse in my absence."

"Done. I'll get my people to organize it," he said with a wave of his hand. "Why do you look so surprised? I told you I wanted you full time."

"I still don't think I'm qualified to help Hermes in the way he needs, but I'll try," Selene replied. "I can't guarantee anything."

"You might not be a mental health nurse, but you have helped Hermes already. He said when you touched him yesterday, he got one of his memories back. *You* did that just by being around him. I can't promise it will be easy, but I can promise you will be safe," said Hades sincerely.

"I don't know how my touching him helped, but I'm not going to spend my time doing it on the off chance that it happens again," replied Selene, her neck going uncomfortably hot.

"I'd never ask you to, and you can ignore Hermes if he suggests it. He's with a psychologist now, shall we see how it's going?" Hades asked, getting up.

"I should've asked for more nursing positions," she said as they got into the elevator.

"Yes, but it's too late now. I got off far more cheaply than I thought," Hades replied. "Thank you, Selene, I'm really glad that I didn't have to force you into this out of necessity."

"Don't thank me until I've helped him," she murmured.

Hermes was sitting at the table opposite a man with glasses. He looked miserable until he glanced up and saw Selene. His expression went from confusion to happiness, to mischievous in a split second as he stood up.

"How is it going, doctor?" Hades asked the psychologist.

"Nowhere, he won't talk to me," he said and looked at Selene. "Who are you?"

"This is Hermes's new friend, Selene," Hades said. "Let's have a break and give them a minute to say hello."

The psychologist closed his notebook and got up. "Might as well, I'm getting nowhere."

Selene put her bags on a chair and tried not to show how nervous she was under Hermes's intense golden gaze. He stepped closer, and she was reminded just how tall and intimidating he could be.

"Cold nurse, I knew you couldn't stay away," he said with a triumphant smile.

"Why don't you want to talk to that guy?" she asked.

"Because he's boring and asks ridiculous questions," Hermes said. "What's in the bags?"

"I bought you a present, but you have to promise not to stab me with any of them if I give them to you."

Hermes's face turned serious. "I'd never hurt you, Lady Moon."

"Okay, then I suppose you can have them," she said and passed him an art book and sets of pencils. "I thought this might help you a little with the boredom. Maybe drawing the things you remember might be easier than talking about them."

Hermes smelled the blank pages of the book.

"Words are tricky. They don't go in the right places that I want them."

He grabbed her unexpectedly, pulling her into a tight hug. Selene froze in surprise at being pressed up against the bare skin of his chest, his heart hammering by her ear.

"Thank you, Lady Moon," he said.

"You're welcome, Hermes," she replied, patting his back awkwardly. "Thanatos said you've been talking to Hades?"

Hermes let her go and tipped out his pencils all over the table. "We played chess. He didn't like it because I won. I told him about Zeus, and he said he killed Zeus, and that made me happy."

"I can see why it would. Hades is very smart, so I'm sure he's going to help undo what Zeus did," Selene said, sitting down opposite him.

Hermes started to sketch in quick lines. "He'll try. Uncle has always been incredibly determined when he sets his mind to something, but I think you're wrong. He won't figure it out, you will."

"Me? What do I know about curses?" asked Selene.

Hermes lifted a shoulder in a half-hearted shrug. "Doesn't matter. You're a key."

"What does that mean, Hermes?" An uneasy feeling was settling under her ribs as he talked. *Maybe this was a bad idea.*

"I meant what I said. You're a key. More specifically, you are *my* key," Hermes said, without looking up from his drawing. It looked like a hallway in a house. "You are going to be my nurse all the time now?"

"Yes, I'm going to keep an eye on you until you are better," Selene replied.

"What if I'm never better? What if the doors remained closed, and I never find out what memories are behind them?"

"Do you really believe that? You said yourself that you are a god of thieves, yes?"

Hermes nodded. "I am. I remembered that much."

"Thieves are meant to be good at getting into places they are not meant to be. If you think your memories are behind doors, then why don't you pick their locks?" she asked.

Hermes's pencil snapped, and he stared at her with his hawk gaze. "What are you, Selene?"

"Here to help?" she suggested her heartbeat in her throat.

"That's not all you are. You have locked up parts too, cold nurse," he said, head dropping to one side as he looked her over. "I'll pick the locks on my doors until they open, oh yes, and then I'll be coming after yours."

Selene wet her lips nervously. "You stay away from my locked doors and focus on your own," she said, far more steadily than what she felt. She retreated to her bags and a safe distance from him.

"You should talk to that doctor when he comes back." She wanted the conversation off her and back on safe ground.

"I'll consider it, but only if you stay," Hermes replied, going back to his drawing.

"Don't worry, I'm not going anywhere," Selene assured him.

She dug into her bags and pulled out her sewing. She had been busy at the hospital lately and had no time to finish her most recent creation.

Least you are going to have plenty of time for hobbies now.

"What are you making?" asked Hermes.

"A blanket for a friend," Selene replied. "I don't sit still very well and I get bored easily, like you."

"Are you going to make me a blanket? I'm your friend."

My very strange friend who just told me they are going to unlock all my secret doors.

"All depends on whether or not you are going to eat regularly from now on."

Hermes selected another pencil, turned the page of his book, and started something new. "Are you back to being a carrot already, Lady Moon?"

"Is it working?"

"You can't trick a trickster, my dear," he said, his voice changing and going smooth.

"It was worth a try, I suppose," Selene said with a grin and pulled another square of fabric from her bag.

"How about you stop trying to trick me, and I'll start eating?" asked Hermes.

"It's a deal," she replied. Hermes was beside her in an instant, holding out his long golden hand.

"Shake on it," he insisted.

Selene put her hand in his, letting his fingers wrap around it. "Deal."

Hermes smiled his mischievous smile, lifted her hand, and kissed her knuckles.

"We have a bargain, Lady Selene." He held her hand for a fraction longer before releasing her and going back to his table, leaving Selene looking at her hand and feeling more out of her depth than ever.

4

Hermes's hands had finally stopped being angry at him. He had something to do with them, and so he was feeling calmer than he had since being dragged from his cave.

The pages in his sketchbook were already filling up. Selene had seen his problem when he hadn't had any idea how to articulate it.

His hands weren't happy unless they were creating something. It was easier to draw the way he saw things in his mind rather than force them into words.

This frustrated him because he knew that he was once good with words and could spin them into beautiful shapes.

He had drawn all day, memories floating to the surface, and Hermes hurrying to catch them, to pin them to the paper so they couldn't run away on him again.

Looking back on the drawings made it easier to hold them in his head without it hurting.

"My clever key," Hermes whispered as he sketched Selene's face, the memory of the smile he got out of her was so vibrant in a sea of grey confusion.

He drew her holding a crescent moon, stars in her dark hair, and a glittering necklace of keys around her slender throat.

Hermes liked her throat. It was pale and soft looking with a small mole behind her ear that he had a strange urge to stroke.

He'd never had such urges the whole time he had been dragged around by Pandora. She was beautiful like a poisonous spider was, something that Hermes could look at but never, ever wanted to touch.

Hermes had a feeling that Pandora had tried to get him to touch her in the early days. She hadn't like it when he had refused, and he'd been put into a small room for a very long time, and then the drugged food had started.

Hermes looked down to where he'd begun to draw the only view out of that small room; bars on the window, lots of rocks and scrubby plants and a blue ocean.

The drawing unsettled him, so Hermes turned back to the page with Selene on it and started to draw a marble temple around her.

Drawing her somehow made her presence close again, and he calmed once more. He didn't know how to tell her how relieved he was when she had arrived that day. It was as if the world was suddenly burning in color, and he felt like a god again, not a broken creature hiding underground. He didn't want to be underground, but everything outside still felt too big, too loud.

"Am I interrupting?" Hades asked, jolting Hermes out of his daze. His uncle was staring at him, and he wasn't alone.

A tall man with dark hair and strong god magic was beside him, a careful smile on his strangely familiar, scarred face.

"Hermes, this is Perseus," Hades introduced.

"Zeus's blood?" Hermes guessed. The face in front of him was familiar because it had the same cheekbones and jawline Hermes had.

"Apparently. It's nice to meet you, Hermes," said Perseus and held out his hand. Hermes put down his pencils and shook it, feeling the spark of power in him.

"What does your power do?" Hermes asked curiously.

Perseus's strange pale eyes widened. "You can feel it?"

"Yes. It's like..." Hermes gestured with his hands. "Fireball? No, sun. Like the sun. Is it burning?"

"Not yet, thankfully."

"Perseus likes painting and drawing," said Hades, looking at his sketch pad.

"Did Zeus hurt your head too?" asked Hermes.

"Not me, my mother. She was very brilliant, like you, and Zeus took it away," Perseus explained as he sat down. "I like to draw and paint because it makes the noise in my head not as loud."

"Me too. I'm glad Zeus is dead, so he can't hurt you too," said Hermes.

"I never met him, but I would've tried to kill him for what he did to my mother."

Hermes gave him a knowing smile. "Zeus never had a child that didn't want to kill him at least once. I always thought Athena would get him, but the prize goes to you, dear uncle."

"One of the best days of my existence," Hades said.

"What does your sun do, new brother?" Hermes asked.

"I'm not sure yet. I used it once, and it healed someone I cared about a lot. I haven't touched it since then, I don't know how," admitted Perseus.

"Selene gave me an idea about picking locks because I'm a thief, and my memories are hidden behind doors. Maybe your power is the same. Are you any good at thieving?" asked Hermes. Hades laughed as Perseus rubbed at his neck bashfully.

"Perseus is shy, but until recently, he was known as the best thief in Greece," Hades said, and Hermes liked his new brother even more.

"Tell me the last thing you stole," demanded Hermes.

"Medusa's heart," Perseus said, and Hermes laughed loudly.

"Wait, really? You're in love with a gorgon? Hades! You didn't tell me we had a gorgon," he said excitedly.

"There are a few you haven't met, but I thought I'd break you in slowly and see how you went. You have the most in common with Perseus, so I thought to try him first," Hades replied. He left Hermes alone with Perseus as they talked about art and safe cracking, and hidden power and potential, mothers and monsters.

"I'd love to have you come to my studio when you are feeling better, Hermes," said Perseus.

"Can Selene come? I feel like I'd be less overwhelmed if she were there," Hermes replied.

"Sure thing. I like Selene too. She has a great aura."

"She has a great everything," argued Hermes, and Perseus gave him a sly smile.

"I've heard that about her too. I hope she can help you quickly, and you can get your mind back the way my mother never did," said Perseus.

"When I do, if you need help getting to your magic, I'll help you. I used to be good at figuring out...potential? Yes, potential. Your sun is potential. It can be whatever you shape it to be," Hermes replied.

"I'd like that a lot. Just as long as we do it somewhere where no one can get hurt," said Perseus.

He might look like Zeus, but he is much kinder, Hermes decided. *Zeus would've destroyed him*. Which made him happy all over again that his father was dead.

After Perseus left, Hermes decided that maybe having siblings might just be enjoyable for once.

∽

Hermes felt the moment that Selene stepped into the villa the following morning; her presence moving like silver light in his mind.

That's new, Hermes thought, momentarily forgetting what he was doing. He was still holding a barber around the throat, pinned to a wall when she came out of the elevator, and yelped in alarm.

Oh, that's what I was doing.

"Hermes! Put him down!" she said, closing in on him.

"He's trying to put a blade to my throat, so I had to stop him," Hermes replied, distracted by the way she had braided her hair and pinned it up that day. Her hand came over his tense forearm.

"He was just trying to cut your hair, please put him down," Selene said, the touch and her voice pulling all the hostility out of him.

He let the barber go. The stocky man scrambled backward, muttering curses as he retreated to the elevator. Selene picked up a pair of discarded hair cutting scissors and a small pair of clippers.

"Was that really necessary? He was only trying to help you, Hermes," she said. There was a small line between her eyes.

You've pissed her off already.

"I don't like people I don't know having sharp objects near me," he tried explaining. "I've had too many people try to kill me."

"What about me? You trust me, don't you?" Selene asked. "I can cut your hair and clip your beard for you. You know I'm not going to hurt you, Hermes."

Hermes hesitated. "You won't make it too short?"

"No, I'll cut it to your shoulders. That way, it's still long enough for you to plait when you're thinking."

"I don't know if I like that you are so observant. I don't know if I want my beard cut either," Hermes said stubbornly.

"I won't shave it, just clip it. You know, the women in the Court have a bet going about which of Zeus's boys are the most handsome: Perseus, Asterion, or you. How are we going to judge if we can't see your face? Erebus keeps telling me you were the most handsome in all of Olympus, I think he's a bit in love with you still," Selene said, a teasing tone creeping into her words that Hermes liked.

"He can't help himself, and I can see what you're doing trying to play to my ego, Selene. It won't work because I already know that I'd win such a competition."

Selene's curved lips twitched. She had some type of a gloss on them that Hermes couldn't stop looking at. He wondered what it tasted like.

"You have an ego? Never would've guessed. If it makes you feel better, my money is on Asterion. I know you haven't met him yet, but he is something else in the big and handsome department," Selene replied deviously. She pulled out a chair and looked at him expectantly. "Come on, don't you trust me?"

"How about I let you cut my hair, and you tell me how you got entangled with Hades," Hermes said. He knew how all the others fit; even the gorgon was a monster and Hades always had a soft spot for those, but a kind human nurse? That didn't make sense. Selene's teasing expression slipped, and he got a quick glance of an old hurt in her eyes.

"Fine, but you need to sit still. It's been a while since I cut anyone's hair other than my own," she replied. She retrieved a comb from one of her bags and picked up the scissors again. "I'm not terrible at it, so you don't need to look so nervous."

Hermes's curiosity outweighed his hesitation, just like it always did.

He sat. Selene stepped behind him and ran the comb slowly through his hair.

Hermes was glad that he'd washed his hair that morning because he discovered that someone combing his hair felt *incredible*.

It had been a long time since he willingly let anyone touch him so intimately, but he sat still and did his best not to make happy sounds at the back of his throat.

"Tell me your story, Selene," Hermes said, closing his eyes as her fingers ran over his scalp.

"My story is one of those that you hear and think, *'fuck me, she really should've known better'*, " Selene said as she began to cut. "It was a bit over two years ago. I was working in my first real job as a nurse, and I met a surgeon called Ezra, who was very handsome and charming. I was young and flattered, and we started dating. He seemed too good to be true, and he was. I didn't know he loved betting on fights and had gotten involved with the pit fighting at the Labyrinth."

"All of Greece's criminals love to solve their problems in that place, so Ezra got noticed by people you should never get noticed by."

Selene sounded upset, but Hermes didn't want to open his eyes and interrupt her. He didn't want to see the hair that he could feel falling to the floor either, so he remained still and quiet no matter how much he hated it.

"To make a long story short, Ezra bet on the wrong guy from the wrong gang. The boss of that gang was going to break his hands if he didn't pay. Ezra called me for money, and I got dragged to the Labyrinth. Hades would settle disputes if he was there and was in the mood. He turned up when I was trying to negotiate to save Ezra's hands. I offered my services as a nurse to the gang, who believe me are rough enough to need a nurse full time."

"Hades...I'll never forget the way he looked at me that night. It was like he was staring deep inside of me and weighing my value as a human as well as a nurse."

"That sounds like him," Hermes said softly.

"Well, whatever he saw must've been good, because he bought out Ezra's debt on the spot. Ezra tried to tell Hades what a shit hot surgeon he was, that he'd be able to help him more than a simple nurse, but

Hades had cleared the debt because he wanted me to work for him only."

"Whatever he saw must have convinced him that I would follow through no matter what. Hades had seen in Ezra all the things I had to learn the hard way. That Ezra's word wasn't worth shit."

"Ezra was so grateful that I had stepped in and saved his ass, right up to the point that I started having the triplets pick me up at all hours. I was allowed behind doors and was privy to secrets that would always be denied to him, and he hated that. He started screwing around on me and got violent when I confronted him about it. Thanatos was going to intervene one night when things were...were bad. He didn't end up having to. Ezra was gone by the time I returned the next day. Last I heard he was in Athens working for some fancy private practice. I still owed Hades, and I liked the Court, so I've stayed working for him."

By the time she was done with her story, Hermes's hands were shaking with anger.

"You should've let Thanatos deal with him," he said, trying to keep his voice from rising. The thought of any man hurting Selene made him want to do terrible and violent things.

"Ezra left, Hermes. I had nothing to worry about anymore. Well, except for having to dig bullets out of Asterion and other such dramas the Court likes to get involved in," Selene replied as her hand brushed the stray hair off his shoulders. "I'm going to use the clippers on your beard now. Is it okay if I touch your face?"

Hermes kept his eyes shut, but nodded slowly. "I trust you, Lady Moon."

Her cool, soft fingers slowly positioned his head, and he was once again overwhelmed at the intimacy of it. He also had a strong suspicion that the deep and lost Hermes was probably laughing his ass off at how awkward he was because of a woman touching him.

Shut up, you bastard. Don't mock me if you can't be bothered to come back and save me from this madness.

Hermes was too aware of everything: Selene's hands, the scent of her perfume as she leaned over him, that she was standing between his knees so she could get close to him.

Her hand went to the back of his neck, so he tilted his head, his pulse jumping to his throat as she moved the clippers carefully under his jawline.

He opened his eyes as she finished, so he could see her close just once. He didn't expect her to drop the clippers in surprise. He caught them automatically, not taking his eyes off her.

"What do you think, Selene? Am I back to being presentable?" he asked softly, face close to hers as he held the clippers between them.

"Definitely an improvement. I'm hungry, are you hungry? Are you eating yet?" Selene replied, taking the clippers and stepping quickly away from him.

"Is Hades cooking for you again?" he asked, pretending he didn't enjoy seeing that he had flustered her.

Good, that makes two of us.

"No, there's no one in the villa at the moment. I'm sure that barber left as quickly as his car could drive him," Selene replied, backing up. "I'll go find something and...and be back."

"I want to come," said Hermes, as he stood up to follow her.

"Upstairs? I didn't think you went up there. It's okay if you want to stay here." Selene pressed the button to the elevator quickly.

"I don't usually, but I feel good today. I want to come with you," said Hermes. They got into the elevator, and Hermes stood behind her.

"Okay, let's give it a go, and if you feel uncomfortable, we can go back down."

Hermes leaned down a little and whispered in her ear, "I don't think I'm the one that's uncomfortable right now, Selene."

"I'm surprised that you're coming upstairs, that's all," she said stubbornly.

"You said the villa is empty. Which means it's quiet for once. It's a good time to try. We are near the ocean, aren't we?"

"Yes, Hades has an outdoor deck that goes out into the water."

"I'd like to see the ocean." Hermes didn't know where the new bravery was coming from, something to do with Selene being close, maybe, but he did want to see the water again.

Hermes tried not to let his panic overwhelm him as he followed Selene through the empty villa, his eyes darting left and right in case it wasn't as empty as she thought it was.

They walked into a kitchen and eating area with glass doors around them. Hermes halted. *Everywhere* was the ocean.

He hurried out onto the dark wooden deck to get a better look. He was struck by the beauty of it, the blue of the waves, the sun turning the edges of the waves golden.

He sank slowly to his knees, the warmth of the sunlight on his back and the smell of salt spray in the air.

Deep in his mind, another door unlocked.

5

Selene put together a platter of hummus and olives and fruit, hoping that Hermes would be more interested in eating if he had lots of different options.

She stole a glance at Hermes to make sure he was still okay and was momentarily struck dumb at the sight of him. He was sitting on the deck and was glowing golden in the sunlight.

Selene had known on a subconscious level that underneath the wild man look would be a god, and brother to Asterion and Perseus to boot, but she hadn't been fully prepared to face the reality.

Hermes had opened his golden eyes and her heart had stopped. She was used to being around the beautiful people of the Court, and she wasn't the type to lose her head over a pretty face.

Hermes was something *else* entirely. There was nothing pretty or soft about him. He was angles, savage lines, and dangerous predator eyes, and for a moment, Selene could see that fierce intelligence that would've been overwhelming if he wasn't mad.

For that brief flash, he was the god that you did not *ever* fuck with.

Now he was staring at the ocean with the fascination and delighted innocence of a child. Selene carried the platter outside, careful not to startle him.

"How are you feeling?" she asked, putting the food down beside him before sitting down on the deck.

"Much better. I can't remember when I felt the sun or saw the ocean. It's been...a long time," he said and noticing the platter, he took all the strawberries.

"It is a great spot Hades has here. If you start to feel overwhelmed, we can go back downstairs. You don't need to stay up here on my account," Selene replied. Hermes smiled sideways at her.

"Thank you, Selene, but your concern is unnecessary," he said, sounding like the calm and confident Hermes there were only ever flashes of. "No, I don't think I'll be returning to the earth any time soon."

"That's a big change of attitude to have in such a short time outside," she said skeptically.

Hermes lay back on the warm wood with a contented sigh. "I had another door open just now."

"What was on the other side of it?" Selene asked, doing her best to keep her eyes on his face and not all the golden muscle that was presenting itself to her.

"A part of myself," he said, turning towards her and propping his head up with one hand. "And Selene, dear, I fucking *hate* being locked up."

"This is really good news. Hades has a large guest wing on the west side of the villa that would give you plenty of privacy if you want to move into it," she replied, trying to ignore the slow, sly way he said her name.

"I feel like a puzzle piece has been put in the correct spot even though there's a lot of blank spaces left to go," Hermes said softly.

"That's a good step in the right direction," Selene replied.

"Selene? Thank you." Something in Hermes's tone made her look back at him.

"I didn't do anything."

"Yes, you did. You do. Don't deny it, it's me that it's happening to so I would know. Also, I don't know how long I'll remain this clear, so let me thank you while I can," Hermes said, the sincerest she had ever seen him. Something flared hot in her chest as she smiled at him.

"In that case, you're welcome, Hermes. I don't know what I did, but it's my job to help you, so I will in any way I can."

"I'm your job? What happened to being friends?" he asked, dark brows drawing together.

"We can be both. I wouldn't have made a blanket for a job, would I?" she said, hating that a slip of the tongue had killed his mood.

"You made me a blanket?"

"I did. I finished it last night. I was going to give it to you after your hair cut, but then we got distracted," said Selene.

You mean you got distracted by his hot intensity.

She cringed. Did she actually just think that about...what was he? A patient? A project? He wasn't a favor because she was getting paid. Paid to hang out, be his friend and keep him talking so that Hades could get Pandora's secrets out of him.

Hermes's smile was strangely knowing as if he could read everything in her mind. *Could* he read minds?

God, please no. Selene would have to ask Hades.

"I'm going to get some juice. Do you want anything?" she said and got to her feet. He lay back on the boards again, hair tousled around him like a curling, dark brown halo.

"Oh, I definitely want things, Lady Moon," he said.

"To drink," she clarified and then got flustered because she felt like she had to.

What is wrong with you today? she complained as she went back to the kitchen. Her phone buzzed on the counter with a message from Hades: *Are you okay there by yourself?*

Selene took a photo of Hermes outside and messaged it back to him. She grabbed a small bottle of juice from the fridge, turned around, and Hermes was...missing.

"What the...?" Selene hurried outside. "Hermes?" There was a splash beneath her, and she went to the railing as his head surfaced. "What are you doing?"

"What does it look like?" he said.

Selene opened the small gate in the railing that led to a ladder. "You scared me. You were just gone."

"I'm sorry...the water looked good," he replied.

"It's fine, really."

Hermes looked ridiculously happy, and if she hadn't been so

distracted by his smile, she would've heard Cerberus barreling towards her. She turned as he let out a happy woof and crashed straight into her legs.

With a startled yelp, she toppled forward awkwardly and into the water. There was a cold tangled moment under the waves when strong hands grabbed her and lifted her up.

"Fucking dog!" Selene shouted as she surfaced, pushing her bangs from her eyes. Hermes was supporting her and laughing his ass off. "Shut up, it's not funny!"

"It's definitely funny," Hermes replied. "Are you okay?"

"No," she said as she splashed him and started laughing. Cerberus was wagging his tail happily above them. Hermes gave him a long look, and then a wide smile broke over his face.

"Oh, Cerberus! I remember you. Why do you only have one head?" He made a flicking gesture, and Selene's ears popped. Light shimmered around Cerberus, and he shook his two other heads free of their glamour.

"How did you do that?" Selene asked, paddling water trying to keep her head above the waves.

Hermes looked down at his hand. "I...don't know." Three different woofs sounded above them before Cerberus dropped a tennis ball into the ocean, and after a few seconds of watching it, the huge dog came in after them.

Selene and Hermes were throwing the ball between them and making Cerberus swim back and forth when Thanatos appeared on the deck with Hades.

"Where was my invitation to this party?" Thanatos asked, leaning casually on the railing.

"You're both welcome to take your clothes off and join us," said Selene as she surrendered the ball to Cerberus.

"No, thank you, Selene. I'm glad to see you in such good spirits, Hermes," Hades replied, "and that you finally succumbed to letting someone cut your hair."

"Selene bribed me," Hermes replied.

"I did not! That's not how it went down at all."

"There was definitely bribery involved. She's very sneaky under her sweet nurse act," Hermes said, taking her hand under the water to help hold her up.

"It's not an act. I happen to be very sweet, right, Thanatos?" she argued.

"I've seen it, but it's buried rather deep," he said, making Hermes laugh.

"Hey, you're meant to be on my side," Selene complained.

"Always, darling Selene. I'm also honest to a fault," Thanatos said.

"That's it, I'm getting out if you guys are going to pick on me." Hermes held onto her, drawing her closer.

"Come now, I wouldn't like you if you were too sweet. I like your mean streak," he said.

"You are going to get well acquainted with it if you don't let me go," Selene replied tartly, and humor danced in his eyes before he released her.

"Allow me," Thanatos said, reaching down to help her up the ladder. Selene grabbed his hand, and he lifted her as if she were as light as a child.

"Thank you," she said before turning to Hades. "I don't suppose I could borrow a towel?"

He gave one of his pleased smiles. "Of course, Selene, let me get it for you." He disappeared, and Thanatos sniggered.

"He doesn't want you dripping on his floor," he said.

Selene stepped back as Hermes pulled himself easily out of the ocean and up the ladder before running his hands through his hair in a casually sexy gesture. Selene looked away quickly, and Thanatos's smile widened.

Oh fuck, he totally just caught you checking Hermes out.

"It's nice to see you looking like your old self, Hermes," he said, and she tried not to cringe.

"Selene told me there's a bet going on about which one of Zeus's sons is the best looking. I had a point to prove," Hermes said, resting his hands on his hips, and then he had the nerve to *smirk* at her.

"I still think it's Asterion," she replied and turned away from them to accept the towel from Hades.

"Liar," Hermes whispered behind her, and Selene carefully pretended not to hear him.

~

HERMES DECIDED that he didn't like watching Selene leave with Charon every day. She had been soaked and had left early, turning down Hermes's offer to wear his clothes.

It wasn't like he could handle wearing a t-shirt all the time anyway, so he had plenty of spare clothes to share, but she had refused.

Selene had left a bag on the couch downstairs, and in it he found a small patchwork blanket in blue and green, the backing an incredibly soft fabric he couldn't identify.

"I'm glad you're getting out of here," said Thanatos as he helped Hermes pack up his clothes and his art books.

"Me too, now that I realize how much I hate being trapped," Hermes replied, wrapping the blanket around his shoulders like a short cloak, and grabbing the stash of small objects he'd pilfered over the last few days: Selene's bangle, one of the pins from her hair, Hades's cufflinks, Charon's tie pin.

He had meant to give it all back but then had forgotten about it. He tucked them in his pocket before Thanatos could see them.

"You are improving more and more now that Selene is helping. It's good for her too. I haven't ever seen her laugh like she was doing in the water today," said Thanatos.

"Why not?" asked Hermes as they stepped into the elevator.

"Selene has been treated poorly by people in the past, so she doesn't allow herself to relax very often. She gets along with all of us, but she hasn't ever socialized with us. When we see her, it's because we need her, and she's protective of her heart," Thanatos explained.

"Good. I know about her old boyfriend. I wish you had hurt him, Thanatos," said Hermes.

"You and me both," Thanatos muttered. "She wouldn't have it."

"I'm her friend, so I won't let anyone hurt her like that ever again." Hermes gripped the blanket around his shoulders a little tighter. He wasn't as clear in his mind as he was when Selene was there, but thankfully, he could still form coherent sentences. Maybe he really was improving.

Thanatos led him through the villa to the large guest wing where Hades's men sometimes stayed if they needed to. It was a separate, small house attached by paths to the main villa.

Inside had its own kitchen and bathroom, and best of all, a deck looking out over the small beach.

"Finally decided to join the living again, did you?" Charon said as he came in a short time later. He flopped down on the couch. "How's your memory going, champ?"

"It's adjusting," Hermes replied and offered him back his tie pin. "You're still too slow, ferryman."

"And you are still a sneaky son of a bitch," Charon said, snatching it back.

"I can't help it. It's just my nature. At least with half my memory gone, we are operating at the same speed."

"Would you listen to this cocky piece of shit, brother? A few days with Selene and he's back to thinking he's the top dog again," Charon laughed. "Mind you, I'd be feeling pretty good about myself too, if I got to spend my days lying about with the lovely Selene. Maybe I should suggest to Hades we take it in turns."

"But I'm actually mad, and *you* are just mad that I still have better game than you," Hermes said as he sat down. "Selene is my nurse, so you can fuck off and find your own."

"*Your* nurse now, is it? I believe you will find Selene would object to such territorial nonsense," Thanatos replied. "Besides, she's not exactly acting like a nurse, just keeping your crazy ass company because we are too busy."

"She might not be acting like a nurse, but I need her. I'm better when she's around and not because she's beautiful," Hermes said quickly.

"Oh, you think she's beautiful now, do you?" Thanatos teased.

Hermes huffed out a breath. "Don't be an idiot. Of course, she's beautiful. You have to have felt that there's something different about her."

"Are you talking about magic?" asked Thanatos.

"Yes? Maybe? She is a healer, not just a nurse. If I wasn't so fucking broken, I'd be able to feel it out properly," Hermes said, running a frustrated hand over his face.

"It's definitely possible. You are the god of magic, so you were always more sensitive to those abilities in humans than others. Get your mind right first, then approach it with her if you need to. I wouldn't want you to complicate her life before you can be sure," Thanatos replied.

"Listen to my brother, and not just because he's particularly protective of Selene. Magic isn't as common in the humans as it used to be, and the possibility of it may upset her," Charon added. "Also, if you hurt her in any way with your trickster bullshit, Erebus, Thanatos, and I will throw you in one of the cells in Tartarus and leave you with only Zeus's head for company."

"I'd never hurt Selene, she's my key and my friend," said Hermes, fingers playing with the corner of the blanket around his shoulders.

"Just don't you forget it," Charon replied. "It is good to have you back. I thought one of the Olympians might have gotten you."

Hermes laughed. "I'm sure they tried their best, but they were always slower than even you, ferryman."

6

It had been a bad morning. To Selene, it felt like a double gut punch because the day before had been so good.

She had gotten more than one breakthrough with Hermes and an unexpected swim that made her laugh harder than she had in a long time. She *liked* Hermes's strange but easy company and getting up at regular hours.

She had woken that morning looking forward to the day and had received not one, but two missed calls from Leo, the Chief of Medicine at the Lethe Hospital.

When she had called him back, she regretted it almost instantly.

"What the fuck is this letter on my desk from Acheron Legal saying they are trading your services for ten nursing positions?" he asked.

"I thought you would be happy to have the funding, not pissed off about it," Selene said exasperatedly.

"I am, don't get me wrong. I just didn't know you ran in such circles. If I had known you had such influence with Hades Acheron, I would've promoted you and gotten you to lean on him for funding earlier," Leo replied.

"Good to know working hard for you for five years meant shit, Leo.

You better let the other nurses know that the only way they will advance is by their social circles."

"Now, now that's not what I meant, Selene. This whole situation has left us a bit bewildered. What kind of work do you even do for Hades?"

"None of your business, Leo. It's confidential and I signed an agreement," Selene replied stubbornly, still too pissed off to want to answer any of his questions. She sure as hell wasn't about to give up the appearance of another god to the likes of Leo.

The thought of the media scum swarming Hermes made a fierce protectiveness rise in her.

"Okay, fair enough. It's personal, I get that. You've really moved up in the world since Ezra dumped you. He's going to be kicking himself that he let you go when he hears about this," chuckled Leo, and Selene's stomach turned to acid.

"For your information, I was the one that dumped Ezra, and he left for Athens to sulk. Acheron Legal will be in touch with the payment details. Goodbye, Leo, don't call me again," Selene said, hanging up the phone before she started screaming obscenities. She knew Leo and Ezra had been close, but she didn't think he'd have the nerve to bring him up.

What a fucking asshole.

It was just another reason that leaving was a good decision. When Erebus arrived thirty minutes later, he looked as pissed off as she did.

"What's happened?" they both asked at once.

"You first," said Selene, not wanting to talk about the phone call just yet.

"Hermes won't get out of the bathtub, and he won't tell any of us what's upset him. My money is on a not so great memory," Erebus replied as they drove to the villa. "You?"

"Shitty conversation with my ex-boss. Hermes in the bath is more important," said Selene.

Thanatos and Charon were sitting outside the guest house where they had moved Hermes. Both looked relieved when she stepped out of the car.

"Has he said anything?" she asked.

"Not a peep, just staring off into space," said Charon, flicking one of his coins over his fingers. Selene had an idea. There was only one cure for a bad day.

"I need you to find a shirt, maybe one of Hades's, something soft or silk so it won't irritate Hermes too much," she said.

"What are you thinking?" asked Erebus.

"I'm going to take Hermes to see my guilty pleasure," she said, and all three of them smiled. "I didn't mean *that* guilty pleasure you perves. The one based outside of Lethe."

"Ohhh," they all said in sync.

"I'll go and talk to him. Find me that shirt," she said, shaking her head at them.

Selene walked through the small house, noting the chaos of drawings already scattered around the kitchen table. She would have to get the triplets to get him more art supplies if he kept it up. She tapped softly on the bathroom door.

"Hermes? Are you in here?" she asked.

"Lady Moon," he said, voice filled with relief.

"Can I come in?" And then as an afterthought, she added, "Are you decent?"

"Yes."

Selene opened the door slowly and saw that he was lying in the empty bathtub, hanging onto the blanket she had made him. He was facing away from her, so she sat on the tiled edge of the tub.

"Looks like you are having a morning as good as mine," she said, and she laid a hand on his head, brushing his dark brown curls from his face.

You are too familiar with him already, a voice warned her, but she drowned it out.

"Do you want to talk about it?"

"Do you want to talk about your bad morning?" Hermes replied but seemed to relax under the touch.

"No," she admitted.

"I don't either."

"I want to take you somewhere instead. You'll have to wear a shirt, but I guarantee it will be worth it," Selene said.

Hermes rolled over and looked up at her. "Where are we going?"

"It's a surprise. The best bit is that neither of us needs to talk," Selene said and held out a hand to him. "Are you coming?"

Hermes looked at her hand a few seconds before taking it and sitting up. "I'm sorry your day has been bad too."

"It happens. Come on, let's get out of here," Selene said. Hermes held onto her hand as he stepped out of the tub and allowed her to lead him out of the bathroom.

Erebus held out a t-shirt to her. "Will this do?"

It was a very soft, dark blue cotton shirt. "Perfect, thanks, Erebus. We are going out, Charon, can you drive us?"

"Sure thing, doll," he said.

They all didn't comment on Hermes, and how strange it was that he was willing to go with them without argument. Selene got in the back seat of the car, and after another long moment of hesitation, Hermes joined her.

"I won't make you put this on until we arrive, okay?" she said, placing the shirt in the middle of the seat between them. Hermes nodded. His eyes were looking at everything around them, soaking in the forest and the city once they reached it.

When it became too much, he closed his eyes, but didn't ask for them to stop or go back.

"We'll be about an hour, Charon," Selene said when they pulled up at a building made of concrete block.

"I'll be close if you need me," he replied.

"What is this place?" Hermes asked, brows furrowing.

Selene tossed the shirt to him. "Put that on and come find out."

She got out of the car and was taking off her shoes inside the front door when Hermes appeared beside her. It was strange to see him in a shirt, but the blue made his eyes glow even brighter.

"Hey, Selene! It's been a while," a woman appeared in scrubs. She looked Hermes all the way up and down. "Though your absence makes sense."

"Jules, this is my friend Hermes."

"Her *good* friend," Hermes said, with a dazzling smile.

Oh, God, just what I need; Hermes in flirt mode.

Jules flushed and let out a chuckle. "I bet you are," she said.

"Is it okay if we are here for playtime?" Selene interrupted before Hermes could give Jules any more wrong impressions.

"Sure thing, we need more volunteers. We have twelve newbies for you to meet, and it's almost time for food, so they will be rowdy," Jules said and waved them through a set of double doors. "Get into position and I'll free the beasts."

They were in a large room littered with toys. Selene lay on the ground and gestured at Hermes. "You need to lie down with me." Hermes's smile was back, the one Selene was starting to recognize as pure, flirtatious trouble. "Trust me, Hermes, this is going to be good for both of us."

Hermes lay down beside her. "You are probably the only person I trust right now, Selene."

Selene didn't have a chance to respond as doors opened and excited yips filled the room. Within seconds, puppies were climbing all over them, biting their hands with their tiny teeth.

Hermes let out a delighted laugh as he picked up a particularly chubby mongrel and stopped it from biting at his face.

"What is this place?" Hermes asked.

"It's a dog shelter. I try to get here once a week to play with the puppies and socialize the other dogs. They are underfunded, so I will sometimes bend the rules and help where I can, stitching up hurt dogs and assisting the vets, or cleaning out cages. Most of the time, I come here for stress relief and because I can't have a dog of my own," Selene explained.

When she risked a glance at Hermes, he was covered with puppies and was stroking their soft bodies.

"I had a dream that I created...bad things. For Pandora. There was an old man in it too who I didn't recognize," Hermes said.

Selene didn't know if Hades had told him about the cage that they had tried to lock Asterion in or the eye mask Acrisius Argos had forced onto Medusa. She wasn't about to bring them up and upset him more.

"I had my old boss ring me and say a lot of things that upset me," Selene said, exchanging one bad morning for another.

His hand found hers, so she entwined their fingers, and let the puppies do their work.

After Jules had come in with bowls of food for the always hungry pups, Selene took Hermes to see the other dogs.

"They all have blankets like mine," said Hermes, pausing to pat an elderly Labrador. "These are your friends."

"Good spot. Most of these dogs come from bad situations and deserve their own blankie. I'm pretty bad at sewing, even though I enjoy it, and dogs aren't fussy," Selene replied. She stopped in front of a pen with a dog sitting in the far corner.

It was an indeterminate mix of mastiff and some other breed and was black and grey. It had a few still healing scars and was missing half of one ear.

"This poor boy was rescued from a dogfighting ring. I sit with him, but so far, he hasn't warmed up to me. I can't say that I blame him after the way humans mistreated him. Jules is hoping to re-socialize him so he can be adopted, but I think it's going to take time."

"Can I sit with him for a little while?" Hermes asked.

"Sure, I'll go and see if Jules needs help cleaning up," said Selene. She drew the bolt of the pen and let him in. "I'll be back soon."

"Okay," Hermes said, sitting down and leaning his back against the wall. Selene left him to it, trusting he'd find her if he had enough.

"Who is that gorgeous man, and where have you been hiding him? Please tell me in your bed," Jules demanded as Selene joined her in the puppy room.

"Hermes is a *friend,* and I haven't been hiding him anywhere," Selene clarified, and seeing Jules's disbelieving look, she said, "He has PTSD. I thought the dogs would help."

"Hot ones are always gay or crazy," sighed Jules. "Where did you leave him?"

"With my favorite boy. They both need company," said Selene. She helped pick up the bowls and the clean out the puppy pens, before feeding the older dogs.

By the time she reached where she'd left Hermes, she heard him whispering. Selene tiptoed and caught him talking with the black dog, who was sitting next to him.

Well. What do you know? Selene smiled at them, two broken creatures that finally found company where they felt like they belonged.

"Selene is here now and is going to give you some food. She doesn't like it if you don't eat, trust me," Hermes said, looking up with a smile.

"I didn't want to interrupt. I haven't seen him this close to anyone." Selene opened the pen and placed the bowl of food down in front of the black dog.

"I told him what humans did to me, and then we decided that it was okay to be friends. Also, he's coming home with me," Hermes said, getting to his feet.

"Really? Are you sure Hades wouldn't mind?" asked Selene.

Hermes gave her a stern look. "I don't care what Hades thinks. I gave him my word."

"Okay, well, I think it's time Cerberus had a friend. What do you want to call him?"

"Nothing. He'll give me his name when he wants to," Hermes said matter-of-factly. "Right now, we've just agreed that he'll come with us without a fuss."

Charon eyed the big black dog that stood between Selene and Hermes. It didn't have a lead or a collar, and Hermes had objected to them being put on, saying that it wasn't necessary.

"You've adopted a baby together already? That's adorable. If it defecates on my seats, you'll be cleaning it up, Hermes," said Charon.

"He would never do such a thing, ferryman, don't insult him," Hermes replied. The black dog sat between them on the ride home, even suffering Selene to pat his back leg. The dog was calmer than she had ever seen it, and she had to accept that maybe Hermes really could talk to animals.

Honestly, nothing would surprise me.

After they pulled up, Cerberus let out a loud woof of warning when he spotted the black dog.

"Be nice, Cerberus, this is my friend, and if you are a jerk, I'll get Selene to neuter you," Hermes told the three-headed dog.

Cerberus gave Hermes a look that was all attitude before sniffing the black dog curiously. Tails wagged nervously, and then both of them exploded into a run.

"They will be fine," said Hermes.

"We've collected another stray I see," Hades called from his side of the villa. "It better be house trained."

Hermes shrugged, but Hades only smiled at Selene and went back inside.

7

His hands were warm against her cold skin. He traced slow, languorous circles over her arms, her stomach, and her thighs.

His lips joined his fingers, trailing hot lines down her chest. She cried out as he took one nipple in his mouth and sucked it hard.

It had been a long time since she let a man touch her, but she wanted him.

Her whole body was on fire, yearning for him, wanting his delicious weight on top of her, skin to skin. His mouth found hers, tongue stroking against tongue, stubble against her lips and chin.

"You're so beautiful," he whispered in his husky voice. "I want to devour you whole."

Lips moved from hers, going down the center of her chest, the curve of her stomach. A thrill of anticipation and nervous fear ran through her as his lips roamed further down, teeth nipping against her hip.

Warm breath moved along her skin, and then his mouth settled between her thighs, tongue and lips and stubble flooding her with pleasure.

"Fuck, Hermes," Selene cried out, and she woke up with a jolt. She was sweating, her hand down her panties, and before she could fully wake, she was coming hard. She whimpered against her damp pillow as the orgasm rocked her.

Then she realized what she was doing and she yanked her hand out.

"What the hell?!" Selene exclaimed. The sun was coming through her window.

She sat up, breathing heavily, as she blindly reached for the glass of water on her bedside table.

Horror and embarrassment coursed over her. Did she just have a sex dream about... Selene downed the water. Her pajamas were scattered around her bed, where she had stripped them off in her sleep, her blanket tangled around her feet.

"Oh, my god," she muttered and dragged herself out of bed.

Having sex dreams about your patient, real classy, Selene.

She climbed into the shower and turned on the water. Her body was still thrumming from the orgasm. She hadn't had a sex dream in years and never about someone she knew. She groaned and rested her forehead against the glass. How was she going to face him and not die of embarrassment?

"You are ridiculous. It's because you've been spending so much time with him," Selene said aloud, and then her treacherous mind went back to the glowing golden eyes between her legs.

You're in so much shit.

By the time Selene got out, she was feeling more or less awake and back to her usual self. She laughed at the absurdity of the dream and dressed in a pair of jeans and a loose singlet.

She was calmly drinking her morning tea in her garden when her phone vibrated with an unknown number. She opened the message and froze.

Hey, I know it's been a while, but I'm going to be in Styx for a few days for a conference. Would love if we could have dinner tonight and clear the air? I miss our friendship...E.

Selene took a deep breath and closed the message. Only Ezra would sign off a message with an initial.

"God, why me?" she asked the plants. She jumped as her phone buzzed again. It was Charon's morning ETA.

Selene finished her tea and toast, brushed her teeth, and grabbed her bag. Her face looked more flushed than usual in the mirror.

She took a deep breath and smoothed her bangs unnecessarily before hurrying down the three flights of stairs.

Charon was leaning against his favorite black Porsche, and there was a small group of women in her building's foyer staring at him.

Not that Selene could blame them, it was rare to see someone that looked like him and a car that expensive on her side of Lethe.

"I'm starting to think Hades should let me use one of his fleet cars, so you don't have to go out of your way every day," she said as he opened the door for her.

"And make you feel like you're not special? Not likely, doll," replied Charon as he got into the driver's seat. "Besides, we have some errands to run before heading back to the villa."

"Like what?" asked Selene. Charon pulled a list out of his breast pocket and passed it to her.

"You were the one that let Hermes bring a new dog home. A dog that he's actually calling Dog by the way. It needs things, and so does Hermes. I figure if it looks like you brought him clothes, he might actually wear them and stop using that blanket as a cape," he said. Selene laughed a little awkwardly, and Charon gave her a strange look. "You okay? You look a little shiny today."

"Shiny? What does that mean?"

"Glowing? I dunno. If I knew you had a guy, I'd suspect you'd been laid," Charon replied.

"Nope. No guy, no lay. Might be that I'm finally getting to see some sunlight," Selene said. Charon didn't look convinced.

They walked through the overpriced stores in the Diogenes, Selene picking more men's clothes of the softest fabrics she could find, Charon giving men's fashion advice as they went.

Selene ignored the strange look the salespeople were giving her singlet and jeans ensemble, but they were polite enough as soon as they saw Charon was with her.

They picked up a dog bowl, bed, and toys for the new addition to the family.

"How was Hermes this morning? No more nightmares?" Selene asked, internally cringing at her own dreams.

"When I looked in on him, he was asleep on the lounge room floor with the dog," Charon replied. "Are you worried about him?"

"No, I just wanted to know what I'm walking into, that's all. Hermes was upset yesterday because he knows that he designed things for Pandora. Maybe Hades should tell him what they found in ARGOS," said Selene.

"I don't think that will make him feel any better. Maybe when he's more back to normal, and when he can process it properly. I know Hermes. He was made to do some fucked up shit for Zeus more than once, and it haunted him even when he was sane. Pandora took advantage of his messed-up state and exploited him. Who knows what she made him do or make? If we tell him now, he'll be confused and angry, and he will have nowhere for that anger to go," argued Charon.

"Okay, but I don't know if hiding it from him will help either. I hope you guys find Pandora soon. I wouldn't mind throttling her myself," she said with a touch of venom.

"Selene, love, I think that's the most violent thing I've ever heard you say," Charon laughed.

"Well, I like Hermes, and it isn't cool what she's done to him."

Charon lowered his Ray-Bans. "That sneaky fucker. He's got to you already."

"What? Don't be ridiculous," Selene said. "Watch the road."

Charon shook his head. "Women have always loved that sly prick. Being mad hasn't changed that by the looks of things."

"We are *friends*, Charon. I have a duty of care for goodness sake," Selene said.

Charon just clicked his tongue. "Whatever you say, *Lady Moon*. I know you aren't friends with men often. I don't think you've had a date in years."

"I was asked out for dinner tonight actually," she said, and then hated herself for bringing it up.

"Oh, really? And what did you say?"

"Nothing yet. I'm making up mind whether or not to respond."

"You'll have to tell me how it went tomorrow when I pick you up," Charon said.

"I will," Selene snapped and ignored his smile.

Stupid nosey titan.

8

Hermes sat outside his small house with one hand on Dog's head.

He had woken up that morning with power vibrating under his skin. He didn't know what it did, but it was making him feel fuller and more complete.

He *was* getting better. He had another two doors open in his mind, and he was feeling steady.

Words were beginning to flow in perfectly coherent lines in his mind again. Most importantly, they were taking hold like seeds on earth. He remembered how much he *liked* words and talking and writing.

Zeus took away my expression. That fucking bastard. He wished he could remember why his father had done it to him.

Charon's black car appeared, coming down the driveway towards them. A strange feeling moved through him as Selene stepped out of the car and smiled shyly at him. He got to his feet and hurried to help her with her bags.

"What is all of this? I feel like every day you arrive with more and more things," Hermes said.

"These are all for you and your new dog," she replied. Her voice sounded a bit breathy and strange. She didn't look upset or angry, so he didn't know what the matter was.

"We can't have you wandering about half-dressed and frightening Selene's sensibilities," Charon said, walking past them with his arms laden with bags and a blue dog bed.

"My bare chest doesn't frighten you, does it, Selene?" Hermes asked.

"No, but you really should get used to wearing clothes," she replied without looking at him, her voice going weird again.

"Are you okay? Did you sleep all right?" Hermes asked.

"I slept perfectly fine. I'm fine. Everything is fine," Selene said and followed Charon into the house.

"Everything is not fine," Hermes commentated to Dog. He found Charon putting food into the small fridge in the kitchen. There were boxes of new kitchen utensils, cutlery, plates, and saucepans stacked on the benches.

"Have you upset, Selene?"

"Not me, champ. She's been peaky all morning. I think it's got to do with being asked out on a date tonight," Charon replied.

"I don't like the sound of that," said Hermes, taking an apple from one of the bags.

"I'm sure you don't, but it doesn't concern you, trickster." Hermes didn't like Charon's tone, so he stole his wallet from his back pocket as he left the kitchen.

Selene was on the deck, setting up metal dog food bowls and taking tags off toys.

"How are you this morning?" she asked before he could say anything.

"Better than you by the looks of things. I woke up, and I could feel my magic for the first time," Hermes said. "And I remembered my staff."

"Your staff?" Selene asked, her ears going red.

"An actual staff, I'm not trying to be lewd," Hermes clarified but was delighted that her mind went there.

"Like a wizard's staff?"

"Don't insult me. I am the god of magic, Selene. All wizard archetypes stem from the stories of me and not the other way around," he said, power flaring under his skin.

Selene jumped backward in fright. "Your eyes just changed, what did you do?"

"Nothing," he said, rubbing at them. "It's my magic. I didn't scare you, did I?"

"Maybe a little bit, but only because I didn't expect it. They flashed with gold light for a second, that's all. It didn't hurt you?" she asked, her hand coming to his forearm.

It hadn't hurt, but Hermes liked it when she touched him, so he kept rubbing at his eyes.

"A little? Maybe you should check them?" he said pathetically. Selene moved to pull his hands away.

"Okay, bend down and give me a look," she replied, going into nurse mode. Hermes obliged her, and she turned his head with her delicate fingers so she could study his eyes.

"How do they look?" he asked softly.

"They don't look red or anything. Maybe it's a god thing you should ask Hades about," she said, hands on his cheeks. Hermes was looking at her lovely shaped lips when Charon cleared his throat behind them.

"There's nothing wrong with his eyes, Selene. It's when his magic flares and it doesn't hurt him. He's full of shit," Charon said, and Selene let Hermes's face go. Hermes was going to *kill* that titan.

"You might know that, but he doesn't," she said, coming to his defense. Hermes smiled smugly at Charon behind her back.

"I didn't remember," Hermes said innocently.

"I think you remember a lot more than you let on, trickster. You better watch out for his games as he gets better, Selene," replied Charon.

"Hermes was telling me about a staff, do you know what he's talking about?" asked Selene.

"Oh, yes. Big, gold, gaudy thing that it was."

"Do you know what it did?"

"He used it for channeling his magic and it could open the doors to the Underworld," said Charon.

"What do you mean doors?" asked Hermes. *Why did it always come back to doors?*

"It's how you used to get around so quickly. It's like you could open a door in reality, step through it and land somewhere else, a bit like

Hades can. You used to need your staff to open the paths of the dead, though."

"So, the winged sandals were just a story?" asked Selene.

"It was humans trying to explain what they saw and couldn't understand," said Hermes, the memory creeping back to him as Charon talked.

"It's a shame really, I think you'd look cute with spangly winged shoes to match your big gold stick," teased Charon.

"Fuck off, ferryman," said Hermes.

Charon looked at his watch. "It is indeed time for me to get out of here. I have things to do for Hades, but text me the time you want to be picked up. I want to give you plenty of time to get ready for your date, Selene. I know it's been a while."

"I agree with Hermes, you can fuck off now," said Selene, eyes narrowed at Charon. He only laughed and gave them a little wave goodbye. "I should go and finish unpacking."

Hermes followed her back inside the kitchen. "What's this about a date?"

"It's nothing," said Selene, putting food into the kitchen cupboards.

"Doesn't seem like nothing, you've been jittery all morning."

"I'm not jittery," she replied. "And if you must know, Ezra is back in Styx and wants to see me. It's not a date, it's a discussion."

Hermes went cold. "Ezra. The horrible piece of shit boyfriend. You are actually going to see him?"

"I don't know. I'm thinking about it. Some things need to be said. It might be good closure."

Hermes couldn't believe what he was hearing. "He doesn't deserve closure, Selene, he deserves a bullet. He's only going to try to use you."

"You don't know that. I'll admit that he was pretty shitty in the end, but we had good times too. He might not deserve the closure, but I do."

"Are you still in love with him?" Hermes asked, closing in on her. Selene halted, holding a bag between them.

"That's none of your business."

"From what you told me, there isn't much to still be in love with. He sounds like he had as much personality as that box of plates over there," Hermes said and lowered his voice. "He probably didn't even kiss you with tongue."

"How he kissed me is also none of your business, Hermes," Selene replied steadily, her hands grabbing the bag like a shield.

"You don't have to answer me; I can see the truth. Something tells me he's not the man you dream about at night," he said. Selene's eyes flashed with anger.

"You know what? I think I *will* text Ezra back and see if he has time for a drink," she said, shoving the bag into his arms and pulling out her phone.

"Don't do it, Selene, it's a mistake."

"Maybe, but it's mine to make and not yours," she said as her fingers typed. "You know, I was on the fence whether or not to see him, but this conversation has convinced me it might be a good idea."

"If you are doing this to prove a point to me, don't, Selene. He's going to hurt you," Hermes replied, hating himself for pushing her.

"He's hurt me before, so I don't have anything to be afraid of, do I?" she said, and her phone buzzed in her hand. "Oh, look at that, drinks at 7pm at the Lethe Loft."

"Why are you acting this way?" asked Hermes.

"Why are you? It's none-"

"Of my business, yes, you said that, but you're wrong, it *is* my business. You're my friend, Selene. Friends don't let other friends date boring plate men who don't know how to pleasure a woman and who have treated them like shit. You're *not* shit. You deserve to be kissed by a man who actually knows what he's doing," Hermes argued.

"It's *not* a date," Selene repeated softly.

"He is going to think that it is, and you've just run to him like he knew you would," Hermes replied, getting in her face. They stared at each other for a long moment, and he thought about kissing her angry lips.

"Have it your way, but don't say I didn't warn you. I'm going to go play with Dog."

"Fine. I'm going to catch up to Charon and go home," Selene said, pushing past him. She grabbed her bag off the table and walked out the door, leaving him more frustrated than ever.

∼

Hours later, Hermes was drinking with Hades down at the villa. Selene hadn't come back, and he'd been angry at himself for the whole day.

"You have to stop her, Hades. You know that guy is trash," Hermes argued, pacing up and down the lounge room. "At least send one of the titans to keep an eye on her to make sure Ezra doesn't try anything."

"Stop worrying about Selene. She is a grown woman and can handle the likes of Ezra. Charon said you remembered your staff and can feel your magic. That's more important right now. Can you see the doorways yet?" Hades asked.

Hermes raked a hand through his hair.

"I don't know what I'm looking for. I can feel the power there, though. We need to find my staff. I need to use it to beat the shit out of this Ezra and get him out of Selene's life once and for all."

"And we are back at Selene again," sighed Hades.

"Of course, we are! It's because she's the reason I can think clearly again. She has magic. Her presence reacts to whatever Zeus did to me, and now my nurse is going to get trampled on by a piece of shit man. How can you be so nonchalant about the whole thing? You *know* what he did to her," ranted Hermes.

"For the god of boundaries, you really need to learn to have some," said Hades. "I know Selene. She's not going to be fooled by Ezra again. She has a reason to see him."

"Yeah, to piss me off."

"Not everything in Selene's life is about you, Hermes."

"Well, maybe it should be."

Hades groaned. "Can you even hear yourself? You're acting like a petulant child. She's not your property, Hermes."

"I am the god of magic and all of its domains! She has magic, so she is mine to protect," Hermes hissed, power racing like hot lightning through him.

"Well, there he is at last." Hades put his drink down and got up. He was taller than Hermes, but not by a lot, and yet, there was something in his silver eyes that made Hermes step back.

"If you are so worried about Selene, go and *do* something about it. Find the doors and find her if you must, but don't whine to me about it when you are the one with the power at your fingertips."

And just like that, Hermes could see the magic in his mind's eye, see the golden seams of light around him just waiting for him to tear open.

Hermes pushed his beer into Hades's hand. "Here, hold my drink."

And he let his magic go, stepped sideways, and was suddenly standing back in his house. Dog barked at his unexpected appearance.

"I'm fine, don't worry," he told him and patted his head. "I've got a date to crash."

9

Selene's stomach hit her shoes the moment she walked into the Lethe Loft. She had been fueled by anger the whole afternoon, and now when she needed it, it was gone.

The anger had forced Selene to take extra care with her appearance that evening, leaving her heavy curls out and putting makeup on for the first time in months. She didn't want to face Ezra looking like the crushed flower he had left behind.

Who did Hermes think he was telling her off like that? She had ranted as she dressed in black high waisted tailored trousers that flattered her curvy hips and a silk top the same pale blue as her eyes.

Selene had been fired up and feeling ready to butt heads with any man who thought it was okay to tell her what to do.

Then she saw Ezra sitting at a booth, and a sickening jolt knocked the wind out of her. He still looked like the perfect poster boy doctor, blond hair carefully groomed, an easy, charming smile and in a suit that screamed wealth.

Get out of here, a voice warned her, but Ezra looked up and saw her. *Just pretend he's Hermes, and you'll have no problems yelling at him.*

Selene straightened her shoulders and made her way to his table.

"Selene, I almost didn't recognize you. You look amazing," Ezra said, standing up so he could kiss her cheek.

He was still wearing the same aftershave, and Selene was reminded of scrubbing her apartment and burning a month's worth of sage to get that smell out.

"Thanks, I think," Selene replied and sat down at the booth.

"Would you like a drink?"

"Sure thing, that's why we are here, isn't?" she said.

Ezra smiled and gestured the waiter over. "Can I grab another gin and tonic, and one for the lady?"

"I'll have a beer, thank you," she interrupted calmly. "I haven't drunk gin and tonics in a long time."

"I stand corrected," said Ezra.

"So, what brings you back to Styx?"

"Speaking at a conference. You know how these things are. You make one new advancement in medicine, and you have to talk about it for the next three years," Ezra said with a dramatic roll of his eyes.

Selene knew that was bullshit. He loved to talk to crowds and have all his peers look at him with equal parts jealousy and admiration.

"What about you? Still working for Leo?"

"I quit a few days ago," Selene replied, as the waiter came back with her beer. She quickly drank two large mouthfuls, hoping that the alcohol would calm her down.

"Wow, really? I never saw that coming. You seemed so comfortable there. What are you doing now?" he asked.

"Working full time for Hades," Selene replied and took a small amount of pleasure in seeing the surprise in his eyes.

"I thought that business would've been dealt with," he said with a careful smile.

"I like working for Hades. He made me a good offer, so I walked."

"Really? What kind of offer? You're a nurse, it's not like he's running hospitals," Ezra pressed.

"Sorry, non-disclosure agreement, so I can't talk about it. I can say it is better pay, better hours," Selene replied.

"I'm surprised but happy for you. Hades Acheron is a hard man to impress. I hoped your...dealings with him would be over by now."

"Why? So you can stop feeling guilty about me being the one to shoulder your debt?" Selene asked and finished her beer while he shifted uncomfortably.

"I have said sorry about that. You know I didn't want it to go down that way. I'm not that person anymore. I got help and made amends," Ezra replied.

"Really? I haven't received my apology yet, or did you miss that step?" she asked. She waved at the waitress for another round of drinks.

"I had to work my way up to you," he said softly, leaning forward to rest his hand on top of hers. "I am sorry, Selene. I would like us to be friends again, maybe more, but I wouldn't push for that."

"Why? It wasn't like our relationship was any good by the time you left, and you know it. Besides, you live in Athens now."

"It's another reason I wanted to see you. I want to start a private practice here is Styx, back to my roots. I'm going to need good people to help me."

Selene moved her hand out from under his and took her fresh beer from the waitress. "I don't think that's a good idea. I'm contracted to help Hades anyway."

"I understand, and it might actually work out in our favor that you're positioned where you are," Ezra said.

Our favor? Selene tried not to choke on her beer. "What is that supposed to mean?"

"Well, no one opens a business in Styx without Hades's blessing, especially in the Diogenes where I'm looking at real estate. I could use your help making this move go more smoothly for me in that area, if you know what I mean," he replied and gave her his most charming smile. She used to fall for it every time.

Now the urgency to catch up suddenly made sense.

"This was what you wanted all along. This isn't about making amends for how you treated me," said Selene.

"That's not true. It's both! You know you weren't a picnic to live with either, Selene. Our relationship didn't break just because of me," Ezra argued, his smooth tone slipping.

"It broke because you fucking hit me," Selene hissed, trying to keep her voice down.

"I told you I didn't mean it."

"It still happened! Now you come back and only want to talk to me because I know Hades," she said.

Hermes was right, this was a stupid mistake.

"What is it between you? Are you sleeping together? Why is he keeping around a nurse? I don't get it," Ezra asked, and downed his gin and tonic.

"You know what? I'm just going to go," Selene said, but as she made to get up, he grabbed her by the forearm and held her in place. His grip wasn't tight, but she froze, fear turning her cold all over as she stared at his perfectly manicured hands gripping her.

"Please don't go. You're still angry, I get that, but please just hear me out okay? If you don't want to be friends again that's fine, just help me out with this one thing for old times' sake-"

"Selene! There you are. I'm so sorry I'm late, I couldn't get away," a warm, husky voice said.

She looked up, and through a thin film of tears, she saw Hermes walking towards their table. He was dressed in dark jeans and one of the white button-up silk shirts Charon had bought him, sleeves pushed up his golden-brown forearms.

Eyes followed him through the bar, the waitress staring dumbly as he breezed past her. Ezra's hand let Selene go in surprise as Hermes slid into the booth beside her.

Before Selene could react or stop him, Hermes brushed a stray curl away from her face before bringing her close and kissing her.

His lips were scorching hot as he expertly coaxed her mouth open and touched his tongue against hers. Something pulsed in her chest in response to him, her entire body breaking out in goose bumps.

Selene's hand came up to rest on his hard stomach, heat radiating from under the silk as she kissed him back.

Kissed with tongue. God, he was right about that too.

Ezra had never kissed her like this, in a way that made her feel the sensation all the way to her toes.

"I've wanted to do that all day," Hermes said against her lips when they broke apart. He turned his head as if he just noticed they had company. "I'm sorry. You must be Selene's old friend."

Ezra's face had gone as cold as Selene's had gone hot.

"Ah, yes, this is Ezra," she quickly introduced.

"Doctor Ezra Adamos," Ezra said in a tone that was all superiority.

"Hermes," he replied, placing an arm around Selene's shoulders.

"Like the god?" Ezra asked with an amused snort. "Your parents must have really hated you."

"*Exactly* like the god," Hermes replied. "And my parents definitely hated me. Sorry about crashing in on your drinks, but I couldn't wait another minute to see my girl." Hermes kissed her temple affectionately, and Selene reached for her beer.

This can't be happening. She drained her drink, so she didn't have to say anything.

"Your girl? Are you seriously out on a date with me when you're seeing someone?" Ezra looked at Selene incredulously.

"This wasn't a date, Ezra, it was drinks like I said in my message," she replied quickly. "I think we should go."

"No, it's fine. I'm just surprised that you're dating, that's all. Tell me, what do you do, Hermes?" asked Ezra, his 'doctor' tone back to set Selene's teeth on edge.

"I'm a magician," said Hermes.

Ezra laughed. "Seriously? Did you guys meet at the children's ward or something?"

"Oh, I'm not that kind of magician," Hermes replied.

"Then what kind are you? Is it even a profession?"

"Ezra! Seriously?" Selene hissed.

Hermes's smile was now a threat that Ezra was too dumb to recognize. Hermes held out his hand and made a small intricate gesture.

"Was that meant to be a trick?" Ezra mocked.

"It *was* a trick. You just weren't quick enough to see it," Hermes replied smugly. "Come on, Selene, we've got a dinner to get to." Hermes stood up and made room for her to get out of the booth.

"Selene, don't go, we haven't finished our conversation," said Ezra as she moved. He went to grab her arm again, but Hermes was quicker, catching him by the wrist.

"Don't you fucking touch her," Hermes growled.

"Hermes –" Selene whispered as the air around him charged.

"Oh, I've already touched her, don't you worry about that," Ezra replied, his tone turning nasty. "I'm sure I'll be touching her again as soon as she grows out of her kiddie clown phase."

"Let me show you a trick you might be slow enough to appreciate," Hermes said, and made a small snatching gesture.

Ezra went to mock him, but no sound came out of his throat. He looked at Hermes, face pale as he tried wrenching his hand out of his grip.

"Now for my next trick, I'm going to break your finger without touching you, and you won't be able to do a thing about it," Hermes said, and Ezra's index finger snapped audibly. Ezra mouthed a soundless scream, tears running down his face.

"Hermes, that's enough," Selene said, wrapping her arms around him. "Please, let's just go."

"You are lucky that she has such a soft heart, and I'm trying to be a better male," Hermes told Ezra and clicked his fingers. Ezra's index finger snapped back into place.

"If you ever bother her again, I'll find you Ezra Adamos, and I'll break every bone in your fucking worthless body. Nod if you understand."

Ezra nodded, his face red with anger and pain.

"Good. I'll give you your voice back now, but do try to be more civil using that tongue, or I'll take it too," Hermes said and let Ezra go.

Ezra breathed in a deep breath and clutched his hand to his chest.

"H-Hermes," he gasped, eyes wide in recognition.

"Yes, like the actual *god*, you piece of shit mortal," Hermes hissed, and his eyes flashed golden. "Let's go, Selene, I'm pretty sure he just pissed himself."

He took her hand, and they walked out together, everyone in the bar carefully looking the other way.

When they were outside, Selene quickly let go of Hermes and took a shaky breath.

"What are you doing here?" she demanded, rounding on him.

"I wanted to keep an eye on you, make sure that fucker didn't try anything. I wasn't going to interfere, but then he fucking grabbed you," Hermes said, his eyes flashing with anger and magic under the streetlights.

"He didn't hurt me. Oh, god, I just...I just panicked," Selene said, pressing a shaking hand to her chest. Tears of shock began falling before she could swallow them down. "I'm sorry, I don't know why I'm crying. It's so stupid."

The anger melted from Hermes's face, and he pulled her into a hug.

"It's okay. You don't ever have to worry about him ever again, hear me?" he said, running his hand over her back.

"I suppose you should say I told you so. Go ahead, I deserve it," Selene sniffed, wiping the tears off her cheeks.

"No, you don't. You wanted your closure. I hope that it's now closed, because I swear, I'm ready to go back and-" Selene put her fingers over his mouth.

"Stop. Don't say it. Let's just go and get something to eat, okay? I don't want to talk about him ever again," she said.

"Okay," Hermes replied and held out a hand. She took it and hung onto it tightly. "Lead the way, Lady Moon."

"I need some carbs in a bad way after this shit. My favorite burger place is this way," she said.

She didn't know how to tell him how grateful she was for him at that moment. She needed to eat and sober up so she could think clearly.

They walked past a silver Audi, and Selene recognized Ezra's personalized plates 'Dr Ez' that she'd bought him when they were dating. Then she noticed that his tires had been slashed, and it was covered in dints.

"Look, there was my other magic trick," said Hermes happily.

Selene burst out laughing. "Oh, my god, Hermes, he's going to be so angry."

"Good, serves him right for being such an asshole," he said, and as they walked past the wrecked car, another shot of magic sizzled out of him, and all its windows cracked.

Selene laughed harder, her stress and anger melting away.

10

Hermes knew that Selene was upset and a little tipsy, but it didn't stop him from enjoying the way she hung onto his hand as they walked through the alleys and back streets of Lethe.

Selene stopped at a burger shop that was only a window in a wall, with a few packed tables on the sidewalk.

"What do you want to eat?" Selene asked, bouncing a little on the balls of her feet. Hermes had never seen someone so excited about burgers before.

"I don't care, order for me," he said and passed her a handful of notes from Charon's wallet.

"Woah, way too much," Selene replied, giving most of it back to him. "I'm going to have to teach you about modern currency."

"I'll learn anything you feel like teaching me," Hermes said, loving the way it made Selene bite the side of her lip to keep from smiling.

Does she have any idea how adorable she is? She didn't if her taste in men was anything to go by.

Hermes had been determined to watch over her and not interrupt her night, but as soon as Ezra had grabbed her and he had seen the fear on her face, Hermes couldn't sit by and do nothing. He had planned to interrupt them; he hadn't planned on kissing her.

He saw the surprise and relief on her face, and he couldn't help himself. He *had* to kiss her, and now he couldn't stop thinking about the feel and taste of her.

Selene was coming back towards him with a broad smile, her arms full of brown paper bags. Hermes vowed then and there that he would say anything to keep that smile on her face and keep her from thinking about the asshole in the bar.

"All the tables are taken, but we might find one at the park around the corner," she said as she joined him.

"I have the perfect place in mind," Hermes replied.

"Really? Where?" Hermes led her to the end of the alley, where there were no pedestrians or watching eyes.

"Down here behind the bins? Gross, Hermes," Selene said, wrinkling her nose.

"Not here. Just try not to scream," Hermes replied and wrapped his arms around her.

"What-" Selene began, but he had already opened a doorway, and they were suddenly standing on the small beach on Hades's property.

"What the fuck, Hermes! How did you do that?" she asked, and her eyes went wider. "The wings of Hermes."

"Yeah, I figured out how to do it this afternoon. I could see the doors again. Okay, wait one second," he said, before stepping through another door and returning thirty seconds later with a blanket from the couch and two beers.

"That is amazing," Selene whispered.

"It's really not as hard as it looks," said Hermes, and he spread out the blanket over the sand. Selene kicked off her heels and sat down.

"You know what? I'm going to eat this burger and then ask you a hundred questions," she said.

Hermes sat down beside her and tried not to touch her dark curls. "I admire your wishful thinking that I'm going to be able to provide you with a hundred answers."

"Give yourself some credit. You're getting better every day, Hermes. I can't believe you turned up tonight," she said and handed him his burger, "but thank you. No one has ever done anything like that for me before."

"What? Kissed you properly?" Hermes asked. "Or break a disrespectful ass's finger?"

Selene tucked her hair behind her ear and didn't look up from her burger. "Both, as it turns out. You might regret that kiss after you watch me eat this."

"I highly doubt it," Hermes said honestly. "If anything, I'm going to be impressed, because that burger is the size of your head."

"I know! Isn't it great?" Selene laughed. After one or two bites, he tried *not* to watch her because the sexy little groans of happiness she was making at the back of her throat combined with her lips wrapping around things made his thoughts turn filthy.

Yes, she definitely has no idea how adorable she is.

Unfortunately for Hermes, Selene didn't stop being adorable after she finished eating.

He wanted the memory back of how to be charming and not awkward in front of the girl he liked.

"I honestly can't remember the last time I had a picnic," Selene said, lying back on the blanket and looking up at the stars.

"Neither can I, but really that's not saying much," Hermes replied, stretching out beside her.

"You are doing incredibly well. I'm starting to think I shouldn't have been so quick to quit my job."

"I still need you. I mean, you're a good nurse, and I'm not as recovered as you think." Hermes looked across at her. "I got my words back, but my mind is a jumbled mess. I have magic with only vague feelings on how to control it. I have nightmares, and I don't know if they are memories or just dreams. I'm confused about everything all the time."

"You didn't seem confused at all tonight when you showed up uninvited," Selene said.

"Oh, no, you've sobered up enough to lecture me," Hermes complained. "I'll go and get you another beer."

Selene laughed softly. "Not necessary, there will be no lecture. As I said before, I'm relieved that you were there tonight. I just don't know why you did it."

Hermes wanted to give her the same line he gave Hades; that he was the god of magic and that she belonged to him. He thought better of it.

"I don't know much right now, Selene, but I do know you're too special to be treated like you're not." Her eyes turned silver with tears, but she didn't let them fall.

"Would it be inappropriate if I hugged you right now? Because I really need a hug."

"You should know I don't understand the meaning of the word inappropriate," Hermes replied, trying to make her laugh.

Selene didn't laugh. She moved to rest her head on his shoulder and put an arm over his chest. He recovered quickly from his surprise and put his arms around her.

Her hair smelled of roses and citrus and something very female, and if he shut his eyes, he could feel the magic swirling deep inside her core.

"Can I ask you something really crazy?" she said.

"You are forgetting who you are talking to again," Hermes replied, and she laughed against him.

"Sorry, let me rephrase. I need to ask you something, and it's going to make me sound as crazy as you, and I don't want to make it weird."

"Ask away, Lady Moon."

"When you kissed me tonight, did you feel something...strange?"

"Define strange." Hermes had felt a lot of things when he kissed her. Mostly that he wanted to kiss her more, a lot more, and everywhere.

She is talking about the magic and not your dick going hard, his newly rediscovered consciousness said.

"Strange, like a pulse? I don't know how else to describe it."

"I felt it, but I don't think you'll believe me if I tell you what it was," said Hermes.

"I saw you steal someone's voice tonight. I'm redefining what I can believe right now," Selene replied, her fingers twisting in the fabric of his shirt. It was distracting and delightful at the same time.

"I'm a god of magic, Selene, what you felt when we kissed was my magic...recognizing yours," Hermes said.

Selene lifted her head up. "But I don't have magic."

"God of magic here, I'm the expert. If you don't trust my word on it, ask Hades. He has felt it too. I'm sure if I didn't have this damn curse on me, I'd be able to tell you what it's for. My guess, though, is that it's to do with healing."

A small, uncertain line appeared between her brows, and he wanted to kiss it away.

"Healing magic? How can you be so sure? I've always liked helping people who are suffering, it's why I chose nursing, but I would have noticed if I were using magic."

Hermes tangled his fingers in the ends of her soft curls. "Don't you think it's strange that out of all the powerful beings around me, that it's only in your presence that I can think clearly. That you were a key to unlocking my doors? All I've done is spend time around you for a week, and I can now form full sentences."

Selene lay back down, and his heart did an unusual thump that he hoped she didn't hear.

"Until I see something magical, I'm going to maintain that it's being around people you know, and not being drugged by Pandora," she said.

Selene hadn't rejected the possibility outright or sounded angry, so Hermes counted it as a win.

They watched the stars in silence until Hermes realized Selene had fallen asleep. Very carefully, he lifted her up, and using her presence as a guide, he stepped through a doorway and into her apartment.

"Sweet dreams, Lady Moon," he whispered as he placed her on her bed and kissed her cheek. He was about to step through another doorway when a light flickered in the corner of his eye.

He turned back around, and Selene, the woman who thought she had no magic, was gleaming like starlight. Hermes watched dumbfounded as silvery grey light pulsed from her skin.

A memory hit him in the face like a slap, and he took an involuntary step backward. He had only ever seen magic like that once before.

"Just what I need," he muttered before opening a doorway and disappearing through the shadows.

∽

HERMES DIDN'T GO to bed that night. He drew and drew and drew until he fell asleep with his head on the table. He was woken up by Erebus charging into the room the next morning.

"Someone had an attack on inspiration last night," the titan said, looking at the haphazard piles of sketches. "What happened?"

Hermes rubbed at his face. "I saved Selene from a bad date and then couldn't sleep because my head decided to explode."

"Wait, you went out? Like outside, out?" Erebus asked. "Does Hades know?"

"He was the one that told me to go."

"Charon said Selene had a date and that you were jealous." Erebus went to the kitchen and turned on the hot water kettle.

"It wasn't like that!" Hermes protested.

"The hell it wasn't. We all know you are crushing on her. I didn't think you were crazy enough to go after her on a date though. How did she take it? I hope she kicked you right in the nuts for being so clingy."

"You are ridiculous, that's not what happened at all," argued Hermes and told Erebus about his night, minus the kiss because the titan would've never shut up about it.

Erebus made coffee and sat down at the table opposite him.

"I can't believe you had a beach picnic and didn't invite me," he complained. "It's rather adorable, even though I hate that she likes you instead of me."

"I don't know if she likes me in the way that you are implying," Hermes said uncertainly.

"If she didn't maim you for crashing her date and then taking her for another one, then it's safe to assume that yes, she does. She likes the Court, and she hasn't hung out with any of us like that. So maybe she likes you that wee bit more than what you think," said Erebus with a grin. "Also, Thanatos and Charon said Selene checks you out when she thinks no one is looking. Cheeky hussy."

"I think I've figured out where she gets her magic from," Hermes replied, wanting to change the subject before it made him feel hopeful and flustered and even more ridiculous.

"Hold that thought, trickster. Hades will want to hear about this because it's been bugging him for years," said Erebus.

"Okay, then you can go and wake him up while I have a shower. I'll meet you down there," Hermes suggested.

"Sure, make me responsible for waking the beast," Erebus muttered in his mug.

"I'll tell Hades you said that."

Hermes showered quickly, thinking over the previous night and what Erebus had said. Erebus was always the flirtiest of the titans, so he knew better than to take anything he said too seriously.

Selene had been emotional the night before and needed comfort, and that was all that there was to it.

You are half a god right now, focus on getting the other half back and not on crushing on pretty nurses.

Once he was back together, then he would pursue it if he thought he had half a chance.

Down in the main villa, Hades was awake and making more coffee. Erebus was chatting to Thanatos, and Hermes felt a strange sensation move through him.

They really were like a family, an easiness between them that was never on Olympus. It had always been so petty and competitive, at least the parts he remembered, and Hades actually wanted to protect those under his care.

"Hermes, there you are. Dressed and all, I think I need to give Selene a raise," said Hades and offered him more coffee. "How was your date?"

"It wasn't a date," Hermes replied, shooting Erebus a pissed off glare.

"What? I never said a thing."

"I felt the moment you left the villa's boundaries and figured you had finally worked out the doors," Hades explained. "You were highly motivated."

"And it was a good thing I was. That guy was as bad news as I said he was," Hermes said, and because he knew Erebus would embellish the story, he quickly recapped for Hades and Thanatos the night with Selene.

"I was taking her back to her apartment, and she was glowing in her sleep," Hermes said, and looked at Thanatos, "It was almost starlight, and it looked exactly like…"

"Hecate," Thanatos interrupted. "Shit."

"My thoughts exactly."

"Selene has magic, but it looks like she's not one of yours, after all, Hermes," said Hades.

"Like fuck, she's not," Hermes snapped before cursing himself as Hades laughed. "I can't think straight, but I know it's been a long time since anyone has seen Hecate. She could be dead for all we know, and Selene being a part of Hecate's chosen doesn't mean the goddess is going to claim her any time soon. She needs guidance and protection now."

"I would know if Hecate was dead," said Thanatos, dark eyes troubled.

"And if she's been marked by Hecate's power, it certainly explains why you've always been so protective when it comes to Selene," Erebus added, looking at his brother and trying to hide his concern.

Thanatos didn't argue with him. Hermes knew that Thanatos had once been friends with the Goddess of the Crossroads, but that was all he could remember.

"Did you tell Selene about this?" asked Hades.

"I told her that I can feel magic in her and left it at that. She was upset last night, I didn't want to make it worse," said Hermes.

"Good, we will need to tread carefully with this. It's a stressful enough time with looking for Pandora. I don't want Pithos targeting Selene because they find out she's got power," Hades replied.

"I got more memories of my time with Pandora and of some people she worked with." Hermes passed him a sketch of two men, one older with mean eyes, the other younger and ambitious. "These two used to come to meet with Pandora too."

"We don't have to worry about this one," said Hades, pointing to the old man. "This is Acrisius Argos, and he's dead. They found his body in a wooden box in the Athens Port."

"That would've been Pandora's doing. She was getting angry with him in the few weeks before you came with Persephone," Hermes replied.

"I don't recognize this other man, but I'll send it to Medusa and see what she and Lola can find," said Hades.

"Of the two, he always seemed the coldest. The one to look out for."

Hermes hugged himself, remembering the man's hungry eyes on him. "He can't ever find out about Selene."

"No one will ever touch Selene. That I can promise you," said Thanatos, the titan of death moving close to the surface of his human form.

"We all need to get together and talk about all of this, Selene included," Hades said looking at Erebus. "Organize a meeting. Hermes, write down anything you remember about this man and anything else about Pandora's associates or your time with them."

"I'll try, Hades, but I don't know if it will work," Hermes said honestly. It wasn't like he could force the memories to come back, and when they did come, they weren't always relevant.

"The sooner we find them, the safer Selene will be," Hades replied. Hermes narrowed his eyes at the deliberate provocation.

"You're still a bastard," he said.

Hades lifted his coffee and saluted him. "Takes one to know one, *Poikilomêtês*."

11

Selene woke the following morning, tucked in her own bed, and wearing the previous night's clothes. She stretched out her hand on the space beside her, searching for...*Hermes*.

Selene went from a doze to fully alert in half a second as she sat bolt upright. The last thing she remembered was looking at the stars and using Hermes as a pillow.

How did I get home? Selene pushed the wild hair from her face. On her bedside table was a small pile of shells and her missing silver bangle.

Hermes must've used his magic and put you to bed. She would have woken up if one of the triplets had driven her. The thought of Hermes carrying her made her hot all over, so she climbed out of bed.

Selene fumbled for her phone and found it still in her pocket. She had six messages, and two missed phone calls from Ezra.

"Boring plate man indeed," she muttered. Then she deleted them all without reading them. There was a message from Erebus that was a confusing series of smiley faces and eggplant emojis, and another from Ariadne asking what time she was coming tonight.

Coming where?

Selene would sometimes work the fight pits if there were going to be weapons matches on, but usually, Asterion gave her plenty of notice.

Selene stumbled to the bathroom and took off her crumpled sandy clothes that somehow smelled more like Hermes than her.

She climbed under the hot water and thought about the night before.

Hermes kissed you, with lots of tongue which you've never liked, and now suddenly can't stop thinking about it. Then you cried on him and fell asleep. Also, you kissed him back. You can't even blame alcohol because you barely had a beer buzz. Oh, my god, Hermes kissed you, and you liked it.

Hermes had kissed her first so she couldn't really be blamed for it, could she? Selene could still feel the sensation of his lips on hers, stubble and soft heat... she shook herself.

Hades was going to kill her. She was supposed to be helping Hermes not kissing him. Hermes might not even remember doing it.

The thought should've comforted her and instead made her feel a little sick. The only way she would find out would be to go and see for herself.

In the mirror, her eyes were looking unusually bright, and despite the awkwardness in her stomach, she couldn't help but smile.

"What's the matter with you? You've only known the guy a week, and he's a freaking god. You must be crazier than he is," she complained to her reflection. Her phone buzzed on her bathroom counter with another waiting message from Charon.

Hey, sleeping beauty, are you awake yet? God of Non-Stop Chatting is asking for you.

I'm awake. Is he okay?

He won't be if he doesn't shut up soon. P.S. Why haven't you ever had a beach picnic with me?

"Just what I need," Selene groaned before she text him back: *Because you've never saved me from a bad date. Come and get me when you have time.*

Selene tossed her phone on her bed, and then went to get dressed. Knowing how Charon drove, he would be outside her door in record time. She left her wet hair out to dry and swiped on some lip gloss.

Selene was determined to treat it like any other day, and completely forget the strange sensation that had pulsed in her chest and other parts of her the night before.

Stop thinking about it.

Outside, Charon's red Ferrari glowed bright in the rainy weather. He waited for her with an umbrella, a knowing smile on his face.

"Morning, doll, how was the date?" he asked as he walked her out to the car.

"Horrendous."

"Really? I can't wait to tell Hermes that," Charon said and shut the door behind her.

"Hermes saved me from it, so he knows," Selene replied when he got into the driver's seat.

"I was talking about your date with him. Two dates on the same night, you minx. I'm so proud of you."

"Hermes and I *weren't* on a date."

"A picnic on the beach is a date, doll." Charon shot her a sideways grin. "Did he kiss you good night?"

"No," Selene said, keeping her eyes fixed on the road.

"He didn't? Damn, he must've lost his seducing skills as well as his mind," said Charon, clicking his tongue.

"I wouldn't say that," Selene replied. "He can be very sweet when he wants to be."

"Hermes has been accused of a lot of things over the years, but sweet isn't one of them."

Selene fiddled with her phone. "He is to me."

"It's because he's a besotted idiot. Really, Hades should have known better than to throw someone as beautiful as you in Hermes's path and not expected the old trickster to have a crack," Charon replied.

"He was in the cave a long time. I'm the only girl he's seen in ages. He'll be fine when he gets out and about again," she said, trying to feel as dismissive as she sounded.

Charon hummed and changed gears. "Yeah, that's not really how gods like to operate. At least not the ones that weren't crazy rapists like Zeus. You've woken something in Hermes, and he's fascinated by you, and you are just going to have to figure out how to deal with that."

Selene played with the ends of her hair. "Any tips?"

"Ha! No, love and obsession ain't exactly my forte."

"I still think you are reading too much into it, Charon. He'll get better, and he certainly won't need the likes of me anymore," she replied.

"You are really fucking cute when you are lying to yourself, Selene. No one is going to think less of you if you end up liking him back. I mean, Erebus will cry because he's been trying to get in your pants for years, but no one else will care," Charon said. "I like that you smile when you're around Hermes."

"He's a crazy, funny guy. That's why," Selene replied dismissively.

A scorching hot, crazy, funny guy. Oh, fuck, stop it, or you're going to make yourself nervous.

When they pulled in at the villa, Erebus was loitering against the front door and trying to keep out of the rain.

"Morning, Selene, how was your romp on the beach?" he asked when she joined him under the awning.

"I don't know what you're talking about," she replied. "Where's Hermes hiding?"

Erebus pointed at the forest. "It started raining, and he lost his shit and took off down the path."

"You let him go on his own?" she demanded.

"If he was in a clear enough mind to talk in full sentences and go after you in the city last night, he can handle a walk in the woods," replied Erebus.

"He might be able to express himself properly now, but he admitted he's nowhere near thinking clearly," Selene said and snatched Charon's umbrella out of his hands.

"You're overreacting, Selene, he's fine," Erebus groaned.

"I am not overreacting! He could get lost or confused or hurt. I'm going after him. If I'm not back in an hour, ping the GPS on my phone," Selene snapped. "Don't even think of trying to deny that you track it. I know you do."

Selene had almost reached the tree line when Erebus called, "Watch out for the big, bad wolf!"

"Up yours!" she shouted back when she saw them both laughing at her.

She wanted to be able to be as chill and blasé about Hermes's safety. Still, she wouldn't relax without making sure he was okay. That he was a god with magic pouring out of him didn't matter.

Selene hadn't ever explored the forest Persephone had created. She knew what the property had looked like before, so she figured it would help her be able to find her way back.

There was a path, so she followed it, hoping Hermes might have done the same. She had wandered for about twenty minutes and was starting to worry when she spotted Hermes sitting on the wet leaf litter and staring at a Cyprus pine.

He was soaked, his white t-shirt sticking to him in ways that made Selene have more inappropriate thoughts that she didn't need.

"Hermes?" she said softly, not wanting to startle him. He didn't move, so she knelt down in front of him, holding the umbrella over his head. "Hey, Hermes, are you okay?"

He looked catatonic. She reached out and rested a hand on his cheek.

"Are you in there?" she whispered.

"Boo!" Hermes said, and she squealed in surprise, dropping the umbrella and slipping backward onto her butt. "Oh, shit, I didn't mean to scare you that badly!"

"Ah, you asshole!" she complained, pain shooting up her back. Hermes's concerned face hovered over her.

"Can you move? Oh no, I hurt my nurse."

Selene gripped a handful of the wet leaf litter and mud and then wiped it down his shirt. "Now, I feel better. If I'm going to be wet and dirty, you are too."

Hermes stared at his soiled shirt with a devilish smile. "I don't like white anyway. Would you like a hand up or do you want to dirty me some more?" he asked, golden eyes shining and tone full of innuendo.

Selene took the edge of his shirt and used it to wipe the mud off her palms.

"It's the least you could do. And to think I came in here because I was worried about you," Selene said, and he helped her to her feet. "What are you doing here, anyway?"

"Enjoying the rain," Hermes replied, taking her hand and stopping her from reaching for the broken umbrella. "Wait, stand here with me. You're already wet, so it won't matter."

"Okay," she said, humoring him.

"Now, close your eyes and tilt your head back," he instructed. Selene did as he asked.

"What now?" she whispered.

"Shhh, just listen."

Selene focused on her breath, the feeling of the rain falling in cold drops on her hot skin, the smell of Cyprus pine, soil and leaf litter in the air.

There was a bird that she didn't know the name of calling through the trees, the branches making soft sounds as they blew in the gentle wind. The whole world seemed to expand and contract around her.

How long had it been since she actually stood still and appreciated something? She had always been so busy, rushing to and from jobs and responsibilities, collapsing at night to start it all again the next day.

The only peace she found were brief stolen moments in her little garden or surrounded by shelter dogs.

Why did she feel like she had to ration that time? For some reason, the thoughts made her feel impossibly sad.

After Ezra, she had shut herself down, locking herself away to protect her mauled heart. She thought it was only just people, but it had been everything.

No one that she knew had tried to save her from it, no one had even noticed. But Hermes had within a week of knowing her.

I'll pick the locks on my doors until they open, oh yes, and then I'll be coming after yours. His words came back to her, and she fought to keep her eyes shut.

She could sense him behind her, like a big shadow of wound up energy stalking her in small circles.

You found the big, bad wolf, after all.

"The rain caught in your hair looks like stars," Hermes whispered. "It makes me want to draw them."

Selene didn't open her eyes, wondering what he would do if she stood there long enough. Long, warm fingers traced through the water droplets on her bare arm, over the strap of her singlet and shoulder.

Selene's breath staggered; the small touch magnified in her hyper-aware state. She knew that her singlet was soaked, and there was no way she could hide her hard nipples that had nothing to do with the cold.

You should stop this before it escalates further.

Selene swallowed nervously as his fingers moved to her throat, following the line of her fluttering pulse.

"Is it okay that I am touching you?" Hermes asked, voice low and husky.

"Y-yes," she stammered.

"Your heart's racing, are you afraid of me?"

"No," she replied as her mind screamed, *Yes*. He was barely touching her, and nowhere that was sexual, but it was the sexiest damn thing she had felt in her life.

Oh, fuck Selene, of all the guys in Greece, why this one? This mad, impossible one that is absolutely off-limits.

Selene knew precisely why; because he wanted to unlock all her doors so he could see her.

"Are you letting me touch you because Hades is paying you to tolerate it?" Hermes asked, a thread of uncertainty in his tone.

"No," she said calmly even though she was fighting not to open her eyes.

"Is it because you like me touching you?"

"Yes," she replied without hesitation.

Hermes was behind her again, his tall body pressing up against hers as his hand moved to wrap around her throat, the other circling around her waist. He wasn't choking her, but Selene felt pinned, locked tightly to him. Instead of feeling afraid or trapped, she found herself leaning back into his warmth, head tilting to one side.

Lips pressed on the skin behind her ear. A tremble that she couldn't hide rocked her, making goose bumps rise on her skin. Hermes kissed her again, her heartbeat racing under the palm of his hand.

"Oh, the things I could unlock in you. I'd let all of that fire out, and you wouldn't be a cold nurse anymore," Hermes whispered, his stubble hot against the curve of her ear.

Selene was shaking, his hands holding her up as she all but melted into him. He tilted her head back and ran his tongue very lightly over her top lip. Selene opened her mouth to kiss him when a sharp whistle pierced the air.

"Hey, you two! Are you still in here?" Charon called through the trees, followed by a loud bark.

Selene's eyes snapped open and she stepped away from Hermes on shaky legs. A huge black dog charged through the undergrowth followed by a heavily tattooed titan.

"There you are! I thought I was going to have to put together a search party, but you found him after all, Selene," said Charon. His sharp eyes took in their wet and muddy state and the broken umbrella. "Are you guys fighting?"

"What? No! I'm really uncoordinated and slipped ass up. Sorry, I owe you an umbrella," Selene replied, picking up the bent and broken remains of the last one.

"That's okay. What about you, Hermes? Had enough of the rain and woods for one day? Your dog was getting worried," said Charon. The big black dog sat down next to Hermes's feet.

"I'm fine. Let's go back," Hermes replied, his voice strained as he started walking.

"What did I just interrupt?" whispered Charon to Selene. She watched Hermes in the distance, his hand resting on the dog's back.

"Nothing. We are fine. He was a bit overwhelmed by nature, that's all," Selene replied, the lie sounding lame even to her.

Charon's black eyes softened. "Okay, let's get you out of the rain and find you some dry clothes."

12

In a sea of uncertainty, Hermes knew two absolutes; he would probably never be the god he used to be, and he wanted to kiss Selene again so severely his body ached. The first he could live with, the second was becoming unbearable.

"I hope you don't mind, but I stole a towel," Selene said, emerging from the bathroom in one of his clean t-shirts and pajama pants. "I might start bringing a spare change of clothes with me, since I seem to be more accident-prone than usual."

She was pressing the water from her hair, and he couldn't look away from her. She had chosen to stay and use some of his clothes to spare Charon another trip into the city, and Hermes had been smug about it until that moment. She looked even more adorable than usual in his oversized clothes.

A heavy paw came down on his leg.

"Cut it out, I'll tell her," Hermes told the black dog at his side.

"Tell me what?" Selene said with one of her small smiles.

That I want to lay you down on the couch and kiss you until you pass out.

Hermes quickly looked away from her and cleared his throat. "He wants to be called Jackal."

"Jackal? What a tough, strong name for a tough, strong boy," Selene said and held out her towel. "You want to get dry too, Jackal?"

The dog's whole body moved when he wagged his tail and hurried towards her.

"Just don't tell Hades I used his fancy towels on you, okay?" she said to the dog.

Jackal gave Hermes a smug dog look from the circle of her arms as she rubbed him down.

Great, now I have three titans, an ex-boyfriend and my own damn dog as competition.

"I knew a god who was a jackal. I met him really late one night on the street in Egypt," Hermes said.

"A real god like you and Hades?"

"Well, he told me he was one. He looked like a jackal. Come to think of it, maybe it was just a random dog. Egypt had excellent beer," replied Hermes. He sorted through the random drawings on his table and gave her the ones of Egypt.

"Last night, I remembered a city that I'm sure is Hermopolis."

"Wow, these are amazing," said Selene, flicking through the sketches. "What were you doing in Egypt?"

"Wandering about and trying to get away from the Olympian's tedious games against each other. The Egyptians used to call me Hermes Trismegistus, the Thrice Great. I'd visit every couple of centuries, and every time I would turn up, they would think I was the reincarnated version of my previous self. I didn't have the heart to correct them because they used to throw the best parties, and I liked having somewhere comfortable to stay," Hermes replied.

Selene laughed. "Sounds like fun. I've always wanted to go to Egypt."

"If you like, I'll take you when I get my staff back. I might even try to track down Anubis and see if he is still running about as a jackal. Gods can get weird in their old age."

Selene hid a smile. "You don't say. I would definitely like to go to Egypt," she said, looking back at the sketches. "You'll be better by then and I'll be out of a job, so I'll have time off. Did you really draw all of these last night after you took me home?"

"Yes, I couldn't sleep. My head kind of exploded, and I was worried if

I went to sleep that I would wake up and would've forgotten everything," Hermes replied.

"Does that happen often still? You forget things that have happened?" Selene's ears were going a little pink, but Hermes couldn't figure out why.

"Not anymore, but I wanted to be sure. I remembered some of Pandora's friends, and I gave the sketches to Hades to try to find out who they are."

"That's great! The sooner we find Pandora, the better. I don't think Hades or anyone else in the Court is going to relax until Pithos is stopped. I'm sure it will help you sleep better at night," said Selene.

"I've slept a lot better since meeting you," Hermes admitted.

"Not last night by the looks of all of these." Selene bit the edge of her lip nervously. "By the way, thank you for... you know. I know I said it last night, but I wanted to make sure I said it today when I was stone-cold sober, so you know I mean it."

"You don't have to thank me for kissing you properly, Selene," Hermes said with a smile.

"I didn't mean that...I was talking about saving me from hitting my stupid ex. You didn't need to kiss me, but it did make the whole thing a lot more believable. I don't think I've ever seen Ezra so shocked," she replied with an awkward laugh.

Hermes frowned. "You think I kissed you only to upset him?"

"I thought it was a part of your act."

"Did it feel like I was acting?" said Hermes, moving towards her.

"Um, no, but you could just be really good at acting," Selene replied, backing up until she bumped into the wall.

Good, now she can't run anywhere. Hermes placed his hands on either side of her, caging her in.

"Do you think I was acting in the forest just now?" he asked, hating the way she wouldn't look up at him. "You think it's just mad old Hermes being fascinated by the only girl around him?"

"I wouldn't judge you if it were. You were in that cave a long time," Selene said, her voice tripping.

"There were plenty of girls in that place, Selene, not to mention Pandora whose beauty was crafted by Aphrodite herself. It's not like she didn't try to force herself on me. If it were just about needing a woman, I'd go and find one," Hermes growled, trying to contain his frustration.

"Trust me, it would be better if it were just that. You're one of Hecate's chosen, for fuck sake, and that is the worst kind of trouble for me."

"I don't know what that means. I do know I work for Hades, and I have a duty of care, so whatever your motivations for kissing me are doesn't matter. I should have better boundaries because I am meant to be the responsible one," said Selene, straightening her shoulders.

"Boundaries, is it? Just you try." Hermes stroked the line of her jaw with an index finger. "I'm the god of boundaries, so all of those are mine too. Every single one belongs to me, even the ones you think you should create."

"Did you ever stop to think that they should be there to protect me from you?" Selene said, finally looking up at him. "Did you ever wonder that you could be attracted to me because I help you feel more like yourself? That I'm your key? Whatever you think you are feeling could be completely null and void as soon as you get all your memories back. And where is that going to leave me if I get any more attached to you? God, this is ridiculous, I barely know you."

"That's not how attraction works. I won't forget everything I've been through. I'll just know what happened in my past," said Hermes.

Selene put her hands on his chest and pushed him back slowly. Hermes didn't want to scare her, so he relented and stepped back.

"It doesn't matter. I work for Hades. I'm here to help you, not make out with you because you make me feel...the way you do."

Hermes felt like he was losing his mind all over again, and then Hades himself appeared in the doorway.

"Interesting fashion choice, Selene," he said, looking her over.

"I fell while looking for Hermes and needed something dry to wear," she replied, her cold nurse face coming up instantly. "Can I help you with something, boss?"

"Yes, I need you to cancel any plans and work tonight," Hades said.

Selene folded her arms. "Why? You never said this would involve night work." Hermes didn't like her business-like tone one bit.

She's back to talking about you like a job.

"I want Hermes to meet Asterion and the others tonight. Medusa wants to talk to him about Acrisius Argos. It's important, Selene."

"He was well enough to be out in the city last night, so Hermes will be fine."

"Stop talking about me like I'm not here," Hermes complained, and Hades gave him a quizzical look.

"He was with *you* last night. We've already established that Hermes is calmer in your presence, and I need you to be there," Hades said. He looked between them. "What's the matter with you two? Are you fighting? Hermes, what did you do?"

"Nothing yet," he said, hating that Selene wouldn't look at him.

"Well, whatever it is, get over it. Selene, tonight at the Labyrinth, someone will meet you at the door," Hades replied.

"I don't have anything to wear," Selene said stubbornly, and even pissed off Hermes loved that she had the spine to stand up to Hades.

"Medusa will have something. I'll have her call you. Take the afternoon and go shopping, I don't fucking care, just be there," Hades said irritably and offered her his hand. "Come, I'll take you home and save you some time."

"I really have no say in this at all, do I?" she groaned.

"None whatsoever," said Hades. He took her hand, and they were gone before Hermes could get a word in. Jackal pushed his head at his hand.

"I know, I fucked up, don't rub it in," Hermes muttered. He only had a few minutes to sulk before Hades appeared again.

"What did you do to upset, Selene?" he demanded.

"Nothing. You're the one upsetting her with your stupid rules," Hermes snapped.

Hades frowned. "What rules?"

"She said I can't kiss her because she's working for you. It's a stupid rule, Hades, she should be able to kiss whoever she wants," Hermes said. He rubbed at his face, trying to focus his words that was always so much harder when he was upset.

"I never said she couldn't kiss you. I would question her sanity in wanting to, but I've never forbidden it. Why is this even coming up?"

"I kissed her last night, and now she's worried about what you will think," said Hermes, collapsing on the couch and putting a cushion over his head.

"Did you even consider that perhaps she doesn't want you kissing her, and she's using me as an excuse to be polite?" asked Hades.

"You're not helping."

"Who said I was going to? If you and Selene want to fool around, that's on you two, but don't try to make out like it's my fault. I like her, I value her, so if you want her just for a screw, find someone else, Hermes. I don't have the time for your drama."

"Fuck, why does everyone think I want her only for a screw?" Hermes demanded, moving the pillow from his face.

Hades crossed his arms. "Don't you?"

"No! I'm not saying I don't want to screw her. I mean you've seen her, how can I not? But that's not all I want her for. She's-"

"Shut up! Save it and tell her," Hades said, holding up his hand. "I barely tolerate my own emotions, let alone want to hear about yours. I won't stop you two from having a relationship if it's what you want. You've both been dancing around each other since you met, and I know you're both different when you are together. Selene has magic, so it might be a good thing to have her close when it starts to manifest, because you know that it's only a matter of time before it does."

Hades dodged the cushion Hermes threw at him and straightened his sleeves.

"And for fuck's sake, stop pouting. Charon will be up in an hour to make sure you've dressed appropriately."

13

Going out and talking to strangers was the last thing Hermes wanted to do, but he needed to make things right with Selene, because knowing that she was pissed at him was the worst feeling in the world.

Even if he couldn't fix it and he embarrassed himself, at least he would be near a bar and could drink himself into oblivion.

He was showered and calm again by the time Charon arrived with a black garment bag.

"Is this necessary? I can dress myself, you know," Hermes said.

"Yes, but I want to make sure you look perfect, because you only get to make a first impression once," replied Charon.

"How did you get like this, ferryman? It's disturbing," Hermes asked, taking the pair of black, pressed trousers that Charon offered him.

"I finally got to live amongst the humans, and found things that I really like about it, such as fast cars, books and as many clothes as I want," he replied. "I know that Medusa will be forcing many beautiful dresses at Selene right at this moment, and I won't have you looking sloppy."

"I don't know what that has to do with anything," Hermes grumbled.

"Hades told me what happened. Not that he had to, you both were acting so strangely this morning I knew something must have sparked it," Charon said, helping him button up his shirt.

He offered Hermes a belt after he finished tucking the tails of his shirt in, and then straightened it.

"Selene is very special," said Hermes, twisting his sleeves so Charon could put his black cufflinks on.

"She is."

"I'm worried I'm going to hurt her, Charon." As much Hermes hated the thought, it was still there. He was a god, and pure bastard did flow in his veins.

"You won't hurt her," said Charon.

"What makes you so sure?"

Charon took a jacket from the bag and smoothed out the sleeves. "Hermes, out of all the Olympians, you were the cleverest, so don't you think that if you are healed enough to worry about hurting someone else, you're going to be rational enough not to do it?"

"But, I am crazy, Charon."

"You and everyone else." The titan straightened Hermes's collar. "Anyway, if you do hurt Selene by being careless with her heart, my brothers and I really will lock you up in the Underworld where no one will ever find you."

Charon took out a tie, but Hermes stepped back to stop him.

"Not in this millennia, titan," he said and put on the jacket. "I won't have a tiny noose around my neck by choice."

"Fine, at least let me fix your buttons up," Charon complained, and undid the first three and arranged Hermes's collar. He took a step back and looked him over.

"Happy?" Hermes asked.

Charon pulled a critical face. "I mean, I wouldn't fuck you, but I'm picky."

"Like I'd have you, ferryman. What now?" Hermes said.

"Now you go get your ass in the car before we are late," Charon replied.

The sun was setting as they drove into the city, Hermes taking the time to look about.

"Do you ever miss the Underworld?" he asked as buildings flashed by.

"I miss the stories the dead used to tell, even though their regrets all used to be variants of the same thing," Charon said as they pulled into an underground car park.

"And what was the thing?"

"Not doing something they should have, like tell someone how they felt about them."

Hermes grinned. "You always were a romantic."

"Get the fuck out of my car," Charon said, "and don't rub up against it and get dirt on your suit."

Hermes followed him through the concrete cave to an elevator.

Now that he was there, he was suddenly nervous and pushed a hand through his hair. Charon tsked irritably and rearranged Hermes's hair against his shoulders.

"If you don't stop fussing, I am going to pull all of this off and run through the club naked," Hermes threatened.

"Do it, trickster, and then Selene will definitely come home with me," Charon replied and stepped out of the elevator.

They were in a set of private rooms, the thrum of the club beating beneath them. Hermes walked to a glass door and looked down at the people dancing, drinking, and kissing.

"Dionysus would've loved this," Hermes said to Charon.

"He's the last person we need coming back," Charon groaned. "Humans are bad enough without his encouragement."

"Saints! There's no doubt you're a son of Zeus," a tall woman said as she walked toward them. She had smooth black hair and a glint of trouble in her grey eyes.

"Hermes, this is Ariadne," Charon introduced.

"The assassin," Hermes remembered, and she laughed.

"Not anymore, I'm retired...well, kind of. Let's get you a drink before Asterion turns up," Ariadne said and took his arm. "You don't seem half as crazy as I was led to believe."

"I'm behaving. Charon gave me a lecture about first impressions," Hermes replied.

"And you listened to him? Bless. Everyone knows that crazies make the most interesting company. If any of the Court claim they are sane, then they are lying." Ariadne went behind the bar and started mixing drinks. "Besides, crazy people are the best in bed."

Hermes laughed loudly, the tension in him easing a little.

"I see you're taking no time in flirting with another of my brothers," said a low voice.

"Oh, honey, like I can help myself when you keep finding more of them. I do have a type," Ariadne replied with a bright smile.

"Hot, violent, crazy?" guessed Charon.

"Bingo," she replied with a wink.

Hermes turned around and got his first look at his newest brother. Asterion was tall and built big. Hermes tilted his head to one side, studying him.

"Wow, a Minotaur. There really wasn't anything Zeus wouldn't fuck, was there?"

"You can see the bull?" asked Asterion curiously.

"Only if I concentrate. You are the one that Selene says is going to win the bet on who is the best looking out of Zeus's sons," Hermes replied, sizing him up.

"What bet? It doesn't matter. The woman is only human, and you boys are, well…you. I think my temperature is going to hit fever point once Perseus gets here," Ariadne interrupted, passing Hermes a glass of something violently red.

"What is this?"

"It's better not to ask, trust me," said Asterion, accepting his own cup and giving Ariadne a doting smile. It was the smile that made Hermes's hackles lower.

Asterion was obviously and unashamedly in love with the woman beside him. Good. It meant he had one less person he had to compete with for Selene's attention.

"Speak of the thief and he shall appear," said Ariadne and went to kiss Perseus as he came up the stairs.

One look at the red-haired woman with him, and Hermes knew she was Hades's gorgon. She was stunningly beautiful, and he could sense the danger radiating off her.

"Daughter of Phorkys, it is an honor," Hermes said with a polite bow. "I am glad to see that the rumor of your death was a rumor only."

"Thank you, Hermes," Medusa replied, her red lips smiling the longer she looked at him. "It's nice to see Selene wasn't exaggerating."

"What about?" Hermes asked.

"Nothing, just girl talk," Medusa said and looked about. "Speaking of Selene, she should be here by now, and Hades for that matter."

"Maybe he's still arguing with her about coming out," Charon replied.

Hermes shut them out and focused on the silvery light that was Selene in his mind. His magic was humming under his skin and coming up blank.

"Woah, Hermes's aura just lit up like a Christmas tree," Perseus said, and Hermes opened his eyes. "What did you do?"

"Nothing, looking for Selene," Hermes replied and drank the cocktail. He coughed. "Oh fuck, that is terrible. Like liquid sugar."

"I'll get you some scotch instead, seeing how you're not adventurous. Come on," Ariadne said, taking the cocktail from his hand and draining it as they went back to the bar. "So, what are you arguing with Selene about?"

"Nothing," Hermes said, sitting down on one of the bar stools. "There's absolutely no argument and nothing at all going on."

"Bull shit. You just went all weird as soon as we started talking about her." Ariadne took out a fresh glass and filled it with something amber.

"I like her company," Hermes replied carefully.

Ariadne placed the drink on the bar in front of him. "That's good, because she just walked in with Erebus."

Hermes took one look over his shoulder at Selene and blood rushed to his head. She was in a low-cut dress of elegant black velvet and had a silver crescent moon hanging between her breasts.

He tore his eyes away quickly, picked up the glass of scotch, and drained it.

"I'm going to need more, assassin."

"I can see that," she chuckled as she poured him another. "I thought you said nothing was going on."

Hermes summoned his old, charming smile and lifted his glass. "Nothing yet, anyway."

"That's the spirit," Ariadne said, tapping her glass against his.

"Hey, Ariadne, do you have a decent beer back there?" Selene asked as she came to stand beside Hermes.

"You know, we got in this lovely craft beer. Let me go ring the bar downstairs to bring you up some," said Ariadne with a smile. "You two wait here, I'll be right back."

Hermes didn't fail to notice the cunning gleam in the assassin's eyes as she walked past.

"I am sorry that I upset you today," Hermes said, looking sideways at Selene and then focusing back on his drink.

"We both have tempers, Hermes, don't worry about it," Selene replied. "You are looking handsome tonight."

"More handsome than Asterion?" Hermes couldn't resist asking.

"I don't know, you won't turn around and look at me," Selene said.

Hermes twisted slowly around on the barstool and looked into her lovely kohl-rimmed eyes. "Charon tried to make me wear a tie."

Hermes tried not to fidget as she looked him over.

"I'm glad you didn't," she said, staring at the space showing the curve of his collarbone. "I'm starting to think I put my money on the wrong son of Zeus."

"Is that so?" Hermes looked at the silver and diamond crescent hanging on her chest. "Very fitting, Lady Moon."

"I saw it and couldn't walk past it. It reminded me of this mad god I know who doesn't like boundaries," Selene said, and Hermes smiled.

"Boundaries are for boring people. Besides, how can you blame me when you wear a dress like that?" Hermes slid off the barstool and into her space.

She held her ground, not giving him an inch even as he bent to whisper in her ear.

"Also, I talked to Hades, so I know for a fact he hasn't imposed any rules on you. We have his blessing to do whatever we like. As if I even needed it. So, whatever happens next is entirely your move, Selene. If you want me, come get me."

Hermes left her standing at the bar and walked back towards Asterion and Medusa, needing to put space between him and Selene before he lost control altogether.

"Hades gave me the sketch you did of Acrisius and the mystery man. Hopefully, it won't take us too long to track him down," said Medusa.

"Sorry, I can't help with a name yet. It's good that Acrisius is dead," replied Hermes. He had always been a scheming rat of a man.

"We have all of his inventions in Medusa's basement. When you are feeling up to it, we are hoping that you might be able to figure out how some of them work," said Asterion.

"Of course. With Selene's help, I'm feeling better every day. I'll help you both, and I'm going to need something to do while we wait to find Pandora."

Hermes saw Persephone arrive with Hades and move to kiss Selene on the cheek. What were they talking about? Persephone saw him watching and gave him a small wave.

"You'd better go and say hello to the queen," said Asterion with a smile. "We can catch up later, Hermes."

"I'd like that. I'm a bit...overwhelmed right now, but I like the idea of having some siblings I don't hate," Hermes replied.

"It's early days yet, and Asterion can be very annoying," Medusa said, leaning her head against the Minotaur's shoulder affectionately.

"Don't act like you don't love me, gorgon," Asterion replied.

Hermes left them arguing and went to pay his respects to Persephone. He could remember her clearly now, the new voice in the darkness of his cave, assuring him that she would get him out. And she had.

Now that he had his magic back, Hermes could feel the vibrant pulse of her own power, so much like Hades's and yet entirely her own. It was so strong it was almost elemental. She definitely was a queen, whether she wore a crown or not.

"Lady Persephone," he said, taking her hand and kissing it.

"I'm sorry, Hermes, but I'm a hugger, not a hand kisser," Persephone replied and wrapped her arms around him. "I'm so happy to see you out."

Hermes looked at Hades for permission, and after a nod, Hermes put his arms around Persephone, returning her hug.

"Thank you for not leaving me behind, my queen."

"Oh, saints above, don't you start with that 'my queen' business as well," she complained, standing on tiptoes and kissing his cheek loudly.

"I'll let it slide, but only because you are so cute. Selene was telling me we have a new dog at home. I swear I go to Athens for a few days, and the whole world changes."

"A clear indication of why you shouldn't leave Styx," Hades said, looking pissed off and terribly in love at the same time. Persephone leaned against Hermes's chest and smiled.

This goddess is about to get me murdered.

"Keep up the attitude, and next time, I'll stay for longer," she said.

"Now I know why you've been so grumpy, Hades," Hermes added because his self-preservation and his need for mischief didn't always go hand in hand.

"This from the god who sulked all afternoon because Selene left early," said Hades. "Have you at least talked to Medusa about the mystery Pithos man?"

"I have, uncle. I have even agreed to go into Medusa's basement tomorrow and look at all of Acrisius's gadgets," Hermes replied.

Whatever Hades said next, Hermes didn't catch. The club beneath them had gone silent, and an eerie voice was rising up in place of the thrumming base. Hermes let Persephone go and moved toward the windows.

There was a band now set up on a stage, a woman singing an intro in Ancient Greek, the audience dead quiet.

"Hermes? Are you okay?" asked Asterion. "Oh, that's the new band, they mix old music to new sounds. Do you like it?"

"I need to go down there," Hermes said and hurried towards the doors.

"Hermes! We haven't—" Hades started.

"I don't remember anything more! Medusa, I'll visit you tomorrow," Hermes shouted and hurried down the stairs.

The club wasn't full to capacity yet, so Hermes had no trouble threading his way through the crowd.

The band was starting to play, blending their instruments in with the singer. Hermes stood in the sea of sound and let himself drown.

14

Selene watched as a strange daze settled on Hermes, and he walked away from Persephone.

"Is he okay?" she asked Selene.

"I don't know. He gets this way sometimes when something grabs his interest," Selene said. Then Hermes was shouting and disappeared through the doors.

"What happened? What did you do to him?" she demanded, closing in on Asterion.

"Me? Nothing! I swear it, Selene. He was fixated on the band and then lost it," said Asterion.

"I need to find him," she said. Hades intercepted her before she hit the doors.

"Please message me and let me know you are both all right," he said.

"I will. If it's too much, I'll make sure he gets home okay."

"Be careful with him. He's more fragile than he appears," Hades said, and she knew he was talking about more than Hermes's sudden strange behavior.

"I will, Hades, I promise," she said. Selene made her way out in the club, searching for him in the crowd.

Hermes was tall, but it didn't help her much in the dim, red light. People were starting to dance as the music picked up around them.

Selene's attention caught on the one person not moving and made her way to him. Hermes was staring at the singer, eyes out of focus, and completely lost in his own head.

"Hermes?" Selene said, taking his hand. He didn't move. Selene placed a hand on his chest to make sure he was still breathing, her irrational panic easing when she felt his heartbeat under her palm.

"Hermes? Can you hear me?" Selene shouted over the noise. She took his face in her hands and not knowing what else to do, she rose on tiptoes and pressed her lips against his.

Hermes shuddered, and then his arms came around her, tugging her close against him. Wherever he touched burned through her, the nervous energy that had been between them finally having an outlet.

"Selene," Hermes said desperately, breaking off the kiss. "Selene, he took the music. He took it away from me."

"Who did?"

"Zeus. Zeus fucking stole it," Hermes replied. The music finished, changing back to club beats, and Hermes covered his ears.

"Let's go, okay?" Selene said, and not knowing if he heard her, she grabbed him around the waist and pulled him carefully through the crowd.

The bouncers recognized her and let her take Hermes out the back doors and into the cold streets. Hermes uncovered his head and took her hand, hanging onto it like a lifeline.

"Do you want to get out of here?" she asked.

"Yes. It's... I need to breathe and walk."

"Okay, let's do it." Selene took her phone out and text Hades, letting him know she was taking Hermes.

"You don't mind? They wanted to see you and-"

Selene wrapped his arm around hers. "They will get over it. I was there to see you anyway."

Hermes went from stressed out to smug in seconds. "Really?"

"Yes, stop looking at me like that," Selene said as they headed down the footpaths of the Diogenes.

She didn't know how long she would last in her high heels, but she'd suffer a few blisters to keep Hermes calm.

She had left him poorly earlier that day and had spent the rest of the afternoon regretting the argument, for not being able to be honest with him, for pushing him away, for being too much of a chicken shit to just kiss him and get it out of her system.

Selene had expected to go the Labyrinth to make Hades happy, have a few drinks, and go home.

That had changed as soon as Selene had seen Hermes sitting at the bar. She was overwhelmed by a kind of desperate want that she wasn't familiar with.

You are so gone on him; it doesn't matter if it's the craziest thing you've ever done.

Hermes in a suit made her want to risk all the crazy that would come with it.

"Do you want to tell me what happened back there?" Selene asked.

"The woman, the singing. Fuck, she was singing Homeric Hymns in Ancient Greek, and I had a big door blow open. Behind it was music. A great, pounding, swell of sound, and then I could feel the shape of Zeus's curse come up and slam it shut again. That hasn't happened before. It's like he took all the things I loved the most just to fucking spite me."

Hermes stopped and took her by the shoulders.

"Selene, I'm the god of memory, poetry, language, writing, music, and he fucking stole it all. Why? Why would he do such a thing to me?"

"I don't know, but he's dead, Hermes. No one will be able to take anything from you ever again. I won't let them," Selene said, trying to keep her voice as reassuring as possible. "The rest of the Court will help protect you too for as long as you need it. I know this might seem scary, but you aren't alone."

Hermes touched her cheek with shaking fingers. "I'm not scared, Selene. I'm so angry I can hardly breathe."

"Hermes, take me home and we can talk about it there. The street isn't the place to discuss curses made by dead gods," Selene said, conscious of their raised voices.

He nodded, checked the streets, and then pulled her through a doorway and into the living room of her apartment.

"Thank you. These shoes were killing me."

"That's a shame, they look amazing," Hermes said, doing his head tilt as she bent to free her feet from the peep-toes.

"They look amazing, but they don't feel amazing if you are trying to keep stride with the god of long legs," she said as she straightened.

She tried not to freak out as Hermes took off his jacket and started looking at everything in her apartment with his sharp eyes.

There was art on the dark purple walls, mostly pieces she had bought from local artists or picked up at op-shops and markets.

She had a collection of colored tins on the bookshelf filled with various lip balms, burn salves, and soaps that she had made for friends or to give to people in her building that she knew would appreciate them.

There was a patchwork blanket on her couch, one of the first she'd made, and a collection of jars of loose tea leaves on her kitchen counter.

"Do you want a beer?" Selene asked, needing to do something other than stare at him in her space.

"Yes," he said, staring at a picture of a ceramic sculpture of a woman, where the artist had filled the cracks with silver. "I like this."

"Beautiful isn't it? It's a Japanese art called *Kintsugi*, where they fix broken ceramics with adhesives of silver and gold instead of throwing it out. I like the metaphor of fixing your broken pieces with something beautiful," Selene explained, pulling beers from the fridge and passing him one.

She opened the door to her garden and turned on the soft solar-powered lanterns to light up the space. She sat down on the white, wicker two-seater couch and sighed.

"This was a much better idea than the club," she said as Hermes studied her herbs, flower boxes, and succulents.

"If I didn't know better, I'd think you're a witch, Selene. This is a witch's garden if I ever saw one," he commented as he picked off a leaf of her overgrown mint plant and chewed on it.

"As if I have enough time to be a witch. I might have to live in a city but having this helps keeps me sane. I like to make and grow things, so I started with cooking herbs, and then it got completely out of control. Are you feeling any calmer or still angry?"

Hermes sat down beside her. "I'm not angry, but I don't know if calm is what I'm feeling. Until the last few days, your presence did level me out, and now it's doing the opposite but in a different way."

"Hades will be pissed when I tell him," Selene said, shifting slightly and having another sip of beer before putting it down on a small table. She wished she wasn't so nervous about being alone with him.

"You don't really care what Hades thinks. Otherwise, you wouldn't have kissed me at the club." Hermes's slow, flirty smile was back. "You kissed me; I suppose that makes us even now."

"I had to do something to get your attention, didn't I? I was afraid you were going catatonic," Selene replied.

"I was lost in the halls of my own mind, trying to find the door with the music again." Hermes leaned forward and rested his elbows on his knees. "I couldn't get to it. My music is gone and now I know what I'm missing."

"It will return, Hermes. You got your words back, and your ability to hold new memories, it's just another thing to work towards," Selene said and placed a hand on his back. "Just make sure if you go into your head, you come home again."

Hermes's smile had returned as he angled towards her. "If I do get lost for a while, at least you know the best way to bring me back."

"I'm not going to kiss you every time you space out, Hermes, I'd be kissing you all day," Selene complained.

It's dark, don't worry, he won't see how red your face is right now.

"Exactly. You aren't giving me much incentive to stay present, are you?" he replied. Selene quickly looked away and tried to get the conversation back on track.

"I'll help you get your music back, Hermes, so don't worry."

"If you do, I'll write an epic ballad of Selene, Mistress of the Moon and Disapproving Glances," teased Hermes.

"Sounds like it would be pretty boring. I don't think I'm interesting enough to have a ballad," Selene replied.

"Then I'll fill it with violence and sex. I'll have a starring role," said Hermes, and she laughed loudly.

"Lots of creative license then," she replied.

"I wouldn't say that," Hermes said and kissed her before she had time to react. It was soft and quick, and when he pulled back, his golden eyes were glowing. "Selene, something just happened."

"Yes, you kissed me-" she tried to say before he was kissing her again, harder and deeper, his hand moving to rest on her neck.

"I saw something when I kissed you, a flash of something. Something important," Hermes said as they parted, his expression thoughtful. Selene put a hand up over his lips to stop him from doing it again.

"Don't. Don't kiss me if it's only to try to unlock your memories," she said, proud that she could keep her voice steady. Hermes gently moved her hand away.

"I didn't know that was going to happen when I kissed you. I kissed you because I think about kissing you more than anything else. I might have gotten a flash of memory then, but it isn't my memories I'm thinking about, it's yours," said Hermes, his eyes heating to a glow once more.

"I want to kiss you to take every memory of bad kissing away from you. I want to make so many good kissing memories that all the other bad ones won't matter anymore, and you'll forget boring plate men that didn't deserve you, and that were too weak to give you the kisses and the pleasure you deserved."

Selene's heartbeat was in her throat and she was hot all over, the pulse of strange magic and desire burning brightly in her core.

"Is that so? And you are so confident of your abilities to do all of that? Because every man has this kind of confidence," she said, trying to make a joke and failing when Hermes took it as a challenge.

His smile was sharp, full of promises, and an intensity that thrilled and terrified her.

"Don't you know who I am, Selene of the Night? I'm a trickster, the master of riddles, and the greatest thief that ever was. What is your pleasure but another riddle for me to solve and lock for me to pick in order to get the treasure inside?" he said.

Selene pulled him to her, kissing him before she could second guess herself. Hermes's strong hands dragged her onto his lap, so she was straddling him, the skirt of her dress bunched up her thighs.

"I don't know why your crazy talk of riddles and locks is doing it for me, but it is," she managed to say between kisses, her hands in his hair.

"Don't you get it? You are my silver, Selene, the precious thing that binds all my broken bits together," he whispered, brushing his lips against her throat.

"And I'm going to be the thief that unlocks every hidden part of you because I want it all, and I don't want you to be ashamed of any of it, even the dark and dirty parts. Come to think of it, I want those bits most of all."

Selene laughed softly as she wrapped her arms around him, burying her face against his neck.

"You are going to ruin me if you keep saying things like that, Hermes," she said.

"Ruination in the best possible way is definitely what I have in mind," he replied, standing up and carrying her through the apartment to her bedroom, kissing her all the way. Selene didn't have time to be nervous as he set her down on her feet and unzipped the back of her dress.

"What's this? A tattoo?" he asked, fingers circling her lower back.

"A birthmark," Selene said, her skin breaking out in goose bumps.

"It looks like the phases of the moon." Hermes knelt to study it. "I'm right, it's a crescent facing left, a full moon in the middle and a crescent facing right. You really are Lady Moon."

He kissed it, and her knees nearly gave way. His hands went to her hips to steady her as he stood, lips dragging up her spine.

Selene reached behind her for his belt buckle, but he caught her hands.

"Stop," he said.

Selene froze. "I'm sorry I thought-"

"Oh, keep thinking those thoughts, because we will definitely get there, but tonight is about you, not about me," Hermes said, kissing her shoulder as he slid the straps of her dress down, letting it drop.

Selene couldn't see his face, but she heard the sound he made in the back of his throat before his hands traced down her bare skin.

"Fuck, you are so beautiful, Selene. This is going to be harder than I thought."

"Isn't that the point?"

"Not tonight."

"Why not?"

Hermes's hand came around to stroke her ribs and stomach. "Memory making."

"Really? Here I thought you were saying that to make me beg," she said, gasping as his hand moved to cup her. Oh, God, she was definitely going to beg.

"Only if you are into it," he replied, "but something tells me that begging isn't your style."

Heat poured through her satin panties and she bit back a groan. He slipped one finger under the side and stroked her, making a growl in the back of his throat when he found her wet.

He moved his finger up to loop around the side of the panties and slid them down her thighs.

Hermes maneuvered her so she lay back on the bed. His golden eyes fixed on her bare breasts and he swore again. No one had ever sworn at the sight of her breasts before, and a smile tugged at her lips.

"Are you *sure* this is only going to be about me tonight?" she asked, stretching an arm up above her head. Hermes's hand came down on it as he leaned over her.

"Wicked woman, stop teasing me. My self-control when it comes to you is bad enough," he said.

Selene's smart-ass reply turned into a gasp as his hand moved up between her breasts and over her necklace. His mouth traced over her collarbone and shoulder. He was stroking her everywhere except where she wanted him, and it was driving her insane.

"Touch yourself," he said against her.

"W-What?" Selene stammered.

"No one knows what a woman likes better than that woman herself. Go ahead, Selene. Teach me," Hermes said, teeth against her earlobe.

Selene tried helplessly to steady her breath and ignore her nerves as she closed her eyes and slid her hand between her thighs.

She had taught herself how to get off after too many disappointing sexual encounters, sometimes doing it as soon as her boyfriend had gone to sleep after sex just to relieve her own frustration.

Not one of them had ever asked her to do it in front of them, though.

Hermes's clever fingers found one breast, his mouth finding the other, and Selene bit down a gasp. She opened her eyes, and the sight of him watching her hand between her legs with his intense concentration nearly made her come.

She was trembling, but she didn't stop as Hermes's hands and lips kept up their slow exploration, his eyes taking in every reaction of her body. He took a nipple in his mouth and sucked it hard, and she came with a surprised gasp and full body spasm.

"I can't believe I just did that in front of you," Selene said. Hermes rested his hand over hers and carefully moved it away from between her thighs, before lifting her fingers to his mouth.

Fucking hell, you are so not ready for this.

"My turn with a few interesting improvements," Hermes said, sliding down the bed and moving between her legs. Selene couldn't stop the shake up her leg as he kissed the skin of her inner thigh. "Relax, Selene, I am a very good student."

She almost laughed, but the sight of his golden eyes between her thighs made her dream come rushing back. She didn't have time to contemplate it as he stroked her wetness with his long fingers.

Selene gripped the sheets, and his other hand came to her stomach to pin her down.

"Fuck, I could watch you like this forever, writhing on your sheets because I'm between your thighs," Hermes said, his voice distant behind the roaring in her head.

His tongue found her clit, moving it with a slow, measured pressure that made sounds come out of her throat that she didn't even know were possible.

His other hand moved from her stomach to grasp one of her breasts and squeezed it hard enough for her to groan and drag her nails down his forearm.

Hermes's tongue pushed inside of her, and Selene's fingers tangled in his hair, thighs tightening around him as her body locked up.

"Breathe, Selene," he said, sliding his fingers in to replace his tongue. He pressed something inside of her, and she cried out. Her burning core exploded, and she came again, hard enough to drive the breath out of her body.

"Holy shit," she gasped, draping one exhausted arm over her eyes. "What did you just do to me?"

Hermes carefully loosened her thighs grip on him, dropping a kiss on the curve of her hip. "I really can't take all the credit, but you should probably know that you are glowing."

"So I should be-"

"No, my dear, you are *actually* glowing," Hermes said, settling on the bed beside her.

"What?" Selene looked up. Her skin was radiating with a sheen of sweat and silvery light. "What did you do?"

"Don't look at me, this is all you, Lady Moon," he replied, brushing her damp bangs from her face. "That is your magic making itself known. As if you weren't beautiful enough already."

Selene held her hand up and studied the glow before looking at the god beside her. "Is it something I should worry about? I mean, can it hurt you if I touch you?"

"No, it's neutral unless you want it to hurt me," Hermes said, stroking her arm. "See?"

"Good," Selene replied and rolled onto him, leaning down to kiss him, her hand going to the buttons of his shirt. He laughed softly, catching her hands.

"This your night, remember?"

"And I'm not arguing, but if you think I'm going to let you keep this shirt on a second longer, you have another thing coming, Hermes," Selene replied, and before he could stop her, she took the ends and ripped it apart, the buttons giving way.

"Okay, have it your way. Nothing below the waist."

Hermes pulled his shirt off and put his hands behind his head, his biceps flexing in a way that made her heart rate go up again.

"I think you want me to beg after all."

"Me? Never!" he said, moving a hand to cup one of her heavy breasts. "How are those new memories coming?"

Selene's smile was a bright and beautiful thing as she ran a glowing hand down his golden muscled chest.

"I'm ready to make more."

15

Using a pen on the back of a shopping receipt, Hermes sketched a picture of Selene as she slept.

She was still gloriously naked, and Hermes congratulated himself on his self-control not to pounce on her again and make her groan his name in ecstasy.

He didn't want her to think that he had run off before the dawn, but as he had dozed in her arms, he had dreamed.

He needed to draw out the horrible things in his head and talk to Hades. He hoped they were only nightmares and not memories. He doubted it.

Need to see Hades and Medusa, sleep sound, sweet Silver, he wrote on the bottom the sketch and placed it on his empty pillow. Hermes leaned down and kissed her bottom lip gently enough not to wake her, but enough to make sure she woke up with the taste of him.

Get out before she wakes up, and you don't leave at all.

Hermes had one last look before ripping open a doorway and stepping back into his own bedroom.

Jackal was asleep on his bed, his heavy tail thumping in greeting. Hermes gave him a pat and the dog sniffed him.

"I didn't fuck it up this time," Hermes told him happily.

They went to the kitchen, and he tipped some food into Jackal's bowl as he fought the uneasy feeling settling in his bones.

He sat down at the table and began to draw the horrors out of his head, the memory of Pandora whispering in his ear. She would always begin with a question.

If you had to cage a monster, how would you do it, my inventor?

And then in his broken and drug-addled state, he would fixate on whatever riddle she posed and would only be calm again once he had solved it. For a minute, he was back in the cave, the damp air smelling of earth and metal and blood. He stopped drawing and shook out his hands.

"Hades and Persephone got you out," he reminded himself. "Selene won't be safe until you stop Pandora. Think, Hermes! Where would the witch hide if not in her cave?"

After Hermes had a small pile of drawings, he went to his bathroom and took a long shower, thinking about Selene to make himself feel better.

Fantasizing about her brilliant smile and luscious body led his mind back to her strange birthmark.

"Hecate's blood. Why did it have to be Hecate!" he groaned.

Selene's magic had made him think that she had an affinity that marked her as one of Hecate's chosen, but the triple moon on her back proved that she had the goddess's own blood flowing in her veins.

Hermes couldn't recall every animosity he had with Hecate or just how much the goddess hated him. He did know they had enough shared godly ground to make them irritate the shit out of each other.

Hermes and Hecate were deities of magic, boundaries, thresholds, and crossroads. She had power over shades and Hermes was their guide. They both spent time down in the Underworld.

They stepped on each other's toes on more than one occasion, and if it wasn't for Thanatos, they probably would have killed each other over one slight or another.

One thing that Hermes had always admired about Hecate was that Zeus was terrified of her enough that he had spared the titaness from a jail cell in Tartaros after the war. He also had never dared try to seduce her or piss her off.

Despite that, Zeus had a special fascination with her. Hecate's presence had never had that effect on Hermes, but Selene did. She possessed that same indefinable quality that made Hermes want to give her anything she liked, in the hope she would want him.

You know better than to fall in love, stupid boy, Zeus's voice boomed in his head, and Hermes flinched.

"Go away, Father, you're not welcome here," muttered Hermes.

Gods were notorious for falling quickly and completely in love with humans, and Hermes knew he wasn't impervious to this strange affliction.

It's too early, you will freak Selene out so calm down, focus on being useful.

HERMES FOUND Hades in his home office, drinking coffee and muttering obscenities at a computer screen.

"What can I do for you, Hermes?" he asked, not looking up.

"No Persephone this morning?" Hermes said as he started going through the objects on Hades's desk, pocketing a fancy pen he liked the look of.

Hades looked up with a smug smile. "She's sleeping off the sex coma I put her in. You didn't come home last night. Is Selene in the same state or did you mess it up?"

"I like to think she's satisfied for the time being," Hermes replied. "My night with Selene isn't why I'm here." He handed Hades his drawings.

"What are these?" Hades asked, taking them.

"I think I made these for Pandora. I can't be sure but-"

Hades put the drawings down. "We need to go to Serpentine and see Medusa now."

"I thought you are working," said Hermes as Hades got up.

"Not anymore. This is more important." Hades placed a hand on Hermes's shoulder, and suddenly, they were standing at what looked like a laboratory.

Hades took out his phone. "Susa? We are in the basement. Can you come down?"

People in white coats gave them quizzical looks or made themselves scarce. Hermes walked slowly through the cavernous space.

Half of it was filled with wooden shipping crates in a range of sizes. The rest of the space was stations of computers, and lab benches cover in equipment and lights.

"It's quite the mess, isn't it?" said Medusa as she joined them. "If I had had gotten a bit more notice, I would've made sure that they at least attempted to clean things up."

"Sorry, Medusa, I had dreams last night," Hermes said with an apologetic smile.

He was staring at a half helmet on one of the benches. His head started to pound when he recognized the 3D version of one of his drawings.

Whatever Medusa and Hades were saying was drowned out as Hermes moved to where a large cage was constructed. He placed a hand on the bars and flinched, releasing it instantly.

They are here. She made them all. Every riddle she put to me to solve. They were to kill and entrap the Court. Hermes was going to be sick.

"Hey, are you okay?" asked Medusa.

"No."

"You recognize them, don't you?" guessed Hades.

"Yes, they are all mine," Hermes replied. He could hope that Pandora never made the rest of them. Hades and Medusa shared a loaded and worried look.

"What does that mean, Hermes?" she asked. Hermes wasn't listening, his vision was tunneling and he swayed.

"No, no, no," he muttered, his eyes burning and his mind breaking. "She can't see them. Silver can't know, she'll hate me if she sees what I've done."

Everything was too big, too bright, and too loud. Hermes climbed into one of the large freight containers, brought his knees to his chest, hands clamping over his head as the world and its horrors rushed over him.

∽

SELENE WOKE to an empty bed and satiated body.

"Hermes?" she called sleepily. She didn't know what time it was, and for once, she didn't care.

She rolled over and spotted the sketch of her. She picked it up and read the note, a big goofy smile spreading across her face.

"So that did happen," she said with a soft laugh. Her whole body felt lazy and happy as she tied on a kimono and made tea.

You feel this good, and you didn't even have sex. Just imagine... Her smile widened further because she *could* imagine, and that was enough to make every part of her tingle.

Figuring that someone would call if she were needed, Selene took a shower and had a lazy morning.

She couldn't stop thinking about Hermes's reaction to the loss of his music and was determined to make up for the lack.

She dug out her iPod and began filling it with songs. She started with her favorite classical and movie scores and slowly moved through all the genres.

She was humming along to a jazz standard when Hades appeared, making her spill her tea in fright.

"Good, you are awake and dressed," he said instead of hello.

"What are you doing here? What's wrong?" Selene asked. She didn't like the frown he was giving her. "Look, if this is about Hermes and me last night..."

"Let me stop you right there. I don't care or want to know what you and Hermes get up to. I'm here because I took him to Serpentine to look at what we recovered from ARGOS Industries, and he's lost it," explained Hades.

"Oh no, he realized what he made," Selene said and put her tea down. "I wondered when that was going to happen."

"He's taken it badly, and I need you to talk to him because he's not listening to Medusa or me," Hades replied.

Selene was already grabbing her bag and stuffed her feet into her boots. In a snap decision, she grabbed the iPod and headphones.

"I'm ready. Take me to him before this gets worse."

"Thank you, Selene. I've never once regretted indebting you to me," Hades said, the closest to a compliment he'd ever given her.

"Me neither, boss," Selene replied and took his hand.

The floor had been cleared and Medusa was sitting at a workstation, idly filing her nails.

"Any change?" asked Hades.

"Not a peep," Medusa said and smiled at Selene. "You're up. He's in there."

Selene dropped her bag and climbed inside the wooden shipping crate where Hermes had curled himself up with his back to them.

Selene sat down, placed her legs slowly on either side of him, and hugged him to her. He shook and then relaxed into her.

"Selene," he murmured, "you shouldn't be here."

"Yes, I should," she replied, resting her cheek on his back. "It's not your fault, Hermes."

"I designed them all! These things that could hurt the Court and Hades. They are going to hate me for it. I didn't know what they would be used for, I swear I didn't."

"They know that, Hermes. No one is blaming you, and they certainly don't hate you," Selene said. She took her iPod out of her pocket. "Here, this will help."

She stroked his hair away and put the headphones in his ears. She wasn't sure where to start, so she chose a soothing piece of classical music.

He stiffened as the music started and then melted back into her, resting his head on her shoulder.

"Oh, Silver, I like this," he said, holding her hands over his chest. She pressed a kiss to his temple.

"Silver, is it? What happened to Lady Moon?"

"I learned that you are no lady," he said, yelping when she poked him in the ribs.

"Are you the god of no manners as well?" she asked.

"You might not be a lady, but you are definitely my Silver, sealing all my broken bits together again," Hermes said, turning his head so he could kiss her softly.

"Do you want to get out this crate?" Selene asked. Hermes tensed again, and she held him a little tighter. "Or not. We can stay here until you're ready."

Selene took one of the earbuds back and changed songs. "Here, I filled it with music for you. I thought it might help motivate some of your musical memories."

She passed him the iPod and showed him how to scroll through it.

"This is kind of you. You treat me better than I deserve, Selene," he said, hanging onto it tightly.

"I'll be the judge of that. You seem to be forgetting that you're the victim and that it doesn't matter if Pandora made all your inventions. The Court has managed to escape them every time. They are safe, Hermes, and now all these things are in their hands. They can't hurt anyone anymore."

Selene stroked his head and he made a happy growl in the back of his throat.

She decided that there were definitely worse places she could be in that moment than having her arms full of beautiful, crazy god.

After a few songs, Hermes shifted, so his back was against the wood, and he could face her properly.

"I'm scared, Selene. There are pieces missing, but I can't remember where Pandora is hiding them. I was taken to another place before the caves. I remember the cell she had me in. She must have found me after Zeus cursed me and I couldn't fight back."

Hermes pulled on the ends of his hair, and Selene carefully untangled his fingers and held his hand.

"Hades is going to find her, don't worry. She can't hide forever, she's too arrogant. She will slip up and the Court will have her," Selene tried to reassure him. "We can't stop her from here."

Hermes traced the lines of her palm thoughtfully.

"What if I never get better, Selene? What if I'm always like this, one good day and then I lose it? That's so unfair to you," he said, and Selene's stomach jolted nervously.

"What are you saying?" she asked, already dreading the answer.

"Maybe I shouldn't have kissed you. I thought I was getting better, but what if I'm not? You don't need someone that's going to burden you with this bullshit," Hermes said.

"No."

"What?"

Selene took her hand from his. "I said no, Hermes. You don't get to decide what I need or feel just because you are having a bad day. It's not just about you. I knew who I was kissing, and it wasn't because I thought you were getting better, whatever that even means. So no, you don't get to push me away when I've only just let you in."

"Selene, I'm trying to give you an out in all this," Hermes said in exasperation.

"And I'm telling you, I don't fucking want one!" she snapped.

His eyes glowed gold, and inside of her, the core of magic pulsed in response.

They stared at each other for a tense, heated second before he was reaching for her, and Selene was kissing him roughly. His hands slid up the back of her shirt and she wrapped her legs around him.

She wanted to be touching him everywhere, needed the feel of his skin in order to know everything was all right.

She moved her hips slowly, groaning when she felt him hard against her. She wanted to return every favor that he had done to her the previous night.

She wanted to touch him the way he had touched her, to have her name on his lips, and... Someone cleared their throat and Selene jumped, banging her head on the roof of the crate. She turned to see Thanatos's grinning face.

"Sorry to interrupt. I was going to see if everything was okay, but by the looks of things, everything is back to normal?" he asked.

"Yes, Hermes is about to take us home," said Selene, her voice shaky.

"Is he?" Hermes asked, and then seeing Selene's face, he added, "He is." They detangled and climbed out.

"Medusa and Hades went back to work. They would like you to go through your sketches for any other hints of where Pandora or the mystery man may be," said Thanatos. "Anything that looks like the beach you drew, for example. Perseus wants to give everything to the Graeae sisters, dubious but effective contacts of his, and see what they can uncover."

"I'll help get them together," said Selene.

"I can't promise any of it will be useful," added Hermes.

"It will be fine." Selene took his hand. "Let's go home."

16

Hermes sat in a bath and did his best not to start counting the bubbles obsessively.

He and Selene had returned to the villa, and she went into full nurse mode, prescribing a bubble bath with lavender oil to help him feel better.

She found a speaker down at the main house and hooked up the iPod to play him music. Having her care for him made him have all sorts of confusingly tender thoughts and feelings towards her.

His Silver, who had gotten so fierce when he tried to let her go. As if he could.

Hermes might be having a bad day, but he knew she was the one thing that he would never sacrifice or give up. He smiled at his reflection in the water.

She wouldn't allow it anyway. Hermes was lucid enough to know he was already in love with her.

Destroy Pandora and Pithos, get the girl, live happily ever after.

That was the plan, and the gods help whoever tried to get in his way. The lavender, hot water, and soft classical music began to do its work on him, and Hermes leaned back and closed his eyes.

THE WIND in Crete blew up dust and rock on the foothills of Mount Ida.

Hermes knew from the urgency of Zeus's message and the chosen location, that his father was struggling with his own immortality again.

Unlike Hermes, who had adapted to the new reality of no longer being worshipped, it still grated on Zeus that Olympus and his petty pantheon were dead, mad, or scattered to the wind.

Hermes removed his staff from its glamored position on his back and went to find his father.

Zeus sat on a rock near a narrow track, waiting patiently for him. He seemed to have embraced the corporate suit look.

Considering the last time Hermes saw him, Zeus had been dressed as a beggar, Hermes assumed that there was a woman around that he was attempting to court.

"Sky Father," Hermes said politely in greeting. He didn't bow. He hadn't for centuries, and Zeus's eye still twitched at the slight, but didn't mention it.

Hermes hated that he had his father's jawline and cheekbones. It didn't bother him until he was forced to see Zeus, and then he would spend weeks afterward wanting to punch every mirror he caught his reflection in.

Hermes was already regretting coming to this meeting, he knew better.

"Hermes, you need a haircut," Zeus said finally.

"You summon me to criticize my fashion choices? You must be bored," replied Hermes, twisting his staff lazily. Zeus's keen eyes followed the movement.

"No, I need a favor."

"If memory serves, you haven't repaid me for the last favor I did for you." Zeus wanting a favor was never, ever, a good sign.

There wasn't much that Zeus couldn't get on his own, which meant it was going to be personal or a particular brand of fucked up that Zeus never wanted to be blamed for.

"Look, son, it's a small thing I ask for. I want to borrow the Caduceus for a single night," said Zeus with an easy smile. Hermes's hand tightened on his staff.

What could Zeus possibly want it for? If it had been anyone else, if Zeus hadn't called him son and used that shit-eating smile, Hermes might have fallen for it.

"No, it's mine, and you hardly need it. You have more power than what it can wield," said Hermes, straightening his shoulders. "What is this really about? Try the truth and I might reconsider."

Zeus's smile changed, losing its polish until it settled somewhere closer to threatening.

"It's for a deal. If I present your staff to the object of my affection, I can fuck her," admitted Zeus.

"That's a very specific request. I wonder why your beloved would want my staff instead of yours?" said Hermes. "Who is the unfortunate lady in question?"

"Pandora," answered Zeus and Hermes bent over laughing.

"You want to stick your dick into a trap of your own creation, even though you know it's a trap? Has life become so unbearable to you?"

Zeus flushed with anger. "She's not like that anymore! None of us are what we used to be. It's nice to be in the company of someone who remembers the old days."

"Really, if she's changed so much, what does she want my staff for, or have you not stopped to question her motivations?" asked Hermes.

Pandora was designed by the gods to be the perfect honey pot, and his father had fallen for her wiles for the chance to get some ass.

No wonder he's no longer worshipped.

"I'm not an idiot, Hermes. I would never let her keep the staff permanently. I only need to show it to her, and then after I've fucked her for a day and a night, I'll return it to you."

"Father, I know you're lonely and you miss the old days, but fucking Pandora won't bring them back. Even if she holds the staff for a minute, who is to know what kind of havoc she will create," said Hermes, as gently as he could.

"I'm strong enough to counteract any harm she could cause. Be reasonable, Hermes. It's only a stick," said Zeus.

"Will you fucking be reasonable? I'll not hand over my most treasured possession so that you can go get your dick wet!" Hermes hissed. "Tell Pandora to ask for something else. I've heard enough of this ridiculous nonsense."

Hermes turned and tore open a door. A bolt of raw power hit him in the back, sending him sprawling across the ground.

"You always have to do things the hard way," Zeus said as Hermes struggled to breathe. The King of the Gods bent down and picked up Hermes's staff from the ground beside him.

"This really is a marvelous creation. I'm sorry, Hermes, but I won't have you disrupt my plans because you don't like to share."

Zeus's voice was fading as Hermes's vision went black around the edges. The curse was streaking through him like poison, and without his staff, he couldn't counteract it.

Fucking bastard.

Zeus's face hovered over him, a satisfied smile on his face.

"You always thought you were so clever. Now you are going to know what it's like to be nothing and no one. Perhaps when I come to change you back, you will have learned to have more respect for your king. If not, then you would have a better chance of convincing the moon to fall in love with you than you'll have getting me to restore you," Zeus said and laughed. "Sleep well, son."

"F-fuck you," Hermes spat as the curse reached his head, and he knew nothing more.

~

HERMES WOKE IN THE BATHTUB, arms and legs thrashing in the lukewarm water. His panic subsided when he realized where he was.

"Fuck," he groaned as he brought his knees up to his chest and took deep breaths. "Zeus is dead, Zeus is dead."

Hermes steadied his breathing and concentrated, reaching deep inside for his power. It took a few minutes, and then he felt the sticky black claws of Zeus's curse.

It was receded in parts and still thick in others. He didn't need more proof that what he had dreamed was a repressed memory.

Zeus had cursed him over a fuck. He knew he shouldn't be surprised, but a part of him had hoped that he had done something to deserve his punishment.

No, it was only Zeus being a fucking asshole as usual.

Despite Zeus never returning to undo the curse, it had begun to lift anyway.

You would have a better chance of convincing the moon to fall in love with you, Zeus had said.

Had he unknowingly created a loophole in his own curse? Maybe the magic didn't differentiate between the actual moon and...

"Selene, my Lady Moon, who shines with the light of the stars and has the blood of the Triple Moon Goddess," Hermes said aloud.

He started to laugh at the sticky hands of the Fates and stopped suddenly as he realized the full implications.

If his theory was correct, then his curse was weakening because he had convinced Selene to fall in love with him. If he told her, would she think he was only pursuing her because he wanted his curse lifted?

Hermes got out of the bath and dried himself off. He needed to find her and talk to her, and to focus on not kissing her outright because she was his key after all.

Hermes wrapped a towel around his waist and opened the door just as Selene was raising a hand to knock.

"Oh god!" she started in surprise.

"Yes, I am," Hermes replied.

"I was coming to check on how you were—" She didn't get to finish her sentence as he pressed her up against the wall and locked his mouth on hers.

Her soft lips opened for him, and he deepened the kiss, slipping his tongue into her mouth to move with hers. Selene pulled him close, one leg going up and around him so he could press his hips up against her.

He moaned, torn between wanting her and wanting to pick the perfect moment to make love to her.

My perfect Lady Moon, full of fire and passion and kindness.

Inside of him, Hermes sensed the darkness of the curse recede further.

"If you keep kissing me like this, Selene, I'm going to lose this towel, and then you'll really be in trouble," Hermes said, moving his mouth along her jaw. "My self-control is only so good."

"Is that so? I was going to say if you keep kissing me, I'm going to *take* that towel and do bad things to you," Selene replied, a gleam in her eye.

She kissed him in the center of his chest and dropped her leg.

"Unfortunately for you, Hades is waiting for me to take him down the drawings. Get dressed and meet me down at the house."

"Here I was thinking I'd stopped you from being a cold nurse," Hermes said, wanting to know in detail what bad things she was considering.

Selene gave his ass a pinch. "Then you really are delusional."

17

While Hermes had been in the bath, Selene had taken the time to carefully sort through the dozens of drawings he had scattered about.

There was one of her standing in a marble temple that made her heart skip a beat.

It was one of the first ones he had drawn, and it made parts of her melt, knowing that he had been thinking of her as much as she had of him.

Selene's lips were still tingling from Hermes's kiss as she picked up the sketches and headed down to Hades's office.

She had planned on waiting for Hermes, but after that kiss, she needed to put some distance between them before she followed him into his bedroom and had her way with him.

"It has to be a god thing," she mumbled under her breath.

Selene had never been with someone where she had felt almost addicted to them. She had never been a wide-eyed, obsessed girl with Ezra, even with his 'hottie doctor' reputation in the hospital.

Hermes conjured a completely different level of feeling in her. She wanted to be touching him if they were in the same room, and she thought about kissing him more than what she would consider healthy.

As Selene entered the back door, she spotted Persephone in the kitchen, making coffee and raiding Hades's pantry.

"Must be sugar in here somewhere," Persephone complained.

"Cookies are kept on the next shelf up. Hades hides them behind the cereal, so Thanatos and Erebus don't eat them all," said Selene.

"My hero!" Persephone pulled the jar out and put it on the bench in front of Selene. "You want? Hades likes to hide how good he is at baking. Really it makes me sick that he's good at so much."

"I'm starting to think it's a god thing," replied Selene, selecting a cookie covered in chocolate.

"Oh, I recognize that smile. Did you find out what Hermes was really good at last night?" asked Persephone, dunking her cookie into her coffee.

"Perhaps," said Selene, trying to keep a straight face. Persephone was so ridiculously friendly, and Selene always seemed to give in to her good-natured pressure.

"It's good to know he didn't forget everything," said Persephone with a filthy laugh. "I do wish you were a details girl. Come on, I'll tell you mine if you tell me yours."

Selene pulled a face. "Sorry, but I don't want to know a damn thing about Hades's sexual proclivities."

"If you did, we'd be here all day." Persephone waggled her eyebrows, making Selene cough on cookie crumbs.

"What are you two giggling about in here?" Hades demanded as he came into the kitchen.

"None of your business," said Persephone sweetly.

Hades's silver eyes narrowed. "Now, I have to know."

"She was trying to get out of me whether or not I've had sex with Hermes," said Selene.

Hades shared a smile with Persephone and reached in the jar for a cookie. "Well, have you?"

"You two are as bad as each other! Here, have your pictures." Selene passed him the pile of drawings.

"Definitely a no then," said Hades to Persephone. "Maybe you should take him on a date. Something tells me that after today, he's going to need an outing to pull him out of his funk."

"I'm hoping the music I gave him is going to help him. That's what set him off last night. He remembered Zeus taking his music away from him. I don't condone violence, but I'm really glad he's dead, Hades," Selene replied.

"Zeus always hated if anyone was better than him at something. He knew how important Hermes's music was to him, so it doesn't surprise me that the malicious bastard stole it from him." Hades took another cookie. "You know, I have a box at the opera house if you would like to take him tomorrow night. They are opening *Don Giovanni*."

"I'd love that! I've always wanted to go to the opera," Selene said excitedly. "Oh, no, I'm going to have to find a dress."

"Medusa will be able to send something over to you. Gods know, she's got enough dresses in her penthouse. The woman is a hoarder, I swear," Persephone replied.

"I might wait and see if Hermes is feeling up to it. He seemed a lot better when he got out of the bath just now."

"Help towel him down, did you?" asked Persephone, hopefully. "I mean, I wouldn't blame you if you did." A growl emanated from Hades's throat and Persephone's smile widened.

"Stop your weird jealous foreplay before it gets out of hand," begged Selene.

"She can't help it. Pissing me off is her second favorite pastime," grumbled Hades. Persephone leaned her head against his shoulder.

"But you're the sucker that still loves me," she said.

"Only because I thoroughly enjoy your first favorite past time," he replied, making sexy eyes at her.

"Gross," Selene laughed.

Hermes arrived in time to save Selene from any more embarrassing questions or the pair's flirting.

He was barefoot and dressed in jeans and a black t-shirt, but there was something about the ensemble and the way his hawk eyes lingered on her that made Selene struggle to look at him.

It's official. He wants me to beg him to take me on this kitchen bench, Hades and Persephone be damned.

"You're looking better, Hermes. Do you want to help me make sense of some of these drawings of yours?" asked Hades.

"The ones I can. I need to tell you something else, too," he said as they walked to Hades's office. "When I was in the bath, I had a vision of the day Zeus cursed me."

Hermes took his drawings from Hades and started laying them out on the carpet. Selene sat on one of the sofa chairs, her heart clenching as Hermes told them how Zeus had summoned and then cursed him.

"Pandora must have stabbed Zeus that night and found you wandering about the mountainside," said Hades thoughtfully.

Selene knew that Hades had been released from the Underworld as soon as he had cut off Zeus's head, finishing what Pandora had started.

"That means Pandora has had you for over twenty fucking years," Selene said, her hands clenching into fists. "She has been tormenting you all this time."

Silvery light began to radiate from her body as hot rage surged through her.

Persephone let out a low whistle of appreciation. "Wow, look at that glow."

"Incredible. Hecate must have had daughters after all," said Hades. "Explains why she's so good with dogs too."

"We'll worry about that later, Hades," whispered Persephone.

Hermes rested his warm palm on Selene's cheek. "I'm safe from Pandora now, Selene, that's what matters. Let the magic go," he said tenderly.

"I am going to kick Pandora's ass," Selene swore.

"Hermes, what have you done to Selene to make her so violent all of a sudden?" asked Hades with a small smile.

He made me fall in love with him. Selene glowed even brighter at the realization.

"Don't worry, Selene, there's going to be a conga line of people to kick Pandora when we find her," assured Persephone.

Hermes hadn't taken his eyes from Selene. "Let the magic go, Silver, you don't need it here," he repeated, and Selene's rage and the glow faded.

"I'm going to kiss you so hard for that reaction later," Hermes whispered with a sly wink.

"I should think so. I don't glow for just anyone," she replied flippantly even though a part of her tried not to freak out.

Hermes finished laying out the pictures and tried to find the memories relating to each one.

"Do you think Pandora has your staff?" asked Persephone.

"I assume so. She wasn't going to fuck Zeus without it, and nothing would've stopped her taking it once she had stabbed the stupid bastard," said Hermes, moving the picture in his hand around.

"I remember a big building, lots of concrete. We had to get on a boat to go there, so maybe it's on one of the islands. I know that's still unhelpful, but I can't pinpoint anything more specific. There were lots of people there like in the caves. I don't suppose you left anyone to interrogate?"

Hades leaned back in his chair. "The triplets talked to a few, but they were all too low level to have any good information."

"What if Pandora is hiding out with the mystery man you drew with Acrisius Argos. If we find him, we could find her," suggested Selene.

"I'll message Perseus and see what he's managed to sweet talk out of the Graeae sisters," said Persephone, pulling out her phone. "It might be worth you going with him to see them, Hermes. Rumor has it they have a weakness for handsome men."

∽

Hermes ended up taking Persephone's advice and going to see Perseus.

There was something about the Graeae sisters that was bothering him since Thanatos had mentioned the name that morning.

It was niggling like him a sore tooth, and the more he searched for a connection to the name, the more frustrated he became.

He knew he wasn't going to get much sleep that night after the horror of the warehouse and the nightmare memory in the bathtub, so he might as well try to get to know his latest brother.

Selene had given him a long hug and a gentle kiss when he'd taken her home.

"You know where to find me if you need me, Hermes," she said, and he had almost stayed with her.

Hermes knew that she had her own busy thoughts about her hidden magic and the chaos of dealing with a mad god.

She deserved a night off after bringing him back from the brink of madness yet again that day.

You know you don't deserve her, and one day she'll know it too, Zeus whispered in his mind.

Maybe you're right, but I'm going to enjoy it for as long as it lasts, Hermes snapped back, and finally, the ghost of his father left him.

Perseus tended to work late at his studio when Medusa was busy filming or had meetings.

He was alone and busy working on a painting when Hermes tore open a door and stepped into his warehouse.

"Persephone warned me you might turn up. I thought you would, you know, use the front door," Perseus joked as he turned his music down.

"Not my style," Hermes said, his eyes taking in the paintings on the walls, half-finished sketches, and pots and tubes of paint. "I like your work. It makes me feel...things. I can't describe it."

"I'll take that as a compliment. There are few benefits to having acid thrown in your face, but it has helped me see the world differently, and that's reflected in my art. Well, hopefully, it is," Perseus said. He looked at Hermes, and his smile changed. "Do you want to paint? Medusa said you had a rough one today."

Hermes knew he probably should say no, but it was a lie. He *did* want to paint.

"I'd like that, but only if it doesn't disturb you," replied Hermes, his hands already itching to touch the brushes.

"Not at all. I don't mind the company, and there's plenty of space and easels around. I started a kids' class a few times a week for all the ratbags in the neighborhood, so I have lots of spare gear." Perseus helped set Hermes up at the other end of the bench, complete with paint and a fresh canvas.

"It's nice of you to teach children. I would never have the patience," said Hermes.

"I don't really teach them, just give them a place to hang out that's not the street or whatever messed up home life they have. I know what it's like to grow up on the streets, and I would've loved a place where I could come and feel safe. I'd rather have them addicted to art than drugs," replied Perseus.

Hermes studied Perseus, so much like Zeus, and yet the complete opposite in his personality. It made Hermes wonder what he would've become if he had never been found.

You still have time to become something else.

Hermes put paint to canvas, keeping up an easy conversation with his newest brother.

He told him about Zeus and the hopeless feeling inside of him that he would never get his memory back or be able to find Pandora.

Perseus was suspiciously easy to talk to, and like Selene, his company was comfortable because he hadn't known Hermes before the curse.

Despite worrying about his past, his staff and Pandora, Hermes ended up painting Selene in black, white, and grey.

She held her hands above her head, cupping the full moon, her neck draped in necklaces of glittering stars and keys.

"Have you heard from your friends about who our mystery man could be?" asked Hermes.

"The Graeaes? Not yet. They will be awake if you want to go and talk to them and put your mind at ease. I can't guarantee that they will have any information for you," said Perseus.

"I feel like I have to. I don't know why. It's going to bug me until I do." Hermes washed out his brushes and tried to search his broken memories of the sisters and found nothing. Yet, the impulse was insistent.

"Okay, let me lock up. I should warn you though, the sisters are charming but can be handsy," Perseus said, laughing.

They took a cab out to the other side of Styx to a quiet neighborhood lit with street lamps.

Hermes had deja vu hit him when they walked up to the door of a pretty house.

Perseus knocked, and a woman's face appeared through a crack in the door. Her eyes went wide behind her glasses and flung the door open.

"Hermes! Where the fuck have you been?" she demanded.

"You know him, Enyo?" asked Perseus.

"God of tricks has done a disappearing act on us for the last twenty years," snapped Enyo.

"I don't...know you?" said Hermes, his mind racing, trying to recognize her face.

"How dare you! Perseus, hit him for me," Enyo demanded.

"Easy now. Hermes has been cursed," said Perseus.

Enyo's pissed off expression became even angrier. "We told you not to answer Zeus's summons! We tried to warn you!"

"Sister! Stop hollering and let them in. Can't you see Hermes is in distress?" Pem said, moving her sister out of the way and waving them inside. "Come in, dear magician, you look like you've been to Tartarus and back."

"I'm so confused," whispered Hermes to Perseus. His brother only shrugged and followed them.

Another sister was in the kitchen, pouring out glasses of wine. She took one look at Hermes and grinned.

"About time you came back for your stuff," she said.

"Don't waste your time, Deino, the god of stupid plans here has been cursed," said Enyo.

"Oh, dear, better have some of this," Deino tutted and passed Hermes a glass of wine. "Go on, this is an old vintage. You'll like it."

"Thank you," Hermes replied and sipped. It was a nice wine and he said as much.

"Well, you stole it for us, and you were never one to take a bad drop," said Pem.

"Ladies, would you mind telling us how you know Hermes?" asked Perseus. The three women studied Perseus and then Hermes.

"Oh, goddess, we are so blind-" said Deino.

"They can't be-" muttered Enyo.

"But they are handsome enough to be-" added Pem.

"Brothers? Yes, we are," answered Hermes.

"Zeus is the worst," said Enyo. "I should've known Perseus was far too charming."

"Thanks, love," Perseus replied. "You can stop dodging my question now." The three sisters looked at each, exchanging a silent conversation of eyebrow raises, grimaces, and nods.

"We've known Hermes since the old, *old* days," said Pem tactfully.

"So, you are oracles! I knew it!" exclaimed Perseus.

"Calm down, young one. Yes, we've been oracles, and now we are just us," said Deino, looking Hermes over. "Hermes has stayed in contact through the centuries, and twenty years ago, he came to visit. He said that Zeus was summoning him for the first time in decades, and he was worried about it."

"You should've ignored him like we told you to, but no. Your damn curiosity couldn't help itself. You were all worked up about war rumors and you wanted to go and see if Zeus was involved," added Enyo.

Hermes chewed on a lip and tried to find something, *anything* that would spark what he was thinking the last time he saw the sisters.

"You said he left his stuff here? Can we see it?" asked Perseus.

"Let me go find his bag. I know I put it somewhere," replied Pem and headed for the basement stairs.

"I thought it was you that killed Zeus, but you died in the effort," Deino said softly.

Hermes shook his head. "Not me, Hades got him. Zeus cursed me and took my fucking staff."

"Bad to worse!" said Enyo.

"Gets even worse than that." Perseus told them about Pithos and Pandora, while Hermes fought with his anxiety of not having a clue who the sisters were.

"Oh, Perseus love, the trouble you have found yourself in," Deino said with a sad sigh. "We've been looking into your Pithos since they threatened Dany. Not much on them, except they like to buy lots of property around Greece through multiple shell companies."

She went into her office and reappeared with a folder of clippings. "This is what we found on the man in the drawing."

Hermes opened the folder and looked at the newspaper pictures of the smiling man in black and white. He passed a few over to Perseus.

"Darius Drakos? That has to a fake name," said Perseus.

"Sadly not. The Drakos family are big money out of Cyprus. His name isn't the strange part, it's the fact that Darius Drakos has been dead for the past ten years," said Deino.

"That's impossible," said Hermes. "I saw him and Acrisius Argos not long before Hades found me."

Deino shrugged. "He's got a legit death certificate in there. Died by misadventure on a sailboat. Both the boat and he went into a storm and never came out again."

"He faked his own death. I wonder why?" said Perseus.

"It's easier to live as a ghost," replied Hermes. Pem came back into the room with a big black duffel bag and dumped it on the floor beside him.

"There you go, Hermes, I knew I had it somewhere," she said cheerily.

Without hesitation, Hermes knelt on the floor and opened the bag.

Inside were thick leather-bound notebooks held together with string, clothes, three guns, passports, money, and a sword wrapped in leather.

"Where did I get a *kopis* from?" he said, studying the blade.

"Sparta, I imagine. You can remember what type of sword it is but not where you got it? Your curse is ridiculous," criticized Enyo.

"Tell me about it. If it wasn't for Selene, I would still be hiding in Hades's basement," said Hermes as he wrapped the sword up and put it away again. It made his hands itch, and he didn't want to be around anyone when he found out why.

"Selene? You mean Hades's nurse?" asked Pem.

"The really pretty nurse," said Deino suspiciously. "How is she tangled up in this?"

Hermes smiled self-consciously. "I'm in love with her."

All three of the sisters groaned dramatically. "Of course, you bloody are. I suppose we shouldn't be surprised that even with half a brain, you still have time to chase tail," complained Enyo.

"Ladies, it's been a revelation, but I have a past to find and people to kill," Hermes said as he got to his feet and picked up his bag. "Once I break this curse, I'm sure I'll be back to apologize for forgetting you."

"You had better. We'll keep digging on our dead Darius," replied Deino. "Try not to get Perseus killed with your bullshit. I like him more than you."

Hermes laughed and took Perseus by the arm and summoned his magic.

"I'm not promising that," he said before pulling them through a door and leaving the three sisters cursing him.

18

Hermes spent the following day going through his bag and the overstuffed journals.

He planned on going for a mystery date with Selene that night, so they decided to spend the day on their own.

Hermes wanted to be alone when he went through his old possessions in case there were nasty surprises that he didn't want Selene or anyone else to see.

Jackal slept on the lounge room floor beside him, a silent comfort as he went through the journals page by page.

Some sections were written in code that a part of him must have understood, but the curse wouldn't allow him to have the knowledge.

Even without the sections deciphered, Hermes pieced together that he had been hunting something when Zeus had summoned him.

There were notes on different artifacts, of mysterious healings in towns, and strange, violent deaths in others.

He had been wandering country to country, searching for old treasures and mysterious figures. There were sketches of a bookstores in Cairo and Alexandria, a temple in Turkey, a photo of a sealed tomb entrance.

Had he been trying to find others like him? Gods and monsters, magicians, and outcasts, they spilled out through the pages.

The last few entries were written in a hurried hand that he thought he was being watched.

Maybe Pandora and her Pithos were already hunting you as they hunted the others?

Hermes flipped through the back of the journal and a photo fell out. It was a hurried shot, the edges blurred, but the man was unmistakably Darius Drakos.

Was he a god or a supernatural being that Hermes had forgotten about? Hermes found the last thing he had written, the ink smeared.

Zeus has summoned me. Maybe he too, has felt the war brewing and is willing to stop fighting everyone and worry about his own for once. If he's not concerned about the threat, I'll find other allies to stop them.

"What war, Jackal? What is this all about?" Hermes said, putting the journal down.

He picked up the Spartan sword, untied the bindings around the hilt, and with considerable dread, wrapped his fingers around it.

The world tilted and swayed as the memory rushed over him.

THERE WAS A MANSION OF MARBLE, and Hermes walked silently through the doorway, right under the guard's noses.

He was the god of thieves and magic, and he'd been drawn to the pulse of power coming from the island and the mansion.

Music was playing outside in the gardens, with people lingering in doorways wearing Greek tragedy masks and drinking cocktails.

The owner of the house would've been incredibly wealthy but was of the rare breed that actually had a decent taste in art. Hermes ignored the beautiful paintings, throwing a glamor up so the people at the strange party wouldn't notice the uninvited guest.

"Do you think this group is actually serious? That monsters and gods are still roaming the earth under our noses. It seems implausible to me. Otherwise, we would know by now. They would be running the whole show," a blond man said, one of the few that wasn't wearing a mask.

"Lander dear, you are thinking about what you would do if you had that kind of power. The gods and supernatural beings wouldn't want to advertise who they are. They would want to creep about and corrupt wherever they went."

"Mankind stopped believing in them because they were redundant, even if half the stories of their magic are true. Maybe this Pithos will be able to harness the unnatural abilities of those freaks for good."

"Can you imagine what medical advances we could make if we had one to experiment on? What abilities we could harvest from them and enhance others with? Fascinating," replied a woman with a cold laugh.

Invisible to their eyes, Hermes leaned over and dribbled spit into her martini and kept on walking.

What the fuck is this place?

Once he had gotten his hands on what he'd come for, he would have to check them out further.

A magical pulse came from beneath him, so he went to the kitchen and found the entrance to the wine cellar.

He dodged a waiter dressed in a white coat and followed him down among the racks of wine. Set into the brick wall was a door made of iron.

After making sure the waiter was gone, Hermes placed his palm over the lock and let his golden magic seep into it, filling the shape and forming a key. Then he twisted his palm and the key unlocked the door.

He expected a treasure hoard. Instead, there was a single Spartan sword displayed on a plinth of stone.

"All of this fuss for little old you," Hermes said.

He picked it up and let the aura of old age and magic tell him the history of the sword. It wasn't just any blade. It had belonged to Leonidas, the king of Sparta himself.

"No wonder you pulse with power. So many Persians fed your steel and legend, and fame has made you into an object of power, bright one."

"I thought I sensed a stranger in my midst," a strong male voice said behind him.

Hermes turned as a human man lifted his mask, revealing a handsome smiling face.

"I do believe that sword belongs to me."

Hermes twisted it casually in his hand. "Not anymore. Those Spartans sure knew how to craft a blade, didn't they? I suppose this is your party of power-hungry, entitled assholes?"

"It is, though I like to call them associates," the man said, giving him a small bow. "Darius Drakos at your service. I can't say I've had the pleasure of meeting you, and I'd definitely remember a face like yours. At least let me know the name of the man that I'll be killing."

He was pointing a gun at him and Hermes laughed loudly.

"I'm no fucking *man*. That little pea shooter won't do you any good, I'm afraid. Don't worry, the story of how Hermes the God of Thieves and Dreams stole from you will make an excellent anecdote at your next cocktail party," Hermes said, disappearing as the gun fired.

HERMES DROPPED the hilt of the sword with a gasp. He quickly wrapped it up again and shoved it back into the bag.

He went into the bathroom and splashed his face with cold water as he fought a battle of wills to keep hold of the memory.

The effort made him shake, but he managed to control it.

He needed Selene; her warm mouth and easy company would steady him. She would know what to say to calm the fear in him.

"Hermes? Are you in here?" Thanatos called. Hermes wiped his face dry and hurried to stop the titan from moving his papers around.

"Don't touch anything," Hermes said as Thanatos knelt to look at the broken journals.

"I wasn't going to, don't worry. Have you found anything interesting?" he asked.

"Does the sword of Leonidas count?" Hermes asked, and Thanatos laughed. "I'm not joking. It's in that bag. I don't want to touch it again." Thanatos opened the bag and pulled the sword out.

"What the hell were you up to, Hermes?" he asked, studying the blade.

"I have no idea. I know I stole that from Darius Drakos during a Pithos party, and that I was worried about a war."

Hermes tugged on the ends of his hair before he forced himself to stop it and started packing it all up again.

"Everything is still in broken chunks. Maybe if Selene were here, I could think more clearly, find how the pieces fit together."

"Speaking of Selene, I bought you a suit for tonight. I thought time might have gotten away from you, so I came to remind you that you have an hour before you meet her," Thanatos said, pointing to the garment bag.

"Get ready and I'll take you into the city. I'm not going to have you being late and stressing her out."

Hermes nervously eyed the crowd of people standing outside a theatre. Thanatos drove down an alley beside the building where a man was waiting beside a door.

"Selene knew the crowd would make you nervous, so Hades arranged a VIP back entrance for you," said Thanatos.

"What is this place? Where is Selene?" asked Hermes.

"You are going to have to go inside to find out. Selene is already waiting for you." Thanatos turned in his seat.

"Hermes? Be careful with her heart. She is Hecate's blood and my friend, so I will defend her even against you."

"You don't have to warn me, Thanatos. I might be cursed, but I'm still determined to take care of her heart as well as the rest of her."

"I hope so with a new war brewing. Now go and have a good night. I trust you will make your own way home."

Hermes got out of the car and the man obediently opened the back door for him. "Straight up, sir. Your lady is already there," he said. Hermes beamed.

My lady indeed.

Hermes hurried up a set of stairs and into a curved hall lined with gilt-framed mirrors and thick red velvet carpeting.

He did a double-take when he saw Selene, his breath catching in his throat.

She wore a dress of shimmering silver that gleamed in the light. Her dark curls were pinned up to show off her long neck, and she was giving him a smile that he wanted to keep forever.

"I was wondering when you were going to turn up," she said, quite unaware of the affect she was having on him. Hermes bowed low and kissed her hand.

"Lady Selene," he greeted, still struggling to think of something to say.

"You like the dress, don't you? I can tell because you're staring," Selene said and moved to press her red lips to his.

"As much as I like it, I'm still going to rip it off you later," he promised.

"Then, my evil plan is working. Come on or we'll be late."

Selene took his hand and opened a nearby door to reveal a private box with a long velvet chaise lounge instead of chairs. They had a perfect view of the lit stage beneath them.

"This is Hades's box, so we won't be bothered," Selene said, shutting the door.

"What are we watching?" Hermes asked, knowing it didn't matter because he would be staring at her all night anyway.

"I thought this might help with your music memories," she said as they sat down.

Hermes didn't get a chance to reply as the lights went out, and the orchestra appeared in the space before the stage. His grip on her hand tightened as the overture swelled loudly, echoing and magnifying around them.

Hermes was drowning again, dragged down by the power of the music.

"Selene, what is this?" he asked, struggling not to cry.

"This is Mozart's *Don Giovanni*," she replied, resting her hand on his heart. "Breathe, Hermes. Let it drag you away if you need it to but keep breathing."

Hermes put his arm around her, needing to feel her with him. Then he adjusted to the overwhelming sensation of it all and let the music take him, leading him down the hallways of his mind to the sealed doors.

After struggling against them for a while, Hermes went back to the present, determined to enjoy the music, and singing. Selene was watching the stage, eyes shining with awe. She really was painfully beautiful, and somehow, he managed to win her when he was at his worst.

Hermes couldn't stand it any longer. He leaned over and kissed the soft, warm space where her shoulder met her neck.

Her eyes fluttered and she tilted her head over a little more, offering it to him like she always did. Hermes pressed another kiss and another, working his way up to her ear.

"I don't know what's ruining me more, the music or you," he whispered. Selene lifted her mouth towards his.

"Don't make me beg tonight," she said.

Hermes kissed her slow and deep, the hand on his thigh sliding up further. He ran his fingers down her collarbone and over the soft curve of her breast.

Selene bit down on his lip, and her hand brushed against his dick, already hard from the combination of music and stunning woman.

Hermes groaned as her mouth moved from his and kissed his neck, her hand continuing to massage him.

"Stop me if it becomes too much," she said, her breath hot on his ear.

"I can never have too much of your hands and lips on me," Hermes replied with a soft laugh. "I have lots of plans for both."

"Me too," Selene said as she undid the zipper on his trousers.

Hermes lifted an eyebrow but didn't stop her. "Aren't you full of surprises? Here I thought you were a sweet and innocent nurse."

"It can hardly be the first time you've been wrong," Selene said, making him laugh, and then before he could suspect her, she went down on him.

Hermes gripped the back of the chair so hard, he felt the polished wood crumble under his fingers.

"Sweet fucking Fates," he groaned, as all his senses went into overload with the music vibrating through him and Selene's warm wet mouth sucking his dick.

His heart was pounding so hard, his breath turned ragged. He wanted to be inside her when he came, and he couldn't do it in the middle of a theatre.

"Wait, too much," he gasped, taking her by the shoulders with shaking hands.

"What's wrong?" she asked.

"Oh, fuck, nothing, I just...we need to get out of here, but I want the music and..."

"It's okay. I downloaded the album onto my phone in case you enjoyed it," she said.

"Good, the music can come. I can't do what I want to you here."

Hermes got up on unsteady legs, pulled her close, and tore open a doorway, landing them in his lounge room.

"That is still going to amaze me every time you do it," Selene said breathlessly. She pressed something on her phone and the music came through the speakers. "There we go. Better?"

"Not quite," Hermes said, before grabbing the front of her beautiful silver dress and tearing it in half, sending silver sequins all over the carpet as the pieces fell off her. He stared at her in black lingerie and high heels.

"*Now*, I'm better."

Selene dropped the small clutch she was holding and collided with him, pulling off his clothes until he was as naked as she was.

Selene kissed him hard, her body pressed against his.

"Fuck, you really are perfect everywhere," she murmured, touching his muscles and the scars on his back.

Hermes dragged her to the carpet, her shoes and lingerie being ripped off on the way down.

"You have all the control, Selene. Tell me what you want," Hermes whispered between urgent kisses.

"I want to fuck you senseless," she said, biting his neck. "I want every part of you, and then I want it all over again."

At her words, Hermes's dick went even harder. "Then do it, Selene. Do whatever you want," he groaned.

Selene surprised him for a second time that night by rolling him on his back, her mouth nipping and kissing him down his chest before mounting him backward.

Hermes ran a hand down her pale back, his hands gripping her hips as he watched her slowly lower herself down onto his dick. She was so tight, hot, and wet that Hermes thought he was going to explode.

Selene gasped as she fit him deep inside of her. She didn't move, her hand reaching back to grip his side and steady herself.

Hermes smoothed his hands down the curves of her perfect ass, swearing softly as she moved her hips. His grip tightened on her ass, moving with the maddening rhythm she was setting, pulling her down harder every time she rocked back.

"God, Hermes," Selene said. Hermes sat up so he could reach her breasts, teasing and massaging. He licked the sweat off the side of her neck, and she trembled.

"Come for me, Selene. Don't ever hold back on my account. I plan on fucking you until you tell me to stop," Hermes promised her, pulling her tight against his chest, his hand curling against her throat.

Like the day in the forest, her heart rate picked up as he pinned her, and she groaned. He slipped his hand between her legs, gently touching her slick clit as she rode him. Her thighs squeezed together tightly as she cried out.

"Don't let me go. I don't think I can hold myself up," she said breathlessly.

Hermes kissed her damp cheek. "Never fear, sweet Silver, I have no intention of letting you go anywhere just yet."

19

Selene felt like she couldn't get enough air in her body to counteract everything she was feeling. Hermes tilted her head so he could kiss her roughly.

"You are incredibly beautiful, sweating and panting on top of me. I thought the dress was great, but this is definitely my favorite look on you," he said, making her laugh breathlessly. "And I'm only getting started."

Selene didn't know how much she could take of his feeling. She had never been a prude in the bedroom, but Hermes could probably convince her to do anything if he kept making her orgasm that hard.

She wasn't shy with him either and loved that he thought about her pleasure before his own.

Hermes kept hold of her as he moved, her forearms bracing on the couch cushions as he bent her over it.

His knees knocked hers out wider so he could settle between them, her ass up so he could reach her.

Selene gasped as he moved in and out of her slow and deep, the change of position hitting new parts of her. His fingers moved down the crack of her ass to where they were joined and back up again in light strokes, making her cry out into the pillow.

She tried to push back faster against him, but he stopped her.

"Easy, I'll get you there, trust me. Let me take my time with you," he said, nipping at her shoulder.

Selene reached behind her, grabbing onto his thigh, pulling him up against her with each slow, deep thrust.

His body was strong and heavy over her, pinning her, overwhelming her with heat and pleasure that radiated from her core.

She didn't know if it was magic or love or getting fucked by someone who knew how, and it didn't matter. She let instinct and sensation take over, let him do whatever he wanted to her until she was crying from the intensity of the orgasm that demolished her.

Hermes swore behind her as he came deep inside of her.

"I feel like that was overdue, but so worth it," he groaned as they both lay panting on the carpet.

"Tell me about it. I've been trying not to climb on top of you for the past three days," she replied as she picked a few stray sequins off his chest before collapsing against him.

Her skin was glowing again as Hermes pulled her closer and kissed her forehead. She knew they would have to get up eventually, but she was too exhausted and happy to move, her body heavy and soft.

Her eyes fluttered closed as she listened to his strong heartbeat.

"I'm so in love with you," she murmured.

"I love you too, my Silver," he whispered. She barely registered his breath catch, and a tremble run through him before she slipped into sleep.

SELENE WOKE THE NEXT MORNING, not on the lounge room floor but tucked up in Hermes's bed, a cup of tea steaming beside her.

She took one of his shirts from the wardrobe, slipping it over her head and brushing off the random sequins still stuck to her skin.

Medusa is never going to let you borrow one of her dresses again.

Selene used some mouthwash in the bathroom and tried but failed to detangle her wild curls. She smiled at her reflection when she remembered that Hermes had said that he loved her.

It was a relief to know it wasn't only her that had been feeling so intensely even before the mind-blowing sex.

Giving up on her bed hair, Selene sipped her tea and went in search of her mad god. Hermes was sitting on the deck outside, his hand patting Jackal as he stared at the ocean.

"Hey, did you sleep at all?" Selene said, leaning down to kiss the top of his head.

"Like the dead. I haven't been awake for long," he replied as she sat down beside him. "I woke up and I could hear music, and now when I concentrate, I can sense my staff."

"Hermes, that's great news," Selene said, wrapping her arm around his waist. "Why do you look so upset?"

"I know I can track the staff now, and we can stop Pandora and Pithos hunting us. I need to go and get it, and it's going to be dangerous. The problem is that I don't want you to come and see that side of all of us, or to be caught in any crossfire, but I'm also worried that if you're not with me, I won't be able to sense the staff either," he explained, golden eyes full of torment.

"Hermes, I know you are a god and that all of the Court is strong and vicious in ways I can't imagine. I'm not like that, but I'm not about to let you go and face your torturers alone. That's not what people who love each other do," Selene replied, tightening her grip on him.

"So, you do really love me? It wasn't just because of an orgasm high?" he asked, a small grin appearing at the corner of his mouth.

"No, I loved you before the high. That's why I'm not going to let you go after your staff without me," Selene said, kissing his shoulder.

"You love me how I am now. What if when I get my staff, and it heals me and turns me back to how I was before, and you don't care for him? I remember enough to know I didn't always do things I was proud of."

"Then take this curse as a motivation to do better. I can't judge what you did or what you were made to do, so you shouldn't either. Get your staff and your memories, then we can go from there," said Selene, reaching up to touch his cheek. "It would take a lot for me to stop loving you, Hermes."

Hermes kissed her softly. "Okay, Silver, let's go get my staff and end this."

∽

Every time Selene said that she loved him, it was like a small bomb went off in Hermes's head.

The previous night, she had fallen asleep as memory and music and magic raced hot through him.

Then he heard his staff calling out to him like a siren's song. It wanted him to find it, wanted to be returned to his hands alone.

Memories of the cell that looked over the beach came back to him. It was on an island near Crete, one that was hidden by the magic that Pandora swore she hated. She had taken him and the staff there, keeping Hermes locked up in the same facility that it was, just in case the staff's power only worked within proximity to Hermes.

When she realized it didn't, he had been shipped back to the mainland so that there would be no way for him to get his hands on it.

Hermes remembered Darius Drakos arriving in a storm and kissing Pandora in welcome and the uncomfortable way he had looked at Hermes.

"I can't believe you got this troublemaker at last. I don't suppose he had my sword on him?" Darius had asked from the other side of Hermes's bars.

"No, I found him wandering about the mountain where I stabbed Zeus. He must've done this to him to get the staff," said Pandora, looping her arm around Darius's.

"Don't worry, I'll make Hermes useful. He's not going to be causing any of us problems ever again."

How very wrong you are, Pandora.

Hermes dug into his notebooks, searching for a map that he had seen the previous day. Hermes had known something was off about Darius and the people at his house that night and he had been hunting for evidence of them.

He had traveled to try to find the lost ones to warn them that stylized monster hunters were loose in the world once more.

"Hermes?" Charon opened the front door letting in Jackal and Cerberus and knocking him out of his memories.

"In here. Don't step on anything," Hermes said, still searching.

"Selene text me to let you know she's ready for you to go and get her. Really, you need your own phone if you are going to have a girlfriend," replied Charon.

"Is everyone else down at the villa yet? I only want to have to go through all this once. Ah-ha! There you are!" Hermes pulled the map out.

It was of Crete, lines, and Xs where he had been searching for Pithos's headquarters. He hadn't known it was an island.

"We are just waiting on Asterion and Ariadne to arrive, but they won't be far away. Can you really hear your staff?" asked Charon.

"Yes, and we are going to get it, and I'll be whole once more," said Hermes.

"It's probably for the best, but I have enjoyed parts of the crazy Hermes." Charon rested his hands on his hips. "All it took was one decent shag and voila!"

"Shut up, it was more than one," Hermes said with a smile, and gathered up his papers. "I'm not cured yet."

"You don't want to have another tumble with the lovely Selene just to make sure?"

Hermes laughed. "Oh, I would, but we don't have enough time. After Pandora is dead or locked up somewhere, then I intend to devote adequate time to making Selene scream."

"She'll probably be screaming at you in annoyance when she learns that you are even more of a smug dick know it all when you have a brain that works," said Charon.

"I love you too, titan. Take this stuff down to the villa. I'll get Selene and meet you there," Hermes replied, handing everything over.

Selene was putting things into a backpack when Hermes opened a door into her apartment.

"Just give me one second," she said without turning around.

"How did you know I was here?" asked Hermes.

"The air change, buzzed, I can't explain it."

"You sensed the magic."

"Maybe, but we'll worry about it later," Selene replied, ever pragmatic. She zipped up the pack and slung it over her shoulder. "Okay, I'm ready."

"What is in there?"

"I'm not going into a fight without medical supplies," she said. Hermes's smile widened. "What?"

He kissed her, full of love and worry. "I love that you thought of it even though the Court is probably going to kill everyone."

"Maybe a handsome trickster god can figure out a way of maybe *not* killing everyone?" she asked.

"I'll do my best for you, beloved. I can't speak for everyone else, though. Pandora has hurt all of them, and her men are fanatics of the worst sort," Hermes replied.

It was another reason why he didn't want her to go with them. How could he convince her to stay behind?

"Whatever went through your head just now, the answer is no," said Selene stubbornly. She gripped his hand tightly. "Let's go."

"I had to fall in love with a bossy one," he sighed and pulled her through a door and back to the villa.

Ariadne and Asterion were getting out of a beautiful black car, both of them kitted out in gear. Ariadne had blades strapped to her everywhere, her hair pulled back in a braid, and wearing her switchblade smile.

"Hey, you two! Ready to go kill some assholes?" she said in greeting.

"Selene's been trying to convince me of a non-violent approach," Hermes replied.

Ariadne reached over and tapped Selene on the nose. "Boop. You're adorable, nursey, that's why we love you. Hope you've been practicing those punches I showed you just in case."

Selene battered her hand away, laughing at her as they went inside. Hermes shook his head at the thought of an assassin and a nurse being friends with each other.

"Were you serious just now, because I don't see this ending up anyway but bloody," said Asterion.

"I'm hoping that if we show up in force and take down Pandora, all her men will shit themselves and surrender," said Hermes.

"You are going to need more than hope. Some of those assholes tortured Ariadne for days, so I can't deny her the revenge she needs for that."

Hermes ran a hand over his face. "I know. I will think of something. Selene isn't naive enough to think that no one is going to die, but she is right in a way. We need to be better than Zeus. If he were in our shoes and had discovered a group like Pithos, he would have slaughtered them all so completely and horrifically that it would be a cautionary tale for a millennium. We are both better than that, Asterion. I *need* to be more than him."

"For her. I get it," Asterion said, patting him on the shoulder. "So, save who you can and let the others die. If nothing else, the ones we let live will be able to warn anyone else who thinks that it's okay to hunt down those who are different."

"I know, but I don't want to be the monster they think we are," Hermes replied.

"I'll try to rein Ariadne in, but if it's self-defense, I won't stop her. Don't look so worried, Hermes, this is going to be fun," said Asterion with a smile.

Inside, Hades's lounge room was packed with the Court chatting and drinking.

Hades watched over them, a small amused smile on his face and his arm around Persephone. Hermes wasn't even going to try to convince his uncle not to decimate Pandora's island.

"Okay, big brother, what is this about?" asked Perseus, where he sat with Medusa.

"A stolen sword and an island that can't be found," answered Hermes and laid out his plans.

20

The next day, the Court traveled to Crete. Hades and Hermes decided the best way to approach Pandora was without magic that she could detect and with the cover of night.

Selene had known about their confrontations with Pithos. She had stitched them up enough times to know that they were violent, but as she sat quietly and listened to battle plans for the past day, she had a whole new understanding of the people she called her friends.

For the most part, Hermes was calm, but as soon as they landed on Crete, he had taken her hand and hung onto it.

They were waiting on a boat to take them from Lentas, and to an island only Hermes could sense.

"Maybe we should have stayed in bed," Selene whispered to him, only half-joking.

"Don't worry, Selene, once I get my staff back, I intend not to leave my bed for a week." Hermes's smile was full of flirtatious trouble.

"Is that so? Am I invited?"

"You'll have to fight Jackal for that side of the bed, but sure, you can come if you still want to," he said, a small note of unease creeping in.

"Unless you turn into a total dick between then and now, I'm pretty certain I'll want to," Selene replied.

"Then it looks like you're sleeping alone, Hermes," said Erebus behind them.

"Jealousy is a curse, titan," Hermes retorted.

"Still more interesting than yours."

With perfect timing, a boat arrived at the docks as the sun disappeared under the waves. Charon was behind the wheel and was the only one that looked relaxed.

"All right, doll?" he asked, as Selene put her bag down.

"Nervous, but okay, how about you?"

"Right as rain. Looking forward to seeing what Pandora has been hatching on her secret hideout. Don't worry too much. We are all going to protect you," Charon promised. He drove them out of the harbor and gestured at Hermes.

"Come on, trickster, this is your shit show. Tell me where to go."

Hermes joined Charon at the front of the boat and closed his eyes.

The air charged around him and Selene stepped back from him, her skin shivering with static. Hermes held out a hand to the darkness and pointed.

"That way, ferryman. The staff's power is covering the island like a cloak."

"Let's hope we don't crash straight into it," said Charon.

"If Darius could find it in a sailboat and not crash, then I'm sure you'll manage," Hermes replied.

His hand found Selene's again in the dim light. She couldn't imagine what he must be feeling as he headed back to a place that had caused him so much torment.

"When it starts, stay behind me, Silver," he said, tucking a curl behind her ear. "*Promise* me."

"I promise, Hermes," Selene replied, leaning into him, the contact taking some of the tension from his face. "Don't get yourself shot and we'll be good."

"I'd heal, you wouldn't. Don't ask me not to get in the way to protect you, because I won't agree to it. Anyone that lifts a weapon to you will die," Hermes said, his voice going cold.

Selene couldn't answer that, a part of her still scared of him, and yet so in love with him that it hurt.

She hated the idea of people getting injured, but it was one argument she would never be able to win against him.

"I love you," Selene replied when their staring competition became too much for her.

Hermes was about to reply, when his head snapped to the front of the boat.

The air was charged again, the core of power thrumming inside of Selene as the boat drove through a wall of magic.

"That's...that's your staff?" Perseus asked, joining them at the front of the boat.

"You can feel it too?" Selene asked, and he nodded.

"It's like ants under my skin."

"We are almost there," Hermes called to the others.

The darkness in front of them shimmered, and lights appeared in the distance, a fortress of concrete and steel rising from the ocean.

Asterion let out a low whistle. "Fuck, would you look at that."

"I'm going to tear it apart brick by brick," said Persephone, her eyes turning black.

"Save some for the others this time, and don't burn yourself out," cautioned Hades beside her.

Black shadows were encircling Persephone. "Don't tell me what to do."

"Don't make me take you back to Styx," Hades replied, and Persephone kissed him.

"Stop fighting, you two! There will be plenty for all of us," hissed Medusa, removing her glasses and pulling down her goggles.

"Hades! I could do with some cover," called Charon and pointed to a patrol boat. Shadows exploded over them, shielding the sound and sight of the boat. The patrol went past them, the men on board not sparing them a glance.

"That's incredible," whispered Selene.

"That's nothing. You wait until I get my staff back and then you will know what incredible is," Hermes said with a cocky grin.

Charon guided the boat into a small bay and threw down an anchor. "Okay, Hades, take us across." They all linked hands and magic poured out the God of the Underworld. Selene gasped as the power reached her and then they were all standing on the beach.

"Good luck, everyone. You know what to do from here," said Hades.

"Cause as much glorious chaos as possible," laughed Ariadne, pulling out her knives.

"Just watch where you throw those things," warned Medusa.

Ariadne rolled her eyes at Selene. "I nicked her once during practice and she's never dropped it."

"Be careful, the both of you," Selene said. Ariadne's smile widened and she saluted her with her knife.

They disappeared in the night, leaving Hermes, Selene, and Thanatos alone on the beach.

The titan refused to leave Selene on her own, and she made a mental note to ask what the hell happened between him and Hecate to make him so protective of her.

"Are you ready for this, Hermes?" asked Thanatos.

"As I'll ever be. At this time of night, most of the men will be at the mess hall, which will leave our path free," said Hermes. They headed up the beach and up to the tall metal gates to the compound. A siren was sounding in the distance.

That will be Ariadne and Persephone.

"There's our way in. Are you ready?" asked Hermes, pointing at the gate.

"We aren't going to sneak in?" Selene thought they would at least try to avoid getting shot.

"No, love, we are going right through the front door, because I intend to make the most dramatic entrance as possible," Hermes replied. His eyes were glowing with gold light and his smile was manic.

Thanatos sighed deeply, his scythes appearing in his hands. "I know that look. Stay by me, Selene."

Hermes laughed, kissed Selene, and then clapped his hands twice. The gates exploded in a rain of metal and wood, and the three of them walked right in.

∽

HERMES WAS THRUMMING with more magic than he had felt in years. The Caduceus knew he was there, its power leading them through the fortress.

He barely registered the men scurrying about, some screaming in terror about a Minotaur.

He knew that Thanatos would protect Selene from anyone getting too close, but they were yet to have anyone raise weapons at them. His shock troops were certainly scaring the enemy in more ways than one.

Hermes opened another door and there was a group of four men, all with guns pointed at him.

"Hello there, I was wondering if you could give me directions to my staff?" Hermes asked politely.

"Surrender now and we won't fill your bitch with bullets," a man said behind his balaclava. Hermes raised a hand to make their heads explode and then stopped.

"You're lucky that she told me not to kill anyone tonight. Listen puppets, we aren't here for you, so put your guns down and I'll let you go free."

"You just said you won't kill us, so why would we?"

Hermes gave Selene a pained glance over her shoulder, but she shook her head. "Fuck. Fine. You know what puppets do best? They dance," Hermes said, snapping his fingers.

The men's guns fell to the floor as their limbs forced them into a rhythm.

"W-what did you do to us?" one of the soldiers demanded as he ground up against one of his horrified companions.

"Saved your useless lives. Go on, fuck off and pass it on," said Hermes, and they partnered up and waltzed away through the corridors.

"That wasn't so terrible, was it?" Selene asked with a wide smile.

"Wasn't nearly as satisfying," complained Hermes as he walked into another corridor.

The fortress was a warren and every damn space was the same. Hermes growled in frustration and then stopped.

"What's wrong?" asked Thanatos.

"Nothing, I'm going to clear a path," said Hermes.

Thanatos moved Selene back behind him as Hermes raised his hand.

He closed his eyes for a split second, centered himself on the pulse of his staff, and blew a kiss of power in its direction.

Concrete bricks and metal framing split open in the wall beside him.

"This way," he said, voice thick with magic.

Hermes walked casually through the new path, ignoring the gunfire and screams in the corridors on either side of him. He spotted men frozen in stone and others torn in half.

"Don't look, Selene," he said firmly, and she gripped the back of his shirt.

"Lead me," she replied and shut her eyes.

The holes in the walls ended and they stepped into a wide circular space with metal sides all around them.

Slots in the metal opened and gun barrels poked through them.

"Come on, Pandora! Let's talk like big kids. This is getting tedious," Hermes called, his voice echoing around them.

A panel in the wall slid back and Pandora walked through it, his beloved staff in her horrible hands.

The staff was as tall as she was, two golden snakes wrapped around the dark wood meeting at the top in the center of a pair of open wings.

"Hermes, I wondered when you were going to come back to me," Pandora said, the purr in her voice making him flinch.

That fucking voice would haunt his nightmares. Selene stepped beside him and took his hand, hiding the tremor in it before Pandora could see it.

"I thought she would be prettier," said Selene, knowing exactly where to prod Pandora's ego.

Fates save me, I love this woman.

"Who is this? Another woman already? You really can't keep it in your pants longer than five minutes," Pandora said.

"I kept it in for the twenty years I was stuck with you, didn't I? That staff belongs to me, so hand it over before the Court decides to decimate this place and everyone in it," Hermes said, forcing his voice steady.

"Zeus, King of the Gods, gave it to me, and you should know that a gift given by a god is yours forever," Pandora replied.

"You really don't care about anyone but yourself, do you? These poor bastards are following you and you wouldn't care if we killed them all right now." Hermes looked at the guns still pointed at them. "You guys really need better role models."

Pandora laughed charmingly. "They don't follow me. They follow the cause to clean up the world from the likes of you. If Hades and his monsters had stayed in the shadows where he belongs, the humans might not have felt threatened enough to want to arm themselves against your kind. We might have a bagged a few for scientific advancements to help mankind, but it escalated when Hades and his freaks refused to return to the Underworld."

"You speak like you are one of them! You are more like the horrible monsters you are so keen to destroy than you are human," Hermes argued. He just needed to get close enough to get one hand on that staff.

"I am not like you. I am the first woman. I am more human than all of them put together," said Pandora.

"How very wrong you are, Pandora. There was nothing ever human about you. You think you are some kind of noble protector, and yet you aren't interested in helping any of them in this building."

"You think this is all of us? We are but a cell. There are so many more-"

"Like Darius Drakos? Oh, yeah, I remember him well. Don't you worry, I'll be finding him next," Hermes promised.

"He always warned me not to get too comfortable with you. That no matter how loyally you performed, you were still not to be trusted, my inventor," Pandora said.

Hermes froze at the title, the memories of a hundred nights of torment flooding back to him.

"Don't you fucking call him that," hissed Selene.

She had a fiercely protective glare in her eyes that Hermes had never seen before. She had never reminded him so much of Hecate.

Pandora's lip curled in a sneer. "Who are you, girl?"

Selene let go of Hermes's hand and stepped forward. "I dare you to drop that staff and find out."

"Hmm, I think not," said Pandora and lowered the staff, sending a bolt of power at Selene.

The blast of magic knocked Hermes and Thanatos backward as it hit Selene squarely in the chest. Hermes watched in shock as the magic bounced off her and back to Pandora, sending her flying across the other side of the room.

Hecate's got a protection on her bloodline after all, Hermes thought in a daze.

Selene was glowing with silver light as she walked towards where Pandora lay bleeding.

Hermes struggled to get up and couldn't look away as Selene bent down and picked up his staff.

She walked calmly toward him with her eyes pale with silver light.

"I believe this is yours, my love," said Selene and offered it to him.

"Thank you, Selene," Hermes replied, but didn't take it.

"It's okay, Hermes, you aren't alone," she whispered.

"Whatever happens, know that I love you."

Selene smiled. "I know."

Hermes took a deep breath, wrapped his hand around the Caduceus and the world burst in golden light.

~

THANATOS'S strong arms wrapped around Selene and dragged her to the ground, shielding her body as Hermes exploded with magic.

"Stay down until it's over," Thanatos warned. Through a gap under his arm, Selene stared wide-eyed as Hermes rose in the air and the golden magic around him sucked back inside of him.

"Oh, fuck, we missed the whole show," complained Erebus as he stepped through the hole in the wall, followed by the rest of the Court.

Hermes looked towards Thanatos and Selene on the ground.

"Unhand my woman, titan," he commanded in a god voice that almost made Selene pee herself. Thanatos wisely got off her and helped her stand up.

"Look at him, back to being his flying sexy Tinkerbell self," said Charon gleefully as he came and stood beside Selene. "I definitely think we need to get him some winged booties just for the hell of it."

"Come down, Hermes, and let's finish this," Hades commanded. A tremble ran through Hermes and his eyes returned to normal as he drifted back down to the ground. Erebus and Thanatos had already lifted Pandora up, one hanging onto each arm.

"You think you've won, but I tell you and all your freaks, this is only just beginning!" spat Pandora viciously. "Go ahead and kill me!"

"And make you a martyr? Not likely, Pandora," said Hades. He shared a look with Hermes. "Asterion, make sure everyone gets out of the building before we return."

"Where are you-" Selene started as Hermes tapped his staff to the ground once, and then he was gone, Hades, Thanatos, Erebus, and Pandora with them.

"Oh, shit, she's going to regret pissing them off so much," said Charon.

"Where did they go?" asked Perseus.

"Probably best not to ask," answered Medusa, taking his hand.

"Come on, we don't know how long they are going to be," Asterion interrupted, his voice frighteningly deep in his bull-headed form.

In a strange daze, Selene followed them out through the wreckage of the building.

"What happened here?" Ariadne asked, bending down and picking up a machine gun. It wobbled strangely in her hand and she burst out laughing. "They are all rubber. How the fuck did this happen?"

"Hermes. He promised Selene he wouldn't let anyone shoot her," said Charon, sharing a smile with her.

"That's certainly one way to take care of it," laughed Medusa.

"You wait to see the ones dancing," Selene replied.

They made it out of the compound's gates before they spotted a group of about thirty soldiers on the road ahead of them, grooving together in a silent rave.

"I wonder how long it's going to last?" asked Ariadne, stroking the hilt of one of the knives in her belt. Selene put a hand over her bloody one.

"Don't even think about it, assassin," she said.

"Aw, come on, you're no fun at all."

They climbed up a small, rocky hill that overlooked the smoking compound beneath them.

Charon sat down on a large rock and started doing coin tricks.

"Now what do we do?" asked Selene, sitting down beside him.

"Now, we wait for them to return."

~

Deep in the darkest pits of Tartarus, Hermes and Hades watched as Erebus and Thanatos dragged a screaming Pandora into a cell of black stone.

"Maybe we should just kill her and be done with it," said Hades.

"I might consider it...eventually. For now, I want her to know how it feels to be locked up in her own personal hell," Hermes replied. He remembered not only who he was, but every single damn day he had been held by the woman in the cell.

"You don't have to do this, Hermes! We can make a deal. I know so many things," Pandora said desperately, straining against her shackles. She turned to Thanatos.

"I know where Hecate is. I could tell you. That woman you protected is of Hecate's bloodline. I could feel her power in the protection around her. I can give you the information you need to reunite them."

"We don't need your help, Pandora. The Goddess of the Crossroads will find us if we don't find her first," said Hermes. "If not, we know where you'll be to interrogate you."

"I-I can give you Darius! You have no idea the power he has. He won't stop with me taken out of the way," said Pandora.

"He can come for us and we will defeat him the same way we defeated you," Hades replied calmly.

"You can't just leave me here!" shrieked Pandora. Erebus, more shadows than man, leaned close to the bars.

"Don't worry, I have one last gift for the Many Gifted one," he hissed and placed Zeus's head outside of the cell to stare at her with lifeless eyes.

Hermes and Hades smiled as Pandora screamed and screamed.

~

SELENE WAS DOZING against Charon's shoulder when the air charged, and Hermes was suddenly crouched down in front of her.

He rested his hands on her knees, his eyes scanning her all over.

"My love, are you hurt at all?" he asked.

"I'm okay, Hermes. Are you?" she said, taking his face in her hands, looking for changes.

He still looked like her mad god, with his hawk eyes and quick smile, but there was something about him that was sharper and even more alert. It was as if he had suddenly come into focus.

"I am back to being me and I still love you. I'm still also a little mad, but I'm sure that's completely normal too," Hermes admitted, his smile growing wider.

"Good, because I don't think I'd like it if you became too normal," Selene replied and kissed him.

It was the briefest of brushes, but magic sizzled through the connection, and she began to glow again.

"What now?"

"Now, I do something that I've been dying to do all night," Hermes said and laughed when he saw her expression. "I meant destroying the compound, not what you're thinking about, Silver."

"I'm only human," she laughed as he helped her up.

"That's debatable. You should be dead after the blow of magic you took," Hermes replied, wrapping an arm around her shoulders.

"Worry about Selene's protections from Hecate tomorrow. I want to go home," Erebus complained.

As the sun rose, Hermes pointed his staff at the compound and turned it to dust. It happened in less than a minute, and Selene had never seen anything so terrifying in all her life.

"Are you going to vaporize the dancing soldiers on the beach too, because they aren't coming home with me," Ariadne asked with a yawn.

"I'd be happy to turn them all into garden ornaments for you," said Medusa. Hermes gave Selene a hopeful expression.

"Don't even think about it," she said, and Hermes groaned.

"Fine, let's give them a healthy dose of amnesia and get out of here," he said. One by one, the soldiers stopped their dancing, collapsing onto the sand unconscious.

"Happy?" asked Hermes.

Selene rose on tiptoes and kissed his cheek. "Yes. Now, I'm ready to go home."

21

Selene spent the next two days curled up in bed with Hermes talking and making plans in between intense bouts of lovemaking.

He was still waking up from nightmares, but at least now he knew what was memory and what was his own fear. She had helped save him from his curse, but he saved her in so many ways too.

They had both healed old wounds and could finally move on. Hermes was still mad and wonderful, and Selene loved him all the more for it.

"I suppose I should look at finding another nursing job now that you are back to your old self again," said Selene, as she sat looking out over the ocean. Hermes placed a fresh beer beside her.

"You are going to be too busy to go back to nursing, Selene," he said, sitting down beside her.

"Doing what? I can't spend all my time in bed with you, no matter how tempting it is."

"I know. I'm talking about your magic and figuring out how it works. Some magic of Hecate's protected you in Crete, and as much as I am loathe to admit it, I can't teach you," he replied.

"I don't understand. You are the god of magic, so how can you not be able to teach me about it?"

"Hecate's magic, and those of her bloodline, answer to her. The magic is completely different, and the women of her line are frightening and formidable," said Hermes.

"But I'm not," Selene replied, shaking her head. "I glow a bit, but I'm just a human."

"I wasn't talking about you, Silver, though I have no doubt that you will be once you're trained. I'm talking about sorceresses like Circe and Medea. They had a power that even I, god of magic, could never understand. Pandora shouted about knowing that Hecate's still walking the earth." Hermes took a notebook from his pocket and flipped it open to a drawing of the ruins of a temple.

"Where is that?" Selene asked, taking the drawing. There was something about it that looked so familiar, like something she had once seen in a dream.

"Lagina. It used to have the largest cult openly dedicated to Hecate. That's the remains of her temple in modern-day Turkey. I traveled there, but I couldn't find any trace of her," Hermes explained.

"And what do we do if we find her? It's not like she didn't know she had some family left alive. Maybe she's never sought me out for a reason, Hermes," said Selene, handing his journal back.

"I knew Hecate for a long time, and there was nothing she was more protective of than her sorceresses and bloodline. Something is keeping her from you, and you are going to need her now that your magic has awakened." Hermes pulled a face.

"You should also know that Hecate and I fought a lot, so don't expect her to be happy about her descendent shacking up with me."

"Oh, no, am I dating an inappropriate boy? The shame," teased Selene.

Hermes pulled her laughing onto his lap and kissed her, and didn't stop until she was glowing like a star.

"What now?" Selene asked, tangling her fingers in his dark hair.

"Now, I need to show you how inappropriate I can be."

"I was hoping you were going to say that. Don't forget you promised to write a ballad for me about all my adventures."

Hermes, the god of tricksters and thieves, gave her his most savage smile that was still somehow full of love and magic.

"Something tells me, this adventure is only just beginning."

EPILOGUE

Thousands of miles away, a pulse of magic rose from the ocean and traveled through the trees and rock and earth.

It had journeyed from Crete, searching and seeking, drawn back to its goddess.

It crept through the mortar in between charmed stone bricks and settled on top of the figure of a woman, locked in an eternal slumber.

The magic covered her, eating away at the curse until it made a small crack in it and slipped between her lips.

It shot through her immortal body and coaxed golden ichor to begin to flow and her ancient, angry heart to beat.

Then after more than twenty years, the goddess breathed in.

ABOUT THE AUTHOR

I believe that all monsters and villains deserve their happy endings. I prefer my clothes black, eyeliner winged, and books full of hot romance. I think heroes are boring, so mall of my books center around dark gods, monsters and villains from my favorite myths.

Come say hi to me on Instagram, or keep track of all of the Court gossip by subscribing to my blog newsletter at:

https://alessathornauthor.com/alessa-news/

Thank you for reading THE COURT OF THE UNDERWORLD (Volume 1), if you loved it please consider leaving me a short review or rating on Amazon as it helps other readers find my books.

The Court's adventures continue in THE COURT OF THE UNDERWORLD (Volume 2) with our favorite triplets, and it's available now!

ALSO BY ALESSA THORN

Please note that the list below is current on this book's publishing day.

I publish every few months so the most up to date list of titles is located on my Amazon Author page.

GODS UNIVERSE

THE COURT OF THE UNDERWORLD

ASTERION

MEDUSA

HADES

HERMES

THANATOS

CHARON

EREBUS

GODS OF THE DUAT

SET

THOTH

ANUBIS

THE LOST GODDESSES

PERSEPHONE

BELLONA

LAVERNA

ERIS

FAE UNIVERSE

THE WRATH OF THE FAE

KISS OF THE BLOOD PRINCE

HEART OF THE WINTER PRINCE

WINGS OF THE NIGHT PRINCE

IRONWOOD

TRASH AND TREASURE

GOD TOUCHED

ELF SHOT

LUNA CURSED

THE LOST FAE KINGS

DANCE OF THE FOREST KING

SONG OF THE SEA KING

ROAR OF THE STORM KING

NOVELLA

FIRE STRUCK

THE GREATDRAKES

DREAM LOST

SMOKE BONDED

MERCENARIES AND MAGIC

DARKEST NIGHT

SHARPEST EDGE

TOUGHEST DEAL

DEEPEST CUT

FEATHER AND STONE

IRON HEART

INFERNO (Ream Stories World)

MERCURY RISING

DANCING WITH DAGGERS

THE BLOOD WOLF

TEMPLE OF MAGIC AND BONE

Made in United States
Orlando, FL
17 April 2025